# DEAD
# KISS

*Also by Daniel Waters*

*Passing Strange*
*Kiss of Life*
*Generation Dead*

# DEAD KISS

DANIEL WATERS

SIMON AND SCHUSTER

A **pulse** book

First published as an omnibus edition in 2011 by Simon and Schuster UK Ltd
1st Floor, 222 Gray's Inn Road, London, WC1X 8HB
A CBS COMPANY

GENERATION DEAD first published in Great Britain in 2008 by Simon and
Schuster UK Ltd, a CBS Company. Originally published in the USA by Hyperion
Books for Children, an imprint of Disney Book Group, New York, 2008

KISS OF LIFE first published in Great Britain in 2009 by Simon and Schuster UK
Ltd, a CBS Company. Originally published in the USA by Hyperion Books for
Children, an imprint of Disney Book Group, New York, 2009

1 3 5 7 9 10 8 6 4 2

Simon Pulse and colophon are registered trademarks of Simon and Schuster UK Lrd.

A CIP catalogue record for this book
is available from the British Library

ISBN: 978-0-85707-450-8

Printed by CPI Cox & Wyman, Reading, Berkshire RG1 8EX

# GENERATION
# DEAD

# CHAPTER ONE

PHOEBE AND HER FRIENDS HELD THEIR breath as the dead girl in the plaid skirt walked past their table in the lunchroom. Her motion kicked up a cool trailing breeze that seemed to settle on the skin and catch in their hair. As they watched her go by, Phoebe could almost tell what everyone was thinking. Everyone, that is, except for the dead girl.

Across from her, Margi shook her head, her silver teardrop earrings dancing among the bright pink spikes of her hair. "Even I don't wear skirts that short," she said before sipping her milk.

"Thank God for that," Adam said from two seats away.

Phoebe risked a glance back at the girl and her long, bluish-white legs. Fluorescent lights were kind to the dead, making them look like they had been carved from veinless blocks of pure white marble. The girl went to the farthest table and sat down alone, and without any food, the way the dead always did during lunch.

Sometimes Phoebe used to joke that she possessed psychic powers. Not useful ones like being able to tell when small children have fallen into wells or anything; more like being able to foresee what her mother was making for dinner or how many bangles Margi was going to wear on her arms that day. She thought her "powers," if that's what they were, were more tele*pathetic* than telepathic.

Phoebe knew as soon as she saw her that the dead girl in the short skirt would get Margi rolling on a whole host of zombie-related topics, none of which she really wanted to discuss.

"I heard that Tommy Williams's eye fell out in homeroom," Margi said, on cue. "I heard that he sneezed or something, and there it went, *splat*, on his desk."

Phoebe swallowed and placed her egg salad sandwich back atop the wax paper wrapping it came in.

"Zombies don't sneeze," Adam said around a mouthful of meatball sub. "Zombies don't breathe, so they can't sneeze."

The girls lowered their heads and looked around to see who was in earshot of Adam's booming voice. *Zombie* was a word you just didn't say in public anymore, even if you were the center on the football team.

Air hissed through Margi's teeth. "You aren't supposed to call them zombies, Adam."

He shrugged his massive shoulders. "Zombies, dead heads, corpsicles. What's the difference? They don't care. They don't have feelings to hurt."

Phoebe wondered if Tommy Williams and the girl in the plaid skirt really didn't have any feelings. The scientists weren't clear on that point yet.

She tried to imagine how she would feel losing an eye, especially losing an eye in public. And in homeroom, no less.

"You could be expelled for saying things like that, Adam," Margi was saying. "You know you're supposed to call them *living impaired*."

Adam snorted, his mouth full of milk. Ten years ago a milk snort would have been the height of biological grotesquerie at Oakvale High. Today it seemed kind of lame next to losing an eye in homeroom.

"Living impaired," Adam commented after recovering. "I think you two are living impaired. They're just dead."

He stood up, his huge body casting a long shadow over their uneaten lunches, and brought his empty tray to the conveyor system that took all of the dishes and garbage away. Phoebe just looked at her beautiful egg salad sandwich and wished that she had any desire left to eat it.

Phoebe's locker popped open on her third try. She figured that her inability to remember the three-digit combination did not bode well for her impending algebra class, which was always right after lunch. Her stomach rumbled, and she tried to tell herself that the spikes of hunger would give her mind an alert sharpness, like a lynx in winter between successful hunts.

Yeah right, she thought.

Tommy Williams was in her algebra class.

The door to her locker shook with a metallic vibrating sound. Inside were pictures of bands like the Creeps, the Killdeaths, Seraphim Shade, the Rosedales, Slipknot, and the Misfits; bands that dressed like the living dead before there were any dead actually living. There was a picture of her, Margi, and Colette in happier times, all gothed up in black fabrics, eyeliner, and boots outside the Cineplex in Winford, ready to be first in line for the premier of some vitally important horror movie she couldn't even remember. Phoebe, the tallest, was in the middle, her long black hair hiding one side of her naturally pale face, and her visible eye closed as she laughed at whatever vulgar comment Margi had just made. Colette had done her eyes like an Egyptian princess, with a single thick line of makeup at each corner. Colette and Margi were also laughing.

There was also a picture of her dog, Gargoyle. Gar was a Welsh terrier and not half as frightening as his name would suggest.

A mirror was on the door opposite the shelf where Phoebe's algebra book lay. On her mouth was a streak of smeared violet lipstick. Her long hair, normally jet-black, shiny, spiky, and tousled, now just looked dull, flat, and messy.

She thought she looked scared.

The lipstick smear was the only flaw that seemed fixable, so she rubbed it away before walking toward Mrs. Rodriguez's class down at the end of the hallway. She arrived there the same time as Tommy Williams, whose eyes, she was relieved to see, were still fixed within their sockets. He gazed at her with the blank stare of the living impaired.

4

children. Apparently, neither did teenagers in Uzbekistan, Burkina Faso, Sweden, or Papua New Guinea, for some reason. But kids from Oklahoma, Rockaway Beach, The Big Apple, Arkansas, or The Big Easy all bore at least a chance of winding up living impaired, as long as they croaked during the delicate teen years. The newest Frankenstein Formula theory was that a certain mixture of teenage hormones and fast food preservatives set up the proper conditions for living impairment. The medical community was still testing the theory, having begrudgingly let go of fluorocarbons and brain patterns rewired by a lifetime of first-person shooter games.

Outside, the dog lifted a matted hind leg on a bike rack where a number of bicycles were chained. Do the dead go to the bathroom? They didn't eat or drink, so the answer would seem to be no.

Mrs. Rodriguez then did a strange thing, strange enough to interrupt Phoebe's train of thought. She called on Tommy for the answer to a problem even though his pale hand wasn't raised.

Tommy looked up from his papers. There was a pause that sucked the air out of the classroom; there was always a pause like that when the dead were called on.

The dead could think, and they could communicate. They could reason, and once in a blue moon, one might even initiate a conversation. But they did so very, very *slowly* . . . a question, even one as simple as the one from Mrs. Rodriguez, could take a living impaired person ten minutes to process, and another five to respond.

Phoebe covertly tried to gauge the reaction of her class-mates. Some were suddenly absorbed in their textbooks, doing anything to avoid the reality—or unreality—that the dead kid represented. Others, like Pete Martinsburg, who was taking Algebra One for the second time and who was normally only interested in football and girls, were rapt with attention. Pete was looking at Tommy with the same expression of manic glee that he wore when he'd tripped Norm Lathrop and sent him sprawling into a bank of big rubber garbage cans in the lunch-room last week.

"One hundred and seventy-four," Tommy said, his voice halting and without inflection. No one hearing his voice could tell if Tommy thought his answer was wrong or right, so most of the class looked at Mrs. Rodriguez for her reaction.

She looked pleased. "That is correct, Thomas."

Phoebe noted that she always called the living impaired kids by their formal first names. It wasn't something she did with the "normal" kids. Pete Martinsburg was just "Pete" when she called his name, which was often, and usually to reprimand him. Phoebe was secretly thrilled to see the leer smacked off of Pete's face.

Mrs. Rodriguez went on with the class like it was no big deal to call on a dead kid. For the most part, the rest of the class reacted the same way.

But Phoebe noticed that Tommy did not go back to looking at his papers. His head remained high for the remainder of the class.

\* \* \*

Margi was waiting for her at the door after algebra.

"How did you get here so quickly?" Phoebe asked. Margi took her arm and pulled her aside.

"Sshh. I've mastered the art of bilocation; I'm really heading off to our English class right now."

Phoebe laughed. "Me too. Let's go."

"Hold on," Margi said. "I want to see that living impaired kid for a minute."

"Whoever told you about the eye thing was yanking your chain. He still has both," Phoebe whispered, and then Tommy walked out of the classroom, the last one to leave.

"I've got something even bigger. I heard he signed up for football tryouts. He's supposed to start practice tomorrow."

Phoebe looked at her friend, wondering just how it was that Margi always knew what was going on with the dead kids.

"Don't look at me like that, Pheebes. I overheard Coach Konrathy arguing with Principal Kim. He wasn't going to let the dead kid try out, but Kim is making him."

"Really?"

"Really. Can you imagine that? Playing with a living-dead kid? Having to shower with one of them? Brrrr."

Did the dead have to shower? They weren't rotting corpses like in all the movies, and they didn't sweat, either. Phoebe didn't think they smelled like anything; at least they didn't smell like anything dead.

"He looks like he could play," Phoebe said, watching him make his patient way down the hall.

"What do you mean?"

"Well, he's built for it."

*"Phoebe,"* Margi said, making a face. *"Ick."*

"He is. He's really, you know, sort of handsome."

"Yeah, if he wasn't, like, *dead,*" Margi said. "Double ick. Come on, we have to get to class."

"What about bilocation?"

"I can't do it when someone is asking me a bunch of questions. Let's go."

Phoebe made one stop after the final bell before she went out to the bus. Adam was methodically stacking books in his locker, lifting half the stack with one big hand.

"Hey," she said, "I hear that a corpsicle is going out for your precious football team."

"Yeah?" he said, not looking up from his task. "Whatever. As long as he can play."

Phoebe smiled. She thought it was cute the way Adam tried to be all gruff around her. She wondered if he even knew he was doing it.

"Listen," she said, "would you be able to give me a lift home tomorrow? I want to stay and get some work done in the library."

"Sure, as long as you can wait until practice is over," he said, pushing his locker closed. "And as long as the STD doesn't take away my driving privileges."

*STD* was Adam's term of endearment for his stepdad, who he got along with about as well as he did with Winford Academy's defensive line.

"Great," she said. "See you. I've got to catch my bus."

Adam nodded. If he really did have an opinion one way or another about playing football with the living impaired he didn't show it. Adam had matured a lot over the summer. Maybe it was the karate.

"Is Daffy coming?"

Phoebe laughed. Adam was more mature around everyone other than Daffy, his nickname for Margi. "I don't think so."

"Okay. See you."

"Later." She watched him walk away. She'd known Adam since she'd moved next door to him years ago, but he was different now—in the way he walked, in the way he talked, in the way his face had slimmed down to reveal a strong, angular jawline. His upper half, always big, had broadened out into a wide V from his narrow waist. Phoebe smiled to herself. If it *was* the karate, it was a good thing.

She almost missed her bus home. Colette was already sitting alone and staring ahead out the windshield. Phoebe saw her, and the familiar pang of sadness and shame flared inside her chest.

Phoebe had grown up with Colette Beauvoir, at least until Colette stopped growing when she drowned in Oxoboxo Lake the previous summer. Colette would be fifteen forever, and yet she was not the same fifteen she used to be. Phoebe had tried to talk to her—once—but the experience had been so disturbing that she'd never tried again. That was months ago. Margi was even worse; she would get up from her seat and leave if Colette entered the room. As gabby as Margi was, she couldn't even bear to discuss what happened to Colette.

The dead always sat alone. The school dismissed them five minutes early so that they would have time to shuffle out to the buses. Every school day since Colette died, Phoebe would pass her sitting there all alone and wonder if she remembered the fun they used to have listening to Colette's brother's old Cure and Dead Kennedys records in the basement.

"Colette." It was the first word Phoebe had said to her since the one failed conversation. The memory of her tears still felt fresh in Phoebe's mind.

Colette turned, and Phoebe liked to think that it was the sound of her name and not just sound that caused her to turn. She regarded Phoebe with a fixed blank stare. Phoebe considered sliding into the seat next to the dead girl. Her mouth opened to say—what? How sorry she was? How much she missed her?

She lost her nerve and moved toward the back of the bus, where Margi was, whatever words she'd hoped to say caught in her throat. Colette's head turned back slowly, like a door on a rusty hinge.

Margi was engrossed in her iPod, or at least she was pretending to be. Colette was like a dark spot on the sun to Margi; she never spoke about her or even acknowledged that she existed.

"Did you hear that the bass player for Grave Mistake died?" she said. "Heart attack after overdosing on heroin."

"Oh?" Phoebe said, wiping her eye. "You think he'll come back?"

Margi shook her head. "I think he's too old, like twenty-two or twenty-three."

"That's unfortunate," Phoebe said. "I guess we'll know in a couple days."

Tommy Williams was the last one on the bus. There were plenty of open seats.

Tommy stopped at Colette's seat. He looked at her, and then he sat down beside her.

That's weird, Phoebe thought. She was going to say so to Margi, but Margi was intent on her iPod and trying furiously not to notice anything about their dead friend.

# CHAPTER TWO

PETE MARTINSBURG ENJOYED THE SUBTLE hush that settled in the locker room when he and TC Stavis walked in. He liked the way Denny McKenzie, their pretty boy senior quarterback, stepped aside to let Pete pass when he approached. He liked the way the newer kids cut their eyes from him when he looked their way.

As the reigning Alpha, he knew that there was no better place to reassert that position than in the locker room before football practice.

"Lame Man," Pete said, making a big show of clapping his hand on Adam's back as Adam sat lacing up his cleats. Adam was the biggest kid on the team, with a few inches and a lot more muscle mass than even Stavis, so a display of force with him was a good way of showing everyone what the social hierarchy of the team was. "What's the good word?"

He felt the larger boy's shoulders tense as Adam shrugged. "Same old same old, Pete. How about you?"

"Same here, horny as hell," Pete said. "You gonna set me up with that freaky chick you hang out with, or what? Morticia Scarypants?"

"No."

Pete laughed. "One night with me and she'll be wearing bright colors again."

"You wouldn't get along."

"Oh, so you're actually admitting you're friends, now?"

Adam didn't reply, and Pete enjoyed the flush that came to the big guy's ears and neck. It was all about finding the weak spots.

"Who's Morticia Scarypants?" Stavis asked. "Are you talking about the new art teacher?"

"No, you moron. Phoebe something, one of those goth chicks. Our boy Lame Man likes them pale and scary."

Stavis frowned, which Pete knew meant he was concentrating. "Is she the skinny one with the long black hair, kind of like a Chinese girl's, or the short one with the knockers and too much jewelry?"

"The first one," Pete said, enjoying that the conversation was making Adam look like he'd just bitten into a jalapeño sandwich. "Why? You interested?"

"Sure I'm interested. I got a thing for boots, and she wears those heeled ones all the time. And dresses. Hell, throw in the short one, too. A twofer."

The look Adam gave Stavis would have silenced anyone

else in the room, but Stavis was too dumb and too big to notice or care.

Pete socked Adam in the shoulder. "Easy, big man," he said.

"You guys are pretty funny," Adam said. "A riot."

Pete smiled. "Don't you think that the whole gothic thing doesn't really make a lot of sense today? I mean, why would you walk around pretending you're dead when you could actually be dead and walk around?"

"It's more than that," Adam said.

"Yeah? Like what?"

"I don't know. Music. The look, whatever."

"The look, huh?" Pete said. "The look sucks. She ought to get some color in her cheeks and start wearing normal chick clothes. She looks like a freakin' worm burger, you know? One of those zombies."

"Then I guess you shouldn't waste your time on her," Adam said.

"Just the opposite, man. I want to convert her before it's too late. Besides," he said, smiling down at Adam, "you know and I know she's a virgin."

Pete laughed and sat down beside him, and from the corner of his vision saw that runt Thornton Harrowwood looking over at them. The kid hadn't played freshman or sophomore year.

"Can I help you?" Pete said to him, sounding anything but helpful. The kid gave a frightened shake of his shaggy head and looked away. Pete chuckled to himself and turned back to Adam.

"You work out this summer, Lame Man?" Pete knew that something had changed over the summer with him and Lame Man, but he had no idea what it was. He, Lame Man, and TC had been the three amigos, the Pain Crew, all through high school, and now they'd barely had a whole conversation since they'd started football practice again.

"Little bit. I took a karate class."

"It shows, it shows. Looks like you dropped a few pounds and got a little more cut."

Adam nodded. "Thanks. You want to sleep with me?"

Pete laughed and peeled off his own tight shirt. He'd worked on his body over the summer as well, and the results showed in the definition across his chest and abdomen, and the lines were deepened by the rich tan he'd cultivated. He made the tight muscles along his arms ripple in case any of the wannabees were looking.

"I would, but I'm still sore from the summer."

He folded his shirt and then folded it a second time when the first fold didn't look right.

"Don't you want to hear what I did?"

"Sure," Adam said, sighing. "What did you do this summer? Go visit your dad again?"

"Yeah. I was in Cali all summer, nailing college girls at the beach."

"Sounds great," Adam said, yawning.

"Yeah, it was," Pete said, trying to ignore his disinterest. "It was like an endless supply, man. Drinking, partying, and sex, sex, sex. Talk about an endless summer."

"Wow."

Adam didn't see his frown, because apparently his sneakers were more interesting than Pete's stories. That hacked Pete off, because this time the stories were true. Partially true, at least. College girls had been populous and friendly to him this summer. But Pete left one key detail out of his oft-told tales; most of the college-age girls he'd hung around were friends of his Dad's newest girlfriend, Cammy—herself a college-age girl. Whatever. Adam's silence was beginning to frustrate him. It took him three tries to fold his T-shirt the way he wanted it.

"Is it just me," Pete said to the room, "or is this stinking hellhole overrun with dead kids this year?"

"Not just you," Stavis said. "There's like fifteen of them this year. I counted."

"Good for you," Pete said, punching Stavis in the meaty part of his shoulder. "Keep up the good work and maybe you'll pass math this year."

TC's grin was a lopsided slash on his round, doughy face.

"There are more dead kids this year," Adam said, without looking up from his laces. "There was an article in the newspaper that said this was a good school for the living impaired. Some of them are bussed over from Winford."

"Just what we need," Pete said, "a bunch of corpsicles shuffling around. Maybe this place really is hell."

"Hell on earth," TC said, shoving his sneakers and pants into his locker. The kid was hopeless, Pete thought. An overweight slob whose flesh hung from his barrel-shaped frame.

"Dead kids are getting up all over the country," a sophomore running back named Harris Morgan added.

Not all of them, Pete thought, giving him a sidelong look. Julie never came back.

Harris caught his look and panicked. Harris had been sniffing around Pete and TC since they'd started practicing in late August, and Pete figured he was looking to join the Pain Crew. He decided to favor the kid with a snicker and a quick nod of the head. With Lame Man acting like a wuss, it wouldn't hurt to round out the ranks.

"Did you see that one dead chick?" TC said, his wide belly hanging over the front and sides of his briefs. "The one in the skirt?"

"Yeah, I saw her," Pete replied. "And I think I could bring her back to life, if you catch my meaning." TC and Harris barked out forced laughter. "If the dead didn't disgust me so much."

His audience, on cue, fell silent.

"Hey, Adam," Pete said, leaning in close so that only Adam could hear, "did you hear who's trying to join the team this year?"

"Thorny? The kid you just terrified?"

"Naw," Pete said. He saw that he was going to have to work on Adam a bit this year. Adam just wasn't picking up on the backfield signals like he used to. "Somebody else."

Adam looked at him, waiting. That was something, too. Adam used to be a nervous sort of kid, awkward and gawky, uncomfortable in his own skin, and now he had a self confidence and poise uncommon in most guys his age. Pete thought that Adam was becoming more like him. He gave Adam his best conspiratorial smile, hoping to rekindle the early days, back when Adam gave him unwavering loyalty instead of grief.

"Somebody dead."

"Oh," Adam said. He flexed his ankle and decided he didn't like how the lace on his left cleat was tied.

"Oh?" Pete said. "Oh?" He looked over at Stavis and made the universal "I'm dealing with a moron" face. Stavis grinned and shook his head. "That all you've got to say?"

"What am I supposed to say, Pete?"

Pete frowned, because there it was again, that *attitude*.

"You don't care that a dead kid is joining the team?"

"I don't have feelings about it either way."

Pete had a temper, but he was good at riding it, turning it into something useful. He wanted to smack the kid, giant or no. Time was, Pete could have slapped him around and Adam would have taken it. But back then Adam didn't have that muscle tone, and Pete wasn't sure this was the right time to test how solid Adam had become.

"Well, Coach has feelings about it. Big time. I heard him arguing with the Kimchi over it." *Kimchi* was his name for Ms. Kim, the much beloved principal of Oakvale High.

"Really?"

"Yeah. He tried just about everything. Not fair to the other kids, practice season already started, blah blah blah. She wasn't having it."

"Well then," Adam said, getting up, "I guess he plays."

Pete rose with him. "Well, I guess we get some say in that."

Adam waited him out again.

Pete flexed his hand. "Coach wants us to take this dead kid off the board."

"He say that?"

"Not in so many words," Pete said, "but his meaning was pretty clear."

Adam nodded. "I'm going to play," he said. "I'm not going in for any assassinations."

"Oh?" Pete said, a wide smile on his face. "Not like last year?"

Adam stared back at him, a look of fury burning through his passive mask.

Pete showed his teeth. "Not like with Gino Manetti?"

Adam didn't reply. He gave each lace a final tug and seemed satisfied with the results.

"I don't think we can hang out this year, Pete," he said.

"Just like that, huh?"

"Just like that."

"Did I say something? Are you pissed because I was talking about Scarypants?"

"It isn't so much the things you say, Pete," Adam told him, "it has more to do with what you are."

Pete looked at him and felt the rage constrict his hands into fists.

"What I am," he repeated. "You want to explain that?"

Adam picked his helmet off the bench and shouldered past Pete.

Pete called Adam an asshole under his breath, but he said it loud enough for just about everyone to hear.

Gino Manetti had been an all-star running back for the Winford Academy Warriors. In a game in which Manetti had already scored three touchdowns on the Badgers, Adam put an end to his season—and his career—with a late and illegal hit to the knee.

Coach Konrathy had ordered the hit.

Not in so many words, Pete thought, shucking his jeans off. But the meaning was clear. He and Stavis had put the hurt on kids before at Konrathy's request; they didn't call themselves the Pain Crew for nothing. But neither had taken somebody out in such a permanent way before.

Pete thought about that kid from Tech he'd knocked unconscious late last season. He'd laughed out loud when he read about the game in the paper the next day and found out the kid had a broken clavicle. The news had him pumped up for days.

Not Adam, though. Adam was never the same person again after hitting that Manetti kid.

"Get back in there, Layman," Coach said, pushing Adam back into the locker room. Pete noticed that if Adam hadn't allowed himself to be moved, Konrathy wouldn't have been able to budge him. Adam had changed.

"I've got an announcement I have to make, and I want the whole team to hear it," Coach said.

"This about the dead kid, Coach?" Stavis said.

"Yes, it's about the dead kid," Coach said, his tone laden

with a level of sarcasm he reserved for only the most boneheaded of players. "But you are never, ever to call him a dead kid if he's within earshot, understand? We are required to refer to them as the *living impaired*, okay? Not dead kid. Not *zombie*, or *worm buffet*, or *accursed hellspawn*, either. Living impaired. Repeat after me. *Living impaired.*"

Pete watched the other boys in the locker room repeat the term.

"I want you to know that the decision to include this kid—" He took off his Badgers ball cap and ran his hand through his thick, close-cropped hair. "—this *living impaired* kid—has nothing to do with me. I have been ordered to let him on the team. So there it is. He'll be at practice tomorrow. Now hurry up and get your asses on the field."

Pete watched him turn on heel and start back up the stairs.

He didn't want any dirty dead kid in the locker room with him. He didn't want dead kids around him anywhere— not in school, not in his classes, and not on his football field. He wanted all the dead kids in their graves, where they belonged.

Like Julie.

Maybe if Julie had come back, he thought. Maybe if she'd come back he'd feel differently, and he'd learn to stand them despite their blank staring eyes and their slow, croaking voices. But she didn't come back anywhere except in his dreams. And now, ever since the dead began to rise, when she returned even to that secret place, she came back changed. She wasn't the girl he'd held hands with at the lake, she wasn't the first girl he'd kissed on the edge of the pine woods. She wasn't his first and only love.

She was a monster. She was a monster much like the one that was about to put on pads and a helmet and take the field with him.

# CHAPTER THREE

THE STD PUSHED THE PHONE INTO ADAM'S chest with the hand that wasn't holding the beer. "It's some girl," he said.

Adam breathed through his nose, catching the phone before it fell to the floor. There were oil stains on his new T-shirt from where the STD's knuckles pressed against him. Adam watched him walk back into the living room, where Adam's mom sat with one of his stepbrothers, watching sitcoms on Fox. The breathing helped.

"Hello."

"Hi, Adam," Phoebe said, "how was practice?"

Adam kept focusing on his breathing when he heard the STD tell his mom to get him some chips. The chips in the kitchen he'd just left with his second beer. God bless America.

"Adam?"

"Hey, Pheeble," he said, "sorry. I was just having a domestic moment with the STD."

"Oh, I'm sorry."

"Me too. What's up? Practice was grueling. Just got home. I was getting sweaty and sore on a muddy field playing for a man who might have been separated at birth from the STD himself. What are you up to?" His mother walked past him, smiled and patted his shoulder.

"Just listening to music, doing some homework. You know."

"Let me guess: the song playing right now has one of the three following words in its title: sorrowful, rain, or death."

Phoebe laughed, and the sound of her laughter relaxed him enough to stop using Master Griffin's breathing technique. Pete, Gino Manetti, the STD's constant harassment. Her laugh blew it all out the door.

"'The Empty Chambers of My Heart,' by Endless Sorrow, actually."

"I was close," he said.

"Death is always one of your three words, I've noticed."

"I've been right most often with it." Adam liked a lot of the music that Pheeble and Daffy listened to, the faster, more guitar-driven stuff, anyhow. The really heavy goth stuff didn't do much for him other than get him thinking about things he didn't want to think about.

"That's probably true," she said. "Hey, did Tommy Williams practice today?"

"Williams? That's the dead kid, right?"

"Yes, Adam. That's the dead kid."

"Oh. No. Coach says he's starting tomorrow. He isn't too pleased with the idea."

"Margi said she heard him arguing with Principal Kim about it."

"I've heard that too," Adam said. His stepbrother John's car roared into the driveway. "From Pete."

"Ah, yes. Pete. He's a big fan of the idea, I'm sure?"

"Why do you say that?"

"Maybe because I've watched your buddy Pete bully and mock just about everyone outside of you and his little band of cronies ever since he moved here."

"Pete has issues," Adam said. "I don't think we'll be hanging out much this year."

He heard her sigh through the phone, or at least he thought he did. Phoebe seemed awfully interested in this dead kid all of a sudden. Johnny walked in and punched him on the shoulder his mother had just patted. Adam caught him with a slap to the back of the head as he went to join the rest of the not-Laymans watching television.

"Really? Why not?"

"Pete and I are on divergent paths."

"I'm so glad you took karate, Adam." He could hear the smile in her voice.

"Really? Why is that?"

"You're different. Not different, really. But more of who you've always been. I can't explain it."

He thought she'd explained it just right, but didn't say so. "That's good, right?"

"I think it's great. Maybe now you'll actually be able to acknowledge me in the hallways if you're with one of your little cheerleader snips."

"Don't count on it," he said. "My cheerleader snips have got pretty high standards."

"Except in men," she said, and they laughed. "So, can you drive me tomorrow?"

"Yeah," he said, dropping the volume of his voice. "The STD is letting me use the truck."

"The beat-up brown thing? That's pretty big of him. What happened?"

"Mom's been working on him. I think she pointed out that it was a little unfair for us to have six vehicles and I was the only one who didn't get to drive one."

"Yeah, your yard looks like a used car lot. Or a 'well-used' car lot, as my dad says."

He heard the amused lilt in her voice and he closed his eyes so he could imagine her expression, one green eye peeking out at him beneath a swath of jet-black hair.

"He must be pretty ticked. We're like a bad cliché." He could picture Mr. Kendall arriving home from work and frowning as he looked over from his front steps at this weeks' crop of rehab vehicles littering the driveway and yard.

"He's okay, really. If we ever get ready to move, he'll probably ask the STD to clean things up until the house is sold."

"Don't ever move, Phoebe," he said. "You might be the only sane person I know."

She laughed. "Then you're in more trouble than I thought. Seven fifteen?"

"It's a date," he said, and hung up. A date. The idea of Phoebe moving left him with a weird feeling, a feeling that had nothing to do with Phoebe being the only sane person in his personal cosmos.

"Layman!" his older and frailer stepbrother, Jimmy, called from the other room. "Get off the flippin' phone! I'm waiting for a call."

"Okay," Adam said, and started his breathing again before heading down the hall to his room.

"About time," Jimmy said, shoulder checking him on his way to the phone. It was pathetic, Adam thought. Jimmy was half his size, but Adam had to pretend that he was intimidated by him to keep the peace in Casa de STD.

Adam lay on his bed and opened *Wuthering Heights*, the first major punishment of the school year, one that he was supposed to have endured over the summer. He closed it again after two paragraphs. There were a lot of things bugging him about his home life and the first week of school, and it took a few moments to identify which one was bothering him at the moment, but then he had it.

Phoebe cared as much about football as he did about the Brontë sisters. What was it about that dead kid?

"Is that a new dress?" Adam asked, observing Phoebe with a scrutiny only a childhood friend could get away with. He forced himself to say something, because if he didn't, he knew he'd be sitting there slack-jawed, his eyes goggling at her. The dress went down to her ankles, but somehow accented her gentle curves despite all the fabric. She had on her calf-high boots and a light gray vest, and her jewelry was all silver or silver-colored. He thought she looked like a gothic cowgirl.

Phoebe might dress a little weird, and sometimes she went overboard on the makeup, but there was no disguising how beautiful she was. She had wide hazel-green eyes that were mirthful no matter how funerary her clothing appeared, and her long dark hair softened her somewhat angular features and framed them in a way that made her face look heart-shaped from a distance.

He realized he might be blushing.

Her glance was quizzical, and he hoped she hadn't sensed the growing shift in how he felt about her. There was a hollow feeling in his stomach even though he'd filled it with eggs and sausage not a half hour earlier. The hollow feeling grew when he realized that the new dress probably had more to do with Tommy Williams than it did with him.

"It most certainly is," she said, brushing strands of her long black hair away from her eyes. It was one of his favorite mannerisms. "Thanks for noticing."

"And black, a completely different look for you," he said, taking refuge in the light banter that was as natural as sleep to them.

"Har-har. See, karate has made you more observant, too."

"All part of my never-ending quest to be more of the person I always was."

"Excellent. I applaud your dedication," she said, and he felt her light touch on his arm. "And how was your date with Emily last night?"

"Emily?"

"Brontë. *Wuthering Heights?*"

"Oh yeah, her. We've kind of hit a rough patch, me and Em."

"Too bad. I always thought that she could help you . . . you know . . . become the person you always were."

"That's just it," he said, mock-punching the dashboard. "She keeps trying to change me!"

They had a good laugh over that, and Phoebe, catching her breath, leaned her head against his shoulder. A clean hint of scent, some island flower that Adam could not identify, wafted from her jet-black hair, and the laughter died in Adam's throat.

"So," he said, "you're hanging out after school today?"

"Yeah. I thought I'd get some stuff done in the library."

"Library closes at four. Practice can go pretty late some days, especially when Coach is hacked off. And I think he'll be hacked off today."

"Why do you think he'll be hacked off?"

"Dead kid walking."

"About that," she said. "How does the rest of the team feel?"

"Oh, they're thrilled. Who doesn't want to hit the showers with a corpse?"

"Adam," she said, and there might have been a warning in her voice.

"I think Williams will have a difficult time," he said, being careful. "Many people are still terrified of the living impaired."

Phoebe nodded, hugging herself even though he had the heater on in the truck.

He stepped out on the ice; why not? "You seem interested in Williams," he said, pretending to glance in the rearview mirror. "In his situation, I mean."

She nodded. "I am. Some of the living impaired kids that moved into town this year are pretty interesting, you know? Like that girl we saw yesterday in the cafeteria."

"Yeah, she sure is."

"Pervert," she replied. "But really, dressing like she does, him trying to play football—I think it must take a certain bravery on their part, you know?"

"That's what interests you? Their bravery?"

"Well," she said, "the whole idea of the living impaired interests me. There's so many questions, so much mystery about the whole thing."

"Like with Colette," he said, and as soon as he said it he wished he'd stuck with the Williams angle.

"Like with Colette," Phoebe whispered, putting her head back on his shoulder. He hoped that she didn't notice how slow he was driving.

# CHAPTER FOUR

PHOEBE WAITED IN THE FOYER FOR MARGI after arriving with Adam at school. At least that's what she told herself she was doing, even as she peered over the top of her history textbook, watching Colette and then Tommy get off the bus. Colette moved with a dragging, side to side motion, her eyes fixed on a single point on some unseen horizon. She had trouble with the steps of the bus and then the steps leading up to the door, and Phoebe knew from previous observations that the motion required to open doors was very complex for her.

Tommy exited after her but reached the school first. He moved more like a student who had stayed up too late the night before, drinking soda and eating pizza, than he did a "typical" living impaired person. There was a pause between the motion of gripping the door handle and the motion of opening it, but the motions themselves weren't all that awkward. He held the door open for Colette and a pair of living girls, who sidestepped him in favor of another entrance rather than allow themselves to be victimized by Tommy's courtesy.

She watched Tommy enter the building. He was wearing a slate-blue polo shirt and jeans and white high-top sneakers. He seemed to stand straighter than the other boys she saw milling around, but that might just have been a side effect of the odd way he walked.

His shirt matched the color of his eyes, she thought.

Margi was the second to last person off the bus, having wedged herself in the backseat with her iPod and a dark, cloudy look on her face beneath her pink bangs. Phoebe waved, hoping to cheer her. No such luck.

"Hi, Margi," she said. Maybe excessive perkiness could win the day.

"Don't you 'hi' me," she said. "You, the traitor who abandons me to ride the doomsday bus. I wish that Lame Man had failed his driver's test. I'm going to fail my spelling quiz today."

"Oh my. You need to relax, girl."

"Relax, nothing."

"Doomsday bus? Come on."

Margi held up one bangle-covered arm. "Colette is really freaking me out."

"I know. Did they sit together again today?"

"I didn't notice."

"Yeah, you did."

Margi pinched her eyes and stuck out her tongue at her. "They sat together. He stepped back so she could get off the bus before him."

"Quite the gentleman, I've noticed."

"You would."

"Of course I would. We have the poet's eye, you and me."

"Please. I don't want to see any of it."

"Margi," Phoebe said, catching Margi's wrists as they waved around in front of her, "we'll need to talk to her sometime. It will be good. For all of us."

She thought that some of the color left Margi's already pallid cheeks. "Not yet," she said. Phoebe barely heard her over the boisterous entrance of another busload of students.

"We're going to be late," Margi said, and shook free of Phoebe's grip before giving her a weak smile. "Come on."

Phoebe got her bag from off the floor and followed her to their lockers, and then to homeroom.

Just eye contact, Pete thought as he leaned back in his chair, stretching and flexing his arms. That's all I need.

"Am I boring you, Mr. Martinsburg?" Ms. Rodriguez asked. No one other than Stavis and that blond bimbette Holly, who had dated Lame Man for a while, dared laugh.

"I'm not bored, Ms. Rodriguez," he said. "I'm just a little sore from yesterday's practice. I'm sorry I distracted you."

Ms. Rodriguez shook her head and went back to the board to discuss some thrilling quadratic equation or whatever.

I bet you were distracted too, you old bag, he thought. It isn't every day you get to check out guns like mine.

He turned quickly toward the windows, where Lame Man's freaky chick sat, and there he had it: contact. He gave her the look that always worked with Cammy's empty-headed friends, and if Morticia Scarypants didn't just melt away, he knew at least that her heart would trip a couple beats faster.

She looked away, just as quickly.

Got you, he thought, making a mental note to follow up on her later. He took a full inventory of her, half hoping that she would glance back and see the look of open appreciation on his face. She was one of the only girls in the class wearing a dress, and her sleek black hair really was striking. It fell past her shoulders, and she was pretty good at using it to keep her pale face in shadow most of the time. Pretty green eyes, but not fake contact-lens green. Her hair reflected the light falling through the windows.

Ms. Rodriguez called on the dead kid a few minutes later— the dead kid who would soon be putting on a nice new practice uniform and some spanking-new pads and helmet. New gear, old dead kid. Pete wanted to puke. He tapped his desk with his pencil and didn't stop until the dead kid answered—correctly, as luck would have it. That would make two questions more than Pete had been able to answer, and the school year wasn't even a month old yet.

He thought that Scarypants was looking over at him again, which was great, just great. It would really frost Lame Man if he were to tag her, even if the big dummy was too emotionally stunted to realize his true feelings for her. Pete thought maybe he'd tell Adam he'd quit with her if Adam would wise up and get his head back in the game. Maybe.

Pete lingered when the bell rang, figuring that if Scarypants engaged in a little more eye contact he'd go ahead and make his play right there between classes. He saw her stand up, and he liked the way her skirt cut in at her waist—she had a nice little figure under all of those layers.

She was taking her time as well, but it wasn't Pete Martinsburg, slayer of college girls, that she was waiting around for. It was the dead kid.

Huh, Pete thought.

She just won't shut up, Adam thought as he nodded his head to every third or fourth point that Holly Pelletier was making, and yet she wasn't really saying anything.

Holly must have noticed the insincerity of attention, because she moved close enough for him to smell the strawberry scent of her gum. Or maybe it was her lip gloss that he was smelling, or her hair spray. Adam realized that there was a time when the smell, and Holly's proximity to him, would have activated certain chemicals and drives in his body, but now all he could think was how artificial the scent was. He knew that if he were to bend down and kiss Holly, as he'd done many times before, it wouldn't be strawberry he would taste but some chemical version of strawberry. And for the first time, the idea of kissing Holly was not exciting; it was faintly nauseating.

What the hell is happening to me? he thought.

Holly never made full eye contact with him during her hallway monologues; she was too interested in who was walking by. Adam was having trouble maintaining focus as well because he'd seen Phoebe lingering by the bulletin board in front of the office down the hall, waiting to talk to him before he headed into practice. He almost missed the sudden wave of disgust that clouded Holly's traditionally pretty face. Adam turned and saw what she was sneering at: the pretty dead girl, she of the risqué hemlines.

"Ugh," Holly said. "I feel so bad for you, having to practice with that dead kid. Imagine if *that* went out for our squad?" She pointed at "that," not caring who heard her.

"Imagine," Adam said, watching the girl pass. She didn't move like a dead girl, that was for sure. Adam realized that her clothes had distracted him from another difference—she had a slight, barely perceptible smile on her lips. A bemused smile, one not so different from the one he often caught on Phoebe's face. Most of the other zombies he'd seen wore blank expressions, as if their facial muscles had hardened into place like old caulk.

Holly watched the girl pass, her fake strawberry lips curling. "It's so gross. Imagine having to touch her? I feel *so* bad for you. I hope the zombie gets cut from the team. There shouldn't be a dead Badger on the field. That would be *so* wrong. Can you imagine?"

I can *so* imagine, Adam thought. He watched Phoebe turn from the bulletin board when the dead girl approached, and he saw Phoebe smile at her before turning back and pretending to read whatever was posted there for the eleventh time.

Phoebe was holding some books against a cocked hip, her opposite shoulder dragged down by a black canvas bag stuffed with still more books. "Get it? A dead Badger?" Holly was saying.

"Hey, Holly. You'll have to excuse me. I need to go talk to Phoebe."

Holly's sapphire-blue eyes narrowed with such speed that Adam thought she would pop out a contact. "Phoebe? Who's Phoebe?"

"She is," Adam said, nodding over to where Phoebe stood, leaning precariously against the weight of her enormous satchel, while at the same time rubbing at the back of her calf with the toe of her black boot. "She's my best friend."

"*Her?*" Holly said. "That goth over there?"

"Yep," Adam replied. "I'll see you later."

People moved out of his way when he cut across the hall to join Phoebe. He wasn't into pushing kids around like Pete and Stavis were, but he'd spent the past two years hanging around them, and he'd never lifted a finger to curtail their actions, either. That was something else that needed to change, he thought.

"Hey, Pheeble," he called, a weird lightness spreading through his chest.

"Hello, Adam," Phoebe said, looking startled. Adam lifted the heavy bag of books off her shoulder.

Phoebe peeked out around him. "Uh, I think you might have ticked off Whatsername. She looks ready to rip the letter off your jacket."

"Yeah, I just dropped a bomb on her."

"Really?" Phoebe said as they started to walk toward the library. "Did you propose marriage?" She giggled, and Adam felt the lightness move out to his extremities. "Or was it something more earthy?"

"Ha-ha. And what makes you think it would be me doing the proposing?"

"Good point."

He heard his own voice slip out of banter mode, and for once he didn't care if Phoebe picked up on it. "I told Holly that we were friends. You and me."

Phoebe stopped. "Really?"

He looked at her. "Really."

She lowered her gaze, but when she looked back up at him her eyes were filled with mirth. "Won't they revoke your charter membership in the cool kids club?"

They started walking again. "Let 'em. The truth has set me free."

She bumped into him, trying to throw him off balance, but it was like a butterfly trying to unsettle an oak tree.

"I wish you'd taken karate a few years earlier, Adam," she said.

"Shut up, Pheeble. Or I'll chop you."

"Kii-ya!" she said, beating him to it.

He walked her to the library, and then headed off to go practice with the living and the dead.

# CHAPTER FIVE

TOMMY WILLIAMS WAS THE LAST ONE TO finish the warm-up lap around Oakvale Field. When he was a freshman, Adam had arrived back at the starting point consistently in the back of the pack, but Coach Konrathy didn't care, because Adam was about as wide as any two students and about as strong as any three. Six-foot-five freshmen were rare enough, but a six-foot-five freshman with muscles was like some exotic animal where Oakvale athletics was concerned.

But now there was an even more exotic specimen on the field. Namely, a dead kid.

Never before had a zombie tried out for any sport in the district. Tommy trotted—and what a weird trot, like someone was yanking his ankle from behind with each step he took— over to the loose cluster of players near Coach Konrathy. Many of the players were covered in sweat beneath their pads and trying to control their breathing, but the dead kid wasn't even winded.

He doesn't breathe, Adam remembered. Adam was sweating freely but his breathing was pretty good. Trying to keep in shape in the off-season with lifting and karate was paying dividends. He knew he'd never be the fastest guy on the field, but there was no reason he needed to be the most out of shape. Karate gave him some techniques that were going to keep him on the field longer, and it also gave him some tricks he couldn't wait to spring on those bastards from Winford. The season couldn't start soon enough, as far as he was concerned. Normally he loved the practice and the discipline of it, but the recent tension with Pete took some of the luster away—and that was before the dead kid joined. Adam tried to avoid getting caught up in the philosophical aspects of the new addition to the team, but it was undeniable that the presence of Tommy Williams cast a hush over what was usually a pretty boisterous event.

Adam liked to be the first one into the locker room, but not today. He found it was eerie to walk into the locker room and see the kid sitting there on the bench, all suited up, his eyes glossy and staring from within the shadow of his helmet.

Focus, Master Griffin whispered in his mind. Adam thought the interior voice was starting to sound more and more like Yoda now that he had cut back his trips to the dojo to once every couple weeks rather than twice a week like he had over the summer. Master Griffin would have to wait his turn behind Coach Konrathy and Emily Brontë.

And Phoebe.

Adam started some post-running stretching exercises, feeling his muscles lengthen and contract. This was Konrathy's first late practice—he liked to do a few a season to get the team used to playing under the lights—and Adam was pleased with the way his body was responding to the shifts.

Coach Konrathy frowned at Tommy as he joined the other players. He took his cap off and put his hand through his thinning hair, and Adam knew that some punishment was coming their way.

"We're going to start out with some tackling drills," Konrathy said. Adam thought he could hear him wheezing; he looked like he needed a shave and his eyes were glassy. "All the rooks line up. We're going to see how you take a hit."

Adam watched Tommy Williams take his place at the end of the rookie line. There were about twelve kids trying out for the team this year; mostly freshmen. Oakvale didn't have enough players to field both a JV and a varsity team, so pretty much all of the new kids would at least get a uniform to wear on the bench. Every year, though, there were a few who washed out, didn't make it through the practices, or decided they didn't enjoy peeling themselves off the ground with a headache and a bloody nose.

Adam watched Konrathy looking over his tacklers. Adam's instincts at the line caused him to read meaning in everything: eye contact, nonverbal cues, the inflection of the quarterback's voice as he called the signals. He watched a look pass between the coach and Pete Martinsburg.

"Look alive, Williams!" Coach shouted, drawing a dark laugh from some of his veteran players. Adam saw Pete watching Coach like a guard dog waiting for the attack sign. Pete smiled before putting his helmet back on, and then Adam saw why. Coach's left hand was held flat at his waist with thumb down.

Adam wasn't grinning at all. He was thinking of the last time he saw Coach make that sign, when he'd ended Gino Manetti's career by hitting him in the knee. He could still hear the tendons pop as he drilled into the side of Manetti's leg with his shoulder, and he could still hear the other boy's shrill cry of pain as he went down. It wasn't until Adam saw Manetti months later at the mall that he realized what he'd done. Manetti, his once-proud shoulders slumped as he gimped along with the old folks, had a cane, and there was a pretty girl, his girlfriend probably, loping along with him, alternately trying to encourage him pick up the pace or slow it down. Watching them—the look of pained resignation on his face, and the look of total loyalty and sympathy on hers— Adam thought that it was one of the saddest things he'd ever seen. He knew as soon as he'd made the hit that Manetti would never walk right again. He damn sure would never *play* again.

A week later Adam had signed up for lessons at Master Griffin's dojo. He had read a little about karate and thought it would help him with control. He also hoped it would help him with his guilt.

"You aren't still mad at me, are you, man?" Pete said, slapping Adam on the shoulder pads and snapping him out of his reverie.

"I'm not mad at you, Pete," he said, although he wanted to hit back. He wanted to blame Pete for his part in making him the ass he'd been for the past two years, but really he just wanted to punch himself.

"You saw it. Coach wants us to take out the dead kid," Martinsburg said. The lines were beginning the drill.

Adam looked back at him.

Pete gripped his shoulder. "Time to pick a team, Adam."

Adam shook off Pete's hand and held his ground without replying. Stavis and Pete weren't shy about using their fists— neither was Adam, for that matter—but he hoped it wouldn't come to that. He hoped Pete would allow Adam to outgrow him gracefully.

Right, he thought. That's how it will happen.

"You take first crack, Lame Man," Martinsburg said. "Case of beer to whoever puts him out."

First crack, Adam thought. There were a lot of things that living impaired people couldn't do—normal things like breathe and bleed.

He didn't think they could heal either.

The hollow resonant sound of Phoebe's heels on the metal bleachers echoed in the cool air of dusk, drawing looks her way from the few spectators sitting in small clusters and watching the action on the field below. Most of the watchers were parents, girlfriends, or kids from the marching band waiting for rides. Phoebe was used to getting stared at. Her all-black wardrobe, an even mix of vintage and trendy clothing, practically guaranteed she would get odd looks from her classmates. Knee boots with heels, long black skirts, dyed hair, and a flowing shawl ensured a raised eyebrow here and there. She didn't mind. She found that her look repelled people she didn't want to talk to and attracted those she did. The goth look wasn't nearly as popular as it once was, probably due to the appearance of the living impaired, but to Phoebe that just gave the style a subtle hint of irony, a private joke to be shared by a special few.

She stood for a moment, scanning the low ridge that rose up behind the bleachers. Koster Field, so named for a scholar athlete who had set track and field records for the state back in the early eighties, was surrounded on three sides by the Oxoboxo woods. A short perimeter of grass ran about twenty feet from the waist-high chain-link fence to the edges of the forest, making the tree shade that reached into the field late in the day appear to be a wall of spectators.

Phoebe sat down by herself. The bench was cold beneath the thin material of her skirt. She took her iPod out of her back-pack and slipped the padded earphones over her ears. She also took a thick rectangular notebook and a silver pen out of her bag and set them on the bench next to her.

At least my ears will be warm, she thought, punching up the new album by the Creeps and drawing her shawl tighter around her shoulders. There were a few girls wearing letter jackets over their cheerleader outfits at the end of her bench, whispering and pointing at the field. Phoebe could fit all of what she knew about football onto the first four lines of her notebook. The only thing she could make out from the action on the field was that some of the boys were running and some of the other boys were trying to knock them down.

Adam was always easy to spot. He was the biggest one on the field just like he was the biggest wherever he was. She looked around for Tommy Williams, but all the boys moved strangely in their padding and helmets.

Then she saw him, his movements stiff, but not because of his padding. He was taking his place in the line of boys about to be knocked over.

Killian Killgore of the Creeps was singing in her ears about being lost on the moors and chased by a banshee. Phoebe tapped on her notebook with her silver pen, the remaining lines of her poem floating somewhere in the air between her and the field, waiting for her to catch them and write them down.

Phoebe set her notebook on her lap and opened it. The first page was blank. She looked up at the sky and then wrote two words. Then she looked at what was happening on the field.

Adam hit Williams cleanly from the side and tried to brush the football out of his grasp. The hit was easy to make, because Williams was pretty slow and didn't try to fake at all. He went down, but Adam thought that if he hadn't jumped into the tackle, Williams might have kept his feet. Tackling the dead kid was like tackling a brick wall.

Dead weight, he thought. Ha-ha.

The ball popped loose and bounced end over end ten yards downfield. If it was the start of the season and Williams was already on the team, he'd offer his hand and lift him to his feet, but in preseason, Adam was supposed to spit next to his head and call him a wuss.

Williams stared up at him with flat, expressionless eyes that reflected the moonlight above. Adam walked away without saying anything. It was creepy, tackling a zombie.

"Layman!" Coach yelled, "did you play with dolls all summer? What kind of hit was that?"

A clean one, he thought, looking back at his old pals Pete and TC. The Pain Crew. It had been funny when they were freshmen and realizing that they were tougher than about ninety-nine percent of the student population; not so funny now that they were juniors and toughness might not be the number-one criteria for success in life.

TC was still grinning, like he was thrilled that he might still win the case of beer, but Pete was wearing that "what happened to you, man?" look that seemed to be on his face a lot when he looked at Adam these days. Pete whispered something to TC, who nodded and took his position at the line.

Adam watched TC hit the dead kid square in the back. With his helmet.

The sound of the impact echoed across the field. Phoebe could hear the hit up in the stands even with loud horror punk playing in her ears.

"Good hit, Stavis!" Coach yelled.

Layman's jaw opened as far as his chinstrap would allow.

Good hit? That was spearing, and it would be enough to get you disqualified from a game, if not the whole season. That sort of hit could hurt or paralyze someone.

It could even kill someone.

TC jogged over to pal Martinsburg, and they slammed each other's shoulder pads.

"I think he's dead, Jim," Martinsburg said, loud enough for most of the team to hear. He was laughing.

Adam walked toward Williams, who wasn't even twitching. He thought that the force of the hit might have shut him off like a radio being dropped on the concrete, but the dead kid pushed himself up from the turf with the knuckles of his hands, brought a knee up under him, and rose to his feet.

Adam couldn't help but smile when the dead kid flipped the ball to Coach Konrathy. A hit like that and he'd held on to the ball. That kind of focus deserved respect.

The attack continued for the rest of the drills. TC and Martinsburg always seemed to line up against the dead kid even though there were more tacklers than runners. Adam watched Pete hit Williams in the knees on his next turn, followed by TC wrapping his apelike arms around Williams for a neck tackle. Every hit was a dirty hit, but the only disappointment that Coach Konrathy showed was when Williams would pick himself off of the turf after each punishing slam.

The drills stopped when the pattern changed. Martinsburg was about to lay in a shot at knee level when Williams's hand came out and hit the tackler on the helmet. The stiff arm sent

Martinsburg face-first into the field while Williams lumbered away untouched. Adam noticed that some of the rookies—who themselves had been taking a beating in the drill—were trying to suppress sly smiles.

"Stay away from the face mask, Williams!" Coach yelled.

Adam shook his head. Williams hadn't come anywhere near the face mask.

Later in the practice Konrathy set up a scrimmage drill. By this time most of the players and rookies were spent and wheezing, all except the dead kid. Adam wondered if it was possible for the living impaired to get physically tired.

The drill was simple. The defensive line was to try and get through to sack Denny, and the offensive line was supposed to stop them. Coach put Williams on the defensive line right across from Adam.

Williams, dead or not, was not one of the bigger guys on the field. Five foot ten maybe, and built more like a wide receiver than a lineman. Layman thought that this was cheap, the same way all those hits from the Pain Crew were cheap. Karate class had taught Adam much about honor, and this didn't seem honorable at all.

But it was also dishonorable not to execute one's duty. Cheap or not, he'd have to hit Tommy Williams just like he would hit any other enemy lineman. He'd hit him cleanly, yes, but no less hard.

No one gets through, Adam thought as he spun the ball on the turf and took his stance. No one.

He snapped the ball to Denny and propelled himself

forward, getting all of his leg muscles into the launch. Williams was slower but he was coming up to meet the charge.

And he did. Adam was peripherally aware of the game; he noticed things at the edges of his vision, like Gary Greene on his right slipping and missing his block. He noticed that no one was helping Williams against him, something that other teams always did to keep Adam from ripping a hole open in their line.

He also noticed that he only moved Williams back about a foot.

The play ended. Greene's slip let one of the rookies through, and the rookie pressured Denny enough to throw an incomplete pass near the sideline. Adam unlocked from Williams, who turned without a sound and went back to his place on the line.

Holy crow, Adam thought. Williams had gone up against him unassisted, and Adam had barely budged him.

He looked around at his teammates to see if any of them noticed the amazing feat that Williams had just accomplished, but for the most part they were all bone tired and shuffling back to their places on the line. Adam knew that very few of them showed any real promise beyond high school—Mackenzie and Martinsburg were probably the best players besides him—and few had the sort of "field radar" that would allow them to notice the important details of the game.

Adam looked over at Coach, whose chubby face was pink with anger, his eyes narrowed to slits. He was shaking his head in disgust.

But it was what Adam saw beyond the coach, out at the edge of the woods, that really caught his attention.

There were a few people standing among the trees, watching them practice: three or four of them just standing like statues, watching. Adam might not have noticed them at all if it hadn't been for the big one, a black guy in a T-shirt as gray as the bark of the large oak he stood beside. Adam couldn't see the others well, but he knew from the way that they stood without moving that they were dead.

Out to watch their boy, he thought, but none of them looked familiar. The black guy had to be as big as he was, and there was no way that Adam would have missed him in the halls.

"Layman!" Coach yelled, taking off his cap and slapping it against his thigh for effect, "are you here to play, or what?"

Adam went back to the line. No one else seemed to have noticed the zombies. The living impaired people, he corrected himself. They were creepy, sure, but he couldn't let their presence distract him from the task at hand. He squared up on the line and looked at Williams. Williams looked back at him with unnerving calm.

He believed in knowing his opponents. On the next snap Adam hit him with equal force and again moved him back maybe six inches. There was no way that Williams was going to get through or around him, but Tommy didn't get knocked over like just about everyone else Adam played against, either.

The play ended with a completion. Coach called Adam a little girl and told him to put some effort into it.

Third time's the charm, Adam thought, and this time when he hit Williams he shifted his hips in the way he'd learned from

Master Griffin. Williams flipped to the side like a gum wrapper caught in a breeze. Denny darted through the Layman-size hole and ran down the field.

Williams was flat on his back. Adam saw light—either that of the harvest moon above or from the stadium lights— reflected in his flat eyes.

He offered Williams his hand, and the dead boy took it.

# CHAPTER SIX

THE LINES PHOEBE WROTE GLOWED WITH a blue electricity on the white page. She read the words a second time and the energy flowed back up through her fingertips. The feeling was something she rarely experienced when writing, despite the pages and pages of notebooks she'd filled. But when it came, the sensation was like the spark of life to her.

She really thought Tommy would not be able to get up from the first bad hit he took. The successive tackles were no less brutal, but up he rose, no worse for wear, that she could see. His resilience seemed to infuriate the tacklers, who pounded and slammed into him with renewed vigor. When he had stopped Pete Martinsburg with an outstretched hand, she had almost started clapping.

She read her poem a third time.

*Harvest moon*
*Above*
*The dead boy on the field*
*Trying to show us*
*What it means*
*To be*
*Alive*

If the cheerleaders saw her smiling to herself and thought she was a bizarro, so be it. It was worth it.

Practice ended with a final whistle from Coach Konrathy. She watched as Adam passed by the bleachers. He saw her sitting in the stands and gave her the most imperceptible of waves. She waved back at him like he was a Hollywood celebrity, hoping she'd embarrass him. But if he really had told Whatsername that she was his best friend, there wasn't much else she could do to tweak him.

Phoebe looked for Tommy and saw him standing at the far edge of the players as they moved in a loose knot toward the locker room. Slower than most, he trailed farther and farther until he was a good five paces behind even Thorny Harrowwood, who was limping along after spending the previous hour being pounded into the turf like a tent spike.

Then Tommy stopped, turned, and began walking in the opposite direction, toward the parking lot.

Or, Phoebe thought, toward the woods beyond the parking lot.

Sudden impulse, perhaps the electric spark pumping

through her blood, brought her to her feet after tearing the sheet of poetry out of her notebook and folding it into a small fringed square. Her book, pen, and iPod went into her bag, and then she was moving.

The sounds of her heels were like gunshots on the bleachers as she ran down to follow Tommy across the field.

"Get in here, Layman!" Coach Konrathy yelled, waving him over to his office door. Adam sighed, thinking that it would have been nice to have gotten more of his gear off than his helmet.

He gave Martinsburg a cold look as he passed, but Pete stared back without flinching.

Konrathy slammed the door. "What have you been doing all summer? Playing with paper dolls?"

Layman breathed deeply. Last year, he probably would have thrown his helmet at the wall if Coach yelled at him that way. There was a locker door that was bent and twisted like a pretzel, wedged so tightly in its frame that it no longer opened. Coach Konrathy had taken Adam out of a game last year for missing a block that led to Denny Mackenzie getting sacked for the first time in the season, so Adam had taken his frustrations out on his locker.

But this was the new-and-improved Adam Layman, he of the zenlike calm. The new-and-improved Adam thought before he struck.

"No, Coach," he said evenly, his pulse and breathing under control. "I was taking karate classes and working out."

Coach Konrathy threw his hands up in exaggerated disbelief. "Karate? Karate? I thought karate was supposed to make you tougher, not make you into a total wussy."

Adam felt his breathing quicken, but he concentrated and reeled it back in. No, Coach, he thought, karate has nothing to do with making you tougher, it has everything to do with bringing more control, clarity, and focus into your life.

*Focus.* When he was ready he answered his coach with a question.

"Is there something wrong with the way I practiced today?"

Coach leaned over the desk so that he was inches away from Adam, close enough that Adam could smell the breath strips that he popped by the dozens during practice.

"You tell me, Layman," he said. "You think there's a problem with your play when you can't even push back a dead kid?"

"I pushed . . ."

"You didn't do squat! You're practically a foot taller than he is, and you couldn't do anything but knock him off balance! And you helped him up! What the hell were you thinking? We don't help rookies up until they make the team, you know that!"

Adam summoned Master Griffin's calm but insistent voice in his head. *Focus, Adam. Focus.*

"He's hard to move when his feet are planted," he said as evenly as he could. "I think he'd be good on the offensive line."

Konrathy drew back like Adam had spit in his eye.

"You do, do you? How about instead of him joining you on

the line, you join him on the list of kids I cut from the team? The last thing I need on this team is an attitude problem."

Master Griffin had taught Adam all about *chi*—the life force that centers all beings—in their studies. Focusing on the chi was good for the breathing. It was good for the heartbeat. It was also good to keep Adam from reaching out and squeezing Coach Konrathy by his fat red neck. Despite all this goodness, he couldn't keep his face from flushing.

"I know your grades, Layman," Konrathy said, getting in Adam's face again. "And I know your stepfather. Without football you've got no hope of getting into or paying for college."

He let his words sink in for a moment, and they sunk deep, plunging through the protective calm that Adam was trying to maintain.

"You'd better straighten up and bring your 'A' game to next practice, Layman," Konrathy said. "Now get out of my office."

There were things that Adam wanted to say and do, but he didn't. Coach was right. Without football he wouldn't be going anywhere; he'd end up staying in Oakvale all his life, working at his stepfather's garage, lifting tires and handing wrenches to his stepbrothers. Oakvale might have an "all-inclusive" approach to their team sports, meaning that they didn't cut kids from the team—but Adam could not take the risk. Excessive bench time would ruin his chances of a pro career.

Stavis snickered as he walked by to his locker. Stavis was another guy destined to be an Oakvale lifer, and if Adam didn't make it to college he'd be stuck here changing oil and replacing brakes for knuckleheads like him for the rest of his life.

He thought he'd rather be dead than live in a future like that. Dead without returning. Not like the Williams kid. *Permanently* dead.

His old locker, the one he'd smashed last year, was next to his new locker. He wanted it that way so that he would have a constant reminder of who he'd been and who he was trying to be. He breathed in stages, and his fists unclenched without him being aware of it.

I didn't think the living impaired were supposed to be able to move so fast, Phoebe thought as she walked through the muddy field. Her boots, as shiny and slick as they looked, weren't helping, either.

There was an economy of purpose to Tommy's movements, like he was walking the straightest line possible from his last position on the field toward his destination. His path would take him directly into the woods that surrounded Oxoboxo Lake. Phoebe's grip on local topography wasn't great, but she knew that somewhere on the other side of those woods was her house. Tommy's as well, somewhere a little farther along their bus route.

Tommy moved between two parked cars and reached the short band of grass before the tree line just as Phoebe made it to the track at the edge of the football field. She closed the distance somewhat, but she wasn't going to catch up to him before he entered the woods, as she had hoped.

The only hesitation in Tommy's purposeful stride was when

he removed his helmet before stepping into the trees. The light of the harvest moon shone on his silvery blond hair in the moment before the darkness swallowed him.

Phoebe's breath preceded her, puffs of vapor like spirits dancing in the light of the moon. It wasn't until she was in the woods and the moonlight had disappeared that she paused long enough to think about what she was doing.

The cover of Oxoboxo woods was nearly total; the canopy of leaves above was like an impenetrable shield against the moonlight.

What on earth am I doing? she thought. Even before dead kids began coming back to life, the Oxoboxo woods was a place of mystery and strangeness, a place where ghosts stories were set and told, stories that had preceded the town and the Europeans who eventually settled there.

But she knew what she was doing, deep down. Tommy Williams was in her head, his white, angular face, the ghost of a smile on his lips, and a pale light in his slate-blue eyes. She knew he would stay there until she summoned the courage to talk to him. And then . . . ?

Phoebe looked over her shoulder, back at the pale parking lot lights visible through the trees. Adam would be looking for her soon, right after he showered and changed. He wouldn't want to be standing around his stepdad's truck, wondering where the heck she was. And if he was too late, the STD would probably flip out like he usually did and ground Adam for the next month of weekends, and it would be her fault.

She looked into the dark shapes of the woods ahead. She could see the vague, grayish outlines of trees now that her eyes had adjusted to the lack of light. She counted fifteen steps and then stopped. The woods were so thick even here at the perimeter that they seemed to swallow sound as well as light. She was aware that there weren't birds or insects making any noise, and how strange that was.

She sighed and stood there a moment, imagining each breath as a piece of her soul, and then imagining each soul fragment rising toward the impervious roof of leaves and seeking a way out to the sky beyond. There was no way she could tell which way Tommy had gone through the forest.

What on earth am I doing? she thought again. A cold wave of fear shuddered through her. She decided that pursuing Tommy through the Oxoboxo woods was a bad idea. She turned around.

And the dead boy reached for her, his pale eyes glowing in the darkness.

Thornton was the only kid left in the locker room while Adam laced up his sneakers. He was standing in front of his locker with a towel around his waist, admiring a huge red bruise that ran the length of his rib cage.

"Wow," the younger boy said, wincing, "I really took a beating today."

"You got up, though," Adam said. "That's the important thing."

"Yeah, I guess I did," Thornton replied, grinning from ear

to flapping ear. The poor kid looked like the guy from *Mad* magazine, but without the missing tooth. Adam smiled to himself, thinking that the season was still young. Thornton walked off to the showers whistling, and Adam thought the kid wouldn't have been any happier if he'd thrown a hundred dollar bill at him.

*With great power,* he thought. The Spiderman clause. Grandmaster Griffin had spent the whole summer drilling that into him, teaching him that being a foot taller and twice as strong as everyone else were not rights, they carried certain responsibilities. He taught Adam that he possessed gifts that could be of great benefit to society or, if abused, could cause great harm to all, including himself.

He was still thinking about that when TC, Pete, and Harris Morgan stopped him in the parking lot.

"Hey, Lurch," Pete said, "where's your zombie friend?"

"I'm not in the mood," he said, waiting for Pete to get out of his way.

"Whose team are you on, big guy?" Pete said, stepping closer instead of aside. "The living or the dead?"

"I play for the Badgers, Martinsburg, same as you. Get out of my way." He looked over his shoulder where his truck was parked but he didn't see Phoebe, which was good. He didn't want her to see this.

And deep down, he knew he didn't want them to see her, either.

"That zombie is coming off the team, one way or another, Layman," Pete said.

Adam was trying to decide if he could take all three of them. TC was the biggest, but Harris and Pete weren't small, and Harris at least was faster than he was. He figured if it came to a head, he should probably try and drop Pete as quickly as he could, because then the other two might lose the heart for it. In fact, Morgan didn't look much like he had the heart for it anyway. Adam was willing his body to stay loose when Pete, either sensing where the situation was heading or having made his point, moved out of his way.

Adam moved past him, his eyes not leaving the senior's sneering face as he walked by. He threw his duffel into the bed of the truck from ten feet away.

"Pick a team!" Martinsburg called after him.

Adam got into the cab of the truck and slammed the door. The engine came alive on the third cough of the ignition, and he turned the radio up. He hoped his three teammates were gone by the time Phoebe showed up.

Phoebe gasped as the dead boy's hand reached out to touch her hair and let the black strands run through his fingers. She was motionless when he brought his hand away and held it in front of her face. He held it close enough so that she could see the leaf he had removed.

Now the only sound was of her breathing. Tommy dropped the leaf, and she watched it hover momentarily before it disappeared in the dark.

"I . . . I was following you," she said, instantly regretting speaking. Her whisper reached her ears like a fire alarm in the silent woods. He was living impaired, not a moron. Of course she was following him, why else would he pull the stealth act and sneak up on her? She wondered if his eyes—eyes the color of rain clouds in the dull fluorescent glow of the classroom, but reflective, like those of a cat—could register the heat she felt radiating from her cheeks.

"I wanted to talk to you," she told him. "I wanted to tell you that I thought you were brave for doing this. For playing football, I mean."

Tommy didn't say anything, which heightened her embarrassment. He was tall, his shoulders broad. He held his helmet at his side by its face mask. What kind of idiot was she to chase after a living impaired kid anyhow?

Maybe all her common sense had flown away along with her breathing. She was aware, as if from a great distance, of reaching into her pocket and withdrawing the square of notebook paper.

"I also wanted to give you this."

She held the square out to him and watched him regard it with his glowing eyes, his face without expression. There was a moment of agony as he looked at the square without moving, and all Phoebe could think about was the time in seventh grade when Kevin Allieri refused her invitation to a couples' skate at a party in the Winford Rec Center.

But then Tommy reached out and took her poem. She inhaled him when they touched; the smell was like a morning breeze drifting across Oxoboxo Lake.

They stood there without speaking for a minute, each

passing second a moment of awkwardness that she felt as acutely as the boys on the field felt their tackles and hits.

"Well," she said, her ears ringing as she was unable to bear the silence any longer, "I've got to go get my ride. Good night."

He didn't say anything—anything at all. Her eyes were downcast as she turned and started walking toward where she thought the parking lot was. But standing in the forest with Tommy, giving him her poem, it was so surreal, so bizarre that she wouldn't be surprised in the least if the Oxoboxo woods, lake and all, went spinning off the surface of the earth and into the stratosphere. Whatever electrical magic she'd had was now engulfed by a cold inky wave of embarrassment and fear. She was about to collide with a tree when she thought she heard her name.

She turned. All she could see of Tommy was a pale shimmering outline and his eyes, two pale disks of moonlight, about fifteen feet away.

"I think," he said, his voice soft and flat, more like the memory of sound than sound itself, "you are brave, too."

The tiny moons disappeared and she was alone. There was darkness all around her, but it no longer flowed within her. She was smiling when she joined Adam in the warm cab of his step-father's truck.

# CHAPTER SEVEN

THE WEEKEND MOVED ALONG WITH A TIRED languor, as though time itself had become living impaired. Phoebe spent long hours sitting on her bed listening to music with her notebook and pen on her lap, writing nothing and talking to no one. Friday night had been confusing in so many ways, but part of her wanted to hold on to that confusion a little longer and analyze it.

Margi called Saturday night, but in typical fashion, the hour of conversation was focused mainly on Margi. Her his-tory report, the show she was watching, the shoes she was planning to wear on Monday, her thoughts on the new Zombicide downloads. Phoebe didn't mind; having a Margi-centric conversation was always entertaining, and it allowed her to not talk about what was on her mind—*Tommy* . . .

She almost gave herself away when Margi asked her if she

was able to accomplish much at the library—she'd forgotten her cover story completely.

"Oh, sure," she said, but really she had just drawn some cartoons in her notebook and flipped through a book she found on the Spanish Inquisition.

"That was convincing," Margi said. "You know, I wish I'd let you talk me into staying, because I'm really having the hardest time doing this history report. Of course, Mr. Adam Lame Man probably wouldn't have driven me home. I swear, Phoebe, he has been crushing on you since the third grade."

"I didn't move here until the fourth grade."

"Well, he probably crushed on you in a past life. Do you ever see him roll his eyes when I tag along?"

"That's ridiculous, Margi."

"Yeah, I know. I'm way hotter than you," she said, and then laughed.

Phoebe had long known about Margi's fascination with Adam, who was the first friend Phoebe made when she moved to Oakvale. They'd hit it off because Adam hadn't known any other girls who liked comic books, and she was a better swimmer and Frisbee player than he was. He didn't acquire his size, or "inflate," as Phoebe liked to tease him, until middle school. Then his taste in athletics started to lean toward contact sports—sports that she had no interest in, despite having a decent outside jump shot.

Adam was a year older but had stayed back in the second grade, so now they were both juniors. High school took them down different paths—Adam was one of the popular ones,

Phoebe drifted on the edges. Neither made a big deal of their friendship at school because the incongruity of it confused their individual circles of friends.

That incongruity, as much as the length of their friendship, was what made it so special. Phoebe still felt that there was no one she would rather play Frisbee or go swimming with in the Oxoboxo.

It was special enough that Phoebe knew neither of them would ruin it with more complicated feelings. She thought Margi was the one who was crushing, but for some reason would never admit it.

"You *are* hotter than me, Margi."

"Right. Is there anything you tell the truth about? You've got the height, the good skin, the cheekbones. What have I got?"

"The wardrobe? And the . . ."

"Don't say it."

"Well, you do. I think they get more attention than my great cheekbones."

More banter, and then they hung up when Margi's father yelled at her to get off the phone. Phoebe went back to scratching in her notebook.

Adam instant messaged her on Sunday night when she was surfing around looking for the latest news on the living impaired. He asked her if she wanted a ride to school on Monday, which was weird because he never asked that. She typed back *Sure* and punctuated it with a goofy emoticon that was the Weird Sisters' trademark, a round, horned smiley with eyelashes, a tail, and tongue wagging moronically out of the side of its open mouth.

*Cool,* was his return message, unadorned. *Seven?*

*Yup.*

*We should play Frisbee sometime.* Then he signed off.

That, she thought, was really weird. The only time they tossed the disk now was when one of them needed someone to talk to. There were things Phoebe couldn't talk to Margi about, and there were things Adam was reluctant to share with any of his friends on the football team. They were an odd pair—but odd pairs were what kept life interesting.

That sentiment instantly brought Tommy to mind. When she switched off the light she imagined his faintly glowing eyes in the darkness of her room, and this time she had no fear at all.

Adam arrived at her house at seven sharp, the STD's pickup coughing in the driveway while he walked into the kitchen and helped himself to a banana. Phoebe, the last one out, wrote a note for her mother telling her not to hold dinner and then locked the door behind her. "Thanks, Adam. How'd you get the truck?"

"The STD's got Mom's car today," he said. "He brought her into work so he could change the oil. We've got time to get a coffee, if you want."

"I'm okay, but you can get one."

He shrugged. "I like the streaks of red. You do it your-self?"

Phoebe reflexively touched the spiked tips of her hair and thought of falling leaves. "Of course. Thanks."

"Yer welcome."

He backed the truck out of her driveway and took a left, which meant he was going the long way, around the lake.

"Soooo . . ." she said, "what's up?"

She now realized how quiet he'd been since Friday. A fair question that night would have been, "Hey, Phoebe, what the heck were you doing in the woods?" But he'd never asked it. He hadn't noticed, and Adam noticed most things around him. She realized she'd been so preoccupied that she hadn't even realized how preoccupied he'd been.

He shrugged again. "Later. I just want to drive around a little."

"Sure, Adam. Driving's good. Smell that clean lake air."

He laughed, and she knew him well enough not to pry it out of him. He would talk to her when he was ready.

The Oxoboxo woods looked different by daylight, and from the outside. She always thought the trees there were set more closely than in other forests, as if they were huddling together to keep secrets from the world outside their sylvan borders. She and her friends had spent a great deal of their young lives in the woods and the lake. The Oxoboxo was a place where one never felt a hundred percent safe, and that was what made being there so exciting.

Exciting, at least, until Colette died there.

"So you never told me how practice was," Phoebe said, turning to look out the windshield. "How was it playing with the corpsicle?"

She'd intended it to be a diversion, but she saw by his shocked look that her words struck close to whatever it was that was eating at him.

"Oh," she said.

"I thought that wasn't PC. Isn't that what you and Daffy were telling me the other day at lunch?"

"I'm *kidding!*" He was fronting and it was obvious, but if he wanted some time before he told her what was bothering him, that was fine.

His shoulders twitched again like they did whenever he was nervous. "You know, the dead kid wasn't so bad."

"Really?" she said, secretly thrilled.

"Really. He's strong as hell. I mean speedwise, he's slow. But he picks stuff up fast. By the end of practice he'd figured out a way to counter me throwing him. It was pretty cool, really."

"Wow, who would have thought?"

"Not me." And that was all he said about Tommy.

He rolled the car into the student parking lot moments later, and then they were out of the truck and making the long trek to school.

"Hey, I've got practice again tonight," he said. "You need to go to the library or anything?"

She smiled at him. "You want to do some midnight Frisbee?"

"Yeah," he said. "I might just need to do that."

Everything was normal on Monday. The living went quickly from class to class, chatting about weekend dates or the hundred subtle liaisons that occurred in the time that elapsed between the morning bell and lunchtime, while the dead moved in straight lines and shared their thoughts with no one, not even each other. Phoebe roamed and looked for Tommy Williams, catching glimpses of him from a calculated distance. He might have the advantage in the Oxoboxo woods with his stealth and his moonlight eyes, but among the living, she held the upper hand. Here in the fluorescent halls she could watch him at all times without him being aware of it.

But that did not mean the dead were incapable of surprises, as Margi proved by dropping the biggest one of all in the hallway after final bell. She was packed and ready to go to the bus before Phoebe even made it to her locker—that's how big it was.

"Sorry, Margi," Phoebe said, "no bus today. I'm hitting the library again."

"You're kidding," Margi said. "I have *got* to talk to you."

"What's up?"

"What's up with *you*?" was her reply, with more than a hint of accusation in her voice.

"Is this twenty questions, Margi? I don't know what I'm supposed to say now, and I don't want to make you miss your bus."

Margi looked at Phoebe, a mixture of impatience and sympathy on her smooth, round-cheeked face.

"Pheebes," she said, "you're my best friend and I love you. You know that. But something is up."

"Right, we've established that. So what, pray tell, is up?"

"Let me ask you: have you ever seen a living impaired kid draw on his notebook?"

Phoebe sighed. Leave it to Margi to bring the melodrama. "I don't think so, no."

"Do they ever contribute to the *Oakvale Review*?"

"No."

"Or take art or music classes?"

"No."

"Pick up digital photography or gardening on a kooky whim? Or basically do anything creative at all?"

"No, not to my vast knowledge."

"Not even decorate their lockers?"

"Margi! Get to the point!"

She did, and drove it home. "Tommy Williams has a poem hanging up in his locker," she said, "and it sure looks like it was written in your handwriting."

The precise moment that Phoebe's mouth opened in response to Margi's statement, the trunk to Pete Martinsburg's car popped up with a click from his key. The car was barely a month old, a birthday gift from dear old long-distance dad.

Pete wasn't stupid enough to think his dad's gift was anything other than an expression of spite for Pete's mom. It was all about getting vengeance on the ex-wife.

But hey, free car.

He led Adam and TC over to the car. It took some convincing to get Lame Man out of the locker room, and even now the big stiff was making a show of how boring this all was to him.

Pete knew how this was going to go, but he felt the need to give Adam one final test of faith before changing his strategy.

He went to the trunk and withdrew his football gear. Beneath the long black duffel bag was a trio of scuffed and scratched baseball bats. Pete took the aluminum one out of the trunk and, gripping it tightly with one hand, snapped it around with his wrist a couple times. His smile was cold and wide.

"Smacked fourteen homers with this baby my last year in the PAL league. I hit .313 that year."

Stavis nodded with appreciation, but Pete could tell that Adam was a hairsbreadth away from making some wiseass comment, and his grip on the bat tightened until his knuckles were white.

"We're going to teach zombie boy another sport after practice," he said, sneering. He dropped the bat back into the trunk, where it landed with a hollow thud, a sound not unlike the one that particular bat would make against a human skull, Adam thought.

Then the trunk slammed down with such force that the thought disappeared.

"Pete," Adam said. He didn't look so smug any longer, which strengthened Pete's resolve to carry the plan through.

"Yes, Lame Man?" he replied. "You have something you would like to contribute?"

"You aren't really suggesting that we go after this kid, are you?"

Pete laughed. "Why not? There's no law against it."

"C'mon, Pete. That's just stupid."

"Stupid? I'll tell you something that's stupid. Your little girl

Morticia Scarypants having the hots for a corpsicle, that's stupid."

"Leave her out of this. I'm talking—"

"You're flapping your jaw, but you aren't talking. Your chick, the one you've had a thing for, for what, your whole life? She's writing poetry to dead guys. She's coming to practice to watch a dead guy. A *dead guy*, Adam. How sick is that?"

"Shut up, Pete." Adam turned a bright crimson shade, and Pete smiled.

"And you're just going to let it happen. You aren't even going to try and get her playing on the right team, are you?"

Stavis, who was still smart enough to catch the signs, moved to Adam's left.

"What happened, Adam?" Pete said, dropping his voice to a low whisper. "What about you is so repulsive that the girl you've been pining after for years turns to a zombie for her lovin'?"

Adam took a step forward, his own hands balled into fists, but that was as far as it went. Pete wished he had taken a swing, because then they could throw a few punches, bloody each other up, and at the end of it they'd be friends again. They'd be the Pain Crew.

"You can walk away, Adam," he said to Adam's back, "but I'm not done. I'm not going to let that charming pale young flower lie down with a corpse. Not while I live and breathe."

Adam continued his walk back toward the school.

Pete said he wasn't done, and he meant it. The rumor making a loop around the school like a brush fire was so absurd that Pete couldn't even get his mind around it. A living, breathing, blossoming sixteen-year-old girl having a thing for a dead kid? It was just plain unnatural. Why not go just go and lie down with a farm animal? At least an animal is *alive*. He decided that he'd better take matters into his own hands.

Pete saw her in the library. He was already late for practice, but what the hell. What was coach going to do, fire him? And lose two interceptions a game? No way.

Besides, getting into this girl's skirt would be well worth the extra wind sprints.

"Hey," he said, sitting across from her.

She looked up and removed a shell-like headphone from one ear. Someone was screaming in pain through the speaker, the volume audible halfway across the library. He liked the way her dark eyeliner made her eyes look even more like a cat's. Slinky. And the best part was that this girl had no idea how slinky she was. She didn't have any friends in Pete's normal datepool, the cheerleaders and other gum-snapping types, the Toris and the Hollys and the Cammys who would have hooked up with him even if he were the ugliest guy on the football team.

He gave her a smile calculated for her to feel it in her toes. Hanging out with the college girls this summer had opened up some new worlds to him, femalewise. This girl was dark, she was serious, and she was bookish. He figured that less experienced guys wouldn't look at her twice, but to Pete, all of those factors were just part of the sweet secret that girls like this held, a sweet secret just waiting to be told to the whole world.

"Hey," he repeated.

"Hey," she said, a hint of question in her voice. He liked that. And she was shy; her pale white skin was turning pink at her throat. He made a point of watching the color spread.

"I saw you at practice yesterday," he said. If there was one thing that girls liked, it was to be noticed.

"You did?"

"Yeah, I did. I'd look up and there you were, watching us."

"I was waiting," she said, "for Adam."

Pete smiled inwardly to himself. Morticia was so far out of her league.

"Layman? He's not your boyfriend, is he?"

She laughed and shook her head, the pink glow hitting her cheeks. Her skin was the skin of angels, he thought, soft and white. He almost reached out to stroke her cheek, but he figured she'd spook. Soon.

"That's good," he said, "because Adam's a good friend of mine, and I'd hate to have him mad at me."

She stopped laughing. "Why would he be mad at you?"

Now it was his turn to laugh, which he did as he leaned back in the creaky library chair, spreading his arms so she could catch the definition of his arms.

"For asking you out."

She looked back down at her history book. Pete leaned forward. Willowy girls liked big guys, and he was a big guy; he made the shadow of his shoulders fall across her like a blanket.

"Because even if he was your boyfriend, I still would have asked you."

She looked like she was having trouble catching her

breath. It made him think of other ways he could make her breathless.

"I need to study," she said, her voice just above a whisper.

You do, he thought. "So is that a yes?" he said, his hand drifting to her arm. She was wearing a light sweater, and he rubbed the black fabric bunched at her elbow with his thumb and forefinger. "I can drive you home if you like. I'll tell Layman we've made some plans. You've probably seen my car around."

"No." Her voice was so soft he almost didn't hear it.

"No, you haven't seen my car? It's the . . ."

"No," she said. "No, I don't want to go out with you."

"What?"

"No," she said again. "Please stop. People are looking at us."

"I don't understand." He really didn't.

"I don't want to go out with you, Pete. Thank you, but no."

"Why not?" he said.

"I just don't want to. Please let go of my sweater."

He did, and leaned back, the chair groaning against his weight. First Layman cops a big attitude, and now this. Pete had been hiding his rage ever since his father packed him off to the airport without even dropping a dime to wish him a good flight, and now it threatened to erupt from his whole being.

"'I don't want to' isn't much of a reason, is it?" he said, his face close to hers.

"It's the best reason," she said, and he was surprised at how poorly he'd misjudged her. "Can this conversation be over, please?"

Pete forced his hands to relax and pushed himself slowly back from the table.

"Hey, I'm sorry," he said. "I thought I was picking up on something that I guess maybe I wasn't. I know I'm a little headstrong, probably because most of the girls I go out with like that. I'm sorry if I offended you."

She softened, but only a little. "It's okay," she told him. "I'm sorry I didn't give you a more graceful answer. Really, I'm flattered."

He gave a nod that he hoped made him appear wounded and crestfallen—as though he really cared what Scarypants thought of him. "Well, I didn't give you much of a chance, did I? Headstrong, that's me."

She smiled. He held out his hand.

"Friends?" he said.

She looked at his hand, and then up at his face, and smiled. "Friends," she said, and held out her hand for him to take.

He was planning on walking away. But something about the feel of her cool, slim hand in his changed everything. She had long, slender fingers, and he blinked and thought for a moment, just one moment, that he was holding Julie's hand. He hadn't had a relationship with anyone like that since Julie died. Julie who died and would not, could not, come back. The rage welled in his mind.

Still gripping her hand, he leaned in close and whispered into her ear. "Layman is tagging you, isn't he?"

She looked up at him then, her eyes more like a cat's

than ever. The color returned to her face and she tried to pull her hand back, but he was too strong.

"Least, I hope the Lame Man is tagging you. Because if I find out that you are passing me over for some dead meat, I might get pretty upset. I might get pretty damn upset that the girl I had pegged for a closet nympho is really a closet necrophiliac, you know what I'm saying? And people, dead or otherwise, could get hurt."

She didn't look away even though he was squeezing her hand hard enough to bring tears to her eyes. After a time he blew her a kiss and stood up, giving her hand a gentle stroke as he let go.

# CHAPTER EIGHT

THE HITS KEEP ON COMING, ADAM thought, watching Stavis rock Williams with a blindside chop block. It would have knocked the wind out of a living kid. Williams was pushed off his feet, and Stavis used his momentum to drill him into the ground.

Williams made no sound. But then, Williams never made a sound.

The play, a halfback draw, was over before Stavis's hit. And it was nowhere near Williams.

Adam was experiencing a tightness in his chest that had nothing to do with his physical conditioning, but with the mental conditioning he'd worked on over the summer with Master Griffin.

He closed his eyes and could see Master Griffin as he met him on the first day of class; his shaved head smooth and glossy in the bright light of the dojo, the merest hint of a smile beneath his thick black mustache.

"We are all gifted with power," he'd said to his students. Adam watched the lithe, catlike way that Master Griffin walked around the practice mat, almost like he was gliding along on the balls of his feet.

"All of us," he'd said, looking at each of them in turn. "It is what we do with that power that is important."

Then he told Adam to try to tackle him. Master Griffin was shorter and more compact than Adam, and much lighter. Adam came at him with a wary confidence. Tackling people was what he did. He moved in low, going for the legs.

Suddenly he was airborne, but it was a short flight. Griffin brought him onto the mat and somehow cushioned his fall. Then instead of letting him go, Griffin maintained a tight grip on Adam's arm with one hand, while his free hand was cocked back and ready for a flat-palm strike. Adam looked at the rigid line of that palm and knew with certainty that Griffin could break his nose or smash his face in with one quick thrust. But he just tapped Adam twice on the chest before hauling Adam to his feet.

"Adam has power," Master Griffin had said to the class. "I have power. Each of you do. What will we do with that power?"

That had been the only physical contact of the first session, Master Griffin tossing his biggest, most athletic student like he'd toss his dirty socks into the laundry hamper. He'd spent the rest of the session teaching them forms and talking about personal responsibility.

"Layman," Coach Konrathy yelled. "wake up and get your ass on the line."

Adam complied and "put his ass" on the offensive line. As he did he could almost hear Master Griffin's calm voice in his head, asking him just how much of his ass he was willing to put on the line for his beliefs.

The dead kid got up the way he always did—slowly—but did not seem injured by Stavis's illegal hit. Adam tried to get into his head. What, if anything, was going on in there? Why was Williams even out here? Did he have something to prove? Was it love of the game? Did he even realize that there were teammates of his working hard to take him out of the game—permanently? There just didn't seem to be any point in offering himself up to the punishment he was experiencing.

And—the thought creeped in like rain through cracks in the ceiling—did Phoebe really have a thing for him? Why would she find him the least bit attractive? How on earth could a dead kid interest her in that way? There had to be some crossing of wires, somewhere.

Back in the locker room, the sudden silence told him that Williams was passing through. Williams didn't shower, at least he never showered with the rest of the team in the gang showers down the hall. He didn't sweat, and one could just as easily wash the mud and turf off one's face at home as in the showers.

Adam shucked off his shoulder pads and covertly watched the reactions of his teammates as the dead kid walked by. The open hostility of the remaining Pain Crew was pretty easy to register: Martinsburg was whispering something to his head thug, Stavis, and to Harris Morgan, who looked to be first on the recruiting list now that Adam had dissolved his membership.

Most of the team turned away, like the presence of the dead kid was an embarrassing secret that no one wanted to acknowledge. Denny Mackenzie, whose neck had been saved today by Williams when he blocked a charging Martinsburg coming in for the sack on Mackenzie's blind side, was pretending to be fully engrossed in something that Gary Greene was saying. Williams opened his locker, withdrew his backpack, and headed for the stairs.

Tommy Williams was a player on the Oakvale Badgers, but no one seemed very pleased about it. Konrathy was leaning in the doorway of his office, watching Williams make a deliberate path toward the exit.

Thornton Harrowwood had the locker closest to the door. He was sitting on the wooden bench with a damp towel wrapped around his skinny waist and was stuffing his filthy uniform into a large green duffel that was nearly as big as he was. He looked up at Williams as he passed and held up his hand like it was no big deal, and Williams slapped it gently without breaking his ponderous stride. Like it was no big deal.

Adam smiled, but then Konrathy called Thornton into his office. Adam became so engrossed in trying to figure out what was being discussed behind the closed door that he almost didn't see his former pals in the Pain Crew skip the showers and follow Williams out the door.

"He's talking to that spooky bitch," TC said as they crossed the lot toward the woods.

"Doesn't change a damn thing," Martinsburg said. He was twirling the aluminum bat, his wrist making swift circles. "Harris, she's your responsibility. If she tries to run or interfere, stop her."

"Aww, man. I ain't hitting no girl."

"I ask you to hit her? Just stop her." Martinsburg pointed the bat at Harris Morgan's chest. Pete outweighed the fit running back by a good forty pounds and Harris took a half step back, but it was Pete's expression more than the bat that did it.

"Stop her," Harris said. "Got it."

"If you plan on punking out like Layman, you'd better tell me now."

Harris shook his head.

Martinsburg looked again at their quarry, who had turned and entered the woods with Little Miss Scarypants.

"Now, what do you suppose they're up to in the woods?" he said, sending a long stream of spit through his teeth and onto the asphalt. "She gonna help him get his pads off?"

The dead kid had knocked the wind out of him at practice today. Pete had been just a few steps away from leveling the quarterback with his shoulder when the dead kid came from *his* blind side and sent him down, driving all of the wind from his lungs.

There was one moment when the zombie stood over him while he lay flat on his back, his closed lungs struggling to draw in air. The dead kid looked down, and Pete felt a moment of breathless panic as he saw the cold gray glare of his eyes under the shade of his helmet.

*Now you know what it feels like to be dead.* He could hear the zombie's voice in his head, and he thought he detected the slightest tic of a muscle by his mouth.

*How do you like it?*

Williams left him there on the turf. Pete's breath was slow in returning, and through it all he couldn't get the image out of his mind of the zombie laughing at him. He was frightened by that image, but fear only served to make him angrier. No one, dead or alive, was going to laugh at Pete Martinsburg and get away with it.

"We'll just come up the path," he said, "and when we get close we'll spread out in the woods. I'll kick it off. Unless they smell Stavis here."

"What?" Stavis said, looking down at his grubby and fragrant uniform.

"You could have at least showered," Pete said. "You reek." Harris laughed, nodding in agreement.

There were a few kids and their parents milling about the parking lot, but no one really seemed to notice them. Pete nodded to his two henchmen.

"Okay," he said, "it's on."

They followed him into the woods.

* * *

Phoebe wasn't sure how she was going to broach the subject of her poetry with Tommy, but he saved her the trouble once they stepped into the woods.

"I have your poem . . . in my locker," he said. "I realized . . . that this . . . could be a problem for you."

Phoebe shook her head and tried to think how she should respond. Funny how the clarity of his speech, which flowed more quickly that the average living impaired person's, was giving her speech troubles.

"No," she said, "I was surprised, I guess."

"Your friend," he said, "with the pink hair."

Phoebe laughed. "Margi."

"I did not think of the . . . consequences," he said, somehow getting all those syllables out in one word. "Everyone . . . knows. I am sorry."

She shook her head and took a step closer to him. He didn't smell like someone who had been at football practice for the past couple hours. He didn't smell like a dead person, for that matter, either. The crisp scent of pine and autumn leaves was all she could smell. His skin was so smooth and white; he looked like a sculpture come to life, someone's idealized version of a young man, without blemishes or flaws.

"Don't be," she said, touching his arm, which felt like smooth stone beneath her fingers. "I wanted you to have it."

He gave a slight nod, his bottomless stare fixed on her. His gaze was disconcerting, to say the least. His eyes did not track when they were talking, and when he blinked, which wasn't often, she could count to three before his eyelids touched. He raised his hand as though to touch her cheek, and she thought of how gentle he'd been when he'd removed the leaf caught in her hair.

He surprised her by turning away, the movement sudden and swift.

"This is . . . difficult," he said, "for both . . . of us. Friendship . . . always is. Much less . . ."

She didn't get to hear what else he had to say, because at that moment two figures moving low ran at Tommy. One swung a baseball bat and hit Tommy in the chest, knocking him off his feet and onto a rotting log. His helmet bounced twice and landed near Phoebe, who shrieked as a third figure came from behind her and leveled a bat at her throat.

"Shhh," Harris Morgan said. Then he smiled.

"So you like sports, do you, zombie?" Martinsburg said. The bat he was holding out at his side came down with a sickening crack. Phoebe couldn't see where the blow landed, her line of sight obscured by Harris and the log that Tommy had fallen over.

"Stop it!" she yelled.

"Shut her up," Martinsburg said over his shoulder as he prepared himself for another swing. Harris looked back at Pete, unsure how to translate that particular directive, and Phoebe used the moment to jump on him, swinging her fists.

She punched him once, and they stumbled, but she ended up on her back, the limbs of the trees high above spinning in a kaleidoscope of fall colors. She was dimly aware of Harris rising from her, cursing and licking his lower lip.

Then she heard the sound of Martinsburg's bat whistling again.

It wasn't easy to rise to a sitting position, but she did. Martinsburg, grinning, was motioning for Stavis to take a turn. She tried to stand, but Harris poked her in the chest with the end of his bat and told her to sit down, swearing. She was gratified to see a thin line of blood where her knuckle had cut his lip.

She saw Stavis hefting the bat with both hands over his head.

"You have no idea how big a mistake you have made."

The deep, even voice belonged to Adam. Phoebe turned to see him looming on the path from where Martinsburg and his cronies had launched their attack. He was speaking to Harris, but he turned to look at the other two as well.

"Stay out of this, Layman," Martinsburg said. Stavis lowered his bat and regarded the new threat. Phoebe noticed that he was actually wider and heavier than Adam, although not quite as tall or as fast, but Phoebe guessed it didn't really matter when Stavis was holding a baseball bat.

"No," Adam said, and took two steps, closing the distance between them.

"I told you to pick a team, Lame Man," Martinsburg said.

"Guess I did," Adam replied, still moving right at Pete.

"Be a shame if one of your knees got busted out," Martinsburg said, but there was a shrill quality to his words, an absence of confidence that hadn't been there before Adam had appeared. "Like your gimp buddy, Manetti."

"A shame," Adam repeated. He was about five feet away from Pete when Harris dropped his bat and dove at him.

Phoebe called a warning as she scrambled for the bat, and Adam's left foot lashed out and caught Harris square in the solar plexus, knocking him flat on his back. But Stavis didn't have the qualms that Harris Morgan did about striking a fellow Badger, apparently, because just as Phoebe turned, he stepped in and gave a short thrust to Adam's stomach, and Adam went down on all fours. Stavis made a move like he was going to hit him again, and Phoebe screamed, throwing the bat Morgan had dropped, which Stavis deflected awkwardly, stumbling backward.

She stood up and faced the two, and saw that behind Martinsburg, Tommy had risen to one knee. Martinsburg caught her reaction and turned back toward Tommy.

"You just stay put," he said, "or I'm going to walk over there and beat your girlfriend bloody." He looked back at her and spat. "I might do it anyway."

Phoebe watched as Tommy looked up at his attacker and did one of those three-second blinks. Then he set his leg down and kneeled on the soft soil of the forest floor.

"Yeah, that's right, dead boy," Martinsburg said, twirling the bat, "she might not come back."

There was such hatred in his voice that Phoebe could almost feel it. Stavis stood between her and Martinsburg; Adam was retching into the soil. Harris was groaning, but she heard him starting to get up.

Tommy was staring up at Pete. Pete walked toward him and readied his bat.

The first figure that appeared out of the woods was nearly Adam's size. To Phoebe's buzzing mind it was as though he had materialized out of the darkness of the forest. A second figure and then a third—the girl with platinum hair who liked short skirts, and a pale boy with a shock of faded red hair—appeared from behind trees and clusters of brush, until there were six figures in a loose ring around them.

Harris, still separated from his bat and rubbing his chest as though to erase the print of Adam's sneaker, made another colorful comment as a seventh figure appeared behind him on the path. The eerie silence with which these new players had appeared sent a chill through Phoebe, one that was amplified as yet another figure walked past to stand between her and Stavis.

"Colette?" Phoebe whispered.

Martinsburg and his cronies milled around, not sure how they should react to this new development. There were eight kids total, standing in a loose ring around them, motionless as tombstones.

The giant one, his movements awkward, helped Tommy to his feet. He regarded Pete with an expressionless stare that still managed to convey a threat that was unmistakable.

He straightened up, and Phoebe saw that he was even taller than Adam. He loomed over Stavis and Pete the way the gray trees loomed over them all, the newly risen moon throwing its shadow over them like a shroud.

"You . . . might . . . not," he said, his halting voice filled with quiet force, "make . . . it . . . back."

The ring of dead kids began to close. The giant spoke, and

each of them took one step forward, tightening the circle like a noose. Harris was the first to run, but Martinsburg and Stavis were close behind.

Phoebe, her eyes wide, thought she caught the hint of a smile on Tommy's lips. But the moment passed, and she ran over to Adam, who was still trying to shake off the effects of the hit to the gut.

"Are you okay?" she said, crouching next to him. Her skirt was ripped and there were twigs and leaves all over her. She was going to have a great time explaining this to her parents.

Adam groaned and spit. "P . . . peachy."

The dead kids had begun to disperse, silently shambling back into the forest in the directions they had come from. One of them, the young-looking boy with the red hair, made an odd high bleating sound, and Phoebe realized he was trying to laugh. Short Skirt Girl smiled at her and said "Bye!" in an amused, perky fashion before skipping away down a pine needle–strewn path.

Phoebe scanned for Colette and saw her just as she turned and melted into the forest. Soon all but the giant and Tommy were gone.

"This is Mal." Tommy motioned. "He is . . . large."

"Hello, Mal," Phoebe said, and Mal began lifting his arm. "Tommy, are you hurt? My God, they were hitting you with baseball bats!" Mal finished lifting his arm, and three of his fingers twitched. Phoebe realized he was waving.

Tommy's head swiveled from side to side. "The blows did not hurt . . . as much . . . as the . . . idea . . . of the blows."

"Tommy," she said. Adam coughed.

"Take care . . . of your friend. And"—Tommy paused, but something made Phoebe think it wasn't the half-speed of undeath that was holding him up, but finding the right words—"*thank* him . . . for me."

She watched Tommy walk into the forest, Mal following him like an enormous shadow.

# CHAPTER NINE

P HOEBE LOOKED OUT THE GRIMY WINDOW of Adam's truck, scanning the woods and thinking about those kids and where they might have come from. Her sleep last night had been restless, and having Adam drive her to school today just made the events of last night seem even more surreal.

Last night Adam hadn't said two words on the entire drive home, and this morning it was she who didn't want to speak.

"Do you understand what happened last night?" Adam asked. "What was that? I don't even know who half of those kids were."

"Colette," she said. Her heartbeat felt like she'd tripled up the caffeine dose in her morning brew. "Colette was there."

Adam was silent for a moment. "Yeah. Colette. And that girl from the lunchroom, I recognized her. But who was that big black kid, and the one that was smiling? Where did they all come from?"

"I have no idea."

"You know, some of them were watching the practice the other night," he said. "They don't go to our school, do they?"

"Some of them do," she replied. "Not Mal, though."

"Colette didn't say anything to you, did she?"

"No. No, she didn't."

Adam nodded as though he understood the significance of that.

"That was weird, is all I can say. It's like they live out there or something. Or whatever you call it."

Phoebe hugged herself. "Not to mention that you were hit with a bat. A *baseball bat*, Adam."

"Yeah," Adam replied. "Yeah, that was a first. Clocked the wind right out of me."

Phoebe looked over at him, and he was actually grinning, like it had been some kind of adventure.

"Adam, has football left you that desensitized to violence? How can you be so flip about what happened?"

"I've gotten into fights before," he said, shrugging. "Never with bats, though."

"Is that all you have to say?" she said. "We watched Tommy get *beaten*. With *clubs*. I think they were trying to kill him."

"He's already dead, so . . ."

"Adam!" she said, her voice loud enough to make him flinch. "You know what I mean!"

"Okay," he said. "Okay, I'm sorry. I guess I wasn't thinking of it like that."

"They could have hurt us too, if Tommy's friends hadn't come."

"I don't think they would have done that, Pheeble. I think . . ."

"So it's okay to beat a living impaired person?"

"That isn't what I mean. I . . ."

"Let's just drop it, okay?" she said, turning toward the passenger window.

"I'm sorry," he said after a moment. "I guess I just wasn't thinking about being threatened. The whole thing was just so weird."

She didn't answer and continued to stare out the window. She thought it was weird, too, and with each passing mile she expected a living impaired person to appear suddenly out of the woods.

"Say," he said, "what were you doing out there, anyhow?"

Phoebe squeezed her eyes shut. "Let's not talk right now, okay, Adam? Can we talk about this later?"

"Sure, Pheeble," he said. His touch was light and brief on her shoulder. "Sure."

Phoebe didn't know why she felt like crying. She opened her eyes and saw dead kids, dozens of them, lumbering through the woods toward the road. She blinked once and they were gone. She looked back at Adam, as solid and sure as an oak tree. He was trying to rescue me, she thought, and the guilty realization cooled her anger.

"I wish I'd gotten some sleep last night." That's all I need, she thought. My mind's playing tricks on me.

"I slept pretty well, surprisingly," he said. "That violent lifestyle I have, always punching guys, living or dead. Gives me inner peace, you know?"

"You're a jerk, Adam," she said, but when her eyes met his, she burst out into a nervous laugh.

She wanted to catch a quick nap in the warm, safe confines of Adam's truck, but when she opened her eyes again, Oakvale High loomed ahead, ready to admit the students coming off the few buses parked in the looping drive. Adam found a space in the student lot, and they started toward the school.

They approached just as Tommy Williams was getting off the bus. He was wearing new jeans, new high-top sneakers, and a navy blue polo shirt.

"He doesn't look like a guy who took a beating last night," Adam whispered.

"No," Phoebe agreed. She thought he looked good. Flawless.

Tommy saw them and tried to smile. Then he waved, and suddenly Phoebe did not feel so tired anymore.

Margi, who didn't have any of Adam's social grace or under- standing, began badgering Phoebe the moment she saw her.

"What's wrong, Pheeb? Ohmigod, you look terrible."

"Thanks, Margi. I can always count on you to help build my flagging self-esteem." Phoebe laughed.

"No, really," she said, her bangle-covered arm looping around Phoebe's shoulder. "What's wrong? Did something happen?"

"Yeah, something happened," Phoebe said, almost instantly regretting her words.

"What? What is it?"

"Nothing." Phoebe tried to play it off. "I'm just kidding." Her locker popped on the first try, and Phoebe wondered if her luck was changing.

"Phoebe, talk to me. Did you have a fight with your parents? With Adam? Did he ask you out?"

Phoebe, having been interrogated by Margi dozens of times, knew that eventually she would build up to "the dead kid."

"Colette," Phoebe said. "I saw Colette last night."

Phoebe's strategy worked; she found the only topic on which she could get Margi to shut up completely, and she didn't even have to lie to do it. Margi's eyes narrowed under the fringe of pink spikes dangling from her forehead.

"We need to talk to her, Margi."

Margi sucked at the corner of her lip, the same corner she'd pierced last summer.

"You couldn't have saved her," Phoebe said. "It isn't your fault she died. It's nobody's fault."

Margi looked away, fellow students passing on either side of them in a rush to get to class.

"We didn't handle it right," Phoebe said.

"I know," Margi said finally, "I know."

"But we have another chance. We can . . ."

"I know," Margi said, her voice rising. "I know, I know, I know! I just can't do it now!"

She turned on her heels and jingled down the hall at a rapid clip.

Phoebe watched her go, wondering just why she'd felt the need to alienate all of her good friends in a single morning. "Wait up, Margi!" she called, hurrying to catch up.

"Not another word," Margi said.

"My lips are sealed," Phoebe responded, following her into the classroom.

Moments later Principal Kim's reassuring voice came on the PA after the morning announcements to let everyone know that there would be a schoolwide assembly immediately after homeroom, and that students were to proceed in an orderly fashion to the auditorium.

Margi, never one to enjoy silence, reached over and gripped Phoebe's forearm. She had pink smiley skulls painted over the black background of her fingernails.

"Yes! No history today!"

Phoebe returned her smile. Margi was always quick to bounce back from a tiff, which was a great equalizer for someone as excitable as she was. The bell rang, and they started to proceed toward the auditorium. The halls were already filled with students. Phoebe saw the pumpkin-like head of TC Stavis bobbing above a sea of students. The auditorium was twice the size it needed to be for the average enrollment at Oakvale High; she and Margi were herded into a pair of seats toward the middle of the cavernous half bowl.

"Slide all the way down," Mr. Allen said in his monotone. "Fill every open seat."

Phoebe noticed that there were some open seats around the few dead kids who were scattered around the auditorium.

"Is this about the fund-raiser?" Margi said. "I hope it isn't the fund-raiser. If it is, I hope it isn't the candles. Who wants to buy a candle anyway? For fifteen dollars?"

Phoebe didn't think this was about candles. She watched Principal Kim, looking bright and energetic in a peach suit, lead two people onto the stage—the first a young woman in a pale blue suit. Her shiny blond hair was pulled back in an unassuming ponytail, and she wore glasses with dark frames and wide lenses. She was simply stunning.

She stopped at the edge of the stage to help her companion, a frail old man who held her arm while being assisted on the other side by Mr. Hill, the gym teacher. Phoebe was terrible at guessing anyone's age over twenty, but she had him pegged as being in his eighties. He turned briefly to the crowd while making slow progress up the short stairway, and Phoebe thought there was something familiar in the beaked nose and shock of sculpted white hair.

"Who's the codger?" Margi asked.

Phoebe, not quite able to place his face, shook her head.

Principal Kim quelled the crowd and made introductions.

"Today we are joined by two people who have dedicated their lives to promoting and educating people on the topic of diversity. Prior to the events of recent years, the term 'diversity' had been most typically used to describe a diversity of culture, religion, ethnicity, or sexual orientation. Today the term may also be applied to diverse states of being. Alish Hunter and his daughter Angela have created the Hunter Foundation for the Advancement and Understanding of Differently Biotic Persons, and are here today to discuss an exciting new opportunity that you will have here at Oakvale High. Please join me in welcoming Angela Hunter to the podium."

The applause was halfhearted, but rose in volume when the hormonal males in the audience realized how gorgeous Angela Hunter was. With her intentionally bookish look, Phoebe thought she looked like a youthful teacher in an eighties hair-metal video, the one who would rip off the trappings of schoolmarmery as soon as the guitar solo kicked in, to reveal a hot-pink bikini and stunning tanned body beneath. Ms. Hunter smiled with pursed lips, almost a smirk, which made Phoebe think that she had calculated the crowd's reaction exactly.

"Thank you, Principal Kim," she said. "And thank you, students of Oakvale High, for your attention and the opportunity to speak to you today about differently biotic people. The people that we at the Hunter Foundation refer to as *differently biotic* are those people that most of you would refer to as *living impaired*. They are the people that some of you, and many outside the walls of this school, would refer to as *zombies, corpsicles, dead heads*, the *undead, worm food, shamblers*, the *living dead*, the *Children of Romero*, and a whole host of other pejorative names designed to hurt and marginalize."

"Wow," Margi whispered. Whatever hormonal restlessness Ms. Hunter had inspired in the auditorium was silenced by the quick, no-nonsense manner in which she had lobbed a mental hand grenade into the room. Virtually every student, Phoebe noted, was as silent as—well, as silent as a differently biotic person.

"We at the Hunter Foundation feel that even the term *living impaired*, although created I'm sure with the best of intentions, is in fact pejorative, as it implies that people who are no longer alive but still with us are broken and or defective. In much the same way that the term *handicapped* was widely recognized as being insulting to differently abled persons, so too is living impaired an insult to those who live differently biotic lives.

"At the Hunter Foundation, we do not believe that the dialogue regarding the understanding and promotion of differently biotic persons begins and ends with its terms and definitions, however. It is one thing to create the appropriate language of discourse; it is another to actually move the culture to a point of acceptance, and we believe that the correct way to do that is through the application of science, both with traditionally hard science and the social sciences."

"Whaaaaat?" Margi said. Phoebe shushed her.

"We believe that differently biotic persons are, in fact, alive—and yet no one knows how they are alive. Part of what we do at the Hunter Foundation is aimed at discovering what makes a differently biotic person tick, for lack of a better term, from a biological perspective. But another part of what we do is discovering what makes them tick from a psychological perspective. Being differently biotic puts these people in a very small cultural group. They are a true minority—and the minority status is one that is sure to have deep psychological implications."

Head shrinkers for the undead set, Phoebe thought.

"Another function of our foundation—and the one in which you can help us the most—is to take the results of our studies and tests and bring them to society at large. Our goal is the complete integration of differently biotic persons into society. We dream of a world where a differently biotic person can walk down a crowded city street without fear. We understand that for our dream to become a reality, everyone else on that crowded city street must be able to walk without fear of the differently biotic person, as well. To that end, we are asking for volunteers among you to participate in our learning lab. Your school is unique among Connecticut schools in that you have the highest ratio per capita of differently biotic persons among you; therefore you have both the responsibility and the privilege of helping teach the rest of the country and the world about what DB people have to offer, and vice versa.

"What we are offering is a chance to learn about yourselves and those who are different from you. The Hunter Foundation, while economically solid, is not an organization that many members of the status quo want to participate in. The topic of DB rights is still politically incendiary. We understand that for someone to join us requires a certain degree of bravery and emotional fortitude. But for those of you who are interested in making a positive social statement, at the risk of attacking the norms of society, working with us can be a deeply rewarding experience.

"We have some friends in the political realm, and we have been able to get our Differently Biotic Work Study program accreditation. For those of you who sign up, you will be given three AP credits, providing you give your full and best effort to the program."

She waited a moment for that to sink in. Phoebe wondered if AP credits were enough of a carrot to interest anyone. Many of the students in the audience were clearly put off by the whole topic, and she looked around to see if any of the *differently biotic* students had any feelings about the proposed course.

"There are two components of the work study. First, you will have to work. We have a variety of positions that we need to staff: clerical, maintenance, and security. You will be paid for your time. The second component is that you must participate in a weekly DB focus group, where traditionally biotic students will meet in a moderated discussion with DB students. The goal at all times will be acceptance; we understand the road to acceptance can only be taken through mutual understanding."

She paused, basking in the stillness of the room. "Are there any questions?"

Very few hands went up. Angela pointed at one toward the front.

"What do you mean by 'differently biotic'? Are you saying that dead kids are alive?"

Phoebe couldn't see the girl who had asked the question, but she could see Ms. Hunter's wry grin.

"No," she said, "I am saying they are differently biotic—that they are alive in a different way than, say, you and a mushroom are alive." Phoebe smiled; the smarter kids in the school laughed.

"In truth, we do not understand the biology of a DB person. It is one of the fields that our foundation is endeavoring to explore."

"Why do only teenagers come back as zomb—as differently bionic?"

"*Biotic.* We don't know yet; nor do we know why the phenomenon seems to happen only to American children. But surely there is a clue there; a popular theory is that there is something that triggers the process in the series of immunizations that American children undergo."

Ms. Hunter nodded to a girl on the aisle near the front of the room.

"My dad says that it isn't natural, people coming back from the dead. He says that there's stuff in the Bible that talks about the dead coming up out of their graves, and that it means the world will end soon."

Ms. Hunter frowned, but Phoebe thought her expression was one of concentration rather than disgust.

"With all due respect to your father's beliefs," she replied evenly, "we have found nothing in our extensive studies that suggests the phenomena of the differently biotic is a sign of the Apocalypse. Of course, we could be wrong, but we prefer to look at the phenomenon as a scientific puzzle to be answered rather than a metaphysical conundrum."

There was a thin pale arm among the few that were raised, and when Ms. Hunter smiled and pointed, the question was slow in coming. Phoebe could hear Margi's sharp intake of breath next to her.

*Colette.*

"Can . . . dead . . . kids . . . join . . . too?"

Phoebe thought she could write all of Colette's post-demise speech on a single Post-it note.

Angela's response was effusive. "Absolutely. As I said, Oakvale High has the distinction of being the first school in the state to commit to creating a DB studies program. I think the experience will be more rewarding for everyone if we get a strong DB enrollment."

She focused on Colette as she spoke, as though the warmth of her smile could bring some color back to her pale dead skin.

"I believe we have time for one more question . . . Yes, in the blue sweatshirt."

"How much do you pay?"

Ms. Hunter laughed. "You could probably make more at the mall. But the educational work study is certain to look better on your college application than a part-time gig at Cinnabon."

Principal Kim rejoined Angela at the podium. She waited for the polite laughter to end, then she said, "Thank you all for giving us the chance to talk to you today. I am hoping to see a good number of you at the foundation."

Principal Kim began clapping and allowed the students to clap for a few listless minutes before talking about how the application process would work, what the qualifications were, and how many would be accepted.

"Applications can be picked up at the front of the stage from myself or Ms. Hunter, or, if you prefer, in the office. The applications are due on Friday."

"Well, that was still better than history," Margi said. "Too bad it didn't cut into English. Phoebe . . . where are you going?"

Phoebe looked back but remained silent as she joined the few differently biotic kids walking against the tide of students eager to make their way out of the auditorium. She saw Tommy, Colette, that boy Evan who was in the woods last night, and a few others. Adam was waiting at the end of an aisle.

"Are you going to sign up?" she asked him.

"Yep. You?"

"Uh-huh."

There weren't many takers, but that fact didn't seem to drain any of the warmth from Angela Hunter's smile as she handed Phoebe an application, which looked to be three grayish sheets stapled together.

"Could I have two?" she asked. "I'm hoping I can convince my friend to join with me."

"Have a whole stack," Ms. Hunter said, peeling off copies. "I don't think I'll need them all."

Phoebe passed Colette on her way back, and Colette seemed to see her for the first time since her death.

Phoebe thought she was trying to smile.


Pete Martinsburg wasn't smiling. He had sat through the entire assembly staring up at the hot blonde.

He hadn't slept well since the debacle in the forest. When he did sleep, his dreams were of Julie, but not the Julie of puppy love, ice-cream cones, and being thirteen. This was dead Julie, returned to the world. He dreamed of Julie holding hands, but it wasn't his hand she was holding, it was Tommy Williams.

*She might not come back*, this nightmare-Tommy told him. But in the dream it was Pete who moved at half speed; nightmare-Tommy was quick in getting to his car, the one Pete had driven around all summer. The one Pete had never sat in with his father.

*Now you know what it is like* . . . he heard the cold, hollow voice in his head say as the zombie brought the car to life . . . *to be dead.*

The car lurched into hyperdrive, accelerating as it approached a brick wall that had grown from the asphalt. The car struck the wall as a yellow blur that blossomed into an explosive flame, and Pete awoke with the sound of Julie's screams and the dead boy's laughter ringing in his head.

But of course Julie, the real Julie and not the ashen, flat-eyed Julie who walked his dreams, had not been able to scream. Good old Dad had broken the news ever so gently in his classic style, over the phone with a continent separating him from his son. He'd called at Christmastime. It was right after Pete had tried to tell him what a football hero he'd been that season, how many tackles he'd made, how many interceptions he'd caught for the Badgers.

"Oh hey, Pete," his dad had said. Pete could remember the conversation in exact detail, the way he could recall all of the conversations he'd had with his father since he'd left them. "Hey, you remember that girl Julie you played with over the summer?"

*Played with*, as though they would be playing hide-and-seek.

"Marissa's daughter? Remember Marissa, that woman I used to date?"

Pete remembered, with growing dread. No news was the only good news Dad was capable of providing

"Well, her daughter, Julie, died about two weeks after you went back home to your mother. Helluva thing. She had a massive asthma attack. They said it was triggered by a spider bite or something."

*Helluva thing.*

He watched Angela Hunter laughing with Layman and Scarypants, and the pen he'd been tapping on the back of the chair in front of him snapped in his hand, spilling a long blue bubble of ink onto his skin.

He smeared the ink bubble onto the seat cushion next to him. Dad was utterly clueless about how Pete had felt toward Julie. Just like he was clueless that Pete would never feel that way about anyone ever again.

The sad tale of Dallas Jones, the original zombie, had hit the media a few weeks after his dad broke the news of Julie's death to him. At first, Pete had secretly clung to the hope that Julie might come back, but when she didn't, that hadn't surprised him either. People hung around the edges of his life, but they never really "came back."

His hand was blue from the base of his little finger all the way down to his wrist. People had begun to leave the auditorium, but not Morticia Scarypants; she was still hanging around where the hot blonde stood trying to pass out sign-up sheets. There was something about Phoebe that reminded him of Julie.

Why Scarypants gave him this feeling, he wasn't sure. Julie had been the furthest thing from a goth and she hadn't been the dress-and-boots-wearing type, either. But there was something— an expression, a smile. Something.

He watched Phoebe for a little while, and then he left to go wash his hands in the big lavatory outside the auditorium. He ran the water as hot as he could stand it and squirted six shots of the thin pink hand soap into his palms and worked up a lather. The restroom door swung open, and he heard someone shuffle in. Frowning, he looked up and saw the blue-gray face of Tommy Williams in the spotted mirror.

"Didn't think you'd have much use for this room," Pete said, smiling and shaking his hands over the sink. "Seeing as how the parts don't really work anymore. They don't, do they?"

He watched Williams clench and unclench his hands.

"Leave . . . me alone," the dead boy said, his strange voice echoing over plumbing and tile. "Leave . . . Phoebe . . . alone."

Pete thought about walking over and drying his hands on the dead boy's shirt, but the idea of coming that close to his body without the benefit of football pads and tape was nauseating to him.

"You should be the one leaving her alone," he said. "Freak."

Tommy took another step toward Pete, and Pete had a moment of panic because he really didn't know what he would do if the zombie reached for him or took a swing at him. There wasn't anyone in the school he was afraid to fight with, from Adam on down—anyone living, that is. He'd tried a half-dozen different ways to hurt him in practice, but the zombie had shaken him off like droplets of sweat off his skin.

"I know . . . what you are . . . thinking," Tommy said, the left side of his mouth lifting in a sick approximation of a smile. "You are thinking . . . what do I . . . do . . . if he . . . hits me? What do I . . . do . . . if he puts his . . . hands . . . on me?"

"You can't get inside my head," Pete said, but he saw Tommy raise his hand and cover the light switch with it. Pete looked over his shoulder at the door. He didn't want to be in the dark with the zombie; not in this bathroom, not anywhere, ever.

"I'm already in your . . . head," Tommy said, his voice a dry whisper. Pete felt the exhalation of air touch his cheek, and he shuddered. "Do your worst at practice. It . . . only makes me . . . stronger. But do not . . . threaten . . . my friends."

Pete was about to reply, but he couldn't find the words, and then the lights went out. He threw a punch in the dark, hit nothing but air, and threw another one with the same result, then covered up, expecting a rain of blows that never came. A moment later the lavatory door swung open and the room was illuminated with light from the noisy hallway outside.

Pete felt along the wall and got the lights on a moment before Norm Lathrop entered. Norm hesitated upon seeing Pete, probably debating whether or not he should just run out the door before Pete had a chance to terrorize him.

"You're in my way," Pete said. He took a paper towel out of the dispenser and wiped his forehead.

"I'm sorry," Norm said, almost jumping on the way to the urinals.

I've got to do something about the freakin' zombies, Pete thought, and punched open the bathroom door.

# CHAPTER TEN

"SO," PHOEBE SAID, SQUEEZING OVER NEXT TO the dirty bus window. There weren't all that many students taking the bus home, but she and Margi usually shared one of the double seats.

"So what?"

"So what do you think?"

Margi was practicing being "obtuse." "About what?"

"About the assembly, brainiac."

"Oh. I don't know." She took her iPod out of her satchel and started to scroll through the long list of bands.

Phoebe sighed. "I'm going to join," she said, "if I can get in."

"I figured you would," Margi said. She selected a song off of M.T. Graves's solo album *All the Graves Are Empty Except Mine* and pushed the volume until they could both hear it, a thin tinny wail, above the chugging of the bus. "You'll get in."

"You figured I would?" Phoebe rocked into Margi's shoulder, applying gentle pressure. "You and me against the world, right, Margi?"

"Yeah. I know why you've been hanging out after school, Pheebes. I know it doesn't have to do with getting your history project done."

"Oh," Phoebe said. "I did get the project done, though."

Margi leaned gently back into her, like she appreciated Phoebe not coming up with some stupid cover story that would have embarrassed them both. Margi's stare normally had a hard edge, but now her eyes were soft and scared.

"What is the deal with you and him, anyhow?"

Phoebe turned to look out the window; they were already on the wooded roads. She saw no zombies—*differently biotic persons*—swaying in place among the birches and oaks.

"I don't know what the deal is. I don't know that there is any deal. There's a connection, I don't know what. We're communicating, and that's rare for you or me to do with anyone. Living or dead."

Margi nodded. "That's our choice, pretty much."

"Pretty much."

They were quiet for a few moments, which was uncharacteristic for Margi.

"Will you join with me?"

Margi shrugged.

"C'mon, Gee," Phoebe said. "Weird Sisters, right?"

Margi leaned her head against Phoebe's shoulder. "Minus one," she whispered.

"Gee . . ."

"No, I know, I know. Maybe it could be a good thing. Like I'll learn how to talk to her or something."

"Colette?" Phoebe asked.

"Yeah, Colette."

"Maybe. Maybe you would. That would be good, right?"

"Sure. But it's still weird, you know? Something is happening. Something is up. Why aren't there any dead kids on the bus today? Colette, or your pal, or the other one? They don't drive."

Phoebe looked around her. The dead kids never missed their ride home. Margi was right. It was weird.

"I didn't even notice."

Margi shifted against her shoulder, like she was nodding. She also rubbed her eye. "I'm not totally brain dead, you know. I see things too."

"I know you do, Gee."

"You'll tell me if you and—Tommy—are more than friends?"

"I'll tell you," Phoebe said. "I don't even know if we are that yet."

Margi sniffed. "Pheebes and Gee against the world, right?"

"That's right," Phoebe said, putting her arm around Margi's shoulder and hugging her.

The old bus groaned to a halt at Phoebe's driveway, and Rae, the driver, said "Goodnight, ladies," same as she did every time they disembarked. Rae didn't discriminate—she said her farewells to living and dead students alike.

Gargoyle met them at the door, his rump swaying back and

forth with doggy glee when Margi stooped to pick him up and let him lick her face.

"Careful," Phoebe said. "Foundation is poisonous to puppies."

"Shut the hell up and get us some snacks. I'm taking my little pretty boy outside."

Phoebe turned the stereo on and filled the house with The Empire Hideous. She took a pot of coffee out of the refrigerator and poured some into tall glasses in which she added too much cream and too much sugar and too much ice, which was how they liked their coffee. There was a bag of potato chips and a box of crackers and some hummus spread.

Margi came back with Gargoyle and began singing along with Myke Hideous, her husky voice blending well with his doleful intonations. Phoebe smiled, filled with affection for her.

"Today's beverage?" Margi asked, setting Gar down and watching him pad over to the couch and hop on.

"Crème brûlée," Phoebe said, holding out the tray for Margi, who selected one of the glasses.

"Mmmmm," she said. "Tastes sweet."

"That would be all the sugar I added."

"Yes. Good choice. So what are we doing, other than getting caffeinated?"

Phoebe brought the tray over to the coffee table and sat next to Gar, who rolled over for a tummy rub.

"I TiVo'd something last week. I thought we could watch it."

"Uh-oh. My spidey senses tell me this is a setup."

"Wow, Margi, I'm really impressed. First bilocation, and

now precognition. Your telepathetic powers are working in overdrive today."

"It's that psychic bond we share," she said. "Because if there is one thing you are not, it's predictable. Goo-goo eyes at a dead kid, even I couldn't have foretold that."

Phoebe tossed a throw pillow at Margi. "The show was on CNN. It's called *The Young Undead in America.*"

"I sense a theme here," Margi said, flopping ungracefully next to her, with Gar in between. "I don't suppose that we could just listen to Empire Hideous and call it a life?"

"Nope. We're going to be socially conscious today. Topical. I hear differently biotic persons are all the rage these days."

"Hmm. Me too."

Phoebe worked the TiVo remote with one hand while using the stereo remote to kill the music with the other.

"You're good at that," Margi said. "You should have been a guy."

"Too cute," Phoebe said. "And I like smelling nice."

There was an opening montage narrated by someone who'd mastered the art of the grim monotone. Then there was a brief clip of the Dallas Jones video with some explanation of the start of the living impaired phenomena, crosscut with some sound bites from Reverend Nathan Mathers, who seemed to think that the dead coming back to life was a sure sign of the Apocalypse. The montage ended with the narrator suggesting that, as with any other new trend in American society, someone would be on hand trying to profit from the phenomenon. The montage ended by showing a well-dressed man with a toothy smile signing copies of a book called *The Dead Have No Life: What Parents Need to Know About Their Undead Youth.*

Phoebe rubbed her temples. "Telepathetic powers, activate," she said, and then attempted to replicate the narrator's delivery: "One thing is clear: the living impaired phenomenon has changed the very fabric of American society."

"One thing is certain," the narrator replied, "the presence of the living impaired has irrevocably altered the American way of life—no pun intended."

Margi laughed. "You totally watched this before."

"I totally did not," Phoebe said. "If you watched the news occasionally you'd be able to do it, too. And you'd be better at doing the voice."

"Deadpan. No pun intended."

"You're dead right. No pun intended."

"He has a better vocabulary than you do. Irrevocably."

"Someone has to. Inevitably."

They sipped coffee as the Dallas Jones video began to run.

"Ugh, I hate this," Margi said as the now-familiar grainy black-and-white image began to click forward. Dallas Jones walked into the convenience store and withdrew a gun from the pocket of his puffy black bomber jacket and pointed it at the clerks. There was no sound, but it was clear he was shouting at the clerk, who started punching buttons on the cash register.

Dallas turned his head to look toward the street, and in the moment he turned back, there was a smoky blur as the shotgun blast caught him high in the chest and blew him back a good five feet into a rack of snacks and a pyramid of soda cans.

"No matter how many times I see that," Margi said, "I will never get used to it."

Phoebe nodded. The image of Dallas Jones being killed was more disturbing to her than what would come later—even though it was what came later that had "irrevocably altered the American way of life."

The shooter—the store owner—came around the counter, clutching the hand of the clerk, who was also his wife. Ahmad Qurati would receive a lifetime of criticism for the risk involved in shooting a robber when the man had a gun pointed at his wife's head. He would also be criticized for not checking Jones to see if the shot had killed him; the video showed him exiting out the door Jones had come in and then locking it behind him—another move that seemed to make little sense. The police department had also come under fire for not arriving until two hours and seven minutes after Jones was shot, even though the dispatch records clearly showed that Qurati did not call 911 until one hour and fifty-three minutes after the locking of the front door.

CNN time lapsed the remaining footage, up until minute 109. Jones was mostly hidden from view by the chip rack, one askew leg clearly visible, as was part of an arm and a dark puddle that spread perceptibly in the first few moments of the time lapse.

At minute 109 the footage reverted to real time, and Dallas Jones's leg twitched. The chip rack fell away, not like it had been lifted and thrown, but like it had been shrugged off. The arm lifted from the floor as Jones apparently—it was hard to tell because most of his body was off camera—pushed himself upright.

"Oh God," Margi said.

A minute later Jones lumbered into frame, the tread of his high-tops never leaving the floor as he shuffled forward. The camera was focused on his broad back, and his jacket was torn and leaking dark down feathers where the shot had ripped through him. He walked forward until he bumped against the glass doorway. He made no attempt to open it, and after another moment he turned and shuffled back the way he had come, toward the camera.

The narrator began talking over the video, giving the sad biography of Dallas Jones, teen hoodlum. Phoebe felt her skin grow tingly with anticipation for the moment that had launched a hundred doctoral theses, and when it came, CNN held it and then panned in, which made the image twice as grainy, but also twice as effective.

Phoebe always wondered why Dallas Jones looked up at the camera at the end of his second aimless lap around the store. The image grew until his eyes filled the television screen, so that individual pixels stood out.

"Dallas Jones was the first," the narrator said, and the image of Dallas's eyes was replaced by some equally grainy home video footage of other dead people moving around, and then some on-location reporters sending back stories about a dozen different undead.

"They didn't show the part where the cops come in," Margi said. Phoebe had studied the full video; after Qurati fumbled with his keys for a minute, two cops came in and tackled Jones. When the EMTs arrived a moment later, one of the cops was covered with blood, none of it his own.

"Repent," Reverend Nathan Mathers was saying. He was screaming, spit flying from his lips. "Repent, for surely the end is nigh. The graves give up their dead and the coming of the Lord is most certainly upon us!"

"I feel bad for whoever is in the first pew," Phoebe said. Next to her, Margi pulled Gar closer.

"I hate when they show this stuff," she said.

The next image was even more hateful. The video jerked around as though the camera were strapped to a hyperactive child, but the image it conveyed was easily understandable, and horrific. Two men with jerricans were pouring gasoline on a sluggish living impaired girl whose arms were bound behind her to a metal basketball pole set into concrete, like you'd see in a school yard. The girl went up in a sudden rush of yellow flame, and her twitching seemed to grow more animated, but that might have been a trick of the flames dancing around her. Mathers was still giving his speech in the background.

"Oh God," Margi repeated, and they were quiet for the remainder of the program, even when Skip Slydell, the young author, began talking about how parents should raise their differently biotic youth and help integrate them into a society that still does not have any legislation that prevents burning them at the stake.

# CHAPTER ELEVEN

THERE WERE THIRTEEN NAMES ON THE list of students accepted into the Hunter Foundation. Phoebe Kendall was the third name on the list, right below Tommy Williams and Karen DeSonne. Colette was next, as was Margi and then Adam.

Phoebe felt a bounce in her step as she turned from the list, but it nearly carried her into the arms of Pete Martinsburg. He pushed her back against the wall.

"You should watch where you're going, Scarypants," he said, looming over her. She had an armload of books, and his hands were free, the left one balled into a fist. "You should watch what you're doing, too."

She could feel her cheeks flush with rage and embarrassment. And more than a little fear, too. This was a person who had no compunction against taking a baseball bat to another student, after all. Margi would already be dragging her hot-pink nails across his face and hissing like a wet cat, but Phoebe was afraid of getting hurt, and she could see in his face that he was not above hurting her.

"That's the most color I've seen on your face in a long time. You scared, dead girl?" he asked, smiling. "You should be."

Phoebe felt like she was shrinking beneath the weight of his stare. She was wearing her knee-high boots, which would have been great if she could have lifted them groin high, but the skirt she had on was tight all the way to her ankles, and barely allowed for a short stride, much less a swift kick.

A clear memory of the sound of Martinsburg's bat as it cut through the air to strike Tommy's flesh rippled through her mind. She noticed that his fists were clenched.

Martinsburg ripped the roster off the wall, tearing a corner where the masking tape held. He folded the list twice and put it in his shirt pocket.

"Everyone on this list," he said, "is going to regret ever hearing about this class."

He walked down the hall, and Phoebe watched him go, tears of frustration and shame gathering at the corners of her eyes. She could go in the office and tell someone what just happened. She could find Adam, and he would probably want to have a chat with Martinsburg. But in the end, all she did was wipe her eyes and wonder what Martinsburg was going to do when he saw Adam Layman's name on the bottom of the list.

Margi found Phoebe in the hall. The flush in Phoebe's cheeks must have subsided since Margi was back to her usual chattering self, relating a brief tale of an atrocity committed by Mr. McKenna in Spanish that morning, something about his failure to announce a pop quiz.

"Isn't that why they're called pop quizzes?" Phoebe asked. "Because they're surprises?"

"Still, it isn't fair. Speaking of surprises, when are they going to post the list for the work study? I mean, not like I want to do it or anything, but I am your best friend, and I guess it will look good on a college application. And they can't be grading very hard. Can they? I mean, the grading is just a formality with these things, right? I don't want to take it if I'm going to get a bad grade."

"They posted the list. It got ripped down."

"Really? Who would do that? Some moron who couldn't get in? I better not say that; what if I didn't get in? Do you know who got in?"

"You got in. Me too."

"Yay," Margi said with false enthusiasm, clapping so that her hundred bangles clinked together in a soft tinny rhythm. "Who else? Anyone as cool as us? As if that were possible."

"Tommy, Adam," Phoebe said, smiling when Margi made a face. "Colette. Thornton Harrowwood is taking it, for some reason. I saw that living impaired—that differently biotic—girl on the list: Karen with the unpronounceable last name. They only accepted thirteen people."

"Once again, the elite," Margi said, touching Phoebe softly on the shoulder that Martinsburg had just shoved. "Of course, only thirteen people applied."

The thirteen became twelve before the first bus ride from Oakvale High to the Hunter Foundation, which was a short drive through the woods near the Winford line.

"I heard that her parents refused to sign the permission slip to let her come," Margi said about the last-minute deletion.

"Is this precognition again?" Phoebe said. "Or telepathy?"

Margi shook her head. "It's called divination if you can reveal something that already happened. But no, it is really because I overheard one of the school secretaries telling Ms. Kim."

"Well, that was progressive of her parents."

"These are progressive times, Pheebes my dear."

In homeroom they discovered that they would be missing their seventh period class—which for Margi was a study hall, so she was none too pleased to be attending an orientation. The feeling that Phoebe carried around with her was similar to the one she'd had in the days and hours leading up to the seventh grade talent show. Sometimes the butterflies were there just to make you queasy; sometimes the butterflies were there to let you know that something good was on its way.

The dead kids were waiting when she walked down to the library for orientation. She saw them through the streaky windows in a loose ring of chairs in the study area. Principal Kim was waiting at the door with a clipboard.

"Hello, Phoebe," she said, handing Phoebe the clipboard. "Please sign on the line next to your name."

Phoebe did. The dead kids had signed in already. Not known for their fine motor skills, their "signatures" were mostly block printing that looked as though they'd slashed the letters across the page with the pen. Tommy's name was the only one that was within the lines provided, and the letters were even and uniform in height.

"Hey, Pheeble," Adam said, taking the clipboard out of her hand, startling her. The old Adam was known more for his lumbering than for his stealth, but it gave him no end of amusement to sneak up on her.

"Mr. Layman," Principal Kim said, "please . . ."

"Sign on the line that is dotted, yes, ma'am," he said, scrawling out a name that wasn't much neater than the marks left by the living impaired kids.

"Why don't you two have a seat?"

Phoebe watched Adam as he scanned ahead into the room. If he was apprehensive, he was doing a good job of not showing it, but she did note the slight shrug of his shoulders as he motioned for Phoebe to follow him into the room.

Tommy was sitting in one of the creaky wooden library chairs, his shoulders back and his head straight. Phoebe thought of the last time she'd been in a ring of living impaired kids and recognized a few of them: Colette sat on a cushioned futon next to the girl with streaky white-blond hair who Phoebe'd seen out in the forest.

"Hi, Tommy," Phoebe said. "Hi, Colette." She waved at the

other kids, making brief eye contact with each. The girl with the white-blond hair returned her wave with barely a pause.

"Hello, Phoebe," Tommy said. "Adam."

"Hey, Tommy. Hello, everyone." Adam took the last of the lime-green lounge chairs, leaving Phoebe one of the wooden ones. Her chair squeaked when she sat on it. He laughed, and she made a face at him.

Margi entered the silent lobby like a small black-and-pink twister, her skirt flapping, her spangles jingling. "Ohmigawd, that was the longest history class ever. I think I actually became a historical figure in the time it took for that class to end."

She pulled up short, as though it had just dawned on her where she was and who she was there with. Her greeting of "Hullo, everyone" was mumbled, and she looked relieved when Thornton Harrowwood entered and demanded high fives, first from Adam and then from Tommy. There was a tense moment when Tommy regarded Thorny's raised hand as though he was wondering what it was for, but then he gave a light slap.

Thornton had been the last to arrive, which meant another person had dropped out. Principal Kim led Angela Hunter and her father, Alish, into the room. Ms. Hunter wore a pale blue skirt that ended at her knees, and Phoebe thought her legs could probably cause even a dead kid's heart to race. Tommy was watching her cross the room. The chair did not even creak when she sat on it.

"Well," Principal Kim said, "I must say that I'm quite surprised and pleased to see two football players in this program. I'm glad to see you boys taking an interest in something other than football. And I have already spoken with Coach Konrathy, so he knows that you will be missing one practice a week."

Adam nodded, and Thornton puffed up as though he had been named running back of the year. Phoebe noticed that Adam hadn't looked up from the spot on the carpet he'd been staring at since he sat down. She looked down. Moss green, slightly variegated with some dark green strands. There was a stain that might have been coffee near the leg of the futon where the two dead girls sat, but Adam didn't seem to be staring at that.

"Three."

She looked up. Everyone looked at Tommy, including the principal.

"There are . . . three . . . football players here."

The principal smiled. "Three. Of course. Thank you for reminding me, Tommy. First, let me thank you all for signing up to participate in what we expect will be a very exciting program for the Oakvale school system. The Hunters are here today to discuss the program in a little more detail with you, as well as to set expectations—yours and those of the school and the foundation."

"Thank you, Principal Kim. And again, thank you for joining our program! I look forward to working with all of you!"

Angela's smile, like her legs, could bring the dead to life. Margi was squirming on the seat next to Phoebe.

Alish spoke next, and his voice was one suited for libraries: dry, raspy, and soft. He smiled, but there was none of his daughter's restorative power there.

"Yes," he said, and Phoebe thought she could hear an extra

"s" in the word, as though the word had been hissed. "Thank you all for choosing to work with my foundation. I am Alish Hunter. I fully expect that the work you do here will change your lives, if not the lives of all persons, differently biotic or not. I know it will change mine."

More smiles from the Hunters.

"I have your files, but I would like to hear from you. I gather some of you are friends, but it will be in the interest of the foundation if we could all become friends. So please, let us all introduce ourselves. And when we do so, let us each give a little of ourselves by saying our names and also something that we like to spend time doing. I'll start. My name is Alish Hunter, and I enjoy wearing a lab coat and conducting experiments like a mad scientist."

There was some polite laughter, mostly from Thornton and Angela, who went next. Contrary to what Phoebe expected, Angela's hobby was running, and not lounging around on Misquamicut Beach in a string bikini.

Thornton liked football. The dead girl with streaky white-blond hair was named Karen DeSonne (de-sewn, Phoebe noted), and she liked to paint. There was almost no pause at all between her words. Adam liked karate. Colette took a full minute and a half to let the group know that her name was Colette Beauvoir and that she liked walking in the woods. Margi liked music. Kevin Zumbrowski was nearly as slow as Colette, and he liked chess, which Phoebe figured probably worked out just fine for him. Phoebe said that she liked to write, as did Tommy Williams.

"Wonderful," Alish Hunter said. "See that? We've already found some things in common."

Evan Talbot, who could not have been much older than fourteen when he died, confessed to being a science fiction fan, especially *Star Wars*. He was wearing a Darth Vader T-shirt and had a shock of wiry orange hair that stood up from his head like a wick. He was pretty quick, too, much quicker than Sylvia Stelman, who agonized in telling the group that she liked her two cats, Ariel and Flounder. Tayshawn Wade told everyone that he liked to watch movies.

"What sort of movies?" Angela asked brightly.

"Action," Tayshawn replied, giving the word an extra syllable, "and . . . horror."

Alish laughed like it was the funniest thing he ever heard. Phoebe expected clouds of dust to billow out of his mouth from somewhere deep in his lungs.

"Well," he said after a moment, "we are about out of time. Angel has a folder for each of you with more information. There is homework inside, as well as another permission slip that says your parents will allow you to be transported from the school to the foundation and back again. There is also a confidentiality agreement for each of you to sign with your parents. There are some other forms that you should be familiar with. Please read everything and have your parents read everything. Provided that Principal Kim receives all of the necessary documents by the end of this week, we will see all of you next Tuesday at the foundation. You will be leaving after lunch, so please remember to schedule time for yourselves to make up any assignments you might miss. Thank you, and see you next week."

Principal Kim stood and walked the pair to the door after telling the students they were dismissed.

Margi sighed beside Phoebe.

"What a lizard," she said.

"Aw," Thornton said, flipping through his sheaf of paperwork, "we've got to write an essay on why we wanted to do the work study."

A thin pink sheet escaped from his folder. Phoebe watched Adam pluck it out of the air with liquid grace and hand it back to Thornton just as Thornton dropped his pen.

"Be interesting to hear what some people write on that one," Adam said, looking at Phoebe.

Karen was the first to rise. She lifted a slate-gray backpack that had a small pink stuffed dog hanging from the zipper. The dog's tongue, equally pink, drooped from the line of stitching that was its mouth. The eyes were closed, making the dog look as if it were sleeping or hanging from a rope. One corner of Karen's mouth twitched up.

"Don't worry," she said. "Only one . . . page. I think you'll survive."

Phoebe watched Karen walk away. Her blond hair looked almost soft under the bright library lights, and she moved without the hitch that was present in the gait of most of the differently biotic.

There might have even been a calculated sway in her khaki-clad hips.

"She's the one who wears short skirts," Margi whispered.

Phoebe nodded. She saw Tayshawn helping Colette off the futon. "We should talk to Colette."

Margi grabbed her forearm, her hands freezing cold. "We should. And we will. But not now. I really want to get out of here," she said, tugging her toward the door.

Phoebe turned long enough to wave at Tommy. Tommy waved back.

# CHAPTER TWELVE

THE FIRST GAME OF THE SEASON WAS against the Norwich Fisher Cats, which was one of the major rivalries for the Oakvale Badgers. Phoebe had read that this was the first year in many that the game was being played in Oakvale. For a long time the game had been played in Norwich as their homecoming game in accordance with the long-standing tradition of giving the Fisher Cats a team they could demolish for that spirit-building event. But now, with Adam on the team, the Badger's were actually competitive.

Phoebe's dad had agreed to drive her and Margi to the game, and Phoebe noticed as he pulled on his threadbare Fordham sweatshirt and an old ball cap, that he might have been a little too eager to volunteer. She knew how much he liked to spend time with her, and he liked spending time with her and Margi even more—mainly because he loved to try and embarrass them. "Bring some color to those pale, pale cheeks" was how he liked to describe it.

"So Margi," he said, "are you as excited as Phoebe is about this Undead Studies thing?"

"Dad!" Phoebe said. "Study for the Advancement of Differently Biotic Persons. Didn't you read the paperwork?"

He looked back at her in the rearview. "I feel like all I've been reading lately is paperwork."

"I'm with you, Mr. Kendall," Margi said. "Too much paper."

"The newspaper called it the Undead Studies Program," he said. Phoebe wished that he would just watch the road.

"Don't believe everything you read," she said.

Her father laughed, and despite the lines around his eyes, he looked younger than his forty years.

He managed to look away from her just in time to notice the stop sign up ahead. "Good advice for everyone, I think."

Margi giggled, and Phoebe hit her with an elbow and a dirty look. "I think it will be interesting, Mr. Kendall. One of the de . . . differently biotic boys likes horror movies."

"Really?" he said. "Nice to have something in common."

"Sure." Phoebe wondered why everyone thought that commonality was the lynchpin to the whole "why can't we all just get along" deal.

She could sense the next question on his lips. She knew he was about to ask about Colette, but then they turned the corner and there was the school. There was a crowd of maybe twenty people near the front steps, some with poster board signs. A few police cars were parked in the loop where the buses would wait on school days.

"Those don't look like football fans," her dad said.

Phoebe read some of the signs: SPORTS ARE FOR THE LIVING; DEAD = DAMNED; LIFE, LIBERTY, AND THE PURSUIT OF HAPPYNESS; and in bold red letters, BURY YOUR DEAD.

"Nice," Margi said. "Look, they spelled happiness wrong."

"Maybe this isn't such a good idea, kids."

"No, Dad," Phoebe said, "we can't let people like this win."

"Win what?"

"Could you please just drop us off in the student lot? We'll walk up."

"I don't know."

"Dad, we'll be fine. It's just a couple of nuts with signs." She knew what was going on in her dad's head. Visions of bombs under bleachers, handguns in belts, vials of acid tucked away in overstuffed purses.

"Phoebe—"

"Dad," she repeated, "we'll be fine."

"Maybe I'll see the game with you after all," he said. "I've always wanted to hear Armstrong speak."

"Right." At least she'd get to see the game.

There were protestors inside the game as well. Many of them wore latex monster masks, even though Halloween was still a few weeks away.

"Are they actually chanting 'Out of life, out of the game'?" Margi asked.

"I'm afraid so," Phoebe said, selecting seats in the heart of the Oakvale boosters section. She and Margi would normally be huddled together in a corner, away from everyone, each wearing earbuds jacked into the same iPod; but the people who normally seemed insane to them now seemed safe and comforting compared to people who actually *were* insane.

"I could think of some better cheers," her dad said.

"Please don't."

Phoebe had seen only one game last year just so that she could tell Adam she'd seen him play. Adam's role seemed to be to keep the opposing team from tackling Denny Mackenzie, the quarterback, and from what Phoebe could tell, he was very good at it. Denny had gone untackled for the game she'd watched, except for a few plays where he'd run downfield from his blockers. With a routine nonchalance, Adam had blocked or knocked down the one or two people who had run into him.

A young girl in a star-spangled dress, her hair done up in a loose mound of blond curls, skipped out to sing the national anthem, the crowd joining in with a sort of restrained mania. Some of the voices were belting out the words, as they held special significance for the day's events.

The announcer asked everyone to please welcome the Honorable Steven Armstrong, state representative. A trim-looking man in khaki pants and a navy blue windbreaker walked to the microphone where little Kayla Archambault had just finished singing about the land of the free and the home of the brave. The applause became listless and interspersed with booing as soon as the little girl was out of sight.

"A man of the people," her father said. "Excellent."

"Look at all the guys in shades," Margi said, pointing to a row of stern-looking characters on the edge of the field. "Are they part of Armstrong's staff?"

"The Men in Black. I guess they're ready for trouble. Maybe they think the undead belong at Roswell."

"Dad," Phoebe said. Her father was a longtime conspiracy buff who liked to make people think he believed in flying saucers but didn't believe that man ever walked on the moon.

"Thank you," Armstrong said, flashing a wide smile. "And thank you to the students and faculty of Oakvale High for inviting me on what is sure to be a historic event. One cannot help but think of the American athletes of the past who overcame obstacles of injustice and hate to go on to greatness. I am thinking of people like Jesse Owens. Greg Louganis. Billie Jean King. These people were willing to suffer through adversity and discrimination to participate in the sports that they loved, and in doing so, left a legacy that is an inspiration to all who would walk—or run—in their footsteps."

Phoebe was marveling at how quickly Armstrong had silenced the crowd, and then someone shouted "necrophiliac" over the silence. Armstrong continued speaking as though he hadn't heard.

"So I ask you, when you watch Thomas Williams take the field today, I ask you not to think of him as a living impaired young man, because clearly he does not consider himself to be impaired in any way. I ask those of you who would shame our country by singing our national anthem with a mask covering your face not to think of him as a zombie or a freak or any of the other hate-filled terms you would seek to tag this brave young man with. I ask that you forget also, for the moment, that he is differently biotic—I ask only that you consider him an athlete, and in that, he is no different than the other young men set to play today. Thank you."

"He's good," Mr. Kendall said, joining the girls in clapping.

Despite the fine oratory, Tommy didn't play the entire first half. Adam did his job well and gave Denny time to pass on most plays, although Denny was sacked for a loss on a play where Adam blocked right and Denny ran left. Pete Martinsburg had one interception and seemed to take a special delight in shoving opposing players into the sidelines. Thornton Harrowwood was allowed to carry the ball on a play and was crushed after a three-yard gain.

"Ow," Margi said. "I hope he gets up."

He did, and strutted as though he'd just carried the ball seventy yards for a touchdown.

"You have to admire his pluck," Phoebe said.

"Yes. He is a plucky young man."

Her dad looked at them, squinting. "What are you two talking about?"

At halftime the score was ten all. Harris Morgan scored on a thirteen-yard pass in the corner of the end zone, and the Badgers tied it up with a field goal just as time expired.

Armstrong came back onto the field after a short but loud performance by the Badger Band. "Wow, what a game," he said. "Let's hear it for these athletes." Most people, even the protesters, were more intent on getting a hot dog or a soda than they were on recognizing gridiron accomplishments, and again, the reception Armstong was given was lukewarm at best. "I'd like to talk briefly about the Hunter Foundation for the Advancement of Differently Biotic Persons. As you are well aware, the foundation is committed to the study—physiological, psychological, and perhaps most important, sociological—of differently biotic persons. The goal of the foundation is, through scientific study, to help create a world where all people, regardless of their biology, can live and learn together. I encourage you to show your support for differently biotic children everywhere through a donation of time or money to the foundation, with offices located right here in Oakvale. Thank you."

Phoebe saw a policeman talking to a guy in a Frankenstein mask in the bleachers across the field. The conversation didn't look pleasant.

"I'm amazed that the coach hasn't put the Williams boy into the game," Phoebe's father said.

*The Williams boy.* At least he hadn't said "the dead kid." Phoebe thought. "I don't think Coach Konrathy is very excited about putting him in."

"Everyone else is."

"That's the problem," Phoebe replied.

"I think he needs to put the kid in at this point," he said. "You've got half the crowd ready to throw a fit if he goes in, the other half ready to riot if he doesn't. You can feel the tension rising."

Frankenstein must have lost the discussion, because he was preceding the policeman down the bleacher steps. Every few steps he'd stop and turn as though tossing insults over his shoulder.

"If I'm Konrathy," her dad said, "I'm putting him in at the start of the half."

But he wasn't Konrathy, and Konrathy let Williams ride the bench throughout the quarter. Oakvale scored again on a quarterback draw after another nice reception from Harris Morgan. Norwich led a gritty march downfield and into the red zone, but Pete Martinsburg picked off a screen pass and ran it back ten yards before being tripped up. It was the play that served to break the spirit and chances of the opposing team, but Phoebe could not bring herself to cheer.

"That was a nice play," her dad said, nudging her.

"Pete Martinsburg is evil, Mr. Kendall," Margi said.

"Ahh," he replied, and stopped clapping.

Phoebe shot Margi a look so that she wouldn't begin explaining just how evil Pete Martinsburg had been.

Margi returned her look, and stuck out her tongue.

The Badgers kept the ball on the ground, and three plays later they had a first down on a six-yard carry by Thornton Harrowwood. Again he was leveled, and again he sprang up as if he hadn't been touched.

"That little guy is pretty tough," Mr. Kendall said, stifling a yawn. The volume of the crowd tapered off and then rose again as Tommy Williams fastened the strap on his helmet and trotted onto the field.

"He finally put him in! And these knuckleheads are booing. That just isn't right." Her dad clapped louder, and Phoebe and Margi joined him. Someone hit Margi in the back of the head with a french fry, and another sailed past Phoebe's face as she turned around.

Her dad stood up and scanned the upper rows, but whoever it was hid the remainder of their deep-fried missiles.

"Coward," he called, and sat down.

"Not worth it, Dad," Phoebe said.

"It never is," he said. "Looks like Williams is on the line next to Adam. This ought to be interesting."

Mackenzie took the snap and dropped back five steps. Adam and Tommy gave him plenty of time, and he completed an out to Harris Morgan, who let himself get pushed out of bounds. The second play went much the same way, but this time with a curl up the middle of the field so as to keep the clock running. The Badgers were past midfield with a first down, so they ran the next two plays and got short yardage. The next play was third and one, and they ran a draw where Denny pitched the ball to Harris, who swept around to the left behind Adam and Tommy. The hole they left him was big enough to drive a moving van through, and Harris sprinted, juking the one tackler who had a chance, and ran forty yards into the end zone without anyone getting close to him.

The Badger fans cheered, but the Badger players were met with a barrage of fruit as they trotted back to the bench. A flurry of a dozen or so tomatoes sailed from the lower levels of the bleachers, most of them hitting Adam, who stepped in front of Tommy the moment the throwing began. Someone tagged Konrathy in the head with an apple.

The stocky cop who had escorted Frankenstein out earlier headed over to that section of the bleachers, waving to a policeman on the other side of the stadium. There was a lot of shouting and pointing and some shoving, but by the time the cops got there, all the evidence was out on the field and it didn't look like the witnesses were planning to go on record.

"That was pleasant," her father said, shaking his head.

The Badgers won, 24–7. Tommy Williams did not take the field again.

"You understand why I am uncomfortable about this," her dad said.

"I'll be careful, Daddy."

"You know it has nothing to do with my trust in you. But some of these idiots in the stands . . ."

"I know, Daddy. I'll be careful."

"Careful doesn't help if some knucklehead has a gun, or a grenade."

"I know," she said, wondering how many people actually had a stockpile of grenades lying around the garage for day-to-day use.

He looked at her and at Margi, who was lingering by the fence, pretending not to be listening to their conversation.

"We didn't come here so Margi could watch Adam, did we?"

Phoebe smiled. "We didn't come here so Margi could *not* watch Adam, either."

"Phoebe, who . . ."

"I'll be back in fifteen minute," she said. "Promise."

He raised his hands in resignation. She skipped away to drag Margi over to the exit where the players, freshly showered, would be emerging from the school. She looked back at her father, but he was already squinting at the people they passed as though scanning for signs of impending mayhem and destruction.

"My dad never would have let me go," Margi said. "You think he knows you've got the hots for a zombie?"

"Margi!"

"Well, does he? He's pretty sharp about you. He pays attention. I think I could set my head on fire in the living room and my dad would ask my mom what we were having for supper."

"I have a very cool father," Phoebe said, "and I do not have the hots for Tommy. I'm just . . . interested, that's all."

"Whatever."

"Dad thinks that we came here so you could drool over Adam. A very plausible cover story, by the way, and one that he swallowed completely. He's sharp, like you say."

Margi made a disgusted noise and slapped Phoebe's arm, and then chased her to the back door of the school.

"Uh-oh," Margi said as they rounded the corner. The protest had moved to the exit, as had the Channel Three mobile news van. The stocky cop was escorting Adam through the crowd. The reporter from the mobile news van walked along-side, shouting questions.

"What was it like playing with a living impaired kid? Were you surprised at the crowd's reaction today?"

Adam was about as big as the cop. He glared at the protestors, but allowed the cop to lead him through without stopping. Thornton Harrowwood was next, and his appearance on the arm of a young female state trooper drew attention away from Adam.

"Do you have any comment about today's game?" the reporter asked. "What do you think of all the controversy surrounding your teammate?"

"I carried for nineteen yards!" Thornton said, smiling into the camera.

Adam thanked the cop and joined Phoebe and Margi.

"Hey," he said.

"You smell like spaghetti sauce," Margi told him.

"Har-har," he replied. "I don't think I'm going to wash my uniform. Maybe opposing teams will think it is the blood of my enemies."

"Where's Tommy?" Phoebe asked. "How is he doing?"

"He didn't say much," he said, and then raised his hands after catching something in Phoebe's expression. "I'm not trying to be funny. He didn't cry or anything. But he was clearing out his locker."

"Sooo . . . what? What does that mean?"

"I don't know, Phoebe. I asked him if he was okay, and he said he was. That was about it. They're sneaking him out of one of the other exits so he can avoid all this," he said, waving his hands at the cluster of restless protestors awaiting Tommy's exit. Stavis and Martinsburg pushed through alongside the stocky cop, but the protestors didn't have anything to say to the other players. Even the Channel Three guy was getting bored. They overheard him ask the cop if they took the dead kid out another way.

"Yeah," the cop said, smiling. "He's long gone."

"I have to get out of here," Adam said. "The STD said I've got to rake up the leaves. Need a ride?"

"No thanks. My dad brought us."

"Okay," he said. "Oh yeah, I almost forgot—Tommy Ballgame asked me to give you this."

He held out a piece of notebook paper folded into an uneven square.

She opened the note and read it to herself, shielding it from Margi's prying eyes.

"He wants to know if I want to go out some night next week." She looked first at Adam for his reaction, but whatever it was, he kept it to himself.

"Ick," Margi said. Phoebe hit her.

"Ouch. *Out*, like as in a date?"

"I don't know."

"That's just weird."

"Shut up, Margi."

"What else does he say?" she said, trying to scan the paper.

"None of your business," Phoebe replied, snatching it away.

"You gals have fun," Adam said. "I'm off to rake leaves."

Phoebe watched him leave, wishing that she could tell what Adam thought about her and Tommy, while at the same time whispering a death threat to Margi should she breathe a word of the note to her father.

Pete Martinsburg watched the dead kid escape out the back door and head out toward the woods, avoiding both the reporters and the food-throwing brainiacs from the stands. Pete debated running after him, but there were a pair of cops making sure he made it without being bothered, so Pete just watched him slip away, undetected by any of the other people who had something to say about a worm buffet playing on a high school football team.

Before the dead kid left, though, he'd made a point of standing next to Pete's locker, blocking Pete from getting to his things. He stood there with his twisted half grin on his face, as though saying to Pete, "What you can do, I can do. Watch out." It was a subtle point and one made for Pete alone.

Pete did something he'd done only once before when faced with a confrontation: nothing.

The zombie was in his head, stomping around with cleats. Pete could only see one way to get him out of there.

After watching the zombie enter the woods, Pete walked back to the locker room, his jersey in hand. Someone had tagged him with an egg just before the game ended. He'd been standing on the sidelines, waiting for the offense to score again, so he could get in and put the hurt on someone, when he'd felt it splat against the small of his back. The dead kid hadn't even been close to him when the egg hit.

He got his locker open and threw the jersey into it, where it stuck to the back wall before sliding down and leaving a viscous trail.

"Yeah, bay-beee!" Stavis yelled, his pale lumpy body nearly plowing into Pete as he stood staring at the yolk trail. "The Badgers win again!"

Idiot, Pete thought. Stavis was holding a blue towel that he'd managed—just—to wrap around his wide waist. He punched Pete in the shoulder, and it took Pete conscious effort not to drive his fist into his grinning moon face.

"Pete, did you see that sack I made?" Stavis said, withdrawing a stick of deodorant from his locker. "Blindside hit, wham! Coughed up the ball and everything."

Pete counted to three so that he could choke back his initial response.

"I missed it," he said. "I was downfield covering that tall kid. Belton, I think his name was."

"Yeah, you shut him down today, man," Stavis replied, chucking Pete's shoulder again with the hand that had been holding the towel while swiping the deodorant onto his pits in a manner that Pete thought insufficient to mask or prevent any odors. "What did he have? One catch the whole game?"

"Two."

"Shut down!" Stavis said, tossing the deodorant back in his locker, where it clanged against the metal walls. He then turned and raised his arms over his head for a double high five.

Pete left him hanging. "Out back," he said. "I want to talk to you. Bring Harris, too."

After they were dressed, he led them outside and back to

the field, taking a seat on the bleachers. Wilson the janitor was going to be pissed, he thought, there was so much food and crap all over the seats and aisles.

As soon as they were seated on the bleacher below, Pete started his speech.

"We're the Pain Crew, right?" he said.

"Hell yeah!" Stavis bellowed, and Harris nodded. This was a promotion for him.

"And the Pain Crew is all about what?"

"Inflicting pain on our enemies," Stavis said, rubbing his thick hands together. "Like we did today."

"That's right, TC," Pete said, smiling. "Like we did today. But we weren't the only ones who inflicted pain, were we?"

TC looked puzzled, so Harris helped him out. "The crowd," he said. "I got hit with a goddam carrot." He shook his head. "Who throws a carrot?"

Pete clapped him on the back. "I got egged, man. Don't feel so bad." He looked at them both in turn. "Yeah, the crowd. But why was the crowd throwing stuff at us?"

"The dead kid," his subjects answered, in unison.

"That's right," Pete said. "The dead kid."

He took the blue paper with the work study students listed out of his shirt pocket. He unfolded the paper and smoothed it on the bleacher between them.

"This paper has the names of a bunch of dead kids, and the living kids that love them. Adam Layman's name is there, as is Scarypants's—Phoebe Kendall."

"Her little friend is in that class, too. Pinky McKnockers," Stavis said. "Thorny is too, I think."

"Yeah," Harris said, nodding. "Coach lets those two and Williams miss practice once a week to go to that thing. And he wouldn't even let me leave early for my grandmother's birthday party."

"Believe me, Morgan, Coach isn't happy about it. Kimchi ordered him to let them go. If he had his way, they wouldn't be going, and the zombie wouldn't even be on the team." He looked at each of them, his fingers tapping on the paper. "Which is why we really need to do something about this."

"You mad 'cause we got punked by those zombies in the woods, huh, Pete?" Stavis said.

Pete wanted to hit him, but he still needed him, so he continued to drum with his fingers on the page.

"Sure, that's part of it. We can't let anybody punk the Pain Crew, ever. But it is more than that. We need to do something because what's going on isn't *right*. Dead . . . *things* walking around, going to school, playing for the Badgers? It isn't *right*. This whole crap about *living impaired* and *differently biotic* is just *crap*. These things aren't even human. I read some stuff that says they're demons or signs of the end of the world or something— and it's probably true."

Stavis, who, Pete knew, had no hope in scoring high on the critical-thinking portion of his SAT, was nodding his head. Harris still looked like he was wondering where Pete was going with this.

"I don't think they're human, and they're certainly not alive.

I'm just waiting for the day they throw down and start shuffling around trying to eat our brains, to be honest with you. But even if that doesn't happen, what's next? Worm burgers making your milk shakes down at the Honeybee? Taking up scholarship money that should be going to kids with a life ahead of them? Just wait until a zombie wants to date your sister, Harris."

"I don't want any zombie sniffing around my sister," Harris said, and Pete knew he'd turned the corner.

"Me neither, pal, and that's why we've got to do something about this list," he said, shaking it in front of their faces before handing it off to Stavis, who pursed his lips and squinted as he read the names. "We've got to do something to . . . discourage them. Whatever they are."

"What do you mean by discourage?" Harris asked.

"I mean we have to take them out of the game," Pete said, "permanently."

"We can't go killing people," Harris said. "That's crazy."

"I'm not talking about killing *people*, man. The actual people on this list—Adam, Julie, and the others—I think they deserve a good beat-down for fraternizing with these monsters, but I'm not talking about killing them." He smiled. "Just the others."

Harris shook his head. "Pete, man . . ."

"Wait up, Harris. I want you to think about it. These aren't *people*. They aren't *citizens*. They don't have any rights at all. Haven't you been hearing all the talk in Washington? What that senator or whatever the hell he is was talking about today before the game, that's all BS, man. They're like mushrooms—

there's no law against killing a mushroom. People destroy these things all the time and nobody cares. It is only a matter of time before these things start to want to get with real girls. And real boys. Then they'll be marrying each other. Can you imagine that?"

"I've got a couple of thirteen-year-old cousins," Stavis said, scratching his stubble-covered head. "I'd kill any zombie that went for them."

"That's why all those zombies crawled out of the forest to attack us," Pete said. "Because that *thing* that they are calling Tommy Williams is trying to get into Julie's pants. And we *cannot* let that happen."

"Who's Julie?" Stavis asked, looking up from his list.

"What?"

"I said, Who's Julie? There isn't any Julie on the list."

Pete felt the heat rise to his cheeks.

"So sue me, idiot," he said. "Phoebe, Julie, Jenny, Katie, Hildegard. Whatever her name is, we have to protect her from them. We have to protect her from *herself*."

Stavis handed back the list and then spread his hands.

Pete held his gaze a moment. "So are you with me on this?"

"Absolutely."

"Harris?"

Harris rubbed his jaw with a nervous hand. "I guess so. Yeah, I guess so."

Pete reached out and clapped them both on the shoulders, the same way he'd slap their pads if they were in a huddle out on the field.

"Good."

His crew leaned in, and he told them his plan.

For the fifth time Phoebe read the note that Adam had given her. Once at the field, once in the car on the ride home, another three times throughout the course of the night, and the last as she sat in front of her computer screen.

There was an e-mail address at the bottom of the note. Phoebe typed a short reply and hit SEND.

# CHAPTER THIRTEEN

ON MONDAY A BLUE VAN PICKED PHOEBE and Karen DeSonne up at the school and brought them to the Hunter Foundation so they could do the work part of their work study. They exchanged brief pleasantries and then Karen took a book out of her satchel and read, and Phoebe stared out the window. Phoebe sneezed at one point and Karen coughed a minute later, and Phoebe thought that the dead girl might have been making fun of her, but she wasn't sure. The book Karen was reading was William Faulkner's *As I Lay Dying*.

Phoebe was certain that in getting the clerical job, she'd drawn the dullest detail of the lot. Margi was selected to work in the lab, and it sounded like Adam had a pretty easy gig on the facilities-management crew. The plan was for everyone to switch every six weeks, but after the first day, Phoebe knew she couldn't wait. They spent the entire four hours of their shift opening mail and sorting it into three piles—support, complaint, and junk. Angela stopped by at one point with two thick stacks of paper.

"E-mails," she said. "Please sort them in the same manner. I hope neither of you is easily offended."

Phoebe said that she wasn't, and as she turned, she saw Karen fluttering her eyelids with mock concern, her long lashes twitching with more movement than some of the other zombies seemed capable of. Karen's eyes had a thin corona of crystalline blue at the far edges of her retina but were the color of diamonds close to the pinprick pupils. Phoebe wondered what they had looked like when she was alive.

Most of the mail was hate mail, and it made for interesting reading, at least in the early going, when it seemed that there was some variety in the letters. Phoebe was initially impressed at how creative the writers were.

*Dear Necrofiliacs,*
*What you are doing is sinful and wrong and deep down you*
*know it. Why don't you just die too so you can be with the*
*dead people that you love so much. Dead people are evil and*
*demonaic and should all be burnt up. Jesus is coming and He*
*will be very displeased at the filthy things you are doing. You*
*will burn in Hell.*
*Sincerely,*
*A righteous soul*

"A righteous soul" wasn't as concerned with spelling as

he/she was with pronouncing judgment, apparently. There were a lot of righteous souls who wrote in with various admonitions, and while Phoebe thought the letters were vaguely creepy, they were nothing compared to the dozen or so that promised threats of a less metaphysical nature.

"Here's a good one," Karen said, walking over from the other cubicle with a piece of yellow notebook paper someone had block printed on. It was a short letter.

*You are just like an abortion clinic but worse. You steal the right to death as they steal the right to life and the explosions will reach you, too. This is your last chance.*

"Oh my," Phoebe said, looking over at the pile of mail in front of her.

Karen laughed. "Why don't you let me do the snail mail?" she said, scooping the pile off Phoebe's desk. "Who knows what sort of spores or toxins the . . . freaks . . . could send through the U.S. postal service?"

"Thanks, Karen."

"No worries, Phoebe. If I say I smell something funny . . . start running."

Phoebe smiled and hoped she was kidding.

At the end of the shift, she had two communiqués, both e-mails, in the positive column. One from a senator in Illinois who "believes in the work they are doing," and another who had forwarded a PayPal receipt of twenty dollars to an edress of the Hunter Foundation.

*I hope that one day I can send my daughter to you good people.*
*I thank you for the literature you e-mailed to me and we are*
*trying our best but it is difficult since my husband moved out.*
*We are still married and trying to be a family but my youngest*
*is too scared to live with Melissa right now. Melissa is able to*
*speak more clearly now but we were worried because when*
*Jonathan took Emily, Melissa stopped talking all together. Any*
*advice you have I would appreciate as always. Bless you all.*

Phoebe didn't know who she felt worse for in the shattered family, the girl who died, her parents, or her little sister. They were all suffering in their own ways, and Phoebe doubted that there was an easy answer for it. She wished she could have read the previous correspondence so she would know what it was that Angela or Alish wrote that had made such a difference for the writer of the e-mail.

She was going to show it to Karen, who had not looked up from her three tidy piles since grabbing the rest of the snail mail, but then Mr. Davidson, the director of operations, came to let them know that the van was ready to take them home.

The encounter group that comprised the bulk of their sessions was led by Angela in a comfortable lounge with a number of cushioned chairs and sofas arranged in a jagged semicircle. There were coffee tables, which usually had soft drinks and bags of potato chips that the living students had taken out of the adjoining pantry. Sometime during the orientation Phoebe had mentioned liking coffee and she noticed that they had added a coffee maker. The cushioned chairs were far more comfortable (and less creaky) than those in the library, and the sofas were long enough to seat two without touching. For the second session Phoebe and Margi plopped next to each other on a sofa.

"Hello," Angela said. "How was everyone's weekend?"

No one answered. The differently biotic kids were silent and still; the living kids, likewise, except for Thornton, who had difficulty remaining motionless.

Angela smiled. "The questions get much harder from here on out."

"I had a great weekend," Thornton said. "We won the game."

She nodded. "That's right. I had forgotten so many of you played."

"Yeah," Thorny added, "Tommy was the star even though he only got in for a few plays."

He meant it as a joke—Thornton didn't have a mean-spirited bone in his body—but the joke fell flat. Phoebe tried to read Tommy's expression but saw nothing there that she recognized. She wished she could tell if he had any feelings whatsoever about their upcoming date—was he nervous, excited, regretful, what?

"Tell you what," Adam said. "Denny would not have gotten sacked in the first half if Tommy had been on the line next to me."

Angela nodded. "No?"

"No. He's better than the kid Coach played instead."

"Why didn't the coach play Tommy more, then, Adam?"

"Come on," Adam said. "Coach was afraid to play the dead kid."

"Differently biotic," she said, still smiling. "A differently biotic kid."

Adam shrugged.

"No," Tommy said, and Angela turned the smile on him.

"No, that wasn't the reason?" she asked.

"No, not . . . differently biotic. Dead . . . is fine."

Angela arched her eyebrows. "You don't mind being called dead?"

"Zombie is fine too," Karen said. "We call each other zombies. With affection. Sort of the way . . . people . . . in cultural and ethnic . . . minorities . . . take back certain. . . pejoratives . . . to use among themselves."

Angela tapped her notebook with her pen. She blinked.

"I see. Is that true for everyone here, or do you see the term *zombie* as a hurtful word?"

Evan gave a slow nod, and Angela called on Tayshawn.

"Depends . . . on who . . . is saying it. And . . . how," he said.

"Living people mean for it to hurt," Thornton said, and when everyone turned toward him he looked like he wished he hadn't spoken. "I mean, sometimes. Not always."

"Do you ever use *zombie* to refer to a living person in a negative way?"

"Don't."

Colette had spoken, and Phoebe thought her voice was nothing like that of the carefree, uncomplicated girl she'd known two years ago. She realized it had taken Colette that long to let everyone know she did not like being called a zombie.

"Why is that, Colette?"

Phoebe shrank into the sofa. What if Colette's answer was that she didn't like being called a zombie because her so-called friends had abandoned her and left her alone in her suffering?

If Colette harbored such thoughts, she kept them to herself.

"People . . . hate . . . us."

Angela nodded, her eyes brimming with compassion. "Thank you, Colette. We appreciate your honesty." She regarded her notepad for a moment. "Which makes this a good time to point out the rules and intent of these sessions. Let me start by saying the goal is to have a greater education and understanding of the rights, thoughts, and concerns of differently biotic persons. We'd like you all to have a better understanding of each other's thoughts and feelings. We want you to leave here able to see through another person's eyes, and for them to be able to see you with greater clarity as well.

"To that end, we need to be able to create an environment of complete openness and honesty. We want you to speak your mind, but please do so respectfully. If you do not understand a person's point of view, please ask them questions. You do not have to raise your hand—we want the tone to be conversational rather than have you feel like you are being lectured to, but we do want to give everyone a chance, so I may interrupt to call on people if the dialogue is dominated by a few."

Phoebe thought that Angela may have glanced at Karen but could not be sure.

"This is the portion of the work study upon which you are graded. The grades you get will be dependant upon the level of your participation. Are there any questions on either the goals or the rules of participation?"

She looked at each person in turn, but no one spoke.

"No? Well, then, I have a question for Colette. Why do you think that people hate you?"

Colette seemed to stare through her, unaffected by her glow.

"Because . . . they . . . have . . . told . . . me."

"Mmmm. Has anyone else been told by someone that they were hated?"

Every hand went up initially, except for Phoebe's. Margi made a face at her.

"What? No one has ever said they hated me."

"Not in so many words," Margi replied.

She spoke for Phoebe alone, but Angela picked up on it.

"What do you mean, Margi?"

Phoebe was taken aback by the intensity of Margi's glare. "People give Pheebes and I a lot of crap because we dress different and act different."

"Hate is a strong word, Margi," Phoebe said. She was surprised at the level of Margi's conviction.

"It's the right one, though," Adam said. "Kids hate at the drop of a hat. People do."

"Who do you think hates you, Adam?" Angela asked.

"I'd prefer not to say."

"Fair enough. That is another rule, by the way. If a question makes you uncomfortable, you don't have to answer it. It won't affect your grade as long as you are participating otherwise."

"The question does not make me uncomfortable. I just don't want to answer it."

"Okay," Angela said, her easy smile remaining on her pretty face.

Adam spread his hands. "Okay."

"Great. Let me change direction here. Who in this room has been told they were loved? By anyone at all."

Most hands were raised except for Colette's and Sylvia Stelman's.

"Sylvia?"

Sylvia closed her eyes. A full minute later one of them opened.

"Not . . . since . . . I . . . died," she said. Her other eye opened.

Angela made a compassionate noise, but it was Karen who spoke up, her white diamond eyes seeming to catch even the pale fluorescent light above.

"I love you, Sylvia." She was seated on the end of the semicircle and she got to her feet and walked over to hug Sylvia. "You too, Colette."

Angela made some marks in her notebook. Colette did not seem to want to let go of Karen.

"Let's take a short break. When we get back, we'll read

some headlines and articles concerning the differently biotic that ran in newspapers and magazines last week."

Phoebe watched Karen hugging Colette. She swallowed twice and turned away, blinking.

# CHAPTER FOURTEEN

I CAN'T BELIEVE YOU ARE MAKING ME DO THIS."
Phoebe smiled. "I know."

"You owe me big time for this, Phoebe. This is big."

"Big," Phoebe repeated. Raindrops glittered on the windshield, backlit by the light of a passing car.

"So," Adam said, "is this like a date, or something?"

"Or something. I don't know."

"You've got feelings for him?"

"I have *feelings* for everyone, Adam." The more Adam talked, the slower he drove. Phoebe expected they would be crawling to a halt at any moment, the STD's truck rolling off into the grassy shoulder of the road.

"You know he's dead, right?"

She turned toward him in the seat, hot words rushing to her mouth. Adam stopped her by laughing.

"Just checking," he said.

"Watch the road," she said, unable to keep herself from smiling. "I don't know what it is, Adam. He's interesting to me, that's all."

"You can't be attracted to him, can you?" He turned toward her. "Just tell me to shut up if you want to."

"You don't have to shut up."

"Okay. So are you attracted to him? *Attracted* attracted?"

"I don't really know what I'm attracted to. I don't know."

Adam nodded. Phoebe wondered what he thought she was explaining.

"You don't date much," he said.

"I don't date much. Not like you, anyway. How is Whatsername, by the way?"

He shrugged. "She is who she is. I'm just trying to figure out where your head is at."

"Well, where is yours? With Whatsername, I mean."

"Nice segue. I dunno."

Phoebe smiled, leaning her head against the window. "Well, there you are. I dunno, either."

It seemed like a good time to be quiet, so they were.

Some minutes later they rolled up to the gates of the Hunter Foundation at the edge of town. Her new place of employment made Phoebe think of a medieval castle. Instead of a moat, there was a high stone wall and a road that was barred by a retracting metal gate.

Adam leaned out his window and pressed the red intercom button.

"Can I help you?" a flat, male voice answered.

"Adam Layman and Phoebe Kendall," Adam said. "We're here to pick up Tommy Williams."

There was a brief pause before the voice answered.

"Drive to Building One."

They waited for the iron gate to separate, the Hunter logo, a large stylized H and F split down the middle and slowly swung inward.

Adam put the STD's truck into gear. "I think that was Thorny," he said

"Could be. He's working security with you, right?"

He nodded. "Yep. But they call it *facilities maintenance*, probably because we take out the trash in addition to delivering beat downs to would-be bioist saboteurs."

"How many beat-downs have you delivered?" she said, laughing. "And just what is a bioist?"

"That would be zero beat-downs thus far, but I'm ever hopeful. And a bioist is like a racist but hates dead folk."

"Aha. Do you get guns? I'd love to see Thorny with a gun."

"No guns. He's bad enough with the Nextel. Duke carries a gun, though. And a Taser, if you can believe it."

"A *Taser*? Who's Duke?"

"Davidson. He's a real piece of work, that guy. Even Zumbrowski has more personality and warmth than that guy."

"Adam!"

"Sorry," he said. "I don't censor my thoughts around you."

Adam drove to Building One. Evan Talbot, his shock

of faded orange hair wicking up like thin strands of copper wire, was standing underneath the porch awning with Tommy.

"Is Evan coming too?" Adam said. "It'll be kind of cramped."

"I don't know," she said, and stepped out into the rain. "Hi, Tommy. Hey, Evan."

"Hello . . . Phoebe." Tommy took his time saying her name, but she wasn't sure that he needed to. "Can Adam . . . give Evan . . . a lift?"

Adam leaned over and called through the open door. "Hey, guys. I don't think there's room in the cab. I guess somebody can ride in the bed, but I think the rain is starting to pick up. It'll be a pretty wet ride."

Tommy nodded. "I can."

"No way," Evan replied. "I . . . get the . . . back."

He moved to the bumper and started to climb. Phoebe watched him awkwardly make his way into the bed of the truck, his arms and legs angular and stiff. He moved quickly for a dead kid, and she wondered what the difference was—why kids like Colette and Zumbrowski seemed to move at half zombie speed, which was like moving at a quarter of regular speed.

Adam got out of the truck and unlatched the lid of the tool kit that ran the width of the bed. "I think the STD has a painter's tarp back here. You're still going to get wet, but it ought to help."

"Gee," Evan said, "I hope . . . I don't catch a cold."

The right side of his mouth twitched. Zombie humor, Phoebe thought.

Adam spread the tarp out over Evan, who waited until he was finished before drawing it all the way over his head. Adam looked at him, a vague teen-size lump under the tarp, and shook his head.

"That's just creepy," he said.

Phoebe saw that the corner of Tommy's mouth was twitching as well. He looked at her, and she had the sensation that his eyes were illuminated.

"Do you . . . like to dance?" he said.

She laughed. "I guess so."

"Great. We . . . are going to . . . a club. The Haunted House."

Phoebe's eyebrows rose and her lips pursed in concentration. She was hyperaware of her expressions and wondered how they appeared to Tommy, whose facial movements were so minimal. She imagined her face a constantly shifting landscape of twitches and tics. If Tommy noticed her sudden self-consciousness, he did not react.

"We don't really . . . dance," he said. "We just sort of . . . jerk."

The thin line of his mouth turned up at the corner. Phoebe laughed.

"Holy crow," Adam said. "This really is a haunted house."

They pulled into the driveway of a home clear on the other side of the Oxoboxo, an old white colonial, faded and blank-looking in the pale light of dusk, with waist-high gray grass that rippled in the light breeze. There was a wide porch that ran the length of the front of the building, the roof of which had collapsed on one side. She saw a huge barn set back a little farther from the road that slouched at a forty-five-degree angle. On the main house, shutters hung askew from the few windows where they hadn't rotted off completely. Most of the windows themselves were broken, leaving glass teeth that shone in the headlights of the STD's truck.

The windows were rolled up, but they could hear music, loud and fast, blasting from the house. There was dim light somewhere deep inside the house, just a few flickers, as though it were lit entirely by two or three candles.

"Is that Grave Mistake?" Phoebe asked.

"A house . . . favorite," Tommy said. "Please come in."

Said the spider to the fly, she thought. Tommy got out of the truck, as did Adam. Phoebe's left side was warm from being wedged in between them; the right side, which had been against Tommy, felt no such additional warmth. She shivered when she left the truck, but it might have been the cool rain hitting the back of her neck.

They followed Tommy up the creaking porch steps. The music was at a near-punishing level now, as Grave Mistake segued into a metal group Phoebe did not recognize, the double bass drum threatening to send the rest of the roof into collapse. She could feel the vibrations through her boots. The air smelled of old wood and, subtly, of decay. Rotten wood or maybe vegetation smells kicked up by the rain from the surrounding woods.

"Is he okay back there?" Adam said, nodding at the truck. Phoebe had forgotten all about Evan, who, on cue, yanked the tarp down, a wide grin on his face.

It was disconcerting. They didn't smile much, the dead.

She and Adam exchanged a look of mild apprehension. She knew that Adam would not allow himself to show fear, and she was pretty good at being unflappable herself, but they were now in uncharted waters.

She felt Tommy's light touch on her arm.

"The music is . . . loud?" Tommy said.

"Very."

"We will . . . turn it down," he said. "It takes much . . . to make the . . . dead . . . feel."

"Must be hard of hearing, too. Do you guys live here?" Adam said above the renewed attack of an old Iron Maiden song. Phoebe poked him in the ribs. It took him a moment to realize why.

"Uh, so to speak. I mean."

Tommy smiled—it almost was a real smile. "Some of us do."

They followed him into the house. Beyond the foyer was a larger room where a number of figures were recognizable only as vague gloomy outlines blocking whatever dim light source there was.

"Kill!" Evan shouted. Phoebe's heartbeat tripped. "The music!"

For an instant, Phoebe's mind flashed to *The Return of Living Dead* and the scene where the punk chick takes off all of her clothes and starts dancing just before all the zombies come rushing out of their graves to claw her to death as they drag her down into the muddy soil.

The music stopped, and the only sound was a hollow thump as Tommy slapped the grinning Evan, Three Stooges style, in the back of the head.

"Welcome to the . . . Haunted House," Tommy said. "I'd like you to meet a few . . . people."

There were a dozen kids in the large room, which was empty except for two mismatched cabinet speakers resting on the floor and a short lamp with an amber lampshade on the fireplace mantel. Wires ran from the speakers, and a thick yellow extension cord ran into an adjacent room that had couches and chairs; there were a few more kids in there, but the room was in darkness, scarcely penetrated by the amber light.

Tommy said, "Zombies, this is Phoebe and Adam. Adam and . . . Phoebe, these are the . . . zombies."

Phoebe waved. Adam said, "Hey, zombies," but he was too far away for her to poke him again.

She recognized a few of them. Sylvia was there, as was the big kid Mal from their little adventure in the woods. He made his fingers twitch at them. Tayshawn came out of the dark room and said hello. Karen was wearing a long white dress that looked made of moonlight. She gave them an easy wave.

Tommy answered Tayshawn's unspoken question with a nod. "But softer. For our . . . guests."

Tayshawn disappeared, and a moment later a Slayer song filled the house, at a volume that was just a notch higher than Phoebe would have listened to on her iPod.

"Where do you get the power?" Adam asked, shouting into Tommy's ear.

"Generator," he replied. "Gas powered."

"How do you get the gas? You all have jobs?"

Tommy smiled. "We do . . . now. Some of us."

Phoebe looked around the room. A few of the kids *were* trying to dance, just as Tommy said. Evan's shoulders were giving a sort of Saint Vitus spasm; Mal, not quite as fast, was trying to bob his head along with the music, but was catching only every fourth or fifth beat. There was a girl with only one arm who was swaying slightly, her fingertips pressed against the wall as though to draw the music's vibrations into her lifeless body.

"'Angel of Death,' huh?" Adam said, picking up the title from the shrieking chorus. He wasn't much of a music guy, and Phoebe's three thousand attempts to change that character flaw had been met with complete resistance. He liked Kenny Chesney and maybe some classic rock. "And calling yourself zombies. You guys are big on irony, aren't you?"

She wondered if it was his size that made Adam confident enough to just start talking, to dive in and throw out one-liners that had all the marks of being insensitive. But that was Adam. She wondered if she were big or beautiful or the smartest kid in the school, would she possess that type of confidence.

"It is an ironic state that we are in, don't you think?"

This was from Karen, who had glided over to them. Like a ghost, Phoebe thought. Now who was being ironic?

"You have to admit, the whole idea of the dead coming back

to life is somewhat ironic. It is sort of the reverse of the . . . goth culture thing, wherein the living . . . romanticize things dead and of the dark."

Phoebe felt her cheeks flush and wondered if their crimson hue could be detected in the amber light. She couldn't tell if Karen was purposefully making fun of her or just pointing out reality as she saw it.

Karen was the only dead girl Phoebe knew that she could say without hesitation was beautiful. Colette, pretty in life, had lost more than a little of her luster in death; her dark eyes were now shrouded and her soft brunette curls looked brittle and mousy. Karen, though, was stunning. The dress she wore was spaghetti strapped and ended just below her knees; her bare shoulders were flawless, as was all of her skin, really. Her voice was free of the glottal hitch that the other dead kids exhibited, and contained all the appropriate inflection and nuance lacking among most of the dead. She was barefoot, and even her feet looked ethereal.

The differently biotic, Phoebe thought. Karen's eyes were white diamonds even in the murky light.

"I'd give up irony for reality any day," Karen said, her eyes seeming to bore deep into Phoebe's head.

Karen blinked. She leaned over and kissed Phoebe on the cheek and turned away. It happened so fast that Phoebe didn't have time to react. She watched Karen cross the room to Sylvia, who was standing motionless against a wall. She took Sylvia's hand and tugged her into the dark room. She realized that Karen's dress reminded her of the one Marilyn Monroe wore in that movie where she stood over the subway grate. *Gentlemen Prefer Blondes*? *Seven Year Itch*? Somehow the cool imprint of Karen's lips brought heat to Phoebe's cheek.

"What was that all about?" Adam said. Phoebe shook her head, words failing her.

"You would . . . think," Tommy said, "that Karen . . . would have it the . . . easiest . . . among us."

Phoebe nodded, waiting for him to continue.

"The reverse . . . is true," he said. "Ironically enough."

"She's amazing," Phoebe said.

"We have more . . . people . . . joining us every day."

"Yeah," Adam said. "I noticed that. There seem to be more zombies around than before. I had no idea so many kids had died around here."

Phoebe watched Tommy look up at him. "Most . . . did not die . . . around here."

"Oh, really? Where do they all come from?"

Tommy might have been smiling; it was difficult to tell in the light. "They come . . . from all around. And there are . . . reasons . . . to come."

Tayshawn cued up a Misfits song, "Dust to Dust," one of Phoebe's favorites, and the sudden shred of guitar cut through their conversation like a saw blade.

"Would . . . you . . . like to see . . . the rest of the house?"

"Okay," Phoebe said. "Adam, are you coming?"

"No thanks. Hey, Evan, you have any snacks here? Chips or anything?"

They all stared at him, and much to Phoebe's horror, Adam

made the corner of his mouth twitch up in a perfect parody of a differently biotic smile. Evan made a sound like the bleat of a small foreign car horn, the DB version of laughter. She wasn't sure what she wanted to kill Adam for more—the unsubtle way he cut her loose with Tommy, or the risks he was taking by offending their hosts.

But Tommy was smiling. "Let's go."

She followed him up a creaking staircase that ended in gloom.

"Uh, Tommy," she said, "you know I can't see in the dark like you guys."

"Right," he said, and offered his hand. It was cold and smooth.

She shivered, partly from his touch, and partly from the thought that in a few more steps she would be in total darkness, with only his hand to guide her.

"So," she said, sounding nervous even to herself, "you said that some of you . . . your friends stay here?"

"Yes," he said, his back now visible only as a vague grayish outline. "Some . . . parents . . . do not approve. Mal stays here. Sylvia. Careful. This is the last step."

"Not you?"

No," he said. "I . . . stay . . . with my mother. We live in a mobile home . . . at Oxoboxo Pines Mobile Home Park. Turn here. There is another flight of stairs."

The darkness at the top of the second set of stairs was complete. The music throbbed through the darkness, but they no longer had to shout to be heard.

"Really? With your mother?" She thought she was being

led along a corridor that must have run parallel to the stairs. She was afraid that if she reached out with her free hand, there wouldn't be any walls. His hand, which seemed to be warming in hers, was like a tether that anchored her to a swiftly crumbling reality.

"Really. In here."

She heard him open a door, and pale light reached her eyes from two huge windows in the far wall. One of the windows was broken, and wind shrieked into the room as though wounded by the jagged glass shards clinging to the frame. It was very chilly in the room.

Tommy wasn't cold. He let go of her hand and walked toward the window.

"I love this view," he said.

Hugging herself against the cold, she joined him by the window. They were high enough so they could see far into the Oxoboxo woods. The clouds above were rolling gray cotton against the dark sky; somewhere behind one of the spooling clouds was the moon. There was a flash, and a forking bolt of lightning cut the sky.

"Wow," Phoebe said. She looked over at him, mainly to erase the mental image of torch-bearing peasants clustering at the foundation of the house. He was staring off into the distance with an intensity that the living could never hope to match.

"The lake is beyond those trees," he said. "On clear nights when the moon is out you can see it glittering. Like the stars, only here on earth."

"I'd like to see that." Pheobe's voice was wavering as the cold began to seep through her skin.

"You're cold," he said. He took her hand, and it almost felt as though his hand were warmer than hers.

She wished she could say something clever and witty like Adam would have, something like *Yep, did ya forget I was still alive?* or *All the dead boys say I'm frigid.* The lines came to her, but she found she couldn't speak them like she would have if she had been with just Adam or Margi.

Tommy led her outside. "I want to show you one other room." They went back down to the second floor and along the corridor. Phoebe's sense of disorientation was now complete; she knew the big windows upstairs faced the backyard of the house, but she thought they had taken a right turn at the foot of the landing, which would put them back in that direction. The music was a dull vibration from somewhere far away.

Tommy stopped.

"Phoebe," he said, his voice echoing in the room.

"Yes, Tommy?"

"Do you trust me?"

*Uh-oh.* "Why wouldn't I?"

"I need you to trust me."

"Okay," she said, "I trust you."

He let go of her hand.

"Good." His voice seemed to recede in the darkness. "Please lie down."

"Uh, Tommy, I don't know . . ."

"Please," he said. "It isn't like that. Trust me."

Phoebe could hear herself breathe in the silent darkness. *What the heck is this?*

"On the floor?"

"Please."

She couldn't see him. She wondered if Adam could hear her scream if it came to that. And what if her scream was the zombies' cue to ambush Adam, to attack him and rip him limb from limb while she was up in the darkness alone with Tommy?

"Please," he said. "I . . . I . . . I . . . am not . . . going . . . to . . . touch you . . . if that . . . is what . . . you are . . . afraid of."

He was hard to read, like all the differently biotic. Their facial expressions were minimal, their body language unreadable, and their voices flat and toneless. She couldn't see him, but Phoebe thought she detected a sadness in his words as wide and deep as the Oxoboxo.

"Okay, Tommy," she said, crouching down until her fingertips grazed the dusty floor, the movement of her body kicking up smells of old paint and mildew. "I trust you."

She lay down and smoothed out her long skirt over her legs. She crossed her legs at the ankles and folded her hands on her stomach. Her eyes were open, and an eternity of darkness swirled above her.

"Thank . . . you," he whispered.

Her lips were dry. She licked them, trembling.

"I will . . . return," he said. "I need . . . to get . . . a flashlight."

"What?" she said. "You're going to leave me here?"

"Trust . . . me," he said. She could feel as well as hear his footsteps on the floorboards as he walked away.

Phoebe, Phoebe, Phoebe, she thought. What have you gotten yourself into now?

Patterns of purple began to pulse out of the darkness, strange amorphous shapes that radiated and spiraled toward her. She wished she'd paid more attention in biology, so that she'd have some rational explanation for the effect, some knowledge of rods or cones or corneal refraction or whatever it was that caused those violet shapes to flow toward her. The stillness of the room let her focus on the sounds from downstairs—Michale Graves, maybe—but the music grew fainter and fainter, as though invisible purple hands were lifting her up into the darkness, faster now, carrying her through the roof and into the sky, somewhere far beyond.

*Tommy, where are you?*

She sneezed, the scent of rotting wood filling her sinuses. Her folded hands were like blocks of ice on her stomach. She was cold all over, and it was like the darkness was drawing the heat from her body. Above the music she could hear her breathing and her heartbeat, but neither seemed normal to her; her heartbeat too slow, her breathing too fast. She closed her eyes when the purpling dark revealed what looked like faces and clutching hands, but when her eyes were closed, the faces were still there.

"T . . . Tommy?" she said, her voice a flat whisper.

She lay motionless—even her shivering stopped. She knew then that she never should have trusted him; that he was never coming back, that he had left her alone in the dark.

She wanted to rise, to lift herself off the cold wood floor but she could not breathe. The dust coated her lungs, and she wanted to move but was afraid. Because what if she couldn't move? What if she tried to move and her body would not obey her? What if she and her body were no longer one because the purpling dark had sucked her spirit out like liquid at the bottom of a glass?

Was this what they felt?

A light cut into the darkness beyond. She lifted her head from the floor, thinking she heard the tendons in her neck creak. And there was Tommy with a flashlight, standing in the doorway. She blinked as he trained the light in her direction, and the force of her exhalation made the dust whirl and spin.

"Thank you, Phoebe," he said.

She watched her breath, a mix of vapor and dust, flow from her. "Can I get up now?"

"Please. I want to show you . . . something."

He waved the light over to the wall behind her.

"Look," he said.

She looked.

The wall was covered with papers that had been taped, or in some cases, nailed onto the crumbling plaster. She got her legs under her and walked closer to the wall. She looked at the papers, some fluttering in the drafty air. Most were digital images printed to computer paper, but there were a few scattered photographs and a couple of slick Polaroids.

The blank stares of a hundred differently biotic kids looked out at her as though in accusation.

"Every one of them . . . felt . . . what you felt just now. The cold. The darkness. The . . . fear."

She could see the fear etched into the blank faces. A young-looking boy in a Boston Red Sox cap looked away from the camera, his expression like that of a beaten dog too scared to meet the eyes of his master. A girl whose face was horribly burned stared straight ahead, her one lidless eye a bottomless well of pain.

"Every one of them . . . died . . . and came back."

There was a boy with a shaved, scarred head who had taken off his shirt and put a large kitchen knife into his chest and was looking with a disturbing placid calm at whoever had snapped his picture. Another dead girl in a party dress stood beneath a poster of Cinderella Castle at Disney World, her face sallow and unsmiling.

"You . . . cannot . . . know . . . what . . . we . . . feel."

She turned away from the wall and the forlorn children upon it, hearing the same hurt quality somewhere in the monotone of his words. There were so many of them on the wall. Dozens. Maybe hundreds.

"Because . . . we . . . do not . . . know what . . . we feel."

She took a step toward him.

"I need to . . . help . . . us."

She hugged him, and although their embrace was not long, she began to feel warmer by the time they joined the kids moving to the heavy metal blaring on the first floor.

# CHAPTER FIFTEEN

ADAM ROLLED THE TRUCK INTO HIS driveway about an hour later. Phoebe thanked him and wished him a good night and hurried across the short stretch of grass that separated their houses. He watched her go, and she must have known he was watching, because she waved again as she worked her key into her front door.

He waved back, wishing that a vampire would swoop down at her from the roof of her house, or a pair of lurking thugs would leap from the bushes, because then he could spring into action. He could launch a flurry of kicks and open-hand strikes to her would-be attackers and beat them into submission, and when he was done she'd know. She'd know that she was protected, and she'd know that he would always be there for her. She'd know everything.

He slapped the hood of the truck in frustration.

There were only three other cars and the truck at the home of the STD, which meant that Jimmy and Johnny were still out, causing chaos. Fix cars, drive cars, break cars. Sometimes Adam looked with jealousy at their lives, which seemed so uncomplicated to him.

Inside, the STD was awake and in front of the television, flipping back and forth between a baseball game and some sitcom, a line of empties on the floor on the side of his recliner.

The STD looked over at him and nodded. "Hey," he said.

"Hey," Adam replied. "Mom in bed?"

"Yeah," came the wheezing reply. The STD's work shirt was open to his navel, and a tuft of wiry black hair poked out at the V of his once-white undershirt. His arms were still stained with grease.

"She was pretty tired tonight. I think her boss was giving her crap again this week."

Adam nodded. His mom worked at a bank, and her boss was an arrogant, brusque little man who had reduced her to tears on several occasions.

"How was your date?"

Adam looked for signs of sarcasm, but saw none in the weathered face. The STD liked watching television with the lights off, and the blue illumination from the screen lent his face a pale, differently biotic quality.

"It was good," he said. "We went to a party."

"Oh yeah? Did you have any beer?"

"Naw."

Adam felt his stare. "Well, you can get one now if you want. Long as you bring me one."

"Okay, Joe. Thanks."

Adam went to the refrigerator and cracked a couple cans of beer, one for him, and one for Big Joe Garrity, the STD. Joe wasn't such a bad guy once he got into his third or fourth beer, which was usually an hour or so after dinner. Adam handed him the beer and lay down on the couch, balancing his can on his wide chest.

"You like this girl, don't you?" Joe asked him after taking a noisy sip.

"Yeah," Adam said. "Yeah, I do."

"This the cheerleader? The blonde?"

"Holly?" Adam said. The Sox were up three to two, but there was one more inning to play. "Naw. I quit seeing her this summer for the most part."

Joe gave a quiet belch and shifted in his seat, almost dropping his can. "Pretty girl," he said. "Not a whole lot of personality, though."

Pershonality, Adam thought. His father, Bill Layman, had been an alcoholic too, but his "pershonality" went the other way when he drank. While the STD grew more tolerable, Bill Layman grew demonic. Adam sipped from his can, wondering why his mom needed to go for guys that drank. He wondered about Phoebe.

The STD swore when the tying run reached first after a grounder bounced off the third baseman's glove.

"You're right," Adam said, after a time.

"So who's the new girlfriend? Is it the one from next door, finally?"

And the truth shall set you free, Adam thought. He took another sip.

"Yep."

The STD was silent for a moment. The next batter chopped the ball right to the second baseman, who ended the game with an effortless double play.

"She seems like a nice kid," Joe said.

"Yeah," Adam said.

Joe fell asleep somewhere in the ninth inning between the careful dissection of the pitch count and the in-depth analysis of the batting order change. Adam listened to his snores until he heard one of his stepbrothers pull into the driveway, at which point he gathered the empties and dumped them into the recycling bin after washing them. Johnny came in, smelling of beer and cigarettes, and thumped him on the shoulder.

"Hey, bro," he said, heading down the hall to his room.

"Hey." Adam drained the remainder of his can into the sink before following him down the hall to his own room.

Phoebe took the bus the next day, so Adam was alone with his thoughts for the drive. He tuned into a sports radio station, something he never got to do when Phoebe was in the truck with him, and within minutes he was reminded that the pleasant glow Joe had been sporting last night would be gone today because the Sox ended up losing in the ninth on a two-run homer. Bye, Joe. Thanks for stopping in. Hello, STD. Adam wondered if any other kids had their home life governed chiefly by the consumption of alcohol and the Sox's record.

He arrived at school early. Some of the teachers were just coming in, and none of the buses had arrived yet. He pulled into the student lot at the bottom of the hill and debated going inside, then decided against it. He went through his backpack and found his creased copy of *Wuthering Heights* and tossed it onto the seat next to him as though he were planning on reading it. The radio personality was discussing the relative importance of the Red Sox game to the cosmos, and he took out his history text-book because they were due for a quiz, and he realized that the only reason he was waiting in his car was so that he could watch Phoebe leave her bus and walk up the steps and into the school.

Dang, he thought. He shoved *Wuthering Heights* back into his pack, got the duffel with his gear out of the truck bed, and started the uphill trek to the school.

He was about halfway up when he watched a green station wagon roll next to the curb in the bus lane, and then he saw a familiar shock of pale orange hair appear over the roof of the car. Evan waved at the driver and watched as the car pulled away. Adam jogged up another half flight of steps so he could get a good look at the driver, who was a woman with hair a shade darker than Evan's.

His mom, Adam thought. Dead kids can have mothers.

"Hey, Evan!" he called. "Wait up!"

Evan turned like he expected the shout to be followed by a thrown rock. Adam called his name again, and then Evan waved a pale hand and waited for him outside the school.

"Hey," Adam said, his breathing even, thanks to the weeks of conditioning, "thanks for a good time last night."

He noticed that Evan had a scattering of light beige spots across the bridge of his nose and under his eyes, the ghosts of freckles. He was about half Adam's size, a skinny little guy in an oversized T-shirt and jeans. He stood there looking up at Adam as though waiting for a punch line.

"That was pretty cool, seeing where you guys hang out. I mean, listening to the music you guys listen to and all." Adam shook his head and whistled. "That sounds really stupid, huh?"

Evan give his weird lamb's bleat of a laugh. "I wish . . . I could still . . . whistle," he said. "I . . . try . . . and try . . . but I can't get it. I used to be a . . . great whistler."

"No kidding?" Adam said, not knowing what to say next, and feeling stupid for having said anything in the first place. A bus roared up along the road next to them as Evan tried to say something, but his words were gobbled up by the guttural engine.

"What?"

"I . . . said . . . that you and . . . Phoebe . . . were the first . . . living . . . kids we've had over," he said.

"Really? Wow, what an honor," Adam said. "So, do you . . . stay there?"

"I stay with my . . . family," he said. Another bus chugged up the hill, and Adam could see Margi's pink spikes through a window toward the back.

"Oh yeah? Was that your mom that dropped you off?"

Evan nodded, and Adam thought he could detect the slightest hint of a smile on his pale face.

"Cool," Adam said. "So hey, I was wondering . . . I've got a question for you. But don't take it the wrong way, okay? I don't mean to be insulting, so please don't be insulted, okay?"

Evan looked like he was trying to shrug, but one shoulder lifted considerably higher than the other.

"Shoot," he said.

"So what I was wondering," Adam said, conscious that behind him the buses had started to release their passengers. "What is it like . . . what is it like to be dead?"

Evan looked at him with his dull, unblinking blue eyes long enough for Adam to think that, despite his precautions, he'd insulted Evan after all, but then the smaller boy spoke.

"I don't know," he said. "What is it like . . . to be alive?"

His expression didn't change as he laughed again, the sound like that of someone heavy stepping on a dog's squeak toy.

Adam felt himself grinning.

He looked over at the buses just as Phoebe got off. He started to wave, but she wasn't looking at him, her face shrouded by a curtain of shiny black hair as Margi talked at her, her spangled arms stabbing the air, emphasizing whatever ludicrous point she was trying to make. Tommy was right behind them.

Phoebe laughed, her hair falling back over her shoulder and revealing her open mouth, her smooth pale skin. Adam smiled, but then Tommy managed to catch up with them, blocking his view.

Adam sighed. "Let's get to class, Evan," he said, hefting his duffel and slowing his pace so the smaller boy could keep up.

# CHAPTER SIXTEEN

"GOOD AFTERNOON, EVERYONE," ANGELA said, her brisk stride carrying her into the middle of the room. As she passed Phoebe, she put a soft, warm hand on her shoulder.

She was followed by Alish and a trim young man who Phoebe recognized instantly as Skip Slydell, the author of many books and articles on the whole undead movement. "Today we have a special guest who you will recognize from having watched the CNN video last week. Please welcome Skip Slydell."

Skip waved. "Thank you, Angela and Mr. Hunter, for letting me come here today. And thanks especially to your students for putting up with me for the next hour or so."

Margi looked at Phoebe and rolled her eyes heavenward, pointing out that every time Principal Kim or Angela introduced a guest speaker to the class they did it with a sort of over-the-top elated gravitas, as though the coming of the guest speaker were both a joyous and serious occasion.

The first thing Slydell did was hand out business cards to all the kids. Phoebe watched Tayshawn grip his in two hands and bring it within inches of his nose, his eyes crossing.

SKIP SLYDELL ENTERPRISES, the card read, and featured a studio head-and-shoulders shot of Skip beaming over a pile of books and products. IN ASSOCIATION WITH THE HUNTER FOUNDATION. There was an 800 number on the bottom of the card.

"Let's get to it, shall we?" he said. "Ms. Hunter has told me that one of the main goals of this foundation that you are all working for and learning in is something I call the successful acclimation of differently biotic persons into society, as well as to acclimate society to a point where it is more fully accepting of differently biotic persons within it. Does that make sense? Any questions?"

He did not wait for either question to be answered. He walked as he talked, with his large, soft-looking hands waving and pointing to accentuate his statements. He took great care to make eye contact with every person, and would hold the contact a few beats longer when he focused on one of the differently biotic people. He spoke so quickly that Phoebe thought it was unlikely that most of the dead kids could follow. She might have had trouble following had she not made herself a coffee when she came in.

"Could you all turn your chairs over here? Would that be okay?" There were two long tables at the back of the room, each covered with a white cloth that hid whatever was stacked from view. He stood in front of them.

"The question then becomes, How can we make that acclimation happen? How *can* we make that acclimation happen? It isn't easy to do, what we are planning. Change the culture. Changing the culture is very, very difficult, even in this country. You and I"—and here he held Sylvia's blank gaze for a pause of nearly twenty seconds—"you and I have not chosen easy work for ourselves. Not at all. It isn't easy to transform culture."

He leaned back against the table, staggering a bit, as though the enormity of their shared task had overtaken him and left him breathless. Margi was making a low humming sound that brought a smile to Phoebe's lips, because it meant Margi had turned on her bullshit detector.

"What we are going to do is not easy. But it can be done. Even here in America. Elvis Presley did it. Martin Luther King did it. Jimi Hendrix. John F. Kennedy. Bill Gates. Michael Jordan. The two guys that created *South Park*."

The American community of saints, Phoebe thought.

"And we can do it, too. Do you follow me? The fact of the matter is that the heavy lifting, the really hard work, has already been done. You know why?" He smiled. "Because the undead are a fact of life. That's a funny phrase, isn't it? Almost an oxymoron. Say it with me: *the undead are a fact of life.*"

No one joined him in the chorus, but a few of the kids looked a little uncomfortable—undead wasn't a word typically used in polite society, especially not in a room full of undead kids.

"How did what I just said make you feel? Think about that for a minute. The undead are a fact of life. How do you feel? Karen, isn't it? Could you share your feelings on what I just said?"

Karen blinked. "It's true," she said, and blinked again. "You've presented a reality that not everyone has chosen . . . to accept."

"Wow," he said, grinning at her. "Wow. A reality that not everyone has chosen to accept. Wow. I'm writing that down."

He withdrew a notepad from a leather case and began to write. "Exceptional. Thank you for that. What about the terminology I used?" he asked. "How do you feel about that?"

"I'm . . . neutral. But it bothers me when certain people use that word," she said, "about me."

"But it didn't bother you when I said it?" he asked, tossing his notebook on the table.

She shook her head, her hair swinging like curtains of platinum caught in a breeze.

"Thank you. That means a lot, really."

"Not yet, anyhow," she said, returning his stare calmly. Evan gave his one-note bleat of a laugh.

"Fair enough,' he said, laughing himself. He peeled back one of the tablecloths like a magician about to reveal a trick. "Angela told me that you kids . . . you undead kids . . . like to call yourselves zombies, too. Is that right? Anybody can answer."

"Yes," Evan said.

"Do the same rules apply? You guys can say zombie, but you might get mad if somebody—somebody living says it?"

"Depends," Tommy said.

"On what?" Skip asked, nodding at him with encouragement.

"Depends on how they say it."

"Okay," he said, turning to the other half of the room, where the living kids sat. "What about you all? Don't just sit there like zombies, especially when the zombies are giving me all the answers! What do you think?"

"About what?" Adam said, the irritation evident in his voice.

"About the word *zombie!* Do you ever call Thomas Williams a zombie?"

"No."

"Well, why the hell not?" he said, throwing his hands in the air. He'd really worked himself into a lather now.

"Because I respect Tommy. I wouldn't say or do something that possibly could hurt him."

Slydell nodded. "What about you, Williams? You care what Mr. Layman calls you? Would you get all pissed off if he called you a dead head or a zombie?"

Tommy shook his head.

"Why?"

"Because Adam . . . is my friend."

"Hallelujah! " Slydell yelled, staring up through the ceiling. "You see that? Do you see that, everyone? Layman here won't call his pal Tommy a zombie because he respects him. And ole Tom wouldn't care if Adam did because he considers him a friend. You see that? Do you understand where I'm going here?"

He walked in front of Zumbrowski with his hands on his hips. "Do you know what those two are doing, Kevin? Sylvia? Margi? Those two are transforming the culture, and that is what it is all about."

He picked up his mystery gear on the table and began unfolding what looked like a black T-shirt.

"How'd you get to be friends, guys? Was it the football?"

"Yes."

"Pretty much."

"So it took a radical act—that of a zombie putting on the pads and helmet—for that to happen, didn't it?"

"I guess so," Adam said.

"You guess so? You *guess*? You'd better know, son, because you and Tommy are on the bleeding edge of a new society. You guys are it. Transformation always requires radical action. Do you follow? *Transformation always requires radical action.* If Elvis Presley had not taken the radical action of singing a style of music traditionally sung by black people, we may never have had the transformation that rock and roll enacted on modern society. If Martin Luther King had not taken the radical action of organizing and speaking around the cause of civil rights, we may have never undergone the transformation from an oppressive state to one of freedom and equal opportunity for all. And that transformation is not yet complete. You kids are living—or unliving, as the case may be—proof of that."

"What radical action did Michael Jordan take?" Thornton asked.

Slydell smiled at him. "Wise guy, huh? No radical action. He was just radically better than everyone else. That alone transformed the game. And that's what we're all about. Transforming the game."

Phoebe wondered how he could just talk and talk like this without ever pausing for breath. She thought that it would be fun—and exhausting—to watch him and Margi have a conversation, if only Margi was in a better mood.

"Okay. A little more philosophy. Then I'm going to get into how you can help me. And when I say how you can help me, I'm really saying how you can help society. How you can help yourselves. Help me do that. Okay? Now—you two, Adam and Tommy. You're friends. Did you have any dead friends before Tommy, Adam?"

"Not really, no."

"How about you, Tomàs? Any blood bags you would call friends?"

Tommy's gaze drifted toward Phoebe. "A few."

"A few. Well, okay. But in this case it took a radical action on your part to *transform* Adam. Without the radical action, the transformation would not have occurred. Adam would have no undead friends."

"Hold up," Adam said. "You can't assume—"

"Stay with me, Adam. We'll get to your thoughts in a

moment. Without the radical action, transformation would not have occurred. Was everyone as thrilled with this action as Adam was? Did everyone embrace Tommy Williams onto the football team and everything was just hunky-dory? No? No! As I recall, it was protest in the streets! If the newspapers were accurate, as we all know they so often are, there were signs, placards, chants! Thrown fruit!"

Phoebe looked over at Adam, sitting slightly apart from the group as he always was. His hands were folded and his elbows on the tops of his knees. He was staring at the floor.

"That's the second necessary ingredient of culture change, people. The second key to transformation. Conflict. Radical action coupled with radical response. Only then can we get true change. There was a reason that I used strong words with you, impolite words like 'zombie' and 'undead' and 'blood bag,' and the reason was not because I wanted to be offensive. I used those words because *right now* they are radical words, and I wanted to provoke a radical reaction in you. Some of you are cool with using 'zombie' to refer to yourselves. Some of you are not cool with using the term at all. All apologies to Angela, but I need your help in figuring out a term we can *all* be cool with, because 'differently biotic' is not going to cut it. Too cold, too many syllables. No panache. Frankly, it just ain't sexy enough. Now, *zombie* . . . I personally think that makes a statement. The first step toward transforming a culture is to give names and definitions to the transformative aspects of that culture. You are *zombies*, kids. And you need to use that term with pride, *regardless* of the reaction that it provokes."

Phoebe wondered if any of the other kids realized that Skip had given them about three "first steps" in his talk. But he was like a train racing to get back to the station before sunset; Colette had raised her hand at some point during the unifying-effects-of-team-sports speech, and Slydell had still not allowed her to speak.

He unfurled the T-shirt he was holding. It was basic black with the words DEAD . . . AND LOVING IT! in greenish lettering that probably glowed in the dark. The word *dead* was written in a creepy movie-poster font, and the rest was in emphatic capital letters.

"What do you think of this shirt?" Skip asked. "How does it make you feel?"

"I . . . think it is cool," Evan said, his mouth twitching.

"Good. It's yours," he said, throwing it in Evan's face. "What about this one?"

The shirt was gray with a white fist and the words ZOMBIE POWER! in the same creepy font as the first. The skin stretched tightly on the cartoon fist so that the knuckles were clearly visible. "I've got a few of those." He tossed one to Tayshawn, one to Sylvia, and one to Thornton.

"This one is a little risky," he said, "a little more radical. Let me know what you think."

The shirt was black with white no-nonsense lettering. It said OPEN GRAVES, OPEN MINDS above a stylized image of an open grave in a cemetery.

"I like that one," Phoebe said at the same time as Karen.

"Really?" Slydell said. "Cool. I've got two."

There were a few other items. Hats, wristbands. Temporary tattoos that would work even on the rubbery skin of the dead.

"Okay, kids," Skip said, "here's my point. Don't be afraid to be who you are. And don't be afraid to tell people who you are, either. Understand that these things I've given you have been designed to provoke a reaction in people, and that the reaction will not always be pleasant. You have to be brave. But being brave is the first step toward transforming the culture."

There it was again, Phoebe thought, another first step. She ran the soft cotton of her new shirt through her hands. It *was* a cool shirt. . . .

"Last thing," Slydell said, "and then I'm going to get out of your hair. As you know, when I started talking to you today, I said I was going to need your help to make a change, and I do. Like it or not, one of the quickest ways to evoke a culture change is to get the message into the hands of the young and the hip. I need a street team, in other words, to help me get this message out. Many of these products are going to be carried in Wild Thingz! stores and at select music outlets. We're putting together a music compilation as well, one that will have the Creeps and The Restless Souls and other bands that you are probably familiar with. I'm leaving you with some homework. What I want you to think on, and write some ideas down to discuss, is what other products—be they fashion, entertainment, whatever—you think we could put out that would help us get our message of radical transformation out there, and really start changing the world. So think on that, and we'll have some fun kicking it around when the delightful Ms. Angela invites me back here. I'll have some more swag for you to take, too. You can e-mail me at skippy@slydellco.com. I'd love to hear from you. I'm out of time, and I'm outta here. Thanks!"

Phoebe watched him leave the classroom. A few kids clapped, and without turning, he lifted his hand above his head as though in triumph. The lounge felt drained and empty now that it was no longer filled with his words.

"We've still got some time," Margi said, glancing at her cell phone and looking bored.

"Hey, Daffy," Adam said, "you didn't get any loot."

Margi shrugged. She was still the quietest one in the group; she spoke even less than Sylvia or Colette, and did so only when called on, a fact that boggled Phoebe's mind.

"Maybe she's unclear as to what exactly our message . . . of transformation is," Karen said. "I know I am."

Margi looked ticked off, like she thought Karen was making fun of her. But before Phoebe could intervene, Adam spoke.

"I think the message is that we can bring attention to the plight of the differently biotic by getting our friends to buy T-shirts."

Evan, who was wearing both the shirt and a black baseball cap that read, simply, DEAD, laughed his abrupt and disconcerting laugh. He looked even paler with his red hair encapsulated by the black hat.

"The way to social change in America is through conspicuous

consumption, hmm?" Karen said. "That zombie theme goes way back."

She paused, and then winked at Phoebe.

"Cool shirt, though."

# CHAPTER SEVENTEEN

P HOEBE DIDN'T LIKE LYING TO HER
parents, but sometimes it was a necessity. No
matter how progressive they might consider
themselves to be—and Phoebe had to admit
they were pretty progressive—there was no way that they would
allow her to spend time alone with a dead boy.

She was sitting in the cafeteria with Adam and Margi, both
of whom were staring at her with a mixture of concern and
anger.

"God," she said, "you two look so much like my parents
right now it scares me."

"I hope not," Margi said. "I'd like to think you'd tell me and
Lame Man the truth."

"Now that you have ensnared Daffy and me in your
impenetrable web of lies," Adam said, "go over again what
we're supposed to say?"

Phoebe sighed. "I went over to Margi's to listen to some new music," she began.

"Ah. The old standby."

"Right. We listened to some music, and then Adam called to see if we wanted to go to a movie."

"Yeah, that's likely," Adam said. "What movie? I don't even know what's out."

"Wait a minute. Why would we go out with Adam?"

Phoebe sighed again. "Because we need to get out of your house in case your parents talk to mine. "

"Why involve me in the first place?" Margi said. "Why didn't you just tell them you were going out with Adam?"

Phoebe shrugged. "I didn't think about it. You know how these stories kind of get away from you."

Margi made a disgusted noise and slapped the remains of her cheese sandwich down on the table.

Adam was shaking his head. "So basically, to cover your tall tales, I need to vacate my house for the evening, lest your dad peek out the window and see the STD's truck sitting in the driveway."

Phoebe shrunk in her seat. "You don't have plans, do you?"

"I was going to get a jump on my English homework. I was going to read *Wuthering Heights* and have a nice bubble bath."

They laughed. "Seriously though, I hope I can get the truck."

"So what am I supposed to do?" Margi said. "Go hide in the woods with your other zombie pals?"

"I was thinking that maybe you and Adam could go to a movie. That way you could tell me the plot when Adam gives me a ride home."

Margi blinked at her and threw her dessert, a wrapped Hostess snack cake, which bounced off Phoebe's chest.

Adam looked at Margi and then back at Phoebe. "You're paying," he told Phoebe.

Margi had a few more questions for Phoebe on the bus ride home.

"I can't believe you just assumed I'd lie for you," Margi said, her pink spiked bangs grazing the window as she made a point of not looking at Phoebe.

"Yes, you can. That's not what is bothering you."

"Oh really, Miss Telepathetic? What is bothering me, then?"

Phoebe closed one eye and touched Margi's temple. "I sense confusion . . . and anger . . . and worry."

"Of course I'm worried, dummy! He's a dead kid!"

"Shhhh!" Colette was sitting three seats in front of them, with Tommy across the aisle.

"Don't shush me, Phoebe. It's weird and you know it's weird. Look, I have goose bumps! Feel my arm."

Phoebe did. "Yep, those are goose bumps. Or a bad case of arm acne. Or as I call it, armcne."

At first, her stupid comment failed to generate the laugh she'd intended, but Margi could no longer choke it back and snorted, shaking her head.

Phoebe clapped her on the back. "Now will you please be

cool? He's just a friend and we're going to his mom's house, okay? His mom gets home at four."

"A lot can happen in an hour."

"Puh-lease. Like you would know." She poked Margi in the ribs and Margi giggled, which only made her more irritated.

"It's creepy."

"Have an open mind."

"Ick."

"Go home and put on your Zombie Power! T-shirt."

"I didn't get one of those. I got Some of My Best Friends Are Dead, and only because Angela made sure that I didn't go home empty-handed."

"That's lame."

"Very."

"I've been thinking of some good ones for next week: Life Is Just a State of Mind, He Who Dies With the Most Toys . . . Is Sitting Over There."

"Funny," Margi said without enthusiasm. "Phoebe."

"Yeah?"

"Be careful."

Margi's stop was early on the line. Phoebe stood to let her out.

The bus rolled to a stop at the foot of the Oxoboxo Pines Mobile Home Park. The coarse driveway sand crunched beneath Phoebe's boots as she walked beside Tommy, who hadn't spoken since they disembarked.

"Where does Colette live?" Phoebe asked, then caught herself. "Stay, I mean?"

Tommy smiled. His mouth seemed more pliable lately; instead of the slight twitch on one side, both corners of his mouth stretched upward.

"The Haunted House."

"Really? When her parents moved . . ."

"The laws . . . do not always protect . . . the dead. And sometimes they do. A parent is no longer legally . . . responsible . . . to take care of their . . . deceased children. Colette was abandoned. As were many of us."

Phoebe thought about Colette's parents, of a day trip they had taken to the beach the year before Colette died. Phoebe remembered being wedged in the backseat between Colette and her brother on the long ride to Misquamicut. Mrs. Beauvoir spent the day sunning herself while Peter tossed the Frisbee back and forth to her and Colette, who had no aptitude, even then, for the game. Mr. Beauvior slept in a lawn chair the whole afternoon. After Colette died, he took a job somewhere down south, and they moved, sans Colette.

"How does she get away with it, though?" she said. "I mean, if I tried to go live in an abandoned house somewhere, they would come and get me and put me in a reform school or something."

"You aren't dead."

They arrived at a mobile home with blue shutters and a well-tended yard. There was a plastic awning above a walkway that led to the front steps. A number of plants and flowers sat in hanging pots from the frame and sitting along the ground.

Tommy withdrew a key from his pocket, a process that was much more involved for him than it would be for a normal kid. Phoebe watched him, unsure if she should offer to help.

"We are . . . inconvenient. No one knows what . . . to do with us. We do not know what to do . . . with ourselves."

He unlocked the door and they entered the living room. There was a couch and a television, and plants were everywhere. There was a small round table with four seats in the corner near a beaded curtain that separated the room from the kitchen. A fat black cat trotted over to them and sniffed at Phoebe's boots. Phoebe bent to pet the cat, and it arched its back in appreciation.

"That's Gamera," Tommy said. "He hates dead people."

Gamera enjoyed having his neck scratched. Phoebe looked up at Tommy, who was smiling.

"There's a shelter in Winford that many . . . zombies . . . stay at. St. Jude's Mission. It is run . . . by a priest who is sympathetic . . . to our cause. Colette stays there sometimes and . . . Kevin. It is not a home. The Haunted House is better, for most."

Phoebe rose, smoothing some cat hair off her jeans. Gamera twisted himself around her boot. "Where do the other kids in the work study stay? Karen and the others?"

"Karen . . . is with her parents. Evan also. Tayshawn stays

with his grandmother, but the situation is . . . different. Sylvia is . . . at the foundation."

"She *lives* there?" she asked. Tommy smiled. "You know what I mean. I thought you said she was staying at the Haunted House."

"We wanted her to stay at the Haunted House. But her need is . . . great. And the foundation is . . . well equipped."

"Huh."

"Yes," he said. "We have concerns as well."

"Who is this 'we' you keep referring to? Is it the royal 'we'? The papal 'we'?"

She thought his smile grew a bit wider. "I want to show you something," he said, and motioned for her to follow him through the kitchen to a closed door, which no doubt led to his bedroom.

"Um, could you tell me where the bathroom is?"

"Back that way. On . . . the right."

"Thanks."

She left her hands under the faucet for a couple minutes, the cool water making her hands tingle and the floral scent of the hand soap filling her nostrils. Margi's words echoed in her head, and she stayed behind the locked door longer than she needed to.

She walked back. Tommy's door was open and his complexion had taken on a bluish cast as he sat in front of a computer screen in the dark. The room itself was a male version of hers, with books and a stereo and posters, the differences being that the stereo was a lot cheaper and there were sports stars mixed in among the musicians on the walls. And the room was a lot neater.

"I wanted to show you this," Tommy said, and motioned to the screen.

Phoebe saw that Tommy was on a Web site called mysocalledundeath.com. The home page was decorated with comic book zombies shambling from graves, and menacing pink people, mostly blond and buxom. Some familiar heavy metal mascots were present as well.

"What is this?" she said, leaning over his shoulder. There was a subtle scent to him, one that she could not quite identify. Something outdoorsy. She resisted the urge to touch his shoulder.

"My blog."

"Your blog? No way."

"Way. I've got close to a thousand subscribers."

"Wow." She leaned in closer. When he typed she could see the muscles of his arms move underneath his shirt.

There were a few hot links on the home page: Archive, Deadline, MSCU Alumni, Links.

"I try to write . . . every night."

"Can I read some?"

He clicked on the Deadline link, and there was an entry for the day prior. She began to read.

*Week three of the Hunter Foundation's necrohumanitarian experiment. The class was subjected to the crass but persuasive arguments of Mr. Steven "Skip" Slydell, with whom all of you are by now well familiar, thanks to his being a good year's worth of blog fodder. Skip's main thesis seems to be that the zombie community can achieve legitimacy through consumerism and sloganeering. He dispensed swag to the class; I myself am now the proud owner of a new* Zombie Power! *T-shirt. There is something almost endearing in his shameless hucksterism, and the gear he showered us with does have a certain radical chic to it. You can't help but question his motives, which almost certainly are profit driven, but at the same time you can't help but be drawn into his circle of "positive transformation." If there is cheesy packaging around a universal truth, does that make the universal truth inside any less valid?*

*In a perfect universe, we would not need the Skip Slydells of the world to sell us the messages that we should be creating ourselves. But the fact of the matter is, until we as a group are able to fully take advantage of the DIY ethic that built this country, we are at the mercy of the Slydells. Until we have a press, a voice, a piece of the media, we need to take what we can get. Until we can get hired and have some economic worth, we need to take what we can get. Many of us by now have been dead for three years, meaning that by human terms some of us are now eighteen and should have the legal right to vote, but of course our death certificates are, for all intents and purposes, a complete revocation of our rights and citizenship.*

*So I'll work with Skip Slydell as best as I possibly can. I'll do so knowing that I am selling myself and all of you out, but that such sellouts are necessary to really make change happen.*

At the bottom, there was a flashing banner ad that read, *Support Proposition 77.*

"What is Proposition 77?"

"A proposal to have the federal government issue a rebirth certificate to anyone who comes back . . . from the dead. It's what would grant us some rights and . . . citizenship."

"So you could hang with the humans, huh?"

He looked up at her. "Poor word choice?"

"I'm cool with it, but you know how us blood bags are. Seriously though, Tommy. This is incredible. You are a really good writer."

"Wish I was a better . . . typist," he said, wiggling his stiff fingers.

Their eyes met, and Phoebe imagined that her pale skin did not look much different than his in the soft blue glow of the computer screen.

Phoebe heard the front door open, and she jumped as though caught doing something wrong. Gamera leaped off Tommy's lap and ran into the living room.

"I'm hooooome!" a high voice carried throughout the trailer. A blond woman in a nurse's uniform walked in and hung her keys on a hook on the wall.

"You must be Phoebe," she said, crossing the kitchen and taking a hold of Phoebe's arms. Phoebe could feel the warmth of her hands even through the thick frilly material of her blouse sleeves. "I've heard so much about you. Welcome."

Phoebe could barely bring herself to say hi as the woman hugged her.

"Phoebe," Tommy said, "my mother."

"Call me Faith," she said, her blue eyes shining at Phoebe to the point where she wondered if the woman was about to cry. Faith released Phoebe and threw an arm around her son's shoulders, stooping to give him a loud wet kiss on the cheek. "Hey, you," she said. "How's life?"

"You tell me. I was just . . . showing Phoebe the site."

"My son, the writer," she said. "Isn't it great?"

Phoebe nodded, still in shock. She hadn't really been able to picture Tommy's mother, and the tiny woman's vibrant cheer wasn't at all what she'd expected.

"Thomas Williams!" Faith said. "You didn't give the poor girl anything to eat or drink. Some of us still have to do that, you know!"

"Sorry, Ma," he said, as his mother walked two steps into the kitchen and withdrew a bag of cheese puffs and a glass from the cabinets.

"What do you like, Phoebe? I have Diet Pepsi, milk, orange juice. I could make coffee. You like coffee?"

"I like coffee."

"Good girl!" she said. Her smile made even Angela Hunter's seem lopsided, maybe because there was a sincerity that was absent in the other woman's.

"She likes you," Tommy whispered.

"What? I heard that, Tommy. Of course I like her. Why wouldn't I like her?"

Phoebe watched her rifling through the cabinets, no doubt in search of misplaced coffee, which she eventually found in the freezer. She realized that Faith was as nervous as she was, but the woman was also so happy, the emotion seemed to be coming off her in waves. Phoebe felt a stab of guilt deep within her.

"My parents don't know I'm here," she blurted.

Faith stopped her shuffling and looked at her, a coffee cup in her hand. Her face grew a bit more serious, but her smile didn't leave her eyes. Tommy forced a sigh of air through his nose.

"We'll talk about that, Phoebe," she said. Her voice was soft and warm. "We have time. Do you like sugar? Cream?"

Phoebe said that she did, and then she followed Tommy over to the round table and waited for her coffee.

"So," Adam said, looking over at his companion, Margi had been sitting with her arms folded across her chest and a stormy expression on her pale face from the moment he'd picked her up. She'd been glaring out the window without speaking as he drove laps around Oakvale Heights and the twisting roads that radiated around the development. "What do you want to do?"

"I can't believe she would do this to me," Margi said, her bracelets jangling as she uncrossed her arms and threw her hands skyward. Adam didn't mind that she'd ignored the question; he was just glad she was talking. "Can you believe she did this to me?"

"We could go to the Honeybee if you want," he said. "Get some milk shakes."

"She's irresponsible, is what she is. Irresponsible. To think that we would just cover for her so she could go on a date with a dead kid."

"Any movies you want to see?" Adam watched her out of the corner of his eye, amused at seeing Typhoon Margi start to blow. He knew that Margi had no problem at all lying to cover for a friend. In fact, it was usually Margi who would suggest it.

"And then to make you do it, too," she said, turning toward him as though suddenly aware that he was in the truck with her. "Bad enough to make me do it, but you—that's just icing on the cake. Talk about insult to injury." Her eyes were fiery and wild beneath her pink eye shadow.

He almost wanted to pursue that line of thought, but Margi wasn't always a reliable source of information, and the last thing he wanted, regarding Phoebe, was misinformation. So he let it go.

"I've got a Frisbee if you want to play Frisbee," he said. "Phoebe and I toss a Frisbee around sometime."

"Phoebe is the sensible one," she said. "She isn't supposed to do stuff like this."

She sniffed, and Adam realized with a growing sense of horror that she might be ready to burst out crying.

"Could we go to the lake?" she said. "I used to like going there."

Adam nodded and headed for the access road that would bring them to Oxoboxo Park, a short stretch of public beach kept sandy by the town.

"I learned how to swim there," Adam said. "The Oakvale Rec used to give lessons."

"Me too," Margi said, reaching into her enormous black purse and pulling out a wadded lump of tissues. "I was in Colette's class. We were Guppies together."

And then she just let loose with deep sobbing cries. Adam gripped the wheel and pressed down on the accelerator.

Like everything in Oakvale, Oxoboxo Park was a short drive away. The entire town was made up of a lopsided hub around the lake and the woods that surrounded it, and the park was nestled in the southern corner where the Oxoboxo River joined the lake.

The parking area was roped off, so Adam parked beside the ropes and paced around in front of the truck while Margi cried a little longer. After a few minutes she must have realized that her makeup was a complete ruin and the only sensible thing to do would be to take off as much of it as she could. Adam watched her rubbing at her cheeks and eyes with the wadded tissue balls. He thought she needed some air, so he opened the door of the truck.

"Daffy," he said, "why don't you come out of there? We'll talk."

"Don't look at me," she said through her sobbing. "I'm horrible."

"No worse than usual," Adam replied, but her wailing indicated that humor was not the answer. He looked out over the Oxoboxo where it met the wide crescent of sand that the town had put in years ago and replenished every year since. There was a cold breeze rippling the water and making it lap gently on the shore. Beyond the crescent and far on the other side, the trees were thick, their branches full of red, yellow, and orange leaves that had begun to fade, as though they'd been bleached out by the grayish sky above.

"Come on, Daffy. I'm just kidding. You'll always be beautiful to me."

She gave a curt laugh, and Adam turned—partly because it was the polite thing to do, and partly because he was revolted as a big saliva bubble blew from her mouth.

"Yeah," she said, "I buy that. I wish I bought that."

"Daffy . . ."

"You and Phoebe should be dating," she said. "Then I wouldn't feel so bad."

"Sure," he said, with no witty rejoinder coming to mind.

"Take me home, please. I don't feel so good."

"Not yet," he said. "You wanted to come here, we're here. Let's talk."

She looked up at him, her eyes red from crying. Then she seemed to catch her breath and compose herself.

Adam held out his hand and motioned for her to come out. She gave her puffy face a final scrub and then took his hand, allowing him to lead her out of the truck.

"Well," she said, "I guess we learned that I'm an idiot. A total, total idiot."

"Nah," he said. "You're just upset. And you were just about to tell me what's upsetting you."

She let all the air out of her lungs in a great rush, and then she leaned back into the cab to rummage through her purse some more. "Phoebe. Colette. Zombies. Wow, it really turned cold today, didn't it?"

"Why don't you start with Phoebe," he said. He could feel a muscle along his jaw twitch, and was glad when Margi returned from her purse with a pack of gum. He accepted a piece, trading it for his heavy letter jacket.

"This smells good," she said, pulling the shoulders of the jacket in. "What cologne is that?"

"My natural musk," he said. "Phoebe?"

"I'm just worried about her," she said. "It's weird, her dating a dead kid. Having us cover for her. Don't you think it is weird?"

"It's weird," he agreed, folding the cinnamon gum up into his mouth and starting to chew.

"She's not talking about it, which is also weird. She isn't really telling me what she feels."

Me either, he thought, but didn't see any point in discussing that. "She probably doesn't know. Not everyone is struck by lightning when they think they have feelings for someone."

"I know, I know. I guess I just find the idea . . . creepy."

"Tommy is a good guy," he said, hoping she didn't notice the caution he felt in his voice.

"Sure," she said. "But he's dead. Where can it go?"

He didn't have an answer to that, so he started loping toward the water.

"Adam," she said, "can we leave now?"

He turned back to her with a wise comment on his lips, but he'd caught the tone of her voice, and he saw that she was shivering within the shelter of his coat.

She looked terrified.

"Daffy . . ."

"This is where she died," she said, her voice barely audible over the leaves rustling in the wind. "Not here, but over on the other side, where we used to hide out. The Weird Sisters, we were *so* spooky. Spoooooky! We had our own secret grotto deep in the woods. That was where she went under, right outside of the grotto."

"Who?" he said, knowing as soon as he said it. "Colette?"

She nodded, rubbing at her eyes, sending her bracelets clinking. "I thought maybe if I came here with you, you know, someone as big as you, I wouldn't be afraid. I know you'll think I'm making fun, but how could a girl be afraid if you were with her? I thought that maybe I could walk down to the water and put my big toe in and it would be all right again. I wouldn't be afraid."

"Margi, I wasn't even thinking when I mentioned the lessons. I'm not a very smart guy most of the time."

"But I still am. Afraid, I mean. I'm still afraid."

Adam looked back at the water and thought the whole surface of the lake had just darkened, like a giant mood ring.

"I haven't been back here since," she said.

"Margi," he said, "her drowning wasn't your fault. She blacked out, had a seizure or something. It wasn't anybody's fault."

"*That* part wasn't my fault," she said, so low he could barely understand her. Two tears rolled down her cheeks, leaving fresh grayish tracks on her skin.

"You could talk to her," Adam said.

"That's what Phoebe says too," she said. "But it's so hard, Adam. It's so hard to see her, to watch her walk or try to get up from her chair when class is over. And the way she looks at me . . ."

"Margi . . ."

"I thought the class might change something, Adam. I really did. I thought I'd have some major breakthrough or something, and just be okay with things. But I'm not. I'm not okay. The more time I spend with dead people, the more time I spend *thinking* about dead people, and I don't know how much more I can take. I start thinking about *being* a dead person. And now with Phoebe ditching us for zombies, I just don't know what to do."

"She's not ditching us," Adam said.

"I didn't let her in," Margi said. "She was calling and I didn't let her in."

"Who was calling, Margi?" he said. Was that some bizarre, Daffy-esque metaphor for what she was going through with Phoebe?

"I'd really like to go home now, Adam," she said. "Please."

Adam nodded. Her crying jag had left her looking disheveled and urchinlike in his jacket, which covered her like a tent.

"Sure, kid," he said, and climbed back into the truck.

Pulling out of the parking area, he realized that she hadn't looked at the Oxoboxo the entire time they'd been there, not even when the only view of the lake was in the rearview mirror.

# CHAPTER EIGHTEEN

"AREN'T YOU COMING, PETE? WE'RE GOING TO be late."

A half dozen scathing retorts bubbled up through his subconscious, but Pete let them dissipate without comment.

"You go ahead," he said, watching from the foyer as Williams got on the bus. "Tell Coach I have diarrhea or something. I'll be out in a while."

"Really?" Stavis said. "You sick?"

Pete turned back to him and shook his head. The dead kid was moving pretty well for a dead kid, much better than the girl that he let on the bus before him.

"You want me to get the nurse, or something?"

"No, TC," Pete said through clenched teeth. "No, I don't want you to go to the nurse. What I want is for you to get out of here and go to practice and tell Coach that I'm sick.

Tell him that I will be on the field as soon as I clear my colon."

"You want me to say *that*?" Stavis said. "I can't say that. He's gonna be pissed."

"TC, make something up. You're a creative guy."

"Yeah? You really think so?"

"Yeah, I really think so. Now go away."

Pete set his backpack down and took out the roster he'd ripped off the office wall. The blue sheet was creased and torn in places, one gummy strand of yellow masking tape still affixed at the remaining corner. There were four of them on that bus. Phoebe Kendall, Margi Vachon, Tommy Williams, and . . . some other dead chick. Either Sylvia Stelman or Colette Beauvoir, because the slutty-looking one was Karen DeSonne. One of the girls, either Sylvia or Colette, got picked up every day by a blue van that also took a zombie who must be Kevin Dumbrowski, because Evan Talbot was the redheaded freak who lived in Pete's neighborhood and Tayshawn Wade was the black zombie. Well, the gray zombie, anyhow.

That left only Adam Layman and Thornton Harrowwood, who were no doubt getting suited up to head out to practice with lunkhead Stavis.

Williams was a missed opportunity, Pete thought. The idea that he and Stavis had had the chance to put the hurt on him and failed to do so still rankled. And he'd tried. Every touch that Williams got, every time Williams lined up for a block or to cover, Pete hit him with everything he had. No matter what he and Stavis threw at him, Williams got up again like it was no big deal.

Pete had heard that the zombie was off the team. He was glad about it, sure, but it would have been much more satisfying had the zombie left with broken bones that had no hope of healing.

*Big talk, Martinsburg.*

That's what Coach had said to him, and the words still rang in his head like a shout in an empty gymnasium.

"Big talk, Martinsburg. I hear you yapping all the time about what a big deal you are, all these girls you've supposedly made. Big man."

Pete had been hanging around the locker room after their first post-zombie game. Most of the other players had already shuffled off to the bus, but Pete was holding forth with Stavis and Harris. He'd been feeling pretty good about himself; he'd gotten a sack, another interception, and made a few key back-field tackles. He'd only been burned on one play, really, but even giving that one up, they'd beat the far weaker Waterford team by three touchdowns.

Something he said must have set Konrathy off, because he'd ordered the rest of the kids off to the bus but told Pete to join him in the hall. Pete thought about it, the tone Coach had taken with him, and he felt the muscles jump along his arms. A week later and he was still angry.

"Yeah, you're a regular god to the rest of these dumbasses—morons like Stavis who don't know any better. But Layman doesn't buy your line of crap anymore, does he? And that dead kid, he never did buy it, either."

Pete was glad that Coach had ordered the rest of the team

onto the bus so that they weren't around to watch him getting chewed on. He was also glad that they weren't there to hear how his voice cracked when he tried to answer. "Coach," he had said, "at least we ran him off the team."

Konrathy gave him a look like Pete was something to be scraped off his cleat. "You ran off nothing. He quit on his own terms. I had hoped that Stavis at least could get the job done, but he was a wash, too."

Pete was humiliated. He'd wanted to tell Coach that he'd been a coward for caving in to Kimchi in the first place, and that he'd been a coward again for not scrubbing Williams from the team. Konrathy had no right to fault him for not obliterating the zombie. At least he tried. What did Coach do, except make hand signals?

Pete walked under a huge handmade banner announcing the upcoming homecoming game against the Ballouville Wildcats, and the homecoming dance that followed.

"You're all talk, Martinsburg," Coach had said. "I've heard you crow about teaching those dead kids a lesson. All you've taught them so far is a lesson in how big a coward you are."

Damn, Pete thought, draining his energy drink in one swallow. He slammed the lid of the trunk of his car, and there she was, the zombie chick with the short skirt, slipping into the woods across the lot.

He sent the bottle bouncing off the hood of some loser's Impala.

Here's some new info for you, he thought, heading for the break in the trees.

He could feel his fury like a tight bubble within his chest as he entered the woods, tendrils of anger coursing through his veins. His fists were clenched and his mouth was dry. What right did this dead slut have walking around the woods in skimpy skirts and kneesocks while Julie lay still in her grave in some California cemetery? Why did she have a face like a porcelain doll, with pure white skin, while Julie was rotting somewhere beneath the earth?

Pete stifled a cough by pressing his fist to his lips. He wasn't sure what he was going to do; it was like a curtain of red fog had fallen across his vision, and it would not dissipate, no matter how many times he blinked. All he knew was that this zombie had no right to be wandering around these woods.

No right at all.

The path was wide enough to admit a small car or a pair of bicycles riding side by side, and it wound like an uncoiling snake after a sharp downward slope. Leaves crunched underfoot as he began walking. He thought about his last trip into these woods, when Williams had summoned his zombie friends from graves hidden within the forest. He stopped at the edge of the forest to watch her walk away.

He watched her plaid skirt twitch left and right. She was wearing headphones, the cord of which was plugged into something hidden within her small gray backpack. With her white kneesocks and patent leather, her boldness infuriated him. Where was she going? Off to some secret zombie lair in the woods, or some undead ritual on the shores of the Oxoboxo?

The dead girl was fast for a zombie. She cleared the slope and was a fair distance ahead on the curving path, just approaching a copse of thin birch trees whose branches leaned over and cut part of the path from view. The branches obscured her from the waist up, but Pete caught a glimpse of smooth white legs. He waited until she disappeared from his view before running. He figured that he would close the gap between them by the time he cleared the birches. There was no way that a zombie could outrun him; he was one of the fastest athletes in the whole school.

I'll catch her in no time, he thought as he began to sprint. Once beyond the birches, the path stretched out in front of him, long and straight.

The girl was gone.

Pete was beginning to tire of hide-and-seek. He peered around a thick clot of brush and then looked behind the remnants of a low stone wall. There she was, lying on the mildewed and mossy ground, leaves and crawling things twined in her hair, the flesh of her face rotting away, and one lidless eye fixing him with a cold empty gaze. He stumbled back because it wasn't the zombie lying there, it was Julie, Julie in the kneesocks, scuffed patent leathers, and a skirt too short for decency; it was Julie waiting for him behind trees and in dark corners.

Pete swore and rubbed his eyes, his rage morphing into another feeling entirely. Maybe if there weren't any zombies, he could leave Julie where she belonged, dead and buried. He cursed again, and when he turned, the dead girl—Karen—was fifteen feet away from him, standing beneath the shading veil of the birch branches, her hands clasped behind her back.

The dead girl stared at him through lowered eyes—eyes whose blankness creeped him out. They were like diamonds without the sparkle. She did not blink.

"You were following me," she said.

Pete nodded, feeling a muscle twitch in his jaw. He wondered if this freak had put the image of poor Julie in his head.

"Why," she said, "were you following me?"

He didn't answer. She didn't look frightened, but what little he knew about zombies suggested that they weren't the greatest at expressing themselves. He could charge her and knock her down before her cold dead lips could speak another word.

"Did you . . . want . . . to hurt me? Is that it?"

He nodded. He took one cautious step forward, as if she were a deer that was about to bolt, or a dog that was about to bite.

"Yeah," he said, his voice a low, soft whisper. "I do."

She lifted her head after a slow nod. "Like you tried to hurt Tommy."

She'd colored her lips a soft peach hue, and he thought he saw a ghost of a smile there. He couldn't tell if she was mocking him or flirting with him.

"Like I tried to hurt Tommy."

She made a sound like a sigh. "Will that make you feel . . . better?" she asked. "If you could . . . hurt me?"

"Oh yeah," he said, taking another step. There was a fallen branch on the side of the path, and he broke it over his knee.

He was left with a sharp, jagged point of new wood at the end of a three foot section of branch. "I really think it would."

She nodded, her spooky diamond eyes never leaving his. "Then hurt me," she whispered.

He laughed and moved forward, holding the stake level with the point of the V formed by the collar of her white blouse.

"But use a rock," she said, nodding at the stone wall. "We aren't vampires."

Pete paused and considered the option.

"It's a start," he said, choking up on his grip.

Her peach lips parted as if she were about to reply, but then she nodded and undid the third button of her blouse.

"Go ahead," she told him.

She's really going to let me do it, he thought. The sick bitch.

He took his time, but was almost to her when he heard a noise behind him that raised the hair on his neck with its tone and volume—he imagined it was like the bellow of a large, pre-historic animal.

He turned and saw two figures at a distance on the path. One of them was the big black zombie, making the noise again—Pete realized he was shouting the dead girl's name. He was moving as fast as his dead legs could carry him, which wasn't very. His right leg seemed locked at the knee, and the left twitched out in a violent spasm with every step. The overall effect was like watching an old drunk trying to evade the police while at the same time having a heart attack.

The other one, though, Pete thought, the other one was scary.

He was moving just fine, an Asian-looking kid with long black hair, black jeans, and a black leather jacket. He was almost running. And he was smiling, which was weird, because zombies rarely smiled, especially not with their teeth.

"Hurry," the dead girl said, and he whirled, intent on doing her right then, and not taking his time like he'd wanted to. But then he saw in her pale dead face that it wasn't her zombie pals she was warning.

"You're last," he said, tossing the stick away. He forced himself to walk, not run, back down the path toward the school parking lot.

"Is it just me," Thorny said, leaning back in his chair as he unwrapped a chocolate-chip granola bar, "or is this the longest shift of all time?"

"It's just you," Adam replied. He was staring at the four monitors that cycled real-time images from the dozen or so security cameras throughout the foundation. Periodically, monitor four would blink in the lab where Alish was explaining something or other to Kevin and Margi in their white lab coats emblazoned with the Hunter Foundation logo—a big gold HF on a black shield. Adam thought it looked like something you'd see on a yacht cap. Tommy sat next to him in the blue work shirt that both he and Thorny wore, the emblem sewn above the left pocket. Adam had been trying to figure out if Tommy blinked when the monitors flashed and switched cameras.

"No, seriously," Thorny said, putting his feet up on Duke Davidson's desk. "We've been here, what? Four hours?"

"Three."

"See what I mean?" Thorny said. "This is an eternity."

"The shifts go by a lot faster," Adam said, "when you aren't with me."

Tommy's smile was reflexive, but it only reached one side of his face. He got up and stretched, and Adam thought he could hear vertebrae snap and pop into place along his spine.

"You stretch?" Thorny spoke through a bite of crunchy granola. Maybe it was his chewing that Adam heard. "What does that do?"

"It . . . helps," Tommy said.

"How?" Thorny asked, and Adam turned toward him. "No, seriously. How can it help? You don't have to get the blood flowing, right? And . . ."

His question died on his lips as Duke Davidson walked in and slapped Thorny's feet off of his desk, almost sending him crashing to the floor. Adam thought that old Duke moved pretty quickly for a guy who looked like an older, less pleasant version of the differently biotic students in his class.

"Don't you three have something to do?" the man said, his words like the cracking of a whip.

"Um, we're watching the monitors," Thorny said. Duke looked at him, his bloodhound eyes causing Thorny to shrink back in his chair and swallow an unchewed hunk of granola bar.

Adam figured ole Duke for an ex-cop. Either that or an

ex-con; he'd read somewhere that a lot of former prisoners of the state ended up in security. For such a tall, spider-limbed fellow, he thought that Duke carried himself with what Master Griffin called "centered balance"—a way of movement that was economical and always enabled the prepared to act quickly to whatever came their way.

"Watching the monitors," Duke said, leaning forward. "Why don't you do a trash sweep?"

Thorny was about to answer that they'd already taken out the trash, but Adam cut him off before his insolence got them even more chores.

"Yes, sir," he said. "We'll get that done."

He led Tommy and Thorny out into the hallway.

"Let's go to the lab," he said.

"What?" Thorny said, quickening his step to catch up. "What did I do?"

Adam noticed that Tommy didn't have any trouble matching his own stride. "Nothing, Thorny. You didn't do anything."

"Except show a lack of . . . ambition," Tommy said.

Adam continued to find Tommy's sense of humor amusing; it was so quiet and wry. So *deadpan*, he thought, smiling to himself.

"What?" Thorny, clueless, asked.

"Forget it. Let's get going."

"I hate the lab."

"Why?" Tommy asked.

"They . . . *do* stuff there." He lowered his voice. Adam would have found Thorny's comment funny if he hadn't looked scared when he spoke. "Experiments."

"Well, this is a scientific facility. At least on paper," Adam said.

"Yeah, but there's more than that."

"What . . . do you mean?"

The smaller boy looked at each of his companions in turn, and then at the ceiling as though searching for hidden cameras or microphones. His voice dropped to a dry whisper.

"I heard Alish and Angela talking about Sylvia and Kevin, about taking 'samples' from them." He ran his hand through his thick mop of hair. "What *kind* of samples, I wonder?"

"Come on," Adam said, although in a sense it didn't surprise him. How else were they going to learn about the dead?

"No, really," Thorny said, "I heard them. He said he couldn't figure out why some of the zombies could walk and talk better than the others."

"He hasn't . . . stuck me . . . with any needles," Tommy said.

"It isn't your shift in the lab," Thorny said. He grew quiet as Margi turned into their hallway, coming toward them with a huge stack of papers.

"Yet," Thorny whispered.

"Hi, boys," Margi said. "I get to make copies."

"Lucky you," Adam said, thinking that she looked a little happier than the grainy Margi he'd watched on the monitor screens. He suspected it had more to do with her getting out of lab duty than it did with seeing them.

"That's a big . . . stack . . . you have there," Tommy said.

Margi's eyes narrowed at him, and she picked up her pace.

"Was that a joke?" Adam asked. "Was that you being funny?"

"What . . . did . . . I . . . say?"

"I don't get it," Thorny said.

But Tommy did, a moment later. Adam could almost see the realization creeping into his eyes. He thought that he'd witnessed the closest a zombie ever came to blushing, and it lightened his mood as they continued on their way.

But his mood darkened again when they reached the door of the lab and it was locked. It was the one room in the facility their key cards could not open.

# CHAPTER NINETEEN

P HOEBE LIKED EVEN MELLOW MUSIC PLAYED loud,
so she was wearing her headphones as she read
Tommy's words on the screen. She was listening
to a This Mortal Coil album, one she'd copied
out of the vast collection that Colette's older brother had amassed
before going off to war. When she heard the violins, it felt as
though the bows were being drawn over the strings that attached
her brain stem to her spine. She shuddered with the sensation,
thinking of Tommy and Colette and everything she was feeling.

She tapped idly on the down arrow, scrolling through the
page. The skin of her bare arms was a spectral white, smooth
and luminous in the dark room.

Like Karen's, she thought.

*We make deals with the devil every day, metaphorically. I know
there are those who would say that some sort of deal with the*

*devil was made for our very existence here. But the deal
I made with one of the many devils in my life was a
literal one.*

*I have written extensively of my reasons for going out for
the football team here at Oakvale High. I would not have
achieved any of my goals had I not gotten a chance to actually
play, and the coach refused to put me in. He was being
pressured internally from the school administration, and also
getting flak from the media and the few political figures
sympathetic to our concerns. But my devil was stubborn, and
he refused to bend under the pressure. So by halftime I hadn't
played a minute of the game. And I would not have been able
to play the three minutes and thirty-three seconds of game time
I did, if not for what I said to him in the locker room during
halftime.*

*I wish I could tell you what I'm sure many of you would
like to hear—that I threatened him, that I frightened him with
the promise of an undead horde visiting him in the night. But I
didn't. I offered to quit.*

Phoebe leaned forward and read the line a second time, but
it read the same. *I offered to quit.*

*"What?" Coach said. He could barely stand to look at me.*

*"I will quit the team if you play me today. Put me in for a
series of plays."*

*His expression was like that of a distrustful dog being
offered a piece of meat.*

"You'll quit?"

I nodded. "All of this goes away. The whole circus. And if anyone asks why I quit, your name won't come up."

He looked at me for a minute, his face full of hate. He didn't answer, and when he walked past me, he made sure that we did not touch.

He put me in, and I played. But real life is not like the movies. The team did not rally around the undead misfit, nor did my spectacular play inspire a sweeping change of attitude. The kid I tackled pretty much fell down because he was so scared of me—and I can't blame him.

Certain attempts to exploit us aside, some of Mr. Slydell's concepts ring true. Transformation is usually a result of radical action, and in today's world, a dead kid playing a team sport is a radical action. What Slydell leaves out is that much radical action leads to violent reaction, and that violence simmered around school the day of the game.

I was never afraid during the game. The protestors could have thrown hand grenades and nail bombs, and I would not have been afraid for myself. I'm already dead.

But I was afraid for my friends who have not experienced what I have. And I was afraid for the other living people who were there, the ones who have compassion mixed in with their fear. I would not want those people hurt just so that I could prove a point by playing football. That would certainly have happened if I'd stayed on the team; the violence simmering through the bleachers would have boiled over at some point, and people would have been hurt.

*I know many of you will think that backing out was wrong, that I had a chance to battle with the demon and I blinked. I won't argue, but I will say that I did what I set out to do, which was to plant a seed. I did not want to water that seed with the blood of the living.*

Phoebe leaned back and stretched. She rested her fingers lightly on the keyboard. There were a few replies posted already, the first of which was a short diatribe from AllDEAD, who called Tommy a coward and said that only through violence and death will the "blood bags" have an understanding of what it means to be dead in a world made for the living.

Phoebe licked her lips. AllDEAD missed the point; Tommy's decision made her admire him even more. She started to go through the process of acquiring a blogsite login so she could leave a post, stopping herself twice. She wanted to post her own experience of sitting in the stands watching Tommy and feeling as though she were seated in the eye of a hurricane, a hurricane blowing over the surface of the underworld. But in the end, she didn't do it.

She dreamed of Tommy that night. He was alone on the football field, in his gear but without a helmet, beneath a fat harvest moon. She was in the stands, clapping, but surrounded by angry people who were shouting and booing. A crowd of dead kids stood in the shadows of the Oxoboxo woods. Tommy was looking at her, walking toward her across the field, and then people began throwing food at him. Heads of lettuce, hot dogs, apples, bottles of soda. A tomato hit him just above his numbers. Phoebe stood as a few of them began shooting. She had an armful of poetry that fluttered around her like dead leaves as bullets tore into his uniform and passed through his body. He still kept walking. A thrown bottle with a flaming rag stuffed in the neck burst against him, sending flames racing up his side. Bullet holes stitched a line across his chest; he was closer now, and she saw black holes in his cheek, his neck, his thighs. The fire began to melt his skin. He took one step onto the bleachers, and she woke up.

The fourth week of Undead Studies class—Phoebe herself had begun referring to the class that way—began with Tommy relating some of the recent acts of violence that had been committed across the country on differently biotic persons. Phoebe had read most of the stories on Tommy's Web site, but hearing him tell the stories aloud lent them an even more harrowing quality.

"They ran down a girl . . . in Memphis," he said. "She was . . . thirteen. She . . . died . . . twice in two . . . weeks."

"Terrible," Angela said, shaking her head in sympathy. Phoebe looked around to gauge the reaction of her fellow students; the dead kids were impassive and the living ones seemed to have difficulty looking at anyone or anything except for the floor, as though they in some way had participated in the atrocities that Tommy was describing.

Phoebe felt it, too, the lurking sense of guilt that they were somehow responsible for the crimes.

"There was another report . . . of a white van . . . in Massachusetts. And the murder . . . of a zombie."

White vans appeared in many of the reports on the blog. Tommy had a theory that many of the random acts of violence committed against his people weren't so random. Angela, Phoebe noticed, neither approved nor condemned the theory.

"Thank you, Tommy," Angela said, after he described how a zombie with two high-caliber rifle bullets in his head was found in his parents' backyard. "Why do you think these stories never reach the national news?" she asked the group.

"Racism," Thorny said. He'd been shaking like a wet greyhound since sitting down, having pounded two cans of soda from the fridge as soon as he reached the class. He'd told Phoebe and Adam that he was trying to OD on sugar to gain some weight.

"I mean, bioism. Is that a word? What I'm saying is that there are a lot of people out there who hate zombies, so the media isn't reporting everything like they should."

"Maybe," Margi said. She was in a mood today, and Phoebe knew that whenever her friend got that way she could say just about anything. "Or maybe all of these stories are just urban myths."

"What makes you say that, Margi?" Angela asked. Tayshawn, cursed, and Margi looked at him before responding.

"I . . . I just mean that it seems really weird that all these zomb . . . I mean all these DB people are being killed and no one would do anything about it."

"Why would anyone do anything about it?" Karen asked. "It isn't . . . illegal . . . to kill a zombie."

"I know. I know. I just can't believe that people would just watch someone get killed and not do anything about it."

"Would you?" Karen asked. "Do something about it?"

Margi's mouth opened and closed with a shocked abruptness. Her face went as pink as her hair.

"Of course we would," Phoebe said, covering for her as best she could. "It is just so strange that Tommy has to go hunting for these stories, though. Especially the white van. What do you think that is? Some sort of fanatical group?"

"The . . . government," Tayshawn said.

"Do you believe that, Tayshawn?" Angela asked.

He nodded.

"I . . . was . . . left," Colette said.

All heads, some more slowly than others, turned toward her, but Phoebe looked over at Margi. There was a small stuffed animal, a black cat, on a key ring attached to her bag, and she was squeezing it hard enough to make her knuckles white.

Angela, apparently less interested in government conspiracies than she was in Colette's feelings and experiences, nodded. "Left, how?"

Colette was a long time in answering. "Left . . . by . . . everyone."

Angela started to speak but then stopped when she realized Colette had more to say and needed no further urging, only the time to vocalize her thoughts. This was their fourth group session, and the slower of the zombies—Colette, Kevin, and Sylvia—never spoke until directly prompted by Angela—until now.

"My . . . parents . . . would not . . . let . . . me . . . in the . . . house. I . . . walked . . . from the . . . hospital . . . morgue . . . in . . . Winford. Seven . . . miles."

Phoebe stared at the floor. If she hung her head just so, her long dark hair might prevent others from seeing the tears in her eyes.

"I . . . knocked . . . on . . . the door. I . . . rang . . . the . . . bell. My . . . mother . . . was . . . screaming . . . for me . . . to . . . go . . . away. I . . . knocked . . . on the . . . window . . . and the . . . window . . . broke. Daddy . . . he . . ."

Phoebe heard herself sob, and she felt Margi shift away from her on the sofa.

"Daddy . . . came out . . . of the garage," she said, her staring eyes like portals into another world. "He had . . . a . . . shovel."

"Jesus Christ," Adam said.

"I . . . left. I . . . stayed . . . in the . . . woods. Three . . . days. I went . . . to . . . my friend's . . . house."

Margi jumped off the couch. "You were dead, Colette! What was I supposed to do? You were dead!"

"My . . . friend . . . would not . . . let me in." She looked at Phoebe. "None of . . . my friends . . . would let . . . me in."

"I was scared, Colette!" Margi said, her voice a thin shriek. "You were all . . . all . . . I was scared!"

Phoebe wanted to say something, but she couldn't move; her own guilt had paralyzed her. All she could do was cry, which she did, the makeup around her eyes running down her cheeks in thin black rivulets.

Colette turned toward Margi and then she stood up. Margi flinched and tripped over the couch, nearly falling down. She ran out of the room.

"This is probably a good time for a break," Adam said, but Angela shook her head. Phoebe found the strength to stand, fully intending to go find Margi. Colette called her name, and she froze in place.

"Stay."

Phoebe turned toward her. Colette was so impassive, so cold and slow. She was blank and expressionless, with none of the tics or inflections attempted by the more functional dead kids. Phoebe felt like Colette's black eyes were boring through her skull.

"Please."

Adam touched her arm as he walked by. "I'll go find Daffy," he said quietly. Phoebe sat.

"What happened then, Colette?" Angela asked.

Colette remained standing. "I . . . hid. In the . . . woods. And then . . . in the . . . lake. Tommy . . . found . . . me."

Tommy lifted his left shoulder—a shrug. "It is a . . . gift."

"What did you do when you found her?" Angela asked.

"I . . . talked to her. I brought her . . . home."

"Home? Your home?"

Tommy nodded.

"Your mother didn't mind?"

"My mother . . . helped."

Angela's eyebrows arched. "You've brought other differently biotics home to your mother?"

Tommy nodded again.

"Do they stay?"

"No room."

"Where do they go?

He gave the half shrug again.

Angela turned back to Colette. "Colette? Where did you go after spending time with Tommy?"

"I . . . left. Went . . . to . . . the . . . house."

"The house?"

"She spent time with me," Karen said. "And with Evan, too."

"You have a house where you stay?"

"Some of us," Tommy said, "stay together."

"Where?"

"It would not be a good thing for . . . everyone . . . to know."

"True," Angela said. "But certainly you can trust the people in this room?"

"Certainly," Tommy said, his mouth twitching. But he didn't say, and none of the other differently biotic kids chose to fill the gap of his silence.

"Very well," Angela replied. "Thank you for sharing your story, Colette. I'm sure that was a very painful experience for you. Sharing, I mean. We're about out of time for the day."

Phoebe felt like her heart was frozen in her chest. The students shuffled past her. She was still crying and couldn't seem to speak.

Colette sat next to her on the couch. Phoebe looked at her,

her eyes stinging and her vision blurred from the makeup that she'd tried to wipe away. Colette's gaze was unreadable.

"Colette, I . . . I'm . . ."

Colette reached for her in the now-empty room.

Phoebe could hear the STD yelling when Adam picked up the phone.

"Yeah?"

"It's me."

"Hey."

"How's Margi?"

"Couldn't really tell. She wouldn't speak to me. We got permission to leave early, and from the shuttle I drove her home. She thanked me, that was about it," he sighed. "How are *you*?"

"Um . . ."

"Yeah, I figured. Frisbee?"

"Okay."

"Give me a half hour. I've got to do some crap for the STD first."

"Okay."

It got dark too early, so Phoebe suggested they go over to the football field, where they could play under the lights. She felt better the moment she was in Adam's truck, and then felt better again as he tossed the moon-yellow glowing disk to her, throwing it in a soft lazy spiral.

"Can't remember the last time I saw you in sneakers," he

said, looking down at her black tennies. "Don't those boots you wear all the time kill your feet?"

She tossed the Frisbee back, wincing as she saw that it was going to drop about five yards short.

"No, they're really pretty comfortable. And I wore these just last week when we were out here."

"Oh," he said, running for the disk and snagging it the moment before it hit the turf. Adam could throw a Frisbee about two dozen different ways, and this time he threw it sidearm. Phoebe caught it on the angle behind her back.

"Sweet," he said. "I was worried you'd lose it after lying around all day drinking coffee and writing goth poetry."

"Oh, you heard about that?"

"Heard about what?" he said with mock innocence, and ran back so he could catch the disk she'd thrown high over his head.

"Never mind."

"Okay." He looped the next one with a quick over-the-forearm throw he snapped from his wrist. She tried the behind-the-back move, and it bounced off her side.

"Awww," he said. "So, what's the deal?"

Phoebe picked the Frisbee off the turf and sailed it over to him chest high, finding the range.

"Colette hugged me."

"Oh," he said, flipping it back to her in the same manner. "That's a good thing, right?"

"Uh-huh. I was crying like a baby."

"It's an emotional thing, her hugging you. A little scary, too."

She had to run for his next throw and caught it on her fingertips. "Yeah. But look how scary everything was for her."

He nodded, easily flagging down her return throw. He moved with an effortless grace uncommon in kids his size. "You can't feel what other people are feeling. You can only try to imagine what other people are feeling."

"We let her down, Adam."

"You aren't talking about the lake, are you? That wasn't your fault."

The next one went right to her, and she admired the back-spin he'd put on it. "No. Her drowning was no one's fault. I'm talking about her return."

"Oh."

"She came to our houses, Adam. And we turned her away."

He was a long time in answering. "Second chances," he said. "She hugged you."

"Yeah."

"Margi will come around."

They played for forty-five minutes, changing topics to give their thoughts about Margi and Colette some dwell time. They had a good laugh at Thornton, who'd worn a *Some of My Best Friends are Dead* T-shirt to school earlier in the week and had gotten a detention from his homeroom teacher, which Principal Kim revoked.

"What do you think of Tommy quitting the football team?" she asked.

"I'm disappointed. He was pretty good."

"Did you talk to him about it?"

"No. I figure he didn't want the protests and stuff getting out of hand."

She smiled. "When did you turn into such an insightful guy, Adam?"

He ignored her. "I like that sweatshirt. You should wear white more often. I didn't think you had anything that wasn't black."

"Not true. I have clothes that are gray, umber, and noir."

"My mistake." He laughed. "Let's get out of here."

The first thing that Phoebe did when she got home was check her e-mail, but Margi hadn't replied. Nor had she answered her cell phone.

"Dad, did Margi call?"

He looked up from his mystery novel. "No calls, I'm pleased to report."

But Phoebe wasn't pleased. She was worried.

# CHAPTER TWENTY

NGELA SAT IN THE OFFICE WITH PHOEBE and Karen as they worked what would be their last shift in the clerical pool. Next week Phoebe would go off to the wild world of facilities maintenance while Karen would get to do some real work in the lab. Phoebe was not happy about the change, having no desire to spend any time with Duke Davidson, who she found to be creepier than just about anyone she knew.

"I wanted to thank you girls for all the work that you did here," Angela said. "You've been a lot of help."

"It's what we're here for," Phoebe told her. "I just wish we could have found more positive comments for you."

Angela laughed. "Eventually. Eventually I think we'll see a begrudging acceptance of what we do. Society will just have to grow."

"What do you think it will take for society to do that,

Ms. Hunter?" Karen asked as she straightened a sheaf of papers.

Angela looked at her. "I wish I knew, exactly, Karen. I think it will be a combination of things. But chief among them will be a great deal of effort from people like you."

Karen looked up with the flat expression of the dead, something Phoebe noticed she could switch on and off at will, a mask for her.

"What do you mean?" she said.

"I'm sorry. I don't mean to make you feel pressured. But I think for the differently biotic—zombies—to ever get true acceptance, it will be because of people like you."

"Like me?"

"High-functioning zombies. You speak with few pauses. You move well. Your face is more expressive," she said. "When you want it to be."

Phoebe watched Karen for her reaction, but she maintained the empty gaze.

"High-functioning," Karen said.

"Please don't be insulted. But surely you are aware that you are different from most of the differently biotic students. You could almost . . ."

"Pass?"

"I was going to say, see the others looking up to you," she said. If Angela was insulted, she hid it well behind her smile. "The differently biotic community needs leaders. Art. Culture. People like you and Tommy could make a difference."

"Because the others . . . could look up to us."

"And because you can communicate well. You could be the public face of the differently biotic."

Karen did an approximation of a frown. "Oh my," she said.

"It's true, Karen," Phoebe said. "You're beautiful."

"What a sweetie you are, Phoebe," Karen said, allowing herself to smile. When Karen smiled, her face was almost magnetic in its beauty, but Phoebe found the rapid transition to such beauty from emptiness somewhat disconcerting.

"Well," she said, "it's true."

Angela nodded. "There's something within you and Tommy that some of the others haven't tapped into yet. A creativity . . . a spirit . . . I don't know what it is. But I know that neither of you show it enough. Especially Tommy."

"That isn't true," Phoebe said, but Karen spoke over her.

"I . . . appreciate what you are saying. But you are . . . assuming . . . that living people want us to act, walk, and talk like them. I don't think that is true."

Phoebe wrote www.mysocalledundeath.com on a piece of paper along with her site login ID and password.

"You don't think that makes it easier for people to listen to you?"

"For some. I think that for others it is harder. The more we act like them the more they are aware we aren't. It makes them paranoid."

"Really?"

"I think it would . . . absolutely blow peoples' minds if they couldn't . . . tell we were dead."

"Hm."

"Tommy is very creative," Phoebe said, interrupting.

"I'm sure that he is," Angela said. "He just doesn't let on that he is."

"That isn't true," Phoebe said. "He has his own Web site."

"A Web site?" Angela said.

Phoebe nodded. "And a blog. Dead kids from all over the country read what he writes. So I don't think you should just assume that people aren't creative or socially conscious just because they aren't blabbing about it in class."

"I'm sorry, Phoebe," Angela said. "You're right. I shouldn't make those sorts of assumptions."

"Then again, you make a really good point," Karen said. "I probably should do more to be socially conscious. I mean, it's clear that the younger dead do look up to me, in a certain sense—Colette and Sylvia, anyhow—and I should probably . . ."

"What is his Web site, Phoebe?" Angela said.

"www.my—"

"Who knows, maybe I could run for student body president or something. Get it? Student body? I can see the headline: 'Karen DeSonne buries the competition by a landslide.' Get it? Buries? Ha-ha."

Phoebe looked over at Karen, who was not only speaking faster than she'd ever heard a dead person speak, she was speaking faster than Margi, even.

"Phoebe?" Angela said. "The Web site?"

"mysocalledundeath.com."

She could have sworn that Karen sighed when she gave the address, but of course the undead didn't breathe.

Angela smiled her ever-present Cheshire cat smile. Phoebe wondered if she'd just made a big mistake.

Adam watched Phoebe and Margi cross the cafeteria, and he saw Margi's hand shoot out in a blur of jangly silver bracelets to grip Phoebe's arm and steer her away from the table where Karen DeSonne sat, alone, her place setting surrounded by a ring of Tupperware.

Karen had spread out a cloth napkin, and on the napkin she'd set a squat Thermos bowl, like the kind a kid would take chicken soup or macaroni and cheese in, and a smaller round container, a bright red apple, and a cup of yogurt. She put out a plastic spoon and popped the lid off the little container. Adam peered over to see a carefully stacked pyramid of carrot sticks. Yet another tub contained sliced strawberries.

Margi steered Phoebe away from the dead girl's picnic, angling over to where Adam sat by himself, munching on the second of his roast beef sandwiches. He watched Phoebe shake free of Margi's grip before they both took seats across from him.

"Hi, Adam," Phoebe said, irritation evident in her voice. Adam nodded, not wanting to stop observing Karen, who sat and stared at the table she'd arranged with serious concentration.

"I can't take it," Margi whispered, slapping her own lunch bag on the table. "I just can't."

"Gee, she's all alone . . ." Phoebe started, but Margi was shaking her head.

"She has food, Phoebe. Food. She has food, and you know they don't eat. I can't take it anymore, it isn't right, it isn't natural . . ."

"Shhh," Phoebe said. "Keep it down, will you?"

Margi pushed her lunch, and an orange rolled out of the mouth of the wrinkled bag, onto the floor.

Adam looked at them for a moment, filling his mouth with another bite of sandwich so he wouldn't be expected to say anything. Phoebe looked at him, signaling that he should step in, as if they were Margi's parents. Margi was busy acting hysterical. Her hands were shaking, and Adam didn't think that this was her normal melodrama at play here. He swallowed.

"Hey, Daffy," he said. "Are you okay?"

Margi bent to the table, her voice dropping to a harsh whisper. "She has *food*, Adam. Soup . . . and . . . and . . . *milk* . . ."

Adam nodded. He reached across the table and placed his hand on hers. "I know. She's got a regular picnic over there. But she isn't eating any of it. See?"

He nodded over at the next table, but Margi would not look up.

"She probably just wants to be normal, Margi. She's probably just trying to act like any other kid in the cafeteria."

"But she can't, Adam! That's what I'm talking about. That's exactly what I'm talking about!"

Phoebe was looking at Margi as if she were the weird one. Adam shrugged.

"I'm quitting the class," Margi said, slipping her hand out from under Adam's, the cool silver bangles and rings passing under his fingertips like water. "I need to go to the nurse." She stood up and all but ran from the room.

"Gee!" Phoebe called after her. "I'll just bus your table for you, is that okay?"

"She's upset," Adam said. He didn't like to see Phoebe get sarcastic with her friend; it wasn't like her at all.

"And she won't tell me why," Phoebe said. "I could kill her."

"Then you could get her to sit with Karen."

She ignored the joke. "There's something she's not telling me, something about Colette. I got Margi to join the work study because I thought it would help her get over this thing, this fear or whatever it is, of Colette."

"It's hard," Adam said. Over at the next table, Karen was staring at her food like she was trying to levitate it from the table. Martinsburg, walking by carrying a tray, turned to his shadow, Stavis, and said something that made the larger boy laugh. "Death is scary."

"But it doesn't have to be," Phoebe said. "Especially not now."

That didn't make much sense to Adam, but he didn't say so. For a moment he watched Phoebe pull the crust off her cheese sandwich before trying to change his approach. "Are you sure that Margi joined to get over Colette? Are you sure she didn't join because of you?"

Phoebe looked up. "What do you mean?" She sounded angry.

"I don't know," he said. But he did. It was why he had joined, too.

From the corner of his vision he watched Stavis and Martinsburg sit down a few tables away, still looking over at Karen. They were leering at her.

"Hey, you want to go sit with her?" Adam asked.

Phoebe brightened. "Sure."

They picked up their things and walked over to Karen. She was perfectly still.

"Can we join you?" Phoebe asked, and Karen nodded slowly. Adam gave Stavis and Pete a meaningful look before sitting down. Pete blew him a kiss.

Karen looked up at them, a smile returning to her face as though someone had flipped a switch inside of her.

"Isn't it pretty?" she said. "The red strawberries, the way they glisten, the bright orange of the carrots. I like my navy blue napkin, too."

"It's very nice," Phoebe said.

"I'm so glad that I can still see colors, you know?" Karen said. "I mean, I wonder sometimes if they are muted, like some of the pigments in my eyes washed away when I died, but at least I can still tell that this is red and that is orange and the milk is white. I can't imagine going through life color-blind, can you? All the colors washed out of the world?"

"No, I can't," Phoebe said. Adam just nodded.

"My eyes used to be blue," she said.

"Now they are like diamonds," Phoebe told her. "They might be the prettiest eyes I've ever seen."

Karen lifted the little cup of strawberries to her nose. "I wish I could smell them," she said. "Sometimes I think I can, just a little. But then I . . . wonder . . . if maybe I'm . . . remembering what they smell like. Which is ironic . . . because they say that . . . smell . . . is most closely . . . linked . . . with memory."

"The soup smells good, too," Phoebe said.

Karen made a noise like laughter. "Soup! Yeah, remember soup? Gosh."

Adam couldn't smell the soup because Phoebe was sitting so close to him that they touched, and the scent of her shampoo filled his nostrils. He wished that he had a third sandwich, if only so he could give his hands and mouth something to do. He thought that Karen was freaking out in her own way, just like Margi. Was it possible for any girl, living or dead, to be sane for more than a few hours at a time?

"I can still . . . hear. And . . . feel." She smiled at them. "I . . . think."

He wanted to tell Phoebe to hug her or something, but then Karen started putting the lids back on her containers.

"Thank you for sitting with me," she said. "And thank you, Adam, for acting protective toward me. It's kind of funny, the idea of protecting a dead girl, isn't it?" She giggled, and the noise was much more authentic than the previous attempt.

"What . . . what do you mean?"

"Oh, I saw you. Those mean boys. I'm aware. Hyperaware, really. Might be because I can't . . . feel . . . as much."

She put her hand on his. Her fingers were cool and smooth. "Don't let them hurt the others. They want to, you know.

There's something there, something in him, the good-looking one. Something beyond fear."

"Who? Pete?"

She nodded. "Just don't let him hurt . . . the others."

"I'll try."

"I know you will," she said. "You always do."

She patted his hand twice.

"So, Phoebe," she said, "where is Tommy taking you on your date?"

Phoebe blushed all the way to her neck. Adam would have laughed if he hadn't had a sudden ache at the pit of his stomach, one that no quantity of roast beef sandwiches could fill.

Pete had almost worked out what sort of public spectacle he was going to make of the dead girl, but then Adam and Scarypants sat down and kind of killed the idea. Not that he was scared of Adam—he wasn't—but he didn't want the final showdown with Lame Man to be in the school cafeteria. Pete was as realistic as Adam was big, and he knew that he might not have what it took to beat the big oaf in a fair fight, so he would need to wait for an unfair fight.

Lunch was almost over when Adam walked over to the table.

"Can I talk to you for a minute, Pete?" he said. "Alone?"

Pete looked up, smiling. "We gonna fight?" he asked.

The Lame Man shook his head. "Only if you throw the first punch."

"Talk, huh?" Pete said. He smirked at Stavis and a few of the other hangers-on. "Let's go talk."

They went to a corner of the cafeteria, which was beginning to empty. Pete watched Scarypants and Zombina leaving, and he made sure that Adam saw him doing it.

"Pete," Adam said, "this has got to stop."

"What?" Pete said, still watching them as they disappeared into the hallway outside.

"This campaign of hate that's going on. Threatening people."

"Threatening people?"

"Tommy. Karen. Thornton told me that you said you and Stavis were going to stomp his ass some day."

"Not threats," Pete said, smiling. "Promises."

The smile widened when he saw his words get through the armor Adam wrapped around himself.

"Pete . . . we were friends."

"*Were*," Pete said. "Like you said. You picked your team."

"All because Coach told you to rough up a kid and I wouldn't go along?"

"Not a kid. That's what you don't seem to get. Not a kid. A zombie. A dirty, rotting, bug-infested zombie. That's who you picked over me."

"I don't get it. Why all this hate?"

Pete licked his lips, and he was close, he really was, to telling Adam all about Julie. But he'd never told anyone. No one except his father knew anything about her.

Pete shrugged. "Civic duty."

"He knocked the wind out of you. So what. And so we had a big fight in the woods. Let it end there. I'm willing to walk away from it now, if you are."

Pete laughed. "Adam, I've got a list in my pocket. It's all the people in your freakin' Zombie Love class. I take that list everywhere I go. And you've got to know, everyone on it, every one of you, is going to get hurt."

"You . . ." Adam was so angry he couldn't even speak, which was good for Pete. He was sick of listening to Adam anyway.

The bell rang. Pete turned and joined Stavis, who was watching from the doors.

# CHAPTER
# TWENTY-ONE

AWKWARD, PHOEBE THOUGHT.

She was sitting in the passenger seat of Faith's PT Cruiser. Tommy sat in the backseat, no more talkative than a piece of luggage. Faith was driving them to the mall, where they were going to see a movie.

The evening grew more awkward before it got better.

"Do your parents know where you are tonight?" Faith asked.

"Um," Phoebe said, "they know I'm going to the mall to see a movie."

Faith glanced at her, but the brief look fell on Phoebe's conscience like the proverbial ton of bricks. "And do they know how you are getting there? Or who you are going with?"

"Um," Phoebe said.

Faith nodded. "I love my son, Phoebe," she said, "but this will be the last time I'll cover for you. You need to let your parents know what you are doing. This isn't fair to them."

Tommy made a noise in the backseat like he was trying to clear his throat. It was a horrible noise, one that Phoebe never wanted to hear again.

"You're right," she said. "I'll tell them."

Faith reached across the seat and patted Phoebe's hand, her touch warm on Phoebe's skin.

"I know you will, honey," she said. "You're a brave girl. There aren't many girls your age who would befriend a living dead boy."

Phoebe returned her smile, but she didn't feel very brave. Tommy was brave. Karen was brave. Adam was brave because he risked getting kicked off the football team for Tommy.

"Mom," came a dry, froglike voice from the back, "I'm not living dead. I'm a zombie."

"Oh you," she said. "You know I don't like that word."

"Zzzzzzzombie," he replied.

Phoebe turned and caught him smiling while his mother laughed.

"I'll pick you up at ten," Faith said, and then she drove away, leaving them at the big neon mouth of the Winford Mall. Phoebe felt even less brave standing there on the sidewalk with Tommy. A woman walked by them, clutching her plastic bag close to her. "Winford Mall" was written in a bold cursive script in pink neon above the doors. Phoebe looked at the letters and frowned.

"We could go," Tommy said, "if you want." He reached for the cell phone on his belt.

Phoebe shook her head, wiping the damp palms of her hands on the sides of her black jeans. She then held her hand out to Tommy.

"No," she said, "we've got a movie to see."

He looked at her for a long moment, the neon making bright streaks of pink and orange on the flat glossy surface of his eyes.

He took her hand and they went into the mall.

There were strange looks directed their way the moment they entered. A kid in a Patriots jersey turned to his friend and said, loud enough for them to hear, "Hey, check it out! *Dawn of the Dead!*"

His quick-witted buddy chimed in with, "Yeah, but he hasn't eaten her yet."

They shared a raucous laugh, and Phoebe flushed, but she grasped Tommy's hand more tightly as he tried to step away, his fists clenched.

"Don't," she whispered. They walked on.

*Dawn of the Dead* notwithstanding, Phoebe knew that actual dead people rarely entered the malls. One didn't see the differently biotic hanging out at the bowling alley or shooting the breeze outside Starbucks. They had no need to go to a restaurant, and apart from Tommy Williams, very few had been seen participating in or observing sporting events. Zombies, for the most part, were homebodies—the few of them who were allowed to stay at home.

They walked down the hall, past a chain restaurant and a jewelry store into an open atrium, where they could look over a chest-high railing onto the level below. A cluster of small, frail birch trees grew from a hole recessed into the white tile floor. The crown of the birch tree was about even with the edge of the railing, the thin branches sporting small, dark leaves. As they approached the rail, a small brown bird flew from somewhere in the rafters and alighted on a nearby branch.

"A sparrow," Phoebe said. "Poor thing."

"I know . . . how she feels." Beyond Tommy's shoulder, Phoebe saw an older woman standing outside Pretty Nails, frowning at them. Tommy turned just as the woman gestured.

"Did she just throw the evil eye at us?" he asked.

"I think so," Phoebe said. "Or something worse."

Phoebe looked around her. Was she just imagining it, or was everyone staring at them?

Maybe it was all in her head.

Either way, it was a long walk to the theater on the other end of the mall.

They walked past a Wild Thingz! store on the way to the theater, and Phoebe pointed at a small display in the front window that had the *Zombie Power!* and the *Some of My Best Friends are Dead* T-shirts, along with a couple of caps, bandannas, and armbands bearing similar Slydellco. slogans. There were also a few bottles and tubes arranged as part of the display. Phoebe started laughing when she realized what they were.

"Oh my God," she said. "Zombie hygiene products!" There were shampoos, skin balm, and two different toothpastes. Her favorite was a body spray that had a large silver Z on a cylindrical black bottle. The fine print read: *For the active undead male.*

"Maybe I should get some," Tommy said, smiling. "I'm pretty . . . active."

"I'm sorry," Phoebe said, still laughing. "I don't know why I think it's so funny."

They went in among the racks of T-shirts and goth gear, Phoebe's mood improving as M.T. Graves's voice wailed from the store speakers. They asked the clerk if they could have a sample of Z. The clerk did a double take at them. She could have been Margi's stunt double except her spikes were purple and she had a wide silver ring through her nose to go along with the bangles and circlets of leather on her arm.

"Oh, wow," she said, smiling. "A real live zombie! Wow, I've been hoping one of you guys would come in, yeah." She explained they didn't have samples but Tommy was free to "take a whiff" from the display bottle in the window. He took her up on the offer and asked Phoebe what she thought.

She inhaled the air around him. The scent was mostly spicy but with a strong hint of something citrusy. Lime, maybe.

"I love that stuff," Purple-Margi said. "I bought my boyfriend a bottle. Jason wears it all the time."

"Thank you," Tommy said, turning to Phoebe. "How does it smell?"

"I like it," she said. He bought a bottle.

The clerk's friendliness toward them lifted some of

Phoebe's paranoia, as did the idea of undead hygiene products. But the more she thought about it, the more it creeped her out. Okay, so the dead didn't sweat anymore, and obviously they weren't rotting or there would be some real problems. Maybe odor-causing bacteria couldn't live off their skin, or something.

"Mom said I had to take you to a . . . chick flick," he said, and she realized that they were at the theater.

"Mmmm. *Strays and Surfboards* or *Mr. Mayhem*," Phoebe said. "*Strays* it is."

Tommy paid for the tickets and bought her a tub of popcorn and a soda. Faith had warned Phoebe in the car that he was going to be paying for the whole thing and not to cause a scene because "you could be causing enough of a scene already." The freckled kid manning the popcorn station looked like he was swallowing a frog when Phoebe turned and asked Tommy if he enjoyed liquid butter substitute on his popcorn.

"I used to love liquid . . . butter substitute," he said. Phoebe laughed. Tommy didn't seem to mind when she forgot about him being dead.

There weren't any dead characters in the movie, a light romantic comedy about a woman dogcatcher who kept impounding the adorably incorrigible chocolate Lab puppy of a guy who designed surfboards.

Phoebe thought the movie was boring, and the idea of sitting in the dark next to Tommy and eating popcorn began to strike her as patently absurd. If you had your life to live over again, Phoebe Kendall, she thought—you'd probably spend it watching the madcap antics of Ruffles the dog and patiently await the release of *Strays and Surfboards II*.

The movie's obligatory bedroom scene brought memories of lying on the dusty floor of the Haunted House in pitch-black darkness, for some odd reason. Phoebe was thankful they played the scene for laughs; Ruffles leaped up on the bed during the festivities, and surfer boy smashed a lamp trying to evict the loveable scamp.

Phoebe glanced at Tommy during the scene. He stared ahead, unblinking, as the dead were prone to do, and she wondered what either of them was doing there.

They went back into the too-bright light of the mall around nine o'clock. The few people who had been in the theater stumbled blearily into the foyer, lurching not unlike the more traditional zombies of movie history.

"Did you like . . . the movie?" Tommy asked.

"The dog was cute," Phoebe said.

He murmured agreement, a long sustained sound. "Me . . . neither."

"Tommy," she said, "is this like football for you?"

Tommy cocked his head to the side, just like Ruffles had when he saw the dogcatcher lying on his spot of the surfer's bed in that awful movie.

"What . . . do you mean?"

"I mean, being with me. You joined the football team so you could prove a point, not because you had any great love for the game. Is that what being with me is like?"

They walked past a clothing store. There were fewer people

in the mall at this hour and, it seemed, less attention coming their way. Maybe night people were just more accepting of the differently biotic.

"Who said," he replied after a moment, "that I don't like football?"

He was joking, surely. Or was he? It was hard to read the humor of differently biotic people, much like it was hard to read real meaning in e-mails sent late at night. He was about to say more but then saw something in the next store and nodded in that direction.

Phoebe followed the line of his vision toward the bookstore, where Margi was reading a book from a stack set on a display table near the front. She saw them at the same time they saw her.

"Hey guys," she said, putting the book down and trying as best she could to be casual—which was one thing that Margi never was. Normal for her would have been to chatter nonstop.

Phoebe looked at the title that Margi had been leafing through. *And the Graves Give Up Their Dead,* by Reverend Nathan Mathers.

"Mathers?" she said. "Good reading, Margi?" She scanned the back cover copy and began to read it aloud: "'In this thought-provoking and controversial book from one of the nation's preeminent experts on the living impaired phenomenon, Reverend Nathan Mathers draws equally from ancient theological texts and today's headlines. Mathers offers a solid argument that the existence of the living impaired is a warning sign of the coming Apocalypse, and he outlines what Christians must do to prepare themselves for the event.'"

"Well, I'm sold," Tommy said, but Phoebe was waiting for Margi to say something.

She didn't, for a while. Instead she flicked her pink spikes out of her eyes and avoided eye contact with Phoebe. "I think there's a lot of fear," she said.

"This is . . . progress," Tommy said, looking over the rest of the wares on the display table. "Look, there's a few of . . . Slydell's books. '*The Dead Have . . . No Life,*'" he read. "'*What Parents Need . . . to Know About Their Undead . . . Youth.*' My mom . . . has that one."

"You aren't really quitting the class, are you, Margi?" Phoebe asked her.

Margi looked away. Phoebe was more nervous asking her that question than she was walking hand in hand with a zombie.

"I need to, Phoebe," Margi whispered, so that Tommy couldn't hear. Not that he would have; he was already turning pages in a book some lawyer had written: *Civil Law and the Dead.* "I can't take this."

"*This?*" Phoebe said, bordering on shrill. "Margi, I . . ."

"I gotta go," Margi said. She mumbled something about having to meet her mom. Phoebe didn't try to stop her.

"Tommy?" she said.

"Hm?" he said, taking his nose out of the book to respond. "Did Margi . . . leave?"

"Yeah," she said, and Tommy put the book down.

He looked at her for a moment. "Mom said I should get you . . . a milk shake. Mom says . . . you like . . . milk shakes."

"I love milk shakes," she said, wishing that he were easier to read.

They went to the Honeybee Dairy, one of the last non-chain storefronts in the mall. Honeybee Dairy was just about Phoebe's favorite restaurant; she'd spent many a time having burgers and shakes with Adam and Margi at the original one in Oakvale.

Colette, too. Colette used to go with them.

They sat down at the long counter on shiny silver bucket stools that were cushioned with red vinyl. They chose the counter because it was empty. A few of the booths had customers: a quartet of rowdy teens, a young couple Phoebe recognized from the movie theater, a trio of blue-haired ladies. All eyes seemed to follow them as they sat down.

"I wish I could help you . . . with Margi," Tommy said. "I can . . . understand . . . what she is feeling."

"Can you?" Phoebe said, but what she thought was, Can Colette?

He said that he could. "I've heard it from people . . . on my Web site. The dead . . . lived once . . . but the living . . . have not yet died."

"You speak of the dead as though they are all the same," she said. "Is it really that way? You're still different people, right?"

"But bound . . . by common experience."

"Really? Did all of you see . . . experience, whatever . . . the same thing when you died?"

He started to answer, but then stopped. Phoebe thought that maybe this common experience wasn't really so common. How could it be when Karen could practically run a marathon and win a beauty pageant, and Sylvia needed a ten-minute head start to make it up a flight of stairs?

A kid not much older than them with a Honeybee T-shirt and a paper hat on his head came over to take their order. Phoebe ordered a maple-walnut shake. She empathized with the kid, who turned beet red and stammered when he turned to Tommy.

"And . . . and for . . . you? Sir?"

Tommy's mouth ticked upward in the lopsided grin Phoebe still had not quite grown accustomed to and shook his head. The boy turned and moved swiftly to get Phoebe's milk shake.

"At least he's trying," Phoebe said. She was angrier than she realized; she thought Tommy's smirk had a hint of condescension in it. "Most of the people here would just as soon pour the shake over our heads."

Tommy nodded, the smile disappearing. "Do you think it would . . . help . . . Margi if she read . . . my blog? It might help her . . . to see . . . that we're just . . . kids . . . too."

A wadded napkin from the rowdy quartet hit Tommy in the back, but he either did not or pretended not to notice.

"It might. It might, actually." She signaled to Mr. Stammer. "Could I get that to go?"

Tommy shook his head. "You have a right to sit here . . . with me." There was strength in his voice, the same implacable strength she felt in him when she held his hand or touched his shoulder.

"I don't want to cause trouble, Tommy. Not tonight."

He looked over at the table just as a second napkin bounced against his shoulder. There were muffled giggles from the quartet that soon died off under the weight of his stare.

"You know," he said, "I have been thinking of the . . . blog . . . as a way to give hope . . . to the dead. But maybe its real value would be to bring . . . understanding . . . to the living."

Stammer brought the milk shake in a waxed paper cup. Phoebe was a little disappointed; part of the whole Honeybee experience was sipping the shake from a wide-mouth glass, the cold metal cup with a refill beside it.

She started to stand, but Tommy gripped her arm.

"I have one question," he said, "before we go."

His eyes betrayed nothing.

"How do you get," he said, "the walnuts up the straw?"

She laughed, and he smiled—a real smile, devoid of smirk. He dropped three singles on the table and they went outside to wait for his mother.

"No torches?" Faith said as they got into the vehicle. "No tar and feathering?"

"You sound . . . disappointed," Tommy answered.

"I can't believe you guys can joke about that," Phoebe said. "It happens."

"That's why we joke," he said. "It is a way of saying . . . thanks."

"Is that maple I smell?" Faith said.

Phoebe apologized and offered Faith a sip. "I'm sorry; we should have gotten you something."

"Can't," Faith said, waving brightly colored nails. "I'm on Weight Watchers."

Faith dropped Phoebe off up the road a bit from her house, on the far side of the Layman's. The STD's truck was parked in the drive, and Phoebe hoped that neither of her parents had spotted Adam, her alibi for the evening.

"Phoebe," Tommy said, climbing out of the car, ostensibly to move to the front seat. Phoebe noticed that Faith was doing her best to appear interested in the bushes outside the window on her side of the car.

"I had a great time, Tommy," she said, her words coming out in a clipped blur. "Thanks so much."

"Phoebe," he repeated before she could turn. Her heart was beating like she'd just had a triple shot of cappuccino.

What would she do if he leaned forward to kiss her?

He remained a respectful step away.

"I . . . just . . . wanted you . . . to . . . know," he said, "I . . . wanted . . . to be out . . . with you . . . because . . . I wanted to be out with you."

She smiled, and then held out her hand.

"Thank you, Tommy," she said. "Me too."

He took her hand. His skin was cool to the touch, so much so that she wrapped his hand in both of hers.

"Don't answer now," he said, "but would you go to the homecoming dance with me?"

He cut off her response by lifting his free hand to his mouth, pressing his index finger against his lips in a gesture of silence.

"Don't answer yet," he said. "For now. . . . I just want to think that you might."

When she let go and began walking to her house, her heart was still tripping in cappuccino overdrive from excitement, fear, or both. She wasn't quite sure.

# CHAPTER
# TWENTY-TWO

TOMMY'S VOICE WAS COLD AND STEADY AS he read the article. Adam watched him from across the room, and he could tell that Tommy was extremely angry.

"'The assailants used shotguns and a flamethrower at Dickinson House, a privately funded shelter for living impaired persons just north of Springfield, Massachusetts. Seven living impaired people and two employees died in the fire. A third employee by the name of Amos Burke is quoted as saying that the assailants were "two men in dark uniforms and glasses that escaped in a white van." Burke also said that "two of the differently biotic persons residing at Dickinson house managed to avoid destruction, but judging from the burns that they suffered, they probably did not want to. I swear the zombies were screaming," Burke said. "But I couldn't tell if they were happy or in pain." Burke was at the shelter to work off some court-appointed community service time after being caught trying to rob a liquor store in Northampton.'"

Tommy set the newspaper down in his lap. The class was quiet for a few moments.

"Thank you for sharing that, Tommy," Angela told him. "I'm sure it was not easy to read."

"I can't believe it," Phoebe said. "Why hasn't this made any news on television? My parents watch CNN for two hours every night, practically, and I hadn't heard anything about this."

Karen shook her head, and Adam watched the platinum waves flow from side to side. "This happens all the time. Zombies are getting . . . murdered . . . all over the country, and it . . . rarely . . . makes the news."

"That's just crazy," Thorny said. "I can't even believe that could happen in America."

Adam wondered if Thorny was really that gullible, or just trying to act like he was. He was also wondering, in light of his recent conversation with Pete Martinsburg, where Sylvia was. He somehow doubted that her social calendar was keeping her away from class.

"What do the rest of you think?" Angela asked. "Do you think this is really happening?"

"Something . . . is happening," Evan said. "How would this . . . make the . . . news?"

"It's why it *didn't* make the news that . . . interests me," Karen said. "*The Winford . . . Bulletin* is a small paper. Why did it run the story and *The Hartford . . . Courant* did not?"

"You ask me what I . . . think," Tommy said. "I think that someone is . . . killing zombies."

"Really?" Angela asked.

Tommy nodded. "This has been happening since . . . Dallas Jones. It has happened for years. But now it seems more . . . systematic. And notice how the writer felt the need to . . . discredit the witness."

Adam leaned forward. "Why isn't this story reported more widely? Nine people died."

"Two people died," Karen said, her voice a soft whisper. "Seven people died again."

"What . . ." Everyone turned toward Colette, who was sitting with Kevin Zumbrowski at the back of the room. "Is . . . being . . . done . . . for . . . the two . . . that . . . survived?"

"We were contacted," Angela said. "And are hoping that they will be sent here so we can help them."

"They were burned . . . severely . . . over eighty percent . . . of their bodies," Tommy said. Adam noticed that anger made his speech more hitched than usual.

"Can you guys really feel pain?" Thornton asked.

"We can feel pain," Tommy and Karen said, as Tayshawn and Evan said, "Yes."

Angela addressed Tommy when she spoke. "Really?"

Phoebe thought that her question was genuine. Angela's ever-present expression of warmth and empathy had given way to one of curiosity, as though a deep-seated assumption had been challenged.

"We do not feel . . . much," Tommy responded, "unless the . . . stimulus . . . is intense."

Angela nodded.

"I was . . . shot . . . with an arrow . . . once," Tommy said. "It hurt."

Now it was Phoebe's turn to be surprised. She hadn't seen anything about that in his blog.

"You feel more," Karen said, "the more you . . . come back."

Angela turned her smile on Adam. "We're hoping that we can help those poor children just like we are doing for Sylvia," she said. "Dickinson House had a wonderful reputation for working with the differently biotic, but I'm sure that suffering this recent trauma has really set them back."

Adam wanted to ask just what exactly it was that the foundation planned to do for them.

"What?" Angela asked, and he realized that he had been staring at her.

"Adam," Angela said, "did you have something you wanted to add?" Her voice took on a slightly challenging tone.

He cleared his throat. "Um, you mentioned Sylvia?"

Angela nodded. "Yes. Sylvia is not in class today because she is participating in some tests that we hope will lead to higher functionality for her." She looked toward the back of the room, where Colette and Kevin were sitting. "If things work out well, it should lead to a higher degree of functionality for all differently biotic kids."

"Hey, that's great," Adam said.

"We think so. But regarding the crimes that Tommy just told us about . . ."

Adam nodded, thankful that Pete had yet to make good on his promise. But the thought of Pete gave him an idea.

"Yeah," he said. "What I want to know is, what if there really were some kind of group out there hunting down dead kids? How would they go about it?"

"What do you mean?"

"Dead kids . . . dead kids aren't citizens anymore," he said. "They don't have rights, right?"

"Adam, you know that the Hunter Foundation is committed to the rights—"

"Yeah, I know," he said. "That isn't what I'm talking about. I mean, your social security card expires when you do, right? So no one is really keeping records on dead kids, are they?"

"I read somewhere that there may be as many as three thousand differently biotic people in the United States," Thorny said.

"Yeah, I did last week's homework too," Adam replied. "And there are two dead kids in Canada now; great. But those are statistics, not records."

"He's right," Phoebe said. "I read something that said the documentation on the living impaired is very poor because so many of our laws were put into question all at once. There was a bill calling for the mandatory registration . . ."

"The Undead Citizens Act," Angela said. "One of the first of many fear-inspired bills to be shot down in Congress. Senator Mallory from Idaho introduced it by comparing differently biotic people to illegal immigrants."

"Many . . . parents . . . do not want anyone to know . . . their child . . . has died," Evan said. "My parents . . . kept my death . . . out of the paper."

"No health care, ha-ha," Karen said. "I can't even get a library card."

"You're making a joke," Angela said, "but this really is a serious issue. You can't legally leave the country. You can't vote or drive."

"They want . . . to draft . . . us . . . though," Tayshawn said.

"That's true. There's legislation that calls for the mandatory conscription of all differently biotic persons within three weeks of their traditional death."

"How can they do that?" Phoebe asked. "Some of them are only thirteen years old and we're thinking of sending them into war? That doesn't make any sense."

"It makes great sense," Tommy said, "if one wants to get rid . . . of us."

"I'm not sure the government wants to wait around for their shadow organization to take us all out," Karen said. "I guess it would . . . be quicker to have us all registered and shipped to the Middle East."

Adam looked at her. "Why do you think it is a government organization?"

"Who else would have the funding or the need? If the undead rights movement succeeds, if Proposition 77 passes, it will mean that the government will be spending a considerable amount of tax dollars to . . . deal . . . with building the infrastructure. It is probably more . . . cost effective . . . to buy some black suits and flamethrowers."

"Do you feel that you can help in any way? Or is the situation completely beyond control?" Angela asked.

Tommy spoke first. "I think . . . we need to continue . . . to remind people . . . we are here. We need to challenge the perceptions . . . of the living."

"We need to get us some guns," Tayshawn said.

Adam wondered if he was the only one to notice the sudden lack of pauses in Tayshawn's speech.

"Let's take a break," Angela suggested.

When class was dismissed and they started heading down the long gray corridor and out to the portico, where the foundation van—the *blue* foundation van, Phoebe noted—awaited them, she decided she would cast a spell to break up the cloud of disillusionment.

"Hey, Tommy." Phoebe bumped into him with her shoulder.

He looked at her.

"Yes," she said.

It took him a moment to figure out what she meant, but once he had it, he gave her a wide smile, and she leaned into him with her shoulder again before skipping ahead of him down the hall.

# CHAPTER
# TWENTY-THREE

PHOEBE BROKE HER BIG NEWS AT THE dinner table, which even she would admit, in retrospect, had not been the wisest thing to do.

"I'm going to go to homecoming this year," she said. "I'm going to go with Tommy Williams."

Her mother was beaming, but only because she didn't see her husband's reaction. He'd just lifted a spoonful of his wife's French onion soup—one of his favorites—to his lips, and was about to slurp it down. Then he lowered the spoon.

"Tommy Williams?" he said. "Isn't that the dead kid?"

Her mom gasped.

"They're called differently biotic now, Dad," Phoebe said, unable to keep from raising her voice.

"I don't care what they are called, you aren't going to any dance with a dead kid."

"What?"

"Honey," Mom said, "is this true? You want to go to a dance with a differently biotic boy?"

"What does it matter what . . . what *biotic* he is?"

"For God's sake, Phoebe, being friends is fine; a little weird, maybe, but fine," her father said. "But going out on a *date*? What is that? Why can't you go out with the Ramirez kid or someone? Or Adam?"

"Because Tommy asked me!"

"Really, Phoebe?" her mom said again. "A differently biotic boy?"

"I knew that something was up when you asked me to take you to the football game," her father said.

"Nothing is *up*. Tommy is just a . . ."

"But I figured I'd go along with it . . ."

". . . a friend, we're friends . . ."

". . . because I hoped that you were finally developing some normal, healthy interests."

"Normal, healthy interests?" she said, her voice shrill even to her own ears.

"Yeah," her dad said, glowering. "Like in boys! *Living* boys!"

Phoebe looked at her dad, slapped the table, and got up.

"You just sit right down, young lady," he said. Instead she got up and stomped off to her room.

She shut her door—barely managing to keep from slamming it, because that was what they would expect her to do. She turned her stereo on full blast and fell onto her bed.

Her mom came in a while later.

"Hi, Phee," she said, knocking on the door as she opened it.

"Hi," Phoebe said, trying not to sniffle. Her mom sat down next to her on the bed and smoothed out her bedspread.

"Your dad doesn't mean to be a bully," she said. "It just happens sometimes."

"I know," Phoebe said, starting to cry again. "It's a lot to take in. But we really are just friends."

"That's good, dear."

They were quiet a moment, and Phoebe closed her eyes and let her mother run her fingernails through her hair.

"My hair was never this black, or as shiny. You know that Dad just wants the best for you. We both do."

"I know, Mom."

"So you know why we would be concerned by you going to a dance with a . . . with a differently biotic. Is that the term?"

"I guess so," Phoebe said. "But really, it's just a dance." She sat up and tried to read her mother's expression.

"Phoebe," her mom began, "high school is a very special time. A very special time, but a very short time. You get a few good years, the last really protected years of your life. Pretty soon you'll be off to college, and then to a career, and who knows what."

Phoebe thought about Colette and the others, and she wondered how much of anyone's time really was protected. But she remained silent and let her mother build up to whatever point she was trying to make.

"Phoebe, can you imagine going through the scrapbook twenty years from now, and looking back on what is supposed to be the best time of your life? Can you imagine sifting through prom pictures and yearbooks, and there you are, standing with a dead boy in a tuxedo? Is that really what you want?"

Phoebe's eyes welled up again. She felt as though she'd been slapped. Almost as if she were *watching* the exchange between her and her mother, and she knew that deep down, this would be the moment she remembered—her parents reaction to one of the first things that really mattered to her.

"Do you understand what I'm saying, Phoebe?" her mom said. "Is that what you really want for a memory?"

Phoebe closed her eyes and waited a long moment before opening them.

"Mom," she said, "I understand what you are saying."

"I knew you would, honey."

Phoebe breathed deeply. "But I think you need some understanding, too. The best times of your life that you are talking about—Tommy and the other kids don't get to have those times, do you see? Those times were taken from them. What will they have for memories? Getting rocks thrown at them by school kids? Spending prom night hiding out because they were afraid somebody might drag them into a field and set them on fire?"

"So this is an act of charity?"

"No. No, it is an act of *friendship*. I keep trying to tell you and Dad that, but you aren't listening."

"Phoebe," her dad said from the doorway. "It isn't just that. Do you remember the crowd from the football game? What do you think they'll do if they catch wind that a living impaired kid is taking a real live girl to a school dance? Then it won't be just him that is getting pelted with rocks. It'll be you."

"Dad . . ."

"Listen to me for a minute, Phoebe. Do you know what it would do to your mother and me if something happened to you? You saw those people. They were nuts. Do you know what it would do to us if you got hurt?"

Phoebe sat up on her bed. At once her tears seemed to dry up.

"I *could* get hurt," she said.

Her dad folded his arms and leaned against her doorway.

"I could get hurt a thousand ways. They could throw rocks. The bus could crash. Someone could dump a bucket of pig's blood over my head, and I could make the school explode with my telepathetic powers."

"Phoebe . . . "

"Wait, Dad. Wait. What if I did get hurt? What if I was killed; what if I died?"

"Don't get hysterical, Phoebe."

"I'm just asking the question. What if I died? I don't think Colette's parents figured they would have to think that one through, either."

Her parents looked uncomfortable.

"Well?" Phoebe said. "Would you want me to come back?"

"Of course we would," they said as one.

Phoebe hadn't been sure of the answer, but now that she had it she was glad she'd asked.

"Tommy's mom wanted him to come back, too. And he did, and that's the way the world is now. We can pretend, but we can't really hide it. And you can pretend that you can protect me so every decision I'm going to make in life is going to be free from consequence, but you can't. Every action has consequences. I could go to the dance, and the worst that could happen is that Tommy could feel normal for a little while. Maybe I'll even have fun. Or maybe I'll get yelled at and shunned and have to sneak out the back. But you know what? I'd rather live with the consequences of my choice than live with the consequences of fear. *Your* fear."

Her dad sighed. "Nice speech."

Phoebe's eyes narrowed.

"No, I'm serious," her dad said. "That's probably the speech I should have given you instead of acting like an idiot."

"Dad."

"You're a responsible kid, Pheebs. You're okay. We've always been able to trust you not to do anything stupid. Maybe I wish you had different tastes in clothes and music, but it hasn't seemed to hurt you." He paused to run a hand through his thick, dark hair. "Do you think you'll be putting other kids in danger, though?"

"We'll be quiet about it, Dad," she said. "No one else needs to know until we get there. If there's trouble, I'll leave. I'll even call you if you want."

"This . . . boy, he can't drive, can he?"

"He's renting a limousine."

"Uh-huh."

She knew he was smart enough to sense another story lurking beneath her reply, but he was also smart enough to decide they'd had enough combat for one night.

"Can we think about it?" he said.

She smiled. "You will anyway."

He hugged her. She felt brittle, as though the wrong word from either of her parents could shatter her into a million pieces. Her parents seemed to sense what she was feeling as they got up to leave the room.

"We saved you some soup," her mother said.

"I'm not hungry," Phoebe said, trying to inject her words with enough perkiness that they would believe her. "Is it okay if I give Adam a call?"

The dead kid was singing, Pete thought. Unbelievable.

Pete was crouching behind a shed with Stavis and Morgan Harris at the edge of the dead kid's property, and the dead kid was singing as he worked, his high voice flat and inflectionless as he belted out the words.

"'Wouldn't it be . . . nice . . . if we could wake up,'" he sang, pausing to run a pale hand through his red hair. Pete laughed, watching him move the Weedwacker around the front gutter, just at the edge of where a ring of tulips lay wilted and browning, snuffed out by the early October chill.

"Can you believe this freakin' kid?" Pete said, watching him swing the whirring cord into one of the tulips, kicking up a confetti of shriveled petals. He didn't bother to whisper, even though Stavis and Morgan both looked like they wished they were somewhere else.

Pete hefted a heavy maul, its blade dull from years of hacking cordwood and years of disuse.

It had taken the dead kid twelve pulls to get the Weedwacker started, and it was almost painful to watch his jerky undead limbs trying to coax the machine to life.

Ha-ha, Pete thought.

Pete had been planning this one for weeks. He'd noticed that the Talbots' cars weren't in the driveway when he got home from practice on two consecutive Thursdays, and the pattern held true today, the third Thursday. He'd watched the dead kid doing yard work on those other days as well; first it was picking up sticks that had blown down, or raking leaves, but the kid always ended with the Weedwacker. He loved that thing. Pete wondered if he could feel the machine vibrating through his dead fingertips.

The Talbots lived at the end of a cul-de-sac in Oakvale Heights, the nicer of the two main housing developments in Oakvale. The woods behind their house had trails that eventually led to the lake, and Pete imagined a nest of filthy zombies somewhere in the dark heart of the woods out there. He dreamed about them, and when he awoke, he fantasized about setting the whole forest on fire.

A noise like laughter escaped the dead kid's throat as he missed one of the high notes by a mile and passed the Weedwacker along the base of an oak tree.

Pete ran toward him, lifting the heavy maul over his head.

Adam reached out to catch the spinning disk.

"You told them at *dinner*?" he said. "Phoebe, that is just classic."

"I know," she said. "Impeccable timing, as usual."

She was wearing a heavy black hoodie, which was big enough to fit Adam, with drooping sleeves that hung down to her extended fingertips. Adam had told her she looked like the Ghost of Christmas Yet to Come.

"What did they do? Did they freak?"

"What do you think?" she replied as the Frisbee bounced off her knuckles. "Made Dad practically cough soup through his nose. French onion soup, no less."

"Now there's an image. Your mom's?"

"Yep."

"That's a shame," he said. "Your mom makes good soup."

He watched her retrieve the disk off the turf. She was sucking her knuckle, which had split open when the Frisbee hit her hand.

"Yes, she does."

"So where does that leave you? They going to let you go?"

She nodded, whipping the disk at him with her special backspin toss. He nabbed it without incident.

"Yeah. I got a big speech about how they were concerned and blahdey-blah, and I thought Mom understood, but I think she's actually worried I'll want to put prom pictures of me and a dead kid on the mantel. Plus, I think she implied she was worried I was a lesbian."

"Ouch," he said, tossing it back. "Are you?"

"Yep, that's me," she said.

He put the next one high over her head just so he could

see her run, the long sleeves of her hoodie grazing the Astro Turf as she sprinted across the field.

"They had some good points, though," she said, her breathing labored. "I hadn't even thought that maybe some people would get all crazy about me going with him."

"Segregation redux," he said. "They're right; I'd keep it quiet if I were you."

"Did you just say *redux*?"

"I've been studying up," he said. "I heard chicks were into big vocabularies, and I don't have a date for the dance yet."

"What about Whatsername?"

"What about her?" he said. "So, are you ever going to tell me if you are serious about the dead kid, or what?"

"Please," she replied, snagging one of his loopy hook throws, "don't go down that road again. I'll let you know as soon as I do, okay?"

"Okay."

"We're friends," she said. "I really admire him. He's working hard to help other differently biotic people, you know?"

Adam did. When Tommy spoke in the DB studies class he transformed into this sort of undead charismatic leader. And the students, living and not living, hung on his every word. It was hard not to admire him.

"You think I'm a freak, don't you?" Phoebe asked.

"Naw," he said, wondering how much his answer meant to her. The Frisbee bounced off his palm, a rare miss. "Truth is, if I had any real guts, I'd be asking Karen."

He couldn't see her expression in the shadow of her hood, but he hoped it made her happy and relieved.

"She's pretty hot," he said.

Phoebe laughed and offered to buy them some milk shakes at the Honeybee Dairy, which seemed oddly perfect on such a chilly night. They passed a pair of police cars speeding the other way toward the Heights, lights flashing and sirens blasting—a sight that was rare in their quiet town.

Adam figured it probably didn't mean anything good, but for the moment he was just glad that he could be with Phoebe and pretend that their time together was something more than it really was.

# CHAPTER
# TWENTY-FOUR

PHOEBE HAD TIME FOR INTROSPECTION ON the bus ride to school the next morning. With Adam taking the truck, Margi wedged all the way in the backseat of the bus with her eyes closed and her headphones on, and Tommy sitting with Colette instead of her, she was alone.

She put on her own headphones and cued up an older album by the Gathering, wondering why Tommy seemed to be ignoring her. Was he regretting inviting her to homecoming?

There were other kids on the bus, but they tended to avoid Margi and her as much as they avoided their differently biotic classmates. Pockets of students toward the back, freshmen for the most part, were hacking around and cracking zombie jokes.

"What do you call a zombie in a hot tub?" she heard one say.

Phoebe watched a paper airplane sail toward the front of

the bus, banking past the seat where Tommy and Colette sat. Tommy turned around, his normally blank expression transformed into a mask of hate. Phoebe sat up in her seat, and the hecklers fell silent, remaining that way until the bus rolled up to the curb outside Oakvale High. No one moved from their seats until Colette and Tommy exited the bus.

She watched them walking toward the school. Tommy was very close to Colette, hovering almost, as they made their way up the steps. She saw him knock the smirks off more than a few kids with his glare.

She hurried off the bus and into the school, trying to catch up. She saw that he'd taken Colette by the arm, and she followed him down the hall as he escorted her to her homeroom. Phoebe knew that Colette's lower degree of functionality meant she'd been placed in remedial classes, even though when she was alive, Colette had been at the top of her classes. But Colette's parents had abandoned her, and Phoebe guessed that no one at St. Jude's Mission really knew how sharp Colette was, or had been.

Phoebe willed herself to turn invisible as Tommy reentered the hall after seeing Colette into her room. She hid behind a bank of lockers and waited for him to walk past. He didn't even notice her as he continued down the hall, and she saw that his hands were balled into fists.

She followed him, an easy thing to do, as other students took great pains to avoid close contact with the zombie. He went to his locker, and it sprung open after three steady turns of his wrist. Her poem was the only ornamentation.

She hugged her books to her as she approached him.

"Tommy?" she said. He didn't turn and went about withdrawing his books from his backpack and stacking them in a neat pile on the top shelf of the locker.

"Tommy, are you mad at me?" she said.

He turned toward her, his expression unreadable.

"I'm confused by the way you're acting, Tommy. Did I do something wrong?"

He stopped to look at her but did not answer.

"What is it, Tommy? Is it about the dance?"

His features seemed to soften.

"They . . . murdered . . . Evan," he said. He slammed his locker shut with a force that echoed throughout the hallways.

She didn't understand at first, but when what he was saying registered, a cold ripple passed through her body.

"Oh, Tommy," she said, and she laid her hand against his cheek, ignoring the snickers of students passing by, making rude comments about the goth girl and her dead boyfriend.

The only thing she could think about at that moment was Tommy, and right then she didn't care who knew.

The casket was closed at Evan Talbot's second funeral. Phoebe stood with Adam, Tommy, and Karen, and stared at the black box in the moments before it was lowered into the earth. She was leaning against Adam, clutching his arm and trying to draw strength from him, the tears running freely down her face.

She half expected the lid to slowly open and for Evan to call for help, his high, sardonic voice echoing in the satin-lined prison. She imagined him popping right out of the coffin the way he had popped out from under the tarp that rainy night they had all gone to hang out at the Haunted House, his orange hair askew and clownish above his grinning face.

But these things did not happen.

She looked over at the Talbots as they clung together at the front of the small crowd that had gathered to pay their respects. Angela and her father, both in well-tailored clothing of the purest black, stood beside them, Alish leaning heavily on his mahogany cane. He was wearing a long, trailing, gray scarf that protected his scrawny neck against the chill wind.

Phoebe tried to imagine the pain that the Talbots were feeling. To lose their only child, *again*—how could they bear it? Right then, Mrs. Talbot looked over her shoulder at where Phoebe stood with her friends. She turned back and slouched against her husband, who held her tight and tried to stop her from shaking. He was not successful.

"The mysteries of death have grown deeper in recent years," the priest said. Father Fitzpatrick was a young, solid-built man who Phoebe had learned was responsible for the St. Jude's Mission. She watched him look each member of the cortege in the eyes before gazing heavenward.

"No one, save the Lord, knows why Evan Talbot was taken from his parents . . . not once but twice."

Phoebe heard herself sob, from a distance. It was as if she had floated out of her body and was now staring down onto the tops of the heads of the mourners and the lacquered surface of the coffin. She saw Principal Kim standing near the back in a reserved gray suit, dabbing at her eyes with some wadded tissue. Father Fitzpatrick resumed his eulogy.

"But I would like to think that Evan Talbot helped to play some small part in God's divine purpose, the purpose that He, in his boundless wisdom and endless love, has set for each and every one of us. I would like to think that He would not wish us to dwell on the fact of this boy's second death, but instead reflect upon his second life, which his parents—perhaps touched by that wisdom and that love—chose to take as the gift that it was.

"We can debate whether or not Evan was truly alive after returning to us. Contrary to the opinions of many, I think that is actually a spiritual question and not one for the scientists."

He paused. Phoebe thought she could see her own reflection in the glossy finish of the coffin, and she thought of Margi, who had broken down in hysterics by her locker when Phoebe suggested that they attend the funeral together. Reverend Mathers would be quick to agree with Father Fitzpatrick on the idea of the undead being a spiritual question; although, unlike Fitzpatrick, he would be unlikely to find anything positive to say regarding that question. There were plenty of religious leaders within the Catholic Church who would agree with Mathers as well; in performing the funerary right, Fitzpatrick was risking criticism and perhaps even censure.

Fitzpatrick slapped a knobby fist into his palm, and the sound of the slap brought Phoebe back into her body.

"One thing cannot be denied. Evan Talbot chose to take

his own return as a blessing. Evan Talbot used his second—call it chance, call it life, call it what you will—to try to bring the world a little understanding. He used his return to try to educate those of us who cannot understand what he and those like him are going through. And he tried to be a positive example to those of us who understood all too well. He did this through his humor. His joy. His happy-go-lucky personality.

"Buoyed by the selfless love of his family and friends, especially that of his parents, Evan tried to make a difference," he said, punctuating each word with another press of his fist into his palm. "And by making a difference, I am certain that Evan Talbot fulfilled God's purpose for him here on earth."

Phoebe looked at her friends through her tears, searching for some sign that they could believe as Fitzpatrick did. She was having trouble imagining a God that would require such a purpose—dying, rising, and dying again—from a fourteen-year-old boy. Karen and Tommy were like statues, Karen's eyes shrouded behind a gauzy black veil. Tommy's tearless eyes stared blankly ahead at nothing at all, it seemed. Did he also wonder what it was like to be in there in darkness, the smell of wood and satin and *rot* filling his nostrils?

Or did he not have to wonder because all he had to do was *remember*?

Adam just looked angry, and he would turn occasionally, as though taking in the rows of headstones spreading out across Winford Cemetery.

"Let us pray," Father Fitzpatrick said.

Phoebe turned her head and saw a single tear trickle out from beneath the hem of Karen's veil.

For a second time, Phoebe felt as if she were leaving her own body. This time her knees buckled, and she fainted dead away.

Adam took her to school the next day, and when she climbed into the truck she tucked her long black skirt under her, thinking that she would never be short of clothing that was appropriate to wear to a funeral. She laughed, a bitter sound that echoed in the stale air of the cab.

"Are you okay?" he asked. When she didn't reply, he turned on the radio. She turned it off.

"No, I'm not," she whispered. "I'm terrified."

Adam nodded.

"It's weird," she said. "All these things you don't think of until you have to. What it all means."

"I was scared when you fainted," Adam said.

She laughed again, and this time without the harshness. "I didn't even fall, thanks to you. You could toss me over the goalposts if you wanted to, couldn't you?"

"Yes," he said. "I'm pretty damn powerful."

He let his words hang a moment, hoping they would make her laugh. They didn't. He wasn't just scared when she fainted. Lately the idea of Phoebe being hurt—it filled him with a vague ache, a frustration that no number of push-ups or reps on the exercise racks were going to take away.

He sighed. "But I get scared, too. I thought you might like to know."

"You're a good friend, Adam," she said. "Even if you refuse to be seen talking to me at school."

He chucked her shoulder—lightly, so as not to launch her bodily through the car door. *You're a good friend, Adam*—that was the line that made him want to cry, nearly as much as Evan's funeral had.

"The best. And it isn't you I avoid; it's Daffy."

Phoebe looked away.

"Aw, hell," he said. "And I was doing so well, too. Open mouth, insert size fourteen foot."

"I'm really worried about her. She can't deal with any of this—Evan, Colette, Tommy—I don't know what to do or to say to her. There aren't any scripts written for this sort of thing."

"I hear you."

She slapped the dashboard, a decidedly un-Phoebelike move.

"Who could have killed him?" she asked. "The description in the newspaper was awful, just awful. What kind of monster would do that? Never mind what sort of monster would write that article. They wouldn't have written it that way if he hadn't been a zombie. They didn't even run an obituary."

"I know," Adam said. The steering wheel squeaked with the force of his grip as his hands tensed.

"I think I know exactly who killed Evan," he said.

As she looked at him, realization dawned in her face, and Adam wished he hadn't said anything at all.

Phoebe set her tray down and slid onto the seat next to Margi, who was picking at a cluster of green grapes. They were in the far corner of the cafeteria and facing the wall, which was painted an industrial gray.

"Nice view," Phoebe said. Margi ate a grape.

"Can we talk, Margi?"

Margi shrugged.

"Look, I know that Colette upset you," she began, not really knowing where to start, but Margi was already shaking her head.

"It wasn't what she said. It's what I did."

"What you did?" Phoebe said. "What *we* did. I turned her away, too."

Margi sniffed. "She was right, what she said."

Phoebe nodded, putting her arm around her friend's shoulders.

"When people die, you always are going to wonder what they went through, you know? You wonder what they were thinking. If they think that you let them down."

"And now I know," Margi said. "But I knew it all along."

"Margi, this is different. You get a second chance. You can talk about it with her, if you want."

"Yeah," Margi replied with little enthusiasm.

"She doesn't blame you for her death," Phoebe said. "Or me, or anyone. She's just upset with how we reacted to her return. But she'll forgive us, I know she will. She'll see that no friend could ever understand something like that."

"Yeah."

"Yeah, really? As in, 'You are so wise and correct, Phoebe,

as usual'? 'I'm so glad that you love me and I love you and we're great, forever friends'?"

"Yeah," Margi said, wiping her eyes. "All of that."

"We haven't talked for like two weeks," Phoebe said, and gave her a sisterly squeeze. "I miss you, Margi."

"Me too," she answered. "You went to the funeral?"

"I did. With Adam."

"I'm sorry I didn't go with you guys. It's so horrible, what happened to Evan. I can't even believe it. He seemed like a nice kid."

"It was sad. His parents looked . . . they just looked lost, you know?"

Margi nodded. "I'm sorry I dropped out of the class, too. I'm so good at doing stupid things."

"I bet you could talk to Angela or Principal Kim. I bet . . ."

"I'm not so good at undoing stupid things. Angela called my parents after I dropped out, and they figured that the class probably wasn't doing my mental health any good—my already fragile mental health. You know how they are, Phoebe. They never got the whole goth thing and the music and all, and my sister Caitlyn is such a girlie girl, with the Barbies and the pink dresses and everything." She was quiet for a moment. "I guess I've been spending too much of my time staring at the walls in my room, and my parents got worried. They want to send me to therapy and everything."

"Again?"

"Again. It worked so well the last time; look how well I'm adjusting."

Margi picked out a grape and popped it into her mouth. Phoebe took two.

"How is everyone?" Margi said after a time. "I mean, Tommy and the others. How are they dealing with Evan's death?"

"Today will be hard," Phoebe said. "A few of us are working a shift at the foundation tonight, and tomorrow is the first class after he was . . . he was killed."

"I wonder what they are thinking. The zombie kids, I mean."

"Tommy and Karen didn't talk about it much."

"They wouldn't." She gave a little laugh. "Did you see what she was wearing today? Another little plaid skirt, a white blouse, and kneesocks. And I swear to God she's got patent leather shoes on, doing the Catholic schoolgirl routine again."

Phoebe laughed with her. "She's crazy. It's like dying has given her a license to act however she pleases, to do whatever she wants. Death seems to have frightened some of the kids, but I think it's freed her in some way."

"She had another apple, Phoebe. I swear to God. She was eating it. What is up with that?"

"You're kidding."

"No, I'm serious. Where does the food *go*? I mean, I thought their bodies didn't like, *work* or anything anymore. I thought the scientists figured it was a mold spore or something living in their brains, and that . . ."

"A mold spore? Where did you hear that? *The Enquirer*?"

"No, seriously, I heard that . . ."

A shadow fell across them, and Pete Martinsburg slapped the table with an open palm. They both jumped.

He placed a wrinkled and torn piece of paper onto the table, smoothing it out, taking great care not to damage it. He leaned over and stared at each of them in turn. Phoebe drew her black sweater tighter around her shoulders.

"Hello, dead girls," he said, taking a black Sharpie out of the pocket of his jeans.

"Leave us alone, moron," Margi said, all traces of the unsure, fragile girl gone.

He laughed. "Just wanted to express my condolences."

He took the cap off the Sharpie and drew a single black line on the page about halfway down. He held the paper up to his eyes and nodded with smug satisfaction, the black line visible through the thin paper. It was then that Phoebe realized that what he was holding was the acceptance list for the undead studies class.

"You're completely heartless, aren't you?" she whispered.

He shrugged, capping his pen. He folded the list back into a tight square and put it away, leaving his hand over his shirt pocket.

"Still beating," he said. "Unlike most of your friends."

Phoebe, her eyes filling with tears of rage, tried to stand, but he shoved her back on the bench, his hands lingering on her for a moment.

"No, don't get up," he said. "I'll see you soon enough."

Adam must have seen them from across the cafeteria, because he was rushing toward them through the milling students. Pete aimed an obscene gesture his way and slipped into the crowd.

"Are you all right?" Adam said. "Did he hurt you?"

"No," Phoebe said, but she didn't mean it.

# CHAPTER
# TWENTY-FIVE

ADAM DRUMMED HIS FINGERS ON THE steering wheel. He fiddled with the climate controls, unable to find a balance of warmth and fresh air. He checked his rearview mirror for the thirty-seventh time.

"Adam, is something wrong?" Phoebe asked.

Adam didn't look at her. Even the sound of her voice was now like a sugar rush, and he had taken it for granted for years.

"Oh, I don't know," he said. "What could be wrong?"

"I know," she said. "I still can't believe it."

She thought he was talking about Evan. But the real "wrong" of the day was that the girl that he might actually be in love with had unresolved feelings for a zombie, a zombie who he was bringing her to be with.

"So we're going to the Haunted House, huh?" he said. "We're just picking him up?"

"That's the plan," she said. She tagged him on the arm. "Hey, I almost forgot. Do you have a date for homecoming yet?"

He swallowed hard. "Yeah."

Phoebe slapped him again. "Karen? Did you ask Karen? You didn't ask Margi, did you? I mean, she would have told me, I think."

Adam shook his head. "No, and no."

"Oh," Phoebe said, all enthusiasm draining away from her voice. "Whatsername?"

Adam nodded.

"Oh."

He wheeled into the dirt turnaround at Tommy's trailer park. Tommy was standing on the little patio in jeans and a chambray shirt. Adam thought that he looked like a well-dressed scarecrow.

"There's your boy," he said, but Phoebe had already rolled down the window to wave. Tommy waved back.

Adam watched Phoebe climb out of the truck and sort of half skip to the zombie. He thought she was going to hug him, or worse, give him a kiss, but she pulled up short. Adam swallowed and closed his eyes tightly, but when he opened them, Phoebe and Tommy were still there, together. There was space between them, but Adam thought it was less space than usual.

"Did you see the white van?" Tommy asked. He was looking at Adam when he said it.

"White van?"

Tommy nodded, and Adam thought he seemed excited about the van sighting. "About ten minutes ago. A white . . . van turned around . . . in the park."

"Must have missed it," Adam said. "I wasn't really looking for one, to be honest with you."

Adam watched Phoebe touch the zombie on the arm. "You think . . . you think it might be one of *those* white vans?"

"I . . . don't know."

"I don't think we passed one, man," Adam said. "I don't think we passed many cars at all."

"Oh God," Phoebe said. "You don't think they know about the Web site, do you?"

Adam turned away. In a trailer a few doors down, an old woman wearing curlers and a green house frock was pouring cat food into a silver dish from a very large bag.

"Only a matter of time," Tommy said. "I think there is . . . a white van . . . waiting to pick a lot of us up."

Maybe. The old woman looked up and saw Adam, and waved. No white vans in her world. Either that or she was half blind and had no idea she was living next to a zombie. He waved back.

"Adam," Tommy said, "if we see a white van . . . please . . . do not go . . . to the Haunted House."

"You got it, captain," Adam said.

Tommy moved pretty quickly when he wanted to. He reached the truck first, opened the door for Phoebe, and helped her to get inside. Adam tried not to grit his teeth as he put the truck in gear.

\* \* \*

There was a slim boy with long black hair standing on the porch when they arrived at the Haunted House. He was wearing a black leather coat with thin, rusted silver chains dangling from the pockets, and there were patches bearing the names and logos of various punk and metal bands stitched into the leather. The patches looked dirty, the jacket worn to a gray smoothness at the shoulders and elbows. He seemed to be studying his scuffed black combat boots, and his hair hung down in a dark curtain, obscuring his face.

"That is . . . Takayuki," Tommy said, climbing out of the truck. "Try not . . . to let him frighten you."

Adam returned Phoebe's confused glance with a shrug. They got out of the truck.

Adam watched her catch up to Tommy and call a perky hello to the boy on the porch. The kid didn't move, apparently too interested in the dull gloss of his boots. But his head snapped up like a cobra's the moment Phoebe set foot on the porch steps. Phoebe gasped, and Adam saw why.

The boy was missing a large section of his right cheek. There was a thin band of flesh on the right side of his mouth and then a glaring absence of skin that revealed his teeth all the way to the back molars. At first glance it looked as if he were smiling, but it was clear from the way the dead boy's black eyes regarded them that he was not.

"It is a mistake," the dead boy—Takayuki—said, the missing cheek giving his speech a strange lisping quality, "bringing the beating hearts here."

Tommy stepped in front of Phoebe. "They are . . . my friends," he said. "Keep your . . . insults . . . to yourself."

"We cannot have . . . friends among the breathers," Takayuki said, and Adam could see his grayish tongue through the hole in his cheek. "How many reminders do you need?"

Karen stepped out of the Haunted House and onto the porch. "Phoebe, Adam!" she said, half skipping past Takayuki. "'Scuse, me, Tak. Good to see you!"

She made a great show of hugging Phoebe. Adam wasn't the best at reading undead body language, but it was clear from the subtle shift in Tak's shoulders that Karen's actions—or Karen herself—had an effect on him.

"Tak makes a heck of a greeter, doesn't he?" she said. "Don't you, Takky? We should pick you up an application from Wal-Mart."

Tak returned to staring at his boots.

"Come on in," Karen said, taking Phoebe's arm and waving at Adam. "Everyone is dying to see you."

Adam watched them go in, and he watched a look pass between Tommy and Tak. He drew closer and saw that the dead boy was skeletal beneath the heavy leather jacket. Both the jacket and his black T-shirt had random holes in them, and there was an unpleasant smell in the air around Takayuki. The other zombies did not have a smell that Adam had noticed, except Tommy and Karen, who wore colognes or used shampoos. It wasn't rot or decay that Adam smelled, but more of an unknown chemical.

He made a point of bumping the dead boy with his shoulder as he walked by.

"Oops, I'm sorry," Adam said. "Smiley."

"Smiley" fixed him with a baleful glare. His left arm shot out with a speed akin to Master Griffin's, and the dead boy's fist opened as though he were welcoming Adam inside the door.

And then he really did smile. The effect was horrific, as muscles high on his cheekbone strained to lift the ragged remnants of skin still hanging on to his face.

Now why did I go and do that? Adam thought, sidling in through the doorway, keeping one eye on the swift zombie. Like I don't already have enough enemies for life.

He turned toward the main room of the Haunted House in time to see Phoebe hug Colette.

Good for you, he thought, glad that Pheeble wasn't frozen with fear after her encounter on the porch with Smiley. Colette sort of smiled back, and Phoebe brushed some lank gray-brown hair out of the dead girl's eyes. Tayshawn was there, as was Kevin, the big dude Mal, and the girl with one arm. There were some new faces (none as striking as Tak's), about thirteen or so dead kids overall.

But no Evan, he thought. The atmosphere of the house seemed changed without the little guy, the court jester of the undead community. Adam thought back to the boy riding around in the bed of his truck, rain pattering on the heavy tarp. Differently biotic kids always had a sullen vibe, but they seemed even more so with Evan gone.

"Let's get . . . started," Tommy said. "Thank you . . . everyone for being here. I wanted to talk to . . . all . . . of you . . . about what happened . . . to Evan."

Takayuki glided into the house like a shadow. Adam could hear leather—or his skin—creak as he folded his arms across his chest. He wasn't sure, but he thought he saw that Tak was missing a patch of skin on the back of his hand.

"Evan was . . . murdered," Tommy said. "There is no other way . . . to say it. I do not know if it was a . . . random . . . act, like so many acts of violence against us . . . are, or if it was . . . part of a . . . larger plan."

Adam saw Phoebe looking at him, and he cleared his throat.

"I know who killed Evan," he said, a cold shiver passing through him as the eyes of the dead turned his way. "It was Pete Martinsburg."

"You know . . . this?" Tommy asked. "You have proof?"

"I know it in my heart."

"He told me he did it," Phoebe said, her voice barely above a whisper.

Takayuki laughed. "You trust these . . . breathers, your great . . . friends, and they kept this from you?"

"I didn't keep it from him—" Phoebe began, but Tommy lifted his hand, cutting her off.

"What will we do about this," Tak said, "fearless . . . leader?"

Tommy turned toward him.

"We will . . . tell . . . the police," he said, and Adam thought that some of the quiet confidence had bled out of his voice. "We will . . . post . . ."

Smiley made a spitting gesture, although he produced no spit. "The police will do nothing. Words . . . will do nothing. How long must we wait . . . for breathers . . . like him . . ." He pointed at Adam, who noticed Tak's long, black nails, which Adam assumed were painted, because none of the other dead kids had nails like that. . . . "to come and . . . exterminate . . . us?"

Tommy shook his head. "Your way . . . will get . . . us . . . exterminated . . . much faster."

Takayuki favored Tommy with his hideous smile. "Certain types of . . . death . . . are preferable to others. Write your words. Maybe someone is . . . paying attention. For those who prefer . . . action . . . come with me."

Tayshawn was one of those who preferred action, Adam noticed. About five of the zombies shuffled toward Takayuki.

Karen was walking toward him as well. Adam watched her place her hand on Tak's arm. He looked at it as though it had the ability to cause him physical pain.

"Tak," she said.

"No, Karen," he said. "Enjoy your . . . prom committee. Keep . . . pretending."

Adam watched her recoil as though she'd been slapped. He thought she would have started crying, if she could. Tak led his band out of the Haunted House.

They were silent for some moments, and Adam looked out the window to the backyard as the zombies trudged around the corner of the house toward the Oxoboxo woods. Adam noticed that Karen was watching them through the window as well.

"I . . . apologize . . . for Tak," Tommy said to the room, although his words were directed mainly at Phoebe. "We react to . . . the mixed blessing . . . of our return . . . differently."

"Sure," Adam said, seeing how uncomfortable Phoebe felt. "No matter how it goes down, it has to be a traumatic experience for you. For each of you."

Dead heads nodded in agreement.

"Yes. Yes," Tommy said. "My point earlier . . . was that there are those . . . who do not want us here. And now that there are . . . many . . . of us . . . there may be more . . . Evan Talbots. We must be very . . . careful . . . in coming and going . . . from this house, and from any of the other . . . places . . . we gather. I have seen . . . a white van . . . in Oakvale. I do not wish to . . . panic . . . you, but the events that the media . . . does not want the world to know about . . . are very real. We must take care."

He waited for the message to sink in before continuing.

"We have talked about the . . . homecoming dance . . . at Oakvale High. We will be having an after party . . . here . . . for all of you. Karen has a few . . . words . . . to say."

Karen turned away from the window. "Yes. Thanks, Tommy. I've spoken to . . . the people at St. Jude's Mission, and they have dresses . . . and suits for any of you who do not have . . . the means . . . of getting them."

So that was what the crack about the prom committee was all about, Adam thought, noticing how off-kilter Karen's speech was. Most people wouldn't be able to tell that Karen was differently biotic at all from the way she spoke, but Smiley's actions clearly had had an effect on her.

"We are going to decorate," she continued. "Our DJ just left with the other Lost Boys, but I'm sure we can . . . convince them . . . to attend. If not, we'll . . . make due. And despite some votes to the . . . contrary . . . we are going to invite some trad friends."

Trad, for traditionally biotic. Adam winked at her, and he thought it reignited the glint in her sparkling eyes.

"I'll bring the soda and potato chips," he said. Karen and Tommy smiled, but the joke fell flat with the rest of the group, including Phoebe, who looked mortified.

Adam felt a stab of regret, and realized that he really would miss Evan and his crazy sense of humor.

"I'm going to go home . . . through the woods," Tommy said. "Karen and I . . . have some things to do."

Adam turned away from the instant disappointment he saw on Phoebe's face.

"Really, Tommy?" she said. "It's such a long walk, and it's getting late. Why don't you come back with us?"

"Thank you, no," he said. "Late means nothing to us. We don't . . . tire. We don't sleep."

"Useful for cramming," Adam said. "Pain-free all-nighters."

"Yes."

"Is Smiley going to be trouble?" Adam asked. Phoebe hit him hard on the arm.

Tommy blinked. "Eventually," he said.

Adam figured as much. "Well, thanks for the invite. See you tomorrow."

"Good night."

Adam turned away so he wouldn't have to see them kiss, if that's what they were going to do. He heard Phoebe say good night, and then she was beside him walking out to the truck. He could feel her irritation with him radiating like heat from the sun.

"What?" he said once they were inside the cab, noticing as she pulled her door shut with extra vigor.

"Do you have to be so rude?"

"Was I rude?" he said, spinning the truck around before heading down the long winding path.

"Potato chips and soda? *Smiley?* God, Adam, did you have to say that? How do you think that makes them feel?"

"Hopefully it makes them laugh. I think they have a sense of humor just like any other teenage kids."

"Smiley? Why don't you just call the girl with one arm—"

"Don't say it," he said. "Don't even say it, because that is totally different and you know it."

"How is it different?"

He knew he should just shut up, because with each word he said he could feel her slipping away from him. No more Frisbee, no more riding around town and going to Honeybee Dairy, no more Emily Brontë jokes, and no more hanging out and talking about anything and everything.

No more Phoebe.

He knew he should shut up, but he couldn't. "Well, she wasn't insulting you and scaring you, for starters."

"Oh, so you were protecting me?"

"Sticking up for you," he said. "And for trad people and breathers everywhere. I should have beat the hell out of him, is what I should have done."

She snorted. "Yeah, that's a great idea. Just beat the hell out of everyone who's a little different than you."

"Since when did this become about differences? This is about one kid acting like an ass."

"Just one?" she fired back. "Don't think you need to protect me, Adam Layman. Tommy was doing just fine talking to him and sticking up for me."

"Whatever," Adam said. "Just like he did such a great job protecting you out in the woods."

"Hah!" she said. "Like you did any better!"

Well, there it was. Only her presence and maybe some restraint molded by Master Griffin kept him from pounding his fist bloody on the dashboard.

He pulled into his driveway ten silent, fuming minutes later, and Phoebe's slam of the truck door was like the lid of a coffin slamming into place, trapping him.

Maybe then she'd pay more attention, he thought.

She didn't wish him good night. He watched her storm across the thin stretch of lawn separating their yards. They'd known each other all these years and never had a fight—not even an argument. Some teasing, some debates, an insult here or there, but never a fight.

That was then. Everything was different now.

Everything.

# CHAPTER
# TWENTY-SIX

MARGI LOOKED AT PHOEBE UNCERTAINLY, as if maybe Phoebe wouldn't want Margi sitting next to her on the bus. She sort of shuffled and stood there like a kid in time-out.

Not another one, Phoebe thought. She made a face and pulled Margi into the seat with her.

"Hey, watch it," Margi said. "I bruise easily."

"Well, toughen up," Phoebe said. She sniffed.

"Ohmigod, you're crying! Look at you! You look terrible!"

Margi began rummaging in her enormous black purse for tissues that were no doubt wadded up into tight balls and smelled faintly of patchouli. Phoebe laughed and felt two big tears roll down her cheeks.

Margi leaned in close to her. "What happened?" she said. "Did that dead kid try something? I knew something was up there, I just—"

Phoebe hugged Margi and told her to shut up. She felt Margi kiss her on the top of her head and hug her back. Then Margi actually shut up.

Phoebe knew her eyes were all red, and she hadn't bothered to put any eyeliner or makeup on this morning, even though she needed it after crying for what seemed like half the night. She'd even cried on her algebra homework, for God's sake.

"Will you come back to the DB studies class, please, Margi?" she said.

"You should drop out, Pheebs. After what he tried, you shouldn't have to sit in class with him."

"It wasn't him," Phoebe said. "It was Adam."

"Adam? Adam got fresh with you?" Margi said, leaning back. "My God, I was right! I knew he had a thing for you! He . . ."

Margi handed her a tissue, and Phoebe gently untangled herself from her friend's embrace and rubbed at her eyes. "No, you goof. Adam didn't try anything. We had a fight, that's all."

"Oh," Margi said, looking disappointed. She gave Phoebe a sly smile. "Well, that makes more sense. You wouldn't be crying if Adam tried something."

"Margi!"

"Adam's hot, Pheebs! Admit it, girl. That body is like some kind of happy experiment. It's like he was manufactured in a nympho scientist's secret laboratory."

"A nympho scientist?"

"Lots more of us girls are going into the hard sciences," Margi said. "I saw it on the news."

Her delivery cracked them both up.

"You're just trying to cheer me up," Phoebe said after getting herself together.

"True," Margi said, brushing Phoebe's hair back from her tear-stained face. "Did it work?"

"Always," Phoebe said. "Please come back to the class."

Margi patted her arm. "My parents are going to ask Principal Kim if I can get back in. I tricked my therapist into thinking it was good for me, which just shows how much a waste of money those headshrinkers are, because two weeks ago I had him convinced the class was making me suicidal."

"You're too much, Margi."

"I know," she said, sitting up straight. "So why the hell don't I have a date to homecoming?"

"Maybe because you're too much?"

"Could be. Norm Lathrop asked me, actually."

"Norm's nice."

"Norm's a dork," she said. "But he's a nice kid. He made a mix CD for me."

"Uh-oh."

"I know. It's a sure sign of infatuation. He actually picked some songs I'd like, some Switchblade Symphony and some . . ."

She stopped as the bus rolled to a halt to pick up another passenger. Colette. She swayed from side to side as she made her way down the row of seats, as if the floor of the bus were pitching on an unsteady sea. Phoebe waved. Colette stopped at the seat before theirs and looked at them, her dark eyes like a starless night.

"Hi . . . Phoebe," she said. There was a long pause as she tried to form her next words. "Hi . . . Margi."

Margi took a deep breath, which made Phoebe wonder if she were about to hyperventilate.

"Hi, Colette," Margi said. Her grip bit Phoebe's arm like a bear trap. "I'm really, really sorry I've been such a bitch to you," she said. "I promise I'll try to stop."

The old, living Colette seemed to rise up like a ghost through the dead flesh of her face for a brief moment, and a shadow of the pretty, happy girl they'd spent countless hours with looked at them and smiled.

"It's . . . okay," Colette said. She sat down heavily on the seat in front of them.

Phoebe felt like crying all over again, but from happiness. Margi turned to her and shrugged as if what she'd done was not the monumental event it was.

"Shut up, Phoebe," she said, releasing the death grip on her friend's arm.

"Margi, I . . . I don't know what to say. Thank you."

Margi squeezed her hand.

They were quiet a few moments, and then Colette's head rose like a balloon over the bus seat, and Phoebe winced as Margi latched on to her arm again. It *was* a bit disconcerting: Colette's staring, emotionless face.

"Hey . . . Margi," Colette said, "would . . . you . . . like . . . to . . . go . . . to . . . a . . . party?"

The grip relaxed, and Margi rubbed Phoebe's arm as though to erase whatever pain she might have inflicted.

"I'd love to," she said.

School was a blur, but Phoebe always found the days they headed over to the foundation to be like that. They got to leave an hour early, which helped, but there was something about the sheer anticipation of heading over to the DB studies class. Anything could happen there, unlike her other classes, which even after only six weeks seemed like a dull and predictable routine.

And then there was lunch, which usually was the fastest time of the day but seemed eternal due to Adam's hulking presence a few tables away. He sat with Whatsername, which gave Phoebe feelings of guilt that she didn't quite understand.

"Have you talked to him yet?" Margi asked as she scraped the final remnants of a chocolate pudding cup with a plastic spoon.

"Talk to who?" Karen said. Phoebe had insisted that they sit with Karen, and Margi had not protested too much, for a change.

"Adam. He and Pheebs got in a fight," Margi said, licking her spoon.

"Oh," Karen said as Phoebe hit Margi. Karen hadn't

brought a lunch today, and Phoebe thought she seemed a bit more like her nonchalant self.

"It wasn't a fight," Phoebe explained. "Just an argument. People argue."

Karen nodded, and reached over to pat Phoebe on the arm with her long, cool fingers. Her nails were painted a fiery red. "Don't waste your time fighting," she said. "Life is too short. Trust me."

"Speaking of that," Margi said, getting the last of the pudding off the spoon, "why do you guys think you came back, anyhow? There are so many theories. Something in the water, something in the inoculations American babies get—"

"Mold spore," Karen said. "Don't forget the mold spore theory."

"Yeah, right!" Margi said, pointing at Phoebe with her spoon. "I told you so!"

"There's even crazier ideas out there," Phoebe said. "Alien abductions . . ."

"Signs of the Apocalypse," Karen said.

"Too much junk food."

"Fallout from Chernobyl."

"The power of prayer."

"First-person shooter games."

Phoebe and Karen looked at Margi, who held up her spangled arms in a defensive posture.

"Hey, I don't write the news, I just report it."

"What is a first-person shooter game?" Phoebe asked.

"You, know, one of those computer games where you go around blasting things."

"Usually zombies," Karen said. "Never played one in life or death. Might explain . . . Evan and Tayshawn, though. And Tak. But that's it."

"Who is Tak?" Margi asked. Karen pretended not to hear her.

"Uh, Karen," Phoebe asked, "as a . . . a differently biotic person, why *do* you think you came back?"

Karen smiled and leaned back in her chair, stretching. She had on a black bra beneath her near-sheer white blouse.

"Well," she said, "speaking as a differently biotic person, I think the cause for my return, and the return of differently biotic persons everywhere, is simple. There is only one answer."

"Which is?" Margi asked, and Phoebe nudged her with her elbow.

"Magic," Karen said, and winked.

"Come on."

"I'm serious, Margi," she said, and Phoebe could not penetrate her expression to determine whether or not she really was serious. "It's magic."

"Well, that's enlightening," Margi said.

"Sorry. You asked."

"Karen," Margi asked, "would it be okay if I asked you a personal question?"

"Aha," Karen said, leaning forward and over the table so that her face was about six inches away from Margi's. "Whenever someone living wants to ask a personal question of the dead, it is either, How did you die? or What was it like when you were dead?"

Phoebe felt herself flush with embarrassment, and even her brash friend looked a little sheepish. "I was going to start with the first one, yeah."

Karen nodded and leaned back again. "You aren't the only ones with telepathetic powers, you know."

"I'm sorry if I hurt your feelings."

"Oh, honey," Karen said, grazing Margi's face with a light caress of her fingertips. Margi, Phoebe noticed, managed to keep from flinching. "Some people say we don't have feelings . . . to hurt. I know that you are trying to understand, not hurt, so don't you worry."

"Okay."

"And I'm going to answer your question. The first one. But just the one, and then this interview is over, okay?"

Phoebe and Margi both nodded, and then all expression left Karen's face. The light that seemed at times to twinkle in her diamond eyes went out. The transformation was so sudden and unexpected that Phoebe was shocked.

"I took . . . pills. A bottle . . . full . . . of them. And I . . . drifted away," she said, her voice growing more and more faint, as though she were drifting away right in front of them. "I killed . . . myself."

"Oh no," Margi whispered. Phoebe reached out to Karen and held her arm, as though trying to tether her to this earth. Karen turned her expressionless gaze on Phoebe and the light slowly began to return to her eyes.

"So now you know," she said. Karen lifted Phoebe's hand to her mouth and kissed it as she stood up from the table. "Don't tell anyone. See you in Undead Studies."

"Oh my God," Margi said as Karen walked away, "I can't believe it."

Phoebe looked down at the peach-colored imprint of Karen's lips on the back of her hand.

"Can you believe it, Pheeb? Karen would be the last person I would expect to commit suicide. And I thought that suicides didn't come back."

Phoebe couldn't take her eyes off the kiss, like a tattoo on her pale skin.

"Hey, Gee," she said, "did you hear her say telepathetic? I've never used that word with Karen."

"She said telepathic," Margi replied.

Phoebe shook her head. "No, I'm pretty sure she said tele*pathetic*. Our word."

"Well, I don't think I've ever had a real conversation with her before," Margi said, "so she didn't hear it from me."

"I know," Phoebe said, resisting a strange desire to bring the back of her hand to her own mouth. "That's what I mean."

For some reason, the fact that Karen had used one of her and Margi's code words seemed more mysterious to Phoebe than the revelation of her suicide. Karen was just plain different—truly more differently biotic—than other people, zombie or otherwise. She contemplated this until the announcement to meet the Hunter Foundation van called her from her sixth period class.

She could see that Adam was already in the bus, making a point of sitting in the back, pretending to be engrossed in a paperback novel. *Wuthering Heights*, Phoebe thought. The three dead Oakvale High students—Karen, Tommy, and Colette— were also on the bus.

Colette, she thought. Karen must have heard the word from Colette. She was happy she had solved the mystery, but sad that she no longer had anything to distract her from her feud with Adam.

"Rotten egg," Thorny said, beelining past her and ascending the steps with two energetic hops. Phoebe sighed and climbed aboard, taking the seat next to Tommy near the front. All the other students but Adam were within a few seats of each other, a fact not lost on the ever-aware Thornton Harrow- wood.

"Hey, Adam," he called as the bus doors closed and the driver pulled away from the curb, "what are you, antisocial?"

Phoebe turned back, but Adam didn't even look up from his novel.

"Something like that," he said.

"Is something wrong?" Tommy asked her.

"No," she said, turning back toward him. "Nothing much."

Phoebe avoided his gaze, which was penetrating even on days when she had nothing to hide.

At DB class, Kevin and Angela were the only two people in the room when they arrived. Sylvia apparently had not finished her mysterious "augmentation," Margi had yet to be readmitted into the class, and Evan would not be returning. Phoebe went to get coffee before sitting down, and Karen followed her over to the counter.

"Hey, where's Tayshawn?" Thorny asked.

Phoebe looked over her shoulder as she made herself a blond coffee and saw that Angela seemed to be having difficulty turning up the wattage on her smile.

"St. Jude's told me that Tayshawn has not been back to the shelter in a few days. They do not know where he is, and he has not checked in at the foundation."

Phoebe sipped her coffee and then realized that Karen was staring at her.

"Could you make me one of those?" she said, pointing to her Styrofoam cup.

"Take mine," Phoebe said. "It's a little too sweet."

"Oh, that's just you," Karen said, taking the cup in both hands as though drawing from its warmth, and then she took a delicate sip.

"So he's what, missing?" Thorny asked. "You don't know where he is?"

"I'm afraid not," Phoebe heard Angela respond.

"Jeez," Thorny said, "people are dropping out like flies."

Phoebe had her coffee ready in time to see Adam hit Thorny in the back of the head with his open palm.

"What?" Thorny said.

"Have a little respect."

"What? What do you mean?"

Phoebe felt bad for him, watching as the realization crept over him. She sat on the sofa between Colette and Tommy.

"Oh. Oh, yeah," Thorny said.

Angela ran her tongue over pursed lips. "Well," she said, "the first thing that I would like to talk about today is the loss of one of our classmates. I must say that I was surprised when Principal Kim informed me that none of you signed up for counseling. I would think that Evan's death has left you confused and hurting, and you should know that the private counseling available to you will help you with those feelings."

"We had mandatory counseling," Adam said.

"Which should have been a start," Angela replied, sounding annoyed.

Phoebe looked around the room. Inappropriate or not, Thorny was right: they were dropping like flies. No one said anything until Tommy cleared his throat with an odd wheeze.

"You should know that Tayshawn . . . is fine," he said, "but he will not be . . . returning . . . to class."

"You've seen him. You know where he is?" Angela asked.

"Yes."

"Can you tell me where?"

"No."

"Can I ask why?" she replied. "You know we are only concerned for him, the same way we're concerned for all of you."

Tommy nodded. "I know. But he has a right . . . to his privacy."

Angela was about to respond when Thorny interrupted her.

"Can I ask a question? I'm not trying to be funny, either. But how do we know he won't be back?"

"Tayshawn?"

"No, not Tayshawn," he said. "Evan."

Adam's hand rose above the back of his chair and tagged Thorny on the head again, a gesture Phoebe thought extremely hypocritical after all of the insensitive comments he'd made at the Haunted House.

"Ow, quit it," Thorny said, slapping back at the larger boy as Angela asked Adam to keep his hands to himself. "I'm serious. How do you guys know that Evan isn't going to come back again? He did once. Is there any chance it could happen again?"

Tommy answered.

"We can be . . . destroyed," he said. "Whatever it is that . . . brings us back . . . we need our . . . brains . . . to survive."

"Oh."

"Evan's brain was . . . was . . . stopped," he said, "with no hope of . . . starting it again."

"Oh jeez. I'm sorry about that. I'm sorry I asked."

Phoebe closed her eyes. It was almost too horrible to contemplate.

"What about other internal organs?" Adam asked. "Do you need a heart?"

Karen slurped her coffee. Angela looked annoyed with her.

"There are different theories on that, Adam," she said. "Some differently biotic persons seem to not have any problem existing without organs that you and I need to survive. In most of the case studies those organs no longer appear to have any real function, and in fact are incapable of function. It is hard to tell, of course, because there isn't a big enough pool of people to study."

"Study me," Karen said.

"Most?" Phoebe said, before Angela could respond.

"Excuse me?"

"You said *most*. In most case studies the organs do not appear to have any function."

"Well," Angela said, leaning back in her seat, "it is unfortunate that Alish isn't here to comment, because he is far more familiar with the work than I am. But there have been a few cases where differently biotic people seem to have, or have developed, some organ uses. There was a girl who had a functioning pancreas, I recall."

"I wonder if my bladder works?" Karen said, taking another sip of coffee.

Phoebe noticed that Angela was all but ignoring Karen—she was that unnerved by her coffee break.

"And . . . there was another case of a boy whose heart began to beat again. He had started to manufacture blood cells."

"How do these guys move their muscles without blood?" Adam asked. "Is that what the augmentation process does? Regenerate blood and organs?"

"No, the augmentation process isn't geared specifically at

regenerating organs," she said. "It is more about surgically enhancing a differently biotic person to have a higher level of functionality."

"I think my taste buds are coming back," Karen said. "I can taste the sugar." She crinkled up the empty cup, and a thin beige trickle ran along her hand. "What is involved in the augmentation process?" she asked, her clear retinas fixing on Angela as she sucked the coffee off of her skin.

"It has . . . something to do with reestablishing neural pathways. I'm not very clear on the science; you would need to talk to Alish," Angela said, and she set her clipboard on the carpet near her feet. "Let's take a break, shall we? Ten minutes?"

"We just started," Thorny said.

Angela's exit from the room was sudden and swift. Phoebe could hear the echo of her heels on the glossy burnished tiles far down the corridor.

"What was that all about?" Thorny asked. "What's eating her?"

"I wonder if I could be augmented," Karen said.

Phoebe lifted her own cup and realized the peach imprint of Karen's lips was still on her skin, fading like the afterimage on a television screen.

"I should . . . go . . . first," Colette said. Kevin, as motionless as a mannequin on the futon next to Karen, nodded

"I'm not sure that . . . the science is there . . . yet," Tommy said.

"Oh, you think?" Karen said. "I wonder if they will let us see Sylvia?"

Tommy shook his head. "I asked," he told her. "So did . . . Tayshawn."

"Maybe they've got a white van parked around back, too," Adam said. Phoebe threw mental daggers at his back as he got up from his seat to get a soda.

They heard Angela's heels tap a staccato beat up the hall.

"Hey, Thorny," Karen said, her diamond eyes twinkling. "Before she gets back, do you want to go to a party after homecoming?"

# CHAPTER
# TWENTY-SEVEN

PETE SAW JULIE OVER BY THE DEAD KID, waiting for him with her books clutched against her chest while the zombie was taking his books out of his locker, one at a time. Leaning against the wall with her ankles crossed, she looked over at Pete and blew him a kiss. Pete cursed and took a step back.

"Makes you sick, doesn't it?" Stavis said in his ear. "Me too."

Pete jerked his head as though reacting to a mosquito. It wasn't Julie after all; of course it wasn't Julie, because she was dead and under the ground miles away. This was Little Miss Scarypants, and the rapturous look on her face as she waited disgusted him almost as much as the mirage of his dead girlfriend.

Williams said something to Scarypants, and she gave a flirty little laugh, her eyes lowered in a falsely coy manner. Yeah, I've got your number, Scarypants, Pete thought.

"You'd think it would be illegal, a boy like him and a girl like her."

"Why do you even talk, Stavis?" Pete said, turning toward him as Williams closed his locker. Pete noticed that he brushed against Phoebe as they sauntered down the hall.

Pete'd been watching for patterns, just as he had watched the Talbot household for patterns. Eventually they would begin to emerge. Sixth period seemed to be their one rendezvous period throughout the week; they'd meet at his locker before algebra, they'd sit through the class, and then they'd walk to his locker and down the hall to separate classes. The information wasn't useful, yet.

Stavis looked hurt, as much as a gargantuan doughboy could. "Pete, I just meant—"

"Forget it," Pete said. "Let's go to class."

Pete shared most of his classes with Stavis; he was a lot smarter, but Stavis tried harder; the end result being that they were in classes a shade tougher than remedial. They were headed to English, a class they shared with a few other under-achievers. Pete knew he could get out of the classes if he tried, but what was the point? He'd never be up there with the braniacs like Scarypants and her friend Pinky McKnockers, and he'd have a cushy job waiting for him after college in his dad's company anyhow. No point in overachieving.

Pete looked up at Stavis's round pasty face, which was knitted with concentration. He made a mental note to try and go easier on Stavis; with Harris backing out of the plan, Stavis was really the last person Pete could count on.

"So is he the one?" Stavis asked, his voice a stage whisper.

"Yeah," Pete answered. "Either him or corpse bride there."

"He's the one that punked us in the woods, right?"

"That was him," Pete said, too irritated to even berate Stavis properly.

He still had his list; he carried it around in his wallet. After taking out Dead Red from the neighborhood, Williams seemed the obvious next choice. The slutty zombie could go last; no one was likely to miss her. Pete figured that he'd put the hurt on living kids a lot better if he took out all their dead buddies first. He could—and did—slap around that puny Harrowwood kid whenever he felt like it, either in practice or outside the locker room. Pete smiled, thinking about the block he'd dropped on purpose against Ballouville so that their big tackle could paste a good one on the kid. He'd sat out the rest of the half.

There was a wide cardboard sign above the corridor archway proclaiming the date and time of the homecoming dance. Pete thought that Oakvale should have waited a week and had it on Halloween, seeing as how a bunch of the students had built-in costumes.

"We still going to do it at the dance?" Stavis asked.

"No, I've got a better plan now."

"Really? What is it?"

"I heard about a party," he said, "and we're going to crash."

That was the one good thing about having a little punk like Harrowwood in the locker room, a guy who had to use his mouth to make up for his shortcomings. Thorny had started running his mouth about this "sweet party" he was going to after homecoming, and how not that many people were invited, and blah and blah. Adam had shot Thorny a look, but it was too late.

Pete had caught up to Harrowwood in the parking lot and had the full story in two slaps. "What party?" *Slap.* "I don't know about any party." *Slap.*

"The zombies are having a big party 'cause most of them can't go to the homecoming. Heck, most of them don't even go to school. . . ."

"Where?" Pete had asked, but that was the one question Thornton couldn't answer.

"They won't tell me," the runt had said. "I'm supposed to follow Layman over there. He's been a couple times."

"If I find out you are lying to me, Thorny," Pete threatened, "I swear you'll be partying with them permanently."

"I'm not." The fear in the kid's eyes told Pete what he'd needed to know. "I swear it."

Stavis's nasally voice brought him back to the present. "A party? What kind of party?"

"A zombie party," Pete said, imagining a whole house full of worm burgers, and then imagining the house on fire.

"No way."

"Way," he said, seeing flames rising, smoke curling up under the moonlit sky. He was smiling as they arrived at their class.

He'd planned on being a little earlier to class than the rest of the pack, which was easy to do, because the nosebleeds weren't too interested in punctuality. There was only one other student in the class, and she looked up at the board as the teacher passed an eraser over the grayish surface, her stare more vacant than school on a Saturday.

"Ugh," Stavis said.

Pete laughed and winked at him. He gripped him by one bulbous shoulder.

"Talk to you later, man," Pete said, and went over to sit next to the girl.

"Hey, kid," he said, smiling, "I hear there's a big party going on after the dance."

Colette swiveled her head toward him with all the alacrity of a slowly oscillating fan, and it took her a while to bend her mouth into a smile, but Pete suddenly felt like he had all the time in the world.


Phoebe jumped as a cat screeched like its tail was being stepped on. Gargoyle leaped off of her bed and started barking at the four corners of the earth.

The unearthly sound was her computer's way of letting her know that Margi had just signed on to the Internet. The name Pinkytheghost appeared next to an avatar of a pink Casper-esque phantom that fluttered like a sheet on a clothesline along with Margi's first message of the night.

*I got my dress 2day. U have yrs?*

Phoebe shushed Gargoyle. His bobbed tail stuck straight up, and his low growl was more endearing than threatening.

Phoebe typed back *Yep*.

*U promised we would both wear black. Is yr dress black?*

Phoebe sighed, because Margi typed like she talked: fast and incessant. Phoebe had been reading the latest installment of mysocalledundeath.com and was trying to decide how she felt about it. Because, unlike a good many of the differently biotic topics it contained, this one was deeply personal to her. The title of the blog, which Tommy had posted earlier that day, was Homecoming.

*Nope*, she typed.

*Promise-breaker*, came Pinkytheghost's reply. And then, *Me neither.*

Phoebe smiled, hoping that if she ignored Margi for a few minutes her friend would get wrapped up in some other Internet diversion.

*So what are U doin?* Pinky/Margi asked. So much for her theory.

Phoebe scrolled down the blog entry and read what Tommy had written.

*I'm going to the homecoming dance at my school. I have a real live date. And when I say real live date, I mean an actual living, breathing, traditionally biotic girl.*

Phoebe frowned and turned down the Bronx Casket Company album she'd been listening to on her MP3 player, on the odd chance that one of her parents crept into her room. She didn't want them to read the screen.

*R U there?* Pinky/Margi typed.

Phoebe typed back *No*. Never mind her parents; she didn't want Margi to read this blog. Or Adam, or Karen, or anyone else. She had a vision of Tommy whisking her around at the party, showing her off to all his dead friends and saying, "Hey, everybody, this is my traditionally biotic girlfriend," and then forgetting her name.

*Don't be a b\*\*\*\**, Margi typed. *Is my special fluffy boy there?*

Phoebe looked over at Margi's special fluffy boy, who had resettled at the edge of her bed.

*Gar says hi*, she typed.

She turned back to the blog.

> *The dance will not be our first date. We have gone to a movie at the mall. She has been to my house and has met my mother, who likes her a lot. I like her a lot, too.*

That's what you get for writing poetry, Phoebe thought, her pulse racing from more than the music. She wanted to call Tommy up—Tommy or Faith—and ask him to pull what he had written. What if the hordes of protestors her father had warned her about were reading this? What about the faceless white van patrol; what if they were monitoring his posts? She wasn't comfortable with this at all; in some ways it was like a kid climbing up on a table in the middle of lunch to declare his love for a girl he barely knew. Uncool. Definitely uncool.

*XOXOXO special fluffy boy*, Margi sent.

Phoebe made a noise of exasperation that caused the

special fluffy boy to lift his head from his special fluffy pillow. She looked over and assured him everything was all right.

"I just wish our friend would shut up," she said under her breath. Gargoyle returned to his reclining position, looking disappointed.

> *What can it mean for a differently biotic boy—a zombie—to "like" a traditionally biotic girl? And what would it mean if the living girl "liked" him as well? Would society crumble? Would nations fall into the sea? Would the heavens open up? Would the falcon no longer be able to hear the falconer?*

Phoebe rubbed her eyes. This was a little esoteric for Tommy, whose typical writing was quite literal except during the times he was speculating on the anti-zombie conspiracy he saw stretching across the country.

*What R U listening to?* Margi sent. When Phoebe rushed a response of BCC back, Margi's response was swift even though she upped the point size of the font and colored it red.

*No way! Me 2! Telepathetic!*

Yeah, Phoebe thought, unable to get too excited.

> *I don't know what will happen. I don't know if anything will happen. I don't know if a mob of traditionally biotic people with minds less open than my date's will drag me bodily from the gymnasium and put me to the torch. All I know is that I want to go to the dance with her, and actually dance. I know*

*this because I know that when I am with her, there are times,
even if they are brief, when I no longer feel like a zombie. There
are times when, for an instant, I forget that I've died and I no
longer breathe and my heart no longer pumps blood throughout
my body.*

    *I forget these things when I'm with her. I think that if
I could dance with her, just once, I might feel like I was alive
again.*

She could feel tears building up, but she blinked them away and forced the air in and out of her lungs in a steady rhythm.

No pressure, Phoebe, she thought, and an escapee from her tear ducts plopped onto the space bar of her keyboard. She laughed and wiped at her eyes.

There were a few posts under the Comments section of the day's blog. The first was a single word from a poster by the handle of BRNSAMEDI666, who wrote a single word, all caps: SELLOUT!

Why should traditionally biotic people have all the fun, Phoebe thought, recalling the naked anger on Smiley's— on Takayuki's— face as she and Adam entered the Haunted House.

On cue, another post from PinkytheGhost arrived.

*R U & Lame Man still fighting?* ☹

Phoebe frowned, signed off, and put her computer into idle mode before sitting on her bed next to Gar, who rolled over in anticipation of a belly rub. It seemed easier than trying to respond to Margi's question.

* * *

"You're late," Pete said, letting Stavis into his room through the garage. He had the whole basement floor of the house—a raised ranch—to himself, while Moms and the Wimp occupied the top two floors. There were three usable rooms in the basement: his bedroom, his exercise room, and his recreation room, which had a thirty-six-inch plasma television, another gift from dear old Dad. Stavis walked to the short refrigerator in the corner and popped open a can of beer. He didn't ask for permission.

Pete lifted the rifle he'd stashed behind the couch and pointed it at Stavis's head as he turned around.

Stavis swore and stumbled back against the fridge, spilling a good quarter can of beer on himself and the floor.

"Easy, stupid," Pete said, lowering the rifle sight. "You spilled all over yourself."

"You scared the shit out of me, Pete!"

"Take it easy," Pete said. "Enjoy your beer."

Pete watched him take a long pull off the beer, and he tried to keep from laughing. Stavis's normally beady eyes were as round as hockey pucks.

"Throw me one of those," he said, hoping to distract Stavis before he wet himself.

"Where the hell did you get that thing?" TC asked, carefully handing Pete an unopened can as though he were afraid a sudden movement would get him plugged. "Is it your step-dad's?"

"Hell, no," Pete said after taking a long drink. "The Wimp doesn't believe in guns. Thinks they should be criminalized, that sort of thing."

"What is it? Where'd you get it?"

"It's just a .22. There's a guy up the street who uses it to shoot the raccoons that come up through the woods to raid his garbage."

"Did he sell it to you or something?" Stavis asked.

Pete smiled at him. "He doesn't know it's gone."

TC downed the last of his beer. "Wow," he said, and Pete told him to help himself to another one.

"It's just me and you this time," Pete said. "Harris is wussing out."

Stavis slumped onto the sofa. He pushed the Xbox to the side of the coffee table and set his drink down.

"That last one was pretty gross," Stavis said, and Pete watched him rub a beefy hand over his close-cropped hair. "Who'd have known those zombies had so much gunk left inside of them? It was like you whacked a rotten watermelon or somethin'."

"Or something," Pete said. Stavis looked flushed, and beads of sweat had popped out on his forehead. "You're with me on this, right?"

"Oh, absolutely, Pete," he said, and belched loud enough to shake the dust off the plasma screen. "You know it."

"I need to know, TC," he said, "because I'm going to take another one of them down. Williams. He's got it coming."

"I know, man, I know. I'm with you."

"They aren't people, TC. You know that, right?"

"Who knows what they are," TC said.

"No one, that's who. I saw on the news that they think

some kind of parasite crawls into their brains and controls their bodies after death."

"It might be hairy," Pete said, drawing on his beer. "They've got this house where they all hang out, over on the other side of the lake."

"Like ants," Stavis said, belching again.

"Yeah, like ants. They'll all be there, too, so I need to know you got my back. If Scarypants or anyone else tries to get in the way, you have to take them out for me."

Pete got jumpy just thinking about it. Williams was like some kind of unofficial leader of the dead kids, sort of like Pete himself was the unofficial leader of most of the school. If Williams went down, it should be pretty easy to get rid of the others, and in getting rid of the others, maybe he'd be able to get rid of Julie, too. She just wouldn't leave his head. It was as if she'd walked out of his dreams and into his waking life. He'd seen her twice since the incident in the hallway.

"I got your back, man," Stavis said, and leaned over to clink his can against Pete's.

*Loser.* "That's good, man. You know I appreciate it."

Pete looked at Stavis and sipped his beer and considered telling him all about Julie: how he met her, what they did, how she died. He thought about telling Stavis these things, and then Stavis belched loud enough to peel paint off the walls.

Pete sighed, all impulses to relieve himself of his innermost secrets gone. "Cool. We still riding together? I'll pick you up around seven thirty."

"Seven thirty," TC agreed.

Pete grinned. "You still going with Sharon, right?" he said. "You know she's a pig."

"Oink, oink," TC said, and Pete laughed as TC launched into an increasingly obscene imitation of snuffling sounds.

"And you know we aren't going to have time for any of that stuff, right? We've got to dump the girls and get over to this zombie house before their party is over, you got it?"

"Aw," TC said, disappointment clouding his sweaty face.

Pete waved it away. "Don't worry about it. I'll get you a makeup call. Maybe a real girl, one of my friends from Norwich."

"Awright!" TC said, leaning over yet again for the can-clinking thing. Pete obliged.

TC crushed his can, his thick, stubby fingers wadding it up like a tissue. "Hey, you steal bullets, too?"

"Naw." Pete chuckled. "I got a box at Wal-Mart."

"Wal-Mart," Stavis said. "That's freakin' classic."

"Yeah," Pete said, reaching for the remote. He'd bought a whole box, but he planned on using only one.

# CHAPTER
# TWENTY-EIGHT

P HOEBE, IN HER HEART OF HEARTS, WANTED to wear black. She and Margi had sworn they would never attend any of the ridiculous dances and socials that the school sponsored throughout the year. But on the other hand, they both harbored a secret desire to at least be *asked* by someone to go. They'd made a half-hearted pact that if they ever went, it would be in dresses of flowing black taffeta, complete with veils; Weird Sisters to the end.

Phoebe turned in front of the mirror hanging from her closet door, admiring the way the sleek fabric—a silky, almost shiny white—cut in and hugged her middle and fell along her hips.

She turned back to face herself, pleased that she'd gone with the white dress in the end. Black looked great on her, but something about going on a date with a dead kid while wearing a dress appropriate for a funeral just didn't feel right. She didn't need the attendant barrage of comments from her parents, either. The worst comment she'd had to endure thus far was one from her dad about the neckline of the dress, which of course was lower that he would have liked. Phoebe was thankful that he kept whatever Bride of Frankenstein jokes, which were surely buzzing around his skull like angry hornets, to himself.

Phoebe scanned herself from head to toe before settling on a staring contest with her reflection. Her skin was pale but not sickly; it was not as free from blemish or as even in tone as Karen's, but it didn't have the bluish cast that hers did in certain light, either. Phoebe was slim, and although her figure, again, was not as stunning as Karen's, it was at the very least attractive. Chasing after the Frisbee in the school yard had helped shape some dangerous curves, she thought, and her arms and legs had some nice definition that they would have lacked had she spent every free hour writing goth poetry.

She looked deep within her eyes, which were a warm greenish-hazel color. She liked to think that they were flecked with gold, and if the candles in her room flickered just so, they were.

She was pretty, she realized. Maybe even very pretty.

The thought made her breath catch in her throat. When she broke contact with the pretty young girl in the mirror, she reached for the fuzzy purple notebook and pen that she kept at all times on her nightstand, opened to the first blank page, and began to write.

\* \* \*

"The limousine left when the driver realized that my son was differently biotic," Faith told them, a hint of apology in her voice. "It looks like the kids will be in the PT Cruiser tonight."

Phoebe overheard her talking in the kitchen as she came down the stairs. Her parents stood off to the side of the kitchen, uneasily talking to Faith and her undead son, who looked uncomfortable looming in the doorway in his blue suit jacket and tie. Faith saw her enter, and her face lit up.

"Phoebe, you look beautiful, honey!" she said. "Just beautiful!"

"Thank you," she murmured in reply. She was wearing enough makeup to mask the color that rose to her cheeks, but there was nothing she could do to ward off the spots of blush that she could practically feel rising along her throat. The plunging neckline was a Pyrrhic victory at best, it seemed.

"Isn't she beautiful, Tommy?" Faith said, but Tommy just stared.

Phoebe blushed, but she stared back. The suit fit him wonderfully, seeming to accentuate the quiet strength that she found so attractive in the way it fell across his broad shoulders. The corner of his mouth twitched up in a smile.

From the corner of her eye, Phoebe saw her father open his mouth, and she steeled herself for soul-crushing embarrassment.

"I'll drive," he said, looking surprised at his own offer. "That is, if the kids don't mind."

Phoebe, taken aback by his sudden generosity, shook her head. He smiled back at her.

"We're being rude," he said. "Can we get you a drink? Mrs. Williams? Some coffee?"

"Coffee would be great," she said, smiling and extending her hand, first to Phoebe's dad and then to her mother. "I'm Faith. I don't think you've met my son, Tommy."

"I haven't," her father said. "Watched him play a little football, though."

Tommy stepped forward and shook his hand. "Mr. Kendall," he said, and Phoebe watched their exchange with growing fascination. She realized that her father had most likely never touched a differently biotic person prior to this moment. Even her mother allowed him to take her hand.

"Tommy," her dad said. "Faith, why don't you come in for a while?"

The obligatory photo shoot was awkward, and Phoebe could see her mom's hands trembling as she snapped a few digital pictures. Very few pictures, Phoebe noted. But Faith snapped away with her camera until Tommy finally suggested that it was time for them to be going.

Her dad invited Faith along for the ride, but she remained behind to talk with Phoebe's mother over coffee and some of those biscotti that Phoebe couldn't stand but Margi loved. Rather, the biscotti that Margi loved to feed Gargoyle, who orbited the kitchen table with a greedy look on his furry face. Phoebe kissed her mother and hugged Faith. Faith winked at her when Phoebe turned and waved from the door.

Phoebe and Tommy slid into the expansive backseat of her

father's car, and laughed politely at his lame chauffeur jokes. Phoebe wondered if maybe in some ways she'd lucked out by going with a differently biotic boy instead of a living one, because she knew that if it was a living boy, her dad would have grilled him relentlessly, developing a sudden interest in the boy's lineage, his address, his father's place of employment, what he liked to do in his spare time. With Tommy, there was a wall of mystery that her dad was too polite to breach.

"Phoebe tells me that you quit the football team," he said. "That is a shame. It looked like you knew what you were doing out there."

"Thank you, sir."

"Mr. Kendall is fine."

"Thank you, Mr. Kendall," Tommy said, and aimed a slow wink at Phoebe, making her smile.

"It couldn't have been easy for you, putting that uniform on. Knowing that you were going to have . . . some resistance."

"I wanted . . . to play. That made it a lot easier."

"You did well," Mr. Kendall said. "Very well."

Phoebe wished that he would drive a little faster so that they could get to the dance before he said something stupid.

"Why did you quit, then?" her dad said.

Too late, Phoebe thought.

"The world . . . wasn't ready for one of . . . us . . . to play a school sport. At least I showed . . . that it could be done."

"I think it is damn shame, and a miscarriage of justice. It must be very frustrating for you."

"Being a . . . zombie . . . can often be frustrating," Tommy told him.

"Is that what you call yourselves? Zombies?"

"Oh, look," Phoebe said. "Is that a deer up ahead in the Palmer's field?"

Her father ignored her. "It just seems a pretty, I don't know, negative thing to call yourself. Zombie. Zombies were never the good guys in the movies, from what I remember, so I doubt the term will win you any points politically, you know what I mean?"

Phoebe squeezed her eyes shut. Drive faster, she thought, trying to send a telepathetic message to her dad. But as usual, he appeared to be immune.

"No burning crosses," Mr. Kendall said, "and I don't see any rotten fruit. I guess that's a good thing."

"Thanks for the ride, Dad," Phoebe said, scrambling to get out. There were rows of cars in the loop where the buses picked up and deposited the Oakvale High students every weekday. There were small clusters of students chatting, boys in new sport jackets and ties, their shoes buffed and polished to a high reflective glow. She stepped onto the curb.

"Have fun, kids," her dad said, accepting a quick peck on the cheek from Phoebe. "I almost forgot, how are you going to get to the party later?"

Phoebe felt her heart sink, and hoped that the feeling didn't show on her face. She'd forgotten all about the party, and with the limousine service unwilling to transport zombie cargo, they were left without a ride. One detail she'd failed to mention when discussing the party with her parents was that it was a differently biotic party.

Phoebe opened her mouth to answer when Tommy interrupted her.

"I called Adam Layman, Mr. Kendall," he said. "He'll give us a lift to and from the party. I hope that is okay."

"Adam, huh?" her dad said. "Be sort of cramped in that truck of his."

"We'll manage, Mr. Kendall. I can always go in the back."

"Don't wreck your suit," her dad said. "Okay then, kids. Have fun."

"Bye, Dad," Phoebe replied, hoping he couldn't see how relieved she was. Adam was perhaps the only boy on earth that her father entrusted her with, probably because he would do random acts of pure goodness like shovel their driveway when Mr. Kendall was away on business, and he'd accept no payment for his deeds other than a movie with Phoebe and maybe a bowl of Mrs. Kendall's French onion soup. Adam was her father's favorite for son-in-law—despite the obviously platonic nature of his and Phoebe's relationship—an idea only sidelined by the fact that the STD would one day become the other grandfather to their children.

"Be home by midnight, okay?" he said. "I don't want you turning into a pumpkin."

"Yes, Dad,"

"Good night, Mr. Kendall," Tommy said. "I'm glad I finally met you."

Her father shook his hand again, and Phoebe noticed that the move was a natural one, free from the hitch of trepidation he'd had the first time they touched. Progress was progress.

"Me too, Tommy. Have fun."

They watched him drive away, and Tommy, smiling, offered his arm.

"Mom was right," he said. "You're beautiful."

She took his arm. "You look nice too, Tommy," she said. They walked toward the school. "Are we really getting a ride from Adam?"

"Yes," he said. "Is that okay?"

"It's fine," she said. "But it might be a little chilly in the cab. Adam and I aren't speaking right now."

"Adam mentioned that," he said. "Actually, he said . . . that you weren't speaking to him."

She looked away. Just the thought of Adam made her sad, and she didn't want to be sad, not tonight. She wished that she could have showed him her dress before Tommy had come over. He would have said something nice, and he would have just stood there, looking at her. She could always count on Adam to be uncomplicated in the way he appreciated her.

Stop, she thought. She squeezed Tommy's arm; it was like stone beneath her fingertips.

The clusters of students loitering around outside the dance turned toward them, but with no more scrutiny than they had for any of the other arriving couples. Phoebe told herself that they were more interested in finding fault with her dress than they were in criticizing her date. They walked into the school unmolested, Tommy's stride less tentative and awkward than many of the flustered boys ambling around in their starched shirts, pulling at their constricting ties.

Tommy handed their tickets to a chaperone at the gym door. The darkened gymnasium was done up in paper streamers and balloons, and there were a number of multicolored spotlights casting a glow over the students as they danced on a low platform that had been brought in for the occasion. Freckles of light appeared on Phoebe's arms, reflected by the large mirror ball above the dance floor. Warm, cologne-scented air washed over them.

Phoebe had never attended a school dance before. She thought it all looked beautiful.

They saw Mrs. Rodriguez talking with Principal Kim by a loose throng of parents and teachers standing guard near the punch bowl. The principal saw them and walked over, excusing herself from a waving Mrs. Rodriguez. Phoebe said hello.

"Karen and Kevin are already here, Tommy," Principal Kim said. "Are you expecting any of your other friends tonight?"

"I expect Adam . . . and Thorny . . . to be here," he replied. "If they were able to raise . . . the money . . . to rent dates."

Her smile was wry and reserved. "I'm sorry," she said, "I meant—"

"You meant any of my dead friends," he said. Phoebe gripped his arm.

Principal Kim nodded. "Tommy, we discussed this. You know I do not mind any of the students coming to the dance.

You know I am only trying my best to ensure your safety and the safety of everyone at Oakvale High."

"I know. I saw all of the . . . police cars . . . in the lot."

"We always have the police present at a dance."

"State Troopers?"

The principal's smile didn't waver. Phoebe had the sense that Tommy was being petulant, a sense that was confirmed when he looked away from her.

"None of the . . . others . . . are coming."

"Thank you, Tommy," Principal Kim said. "And just to remind you of some of the finer points of our discussion, seeing as you seem to have forgotten them: if the media or any protestors arrive, we will promptly escort you, your date, and the other differently biotic children out of the gymnasium and then out of the school."

Tommy nodded.

Principal Kim smiled at them with genuine warmth. "Good. Now go have some fun."

"What was that all about?" Phoebe asked as the principal drifted away from earshot. Tommy untangled his arm from her, his hand brushing hers as it fell.

"When they . . . counseled us . . . after Evan was murdered," he said, referring to the mandatory sessions that each participant in the Undead Studies class had had with the principal, the school psychiatrist, and a pair of lawyers, "she asked what we . . . what I would do. I told her I would live . . . my life and continue my work. I told her you and I were going to homecoming. I told her you and I . . . would dance."

Phoebe let his words sink in for a moment. "But she was afraid there would be a protest?"

"Or worse. I agreed . . . that we would leave at the first sign . . . of trouble."

Phoebe sighed. "So I guess I could turn into a pumpkin after all."

"What?"

"Never mind."

Phoebe caught sight of Karen over his shoulder. She was at the perimeter of the dance floor, dancing with a fluid grace that most of the living students would envy. She was wearing a clingy blue dress that had a wide yellow belt cinched at her waist and a hemline that ended just above her knees. When she spun, which she did often, the hem rose to an almost indecent level and showed off her stunning smooth legs. Kevin was standing in front of her in a sacklike black suit with a horrible brown knit tie, his arms lifting and falling with every seventh or eighth beat. His left arm seemed more motile than the right.

"Oh, look," Phoebe said. "How cute!" But Tommy was already moving toward them.

"Hi, kids," Karen said, a swarm of silver lights crossing her face as a strobe glanced off the mirror ball above. "Phoebe, you are absolutely stunning. And what a handsome date you have." Her eyes seemed more crystalline, and they glittered like stars in the flashing dance hall lights.

"Thanks, Karen," Phoebe said. "You might actually be the most beautiful girl I've ever seen."

Karen laughed, caressing Phoebe's arm with a hand that

glided in time with the music. "You're sweet. I'm just trying to bring my date, Kevin here, back to life." Her hand left Phoebe's skin, which tingled where the dead girl had touched her. Karen did a lazy wave that took in the rest of the dancers.

"And the rest of these boys," she said. "I'm trying to knock dead."

"Well," Tommy said, "you are drop dead . . . gorgeous."

"Funny," Karen said, batting her eyelashes, "You aren't so bad yourself."

Phoebe's experience in such matters was rather limited, but it felt as though they were flirting right in front of her.

"Killer," Kevin said. They all laughed.

Karen grabbed Phoebe's hand. "Dance with me." And Phoebe did.

Margi arrived twenty minutes or so later, her dress mostly pink with black accents—black ribbons in the front and back, a wide black belt, and black shoes. She had a puffy black flower pinned in the pinkish nest of her hair.

The dress was snug in an attractive way, and if Phoebe's dad had found *her* neckline risqué, he would never have let Margi leave his house with what she was wearing. Phoebe thought she looked great. So did Norm, judging by the way he stood wiping sweat off his forehead with the back of his bony hand.

"Norm's car wouldn't start in my driveway," she said. "Dad had to jump-start it." Norm Lathrop looked gawky and nervous lurking behind her; he was swimming in his suit. His eyes were wide behind the thick lenses of his glasses.

Phoebe opened her mouth to reply, but Margi was quick and sharp.

"No jokes, please!" she said. "I have the rest of my life to look forward to those!"

Phoebe laughed and hugged her.

"Norm," Margi said, "these are some of my friends I was telling you about. You know Phoebe. Tommy, Karen, and Kevin. They're all dead."

Phoebe was shocked, but Kevin waved and Karen blew a quick kiss, unfazed by Margi's bluntness. Neither had stopped dancing.

Norm waved back, and was drawn out in the front only by Tommy's offered hand, which he shook like it was a snake he was trying to kill.

"Careful, Norm," Tommy said. "We break . . . easily."

"Oh God, I'm so sorry!" Norm said, dropping Tommy's hand like it had bitten him. Margi patted him on the shoulder.

"They're kidders, Norm," she said. "Take it easy."

A popular club hit came on, and Margi began to sway, her hips brushing against Phoebe and then poor Norm, who looked like he was about to melt into a puddle at her feet.

"Remember what I told you, Normie. When you are with me, you have to be prepared to dance."

Norm tried his best, and managed to work himself through their loose circle to practice his moves next to Kevin, probably because he figured he couldn't possibly look inept next to him. Phoebe smiled at the thought, because he was wrong.

A half hour later, Phoebe was breathless and sweaty while her zombie companions looked about as unruffled and energetic as they ever did. Which wasn't very, in Kevin's case, but Karen and Tommy were doing just fine.

She excused herself and went over to find a chair with the wallflowers. The DJ cued up a popular rap tune with an aggressive BPM count, one that made Phoebe glad she'd taken the moment to sit a spell. She found a seat and watched Tommy and Karen share a joke, their bodies moving almost but not quite in time with the rhythm—just like most of the living students. Kevin, a huge smile on his round face, was trying his best, even though he was occasionally jostled by Norm, whose dancing was becoming more and more daring, or more and more spastic, depending on how one chose to look at it. Margi waved at Phoebe and then laughed at something Karen said as Karen executed a sinuous move that Phoebe thought really might be able to bring the dead to life.

Phoebe wasn't sure if she was happy or sad in that moment, so she decided she felt a bit of both. At least they'd been there nearly an hour and no one had poured pig's blood on them.

She looked around the room for Adam, surprised that she hadn't yet spotted his massive form looming over the rest of the puny student bodies. No sign of Whatsername, either. Adam was too good a guy to waste his time with a gum-snapping bimbo like her.

Speaking of wasted time, she wished she hadn't blown up at him. It wasn't fair. Besides, it had been barely a week since her snit fit, and she already missed him. It didn't seem right to be here at a dance and not at least see him and share a joke together.

"Hey, Phoebe," a low voice said, cutting through the bass beats and her thoughts. It was Harris Morgan, Martinsburg's crony, the one whose nose she'd bloodied in the forest. He stepped toward her.

"Hey," he repeated.

"Leave me alone," she said. She tried to rise, but he stepped in front of her chair, meaning she'd have to brush against him if she wanted to stand up. The chair was flush against the wall, so she wasn't going anywhere.

"It isn't like that," he said.

"What's it like, then?" If she called for Tommy, would he hear her over the sound of Karen's laughter? Maybe he'd be too caught up in the bass beat that seemed to give him and his friends a quicker step. Or maybe he'd be watching Karen too intently, intoxicated by the subtle scent of lavender that Phoebe smelled wafting from Karen's hair when she spun.

"I'm just trying to talk to you," he said, "to warn you."

"Go away."

"I think Pete and TC are up to something," he said.

"Really? Are they rolling freshman for soda money in the little boys' room?" Her tone was belittling, but she was certain that Martinsburg—and probably this jerk in front of her—had been responsible for the retermination of Evan Talbot.

She decided she wouldn't call for Tommy, no matter what happened. If Harris tried anything, she'd stand up and shove him as hard as she could.

Morgan shook his head and held up his hands. "No. No, I think they're planning something serious. Something that is going to hurt people. You and your friends."

"What do you care?" She rose, brushing him back with her body. She'd dropped him once, she'd do it again, pretty dress or not. And then she'd leave and let all the zombies and living zombies have all the fun they wanted.

Morgan shook his head. "I'm just telling you, is all." He turned away.

"Hey," she said, and he stopped. "Is he here? Pete and the big one? Are they here at the dance?"

"They're coming," he said.

They stared at each other a moment longer, until Harris looked away and drifted back into the stream of students milling around the edges of the dance floor.

Phoebe remained standing, and she didn't really notice that the flashing lights had been lowered and turned to blue as the first slow song was spun by the DJ.

"Phoebe," a voice called. It was Tommy, looking awkward for the first time that night as he shouldered his way through the kids, many of whom were escaping the dance floor while others were just setting foot on it.

"Will you . . . dance with me?"

Phoebe smiled and took his hand.

"Gross," Holly said. Adam saw what she was commenting on: Tommy Williams leading Phoebe out onto the dance floor so that they could slow dance to an old Journey song. His reaction was far different, but he kept it to himself.

"What's with your friend, anyway?" Holly said. Adam thought that if she was angling for an invite to dance, she had a funny way of going about it. He didn't bother to answer. He watched Thorny pull his giggling date out onto the dance floor. Haley Rourke was a junior and nearly a foot taller than Thorny. She was the star forward of the Lady Badgers basketball team, and Adam thought they were a great match, personality-wise. She was very athletic but shy, and Thorny did his best to be athletic and was one of the least shy people he knew.

Thorny had tried to pal around with Adam, but Holly was making it difficult because she didn't approve of either Thorny or his date. She'd much rather be hanging around people like Tori Stewart and Pete Martinsburg, who'd breezed into the dance about five minutes ago.

Adam watched Phoebe loop her hands around Williams's shoulders as the dead boy placed his hands on her hips. He wanted to look away, but found he couldn't take his eyes off her.

She looks happy, Adam thought.

"Why would she want to dance with a dead kid, anyway?" Holly was perfectly capable of carrying on a conversation with herself, Adam knew. "I'm surprised they even let dead kids in here, it's so gross. That one kid dances like a bug that has been stepped on. And the girl . . ."

"Hey, Holly," Adam said.

Holly looked up at him. "Yes, Adam?"

There was an expectancy in her eyes that he felt bad about, but not enough to change his mind.

"Do you think you could get a ride home from Tori or someone else?" he asked. "I'm not feeling so great, and I think I'm going to take off."

He didn't wait for her answer; he just turned and left her standing there in her pretty yellow dress, her mouth open but for once not producing any sound.

"Okay," Pete said, "we've made our appearance. Let's get out of here."

TC nudged him in the ribs. "Hey, what about the zombie?"

TC pointed right at Williams, who was spinning slowly with Scarypants. Piggy Sharon and Tori were giggling behind him, and Pete found himself really regretting giving them the bottle of schnapps for the ride.

"You want to go mess with him?" TC asked, his voice carrying over the music.

"Not now," Pete said. "Soon."

It wasn't just Williams. Dancing next to them was the slutty dead girl and the other zombie kid on his list. Pete thought he moved like a twitching bug.

"'Kay, girls," he said, turning back to Tori because Sharon was a little sloppy, "TC and I have to go do that little trip I told you about. We'll see you later at Denny's party."

Tori pouted up at him, stumbling a little as she presented herself to be kissed. Pete obliged, tasting the peppermint alcohol on her lips. TC and Sharon locked up like a pair of wrestling octopi. Pete wondered if they had killed the whole bottle.

"Whereya guys going?" Tori asked.

"Special mission," he replied.

"Got a prank to pull," TC said, squeezing Sharon to him with one heavy arm. "We're gonna get—"

"More booze," Pete said, and gave TC a look intended to sober him in a hurry. TC shut his mouth and let go of Sharon.

Pete kissed Tori a second time. "We'll see you later."

As they were leaving, Pete saw Adam across the floor, walking toward them. Adam saw them and drew up short.

Pete smiled and pointed his finger like a handgun at Layman, who looked as if someone had just kicked him in the gut. Pete winked and dropped the thumb hammer, mock shooting Adam in the head. Then he led TC out the door.

# CHAPTER
# TWENTY-NINE

THE PLAN WAS TO MEET ADAM OUTSIDE AT ten, but Phoebe hadn't seen him all night. Whatsername was there, clustered in the corner with two other cheerleading harpies. Phoebe wondered what the deal was.

"What are we going to do if Adam didn't come?" she asked Tommy, who danced next to her in a loose circle with Karen, Kevin, Margi, and Norm.

"He came," he said. "I saw him talking with his date earlier."

"I haven't seen him all night," she said. "He's sort of hard to miss." But she missed him a lot, actually. All night she had been wishing that he was there, dancing with them. She couldn't even imagine him dancing, but she wanted to see it.

"Norm has . . . a car," Tommy said. "So does Thorny. Or his date, I forget which."

"I'm going to see if Adam is outside," she said. "I'll be back."

Oakvale had a strict no-reentry policy aimed at foiling parking lot shenanigans of various stripes, but Principal Kim was a sucker for kids as well behaved and academically achieving as Phoebe was, so she was able to get an exception after only five minutes of wrangling. She hurried out the door. There was a girl sitting on the stone steps. She was crying under the wary eyes of a pair of cops standing watch at the curb. There were a few cars parked in the loop, one of them being the STD's truck. She could see Adam slouched in his seat, staring off into the night sky. The sight of him sitting there by himself, so solid and dependable, erased all of her anger at him.

Phoebe ran over to the truck as fast as she could in her heels. She called his name.

He rolled down the window and turned his Van Halen CD down.

"Hey, Pheeble," he said without enthusiasm.

"What's going on?" she said.

"Lost my date," he said.

"Really?"

"Really. I like that dress. It looks like moonlight. Ghostly. Maybe even spectral. Shimmery."

Phoebe smiled. "Flatterer. Thanks."

They looked at each other in silence for a moment, and Phoebe thought it was strange, this distance between them. She'd almost forgotten what a judgmental jerk she had been.

"Listen, Adam . . ." she began.

"I'm sorry, Phoebe," he said; and she had never noticed how like a little boy's his face could become. Adam was so big, so quietly confident and mature, she'd always thought of him as being much older than she was, but there was something in his eyes, something hurt and vulnerable, that she'd never seen before.

"No, Adam," she said, "I was really . . ."

He shook his head. "Don't even. And don't worry about it. You'd better get your dead pals soon, though, because these cops have tried to roust me a few times."

She laughed; it was like his strong arms had just lifted a big weight from her back. "*Roust*? They actually tried to roust you?"

"Roust," he answered. "What I said."

"You know, you have a pretty good vocabulary for someone who can't get through *Wuthering Heights*."

He lifted the battered paperback off the seat. "I just now finished it," he told her. "I'm a changed man."

"Well, good for you."

"Absolutely. And hey, I was just kidding about the rousting. Stay longer if you want. You looked like you were having fun."

Something about his comment seemed off-kilter, but she couldn't identify what it was. He'd seen her, but she hadn't seen him?

"Yeah, I am," she said. "The dead kids are, too. You should see Kevin dance."

"I did. He's a better dancer than I am."

"I doubt it. Especially after karate and *Wuthering Heights*.

Grace and romantic prose? You'll be the terror of girlhood everywhere if you get on the dance floor."

"Yeah."

Something was bothering him. He was acting like he had that night he'd asked her to play Frisbee, when he didn't want to share whatever it was that was weighing on him. But she knew him well enough to realize that no amount of prodding would pry loose whatever it was; he'd share it in his own good time—if ever.

"Okay," she said, and knocked on the door of the truck twice. "I'll go do some rousting and get this party started."

"Great. See you in a few."

"See you."

She was halfway up the steps when her friends came out en masse from the building. Kevin's shoulders were still rolling and twitching as though permanently infused with rhythm. Tommy jogged ahead to her.

"Margi said that Norm would like to take us," he said. "Margi . . . said that he is more socially . . . inept . . . than most zombies, even."

The last bit he did in a fair approximation of Margi's signature machine-gun delivery.

"God love her," Phoebe said, looking over to see Margi and Karen goofing on something poor Norm had said. "But Adam's right over there."

"Oh, I'll go with Adam!" Karen called, waving at him as he sat in the now-warming truck. "I'll see you all at the Haunted House. Maybe."

Kevin didn't seem to mind; he looked like he was trying to perfect the undead version of the Robot, which was very strange to watch without any music playing, so Phoebe followed Tommy and the others out to Norm's car.

Phoebe looked back once, to see Karen practically bouncing into Adam's truck.

That will be good for him, she thought, but really she wasn't sure. She wasn't sure what she thought about it at all.

Norm was a much more cautious—and less-skilled—driver than Adam, and he might have had some additional nervousness about having a pair of zombies in the backseat; but it wasn't often he got invited to parties, so he managed to get them there in one piece. They arrived just as Adam and Karen were heading up the porch steps.

Phoebe was the first one out, and she saw Mal, his huge figure filling the doorway, waving his absurd four-fingered wave.

"How . . . was . . . the . . . dance?" she heard him say.

"Great," Karen said, grabbing Adam's hand and pulling him along. "No one threw rocks or bottles or even insults. I think Kevin might have . . . stepped on a girl's toe, but that was as violent as it got."

Inside, the dead were dancing to a loud club mix that blared throughout the house. Phoebe had never seen so many zombies in one place before There had to be at least two dozen of them, just in the foyer and the front room, all swaying and jerking beneath an array of decorations and lighting.

"You like it?" Karen said, detaching herself from Adam for the moment. "I got my parents to buy the lights. And look at the little disco ball. Isn't that just the . . . cutest?"

"You did a great job, Karen," Phoebe said. She caught sight of Colette dancing in the corner by herself. She reminded Phoebe of the blissed-out hippie girls from the Woodstock movie her dad had made her watch a few years ago. Karen hadn't waited for her answer, though. She'd whisked Adam to the center of Club Dead and was spinning around him, the hem of her short skirt rising in a provocative floret of silky material. To Phoebe's surprise, Adam started moving his arms and feet.

"Oh man," Norm said. He was as pale as any of the dead people in the room.

"Breathe deeply," Tommy said. "I'll introduce you . . . around."

Tommy introduced them to a few of the people lingering in the foyer, most of whom were expressionless and seemingly blasé about the introductions. The music was incessant but the strobe light flashed in intermittent waves, making the dancers look even more halting and bizarre. The scene threw Phoebe's perceptions off. She said hello and shook a cold hand or two, but it seemed as though some of the zombies were less than happy to meet her. Conversely, she thought Tommy was a little too happy to be showing her off.

It could be the lights and the music, she thought.

Someone grabbed Tommy's shoulder from behind.

"Tayshawn!" Phoebe said. "How are you?"

He didn't answer her and spoke directly to Tommy.

"Takayuki . . . wants to talk . . . to you," he said. "More . . . are arriving . . . daily."

Phoebe watched Tommy go from festive to serious in a heartbeat. "Where is he?" he asked. "Upstairs?"

Tayshawn nodded, and Tommy turned back to her. "I'll be right back," he said.

She watched them go up the dark staircase, where she pictured Takayuki hanging upside down and hidden in an empty closet somewhere.

*Brr*, she thought, and went back to watching the dancers, squinting whenever the too-bright strobe flashed. Pretty much everyone was moving, but she couldn't tell if any of them were having fun, because most of the zombies wore no expression as they twisted and shook. The exception was Colette, whose smile looked more and more natural each time Phoebe saw her. She was chatting in the corner with Margi and Norm.

Thorny arrived with his date just as Tayshawn came back down the stairs, alone.

"Tayshawn!" he called, raising his arm for a high five. "How are you, man?"

Tayshawn left him hanging, making his way with purpose through the dance floor to the other room, where the stereo equipment awaited him.

"Dang," Phoebe heard Thorny say, and then he caught sight of her. "Hey, Phoebe. Do you know Haley Rourke?" he said, leading Haley deeper into the room. Phoebe thought she looked terrified; Phoebe said hello, but the tall girl was frozen in place.

"Thorny," Phoebe said into his ear, "did you tell her that there would be mostly differently biotic people here?"

"Huh?" he said, swinging his arms to the new tune that began to blare through the speakers. "You think I should have?"

Phoebe started to reply when she saw Tommy and Takayuki coming back down the stairs. Tak kept walking out the front door.

"Is everything okay?" Phoebe asked him.

"Yes," Tommy said. "We have had . . . new arrivals. Some for . . . the party. Others . . . to stay."

"That's good, right? The more, the merrier?" She wanted to ask about Takayuki, but didn't.

"Yes," he said. "But it might get us . . . noticed."

"Isn't that what you want? To be noticed?"

"What do you mean?"

"The blog," she said. "Playing football and all that. Aren't you just trying to get people to notice your cause?"

She wanted to add *dating a trad girl*, but she didn't need to. The sentiment was obvious; it seemed to hang unspoken between them during every conversation.

He took his time answering. "It is . . . important," he said, "for . . . people to understand our situation. What we go through."

"Won't this help?"

"It could. But not everyone sees . . . the same opportunities that I do."

"Tak?"

"Yes. And Tak . . . is not alone."

An old power ballad began, and many of the couples, zombie and otherwise, began to break off into pairs. Phoebe watched as a pair of zombies, the boy in a suit jacket two sizes too big for him, moved toward each other into an awkward, spidery embrace. Norm was crouching so that his head rested on Margi's shoulder, some of her hair spikes poking behind the frames of his glasses and into his closed eyes. Haley Rourke was clinging to the much shorter Thorny as though he were the last free rock in a stormy sea.

She looked back to Tommy, who was scanning the room, watching his people reach for each other in the muted light beneath the glittering mirror ball above them. His invitation to dance seemed to her an afterthought.

"Actually, Tommy," she said, "could we go somewhere and talk a little more?"

"This house . . . is full of zombies," he said, managing to affect a disgusted expression. It made her smile.

"Yes, it is."

"A walk in the woods? Like when we met?"

"Like when we met," she said. "I'd like that. It's a little chilly, though."

He gave her his jacket, which carried a subtle scent that she had a hard time placing at first but then recognized as Z, the cologne they'd laughed over at the mall—the "scent for the active undead male."

She followed him out the back door and into the woods.

Adam gently guided his dance partner around so he could peek out the living room window and watch Tommy and Phoebe enter the Oxoboxo woods. Karen's grip on him was tight.

He held his breath as they disappeared into the tree line, their bodies swallowed up by the darkness. He wondered if that's what it felt like to be dead.

I hope you know what you are doing, Pheeble, he thought. No wait. I hope you have no idea what you are doing. I hope you . . .

"She doesn't know, does she?" Karen said, breaking his train of thought.

"What?"

Karen's diamond eyes glittered like the stars.

"Phoebe," she said. "She doesn't know how you feel about her, does she?"

"No," he replied. "How do you?"

"Telepathetic," she said, shrugging. Beneath his rough hands, her body felt airy and fragile, her bones like those of a bird. She pressed her face against his chest.

"Actually, it is a combination of things. Your body language. The way you look at her when you are with her, the way you look at her when she doesn't know you are looking. The way you look when you aren't with her. The way your overly serious face softens when you are speaking to her. That sort of thing."

"Ah. My overly serious face. It betrays me every time."

"Sorry. I meant to say your overly cute and serious face."

"Okay," he said. "That helps."

"Adam, look," she said, fixing him with her cut-diamond eyes. "Take it from me. Don't wait around to die for love."

"Great advice. What exactly does it mean?"

"It means you should find the right time and tell her how you feel."

"The right time for her? Or for me?"

Again he felt the subtle shift of a delicate skeletal structure beneath his hands.

"Just the right time."

He looked out the window, where shadows seemed to move among the trees.

"What about Tommy?"

"Tommy is Tommy," was her quick reply. "And your feelings aren't really Tommy's concern, are they?"

He thought there was an edge in her voice. "What about your feelings? Do you have feelings for Tommy?"

She laughed and squeezed him again. "I've got feelings for a lot of people. Dead people, trad people, whatever. . . ."

He laughed and smoothed her silvery hair.

"You're a special girl, Karen." And without thinking, he brushed her hair behind her ear with his fingertips and bent low so that he could kiss her cheek. It was an act of pure impulse, one that he was scarcely aware of doing until the cool smoothness of her skin against his warm lips reminded him of who he was, and what she was.

"Oh," she said. "Oh, thank you, Adam."

The glittering stars in her eyes were going nova, like they weren't merely reflecting light but, instead, projecting it.

"No," he said, hugging and then releasing her. "Thank you."

The song changed into something more frenetic, and he pressed through the dead with deliberation toward the back door.

# CHAPTER THIRTY

PETE COULDN'T BELIEVE HIS GOOD LUCK. Even with TC half in the bag and reeking of peppermint, they'd managed to find the place—a short hike through the woods after stashing the car in one of his old make-out turnoffs. The roads around the Oxoboxo were full of these bootlegger turns, and he knew each one.

They'd just arrived when Adam's battered truck and the second car with Scarypants and Williams arrived. For fun he'd sighted along the barrel and aimed at the big zombie on the porch. At his head, specifically, which sat on his wide shoulders like a lump of melted candle wax.

*Pop*, Pete thought, and then aimed at Karen and Adam in turn as they went up the stairs. Then TC almost gave them away with a loud sneeze.

"Shut up, you idiot," Pete had said through clenched teeth.

"What?" TC said, grinning. "The music is wicked loud, and they can't hear too well anyhow."

Pete wanted to crack him with the rifle butt, right in his grinning moon face. He turned back, and Tommy was halfway up the steps, at the center of a loose knot of people. Scarypants was with him, and their usual crowd. Also some dweeb who Pete vaguely recalled roughing up on a few occasions.

Pete aimed at Tommy. While other kids had been day-dreaming about all the wholesome fun they'd have at the big school dance, Pete had spent the week shooting cans and assorted woodland critters behind his house. He even put a round into the Talbot's chimney, just for fun. His finger was loose around the trigger.

Head shot, he thought, squinting.

"Why didn't you shoot 'im?" TC asked as they watched Williams enter the house.

Pete was sweating; he felt damp at the armpits and on his neck. He and TC had shucked their semiformal wear and put on dark sweats and sneakers for their mission.

"I didn't have a clear shot, stupid," he said, leaning back against a tree.

"So what do we do now?" TC asked.

"We wait."

"But I've got to piss," TC said, whining.

"So go piss! Just be friggin' quiet about it!"

TC lumbered off to relieve himself, moving with all the grace of a moose.

He returned and they waited, watching that little runt

Harrowwood and his freakishly tall date arrive, and then they saw some way-too-happy metalhead dude leave and walk into the woods in the opposite direction. Pete thought he looked familiar.

"Was that a zombie?" TC asked.

"Couldn't tell," Pete answered. "Probably."

"Look!" TC jumped up and pointed.

"What?"

"They just left! They went out the back door!"

"Who? Williams?" Pete said, picking the rifle off the ground and rising.

"Yeah, and the goth chick! They walked off into the woods."

"Okay," Pete said, "there must be a path back there. We'll move along the tree line until we find it. When we catch up to them, you grab Julie, and I'll bust a cap on dead boy."

"You got it, Pete," TC said, but Pete was already moving, glancing at the house every few steps just in case any more zombie lovers decided to take a moonlight stroll.

"Hey," Pete heard TC say as they circled, "who's Julie?"

A muscle in Pete's jaw twitched, but he didn't answer.

The moon wasn't helping much, its reflected light casting only a murky gloom through the bare trees, but Phoebe didn't want to ask Tommy for his hand. She didn't know what signals she wanted to send him. She was already wearing his Z-scented jacket, and that was signal enough, even though all it really signaled was that she was cold.

"The woods aren't made for heels," she said, pausing to slide her shoes off.

"They are unkind to nylons, as well," he said.

She agreed, but thought twice about taking those off.

He was faintly luminous in the poor light.

"Did I ever tell you how I died?" he asked.

She shook her head, not sure if he could see.

"It was a car accident. My father was driving. A drunk driver ran a red light and . . . plowed into us. He survived, but he killed my father." He made a noise that was either a humorless laugh or a sigh; Phoebe couldn't tell in the darkness. "Me too."

"I'm sorry," Phoebe said.

"Dad was killed instantly. I took a little longer. One of my ribs had broken and punctured my lung, so I ended up . . . drowning in my own blood."

"Oh, Tommy," she said, "that's horrible."

"No picnic," he said.

She felt his hand slide over hers, and he led her to a stone bench alongside the path. She let him guide her.

"It happened at night, at an . . . intersection in front of a big church. I could see the steeple through the shattered windshield. We'd spun around a couple times and ended up in line with that steeple. I looked up at the steeple and . . . prayed that my dad was still alive. I remember praying for that because I knew I was a goner and I didn't want my mom to be all alone."

Phoebe, mixed signals or not, squeezed his cold hand. Tommy had never seemed so vulnerable before.

"The first thing I thought when I . . . came back," he said, "was that God got it wrong. I was thinking, no, God, not me. My father. You were supposed to save my father."

"Faith must have been happy that you came back," Phoebe said.

"She's . . . well-named," Tommy said. "Dallas Jones was . . . famous . . . by then, and she says she knew I would . . . come back."

"Faith has faith," Phoebe said. "What about you?"

"Coming back," he said, turning to face her, "explains . . . certain things. And it makes others . . . more of a mystery. I'll try to tell . . . you . . . someday."

Phoebe felt herself growing warm. She turned away and looked off into the dark woods, but her grip on his hand tightened.

"Why do you think that . . . zombies . . . like you and Karen are so different from the others?" Phoebe said. "I mean, why are you able to run and play football, and Karen can dance and drink coffee, and poor Sylvia has trouble walking? Your death was as violent as anybody's."

"I thought it was obvious," he said.

"I guess I'm slow, then," she said. "What?"

"Love."

"Love?" She wished that she could see more of his face than his faintly glowing eyes.

"Love. I live with my mom, who loves me. Karen has her parents and her sister. Evan's parents loved him . . . unconditionally. That's the whole and only difference between us and kids like Colette. Her parents skipped town when she came back."

"Yes," Phoebe said, at once amazed and embarrassed that she'd never really made the connection. "Sylvia? Tayshawn?"

"Sylvia was at St. Jude's, along with Colette and Kevin, and now she's at the foundation getting augmented. They are taken care of at St. Jude's, but I wouldn't call it love. Tayshawn stayed with his grandmother in Norwich . . . for a while. But it didn't work out."

Phoebe's pulse was racing through her as she struggled for a response. She wanted to say something to Tommy, something that would make things better for him, but the only response she could come up with was one she was not ready to give.

She thought that Tommy might have sensed it, too.

"I . . . I just . . . thought," he began. "I thought that . . . if . . . I . . . could get a girl . . . a real girl . . . to love . . . me . . . to kiss . . . me . . . I'd come back . . . even more."

And there it was again, Phoebe thought, turning back toward him. "A girl," he said. Not "Phoebe." *A girl.*

"Tommy . . ."

"I know," he said. "Believe me . . . I . . . know . . . what I'm asking."

He turned and looked at her with his strange eyes, and she thought that she could see all the pain and hurt deep within them. All the pain and hurt of someone whose life had been taken too soon. Before he could experience any of the things that young men experience.

"I just thought," he said, leaning closer to her, "if I . . . could . . . kiss . . . you . . ."

She opened her mouth to answer, but then there was a crash

in the woods behind them, and she felt herself being lifted from the bench by strong, unyielding arms.

She had been about to kiss him, Pete thought. That cheating bitch Julie had been ready to give herself over to that maggot-infested corpse.

"How could you, Julie?" he said, his voice just above a whisper as he stepped to the edge of the path a few feet away. He'd sent Stavis around back of them, hoping that if they heard him stumbling they'd run right toward where Pete was creeping up. But Williams and Julie had been so into their little pillow talk that they hadn't even heard Stavis until it was too late.

"Pete," she said, her voice shrill and scared as she wriggled in Stavis's grip. Pete watched her try to kick him in the shins or higher up, but Stavis put a knee into her backside.

Pete lifted the rifle and sighted down the barrel, focusing on the center of the zombie's forehead. The zombie just stood there, looking at him with his empty eyes.

"Pete, please," she said. "We—"

"Quiet," Pete told her.

"Pete, please, this is—"

"I said shut up!" he screamed, and he shifted his aim from the zombie's face to hers. Her eyes grew wide, and she stopped struggling.

"Hey, Pete," Stavis said, "the zombie . . . I think the zombie—"

"You too, Timothy Cole," Pete said. He only used Stavis's

real name when he wanted instant obedience. "Put her down and shut the hell up. Step over there so you don't get messy."

Stavis hurried to comply, tripping over fallen branches.

Pete watched her look over at her undead lover, the final insult. He was tired of them mocking him in his dreams, mocking him in his waking life. She was probably already infected with the zombie disease. And if he let her go, she'd probably infect even more people.

The barrel of the rifle quivered, but he forced it to remain steady. She looked back at him, and her eyes were wide with fear.

Head shot, he thought. Only way to take out the undead.

"I loved you," he whispered. Then he pulled the trigger.

Adam paced along the dead grass in the backyard, trying to decide if this was the right time, and exactly what he should say.

Hey, Pheeble, he thought. Before you go and kiss this dead guy over there, you ought to know something. You mean more to me than Frisbee and lame jokes about the size of my vocabulary. You mean more to me than a thousand Whatsernames ever could, even if I did ignore you in the hallways for most of our school years together. And Pheeble, if I need to, I'll listen to groups like the Restless Dead and Zombicide and the Drumming Mummies or whatever, and I'll wear black and burn incense if I have to. I'll go have my tarot cards read and I'll pay attention to Daffy like she was an incredibly interesting and insightful savant instead of just some chattering goof. I can do it, Pheeble . . . Phoebe—

He heard a crash somewhere in the woods down the path, and then he heard Phoebe shriek.

He ran down the path, calling her name. At first he thought maybe Tommy did something he shouldn't have, but then he saw Phoebe standing with Tommy, and he saw Pete Martinsburg standing at the edge of the path, training a rifle on them.

On Phoebe.

He ran, calling her name. He ran as fast as his legs could carry him.

He heard Master Griffin's calming voice in his head.

*Focus*, he said. *What will you do with your power?*

Adam reached Phoebe just as Pete pulled the trigger.

When it was over, and Phoebe was once again surrounded by people who loved her, she would remember his moment of hesitation. It might have been that his undead limbs just did not have the reaction time that was required to come to her aid, but when she looked over at him, Tommy Williams, leader of the zombie underground, had hesitated.

Pete Martinsburg hesitated only as long as it took to pull the trigger.

Adam didn't hesitate at all, and that was why he fell.

# CHAPTER
# THIRTY-ONE

THE RIFLE SHOT SPLIT THE SILENCE OF THE woods. Pete saw someone step in front of Julie, and he watched that someone fold in half as if he had been leveled by a squad of invisible tacklers. Adam. He'd shot Adam Layman.

"Jesus Christ, Pete!" Stavis yelled, looking at Pete, his fat face a mask of shock and fear. He took off into the woods.

Scarypants screamed Adam's name and dropped to his side.

Pete aimed at her another moment before throwing the rifle into the brush, and then he also started running. He ran without thinking, tripping and almost breaking his ankle on a low stump. He ran until he found what appeared to be one of the many paths that twisted through the Oxoboxo woods like drunken snakes. Breathing heavily, he slowed his pace to a loose trot, his racing mind, trying to figure out which direction he'd left the car. He had no idea where he was.

"Leaving . . . the party," a voice said from behind him, "so soon?"

He turned; it was the guy who had left the house earlier, and then Pete realized where he'd seen him before. It was the zombie from that day when he'd let the slutty zombie go. The happy guy, the metalhead. Pete saw the glint of chains that hung from his leather.

"Screw . . . yourself," Pete said. The other only smiled as he approached.

Pete turned and tripped over a rock in the path. He rolled onto his back, and the zombie leaned over him, burning the image of his ruined face into Pete's brain.

"Did you think I would . . . kill you?" the zombie asked him, his voice a reptilian rasp and his dark hair hanging down like the tendrils of a jellyfish. "Death is . . . not for you. Death is . . . a gift."

Pete saw then that he wasn't smiling, even though he could see all his teeth. That's when Pete screamed.

Phoebe fell to her knees in the dirt beside Adam's body, tearing the hem of her pretty white dress as she did. Adam had gone over as if leveled by an invisible tackler. It looked like the wind had been knocked out of him, and his big body seemed to deflate as he'd hit the ground.

"Adam?" she said. "Oh my God. Adam, are you all right?"

She had her hands on him now, feeling his arms and shoulders for a sign of injury, and when her fingers touched his chest, she watched a roseate bloom appear and spread in the center of his clean white shirt.

She screamed. "Adam? Adam can you hear me?" Tommy was kneeling next to her, his hand on Adam's shoulder as he started to shake. Adam's mouth opened and closed and his eyes rolled up in his head. He coughed, and a thin trickle of blood appeared at the corner of his mouth. Phoebe pressed her shaking hands against the stain spreading on his shirt and asked God to help her hold Adam's life inside him until help arrived.

"He's going . . . into shock," Tommy said.

She could feel his life ebbing through her fingers.

"No, Adam!" she said, "Don't go! Please, God; don't go, Adam!"

Then his eyes focused and he looked right at her and opened his mouth to speak. He was trying to say something but he was choking, and she was telling him, "Shh, help will be here soon."

He smiled at her, but then she saw the light leave his eyes. His large frame gave a massive convulsive shudder, and then he died.

She held her breath. Adam was motionless.

"Don't go," she heard herself cry, but it was like she was outside herself, like she had left her body behind the moment Adam left his. She looked down at herself, slumped over Adam, her body convulsing with sobs. Tommy knelt beside her, his face cast in shadow.

She looked around her, but Adam—his spirit—was nowhere to be seen.

Then Tommy touched her arm, and she was back inside her body. The stain was still spreading on Adam's white shirt, and she could still feel his life ebbing through her hands.

She heard voices coming up the path, but it was too late. Adam was gone.

The dead gathered around Phoebe. Karen and Colette and Mal and Tayshawn and the ones she didn't know—the burned girl and the girl with the missing arm—they stood in a loose circle around where she and Tommy knelt beside Adam's lifeless body. She thought it was like a funeral, in reverse. The mourners were all dead, and she, the sole living person, was about to be lowered into the earth.

She looked up at them as they stood as still and silent as the trees, and she wanted to scream at them to help her, to use whatever strange powers they had to bring Adam back.

She saw Margi standing among the dead, her hands shaking as she punched numbers into her cell phone.

"How can you just stand there?" Phoebe said, looking at Colette, looking at Mal. She tried to lift Adam up by getting his arm around her neck, but he was too heavy. "Why aren't you helping me? Karen, please!"

She heard Margi talking into her phone, and she tugged at Adam's arm with newfound hope, remembering how many policemen were a short drive away, outside the homecoming dance. The Oakvale fire department always responded to emergencies with immediate attention. She pleaded again, looking up as Takayuki drifted in among his fellow dead.

"Please!" she said, stumbling as Tommy tried to help her lift Adam's body to a sitting position. "Please help me!"

"They're coming," Margi said through her tears.

Karen walked forward and knelt down, putting a cool hand on Phoebe's shoulder. Her diamond eyes twinkled like far-off stars as she placed her other hand flat against the center of the red stain spreading on Adam's shirt.

"There has to be something you can do, Karen," Phoebe begged. "You can, can't you? Can't you help him?"

Karen blinked, snuffing out the stars for a moment, and shook her head.

"I'm sorry, Phoebe," she said. "I'm so, so sorry."

Phoebe's mind cycled through a range of responses. Rage was the first; she wanted to hit Karen, to slap her face, to call her a liar, then she wanted to throw her arms around her and cling to her until the police came and Adam's body was taken away.

"I . . . have him," Tommy said, and Phoebe let Tommy bear his weight gently back to the earth.

"No," she said. There had to be some hope. The police were coming, they could bring him back.

Not knowing what else to do, she hugged Adam's body to her, trying to keep him warm.

Adam opened his eyes.

He thought he felt rain on his cheeks, but when his vision cleared and became acute, even in the gloom, he saw that Phoebe was leaning over him and crying.

He watched her as she caught her breath.

"Adam?"

He laughed, and he made some lame joke about what a hero

he was. Two trips into the woods to rescue her, and he had been knocked flat on his ass for both. Phoebe smiled, but she only seemed to cry harder. He realized that he must be a little dizzy from having the wind knocked out of him, because what he tried to say and what came out were two totally different things.

She shushed him and put her finger against his lips. Funny how much warmer her finger was than Karen's cheek. He tried to make another joke, but he still hadn't gotten his wind back, so all he could produce were short gasping sounds. No big deal. He'd had the wind knocked out of him plenty of times on the field. Just sit back and relax.

He didn't like seeing Pheeble cry, though. He raised his right hand with the idea of brushing away her tears, but—funny thing—it was the left that moved. He watched his hand as it sort of twitched and then lay still on his chest.

His wet chest.

His *really* wet chest. He tried to lift his hand out of the wetness, but his hand wouldn't obey. Phoebe lifted her hands from him in a gesture that she no doubt meant to be reassuring, but as her hands were covered with blood—his blood—she didn't quite get the effect she wanted.

Pete, he thought. The freaking idiot.

Phoebe was still sobbing, and Adam was aware of other people around him. Tommy and Karen were at his side. Daffy was on her cell phone, apparently unable to stop talking even for a few minutes.

He saw that Daffy was crying too. Karen, maybe. Karen Starry-Eyes, that would be his new nickname for her. Her eyes winked like penlights even in the darkness of the Oxoboxo woods. Of course she couldn't really cry, even though Phoebe insisted she'd seen a tear roll down her face at Evan's funeral.

Poor Evan, Adam thought. He'd really liked that kid.

Adam knew then why they were all crying. He opened his mouth to tell them they didn't have to.

"I'm okay," he said. Or tried to, because that wasn't what anyone heard.

"Shhh," Phoebe said, and she actually leaned forward and hugged him to her. He thought he'd be thrilled if he weren't numb all over.

"Don't try to talk," she whispered, her lips close to his ear.

He tried anyhow, before she could say what he knew she would say next, but the noise he made just sounded like a long choking wheeze.

"You're dead, Adam," she whispered.

He tried to turn, but the flesh was both unwilling and weak.

He heard the catch in her throat as she tried to get the words out. "Pete killed you."

The realization hit him with a force almost equal to that of the bullet. His first thought was to protest, to tell her that she was wrong, but he knew in his heart, the heart that was no longer beating, that she was right.

"I love you, Phoebe," he said as she cried, but the only sounds that came out of his body were strange, strangled noises, nothing like human speech at all.

\* \* \*

Phoebe stayed with him until the police came. Her pretty white dress was neither white nor pretty any longer; the hem was tattered and dirty, and it was covered with Adam's blood. He'd taken the bullet high in the chest because Pete had been aiming at her head. The thought should have terrified her, but all she could think about was Adam and how different everything was going to be between them.

Seeing him lying there, his eyes unblinking as he tried in vain to form words she could understand, she could only think about how bad she'd felt in the few days they hadn't been speaking. She was crying and she couldn't stop crying, and although it was absurd, she knew that some of her tears were for those few lost days. She wished that she could rewind to the last time they'd been together at the Haunted House, and she wished that she could take back the things she'd said. She wished he had let her finish her apology.

Most of the zombies dispersed into the woods, melting into the forest like phantoms the moment the flashing lights of the cruiser began to cut through the darkness. Phoebe watched them disappear, thinking back to the night when some of them had seemed to form out of the very darkness and woods to rescue them.

Tommy and Karen stayed until the police came, as did all of the traditionally biotic kids. Colette stood with Margi, and they held on to each other after Margi finished making the calls on her cell phone. Haley said she knew some first aid and CPR, but everyone there knew it was useless; Adam was gone and then he wasn't.

Phoebe wasn't sure, but she didn't think many differently biotic people came back as fast as he had. He'd only been gone a few minutes. The longest minutes of her life, but maybe that was something to be hopeful about. Maybe his rapid return from the shores of death meant that he would gain control of his voice and body faster than some of the others. Maybe.

Tommy tried to console her, but she didn't want to be consoled. Margi and Karen both tried to talk to her, but she didn't want to talk, either.

Adam had run into the woods to save her. Not once but twice. Seeing him lying there, looking up at her trying to speak, she knew that it was her turn to enter the woods for him. She took a deep breath and dried her eyes on the bloodied sleeve of her dress, the dress he'd said looked like moonlight.

Even when the ambulance arrived sometime later and the paramedics gently pried her arms from Adam, who twitched and coughed unintelligible sounds as they lifted him onto the stretcher, Phoebe could only think of this one thing:

Bringing him back. Bringing him back as far as she possibly could.

# Acknowledgments

I'd like to thank the following people for their help in bringing *Generation Dead* into print:

For their invaluable advice, assistance, and guidance: Al Zuckerman, for *everything*; Alessandra Balzer, with whom I shared a wonderful "telepathetic" link throughout the editorial process; F. Paul Wilson, Rick Koster, Elizabeth and Tom Monteleone, and all of the instructors and students at Borderlands Boot Camp; my first reader, Rosina Williams; Robin Rue, Matthew Dow Smith, Tom Tessier, Scott Bradfield, and Doug Clegg.

For their love and support throughout: my parents, Elaine and Jeff Waters; my brother Mark Waters and family; the entire Pepin lineage; Linda Waters, Sandra and Ted McHugh, John Fedcli, Mark Vanase, Dan Whelan, the staff at P.G.'s for the office space; all my friends at SM; Thor, and Bonny.

And just for being: Kim, Kayleigh, and Cormac.

# KISS OF
# LIFE

# ACKNOWLEDGMENTS

Al Zuckerman, Arianne Lewin, Jenn Corcoran, Ann Dye, Elizabeth Clark, Jennifer Levine, Angus Killick, David Epstein, Nellie Kurtzman, Christian Trimmer, Colin Hosten, and all of the great people at Hyperion who helped launch *Generation Dead*, and all of the booksellers, librarians, and teachers that we met on our travels. Also Alessandra Balzer, and always, Kim, Kayleigh, and Cormac.

And special thanks go out to all of the book-loving zombies who visit Tommy at his blog *mysocalledundeath.com*.

*For Kim, the story continues*

# CHAPTER ONE

PHOEBE.

*Beautiful Phoebe.*

*Through the glass watch Phoebe leave bus walk to house Phoebe green skirt green eyes skirt trailing hair flowing black and shiny in the sun. Brown leather boots beige scarf wearing colors no black Phoebe beautiful Phoebe. Halloween Phoebe in costume no costume.*

*"Hey, Frankenstein. Get away from the window before the villagers go and get their torches."*

*Jimmy. Turn. Turn. Want to hit evil stepbrother Jimmy pound Jimmy turn can't turn. Turn left move right. Left left left.*

*"Don't strain yourself. It's your special day, Frankenstein! Happy Halloween!"*

*Turn can't turn Jimmy shoves fall falling heavy land hard head crack coffee table loud heavy body crash loud don't feel don't feel anything Jimmy grinning kicks ribs can't feel get up can't get up Jimmy laughs. Mom yells at Jimmy Jimmy yells back want to pound Jimmy. Hard. Get up. Can't get up.*

*"I said don't strain yourself."*

*Standing over FrankenAdam laughing ceiling is the sky get up can't two bulbs in ceiling skylight one burned out out get up Jimmy Jimmy sprays spits when he laughs get up can't.*

*Jimmy laughing. Mom cries get up can't holds arm pulls can't get up Mom crying can't feel. Feel feelings Phoebe. Get up get up can't get up.*

*Get up.*

*Get.*

*Up.*

# CHAPTER TWO

ALL PHOEBE COULD think about before going next door to Adam's house was the night he died in her arms. The rose of blood blooming on the white shirt he'd worn to homecoming, his strangled cry as he came back from wherever it was the dead went.

He'd only been dead for a few minutes, but despite the rapid return, control over his body wasn't coming back quickly. Phoebe debated changing out of her school clothes before leaving, but didn't want to waste the time. Since Adam's death she'd become acutely aware of its value.

Other zombies, or "differently biotic persons," to use the politically correct vernacular, seemed able to overcome their physical issues as "life" went on. Tommy, who she had dated, and gorgeous Karen DeSonne walked and talked so well that they could practically pass for traditionally biotic. Even Colette Beauvior had "come back" at a much greater rate than Adam, partly due to her reconciliation with their good friend Margi Vachon. Somehow Margi had even convinced her parents to let Colette move in with them, and now the two were as inseparable as Phoebe and Adam.

Adam, however, didn't seem to be getting any benefit from Phoebe's constant presence, which left her wondering what she was doing wrong.

Phoebe dumped a half inch of sugar into a glass, took the rest of the morning's coffee from the refrigerator, and poured it over the sugar. She stirred it with a spoon, then drank half in one swallow, hoping it would make the world look a little brighter.

It had been nearly a month since Adam's murder. His movements were still random, his speech only occasionally intelligible. Adam, her tower of strength, had been laid low, reduced to the helplessness of an infant. His long, once-athletic body was now awkward and shambling, and his thick limbs jerked as if they were being pulled by unseen strings. His broad shoulders slumped when he walked, which he was able to do only with great concentration.

Phoebe took another sip and closed her eyes, rolling the cool vanilla-flavored coffee on her tongue. When they'd lifted Adam onto the stretcher, he'd looked at her, his arm flailing out helplessly as though he was trying to grasp something that would be forever out of reach.

Phoebe dumped out the rest of her coffee. She scrawled a quick note to her parents and got her backpack, which she'd stocked with a few bags of Halloween candy in case any kids came to Adam's house.

Adam's stepbrother Jimmy was leaving his house as she locked her door. He gave Phoebe a dirty look and muttered under his breath when she waved. She didn't know what it was about Jimmy; he'd been unpleasant enough when Adam was alive, but now that Adam was dead, he was *impossible*.

"Welcome to the morgue," he said, slamming his car door and backing out so quickly his wheels kicked gravel.

Phoebe let herself in. The kitchen smelled of this morning's fried eggs and burned coffee. Dirty plates and pans were stacked up on the counter by the sink, and there were thick yellow smears on the vinyl cloth that covered the kitchen table.

"Don't mind Jimmy, Phoebe," a voice called out from the hall. Adam's mother walked into the kitchen, her once pretty face drawn, her cheeks sunken, and her eyes ringed with gray. "We all deal with life differently."

Phoebe nodded. The phrase was a mantra with the ex–Mrs. Layman, now Mrs. Garrity, and there didn't seem to be an appropriate response to it.

Phoebe watched her walk to the sink, where she moved one of the pans from the stove to the counter. Then she walked to the table with a sponge, went back to the sink and wet the sponge under the faucet. She made a single pass at one of the clotted stains, then dropped the sponge and made a half-hearted attempt to straighten a pile of newspapers that sat on the table.

"Phoebe," she said, "I've got to do some shopping. Some grocery shopping. Would you mind staying with Adam for a few minutes? A couple hours?"

Phoebe tried to keep her smile even as she looked at Mrs. Garrity, whose hands were shaking like leaves. "I'd be happy to, Mrs. Garrity."

"Good. That's great. Adam's in his room. Great."

"Are you okay, Mrs. Garrity?"

"I'm fine," she replied. "Adam had another fall, that's all. I'm okay now. He's fine. I guess it doesn't really hurt him. Falling, I mean."

It took her twenty minutes to find her purse, time Phoebe spent washing the stack of dishes and bundling the papers so they would fit in the recycling bin. She wanted to run down the hall to see Adam, but she wanted Mrs. Garrity to leave first. She was scrubbing the crusted layer of sediment from the table when Mrs. Garrity bustled back into the room.

"Damn that Jimmy," she said, oblivious to Phoebe's efforts. "He took my cigarettes." She walked out the door without saying good-bye to either Phoebe or her son.

When Phoebe was finished and the dishes were left drying in the rack, she walked down the hall to Adam's room. He was sitting on his bed, his back straight against the wall behind him and his long legs stretched out on top of the covers. His large hands rested on his thighs, and although he was staring at her, it didn't seem like he was seeing anything.

"Hi, Adam," she said, aiming for a high level of perkiness, knowing that even on her best days she fell far short of bubbly—and this was not one of her best days. Seeing him there—his face and his big graceful body frozen into immobility—was heartbreaking.

He would have been a professional football player, she was sure of it. Just one summer of karate lessons had given him a fluidity that, combined with his incredible size and strength, made him a force of nature on the field. He'd been the proverbial hometown hero, universally expected to get a free ride to the college of his choice on a football scholarship. All gone. Spent, along with his life.

Because of her.

She sucked in her cheeks and ordered herself not to cry. She'd vowed, along with her promise to bring him back, never to let him see her cry.

"You're looking big, as usual," she said once she had regained control of her emotions. She walked to the bed and bent to give him a kiss on the cheek, letting her lips linger on his cool skin for a few heartbeats.

"I brought bags of candy," she said, "in case we get any rug rats tonight. Hershey's minis, Reese's cups, the good stuff. You know it's Halloween, right? I know we don't get many trick-or-treaters out here; most of the little ones hit either the Heights or Oakvale Manor. But maybe we'll see a few."

He was centered on the bed and there was no room to sit beside him, so Phoebe climbed over his legs and sat across from him, her bent knees tenting over his calves. His head tilted toward her with slow purpose, like a door improperly set in its frame.

She gave him what she thought was her winningest smile.

"Remember that year you and I went out with Margi and Colette? We were all Catwoman and you were Batman? What were we, like, ten? Eleven?"

She searched for any sign of remembrance, any flicker of recognition in his eyes, but they were flat and glassy.

"I'll say eleven. We got my dad to bring us to the Heights *and* the Manor that year. What a haul that was! I think Margi and Colette ate about a hundred SweeTarts just going from house to house. I didn't have a single piece of candy until the next day. My parents wouldn't let me have any until they'd gone through it all; they were fanatics about doing an inspection. Like they could detect by sight the myriad of deadly poisons, razor blades, and broken glass hidden in my Charleston Chews."

She thought she saw a faint twitch of his upper lip, but she wasn't sure. The light in Adam's room was terrible and her eyes stung. She slapped his leg, almost knocking one of his hands into his lap.

"You like how I used 'myriad' in a sentence, huh?" It was a game they used to play, dropping little-used words into their conversations to try to get a laugh out of the other. A twitching lip wasn't exactly evidence of high hilarity, but Phoebe chose to take it as a positive sign.

"Then there was the year Margi threw her haunted house party," she said, her voice trailing off as she thought of the other Haunted House, the one where Adam died.

They had been having a party, Phoebe and her friends—the zombies who "lived" there. Karen had hung streamers and a disco ball. The zombies had been dancing and laughing and having fun, able to forget, at least for a little while, that they were dead.

Tommy asked Phoebe if she wanted to take a walk, and

she'd gone outside feeling happy, not only because her friends were enjoying themselves, but because she was with Tommy. Once they were alone in the woods he'd told her that the more loved a zombie was, the more alive they became. He'd been about to test his theory by kissing her, but his chance was ruined when Pete Martinsburg and his henchman, TC Stavis, came crashing through the brush. It turns out they hadn't been alone after all.

Adam looked up at her as though he could sense what she was thinking. His mouth opened and he struggled to speak, a guttural vibration humming up from his throat.

He usually *could* tell what she was thinking, like they really did have the "telepathetic" bond that she had always joked about. Maybe that was why he'd suddenly appeared that night in the woods, as Pete had taken slow and careful aim at the center of her forehead. Pete had sworn to destroy Tommy, but when he'd raised his rifle, it was her that he'd aimed at. When he'd pulled the trigger, Adam was there. Being there for her had cost him his life.

"Ev . . . ry," Adam said, his low, croaking, and dead voice filling his bedroom and calling her back to the present. Phoebe could count the number of words he had managed to say in the two weeks since his return—literally count them—because each night she'd gone home and inscribed them in her journal.

She watched him try to open and close his mouth for the next two minutes before completing his thought for him.

"That's right, Adam," she said, her voice soft. "Every day is like Halloween now."

She took his hand in both of hers and helped him off the bed and onto his feet.

Tommy never got his kiss. Had she been about to kiss him? Among the many things that were unclear in Phoebe's mind, that was chief among them. She'd been attracted to him, but she'd also been worried that he was using her, that it wasn't her, Phoebe, that he'd wanted to kiss, but a living girl. Any living girl.

Even so—what could a little kiss have hurt?

She'd never know, not with Tommy, at least. She'd avoided him since that terrible night, when he'd just stood there like a graveyard statue while Pete Martinsburg leveled his gun at her head. Maybe she would find out with Adam. Holding him as his life drained away, she'd realized what she'd always known in her heart. That Adam Layman loved her, loved her so deeply and selflessly that he was willing to give his life for her, even when, to all outside appearances, she'd chosen another over him.

And she'd realized that she'd loved Adam all along, but she hadn't been *in love* with him. She'd always thought of him as a big brother, someone who was solid and dependable, someone in whom she could confide her deepest thoughts and secrets. Margi was always telling her that it was obvious to everyone in the world *except* her that one day she and Adam would be together. She herself couldn't understand how she'd been able to overlook their connection for so long.

And now?

Adam loved her. He did. And she'd promised herself that she'd do everything she could to bring him back.

She led him to a seat in the kitchen and started getting things ready for dinner. Phoebe didn't know what she could do to hasten Adam's "return," but she did what she could to keep the Garrity household running as smoothly as possible as each member dealt with their grief.

She cooked spaghetti for Adam's stepdad, Joe, and Adam's other stepbrother, Johnny, when they came home from the garage reeking of cigarettes, sweat, and crankcase oil. Unlike Jimmy, the remaining Garritys were kinder to Adam in death than they had been in life.

Mr. Garrity, Adam's stepdad, who he used to call the STD for short, surprised everyone by the way he'd responded to Adam's death and return. Prior to Adam's death, Joe had treated him with all the affection one reserves for the proverbial redheaded stepchild, seeing him as an inconvenient interloper in a house already cramped with two other teenage male bodies. It was as if Joe did not want to spare the extra percentage of his wife's love. The STD exhibited a complete change of heart after Adam's death, which seemed to galvanize him into a frenzy of parental activity and responsibility. He drank less. He insulted less. He threw reporters off his front lawn, then pursued them in one of the many rusted hulks clustered in and around his driveway, literally chasing them out of the neighborhood.

He began to refer to Adam as "my son" instead of "my wife's moron kid." Adam did not appear to mind Joe's new name for him, but Phoebe wasn't sure if it was because it was something he'd longed for, or because it was too much effort to correct him. Confusing as his epiphany was, Joe's new 'tude was refreshing in an age where many biological parents refused to let their undead youths return home.

"Where's Mary?" Joe asked, a line of sauce trickling from the corner of his mouth like stage blood. He'd gotten so used to Phoebe's presence that the whereabouts of his wife were no longer the first thing on his mind when he got home.

"Grocery shopping." Phoebe refilled Johnny's soda on her way to get herself some spaghetti.

Joe's tanned and weathered face crinkled around the eyes, his fork halfway to his lips, and Phoebe was aware of his scrutiny.

"You're a good girl, Phoebe," he said. "I can't tell you how much we all appreciate what you're doing for my son. He does too."

There it was again. Joe called him "son." Phoebe turned back to the stove and dug her lime green fingernails into her palm until the pain allowed her to push her emotions back down. She couldn't believe this was the same man who used to belittle Adam and push him around.

After dinner, Johnny and Joe lumbered off to watch TV. Phoebe helped Adam down the hall to the kitchen, sitting him where he could see the costumes of any trick-or-treaters. Little kids in costumes could cheer just about anyone up, and if Phoebe's attention couldn't bring Adam further into the world of the living, then maybe candy-snatching children could.

A handful came: a Disney princess, a pirate, a lion in a stroller who giggled without cease when Phoebe dropped a Krackle inside the grinning orange sphere on her lap.

Adam was far enough away that he was hard to see in the dim light of the kitchen, but there was a pint-size vampire who spotted him when Phoebe turned back from the door to get her bag of candy.

"That a dead guy?" he said through the screen door, nearly tripping on his cape as he pointed at Adam with chocolatey fingers.

Phoebe considered her response, wondering where the little boy's parents were. She didn't think that anyone let their kids out without a phalanx of parental guardians swarming around them.

"That's Adam," she explained, opening the door and dropping a couple of Special Darks into his pillowcase.

"Hey, Adam," the kid yelled. The little vampire turned back to her. "He's dead. Like me!"

Then he leaped down the steps, cape flapping behind him.

She looked back at Adam and again she saw the lip twitch, which lightened her heart. The doorbell announced a new group of trick-or-treaters.

Phoebe opened the door, and was startled to see three teenage boys in horrific zombie costumes. Except they weren't wearing costumes.

"Trick . . . or . . . treat," the closest said, a strange mirthless grin on one side of his face.

"Takayuki," she said, taken aback but still reaching automatically for the bag of candy. Takayuki had always gone out of his way to make her feel uncomfortable, and she hadn't seen him since Adam's death. "How have you been?" Her voice broke, betraying her nervousness.

"Dead." The comment put a mirthful, malevolent glint in the dull eyes of his companions. One of them was Tayshawn, who had dropped out of their Undead Studies class, but Phoebe didn't recognize the other two. Zombies were always showing up at the Haunted House, attracted mostly by the writing on Tommy's blog, mysocalledundeath.com. Phoebe hadn't been back to the house since Adam died.

The boy next to Takayuki was wearing a long silver earring and sunglasses with dark lenses. His shaved head gleamed like a second moon in the porch light. When he smiled, he revealed teeth that had been sharpened into rough points. He was wearing a leather jacket similar to Tak's, but the cuffs were stained and spattered with red, as were the tips of the fingers on his bone white hand. There was a very tall fourth boy lurking behind them, his face cast in shadow.

Phoebe reached into the bag and withdrew a few pieces of candy. Tak was the person who had "avenged" Adam, but his presence generated no warmth in her. Whatever it was that drove him to hunt Pete down, his motives were unlikely to have had anything to do with her, Adam, or any of the other "beating hearts" that Takayuki disdained.

"Where are your Halloween bags?" she asked, holding the candy in front of her, feeling foolish. The dead had no use for chocolate. They had no use for her either.

Tak looked over his shoulder. "George," he said, "come trick . . . or-treat from the nice . . . soft . . . beating heart."

Tak and the other boys moved aside so George could ascend the steps. The boy wore a tattered brown jacket, jeans with shredded cuffs, and a soiled T-shirt with holes big enough for Phoebe to see where patches of flesh were missing from his rib cage. He looked at her as he limped up the stairs with a big plastic trick-or-treat bag that had a garish jack-o'-lantern blazing beneath a green and warty witch. The boy was not a pretty sight. He was missing an ear and half his nose, and his hair looked as if it had been washed with sewage. He *smelled* as if *he'd* been washed with sewage.

But the scariest part of him was his eyes. They were like no other zombie eyes she'd ever seen. No matter how flat or glassy the eyes of the differently biotic were, there was always at least a glimmer of intelligence within. Not so with George. There was nothing in his eyes. Nothing at all.

Holding her breath, she forced herself to hold his non-stare. Some of my best friends are dead, she told herself. This boy may be more dead in appearance, but he's no less a person than they are.

He looked at her, or looked through her, she couldn't tell, and opened his bag. She dropped in a piece of candy, but the noise that it made when it landed was not the familiar paper on paper sound wrapped candy made. She glimpsed inside the bag and saw a round wet lump of red and gray fur, and a curling tail.

She shrieked, jumping back.

The dead pretended to laugh. "Can Adam . . . come out . . . and play?" Takayuki asked.

Her heart was beating wildly as she looked over her shoulder to where Adam sat with his back to the wall. He looked like he was trying, but failing, to speak.

"No," she stuttered. "We're spending the night at home, thank you."

Takayuki cracked his knuckles, making sure she could see the ones that were no longer covered with skin.

"Someday," he said, "he will . . . want . . . to be with . . . his own kind."

"He is," she said, regaining her composure. Tak was just another bully, and she was sick of bullies. "I'm his kind."

"Sure," Tak said as he and his companions began to fade into the night. "Happy . . . Halloween."

# CHAPTER THREE

SPEAKING WITH the dead was always disconcerting, but speaking with Karen DeSonne was positively otherworldly. Karen's eyes were like diamonds; Phoebe swore she could see refracted rainbows in them when they were out from under the fluorescent wash of the school's lighting. Even in darkness they seemed to twinkle like far off stars.

Phoebe started eating and was about to ask Margi if she would trade her peach for a yogurt, when she saw Karen from across the crowded cafeteria, her long mane of platinum hair bouncing with each clipped step. Phoebe looked down at her food with sudden interest, even though she knew staring into her salad would not ward off the conversation to come.

"Here's . . . Karen," Colette said, after peering into Phoebe's yogurt as if she couldn't believe she'd ever eaten anything that looked like that. "She's on . . . a . . . mission."

Even with her head down, Phoebe was aware of boys from the surrounding tables craning to get a better look at Karen and her micro skirt and high boots. At one time it was considered impolite to stare at the dead, back in the days where the term of choice was "living impaired." Impaired no longer, the differently biotic could be gawked and leered at just like any other teenage girl. Phoebe wasn't sure if Karen liked the attention or thought it perverse, but if she had to guess, she'd go with liking it.

Halloween had been pretty much a nonevent at Oakvale High. In years past there might have been jokes about the differently biotic already being in costume, but no longer—maybe because Halloween seemed superfluous in an age where the dead walked the earth. But a subtle shift was taking place among the students in adapting to what some called "the second chance" and still others called "the undead plague"—an acceptance. There were still those like Pete Martinsburg who feared or hated the differently biotic kids, but most regarded them with no more interest than they would anyone else.

That was the reaction they had for most db kids, anyway. The reaction they had for Karen was special, and no different than they had for any other girl as flat out *hot* as she was. Phoebe thought of the grisly quartet that had stood on Adam's doorstep last night and couldn't believe how far ranging the differently biotic experience could be.

"Phoebe," Karen said, her voice breathy, as though it had taken her effort to cross the room at such a speed. "Hi, Margi. Colette."

"Hey, K," Margi replied, lifting her diet soda in a silent

toast. The usual clinking of her dozen-odd silver bangles was muted by her newest fashion fad, which was to twist thin wristlets out of electrical tape. Colette waved.

"Phoebe," Karen repeated, and Phoebe lifted her head. "How much longer are you going to ignore Tommy?"

"We're fine, K," Margi cut in. "Thanks for asking. And yourself? Really? No, I didn't watch the game last night. Colette and I handed out six bags of candy. We were both Hannah Montanas. I'm afraid I did not know that you were such a fan of NBA basketball. Isn't that interesting, Pheebes?"

Phoebe watched Karen swivel toward Margi, imagining her diamond eyes flashing into life like twin lasers.

"I'm not in the mood, Margi," she said. "I just had to endure about an hour of . . . interrogation about whether or not I . . . defaced the school last night."

"Did you crack?" Margi said. "Did you sing like a canary?"

"Funny. I don't even know who did . . . it."

"Yeah, you . . . do," Colette said, frowning.

"What did 'they' do?" Phoebe asked.

Karen and Colette exchanged a glance before Karen answered.

"They . . . spray painted the side of the school."

"What did they spray?"

"'Adam Laymon . . . no rest, no peace.'" Karen's crystalline gaze was steady and unflinching. "Over a drawing of a . . . tombstone . . . and an open grave."

Phoebe frowned, thinking of the boy with the stained cuffs and hands.

"Did they use red paint?"

Karen nodded. A tense silence followed until Colette broke it a few moments later.

"I guess they . . . will be . . . talking to me . . . next."

"Could be," Karen said. "They already spoke to Tommy and Kevin. Strange how they don't even . . . consider . . . that a trad may have done it."

"A trad . . . didn't do it . . . and you . . . know it," Colette said. Karen shrugged

"You know who did it?" Margi asked. None of the other girls answered her.

Karen sighed, turning back to Phoebe. The sigh sounded realistic even though Karen didn't need to breathe.

"Phoebe, don't you think you've left you and Tommy . . . unresolved?" she asked. "Don't you think he . . . deserves . . . a conversation at least?"

"Deserves," Phoebe said. She didn't feel good about avoiding him, but that didn't mean that she thought that he "deserved" anything.

"He hasn't . . . been himself . . . since you stopped talking to him."

Phoebe poked at her wilted salad. She didn't like the hitch in Karen's speech. Karen wasn't like most differently biotic people. She could usually converse without any of the pauses and stops that marked typical zombie speech patterns. Phoebe had noticed that with "highly functional" db kids like Karen and Tommy, pauses meant they were feeling emotional, or as close to emotional as the dead could be.

"I've been really busy, Karen," she replied. It sounded lame even to her. "I go over to Adam's every night, and I . . ."

"I know all about Adam, Phoebe," Karen said. "Adam isn't here, and there's no reason why you couldn't give Tommy five minutes of your time. You know, like you used to every day before algebra class back when the two of you were . . . dating?"

Phoebe blushed and set her fork down. She heard Margi tell Karen to take it easy, but she lifted up her hand before Karen could say more.

"I'm sorry, Karen," she said. "It's just really hard."

"It's hard," Karen repeated, her voice growing husky. It was amazing, what Karen could do with her voice, altering the flat monotone that marked the speech of the dead. Phoebe raised her head so she was staring into the blank lights of Karen's eyes. "You think it's hard."

"I know what you're going to say, Karen. I know."

Phoebe knew that the differently biotic had to work at expressing emotions on their faces. She knew from being with Adam since his death that he could have emotions trapped deep within his still heart that his body would no longer convey. She'd spent long hours helping him walk or exercise in the hopes of bringing back a range of motion to his stiff limbs, long hours just sitting holding his hand or leaning against his arm. The time together might make him happy, or grateful, or sad, but Phoebe didn't know. Adam couldn't show it. Yet.

Karen was better at nuance than any of them, as good as some living kids, almost. But if Karen felt any pity for Phoebe, there was no sign of it on her cold, beautiful face.

"Adam needs me right now, Karen," she said. "His mom said he fell again. . . ."

"He fell?" Margi asked. "I didn't think he could, like, walk yet. Without help."

"He can't. He tries, of course. He's stubborn."

"That isn't being stubborn. It's being smart. He isn't going to . . . come back . . . by sitting around on his can all day and night."

Phoebe wasn't sure if Karen was being practical or cruel. "He needs me, Karen. I just don't . . . I don't think I have anything left for anyone else."

Tommy never needed me the way Adam does, Phoebe thought.

Karen put her arms on the table in front of her, palms up. Phoebe couldn't help but notice how smooth and white they were, like she had been carved from a single piece of white stone.

"I know Adam needs you, honey," she said. "He always did."

Phoebe hesitated, then placed her hands on Karen's open palms, relieved that the subject of Tommy was dropped for the moment. Karen's hands felt warmer than hers, which Phoebe could never understand no matter how many times she experienced it.

"Awww," Margi said. "See, we can all play nice."

Karen smiled, looking embarrassed. "I know it's hard, sweetie. I guess I should be asking how I can help instead of bullying you."

Phoebe felt a tear roll down her cheek, but Karen was holding her hands so it made it all the way to her jawline before Margi leaned over and wiped it away with the edge of her napkin.

"I don't know," Phoebe said, crying openly now. "Adam . . . Adam isn't like you, Karen. Or like Tommy. Tommy told me that you and he came back more because . . . because you were loved, and I'm trying with Adam, but it just isn't working."

"He's more . . . like me," Colette said. "It will . . . take time."

The girls fell silent as Principal Kim walked over to their table and asked Colette to follow her. As Colette rose, Principal Kim looked at Phoebe and noticed she'd been crying.

"Phoebe?"

She turned, embarrassed.

"Um," she said, "yes, Principal Kim?"

"Are you all right, Phoebe?"

"Yes. I'm fine, thank you."

Principal Kim gave a slow nod. Phoebe prayed that she wouldn't bring up counseling again: counseling for this and that. Because your friends are dead, because your friends aren't dead. Because they are dead and then they aren't dead and how do you feel about that? How do you feel? How do they feel? How *can* they feel?

Principal Kim's silence was worse even than the mandatory counseling that they'd made Phoebe go to for the first week after Adam was killed. Margi and Karen were looking at the table, compounding the air of guilt that seemed to hang over their lunch.

"Um, is there anything else, ma'am?" Phoebe said, finally.

The principal thought a moment before answering her question. "You wouldn't know who vandalized the school last night, would you?"

"No," she said, the lie passing her lips with surprising ease.

"I know you spend a lot of time with the differently biotic students," she said, looking at Karen apologetically. "With Adam, and with other kids that don't go to our school."

"You don't know that a zombie did it."

"No, I don't," she said. "But I thought you might know if someone was . . . upset with the situation."

"Everyone should be upset." Phoebe's eyes were burning, but she refused to cry again.

"Of course," Ms. Kim's voice was soft. "Understand, I'm more interested in getting people the help they need than I am in punishment. You realize that, don't you? All of you?"

Karen said she did, and Phoebe nodded. She was afraid to use her voice.

Ms. Kim held her gaze. "Well, I'm sure you'll let me know if I can help. Let's go, Colette."

They watched her leave, Karen shaking her head. "You get a few questions, we get interrogated. That's fair."

"I'm sorry," Phoebe said, rubbing at the corners of her eyes. "Thank God, I don't have mascara on today."

"Yeah, what's up with that?" Margi said, as eager to derail the conversation as she was. "And what's with the new wardrobe too?"

Phoebe looked down at her light green blouse, shrugging. "I just thought it was time for a change."

"A change?" Margi said. "I barely even recognize you half the time now. What are those—*slacks*? Blue jeans? And all the colors . . ."

"She doesn't want to look like she's in mourning," Karen said.

Phoebe, her tears under control, pursed her lips. Sometimes it really did feel as if Karen was walking around inside her head, because she'd nailed her motivations exactly.

"Whaaaat?" For someone as fashion conscious as their pink-haired friend, Margi had a tendency to overlook the obvious.

"She doesn't want to look like she's in mourning. When she's with Adam. Out with the blacks and the grays, good-bye gauzy skirts and ruffled sleeves. Good-bye, Morticia Addams, hello, girl next door."

"I didn't think it was that obvious," Phoebe said,

Karen conveyed sympathy with a slight turn of her eyebrows. She really was amazing. Such an actress.

"Don't get me wrong, honey. Earth tones work for you. But you have such nice creamy skin, and that beautiful black hair— you're a knockout in black. White, too. And you could give red a chance."

Phoebe thought of the dress she wore for homecoming, a simple, straight sheath so white it shimmered. She ruined it on the muddy earth kneeling over Adam's body as he died. Tommy knelt with her, and he might have held her, or he might have tried to help Adam. She couldn't remember much about that night except for her dirty dress and the blood spreading across Adam's chest.

He'd said her dress was like moonlight.

She shuddered.

"I'll try, Karen. I'll try to talk to Tommy."

But later, when she saw him lingering by the doorway to their algebra class, the one that they'd once shared with Adam's killer, Pete Martinsburg, and Pete's flunky, TC Stavis, she found she couldn't try at all. He stood so straight and tall, with his shoulders broad and his face strong and angular. He looked like a sculptor's idea of a young god. Like Karen, he looked as though physical perfection could only be achieved through death.

She watched him for a moment. Watching him, with him not knowing she was watching, gave her a weird feeling in her stomach.

You should have saved me, Tommy, she thought. *You.* But you didn't.

Her breath caught as he turned suddenly and saw her, his gray-blue eyes finding hers even through the passing crowd. Her insides did a somersault, and she turned around in a hurry and marched off toward the nurse's office.

But he caught up to her. Even Adam had talked about how quick Tommy was for a dead kid.

"Phoebe . . ."

"Oh hi, Tommy," she said, not stopping. *I'm not ready for this.*

"Phoebe, can we—"

"I'm not feeling very well, Tommy. I'm headed to the nurse's office."

"You're . . . sick?" his said, his face a mask of concern. Literally a mask, as expressiveness did not come as easily to him as it did to Karen.

"I'm sick," she said. What right did he have to be concerned for her?

"I'll . . . walk . . . with you."

"So now you want to move," she said, her anger flashing, the words out before she could stop them.

"What?"

"Forget it."

"No," he said, "what . . . did you mean?"

The anger engulfed her like a hot wave pitched by a boiling ocean. She felt it wash over her and carry her out to sea.

"I said, *now* you want to move! *Now* all of a sudden you can move!"

She was shouting, and everyone in the hall stopped what they were doing to stare. She didn't care. They'd stared when they were dating, when they touched hands in the hallway. The only difference now was that they stared openly, instead of hiding behind books and locker doors. Hypocrites, every last one of them, a world full of hypocrites.

"Phoebe, what . . . ?"

"You didn't move, Tommy! He pointed the gun right at me and you didn't do anything!"

"I . . ."

"All you had . . . had to do was . . . *move*," she said. "It wouldn't have hurt if he shot *you*. But you just stood there, and . . . and Adam's *dead*! He's *dead*, Tommy!"

She looked at him, her eyes blurry with tears. He'd stopped trying to talk, and the mask of concern had fallen away from his face as he stood there.

Just stood there.

"He'd be alive if it weren't for you, Tommy," she said, whispering so the gawkers wouldn't hear.

He'd be alive, she thought, and you and I would be together.

Tommy didn't try and stop her as she fled down the hall.

# CHAPTER FOUR

"H APPY" BIRTHDAY," Gus
Guttridge, the lawyer, said
with all of the warmth of a
day-old cup of coffee.

"Gee, thanks," Pete replied.

"Cheer up. If you were born a few months earlier you could
be tried as an adult instead of a juvenile, and then the circus
would really come to town. We're in good shape."

Guttridge sat down at the head of the table facing Pete, his
mother and her husband, the Wimp, and the social worker.
They were in a conference room at the Winford Juvenile
Detention Center where Pete had been living for the past two
weeks. There were two wrinkled posters in the room, one
that said drugs were Uncool and one that said gang violence
was Uncool. Pete didn't mind the detention center. The food
was better than what he got at home, and they delivered it right
to his room because he wasn't allowed to mix with the other

kids being held there. Other kids would probably think that was Uncool, too, but Pete thought it was pretty Cool.

"The downside is I don't think you returning to school is an option at this point," Guttridge said. "The best we can hope for is that you'll be sent home, remanded to your mother's custody, and homeschooled by a state-appointed instructor."

Pete thought the downside was looking up. He ran the tips of his fingers along the scar on the left side of his face, the tips of his index and middle fingers tracing the ragged stitch marks where the zombie had cut him. The wound was still capable of flaring into a sudden pain or a steady dull throb, but Pete didn't mind either sensation. The time when his cheek was numb and he was drooling all over the place was worse.

"Typically, murder by a juvenile offender means you get tried as an adult," Guttridge said. "The fact that Mr. Layman is still able to walk into the courtroom himself means that the court is already thinking that this isn't really a murder. We can work with that."

The Wimp, motivated no doubt by a desire to posture for his wife rather than by any real feeling for Pete, asked a question, but Pete wasn't listening to him. He was listening to the voice of the scarred zombie in his head.

"Did you think I would kill you?" the zombie had whispered, its fetid breath like the air from an open grave. "Death is a gift."

In some ways Pete was glad that the zombie had maimed him, because his scar was visible proof that worm burgers were evil monsters that delighted in the pain and disfigurement of the living.

"Well, Mr. Clary," Guttridge was saying, "the idea is that Pete should not be tried for manslaughter, because Layman doesn't meet the legal definition of 'dead.' He's differently biotic, but if he is still 'biotic,' he's alive and therefore Pete did not commit manslaughter. Assault, maybe. But I think even that's a stretch at this point."

One of the stitches was protruding from Pete's cheek like a small thorn or the sting of a hornet. He worked the stitch back and forth, ignoring the sharp bright pain that accompanied the movements. He realized that the lawyer, Guttridge, was saying his name.

"Mr. Martinsburg? Pete?"

Pete looked up. His mother and the Wimp were sitting with looks of false concern as Gus Guttridge tried to get his attention. Pete leaned forward in his chair.

"Sorry," he said, "what were we talking about?"

"We were discussing what should and should not be said on the stand."

"Right," Pete said. "Right. Just be honest, is what you said."

"Correct." Guttridge said. Pete didn't trust guys with beards, and Guttridge had a hell of a beard, a big wooly thing as thick as the curly hair on his head. But Guttridge was his father's choice, and his father went with the best that money could buy, so Pete went with the flow.

"So, again," Guttridge said, "you understand that when Ms. Lainey asks you a question, it is in your best interest to give her short, succinct answers."

"Succinct, right." Pete felt his fingertips drawn back to the loose stitch like a magnet. They'd come out in a week if everything went as planned, and good old Dad Martinsburg was going to pick up the tab for whatever cosmetic surgery Pete required to get rid of the scars. Pete wasn't so sure he wanted to be prettied up just yet.

"Yes," Guttridge continued, his baggy blue eyes regarding Pete. "So when Counselor Lainey asks you why you went to the property on Chesterton Road, how will you respond?"

"I heard there was a party there."

"Were you invited to this party?"

"No," Pete said.

"Were you under the influence of drugs or alcohol?"

"I had a few sips of schnapps. Peppermint."

"Were you drunk?"

"No."

"So you went to crash the party?"

Pete sighed, his fingertips drifting once again to the cut on his cheek.

"I heard that the zombies were having a party and that some real people were going to be there too, and I didn't like what I heard the zombies were going to do."

Pete watched Guttridge pooch out his lower lip as he peered down at him through his glasses. The glasses were light frames of gold wire, the kind a lot of overweight guys with big faces wore.

"Don't call them zombies," Guttridge said. "Say 'differently biotic.'"

"They call themselves zombies," Pete said, just to see if he could get a rise out of Wooly Face. No luck.

"Doesn't mean you can. Don't say 'real people,' either. If you could remember to say traditionally biotic it would be helpful also. Understand that you may hear *me* use other terms, but that doesn't mean *you* should. You need to project Wholesome and Respectful. Let me do Outraged, if I need to."

"Why should you have all the fun?" Pete tapped the edge of a fingernail on the heavy tabletop.

Guttridge gave him a thin smile. "Because you already had yours. Now, back to business. Did you go to the party alone?"

"No."

"Who were you with?"

"TC Stavis."

"I see. What did you and Mr. Stavis do, once you arrived at the party?"

"We parked the car at a turnoff a half mile down the road, and then we walked through the woods until we got to the house, and then we waited."

"Don't volunteer the info about the car unless asked a direct question," Guttridge said. "Why were you waiting outside?"

"We weren't invited."

Guttridge frowned. "Very funny. Please answer the question."

"We were waiting to see if Phoebe was at the party."

"About Miss Kendall," Guttridge said, shuffling a file to the top of his deck.

"Morticia Scarypants," Pete said, smiling.

But Guttridge's well of patience seemed bottomless, probably because good old Darren paid him by the hour. "Please forget you ever invented that name," he said, "unless you want to be tagged something similar when you get sent to prison."

Pete laughed, and he could feel the skin around his stitches grow taut with the movement. "What happened, Your Honor, is that I saw Julie with the differently biotic boy, and I remembered what he told . . ."

Guttridge lifted his fleshy hand, cutting Pete's thought short. The ring on Guttridge's finger was the size of a cherry tomato, with a large onyx set in the center.

"Another thing," Guttridge said. "You need to stop calling her Julie. There is no Julie I see associated in any way with your case, and the last thing you want is anyone in the courtroom to be confused. Don't confuse them. Call her by her first name. Phoebe."

"Phoebe," Pete repeated. He wasn't smiling any longer, but he wondered if the scar and its stitching made him look as though he was. Julie had been his girl back in California, but she died. She died, and she did not come back. Life wasn't fair sometimes. "Yeah, Phoebe."

They sat there, a patient and concerned audience, and he told his version of what happened on that night.

# CHAPTER FIVE

"WE'RE READY, right, Adam?" Joe said. "I mean, you don't want to wait, do you?"

Nod. Nod open mouth no Joe don't ask two questions wait until first answered patience all need patience not ready but ready as can be can't wait around right leg can't stay in room any longer go more insane than already am left leg freaking leg Frankenstein must go to foundation could help mouth open speak speak speak.

"Red . . ."

Speak right leg Joe open the door don't just stand there waiting waiting to speak not used to you paying attention easier when you ignored go see Tommy go see Karen learn learn how they do what they do did what they did left leg goal walk normal one week no three speak speak speak.

"Dee."

Joe opened the car door, frowning. "You sure?"

Speak speak no stop speak nod nod right arm hold door left leg step left knee bend bend push left arm right leg damn body push damn teenage Frankenstein.

"You need some help?" Joe asked.

Help Phoebe help see Phoebe at Undead Studies see Angela Alish move body move left leg see Kevin Sylvia not Sylvia see Thornton see Margi Colette help learn bring back help push Joe yes FrankenAdam am too big heavy push shoulder yes push.

Ignition gear miss driving goal two months no two years driving accelerate stop turn miss friends miss football miss baconandeggs miss karate Master Griffin miss Frisbee God miss Frisbee goal one month no three months.

"Are you nervous?"

Nervous not nervous stop miss Frisbee spinning arc disc flying across surface of the moon topspin backspin overhand underhand Astroturf miss running Phoebe running hold out hand the hand obeys hold out your hand catch spinning floating thing don't let it get away pull it close into the body.

"Phoebe said she'd meet us at the front," Joe said. "I told that girl there, Angel? Angie? I told her I wouldn't be coming in. That okay with you?"

Nod. Nod speak stop speak miss Phoebe miss Phoebe sad Phoebe waste time with teenage Frankenstein myriad of problems heh Phoebe sad said change needs to live not live with teenage Frankenstein miss Phoebe help Hunters help.

"That girl has been such a help to us," Joe said. "Not a bad little cook either."

Miss Phoebe said unsaid pity unsaid too late waited too long to live Karen right too late Phoebe become who you always were not what you are now spinning disc Phoebe why why didn't anyone take the bullet out of my heart?

# CHAPTER SIX

"WELCOME BACK, Adam," Angela said as Phoebe led him into the classroom by the hand. Phoebe realized that despite its radiance, Angela's megawatt smile could not bring the dead back to life.

And I had such high hopes, she thought. The Hunters, Angela and her father, Alish, were watching Adam with undisguised interest. Phoebe couldn't help but think that they were wondering how they could use Adam's murder and return from death to advance the stated aims of the Hunter Foundation, which were to "integrate the differently biotic into American society and culture through the application of the sciences." Phoebe knew that Angela had real concern for Adam, but she still found their scrutiny creepy.

She led Adam to the wide vinyl chair he usually occupied in Undead Studies class. She supported him as he bent at the knees, falling back into the chair with a heaviness that drove all the air out of the cushioning. Phoebe didn't let go of his elbow until he craned his neck upward to look at her.

She was aware that everyone in the room was focused on them.

"Thank . . ." he said, and she could feel him concentrating on the word, concentrating on making his lungs move and his mouth open, his tongue like a piece of cold rubber as he tried to form the word. She could feel his awareness of the seconds ticking by into minutes as he tried to complete his sentence. The trad kids in the class were used to being patient with the db kids' mode of speech—Adam himself had been infinitely patient— but she knew that his patience would not extend to himself.

He's so helpless, she thought, and hated herself for thinking it. She couldn't understand why Adam wasn't coming back faster. Even terminally slow Kevin Zumbrowski, who sat next to Colette on the futon, was more "returned" than Adam. Colette was changing, her limbs were more pliable, her skin less ashen. Her hair was closer to the dark brown it had been when she died. Phoebe knew that Margi was spending a lot of her time with Colette. The time together seemed to be doing both girls good. Phoebe was happy for them, and she did her best to tell herself that she wasn't a little jealous too.

In contrast to the slowly returning, there were Tommy and Karen, whose stillness now seemed more like a mark of maturity than a sign of death.

". . . you," Adam said, finally completing his response.

Phoebe sighed with relief. She saw that Angela's smile, at least, was free from the pity she'd seen on so many other faces.

Adam could take the disgust and hatred, but she knew that the thought of someone pitying him filled him with fury he was not capable of releasing.

Angela nodded. "You're welcome."

Phoebe looked up at the sound of a shuffling noise coming from the hall outside, and wondered if a new student was joining them—the ranks were certainly depleted from the last time that Adam had been in class; even with Margi back the class was still down a few people. It was like an episode of some bizarre prizeless reality show; Tayshawn Wade dropped out, Sylvia hadn't come back yet, and Evan Talbot would never be returning again, thanks to Pete Martinsburg and his cronies. They'd reterminated him and got away with it.

Alish Hunter, his lab coat hanging loosely over his spidery, skeletal frame, entered the lounge. The old man's rubber-soled loafers slid along the thin beige carpeting in short, arthritic movements. Phoebe watched his feet and wondered at the static charge the old man must be building; in her mind's eye she could picture him throwing his hands to the sky and shouting "Life!" as he shot Adam with a bolt of pent-up static electricity from the metal head of his cane.

"My boy," Alish said, his bushy gray eyebrows knitting as he stared down at Adam. "I'm glad to see you haven't left us. We can learn a lot from you, Mr. Layman."

Adam didn't even try to respond to that.

"Welcome," Alish said, beaming as though he were reuniting lost relatives over an expansive meal. He led two new students, zombies, into the room. They sat next to Thornton

Harrowwood on the long orange futon. Thorny, who still played on the football team even though Tommy had quit and Adam was no longer able to play, looked especially glad to see Adam back in class. Thorny was the smallest kid on the team, but Phoebe'd heard he was getting a lot of playing time, not only because of the Undead Studies kids dropping out, but because Pete Martinsburg and TC Stavis were kicked off. She was surprised, actually, that Thorny hadn't been injured yet.

"Welcome, students," Alish was saying. "Please help yourself to refreshments. We have coffee and soft drinks."

Phoebe watched the two new zombies. The boy looked typical enough as far as zombies went, a pale, thin kid with gray-black hair, wearing a flannel shirt, jeans, and scuffed work boots. The girl next to him was different, starting with the mass of hair that billowed around her head like a bright red cloud. It reminded Phoebe of Evan, the only other zombie she'd known with red hair. His had been a faded red, but the new girl's was rich and coppery. But that wasn't even the most striking thing about her.

She was wearing a mask. A bone white mask that covered her entire face; it was similar to one of the comedy and tragedy masks that Mrs. Dubois, the drama teacher, had hanging in her office, except this one had no expression at all, the thin lips a carved straight line.

"I'd like to introduce to you Melissa Riley," Alish said. Melissa was wearing a long brown skirt that went past her knees, and a heather green sweater that bunched at her wrists. She sat with her hands folded in her lap and her head bowed, her eyes hidden behind the almond-shaped eyeholes of the mask. Phoebe could see pale beige dots, the ghosts of freckles, on the backs of her hands. Next to her on the couch was a whiteboard the size of a large notebook, and a black marker.

There was a bright chorus of welcomes from the students, but Melissa did not lift her head or respond in any way. Alish waited a moment before continuing, his smile unwavering despite Melissa's apparent shyness.

"And this young man to the far left is Cooper Wilson," Alish said, and as Alish gave a fluttery wave toward the boy, Phoebe noticed that the old man had pale brown spots on his hands as well, but his were liver spots.

"Hey . . . everybody," Cooper said, "call . . . me . . . Coop."

"Hey, Coop," replied most of the class, nearly in unison.

"Yes," Alish said. "You may recall that our Mr. Williams read an article about a tragic fire at a place called Dickinson House, in Massachusetts. Melissa and Cooper were made homeless by that fire. We are thrilled that concerned parties helped them find residence here."

He hesitated. The article that Tommy read indicated that the fire was more of a massacre than an accident, with seven zombies being reterminated in the flames and just the two on the couch surviving. Phoebe looked over at the girl and wondered what the mask hid.

"Well," Alish said finally, "please do what you can to make our newest students feel welcome."

"You are probably all wondering how our fair Ms. Stelman is doing," Alish continued. Phoebe and the other "veterans" of the Undead Studies class snapped to attention. Sylvia Stelman was a zombie classmate who had been taken for a special "augmentation" procedure. All they knew about the "augmentation" was that it would supposedly restore Sylvia to a near-living state. They had no idea how it was performed or what exactly it entailed, and the Hunters refused to elaborate. Sylvia had been gone a number of weeks, and naturally everyone in the class was worried about her.

"I am happy to report that the first phase of her augmentation is complete and that she's doing quite well. If she continues to progress at this rate, we should soon have her back in class."

"That's great," Margi said. Kevin's head lolled forward and back, probably in eager anticipation of being the next in line for an augmentation. "Can we see her?"

"Not yet." Alish's smile remained fixed on his face.

"Well, that's our news," Angela said. "I have a new project, which we're going to have you all work on, but first are there any topics you would like to discuss?"

"There were more killings," Tommy said. "Of zombies. In Texas . . . a mob of . . . people . . . tied two of us to the . . . tailgate . . . of a pickup truck. The killings were . . . soon after . . . a talk given by . . . Reverend Nathan Mathers. They . . ."

Phoebe couldn't look at him as he told the rest of his grisly story. She knew that part of what she was feeling was akin to "survivor guilt," something she'd overheard Angela talking to Margi about: a feeling that one was somehow complicit in acts of violence that one had nothing to do with. Phoebe listened to Tommy talk about how the mob tracked down the zombies and tortured them, and she couldn't help feeling as if she'd helped tie the knots.

She'd certainly tied them around Tommy. Her guilt went beyond survivor guilt, however. There was a hopeless quality to Tommy's reporting today, and she knew it was because of the way she'd treated him.

When he was finished, there was a moment of stunned silence, and then Colette spoke.

"Tommy," she said, "why don't you . . . ever . . . talk about . . . the good news? Your site would be . . . so much . . . better if you had some . . . good news."

Phoebe looked for his reaction, but all he did was blink.

"What . . . good news?" he finally said.

"You never . . . talk about . . . the good . . . things. Like Z," she said. "You . . . wear Z."

Phoebe smiled because Tommy bought a bottle of Z, "the body spray for the active undead male," when they were on their first date. She smiled, despite the conflicting feelings the memory brought up. Tommy started to reply but Colette interrupted him.

"And . . . Aftermath," she said, "you haven't . . . ever mentioned . . . Aftermath either."

Tommy managed a sardonic grin.

"You want me to talk about . . . cologne . . . and dancing . . . when . . . our . . . people are being killed?"

"What is Aftermath?" Alish asked, looking even more confused than usual.

"It's a club," Margi answered.

"A club?" Alish leaned over and put a skeletal finger to his dry lips.

"A zombie club, in New York City," Margi said. "Music, dancing. It's open twenty-four hours a day."

"In New York City?" Karen said. "I've never heard of a club like that."

"Margi found an . . . article . . . in a music magazine," Colette said. "It was started . . . by Skip Slydell."

Skip Slydell was the entrepreneurial founder of Slydellco, the company responsible for launching zombie hygiene products like Z body spray (for the active undead male) and a line of T-shirts with slogans like "Some of my best friends are dead" and "Open graves, open minds." Phoebe had heard Margi refer to the clothing line, which Colette often sported, as "inactive wear."

"I'm kind of surprised you don't know about it," Margi said, probably because there was some sort of relationship between Skip and the Hunter Foundation, as he had been a guest speaker in their class. "He opened it as a not-for-profit, so it's classified as a charity or something."

"Really?" Alish said, intrigued, looking back at Angela, who shrugged. "He made no mention of this. It isn't easy to get the government to recognize the differently biotic as being a group deserving—or even in need of—charity. And what do the differently biotic do there?"

"Dance," Colette and Margi responded in unison.

"Dance?"

"Well, and listen to music," Margi said. "Sometimes Skip gets live bands to play."

"Live bands," Colette said, and Phoebe watched the corners of her mouth twitch upward. Margi busted out giggling, her snorty laughter made musical by her jangling bracelets and dancing spikes of pink hair.

"Amazing," Alish said.

"Skeleton . . . Crew . . . plays there," Colette said. "They have . . . a zombie . . . in the band."

"DeCayce," Margi added, in a teasing voice that made Phoebe think that Colette was a big fan of Skeleton Crew.

"Amazing," Alish repeated.

Angela cleared her throat. "Does anyone else have anything pertinent to discuss before we start today's assignment?"

"I've got something I want to talk about." Thornton 'Thorny' Harrowwood III said. "Something that really made me mad."

"Mr. Harrowwood," Alish said, making a sweeping gesture with his liver-spotted, knob-knuckled hand. Phoebe thought it was kind of cute the way he was enjoying the class so much. It made her wish that he attended more often, but he was probably too busy with all the important lab and scientific work the foundation was doing. "You have the floor."

"I got a detention yesterday for saying the word 'zombie.'"

Everyone in the room, even Tommy, who Phoebe hadn't seen crack a smile since homecoming, seemed to think that was pretty funny. Alish laughed out loud, unmindful of his daughter's warning glance.

"It isn't funny," Thorny said, but a moment later he was laughing too. "Honestly, it made me pretty mad. You guys call each other zombies. We use the word here in class all the time and nobody gets offended."

"Colette said that she didn't like the term," Angela said gently, reminding him one of the earliest discussions they'd had as a group. Phoebe saw Melissa reach for the whiteboard, but she put it in her lap without taking the cap off the marker. She wondered if the girl was able to talk, or chose not to.

"I've . . . mellowed," Colette said. "Like . . . cheese."

Margi cracked up all over again after adding something about how well Colette would go with Thorny's "wine." Phoebe wondered if the two of them had been sucking the air out of helium balloons prior to class.

"Har-de-har," Thorny said. "Go ahead and laugh. We've lost every game since Adam and Tommy left the football team; my girlfriend, Haley, broke up with me because all my zombie—oh excuse me, my—'differently biotic' friends are too creepy; and now I get a detention for saying a single stupid word."

He looked up at his classmates, shaking his head as though overwhelmed by the sheer enormity of ruin that had been heaped upon his bony shoulders.

"Life sucks," he said, and the dead kept laughing.

# CHAPTER SEVEN

"THE VAN IS waiting," Phoebe said, taking arm. "Let me help you."

No. No help. Right leg left leg no help Phoebe helpless no help.

"I've got your arm. Lift your leg, the left one. That's it. Almost there. Good."

No help. Phoebe touching holding arm can't feel. Can't feel Phoebe holding arm can't move no helpless baby invalid.

"I'll get in on the other side," Phoebe said, "don't worry."

Worry not worry Phoebe Karen in back Margi Colette. Girls girls not worry speak speak speak not worry.

"Don't . . . worry."

Phoebe smile smile Phoebe Adam two words together pretty good good progress Frisbee in three weeks. Three weeks, final.

"You can't really rush it. It isn't like . . . physical . . . therapy. It will come."

Turn. Turn can't turn. Karen can't see Karen Karen in back. Turn Phoebe leaning leaning on shoulder like she used to Phoebe can't smell her hair her shiny hair smelled like gardens remember hair like lilacs.

"How long did it take you to . . . develop?" Phoebe asked Karen.

Margi giggle Colette giggle in front seat develop heh funny. Phoebe blush heh funnier. Karen's voice from back like music.

"I don't know what's got into those two," Karen said. "Don't go by my experience. The timing is different for everyone. And for some it's overnight, for other it has been years."

"But how long?"

Breathe breathe breathe can't breathe try can't Karen laugh and sigh smile walk and talk. Sigh two weeks. Smile one week. Walk one week no ten days.

"I was pretty close," said Karen, "when I woke up."

Awaken. The great awakening awaken the awakened. Why are we here and why did we come Karen's hand on shoulder can feel it?

"But I'm not saying you should stop . . . trying, Adam sweetie," she said. "Just don't get . . . angry . . . if it doesn't work right away."

Try. Try hard trial in a few days. All in van ready to roll. Thorny and Kevin back with Karen Margi Colette up front Phoebe. All but Tommy look see Tommy walking toward woods Tommy alone. Tommy alone. Van coughs starts Tommy turns waves lift arm lift arm lift arm lift arm!

Wave.

# CHAPTER EIGHT

PHOEBE SMOOTHED out Adam's tie on his chest and saw him watching her. She wondered if he was aware that her fingertips grazed over the bullet hole through which his life had drained away.

"You look great," she said, going on tiptoes so she could kiss his smooth cheek. A strange benefit of death was that his beard stopped growing, even though the hair on his head still did. It was strange.

She wondered if he could feel her kiss. She tried to imagine what the kiss would feel like if he were still alive. Did her mouth feel warm to him? If he weren't dead, would there be more texture to her kiss, sensation beyond a vague sense of pressure?

"I bet you'll be glad when this part of it is over," she said, taking his arm. "I know I will."

He nodded. His answer arrived a few heartbeats later.

"Yes," his voice ghostlike.

She had his arm with both of hers now, hugging it like she was dangling over a cliff and it was the last handhold available.

"He'll go to jail, Adam," she said. "He has to."

She was really putting some strength into her hug. She was beginning to think that no matter how tight she clung to him, it wouldn't change anything.

Her guilt was crippling, sometimes. Standing there, gripping him tightly, she wondered if things would change between them if and when he started to "come back." Would they be more than friends? Did he still want that? Did she?

She rested her head against his arm the way she used to when he drove her home from school and she had had a bad day or there was something that she wanted to talk about. She knew he used to be able to curl fifty pounds with that arm— Thunder, he called it. Thunder was the left and Lightning was the right; he named them just because it hacked his stepbrother Jimmy off so much. Now he was lucky if Thunder obeyed him enough to bend at the elbow.

Phoebe let go of him when Joe called from the kitchen down the hallway to see if they were ready.

"We're coming, Mr. Garrity," she responded.

Phoebe led Adam into the kitchen where his mother and Joe waited, both of them looking stiff and uncomfortable in their coats and ties. Phoebe couldn't help but think they looked like people going to a funeral. Joe's suit looked as though it might have fit him way back in the Clinton administration but was straining at the seams today. He'd tried to clean the grease off of his hands, but Phoebe could still see it embedded in his fingernails and in the ridges of his fingertips. He didn't smile often, but his eyes softened at their weathered and wrinkled corners as she led Adam by the hand into the room.

"Johnny's warming up the car. You look good, son," Joe said, his voice like the starting rumble of the '66 El Dorado parked on the front lawn that he tinkered with on occasion. He clapped a thick, calloused hand on Adam's shoulder.

Phoebe waited for Adam to respond, but he didn't.

"Blue is a good color for you," she said, as much to distract herself from her thoughts as to cover up the awkwardness. She patted his arm, and in doing so was reminded that he was wearing the same suit he'd worn at the homecoming dance on the night he died. The jacket and tie came off sometime at the Haunted House, which saved it from being ruined when Pete Martinsburg killed him.

Mrs. Garrity moved to hug her son. Phoebe turned away, because there was something in the way that Mrs. Garrity hugged him—which she did often—that always brought tears to her eyes. She'd make furtive touching motions on his arms and shoulders, the movements of her hands like the fluttering of butterflies unsure of where to alight, and then she would seem to collapse into his broad chest. Adam was at least a foot taller than his mother, and although his body wasn't fully under his control, Phoebe thought she could see his shoulders hitch forward whenever his mother embraced him, as though he were trying to will his arms to enfold her.

Phoebe stopped watching, because it wasn't her tears that

Adam needed now, it was her strength. Adam had enough people crying and showering him with pity, and he didn't need either from her. She wiped her eyes as Mrs. Garrity's sobs became more audible.

"Let's go," Joe said, shoving open the door. Phoebe followed him down the front steps, noticing as she did that Joe was wiping at his eyes with an oil-stained thumb, flicking away an invisible tear. Johnny saw them coming and turned down the heavy-metal CD he'd been listening to.

Joe turned back to Phoebe and gave a mirthless laugh.

"Every day is a goddam funeral," he said so that only she could hear. Then he called up for his wife and son to get moving, and as he climbed into the front seat of the waiting car, he yelled at his living son to not play his goddam music so goddam loud. There were two groups of people outside the steps of the courthouse. Three, counting the thin row of policemen standing between the two main groups. On the right, a dozen or so people clustered around a middle-aged man in a suit. He was shouting into a megaphone and holding a placard that said "Free Peter Martinsburg." Beside him a woman wearing equally conservative clothing had a sign that said "Pro Life" in bold black letters. There was a biblical quote or two which, bizarrely, were accompanied by a photograph of Reverend Nathan Mathers, who had a number of books out condemning the zombies as evil harbingers of an impending apocalypse. Phoebe wondered if the protestors thought the quotes they bore were actually attributable to Mathers and not the authors of the Bible.

Across from them were a loose collection of mostly young

people, some dead, most of whom were sporting black Slydellco T-shirts, the ones with semi-humorous, semi-political sayings like "Some of My Best Friends Are Dead" or "Got Zombie?" Karen was there, along with Colette and Margi. Thorny and his supposedly ex-girlfriend Haley were holding hands. Phoebe spotted Tayshawn toward the back, talking to Kevin Zumbrowski. The zombie contingent didn't have any signs, unless you counted the slogans on their T-shirts, and spent most of their time watching the more organized, vocal demonstrators along the way. One surprise was that a few of Adam's football teammates were there, wearing their Badger letter jackets.

"Look, Adam," she said, pointing to them, "look at all your friends."

Adam stared out the window. One of the football players was taking pictures of the protestors with his cell phone.

"Get . . . hurt," he said. Johnny had already found a parking spot by the time he finished his sentence.

"They won't get hurt," she said. "The police will keep things quiet." She was trying to believe that, but there was real anger in some of the faces in the "Free Peter" crowd. That killing a teenaged boy could be in any way justifiable seemed an insane concept, but she knew that Pete had plenty of supporters because of his stated intention, of "protecting a living girl" from a zombie.

She didn't know if prison was the right answer, but Pete Martinsburg definitely needed help of some sort.

"There's a side door over here," Joe said. "Let's try to avoid the crowd."

Phoebe looked back, praying that no one on either side would do anything foolish. She was looking at Tayshawn as she whispered her prayer.

She led Adam into the empty courtroom, where a lone, unsmiling bailiff stood by the American flag at the front of the room.

"There's a step," she said, leading Adam toward the front row, just behind the tables where the defense and the prosecution set up. A low hum came from gratings high in the wall where ductwork pumped warm air into the room. Outside, it was chilly, even for a New England November. Adam was still taking his seat when Joe, Adam's mother, and his stepbrother Johnny entered the courtroom in a noisy bustle. They were followed by State's Attorney Lainey, who looked like she already had a headache as she fielded questions from Joe and his wife.

The springs on the stadium-style seat squealed as Adam sat. Phoebe tapped his arm.

"Are you nervous?" she asked.

The shake of his head was barely perceptible.

Tommy appeared at the door of the courtroom with his mother, Faith. His appearance startled Phoebe into giving him a quick wave. She hadn't expected to see him. She should have known, though, that if anything powered Tommy, it was his conscience. He and Faith crossed the courtroom and took seats a few rows from the Garrity family, Faith pausing to say hello to Phoebe with a smile that seemed tinged with sadness. Phoebe felt herself flush.

TC Stavis arrived next, sweaty and uncomfortable in a tight sport jacket and knit tie that was too short for his long, wide body. A large, wheezing man was with him. Stavis didn't look at anyone as he took his seat.

Pete Martinsburg had no problem looking at anyone and everyone. He entered the room with his parents and the rest of the defense team, glaring at Phoebe and Adam as he did so. There was nothing in his expression, not malice, hatred, or regret.

She held Adam's ice-cold hand and prayed that he'd be able to speak when it was his turn.

# CHAPTER NINE

LEFT LEG. RIGHT LEG. Joe help don't want help. Light all wrong. Amber. Sick. Light hot can't feel heat Phoebe sweating. Pete not sweating. Like a lizard.

Step. Right leg. Left. Face in mirror one pupil wide one smile. My face not my face right leg. All looking. All watching FrankenAdam right leg left right. Waiting to fall. Won't fall. Staring right leg walk walk.

"Bailiff," judge says. "Please help Mr. Layman to the stand."

Bailiff takes arm can't feel feel only his disgust. Steers pulls right left leg turn. Sit. Sit Sit.

"Please sit, Mr. Layman."

Sit. Sitting.

Right arm. Right arm.

"Please raise your right arm. "Do you solemnly swear . . . Mr. Layman?"

Right arm. Right arm!

"Mr. Layman, please raise . . . thank you. Do you . . ."

Speak. Speak. Speak. Speak.

". . . so help you God?"

Speak. Speak.

"Miss Jensen," said judge, "please enter in the record that Mr. Layman nodded, indicating that he does intend to tell the truth, so help him God. Thank you."

Light all wrong. Amber light. Sick like flypaper film on eyes. Eyes one dilated one not. Fat man approaches bench. Guttridge. Guttridge in suit.

"Mr. Layman," says Guttridge, "please, in your own words, tell us what happened on the night of the Oakvale homecoming dance."

Speak. Speak. Speak!

"Mr. Layman?"

Speak. Speak.

"Mr. Layman?"

Speak.

Guttridge turns. "Your Honor, Mr. Layman is behaving as an uncooperative witness."

Speak.

"He is trying to speak, Counselor. Give him a moment."

Guttridge throws hands in the air. Speak. Speak. Guttridge turns. Looks in eyes.

"I withdraw the question," Guttridge says. "Let me ask something simpler. Mr. Layman, we are here to determine whether or not my client, Pete Martinsburg, is guilty of murder, are we not?"

Speak. Speak. Spoke.

"I'm sorry. I didn't quite understand your comment just then. The question is, are you aware we are here to determine whether or not Pete Martinsburg is guilty of murder."

Nod.

"Do you believe that Pete Martinsburg went into the Oxoboxo forest with any premeditation of killing you?"

"Objection. How could the witness possibly know what was in the defendant's head?"

Guttridge puts on an angry face. "Your Honor, if we have to go through the charade of a murder trial when the supposed victim walked into the room under his own power, can't I at least ask whether or not he felt he was murdered?"

"I think 'under his own power' is an exaggeration," says judge, "but I will allow the question. Mr. Layman?"

Speak. Speak speak speak speak.

Speak. "No."

Didn't sound like "no" sounded like crack crash like explosion deep inside a mountain.

Someone screamed.

# CHAPTER TEN

**T**AK WATCHED George drag his carcass over to a squat mausoleum, following Popeye around the graveyard like an imprinted duck. George held his arms in front of him, his fingers grubby, his nails long and black. He was carrying a box of paper sheets that bore his likeness.

Wind whipped through Tak's smile as he ripped off a thick band of electrical tape and slapped another sheet onto a tombstone. He stepped back to view Popeye's creation.

I WANT YOU, the flyer read, over a murky picture of George he'd taken at the Haunted House. George's head was cocked to the side, his ragged corduroy jacket open, revealing a shredded T-shirt that gave glimpses of his rib cage. The flash of the camera had put a maniacal glint in his eyes, and he looked like he was smiling. He was pointing at the camera, his obviously broken pinky askew at an impossible angle, some of his knucklebones visible beneath skin that looked ready to slide off his hands. The words FOR THE U.S. ARMY! were in the same red, white, and blue lettering below his picture.

And beneath this, in a smaller blocky type, SPONSORED BY THE UNDEAD STATES OF AMERICA ARMY.

Tak thought the flyer was genius. In addition to plasteing the cemetery with the flyers, Tayshawn and other trulydeads—zombies who had no interest in rejoining beating heart society—were putting up still more of the copies at local funeral homes and at Oakvale High.

When they were done, Popeye and Tak met beneath a stone angel, waiting for George to catch up.

"Does he . . . have any copies . . . left?" Tak asked.

Popeye nodded. "We've got a quarter box, maybe. You know, there is . . . a real . . . recruiting station a couple miles up."

"Let's do . . . it," Tak said. Popeye had fewer gaps in his speech when he was in the act of making one of his art pieces a reality. "We have a few hours . . . until the breathers awake."

Popeye called for George, who was rooting around in a pile of leaves that had collected in the doorway of a mausoleum. George lifted his head at the sound of his name and shuffled toward them.

"What has he . . . got there?" Tak asked. George had the box of flyers under one arm and was holding something in his other hand.

George tripped over a low headstone and went face-first into the frost covered earth. The box of flyers tumbled open, some of them blowing across the cemetery. Popeye shook his head.

"We haven't got . . . all night," he said. He and Tak went to salvage what flyers they could as George slowly got to his feet. When he rose they saw that he was clutching a dead squirrel by the tail.

"Nice," Popeye said, smiling. "Did you just . . . catch him, George? Or was he already dead?"

They watched as George brought the squirrel to the ragged slash of his mouth and bit into it.

"Why does he . . . do that?" Popeye asked. George was munching on the creature, bones, fur, and all, with a suspicious, greedy expression on his face, as though he were afraid that Tak and Popeye might want to take it from him.

"He thinks he's . . . supposed to," Tak said.

"Dying must have . . . fried his brain," Popeye said as George looked up at him, the squirrel clenched firmly in his teeth. "Now there's the picture . . . we should have used on the flyers."

"Who's to . . . say?" Tak said. "Maybe . . . George . . . is doing what he's supposed . . . to be doing."

George stared back at him, and Tak thought there may have been the briefest flicker of emotion on his gray, puttylike face as he chewed, but probably not. George was the least expressive zombie that Tak had ever seen. It was almost as if George had no interest in trying to become more like the traditionally biotic boy he'd been prior to death. Tak didn't know if he walked with his arms outstretched because he had to, or because he wanted to. Nobody knew where George came from or how he'd found the Haunted House. He just showed up on the front porch one day, beating on the door with his arms. Tayshawn had called him George, and the name stuck.

The sounds George made as he gnawed on the rodent were not pleasant. Tak watched him eat, and wondered if George would be able to talk if he tried.

"Nice table . . . manners," Popeye said, speaking in front of George as though he were too stupid to understand. Tak held his comments and waited for George to complete his meal. He suspected that George wasn't as stupid as Popeye thought. George could obey instructions for the most part, and seemed perfectly willing to allow any zombie who was around to order him about like a servant. Especially Tak.

George took another bite and flung the broken body over the tombstones. It went surprisingly far. He dragged the muddy sleeve of his jacket across his face and slouched toward them.

"Had enough, George?" Popeye said. He leaned over to Tak. "Can you smell him? I think I can . . . smell him. I think he has actually renewed my sense of smell."

"I can smell him."

"He smells . . . dead."

"It isn't Z, anyhow," Tak said, which Popeye thought pretty funny.

"George," Tak said, "Go back to . . . the house. The sun will be up . . . soon. Go back to the house and . . . wait . . . for us."

They watched him dragging himself over the old graves toward the woods.

"I might be . . . an artist," Popeye said with admiration, "but that boy . . . is *art*."

* * *

Phoebe woke up in a bad mood. She could feel herself emitting a dark cloud of negativity; it poured from her in thick, invisible vapors.

Her terrier, Gargoyle, looked up from the foot of her bed, turned, leaped, and scampered away before her fog swept over him.

She didn't have the energy to argue with Mrs. Garrity when she said that Adam was "too sick" to go to school that day. "Dead kids don't get sick, Mrs. Garrity," is what she should have said, and then she should have asked if she could speak to Adam. Instead she sighed and walked out to the end of her driveway to catch the bus, pushing her hat down lower over her ears against the cold that seemed to be seeping into her.

The bus was seven minutes late. The first thing she heard when she stepped on was Colette's shrill, catlike laughter. Because she wasn't in the mood, she took a seat in the front across from a freshman boy with glasses. He was obviously terrified of her. Phoebe, was self-aware enough to notice that many of the younger kids regarded her with fear. Margi said they gave her the hairy eyeball because of her goth stylings and perfect skin; Phoebe was inclined to think it had more to do with her presence at Adam's murder—either that or being the cause of the murder. She looked over at the boy, who clutched his backpack and stared straight ahead.

Bride of Frankenstein, they called her. She was sure of it.

"Phoebe, Phoebe!" she heard Margi call from the back of the bus.

Phoebe ignored her. She made sure that she was the first one off, sliding into the aisle while the younger boy remained crouched in his seat.

"Where's Adam?" Mrs. Rodriguez asked her at the start of algebra, and if Phoebe had possessed the power to petrify, she would have used it then. She mumbled that she didn't know.

"Tommy isn't here either," Mrs. Rodriguez said. "Do you have any idea where he is?"

Phoebe had to hold back the answer that came to mind, which was to ask Mrs. Rodriguez if she thought she was the den mother for the morgue.

"It isn't like Tommy to miss a day of class," Mrs. Rodriguez said. Phoebe shrugged and went to take her seat. She glanced over to where TC Stavis sat, studious in his attempt to avoid looking at her.

I'm the Gorgon, Phoebe thought, looking over at him, squinting. My stare is death.

TC leaned over his algebra book and seemed to flinch.

Later in the lunchroom Phoebe unwrapped a lackluster lunch of milk, carrots, lukewarm macaroni and cheese, and an apple with a bruise as big as the Tycho crater. Margi came and sat down next to her with such a haphazard flop that she made Phoebe spill milk on the front of her blouse.

"Hey, hey," Margi said as Colette and Karen took chairs on the opposite sides of them. "Baby's in black again."

"Well, I *was* in black," Phoebe said, frowning. "But now I'm in milky black." She rubbed the front of her shirt with a napkin.

"Here, let me help you," Margi said, grabbing another

napkin and thrusting it at Phoebe's chest. Phoebe slapped her hand away, the sharp sound of it making the dead girls laugh.

"Jeez," Margi said, a wry smile on her face, "ease off on the jiujitsu. I was only trying to help."

"Yeah," Phoebe said, "thanks for that 'help.'"

"Still thinking about the trial, huh?"

"No," Phoebe said.

"Adam really freaked, huh?"

"No!" Phoebe said, her voice rising above the boisterous din of the lunchroom. "No, he did not 'freak.' Who told you he freaked?"

"Um," Margi said, looking back to Karen and Colette, but she didn't find any help there. Karen took the lid off a cup of sliced strawberries. "I heard it from Norm. Who heard it from Gary, who I think talked to Morgan Harris, who must have gotten it from TC."

"TC," Phoebe said. "A necessary link in the daisy chain of idiots."

Margi knew that she was being included as a link in the "daisy chain of idiots," so she let the comment slide. "What really happened?"

"I don't know why I even talk to you sometimes."

Margi crossed her eyes. "Because I'm such an insightful listener?"

Phoebe turned to look at Margi, who had now added a wagging tongue to her crossed eyes, completing her performance art piece of congenital idiocy. The dead girls kept their silence, as though they could sense the storm brewing inside Phoebe.

And then a strange thing happened; looking at Margi's display, Phoebe felt the dark cloud dissipate.

"Oh, Margi," she said, laughing.

"See?" her friend said. "*That's* why you hang out with me."

"That must be it."

"Come on, Pheebes," Margi said, leaning over so that Phoebe could feel the points of Margi's spiky hair tickling her cheeks. "Talk about it. Let it out. We're your buds."

"I know you are," Phoebe said. Karen and Colette looked as though they would breathe a sigh of relief if they could. "You really are."

The questions came at a rapid clip, tumbling on each other like a free-verse poem.

"What did he say?"

"Is he okay?"

"What did Pete say?

"Was it really so bad?"

Phoebe held up her hand. "Did they really say that Adam freaked?"

Margi nodded. "Kinda."

"I didn't hear anything," Karen said, holding out the cup of strawberries so Colette could try to smell them. "No one talks to me. I just assumed . . . it went badly because you looked like you wanted . . . to kill everyone."

Phoebe sighed and rolled the bruised apple on the table with her fingers. "He didn't 'freak.' Martinsburg's lawyer asked a million questions, and was being as condescending as he could. Adam tried so hard, but he just couldn't speak."

"Oh, man," Margi said, "poor Adam."

"I felt so bad for him," Phoebe said.

Karen looked like she wanted to say something, but she put a slice of strawberry on her tongue instead.

"What did he do?" Margi asked.

"He tried to answer a question. He did answer it, but his answer wasn't . . . understandable. And it was loud."

"I still . . . do that," Colette said, "sometimes."

"Really?" Margi said. "I thought that was you trying to sing."

"Shut . . . up." Colette shot Margi a dark look.

"It doesn't matter," Karen said.

"What do you mean?" Phoebe was stunned.

"Well, Phoebe," she said, "of course it matters to Adam, and to you. But it wouldn't have mattered how . . . eloquent . . . Adam was on the stand. That boy wasn't going to get punished, no matter what."

"He got community service," Phoebe said. "And he has to get counseling."

"Big deal," Karen said, selecting another slice of strawberry. "Counseling. And they didn't even let Tommy speak. It wasn't . . . easy for him to go, you know."

Phoebe looked at her to see if she was being accused of something, but Karen's strange eyes were guileless. "I would have liked to see him get a tougher penalty too."

"Like a beating," Margi said. "Or worse."

"Some would agree with you," Karen said. "Only they would not be . . . joking."

She smiled and licked the strawberry juice from her lips.

"Are you okay?" Phoebe asked, watching Karen slice into an orange with the edge of her fingernail.

"Well, that's a funny question, isn't it," Karen said, husking the fruit with a sudden violent twist of her hands. "Considering the circumstances."

"You seem like something is bothering you," Phoebe said. "Is it something I said? Or is it the trial?"

Karen looked up at her, and for a moment Phoebe could swear she saw a coppery light in the glittering retinas of her eyes.

Karen lifted the orange to her face and inhaled deeply. She was even weirder than usual, Phoebe thought. She came to school wearing jeans and a heavy sweatshirt with a school logo on it, instead of her usual skirts or dresses. *Short* skirts, and *short* dresses, ones that showed a lot of her ice-white skin, even now when the weather was getting colder.

The light left her eyes. "I'm sorry, Phoebe," she said. "I'm a little off today, aren't I? But why is that, do you think? Don't you need hormones and blood sugar and all those chemically things to be moody?"

"Must be the . . . formaldehyde," Colette said.

Margi's cackle cut across the whole cafeteria.

Karen turned toward Colette and broke the orange in half, offering it to her.

"I'm so glad you're . . . progressing," Karen said. Colette refused the orange, and when neither Margi or Phoebe wanted a piece she set it on the napkin in front of her.

"Speaking of progressing," Phoebe said. "I was thinking that we should do something nice for Adam to try and cheer him up. Maybe we could have a party for him? At the Haunted House?"

"That's a great idea!" Karen said. "Really, Phoebe. I think having a . . . party for Adam is a great thing. Being surrounded by people who love him . . . can only help."

"I . . . think . . . it is a good thing . . . too," Colette said, "I wish . . . someone . . . had done . . . that for me."

Margi rolled her eyes, reaching for the orange slices. "You *had* to go there again. When will you give it a rest?"

Colette looked at her, the nervous ticking smile pulling at the corners of her mouth. "I will . . . never . . . be . . . at rest," she said, which sent Margi off again. Colette's laughter was a lot different from Karen's, which sounded realistic. Her's sounded more like a choking mirthful hiccup, like the sound someone would make if they started laughing with a mouthful of milk.

"Hey," Colette said, still smiling, "did you guys . . . see the newspaper . . . this morning?"

Margi snickered, but neither Karen nor Phoebe had seen it.

"The . . . boys . . . played another prank," Colette said. "Their idea of . . . reprisal, I guess. Did you bring it?" she asked Margi, who was rooting around in her purse.

"Really?" Karen asked, too innocently, Phoebe thought.

"Yeah. It's . . . hilarious," Colette said.

Margi produced a wrinkly square of newsprint and dropped it on the table. George stared out at them from the photo.

Phoebe laughed. "That's great! Better than marking up the school, anyhow."

"Tak and Popeye can be pretty clever," Karen said.

Phoebe saw right through Karen's enigmatic expression and was about to call her on it when Margi asked a question.

"Is Tak the guy with the perma-smile? And who is Popeye?"

"You'll meet them when you come to Adam's . . . party," Karen said.

"Ugh," Colette said, "do they . . . have . . . to be there? I like their . . . tricks, but . . ."

"Don't you want to meet the artists?" Karen said. "Besides, it isn't like I can . . . uninvite them. It's their home."

"I . . . know, I . . . know. They're just . . . unpleasant . . . sometimes. Especially to . . . trads."

"They *are* pretty bold," Margi said. "Speaking as a traditionally biotic person."

"I just hope they don't go . . . too far," Colette said.

"At least they're going . . . somewhere," Karen said, waving her hand. "Tak probably won't want to come, anyway."

And that would be just fine, Phoebe thought. "Maybe we could decorate the Haunted House?" she said. "Sort of like you did for homecoming?"

"Okay, Phoebe," Karen said. "That sounds good."

"I'll invite Thorny," Phoebe said.

"What about the rest of the football team?" Margi asked. "All his old buddies?"

Phoebe thought of some of Adam's "old buddies": psychotic Martinsburg and the mindlessly violent Stavis. "I don't know . . . I don't think many of them would be interested in going. Maybe Thorny would have some ideas."

"Let's call it . . . a wake," Colette said. "I really . . . wish . . . I'd had . . . one."

"There she goes again."

"I'm choosing to ignore you too, Margi," Phoebe said. "What do you think, Karen? Is Saturday too soon?"

"Saturday is good," Karen replied. "We've got all the time in the world."

"Speaking of time," Phoebe said, looking at Karen and with a nervous pout, "there's something I need you to do for me."

She didn't want to drag the apology out any longer than she had to. If she hadn't put off talking to him for so long, things might not have gone the way they did in the hallway. And Karen was right; she did owe Tommy an explanation, at least.

Even so, she was almost surprised when Karen told her that Tommy would, in fact, meet her after school. She'd been so rotten to him she'd understand if he never spoke to her again.

And she knew, no matter how things turned out, that she didn't want that.

"Hi," Tommy said. He was wearing khaki slacks and a white-and-blue Oxford shirt with the sleeves rolled up. He looked, Phoebe thought, like one of the models out of the L.L. Bean catalogue, but a lot paler. She was in a heavy black padded coat that had fake fur lining the hood. Tommy was never cold.

She knew he'd been watching her from the moment she left the school, tracking her with those clear gray-blue eyes of his, eyes that were the color of an early morning sky before a perfect day.

"Hi, Tommy," she said, and took a seat next to him, even though she could feel the icy cold metal of the bleachers through the seat of her skirt. "Thanks for meeting me. And thanks for going to the trial."

"Glad . . . to go . . . though they wouldn't . . . let me . . . speak." He smiled at her, but it was a sad smile, like he already knew what she was going to say. "Are you . . . feeling better?"

She looked at him, eyes narrowing, wondering if it was going to be *that* kind of conversation.

"The other . . . day," he said, "you went . . . to the nurse. I heard . . . she sent you . . . home."

"Oh. Oh, yeah. I feel much better. Too much Halloween candy, maybe."

She knew then that if it was going to be *that* kind of conversation, it would be because of her. He was way too calm and self-possessed to give into whatever emotions he was feeling.

His eyes—eyes that had such a strange, hypnotic effect on her—were clear. She looked away.

"I wanted to apologize," she told him, and it seemed as if she was swallowing with every third word. "I had no right to say those things, they weren't true, and I'm sorry."

"You were . . . right, though," he said. "If I could have . . . moved . . . Adam might . . . still be alive."

The tears she had been trying to blink back started to escape. Adam might be still be alive, but Tommy might have been irrevocably dead. Or she might be—there was no telling. What happened, happened, and could not be undone.

"I'd have given . . . anything . . . to have been able to move."

"You couldn't have done anything," she said. "I'm sorry I blamed you. I really am, Tommy."

He nodded.

"So we're both . . . sorry," he said, looking up at the sound of the buses pulling away. Soon what remained of the Oakvale High football team would be taking the field for practice.

She hugged her knees, hiding her face so he couldn't see. She wanted to get up and hug him and let him know she really meant it, but she was afraid that he'd get the wrong idea.

She was also afraid to touch him because she was afraid that the "wrong idea" would feel like the right one.

It was Tommy who spoke first, his voice husky.

"You are . . . haunting . . . me . . . Phoebe."

"I'm sorry," she said again. "I'm sorry, I'm sorry, I'm sorry."

"Don't be . . . sorry," he said. "Be with . . . me. Give me . . . another . . . chance."

She sobbed and pulled away as he touched her arm.

"I can't, Tommy," she said, "I'm with . . . Adam needs me now."

He was silent, but she thought she could feel the weight of his stare on the back of her head. She dried her eyes with the back of her sleeve.

"He died for me, Tommy."

He didn't answer for some time.

"You love him?"

Phoebe looked into the trees far beyond the field. She wasn't certain of the answer to Tommy's question, not yet. She had feelings for Adam that she had for no one else. Were those feelings love, or an acute pity wrapped in the guilt she felt over his sacrifice? It was so hard to be sure, especially in Adam's diminished state.

*Did* she love Adam?

Her heart told her she did, in the rare moments that her brain was quiet, but she couldn't say it out loud. Not to Tommy.

"I . . . he needs me, Tommy. I can't . . . I can't have time for anyone else right now."

She stood up and looked over her shoulder at him, sitting there in shirtsleeves in the chill air, as implacable as death itself. If only she knew—really knew in her heart—that what Tommy wanted was her, Phoebe, and not just any willing, living girl, things could've been different.

But she didn't.

"It's over, Tommy."

She turned away and started walking down the steel steps.

"Phoebe," he said, and she stopped.

"When he . . . pointed . . . the gun . . . at you it . . . felt . . . like this."

Part of her wanted to apologize again, another part wanted to scream. She wanted to scream, "Well, isn't that what you wanted? To feel? This is what feeling is."

But a third part, the part she kept hidden, made her want to give into her other feelings and rush back to him, to take him in her arms and give him the kiss that he imagined would bring him to life.

But she didn't.

She walked away.

# CHAPTER ELEVEN

"D O YOU KNOW why you're here?" the smiling woman asked. Pete gave two frog-like blinks and waited for his breath to return. Angela Hunter was one of the most beautiful women he'd ever seen, a stunning blonde in a dark blue dress whose conservative style only emphasized her sexy features. Her smile took him back to California, back to the beaches and hanging around his sisters' friends, away from Connecticut, the land of big coats, cold ground, and the dead.

"Mr. Martinsburg?" she said. "Peter?"

"I'm sorry," he said. He couldn't believe this was the same woman who spent her day with the corpsicles in that stupid class of theirs. What a waste of warm flesh. "What was the question?"

Her smile was patient. "Do you know why you're here?"

He nearly laughed. Why are any of us here, he wanted to

say. Why are the worm burgers here instead of quietly rotting in the ground, away from human sight?

"Yes," he said instead. "I was sentenced to therapy and to community service for my involvement in a crime of negligence."

She tapped the lined pad in her lap with a ballpoint pen, and he used the movement as an excuse to lower his eyes to her legs. The blue skirt fell below her knees, but what he could see of them was stunning.

"By crime of negligence, do you mean an accident?"

"Yes," he said, his gaze returning to her eyes. "A tragic accident. I really didn't want it to turn out that way."

"What way did you want it to turn out?"

He started to reply, but the answer caught in his throat. Her beauty was making him dizzy; he forced himself to choose his words with care.

"I don't know how I wanted it to turn out," he said. "I just know that wasn't it."

She nodded. "You know I'm not here to prove or disprove what the state found you guilty of," she said. "That isn't my purpose."

"What is your purpose?" His hands were sweating.

"Just to talk to you," she said. He thought from her tone that she was going to add more, but she didn't.

"Just to talk to me," he said. "Is that what therapy is?"

"It can be. Do you think you need therapy?"

"No."

"Why do you think the state thinks you need therapy?"

"I don't know," he said.

She waited, smiling. He sighed.

"They probably think I'm still a risk to zombies."

"Why would they think that?" she said. "You didn't hurt any zombies."

For a moment he thought of the red-headed zombie, the one that he and Stavis put back in the ground. The look on his face when he saw his second death coming. Pete wasn't sure what that look had meant, but he liked to think it meant "finally." He decided the kid had been grateful in the end.

"No," he said. "But they know I wasn't trying to hurt a real person. Layman got in the way, and then the gun went off. I never meant to hurt him."

"A real person," she said.

"Right."

"So zombies aren't real people?"

Pete looked at his shoes, and then he looked at her legs and up, until his eyes met hers again, taking his time. So she would know.

"I didn't say that."

She nodded. "Well, what do you think? Are zombies real people?"

"No," he said, holding her gaze.

"Did they used to be real people?"

"I don't know." Who cares if they used to be real people? They weren't anymore, that was certain.

"You don't know."

"Nobody knows, do they?" he said, moving his hands fast

to see if she would flinch, and then trying it again when she didn't. "I mean, that's what this whole place is about, isn't it? Studying the dead? I don't know if they used to be people. For all I know they're something else entirely."

"Have you seen Adam since he died?"

Pete looked away in spite of himself. "Yes."

"Is he the same person he was before he died?"

"I don't know."

"You don't? I heard you used to be friends."

"So?" he meant it to sound hostile, but she didn't react.

"Tell me about when you were friends."

"What happens to me if I tell you to go screw yourself instead?"

Her only reaction was a blink, which Pete thought was pretty impressive.

"I'm not sure," she said. "I suppose if you don't participate in the court-assigned therapy, you will be held in contempt and resentenced or something like that. I can find out for you if you want."

"Why do I have to talk about Adam?"

"He's why you're here," she said. "It seems like a good place to start."

"It was an accident. He and I were good friends once."

She nodded.

Pete sighed. "He and I were on the football team together; that's where we met. He was the biggest kid my age I've ever seen. You know. He's in your class."

"Yes," she said.

"We just started hanging out, him and Stavis, lifting weights and stuff. He used to be gawky, a big lummox, but he's gotten really quick since then."

"Stavis was the boy who was with you when Adam was killed?"

He almost snapped at her, but again held his thoughts in check. It hadn't taken her long to get inside his head, but he knew he would have to play along at least a little to keep her happy and get through this.

"Yes. TC. We were the three amigos for a while. We were called the Pain Crew, because when we played football we could dominate the field, especially on defense. Coach played us on both sides of the ball usually, but we were together the most on defense."

"The Pain Crew," she said. "Who called you that?"

"Everyone," he said. "I think I made it up."

She nodded.

"We hung out. Usually at school. We sort of drifted apart at the beginning of this year, though. I came back from spending the summer at my dad's place and we just didn't seem to get along after that."

"Why? Is it because you were apart for the summer?"

"No. We didn't hang out on weekends or anything—just on game days. I made a comment about a girl he liked, and that was the start, I guess."

"You said you spent the summer at your dad's place?"

"Yeah," he said. "My parents are divorced. My dad lives in California, so I stayed with him."

He looked up and saw in her eyes that she thought she had caught something there, some little clue she could use to break his whole head open. And why the hell had he said all that stuff, anyhow, running his mouth like a little girl? He was smarter than that.

"The girl you made the comment about. She was someone that Adam was interested in?"

"Yeah. Tori Stewart," he said, giving her a name of someone that Adam—and half the football team—had casually dated. The lie came easily. "I mean, they went out a few times, but how was I supposed to know he was that way about her? I didn't even say anything that bad, just that I was thinking about asking her to the homecoming dance. He flipped out."

"Flipped out?"

Pete nodded. "Threw his helmet and everything. When a guy that big gets pissed off, you kind of get ready for anything. He said he'd rip my legs off if I so much as looked at her funny. I said, Take it easy, no problem."

"I see," Angela said.

"That was about it, really. We just didn't talk a whole lot after that. I tried, but I think he was jealous or paranoid or something."

"Was this before Tommy Williams joined the team?"

"After. No, before. I'm not really sure."

"What did Tommy joining the team do to your friendship with Adam?"

"Nothing, really," he said. "It was kind of over by then, anyhow."

"What did you think about Tommy joining the team?"

"I can't lie," he said. "I wasn't really happy about it. I don't think it was the right thing to do. I still don't."

"Why?"

"Because," and again Pete chose his words carefully, "because he couldn't play. I didn't think it was fair. Kids work really hard to get some playing time and qualify for the team, and this guy gets to play just because he's dead? Just because the school wants to prove how liberal and politically correct they are? It wasn't right."

"So you're saying Tommy was given playing time just because he was differently biotic?"

"Of course," Tommy said. "He couldn't move, he couldn't run. Last one around the track every single time. No disrespect intended, kids who can't play shouldn't be allowed to suit up. It isn't right."

"Do lots of kids get cut from the team?"

He knew by the way she asked the question that she already knew the answer.

"No. Not really."

"The one game he played," she said, "did he play much of the game?"

"It's the principle," he said. "If you can't play, you shouldn't be allowed to play."

"So it made you angry."

"Sure I was angry," he said. "But he only played the one game, so I let it go."

"Why do you think you were so angry?"

"Because it wasn't right."

"What wasn't right?"

He considered throwing it out on the table. It wasn't right that the dead could pretend they were alive. It wasn't right that Julie was dead and Tommy was not completely dead. It wasn't right that little Miss Scarypants would choose a worm burger over him. None of it was right.

But what he said was just a reiteration of what he'd said before. "Like I said. It wasn't right that he got to play while a more deserving kid had to sit on the bench. People work too hard for that playing time."

"Like you."

"Yes, like me. I busted my ass to make sure I would be on the field for game day."

"You've worked hard today, too," Angela said. "I think this was a good start. Let's go out into the office and I'll call Mr. Davidson so you can start on the community service portion of your sentencing. Wait here a moment."

Pete watched her leave the office, wondering how he was supposed to be able to survive another twenty-three weeks of this. He heard Angela's voice over the intercom asking for Mr. Davidson. He looked around the office—shelves of books, the two chairs, a low table with a pitcher of water and two cups. A print on the wall of a New England coastline, a ship in the distance.

She returned with a tall man who had a bald, lozenge-shaped head. The man looked down at Pete in his chair with all the expression and warmth of the living dead. He was wearing a blue windbreaker with the Hunter Foundation insignia on it, and he wore a belt which had a Nextel clipped on the left hip and a handgun clipped on the right.

"Pete," Angela said, "this is Duke Davidson, the Director of Operations here at the foundation. He will be responsible for overseeing your community service hours."

Pete wasn't sure if he was supposed to get up and shake his hand, but Davidson's narrowed stare kept him in his seat. It seemed like the tall man was licking his lips at the prospect of putting him to work.

Pete considered making a crack about the handgun, but in light of his reasons for being there, it didn't seem well-advised.

"Hi," Pete said, and he said it in a way that he hoped conveyed that he didn't intend to be any trouble.

"Two hundred hours," Davidson said. "The clock starts now."

"I'll see you next week, Pete," Angela told him as he followed Davidson out of her office.

"Thanks," he mumbled.

"The term 'Operations' has a broad context here at the Hunter Foundation," Davidson said, his long strides echoing in heavy, booted footfalls that resounded off the shiny tiled floors and concrete corridors. Davidson liked people to know he was coming, it seemed. "It means security. It means care and maintenance of the physical plant. It means utilities, it means plumbing, it means groundskeeping and whatever else it takes to keep the foundation running as seamlessly as possible."

He stopped at a door, withdrew a ring of keys and keycards

from his belt, and plugged one of the cards into a slot beside the door, which clicked open. Davidson pushed the door open and flicked on the light, revealing a walk-in supply closet, rows of cleaning supplies, lightbulbs, and packs of C-fold towels on gunmetal gray racks.

"It also means janitorial work," he said, wheeling out a yellow mop bucket and wringer. "Especially in your case."

"Pretty high security for some cleaning supplies."

Davidson reached for some of those cleaning supplies. Pete, standing behind him in the frame of the door, looked at the heavy weapon on the man's hip, a single leather strap securing it in place.

"You ever want to cause some damage to a place," Davidson said without turning around, "start a fire in the janitor's closet."

"I'll keep it in mind," Pete said.

"Good," Davidson, pouring some liquid into the bucket. "Use this stuff whenever I tell you to mop out the bathrooms. If you reach for my sidearm I will break your wrist. For starters."

"I . . . I wasn't going to," Pete said.

Davidson looked up at him. "Just so we're clear." There was a sink at the back of the closet with a spray hose that Davidson used to spray hot water in the bucket, sending a lemon-scented steam up from the bucket and into Pete's nostrils.

"A few glugs of the stuff will do it. I don't care how exact you are; we aren't the scientists here."

"Right," Pete said.

"There are cameras all over the facility. Most of them you

will never see, and some of the ones you do see don't really work. I watch the monitors. My staff watches the monitors. Some of your school chums get paid to watch the monitors while they're earning college prep credits. They'll be watching you mop the floors to pay off your debt to society. I'm sure some of them would like nothing better than to catch you doing something that you're not supposed to be doing. I'm sure some of them would like nothing better than to catch you doing something that would actually get you sent to prison, instead of working out your sentence by mopping the floors and cleaning the toilets that the living ones use."

Pete thought that Davidson must hang around dead people a lot: there was sarcasm in his words, but you'd never know it from his inflection.

Pete thought that there was something else in Davidson's words as well, some message hidden beneath his flat stare and deadpan delivery, something waiting for Pete to decode.

"I'll be careful," Pete said.

Davidson tossed a pair of green latex gloves against Pete's chest.

"Careful," he said. "Yes. You be careful. Get that mop over by the wall and wheel the bucket out into the hall. We're going to take a walk to the monitor room so I can get you a jacket."

Pete obeyed without comment. Davidson followed him out and popped his card back into the slot. The lock clicked.

The corridors at the foundation reminded Pete of the corridors at his grade school: long windowless tunnels of gray, the illumination from the fluorescent lighting above dim and shadowy. Every other panel was out, Pete noticed, and he wondered if the foundation was trying to save on its utility bill or that maybe the dead didn't need all that light.

The dead, he thought.

They only passed one office on their long walk. Pete glanced into the open doorway and saw Angela talking to his old pal Pinky McKnockers, the chubby and chesty friend of Phoebe Scarypants. There was another girl in the office, but all Pete could see of her was a billowing cloud of flaming red hair as she sat in front of a computer screen on the wall opposite the door. Pinky's own hair, a thick nest of rigid pink spikes, made it look like a huge sea urchin was sitting on her head.

She looked up as they passed, and he caught the look of sudden recognition under the shellac-thick makeup around her eyes.

He winked at her.

I've still got my list, honey, he thought, remembering the expression on her face as he'd spread out the Undead Studies student list where the name "Evan Talbot" had been crossed out. She looked down at her desk so swiftly that his new boss noticed and glanced up at him. Pete suddenly took a great interest in steering the mop bucket to its destination.

"You aren't listening," Davidson said.

"Excuse me?"

"Cameras everywhere. You think punk stuff like that is going to endear you to anyone?"

"What do you mean?"

Davidson stopped and turned with such abruptness that

Pete almost plowed into him with the bucket. That's all I need, he thought, to slosh my boss's shiny black boots.

"I don't think you're getting it," Davidson said. "Do you want to get away with murder or not?"

Pete looked up at him, not sure how he should respond to that.

"You have an opportunity here," Davidson said. "Don't squander it."

"Okay," Pete said. "Okay."

Davidson regarded him a moment longer before turning on his heel.

# CHAPTER TWELVE

WHY DOES HE always have to be the welcome wagon? Phoebe thought, seeing Takayuki perched like a vulture on the railing of the slumping porch. He lifted his head enough to glare at their approaching car, his dark hair brushed back from his face.

"He looks friendly," her dad said.

"That's Takayuki," Margi said from the backseat. "He's not."

"I was being sarcastic."

"I know."

He rolled the vehicle to a stop, then got out of the car to help Margi and her extract Adam from the backseat. Phoebe thought she heard Takayuki make a noise of disgust, but when she turned toward him he dropped to the ground and headed off into the woods, the rusted chains of his motorcycle jacket somehow failing to make any noise as he passed.

"Hey, Adam!" came a cheer from the house, as some of the

zombies—Karen, Colette, and Tommy among them, all wearing absurd pointed party hats—came out to welcome him. Tommy made fleeting eye contact with her, and she recalled their conversation—all of his questions about how she felt about Adam. Turning, she waved at Mal, a zombie who rivaled Adam in sheer size, and he waggled his fingers back at her. She leaned into Adam, wondering if Tommy was still watching but refusing to look at him.

Thorny was already at the house, along with Norm Lathrop—who had been Margi's date on homecoming night—Denny Mackenzie, and Gary Greene. Phoebe saw Gary hide a can of beer behind his back upon seeing her father.

Holding his hand, Phoebe looked for Adam's reaction, and for a long time there was none—but then she saw his mouth tic upward.

She breathed a long sigh of relief. Thank you, God, she thought.

"I didn't know Norm was going to be here," Margi whispered. "We haven't talked much since the dance."

"Hi, Margi!" Norm said, waving at her.

"No better time than the present," Phoebe said, nudging her forward.

"Phoebe," her dad said. "I need to talk to you for a minute."

Phoebe didn't want to let go of Adam, not even for a second, but she joined her father over by the car, watching as Karen and Colette each took one of Adam's arms and guided him up the rickety porch steps.

"Phoebe, was that beer I saw in that boys' hand?"

She held her breath as Adam tottered at the top of the stairs near Takayuki's perch, then let it out when a gentle tug from Karen righted him again. She was about to say "what beer?" But she decided to go with honesty.

"I think so."

"You know how I feel about you going to parties where there's going to be drinking."

"I do. I didn't know that there would be drinking. I really didn't think there would be any trad biotic kids here except for Margi and Thorny."

Her dad looked at her and she could almost hear the wheels of his mind whirring.

"The living impaired kids don't drink, do they?"

"They're called differently biotic now, Dad." she said. "And no, they don't drink, or eat, or sleep. Except Karen. She'll eat a piece of fruit every so often, but I think she does it just to be weird."

Her father opened his mouth and abruptly closed it.

"Do you know that boy?"

"Gary Greene," she said. "Thorny must have invited him— they're both on the football team. I've maybe talked to him twice."

He nodded, looked back at the house, then at the woods where Tak had disappeared.

"Dad," she said, "I'm not going to have anything to drink. I don't drink. I'm here for Adam."

He nodded. "This is where Adam died, isn't it? In the woods here?"

She lowered her eyes, nodding. Inside they cued up an old

Van Halen song in Adam's honor, at a volume that threatened to shake loose the few shingles that remained on the roof.

"Okay," her dad said, and he did something he didn't often do when her friends might be around: he hugged her. "You know I trust you. And I want Adam to have a good time too. If anyone gets crazy you call me, okay?"

She hugged him back even tighter. "Okay."

"Easy," he said, kissing the top of her head. "Aren't you worried that all of your zombie friends will see you hugging your uncool dad?"

"Not worried at all," she said, releasing him, "and you're not uncool. Usually."

He exhaled, and she knew that he would probably drive slow circles on the streets surrounding the Haunted House, just on the chance that there would be trouble and she would call.

She waved as he got back into the car. "We'll be fine."

Most of us, anyhow, she thought, running back to the house. She saw beams of light from inside rake across the cracked windows as the music blared, meaning that the zombies managed to re-rig the disco ball and lighting like they'd done for the homecoming after-party. A chill passed through her and she wondered if Adam was experiencing the same sort of déjà vu in returning there. She ran up the stairs, afraid that she would peek into the open area the zombies used as a dance floor and it would be a bizarre replay of that night—she would see Adam dancing with Karen, his suit jacket off and his tie a lank band of blue silk around his neck.

He *was* dancing, or rather he was standing as others danced near him. Colette and Margi twirled around him like he was a maypole, tugging at his arms and touching his shoulders as they spun.

She watched him turn his head, trying to track Colette as she circumnavigated his wide body. Phoebe couldn't read his expression, and for a moment she was afraid that he felt as if he was being mocked, but then Margi did a pirouette in front of him, her arms high over her head and her flouncy dress twitching. Adam raised his hand as though to catch hers, but she had already spun past. Phoebe decided that the gesture meant that Adam was on his way to enjoying himself, so she went to join them, trying not to blush at the immediate chorus of catcalls from Colette and Margi.

She leaned against him, her mouth close to his ear.

"I'm sorry I was away," she said. "I had to talk to Dad."

The look he gave her was a strange one, and she decided she wouldn't let anything else take her away from him that night.

A few of the other differently biotic kids were doing the zombie hop—a twitchy, jerky set of movements that looked like they were having seizures. Kevin Zumbrowki, who had recently learned how to smile, was a master of the zombie hop, and at times moved as though he was being electrocuted. No one seemed to care if his motions had nothing to do with the rhythm or the tempo of the song, especially not the dead girl beside him, whose entire dance repertoire seemed to be a dip of her right shoulder.

Tommy was talking with Thorny, Denny, and Gary Greene.

Denny and Gary were each holding a can of beer. Karen was watching the boys talk, her arms folded and a quizzical look on her face.

Margi hip-checked Phoebe, and because she wasn't paying attention, the sudden jolt almost sent her sprawling to the floor.

"You're going to talk to him, right?" Margi said, her voice a high shout above the heavy throb of the music.

"Talk to who?"

"Tommy, stupid."

Phoebe's eyes flicked up at Adam, who managed to shuffle one of his feet forward. She gave Margi the look of death.

"What?" Margi said, sweat already beginning to wilt her spikes. "*Are* you?"

"I already talked to him," Phoebe said, leaning closer to Margi so maybe, just maybe, every dead kid in Oakvale didn't have to listen in. She felt weird even having the conversation, because these were the sort of details that she and Margi passed to each other almost intuitively prior to Adam dying. Now that she was spending all her time with Adam, they had to play "catch up" more.

"You did? What did you tell him?" Margi, oblivious, shouted, pausing to screech as Colette tried to dance.

"That it's over," Phoebe said, silently cheering Colette on. The upside of Phoebe's absence was the renewed closeness between Colette and Margi. "And that I'm with Adam now."

Margi gave her a quizzical look. "With Adam? Like *with* with Adam?"

"Well, yeah. Sort of." That was how Phoebe thought of her

and Adam, anyhow—as a couple. It was like an understanding between them, even though neither had actually said as much out loud.

"Does *he* know that?"

Phoebe started to reply when a shadow fell across her. She looked up, and Adam loomed over her like a tree. She was going to ask Margi what she meant, but she'd already moved away to dance with Colette. Phoebe stepped forward and put her arms around him as the song ended.

"Are you having fun?" she asked. The nod was slow in coming. He opened his mouth to say something but was cut off as another song began tearing through the speakers.

Phoebe put her head against his chest and pretended that the bass was the beating of his heart.

"This turned out well, Phoebe," Karen said.

They were standing in the backyard of the Haunted House, in the shadow of the slouching barn. A few songs ago Adam pointed through the unliving room window at the forest, and Phoebe knew what he wanted. She'd taken his hand and made the laborious process of helping him across the house and out the back door. Karen caught up with them just as they were going outside.

"Thanks, Karen," Phoebe said, pausing as Adam took another lumbering step toward the tree line. Phoebe bit her lower lip.

"It's too bad the new kids didn't want to come."

"Yeah," Phoebe said. "Cooper told me they were still a

little nervous about being in crowds of zombies because of what happened at Dickinson House. The fire."

"The massacre, you mean," Karen said, then changed the subject. "Those boys that Thorny brought came to ask Tommy if he wanted to rejoin the football team. They meant it, too."

"Really?" Phoebe replied, swallowing. "Is he going to do it?"

"No," Karen said, "but I think it made him feel . . . good to hear it."

Adam took another step. Phoebe wanted to go back inside the house and tell Tommy that he should rejoin, that it would be good for him and for everyone who looked up to him. She didn't, though, because she had to be with Adam, especially now, especially because of where Adam clearly wanted to go. He took another step and she thought it was strange that the closer he got to his goal the faster he moved. She was frightened; she wasn't sure that she could bear going there, but she knew she had to.

"It's always nice to feel . . . wanted," Karen said.

"What is that supposed to mean?" Was she making some kind of obscure comment about Tommy? Or something else?

"Oh, nothing. Adam, honey," Karen said, "why do you want to see where you died?"

Phoebe's breath caught in her throat, and Adam turned to Karen.

"Don't answer that," she said, "I . . . know why. We can't help it, can we? But it isn't really a good thing. We . . . moved . . . out of my old house because that is where I . . . I died."

Phoebe's grip on Adam's cold hand was tight. She

wondered if Karen was going to tell Adam what only she and Margi knew, which was that Karen had committed suicide.

"When I came back, I . . . would go there . . . everyday. The upstairs . . . bathroom. I'd go and I'd stand next to . . . the tub. For hours. That's where . . . I died. My parents would come home and I'd still be . . . standing there, staring at . . . the tub. Sitting in it, sometimes."

Adam gave a slow blink. Karen sighed.

"It wasn't healthy," she said. "I'm glad we moved."

"Want to . . . see," Adam said.

Karen shook her head. "It really isn't a good idea."

"Maybe we should listen to her, Adam," Phoebe said, holding his arm and looking up at his face for some sign, some expression that told her what Adam wanted from a return to the spot where he breathed his last. "Maybe we should go back to the house, listen to some more . . ."

No," he said, without turning to look at her.

She was hurt, but she managed to keep it from her voice.

"Okay, Adam," she said. "We can go there if you want."

His arm twitched and slid out of hers. "A . . . lone."

She let go of his arm, shocked. She looked at him, wondering why he wouldn't look at her, wondering why he didn't want her with him. She started to protest, but it died on her lips when he finally turned toward her.

"Alone," he said again, and despite the lack of inflection in his monotone, she thought she detected a tone of gentleness there.

He stared at her, his face an unreadable mask.

"Okay," she said after a time. "I'll wait here."

He didn't speak as he began his slow progress toward the woods.

She felt the weight of Karen's arm around her shoulders as Adam's hulking form disappeared into the thick shadows.

"Don't worry, honey," Karen said, her voice a cool whisper against Phoebe's ear. "He'll be . . . fine. Nothing can . . . hurt him now."

Phoebe shook her head, her cheek brushing against the dead girl's.

"That isn't true," she said. "It isn't."

But even as she said it, she knew she was really talking about herself.

# CHAPTER THIRTEEN

RIGHT LEG. LEFT LEG. Right hurt saw hurt Phoebe hurt bastard left leg. Right leg hurt Phoebe sad I'm sad too Phoebe is it guilt or is it more there never was more so it must be guilt. Stop. Sad Phoebe.

Stop. Ran down this path That Night. That Night ran and ran like wind ran Phoebe screamed ran saved Phoebe saved my love Phoebe shot shot dead run run left leg right leg run run.

Fall. Get up. Get up.

"How the mighty . . . have fallen," voice said. "Literally."

Get up.

Smiley. Get up. Right arm left arm push right leg push. Right and left arm right leg push.

"Let me . . . help you," said Tak. Tak Smiley.

Speak. Stop speak speak.

"Can't."

"Of course . . . I can," said Smiley

Smiley strong lift help no help haul up Smiley not smile. That Night Smiley found Pete Smiley stopped Pete I stopped Pete stopped Pete's bullet.

"It happened right . . . over there," said Smiley, Smiley pointing. "That . . . is where . . . you died."

Look. Look right leg left leg. Look blood gone leaves and dirt and blood blood gone blood seeped into earth life gone.

"We all . . . do it . . . some time," Smiley said. "Like swallows . . . to . . . Capistrano. Revisit . . . our . . . death."

Look. Look no blood blood in the earth seeped into soil Phoebe's tears seeped into skin dead skin. Phoebe held me she held me and she cried and she cried and I died. Gone gone where one door closing one door opening. Whose hand turned the knob?

"I died on the . . . Garden State . . . Parkway," Smiley said, "truck . . . sideswiped my bike. Broken neck."

Smiley look Smiley crack Smiley's head on shoulder head angle leaning on shoulder Smiley lift head crack crunch head back Smiley smiling.

"They hate us . . . you know," said Smiley. "The beating hearts. Hate."

Smiley lifts shirt Misfits shirt ribs look ribs actual ribs white white bones last cracked flesh gray gray skin hangs.

"They hate us because . . . we . . . remind them . . . of the . . . future."

Look. Look. Smiley lets shirt down Smiley lifts hand

spreads bones spread white bones Smiley dead dead like me like me dead.

"They hate us . . . and they will try . . . to destroy us," said Smiley. "Soon."

Hate not hate. Joe not hate STD not hate Johnny hate not Jimmy hate Phoebe Thorny Margi not hate Phoebe love Phoebe. Speak love speak speak.

"Love . . ."

Smiley laughed the dead can laugh can't laugh Smiley not Smiley dead.

"No," Smiley said, "not love. She . . . doesn't love. She . . . didn't love . . . him . . . and she doesn't . . . love you."

Right arm. Right arm right arm right arm. Miss. Smiley quick Smiley swift Smiley laugh.

"I know . . . it hurts. It hurts . . . being dead. The pain . . . gets worse."

Stop. Speak stop speak stop.

"It gets worse. It gets worse because you . . . start to feel. You start to . . . remember what it was like to . . . feel. Really feel. You can get . . . angry."

Smiley smiled.

"Like you . . . just did. You will feel . . . just a little. You will remember . . . feeling. And you will . . . hate . . . as they hate."

Not hate love not hate love Phoebe love.

"You will . . . hate . . . even her . . . because she will remind you . . . of the past."

Not hate Phoebe love not hate hate.

"There is no past. There is . . . no future," said Smiley, "there is only . . . the . . . endless present."

Smiley walk walk into darkness into forest no path straight into darkness right leg Smiley quick gone in darkness.

"When you are ready . . . to hate . . . I'll be waiting for you . . . in the present."

Gone. Not hate.

Not.

Hate.

# CHAPTER FOURTEEN

"**D**ID YOU SEE the plastic surgeon yet?" his father asked from the opposite coast.

Pete sneered into his cell phone. He would rather his dad call up and say, "Does your face hurt? It's killing me," than have one more question about the plastic surgeon.

"No."

"Why not?"

"I just haven't wanted to."

Since his injury, Darren had called almost every other day to check to see if Pete had gotten the surgery. That was the most attention he'd paid Pete since abandoning him and his mother. Even the summers he spent at his dad's place didn't provide as much contact with his father as the scar did.

"You should get that fixed."

"Yeah." But if I got it fixed, you'd stop calling me, wouldn't you?

"Well," Darren said, "I've got a conference call in five

minutes I have to get ready for. How's the community service going?"

Darren never asked about the therapy; just the community service.

"Fine. I'm on my way to work off hours thirty-one through thirty-five," Pete replied. The sound of the admin assistant's voice on Darren's pager told Pete that his father had already mentally disconnected from their conversation.

"That's great," Darren said, with all the enthusiasm of a zombie. "Gotta run. Get your scar fixed."

"Yeah."

"Bye," Pete said, but his father had already hung up. He saw a zombie through the windshield of his car, a pasty-looking freak in a blue jean jacket.

"Was that your father?" Pete's mom asked from the drivers' seat. She hadn't let him drive since his arrest.

"Yes, it was Darren," he said.

"Oh. How is he?"

Pete didn't answer. Duke Davidson opened the front door to the facility as soon as his mother pulled in front of the building. Pete got out when she stopped and said good-bye over his shoulder.

"Ready for more custodial work?" Duke said, smiling thinly and waving to Pete's mother as she drove away. "I'm going to have you do the bathrooms today."

"Great," Pete said. He was looking behind him at the zombie, who seemed to be shambling down the hill toward the security fence. "I have to get my head shrunk first."

Duke laughed. "Don't stare."

"What?"

Duke handed Pete his security badge, which had a small unsmiling photograph of Pete on the right-hand side. "I said, 'Don't stare.' Angela wouldn't like it if she thought you were trying to intimidate the residents."

"Intimidate . . . ?"

"That's Cooper Wilson. He stays here now. He was one of the survivors of a zombie purge in Massachusetts a few months ago. Maybe you heard about it? The Dickinson House Massacre, they call it."

Pete shook his head. He noticed that Duke, who normally kept a brisk pace as he roamed the shiny halls, had slowed to talk to him.

"There's a girl who came from there. Melissa."

"That the one in the mask?"

Duke looked at him, grinning. "See, you do pay attention. She wears the mask because she was horribly disfigured in the fire."

"That's rough." Pete's hand drifted up to the stitching in his face.

"You ever catch up to the guy who did that to you?"

"What?"

Duke stopped, and Pete looked up at him, jerking his hand away from the stitching.

"Do you know who did it?"

"I know who did it."

Duke nodded. "There's some zombies in town," he said,

"they like pulling pranks. Petty vandalism, stuff like that. Some of them are into roadkill."

"Roadkill?"

"They chew on it. Disgusting, huh? But it's the pranks that will get them in trouble."

"I heard about a prank. Zombie recruitment posters, or something."

Duke nodded, his hands on his hips. "That's right. What do you think about that?"

Pete thought that it really pissed him off when he heard about it. Stavis called him up, acting like the posters were a big joke or something, but Pete didn't think it was funny at all. Thinking of Williams and his sick designs on Phoebe, he thought that the posters were too close to the truth—that the dead really were trying to recruit the living for their sick enterprise.

But he didn't know what Davidson was looking for from him, so all he did was shrug. Duke looked at him as though Pete didn't have to say anything, like Duke could see right through into his heart.

"Okay," Duke said, as though satisfied by whatever he saw there.

Pete felt Duke's stare the entire trip down to Angela's office.

# CHAPTER FIFTEEN

"I'M GOING OUT, Adam," Mom said. "Do you want me to call Phoebe so you have some company?"

Speak.

"No."

"Okay," she said, "I'll be back in a couple hours."

Left leg. Right leg. Right arm. Through the window Mom looks scared looks relieved to be out can't blame her can't. Phoebe next door with homework with books with music with Phoebe miss Phoebe.

Phoebe.

Phoebe clings needs to live not cling needs to live can't live hurts. Can't live. Phoebe needs to forget forget me can't forget Phoebe needs to forget me. Tak Smiley is right. Forget.

Can't forget Phoebe said Phoebe become who you always were become. Can't become anything. Can't.

Dead.

"Hey, stupid."

Jimmy. Stupid Jimmy. Meet Takayuki Jimmy.

"There's someone here to see you, stupid," said Jimmy.

Right leg. Left leg. Right leg. Moving faster moving better was slug now snail soon be turtle. Hope. Left leg. Hope Phoebe hope not Phoebe Phoebe needs to live can't live with me.

"I'm out of here, stupid," said Jimmy. "Don't let the maggots catch you."

Jimmy out the door past visitor visitor not Phoebe.

Master Griffin.

"Your stepbrother is a rude individual," said Master Griffin. "Not centered at all."

Speak. Speak.

"Come . . . in."

"No," Master Griffin said, shaking gleaming bald head. "Let's go outside. It's almost warm today. I'm very sorry I haven't come sooner. I'm afraid I'm not very big on newspapers or the like, a side effect of being too long on foreign soil. One of the consequences of having a rich interior life is that you can sometimes lose connection with the outside world."

Smiles. "Which is why you need to come outside with me."

Speak. "Glad . . ."

"I'm glad to see you too, Adam. That's right, bend your knees a little more as we go down your steps."

"Can't . . ."

Master Griffin shook his head. "That word is to be stricken from your vocabulary, effective right now. Remember what Yoda said? 'Try not.' The word 'can't' has no place in your recovery. You can and you will. Time is all it will take."

Quoting Yoda? Can't. Can't speak. Speak. Can't.

Master Griffin's eyes narrow, tone serious.

"I know that it is difficult, and I know that your body is not obeying your instructions right now. But it would not obey your instructions when you first began to work with me, if memory serves. You could not do the Bow. You could not do the Crane. There were other forms that you had yet to master. This is no different."

Right leg. Left leg. Master Griffin's hand on my arm pressure is there pressure stars in the sky breeze can't feel no shoes can't feel cold ground beneath my no shoes feet can't feel.

"Good," said Master Griffin. "We are going to relearn the forms, and your body will begin to obey you. The body will remember. You will regain control through the discipline of practice. Do you remember your forms?"

Master Griffin moves moves like water arm rigid crosses body right arm right arm right Master Griffin bends knee drops shoulder arm down lift arm lift arm lift arm.

"Again," said Master Griffin.

Again, again said Master Griffin can't move didn't lift arm lift arm lift arm.

"Again," said Master Griffin.

Lift arm lift arm lift arm look Phoebe's light is on Phoebe books and music Phoebe's hair the memory of the smell of her hair lift arm.

"Good," said Master Griffin, "feel your focus return."

Lift arm. Lift arm move arm focus move arm. Arm, motionless.

"Excellent," said Master Griffin. "Focus. You are the only one that can do this."

Focus. Lift arm. Move arm bend knee bend knee drop fist. Lift arm.

Lift arm.

Lift arm!

Hand moves.

"Excellent." Said Master Griffin, smiling. "Again."

Lift arm.

"You know, I've missed you at the dojo."

Focus.

Lift arm.

# CHAPTER SIXTEEN

S HE'D JUST SAT Adam down in the back of the van when she felt a light touch on her shoulder. She turned and saw that Tommy, who, driven by an old-world sense of chivalry, was normally the last one on.

"Hello, Phoebe," he said. "Adam."

Phoebe hesitated. Adam tried to wave in the cramped quarters. He got the arm motion right, but the wrist and fingers weren't really bending just yet. Progress is progress, she thought.

"Can I . . . talk to you?" Tommy said. "Alone?"

He motioned to the pair of seats behind the driver. Looking at Adam, she hoped he'd shake his head, or reach for her hand, but instead he nodded.

"Okay," she said, crouching as she slid into the seat before Tommy. He had to lean so the other students could climb in, and she was acutely aware of her pulse as he pressed against her. He was so solid and unyielding; his arm like a rock against her.

"I've been thinking about what you said . . . Phoebe," he said, shifting back as Kevin climbed aboard.

"Oh?" she replied, glancing over her shoulder as the rest of the class settled in their seats. Her skin was tingling from where Tommy had leaned against her. Karen had taken Phoebe's usual seat and was leaning against Adam, whispering something that brought a phantom smile to the corner of his mouth.

"I've thought . . . about a lot," Tommy said. "I want you . . . to know . . . I still have feelings . . . for you."

"Tommy," she warned, turning to face him as the van started up. "Let's not do this here, please?"

Thorny and Margi were complaining loudly about some experiment gone awry in their biology class. Colette's shrill laughter filled the vehicle.

"I'll be . . . brief," he said. He was whispering, at least. Even so, she couldn't help but risk a self-conscious glance over her shoulder. Karen was still talking to Adam, but he was looking right at her.

"I just wanted . . . to . . . thank you."

"To thank me?" She was conscious that he hadn't taken his eyes off her from the moment they sat down. If he was angered by her darting eyes he didn't show it.

"For trying," he said. "With me. It was . . . a . . . brave . . . thing to do."

"It wasn't an act of *charity*, Tommy," she said, anger raising her voice. "I was just as . . ."

She didn't get to complete her sentence, because Thorny shouted to Tommy from the last row of the van..

"Hey, Tommy!" he called. "What do you think, would you let us dissect you for a differently biotic class?"

"Why . . . not?" he said, trying to smile. "Learn more than . . . with . . . a fetal . . . pig."

Phoebe looked away, out the window at the trees whose yellow and red leaves were muting to brown. Won't be long, she thought, before they started to fall. Last year there were storms in mid-October that knocked all the leaves down. She remembered raking them up into wet piles, sad that her favorite season had been compromised by the fickle New England winds.

Adam was looking at her. She wished she knew what he was thinking.

The van arrived at the same time as a sputtering compact car that followed them around the turning circle in front of the foundation. Phoebe could see Melissa riding along in the passenger seat, her coppery hair high enough to press against the car's roof. The girl turned toward the van. She had a different mask on today, still a blank white but this time with the corners of the mouth turned up in a slight smile.

The car pulled to a stop, and the driver got out of the still-running vehicle to trot around to help Melissa out. Phoebe could see that it was Father Fitzpatrick, the Catholic priest that had performed the funeral service for Evan Talbot. She would have liked to have said hello to him, but by the time she'd helped Adam out of the van, he was back in his car, speeding off. Must have some souls to save, Phoebe thought.

Melissa waved to her, holding the whiteboard in front of her like a shield.

"Hey, Melissa," she said, watching the girl hitch from side to side as she walked to the doors. Father Fitzpatrick was late; usually Melissa was already in her seat by the time they arrived at the class. The girl walked with great difficulty; her left leg especially seemed unwilling to move at the appropriate pace or bend at the appropriate angle.

Adam took a shuffle-step forward, and Phoebe tried her best to steady his massive frame.

"Good job, Adam," she said.

He looked down at her, his expression unreadable.

Cooper Wilson, Alish, and Angela were already seated as the students went through the motions of retrieving assignments and notebooks, stowing gear, and, in the case of the few traditionally biotic ones, helping themselves to the refreshments from the back table. Angela spoke over the din.

"Cooper has asked for class time today," she said. "He'd like to tell everyone the story of the Dickinson House fire."

"I've been . . . waiting for a chance . . . to tell . . . this story," Cooper said, managing to look shy as he brushed a lock of gray-black hair out of his eyes, "to . . . people . . . who will actually . . . listen."

Melissa, her arm swathed in loose green fabric ending in a tight cuff at her slender wrist, raised her hand.

"Yes, Melissa?"

The girl wrote on her board with as much alacrity as she could muster.

MAY I B XCUSED?

"May I ask why?" Angela asked.

"Mel," Cooper said, "they've got . . . to . . . know. It's why . . . we . . . came here." He was tall, rail-thin, and usually had a clownish half smile on his face, but Phoebe could see that his goofy demeanor masked a more serious nature. Melissa's presence in the room was very important to him.

Melissa shook her head, her hair bouncing as she erased and wrote.

"Mel . . ."

CANT.

Angela said that she could leave. "I understand, Melissa. I'm sure all your friends do too. You can do work in my office for now, if you'd like. I'll come get you at the break."

Melissa rose, with effort, and dragged her feet across the carpet and out the door. Cooper didn't look like he understood.

"She should . . . hear . . . this," he said to Angela.

"She isn't ready."

"What is she . . . scared of?" he said. "She's already . . . dead."

"Cooper," Angela said, her voice as close to reproach as it ever got.

"Okay . . . okay. Dickinson House," he said, and everyone was rapt. A few weeks prior Tommy had read a news article he'd found on the torching of Dickinson House, which was a sanctuary for the differently biotic, similar to St. Jude's mission, but secular. According to the article, the fire had destroyed seven zombies and taken the lives of two employees.

"The article that you . . . saw . . . was a bunch . . . of crap," Cooper began. "Almost nothing in it . . . was . . . right except . . . that . . . there was a fire.

"The body . . . count . . . for example," he said, "ten zombies . . . burned to . . . a second death. No . . . trads . . . died. Amos Burke . . . was the alcoholic . . . janitor . . . and the only one . . . who talked . . . to the press."

"How did the fire start?" Tommy said.

"Oh . . . yeah," Cooper answered. "That was the other . . . thing in the article. . . that was right. There were . . . white vans."

Phoebe was a little shocked. She'd heard of the white vans so often without seeing any actual evidence of them that even she had begun to think that they were Tommy's personal conspiracy obsession, like the single gun theory or the alien autopsies at Roswell.

Cooper spoke to Tommy. "I know . . . people . . . think you are . . . nuts. Even zombies . . . I've seen them . . . call you a crank . . . on your own . . . Web site . . . but it is true."

If she expected Tommy to look smug or self-righteous, she was disappointed. He looked intent and serious, maybe a little sad. But Cooper was right, there were a number of surprised faces in the room, including, for a moment, Angela's.

"Tell us what you saw, Cooper," she said, covering well.

"I was in . . . the house," he said. "Because I didn't . . . feel . . . like dancing."

He must have noticed the looks of confusion. He closed his eyes and continued.

"There was a . . . dance. Miss . . . Mary . . . she was a volunteer . . . from the college . . . who spent . . . a lot . . . of time . . . with us . . . had arranged it. Miss Mary would bring . . . art supplies . . . puppets . . . and scripts from . . . plays. She was always

. . . trying to get us . . . to have 'fun.' Her idea of fun, anyhow."

The voice was a dead one, but Phoebe could hear a note of sadness there.

"She brought . . . a radio . . . and CDs and hung . . . ribbons . . . in the barn. The other . . . employees . . . did not . . . like her. Or . . . us. We were there . . . to work. On the . . . farm.

"I . . . wasn't going . . . to dance. But Melissa . . . came to . . . the zombie . . . room . . . and . . . asked me. Told her . . . I'd think . . . about it.

"I read . . . a comic book. Batman. Then . . . went . . . upstairs. Saw the vans. Two vans, white. Four men . . . the men . . . wore sunglasses and white suits . . . Tyvek suits. Two had shotguns like . . . Burke . . . said. I saw them shoot . . . inside the barn. The others had . . . Super . . . Soakers . . . not . . . flamethrowers."

"Super Soakers?" Thorny said.

Cooper nodded. "Filled with . . . gasoline. They sprayed . . . inside . . . the barn . . . I couldn't see . . . inside . . . where I was but . . . Miss Mary . . . came out. She was . . . screaming. Covered in . . . gasoline. One of the men said . . . she should . . . shut up . . . unless she . . . wanted to . . . burn . . . with the dead."

"She wasn't mentioned in the article," Tommy said.

"Conspiracy," Cooper said, something like a rueful smile on his face. "The other . . . employees . . . had . . . mysteriously . . . vanished. One of the . . . men . . . punched her . . . in the stomach and . . . threw her down. Then his . . . friend . . . threw . . . the bottle . . . with the rag . . . in it. It went up . . . so quickly."

"So it was the . . . barn . . . not the house?" Tommy asked.

"The house . . . is still there," Cooper answered. "Free of . . . zombies."

"What happened then?"

"The killers . . . watched. The flames . . . threw . . . shadows . . . across the lawn and I heard . . . silence. Nothing but the . . . roar and . . . rush . . . of the fire. My . . . friends . . . didn't scream"

He looked at the floor, his eyes unfocused, as though he was staring at the ashes of his friends. "Later . . . there were . . . sirens. The men . . . got in . . . their vans."

"How did . . . Melissa . . . escape?" Tommy asked, his voice low, almost a growl.

Cooper looked at him a moment, and Phoebe felt like something electrical was passing in the air between them as he answered Tommy's question.

"She . . . didn't."

No wonder the poor thing couldn't stay, Phoebe thought. She felt her fingernails biting into the skin of her palms.

"Miss Mary . . . got up.. The flames . . . were covering the . . . barn like . . . a coat of paint. A part of . . . the roof . . . gave way. She . . . ran in . . . used her jacket . . . on Melissa. I helped . . . drag them out. None of . . . the . . . others . . . made . . . it."

"What did the police . . . do?" Tommy asked.

"They took . . . a statement . . . from . . . Miss Mary. And from . . . Burke . . . who was . . . passed out . . . in the . . . supply room."

Thorny was incredulous. "They didn't talk to you?"

Cooper shook his head. "One of the firemen said . . . 'they missed . . . one.'"

"How did you get . . . to the foundation?"

"Miss Mary . . . drove us. She was . . . afraid . . . they would try . . . to kill us . . . again. She was . . . arrested . . . for helping us."

"Really? For helping you?" Phoebe could almost see the wheels spinning in Tommy's mind; Cooper's story was hitting him on a number of levels, all of which he would be compelled to write about and act upon. Maybe it was hearing the story firsthand and not through the filter of a computer screen that made a deeper impact. That and seeing the evidence of the atrocity—Melissa—with his own eyes.

"The owners . . . of the farm . . . claimed we were . . . their property. An . . . asset."

"Because you worked there?"

"Because they . . . housed us," he said, looking at his hands. "I don't even know . . . if my friends . . . tried to get away. Or if . . . they let the gasoline . . . and then the flames . . . hit them. I don't know . . . if they tried."

He didn't take his eyes off Tommy as he spoke. "Melissa was almost . . . happy . . . before they came. All they wanted . . . was to dance. That's . . . all."

Angela suggested that they take a break after a moment of silence. Tommy volunteered to go get Melissa. When they returned ten minutes later, Tommy was guiding her gently by the elbow. Angela spurred on a discussion about an article that had appeared in *Time* magazine about Slydellco and Aftermath, trying gamely to steer the class in a more upbeat direction, which worked for a little while until Tommy pointed out that the magazine had given equal time to Reverand Nathan Mathers. Melissa sat quietly throughout their discussion without making a single mark on her whiteboard.

There was less than a half hour to go when Angela brought the class to a halt.

"Tommy," she said, her voice soft, "don't you think you should make your announcement before the end of our session?"

Tommy looked up at her and Alish, as surprised as the dead could look.

"I am . . . leaving . . . the class," he said.

There was a moment of protracted silence in the room, like that after a prayer at a funeral.

"Mr. Williams," Alish said, leaning forward on his cane and clearing his throat "has stated his intention to pursue his studies elsewhere." He smiled, in what Phoebe thought was supposed to be a reassuring manner. "Fieldwork, if you will."

"I'm leaving school," he said. "Dropping . . . out."

Thorny was the first student to speak. "Aw, man," was all he said. "Dude," Cooper said, "I am . . . bummed. I . . . am a . . . big . . . fan. I read . . . My So-Called . . . Undeath . . . every . . . day . . . even before . . . we came here."

"I'm really sorry," Tommy said. Phoebe was aware of her own breathing, how fast it had become. "I . . . really am. I will . . . keep writing . . . though."

Kevin was looking at the floor, which is as close as his dead face could come to crestfallen. Margi and Colette watched Phoebe, afraid she was going to freak, but she remained calm.

Karen was another matter.

"Tommy," Karen said, an edge to her voice. "I'm mad at you."

He tilted his head in response.

"I . . . am . . . very . . . mad at you," she went on. "Very. Don't you think . . . you should have . . . discussed this with us?"

Tommy's lip curled up in a fair approximation of sarcasm.

"It's my . . . life," he said.

"It is . . . a lot more . . . than that . . . and you . . . know it," she said.

"Karen, maybe this isn't the best time to discuss this," Angela said.

Karen's eyes flashed as though there were a flurry of hot responses blazing up inside her.

"May I be excused?" Karen asked. "May I go . . . to . . . to the bathroom?"

Angela sighed and gave her permission to go.

Phoebe watched her short blue skirt waving like a flag as she hurried away. Margi raised her hand.

"Can I . . . ?"

"By all means," Angela said, fluttering her hands in frustration. "Maybe the rest of you would like to start discussing how differently biotic people are represented by the entertainment industry today. Would that be okay?"

There were a few nods. Phoebe watched as Alish made his way over to a wide square table that the students used to complete written assignments. He sat in one of the padded rolling chairs, leaning his cane against the table, and tapping his smooth chin with one long and wrinkled finger.

# CHAPTER SEVENTEEN

"SIT ... BY ... MY ... SELF," Adam said, just before he preceded Phoebe on the bus.

As slow as his words were, it took them a moment to register.

"Oh," Phoebe said. "Oh. I'll just sit over here, across . . ."

"No," Adam said. She realized he was trying to point. "Sit . . . with . . . friends."

Phoebe looked at his pale gray face, searching for the meaning that he used to be able to convey with the slightest movement of his eye or mouth. Now he was an enigma, as unreadable to her as an ancient Aramaic scroll.

"Oh," she said, knowing that he could still read her feelings and there was nothing she could do to hide them. Was he mad at her for talking to Tommy? Is that why he wanted her to go away? His stare was impassive and cold, and she couldn't help but shrink from the blankness of it. She let go of his arm.

"Okay, then," she said. "I'll catch up with you later."

She turned and walked toward the back where the Weird Sisters held court, their voices audible over the dull rumble of the bus engine.

Margi and Colette were in the last seats of the bus, and Margi stepped out of her seat to let Phoebe slide in. Margi was already into full monologue, so if she noticed that Phoebe and Adam weren't together she didn't say anything.

"I am *so* glad to be out of the lab," Margi said, her hands a blur of motion as she went on. Colette winked at Phoebe, her mascara'd eyelid dropping and raising lazily, at half speed. "I just thought that was the creepiest thing in the world. Sorry, Colette, but it was. Batty old Alish sticking you guys with pins like you were life-size voodoo dolls or something, that was totally nasty. Totally nasty. Not that the letters are much better. Hell this and hell that, monster this and evil that. Can you believe some freaky mortician is *marketing* to the foundation? Every week we get an e-nouncement where he sends us pictures of all the coffins he has on sale. Phoebe, why didn't you warn me about stuff like that?"

Phoebe shrugged, her gaze drifting outside as the bus rolled to a stop in front of the Oakvale mobile home park, where Tommy usually waited for it.

"Probably . . . could not . . . get a word . . . in . . . edgewise," Colette said.

"Har-de-har," Margi said, "you are such the little comedienne. She should have said something, though. I haven't read that much profanity since I had to use the bathroom at El and Gee club when we went to see the Shadowy Organization last month."

Phoebe listened to Margi laugh and Colette pretend to laugh. She forced herself to smile, but she wasn't quick enough. Margi looped her metal-sheathed arm around her shoulders.

"Aw, what is it, Pheebes? Are you still upset about Tommy?"

"I am not upset about Tommy."

"Is it because he's leaving? Or because you still have feelings for him?"

"I am *not* upset about Tommy!"

"Okay, okay," Margi said, squeezing her tighter. "Jeez, sorry I mentioned it. Bite my head off."

"I didn't bite your head off," she said, knowing that she did. Margi was right on both accounts.

Margi looked at her, pink lips wrinkling. "Clearly, I have erred. There is obviously nothing bothering you, so let's just move on, shall we?"

"I'd appreciate it."

"Good."

"Because it isn't like it's my fault or anything," she said, but her hands were shaking in the frilly sleeves of her blouse.

"That's right. We all agree that it wasn't your fault. Don't we, C.B.?"

Colette was also wearing her hair spiked lately, but no matter how much product she and Margi put into it, the lank strands wouldn't stand up like they did on Margi's head. Margi's spikes swayed, Colette's gave a limp bounce.

"We . . . agree."

"Good," Margi said. "See? We agree. What exactly are we agreeing on?"

Phoebe blew the bangs out of her eyes with a huffy breath. "That it isn't my fault. Tommy leaving."

"Ah. No. No, that definitely isn't your fault. You breaking up with someone is not to say you are responsible for them going on a zombie vision quest."

"A zombie vision quest?" Phoebe said. "So you *do* think I'm responsible."

"Didn't I just say the opposite?" Margi looked out the window, then she asked, "Are you and Adam fighting?"

"Why? Just because I'm not sitting with him you think we're fighting? Am I such a terrible monster that you think I just go around picking fights with people?"

"You mean like you're doing now?" Margi said, poking her in the ribs as though trying to puncture Phoebe's cloud of gloom. "No. It's just when you turned away from him, he reached for you, like there was something else he wanted to say. But he was too slow, and you kept moving."

Phoebe looked at her friend. "He reached for me?"

"Yeah," Margi said, "like he was afraid you were upset or something. It's so hard to tell what he's thinking now, he just hasn't got the 'expression' thing or the 'inflection' thing down yet. What do you think he was doing, C.B.? Can you give us a little help with the zombie-to-English translation?"

Colette tried on a smile. "I think . . . he was . . . going Romero."

Phoebe, being a great fan of *Night of the Living Dead* and all of George Romaro's movies, couldn't help but smile even though she knew what was coming.

"You mean he was reaching for her brains?"

"Yes," Colette said, "delicious . . . brains."

Margi giggled.

"There's a flaw in your thinking, C.B. Even Adam is smart enough to know Pheebes doesn't have any."

The Weird Sisters cackled.

"You guys really need to take this act on the road," Phoebe said, but was suddenly serious again. Margi and Colette caught the vibe as well.

"Like Tommy," she continued, leaning her head against Margi's shoulder.

"Aw, Pheebes," Margi said, kissing the top of her head. "He's coming back, right? This is probably just something he needs to get out of his system."

"I don't know." She thought about how solid he'd felt leaning against her. Tommy wasn't one to change his mind easily.

"I think so," Margi said. "I heard him talking to the Hunters. It sounded to me like he was coming back."

"What was he talking to the Hunters for?" Phoebe asked, sitting up.

"I was working a shift in the office and they were talking to him about the Web site, and how important it was for it to continue. They said that the foundation would pay for the site and for the hosting. Tommy said that was cool, but that he wouldn't let Skip Slydell put banner ads for Z on it."

"You're kidding."

"No, really," Margi said, "they said Slydell wanted to do . . ."

"No," Phoebe said, "I meant about the foundation funding it."

"For real. They said that the site was critically important

for the survival and advancement of zombie rights and culture. I remember because I thought it was weird that they said 'survival.'" She thought for a moment. "They didn't say 'zombie,' though. 'Differently biotic.'"

"That is really weird. What did Tommy say?"

"He said he would still write for the blog, but that he couldn't manage the site anymore. He said if the Hunters could ensure that the people he chose to run the site for him got paid for their work, he would consider letting them fund it."

"Wow," Phoebe said. She had so much going through her head just then it was difficult to focus on one thing. She wasn't so certain it was a great idea to give the foundation or Slydellco access to mysocalledundeath.

"I know," Margi said. "Pretty cool, huh? I guess that would make Tommy the first zombie entrepreneur."

Colette shrugged one shoulder as though to say "imagine that."

"He said he was coming back, though?" Phoebe said.

Margi gave her a quizzical look. "Not exactly. Not in so many words. It was sort of implied."

The bus rolled to a stop at the curb, and the students, some of the living as sluggish as the dead with morning fatigue, began piling out of the bus. Phoebe watched Adam rise from his seat and shoulder his way into the line. He didn't look back. She slipped past Margi with the intention of talking to him before he entered the school. She caught up to him on the second short flight of steps.

"Hi," she said, taking his arm.

"Hell-o," he replied without breaking ponderous stride.

"I haven't seen you in *forever*?" she said. "I missed you."

She was pleased to see the corner of his mouth twitch upward.

"Phoebe," he said.

"I know," she said, "I'm clingy. I'm hovering. I'm altogether a huge pain in the butt."

"No," he said, almost managing to shake his head. He was walking, talking, and trying to shake his head at the same time. This was good, she thought. This was very very good.

"No?" she said, giving him a gentle nudge. "No? Don't tell me we're going back to the old days where you were afraid your friends were going to see you with me. I don't know if I could take that."

They reached the doors, and she sprang ahead to open them for him.

"No," he said.

"Thank goodness. You just want a little space, is that it?"

He stopped, and Phoebe could see a whole flock of emotions lying below the dead skin of his face. He opened his mouth and she thought he was going to say yes, and then she thought he was going to say no, and then she had no idea what he was going to say at all. He reached out a hand as heavy as a ten-pound weight, and clamped it on her shoulder.

"Phoebe," he said, the effort appearing painful. "Live."

He released her, staring down with glassy, lifeless eyes.

She thought that was his way of pushing her away, but then he held out the same hand for her to take. She walked him to his locker, holding his hand on the dial of the combination lock so he could feel the movement of her fingers.

# CHAPTER EIGHTEEN

ANTED TO TEACH her, not Joe teach her.

"Let up on the brakes, kid," said the STD not the STD Joe. "You don't want to hit the brakes when you're going into a curve. If anything you want to give it a little gas."

"I feel like I'm going too fast, Mr. Garrity," said Phoebe. Phoebe's eyes in the rearview mirror look scared but excited too.

"Nah. You're fine."

"Phoebe live," said to Phoebe not sure Phoebe understood. Don't understand. Joe the stepfather formerly known as the STD teaching Phoebe to drive now that's living. Now that's entertainment.

"I can't believe my dad is letting me do this," said Phoebe.

Joe laughed. "I just told him I had plenty of cars, so it wouldn't matter if you crashed one. And if you did I could fix it."

"He's so uptight when he tries to teach me," she said.

"Stop sign coming up. That's it. Ease on it. Good."

Good. Phoebe driving good, Joe acting good. Franken-Adam moving not good not good but better. Better. Turtle. Turtle not snail.

Dojo ahead. Phoebe parks like FrankenAdam gets into the car; slow, sloppy, and with sixteen-point turn. Gives up, parks at entrance.

"Thank you, Mr. Garrity," said Phoebe, handing keys.

"Least I could do," said Joe. Said Joe warmly. Actual warmth. Joe human. Adam not.

"Let . . . me . . . out,"

Phoebe laughed. Phoebe laughed like music, Phoebe live. Live.

"Come on, Adam," Phoebe said, "I wasn't that bad."

Speak. Speak.

"Yeah, son," said Joe. So weird name son. "She's doing all right."

Speak.

"Life . . . flashed."

Phoebe laughs hugs FrankenAdam, Phoebe lives. Her black hair perfect shiny black hair underneath my nose lungs breathe breathe breathe maybe flowers. Maybe. Miss flowers.

"Thanks for the vote of confidence, Adam," said Phoebe, laughing. "That helps."

"See you in forty-five," said Joe, waves. Phoebe waves. Wave.

Walking. Walking with hitch but walking. Phoebe skips

ahead, holds door. Hold door, one week. No, one day. Tomorrow at school.

ahead, holds door. Hold door, one week. No, one day. Tomorrow at school.

"Adam," said Master Griffin, bowing. Bald head shining, beacon. Bow. Bowing.

"And you are Phoebe Kendall."

"Yes," said Phoebe, looking at walls. Photos of Griffin in ghi, in tournament, in Gulf. Had hair. Photos of Griffin kicking ass.

"Would you like to work out today as well, Phoebe?" said Master Griffin. "First trial session is free."

Smiles. "I'm not really dressed for it."

Phoebe in black. Boots and all. Phoebe is back in skirts and ruffles and frilly lacey cuffs. Filled with life.

"You can borrow a ghi," Master Griffin said, "no shoes required."

"Maybe next time," said Phoebe. "I'll just watch if that's okay."

Griffin nods, light reflecting off bald dome head. Turns, bows to the dojo. Walk. Bow.

"We will do the basic forms again, Adam," said Master Griffin. "Please do not be shy in front of your audience."

"No."

"Maintain your focus," he said.

Nod.

Move. Moving.

See Phoebe, in mirror. Phoebe happy and sad. Both.

Moving.

Phoebe loves. Love Phoebe.

"That's it, Adam," Griffin says, "Focus. Try to feel your body as it moves."

Phoebe loves, but doesn't *love*. Loves Tommy?

"Focus."

Live, Phoebe. Forget. Just forget the dead and live. Forget, Phoebe. Phoebe, forget.

"Again."

Forget Phoebe. Try.

"Ha . . . iiiiii,"

"Good," said Master Griffin.

# CHAPTER NINETEEN

"YOU'RE DOING really well," Phoebe told Adam. He walked to the refrigerator, opened it, then withdrew the creamer, which he set on the table in front of her. "I can't believe how mobile you're getting. It was so much fun watching you."

He half smiled at her, then slumped into his chair with enough force to bump into the table and spill her coffee, sending beige liquid onto the plastic tablecloth.

"Oops," she said, and he smiled instead of getting frustrated like he would have a few weeks ago.

He'd made the coffee almost entirely himself, needing her help only to spoon enough of the grounds into the filter. He poured the water and added the sugar after getting her a mug from the cabinet.

"It's good," she said after taking a sip. "Master Griffin has really helped you."

Adam nodded. "More . . . focused . . . already"

"He's an interesting guy," she said, taking another sip. The coffee was actually a little weak because Adam's hand shook when he poured the water. She set her cup down and got up. "How long was he in the military?"

"Five . . . years," Adam said. She went over and stood behind him. "He was . . . wounded."

She started kneading his shoulders, which felt like tractor tires beneath her hands. "I didn't know that."

"Just . . . told me," he said. "Shot . . . in the . . . leg."

"You'd never know," she said. His shoulders weren't budging, so she ran her fingers through his hair. It was dry and crackled under her fingertips. She scratched the back of his neck with her fingernails.

"He told . . . me . . . because . . . thought . . . would help . . . rehabilitation."

She leaned in close, so close that her mouth was near his ear.

"Something's helping," she whispered.

There was no reaction. She hadn't really expected one, but she'd been hoping.

Time to test Tommy's theory, she thought, and kissed Adam on the neck, just below and behind his ear, where a pulse would beat if he were alive.

It was like kissing a rock, she thought. Then she thought about how much Adam loved her. He loved her so much that he suffered in silence while she was dating Tommy.

He loved her so much that he *died* for her.

She kissed him again, lower on the neck, stifling a giggle as she thought about how she could help him with his "rehabilitation." Her hand rubbed his broad shoulders and she turned and slid into his lap, kissing him on the cheek. She felt his arm and it was like steel.

He turned toward her and she looked up at him, smiling, then kissing his cheek. It would be so much easier if he could just grab her and hold her and plant his mouth on hers. Maybe he couldn't now, she thought, but perhaps with proper encouragement, he would, soon.

"Phoebe . . ." he said, his voice a husky rumble.

He died for you, she reminded herself, lifting her lips to his open mouth. *First kiss.*

"Stop!" he said, his voice loud enough to rattle the dishes in their cabinets. His arm uncoiled like a spring as he tried to stand up, shrugging Phoebe out of his lap. She fell on the floor with a loud bump.

"Stop," he repeated, looking away.

Phoebe was stunned. She sat there on the floor in the Garrity's kitchen, looking at Adam, not knowing what to say.

"I thought," she said. "I thought you . . ."

Adam shook his head, unable to meet her eyes.

She stood up, got her bag from the corner of the kitchen, and went home, her cheeks burning.

# CHAPTER TWENTY

"Y OU WANT ME to go in with you?" Margi asked as she parked.

Phoebe shook her head and opened the car door. She still wasn't entirely comfortable with her friend's relative lack of driving experience.

"No thanks, Margi. I really appreciate this."

"No worries," she said, "I need the practice. Buzz my cell when you want me to get you, I'm only fifteen minutes away."

"Okay. Thanks."

She waved good-bye, wondering if she'd even be here if Adam hadn't dumped her. Literally.

Phoebe's heart was in her throat as she walked up the narrow steps, too afraid to knock on the door. She knocked anyway.

Faith answered a moment later. "Oh hello, Phoebe," she said, somehow managing to look and sound happy and sad at the same time. "Please come in."

"I wanted to talk to Tommy," Phoebe said, stepping into the mobile home. She was annoyed at the hint of apology in her voice. She had nothing to feel sorry for.

"Certainly," Faith said. Then she hugged her.

When Faith released her she stood back and Phoebe thought that she was on the verge of tears. Her sudden show of emotion made Phoebe feel like crying too.

Faith brushed at the corner of an eye. "He's in his room. Karen's already there."

"Karen?" she said, an unexpected jealous flash bringing warmth to her skin.

Faith nodded. "Trying to talk my son out of his quest, or something," she said. Her next smile brought real warmth to her worry-lined face. "But you know Tommy's mind can't be changed once it's made up about something."

Phoebe smiled. She knew. His singularity of purpose was one of the things she most admired about him.

"Sometimes I think what makes these kids come back from the dead is just plain stubbornness," Faith said, laughing. "Do you want something to drink?"

"No thanks." She could hear Karen's voice from down the hall.

"Well," Faith said, getting out the milk and a bottle of chocolate syrup for herself, "if you change your mind, help yourself."

Phoebe said she would and walked through the living room to Tommy's room. Karen was standing by Tommy's desk, her hands waving, telling Tommy that he was wrong. A hot spike of anger bloomed inside her as she watched Karen berating Tommy, who sat in passive stillness on the edge of his bed. Despite the harshness of Karen's delivery, Phoebe felt as if she was intruding on a moment of deep intimacy between them, and almost stepped away. Before she could, Tommy saw her in the doorway and the blue of his eyes seemed to brighten. A moment later he willed himself to smile. Phoebe knocked lightly on the doorjamb.

Karen turned. "Phoebe," she said after a pause. "Thank heavens, another sane person in the room. Will you please help me talk some sense into him?"

"I don't think I could do that," Phoebe said. Tommy rose from his seat. He was wearing faded blue jeans, a dark blue T-shirt, and battered white high-tops. His room smelled like Z. Phoebe liked it.

Karen grunted in frustration and turned away.

"I was afraid you'd go without saying good-bye," Phoebe said, holding her left elbow in her right hand. Tommy looked at her, and she was having a difficult time looking back, not because he was dead, or because he could stare without blinking for hours at a time. She had trouble returning his stare because there was something there, something that wasn't longing exactly, but longing and love and sadness and understanding all wrapped together. No one ever looked at her with quite that combination of emotions. It was this look and the feelings it caused in her that first attracted her to him, but now she found herself wilting before the intensity of it.

"I . . . will never . . . say . . . good-bye . . . to you," he said.

Phoebe held out her hand. He took it.

"But I thought . . . you said . . . good-bye . . . to me."

Phoebe was aware of Karen taking a seat on the edge of Tommy's computer desk, her arms folded across her chest and a chagrinned expression on her flawless face. But Phoebe didn't care.

"I did," she said. "I did, Tommy, but . . . but I didn't want it to be forever."

Tommy looked away. "But you . . . don't know . . . what you . . . wanted it to be."

"No. No, I didn't. I don't."

He let her hand slip from his. "I don't know when I'll be back."

He looked sure of himself again, Phoebe thought. It was something that was missing in the weeks since Adam's death, that sense of purpose.

Phoebe bit her lip.

"I know," she said.

"You know?" Karen said. "You know? What is the . . . matter with you, Phoebe? He can't . . . leave. He's our . . . leader . . . for heaven's sake! King . . . Zombie. Baron . . . Samedi."

She took Tommy's arm, and Phoebe's. Her grip was cold but insistent.

"You can't . . . go, Tommy. I'm . . . sorry it didn't work out . . . between . . ."

Tommy raised his hand, cutting her off. "I have to go," he said.

"They all . . . look up to you, Tommy. They . . . *need* . . . you. They . . ."

Horrible choking sounds came somewhere deep within Karen. Her grip on Phoebe's arm tightened painfully.

"Karen," she said, reaching for her with her free arm as the other went numb in Karen's unbreakable grip. Karen's eyes looked pained and scared—lost, the lights behind the crystals fading. Phoebe ignored her own pain and stroked Karen's cheek.

"Shhhh," she said, and repeated it until Karen focused on her. She began to calm down, finally releasing Phoebe from her death grip.

"You . . . can't . . . go . . . Tommy," Karen said, her "breathing" ragged, the sound of a slow fan with a piece of paper caught in the blades. "I . . . they . . . need you."

Tommy took her face gently in his hands.

"Karen," he said, his voice a calming whisper, "that's why I need to go. Because you need me."

And Phoebe knew, watching him, that that was the truth. If he really was "Baron Samedi, King of the Zombies" as they all suspected, he wasn't going to be able to rule his kingdom from Oakvale, Connecticut. He'd have to go elsewhere— Washington, probably. Somewhere he could get government recognition for the undead. The guilt lifted from her shoulders. He wasn't leaving because of her.

Faith appeared in the doorway. "Is everything okay in here? Karen, honey, are you—"

"We're fine, Mom," Tommy said, still holding Karen, still looking at her as though he could pour his own strength into her simply by staring. "Thank you."

Faith looked at Phoebe for confirmation and received it.

"Okay, then," she said. "Can I get anyone anything?"

"We're fine, Mom. Really."

When she left, Karen sat on the edge of the bed. "I can't," she said. "I can't do it, Tommy. I'm not . . . you."

"You don't need to be," he said. "Just be . . . yourself."

She gave an ironic laugh. "Sure."

"They look up to . . . you," he said, "and the living too . . . more . . . than me."

Phoebe saw an odd expression cross Karen's face.

"For all the right reasons, I'm sure," she snapped, running both her hands through her long platinum hair, which seemed to frizz out in her distress. "What about . . . the Web site? How are you going to do the Web site?"

"I'm not," he said, a smile stretching one corner of his mouth. "You two are."

Karen looked at Phoebe and back again.

"What?" they said in unison.

He smiled. "You are. It will be part of your work-study credit at the foundation. They are going to . . . pay . . . for everything. The hosting, the fees. Advertising, even, so we can reach more of . . . our people. They are going to pay . . . you . . . for your work."

"Tommy," Phoebe said. "We can't do that. It's your site."

He shook his head. "That is . . . the problem. It needs to be . . . more than that. You are a . . . great writer, Phoebe. I think if . . . you . . . did a blog, it would be as helpful for . . . the dead . . . as it would be for the living."

Phoebe thought of the poems she'd written for him, and let

the full weight of the compliment settle upon her. Tommy used the moment to turn his attention to Karen.

"And you . . . could be too . . . Karen. If you bothered. You are one of the most . . . gifted . . . people I've ever known. In every . . . sense of the word."

"But mysocalledundeath, Tommy," Karen said, ignoring him. "You can't stop . . . doing that."

"I won't," he said. "The foundation bought me . . . a laptop. Wireless . . . Internet."

"Wow," Phoebe said. "What will you do for power?"

"Libraries, bookstores. Bus stations. Wherever I can find . . . an outlet. I'll e-mail the . . . road reports . . . to you . . . and you . . . can post them."

"So we are going to be your employees?" Karen said. "I've already . . . got . . . a job."

"This is . . . more fun . . . and it will get . . . you out of the lab. Or Davidson's . . . office."

"Well, that's pretty . . . cool," Karen said. "But . . . do you really think it is a good . . . idea for the foundation to fund this? And have access to all of your subscribers?"

Tommy sat on the bed next to Karen. "I . . . put a lot . . . of thought into that question," he said. "It is . . . a risk. But I think the benefit . . . of the risk . . . is great. I think with their . . . backing . . . we can really reach a lot of people. Traditionally biotic, too, especially with Phoebe . . . writing. The foundation has resources to get the site more . . . media . . . attention. We have an opportunity to make . . . our cause . . . a real youth movement."

"A youth movement," Karen said with a wry smile. "In this country, only the young die good."

"That's funny," Tommy said. "You come up with that one yourself?"

"Pretty clever, aren't . . . I?"

"Yes, Karen. You . . . are." Tommy said, and again Phoebe felt like an intruder.

As though he could sense this, Tommy turned toward her. "What do you . . . think, Phoebe? Will you help . . . us?"

I'll help you, Tommy, she thought. "You know I will. I joined the program so I could learn more about the differently biotic and how I could help."

They talked a little more after that, about what needed doing and how it could get done. Tommy spoke with unrehearsed passion about how good this project was going to be for the community of the dead. He was leaving in the morning.

She and Karen left into the chilly night air after hugs all around. Phoebe had on her puffy black coat with fake fur; Karen wore her usual uniform of short plaid skirt and white blouse. "I'm sorry I freaked out on you in there," she said.

"Oh." Phoebe was amazed at how her friend seemed to shimmer and glow in the moonlight. "I'm a little freaked out too."

"He's still totally in love with you." Karen said. "Adam too. You get all the good ones."

Karen wouldn't have believed that if she'd seen Phoebe flat on her butt in the Garrity's kitchen, she thought.

"No, I . . ."

"Shh. Denying it will only make me more jealous. You know it's true and it's okay. They aren't wrong to fall in love with you. I'm a little in love with you myself."

A reply caught in Phoebe's throat, and her cheeks went warm in the cool air. She wasn't sure if Karen was kidding—should she make a joke of it, or tell Karen not to worry, there was someone out there for her too and all that jazz? She hadn't told anyone what had happened between her and Adam. She wasn't at the point where she could talk about her relationships with anyone, because she felt so many conflicting things.

"Oh, I know what you're thinking," Karen said. "Someone's out there for me too. Don't worry, I've got plenty of them chasing me. Just not the right ones. Hey, looks like your ride is here."

Phoebe looked over at the entrance of the trailer park, where the headlights of Margi's mom's car swung a wide arc and cut through the darkness to illuminate the patch of dirt where Phoebe and Karen were talking.

"So, we partners on this?" Karen said, holding out her hand.

"Partners." Phoebe clasped it.

"You want a ride, Karen?" Phoebe asked as Margi gave the horn two quick beeps.

"No, thanks. It's a beautiful night and I promised Mal I'd go over and read to him for a little while. I want to say hey to Margi over there, though."

Phoebe thrust her hands into her pockets as Karen skipped over to the car, smiling as an old Echo and the Bunnymen tune from back in the day wafted out along with the heat that Margi kept on full blast whenever she drove.

*How does she keep those patent leather shoes so shiny?* Phoebe wondered, her hands seeking warmth in her pockets but finding only a scrap of paper. She withdrew it and saw that it was a carefully folded piece of lined notebook paper, the paper on which she had written her first poem for Tommy. He had written a note at the bottom of it, his words a squat and blocky blue print. He must have slipped her the note when they hugged good-bye.

HOLD ONTO THIS FOR ME, he wrote, I'M GOING TO WANT IT BACK SOMEDAY.

Margi and Karen were chattering away, and neither noticed as she folded the note back into a tight square and put it back into her pocket. She decided she was not going to be sad about this; Tommy was going out to make the world a better place for zombies everywhere, and she would be helping him to do it. Getting the note back only meant that he intended to return someday.

*But I miss him already,* she thought, getting into the sauna that was Margi's car.

"It's pretty late," Margi said after they said good-bye to Karen, who headed straight for the woods.

"It is," Phoebe agreed.

"So Karen was already over there, huh?"

"She was."

Margi sighed. "You aren't going to tell me what happened, are you?"

"I'm not," Phoebe said, "at least, not tonight." She knew she'd tell Margi in time, but right now she felt too raw, with Adam rejecting her and Tommy going away. Margi, like Karen, was always joking about her many options—and now she had none. She just didn't want to talk about it,

Margi shook her head.

"Phoebe Kendall, Queen of the Mysterious Silences. Can you at least tell me if you and Tommy are okay? I mean, it kind of ended quickly between you two, and I know I was weird about it, but he is a really nice guy, and . . ."

"Yes," Phoebe said, the paper smooth and cool in her hand. "Yes, we're okay."

# CHAPTER
# TWENTY-ONE

PHOEBE, LIVING. Watched, waited. Margi came driving shock fear Margi driving! Margi and Phoebe left, gone who knows where. Live, Phoebe, live.

FrankenAdam trying. Walking. Talking. Opened door yesterday and this passes for thrills in realm of the undead. Turning a doorknob not so easy. Thinking. I'm thinking. Thinking more clearly, more quickly. Why?

"Are you okay, son?" said Big Joe. STD gone, Big Joe. Watching television, hockey. Like basketball Joe likes hockey we watch basketball. Don't mind. Joe on third beer. Brought him third beer walked opened door got beer closed door walked could not pop tab. Oh well. Next time.

"Okay." Dead but okay. Can do most of Master Griffin's forms. Can bow and raise.

"You seem awfully quiet tonight," he said.

Laugh! Laugh! Laugh!

Can't laugh. Yet. Turn. Look. Joe watching game, sipping beer. Intent. Comedy unintended. Speak.

"Okay."

Much later, knock on window. My window. Bedroom window. Drop book, get up.

Tommy.

Walk to the door. Kitchen door. Walk to the door on quiet feet. Tommy makes me feel stronger. What he accomplished. Braver.

Open door. Cold night, no coat. Don't feel it. Join Tommy in backyard. He's got a backpack, looks heavy. Moonlight. Feel smarter, faster around Tommy. Tommy or the night air.

"Adam," said Tommy. And then remember: Tommy is leaving.

"I'm leaving tonight," said Tommy. "I wanted to come to say good-bye. And to . . . thank you."

"Thank . . . you?" Speaking. A hitch but not a pause. A gap but not a chasm. Night air. Will miss Tommy. Will miss Tommy even though Phoebe is in love with him, not FrankenAdam.

Probably still be alive if never met him. Miss him, maybe. Maybe not.

Tommy nods. "For being my friend, Adam. For accepting me on the . . . football team. For standing up for me in the woods . . . twice."

Smile. "Phoebe."

Tommy smiles too. "Yeah, I know it was for Phoebe. Mostly. I know what she means to you."

Do you? Think about it. Do you know how much love have

for her and how much it hurts? Thinking this. Thinking that maybe he does.

"But I know it was for me too. I appreciate it. Which is why I feel . . . guilty . . . for the favor . . . I'm about to ask of you."

"Favor?" Can speak more quickly if just repeat the last thing everyone says. Tommy looks at Phoebe's house, the house where Phoebe is Living. Do you know the feeling, Tommy?

"A favor. I'm asking you . . . to watch out for them. Our friends. The . . . people . . . at the Haunted House. The kids in the class. Watch out for them for me."

"Real . . . useful." When alive and "watching out" for people managed to get clobbered with a baseball bat and then next time managed to get killed. Unqualified when alive. Now? Have trouble getting in and out of a car and wants to "watch over" people? Maybe not so smart.

"You are really useful, Adam," he said. "You've got a strength to you . . . not just physical. You do what's right. You could really . . . help people."

Waited. Wait a lot now.

"What I'm really asking, Adam . . . I'm asking you to step up. It's not just because I'm . . . leaving. The dead kids . . . need strength. You have it. Step up and let them see it."

"Trying."

"I know you're trying," he says. "Sometimes trying is enough, and sometimes it isn't. You need to step up."

Want to argue. Throw a punch even. Sort of. Don't.

He's right.

"You can do it, Adam," he said. "I know you can do it. But

more . . . important . . . we need you to do it. Things are going to get . . . rougher . . . for our people, Adam."

Saw something in his eyes that scared me, scary as the thought of Phoebe living her life without me. Reminded of Smiley.

"We won't be able to . . . live . . . at the fringe much longer. They won't let us."

"They?" Doing it again. FrankenAdam.

"The trads," he said. "The 'beating hearts.' But also our own people, Adam. Most don't want to stay in the shadows forever, and the others want to see shadows covering everyone."

"Tak." Thinking out loud. Thinking, like the brain energy or whatever making body bend its knees or swing its arms was freed up, free to think higher thoughts and larger concepts. Saw that Tommy agreed.

"Yes, Takayuki," he said, "and he isn't alone."

"I'll step."

"I know you will, Adam. She'll need you to. We all will." He clasped my shoulder.

Shook hands, wished him well on his travels. Watched him walk down the road until the moonlight didn't touch him anymore. When he was gone thought of Phoebe looked up at her window hoped her bed was warm and her dreams untroubled and was thankful very thankful that she was alive. That she was living. Thankful gave my life for her and that despite all the heartache and frustration would do it again in a heartbeat if had a heartbeat to give. Even if she loved but didn't *love* me.

Worked out practiced forms until the sun came up, until red fingers of light reached over frost-covered skin.

# CHAPTER
# TWENTY-TWO

"SO," PETE SAID, "do you have a big holiday planned?"

Davidson didn't look up from his magazine. He'd brought in a large stack, which he'd been reading in silence the entire three hours that Pete had been watching the bank of monitors continue to reveal nothing.

"Holiday?" Davidson said, turning a page. *Time, Newsweek, Psychology Today*—Davidson was a magazine-reading fiend.

"Yeah. Thanksgiving, in a couple days."

Davidson looked up, his pale blue eyes empty of expression.

"Oh," he said, "I'm working."

"That sucks," Pete said. "Will your family send over some leftovers, at least?"

He didn't know why he was bothering; talking with Davidson was like talking to a tree stump. But the boredom of staring at the monitors had grown to soul-crushing proportions; the only movement of the whole day was the geek zombie from the dormitory taking a short walk from his room outside. Pete had watched him walk twenty paces toward the fence, stop, walk ten paces to his left, stop, and then walk back to the dorm. This took the geek twenty minutes.

"I don't have a family," Davidson said. Pete wondered if he was just pretending to read, because his eyes didn't seem to move at all while the magazines were in front of him.

"That sucks." Pete said. "I feel that way too."

He didn't know why he was running his mouth, anyhow. Davidson didn't give a rat's heinie about his personal problems, and Pete wasn't used to sharing. Thanksgiving at Casa de Wimp was a theater of pain to him; the Wimp had his parents over—they showed their gratitude for his mother's efforts in the kitchen by criticizing every little thing, right down to the way she'd organized the pickle tray.

"You have a difficult home life," Davidson said. Pete couldn't tell if it was a statement or a question.

"Not difficult," Pete replied. "I just hate it."

"Your mother? Your stepfather?"

"My mother's second husband," Pete said, aware of how churlish he sounded.

"Why don't you like them?"

Pete wanted to tell him to forget it, to just read his stupid magazines. "They're weak," he said.

Davidson flipped another page.

"He's the biggest wuss on the planet. An accountant that wouldn't ask for his money back if he found rat turds in his dinner at a restaurant. And she's weak for being with a loser like him."

"And you're strong."

Again, Pete couldn't tell if it was a statement or a question, nor could he tell if Davidson was mocking him.

"Strong enough," he said.

Davidson looked up again.

"Strong enough to go mop the lab," Duke said.

Pete wheeled the mop bucket down to the lab, gaining access to the room via the keycard that hung on a clip from his uniform shirt. The keycard had his name and a mug shot.

The lab was full of odd sounds, random blips, and tones from a host of indecipherable computerized machines that were conducting experiments while the experimenters themselves were at home baking pumpkin pie. Pete wondered briefly what Thanksgiving was like at the Hunter home. Did pretty little Angela make a big bird for her scarecrow of a father? Did they invite a bunch of dead friends over for a gnaw on a turkey leg? Did she sit around psychoanalyzing everyone at the table?

What a fraud, Pete thought as he wrung out his mop and started in the far corner of the lab. He hip-checked a table on which a machine that looked sort of like a coffeemaker was humming, a beaker of greenish liquid cooking or electrolyzing or whatever behind a glass door. He hoped the jostle ruined whatever mad science Alish was trying to conduct, just as he hoped tripling the amount of bleach he normally used on the floor would cause some of the findings to go awry.

When he really thought about it, none of this stuff made any sense to him. The lab wasn't climate controlled—Pete knew from experience that it was normally much warmer; today the lab would seem cold if he weren't moving around. He thought that if it was really a scientific lab, people would be here in masks and hairnets and clear plastic gloves and all that, instead of just the too-big stained lab coats that the scarecrow gave to everyone. It didn't make sense.

He mopped a section, then went to work on one of the stainless-steel tables, using a laundered white cloth and some spray cleaner from a bottle he hooked on the edge of his bucket. He spritzed the table in three places, then aimed a forth spritz at a rack of open test tubes before making lazy circles on the table with his less than clean cloth.

"Take it your father didn't call," Davidson said from the doorway.

Pete grunted with surprise, wondering if Davidson was onto his little acts of scientific vandalism. The baleful eyes revealed nothing.

"Isn't anyone worried about these cleaning products affecting the experiments?" Pete asked, ignoring Davidson's question/statement. Of course Darren hadn't called. All Darren called about was to see if Pete had gotten his scar fixed yet, and Pete was pretty sure he'd even lost interest in that.

"I don't think you could ruin any of the experiments if you tried," Davidson said, the ghost of a smile on his bloodless lips. "None of the real experiments are done here."

Pete leaned his mop against the wringer. "What are you talking about?" he asked. "I've seen the . . . I've seen Alish take blood or whatever it is from the zom . . . from the living-impaired kids."

"Would people know that you're a murderer just by looking at you?"

"What?"

"Or would they have to talk to you a little? Watch you. See the look on your face when a zombie walks into your field of vision, like the look on your face when Cooper takes his pointless stroll? I wish I could hold a mirror up to you every time you see our resident zombie leave his room on the monitors."

"What the hell are you talking about?" Pete said. His palms were sweaty, his mouth dry. His heart was racing and the lab equipment chirped like a field of crickets on a hot day late in the summer.

"Sometimes you have to peel the skin back," Davidson said, and now he really was smiling. "Sometimes you have to go beneath the surface. Sometimes you have to dig."

Pete opened his mouth and then closed it. The look on Davidson's face was like the look on the half-faced zombie just before he'd cut him. It was a look that held nothing, not hatred, not anger, nothing.

"I'm not sure what we're talking about right now."

"You will," Davidson said. "Keep the cleaning chemicals out of the experiments. We wouldn't want you accidentally discovering anything."

He left, leaving the sliding lab door open behind him. Pete heard the arrival of the Undead Studies students down the hall; Pinky's voice was shrill enough to grind steel.

Pete didn't realize he was shaking until he took hold of his mop again.

# CHAPTER
# TWENTY-THREE

"MS. HUNTER?" Margi said, "I really, *really* have a problem with Pete Martinsburg doing his community service here."

Phoebe stiffened on hearing his name, but Adam remained motionless on the seat beside her. Margi had pointed out Pete lurking in the shadow of one of the labs, leaning on his mop and looking at them as they entered the building. She'd wanted to take Adam's arm and rush him down the hall before he saw Pete, but she'd been too embarrassed after her smooth moves in the Garrity's kitchen to do much more than say hello to him when he climbed into the van.

"I can understand that," Angela said. "And I'm sure you're not the only one here who feels that way. The court thought that it was a good way to bring him face-to-face with the consequences of his actions."

"He threatened all of us," Phoebe said. "He said he was going to hurt everyone on the Undead Studies list."

"He . . . killed Evan Talbott," Colette said. "And . . . Adam."

"We don't really know about Evan, Colette," Angela said.

"He *told* me he did it," Phoebe said. "When they asked me for a statement after Adam was murdered, I told the police. I told the prosecuting attorney. I told everybody who would listen, but they all said there was nothing anyone could do about it. There isn't a law to prevent someone from killing the dead. The attorney actually told me it might hurt their case against him for Adam's murder if she were to bring it up."

"He winked at me when he walked by the office," Margi said. "He's dangerous, Ms. Hunter."

Angela frowned and made a notation in her pad. "I'll try to see that he's kept away from the students."

"Is it true that he is getting counseling?" Margi said. "With you?"

"It is."

"What are you talking about with him?"

"I can't tell you that, Margi."

"Sure," Margi said, shifting her seat. "It wouldn't be proper for poor Pete's rights to be infringed on."

"Margi . . ."

"He killed Adam!" she said. "It doesn't feel safe to be in the same building as him! What about our rights? Why can't dangerous kids just be taken away from the rest of us?"

"I'll do what I can, Margi," she said. "I'll see to it that he only works and does his therapy here when you're all out of the building."

"How can you do that?" Phoebe said, wishing that Tommy was there to fight this. "Sylvia is still here in the building, isn't she? And Cooper, you're staying here too, aren't you?"

"I don't . . . know the guy," Cooper said. Beside him Melissa, her mask incongruous with the heavy weight of the conversation, began writing on her whiteboard.

"You didn't know those white van guys, either," Thorny said.

"Watch out for him. I think he would find you . . . guilty . . . by association," Karen said. "Angela, you know that this is a big part of the reason why Tayshawn refused to rejoin this class, don't you?"

"Because he was worried that Pete would be coming here?"

"He wasn't worried," Karen said. "He was furious. In his words, it was the biggest display of hypocrisy that he'd ever seen, an organization supposedly . . . created . . . to help the undead harboring someone who has sworn to destroy them . . ."

"We aren't *harboring* him. We're—"

". . . and has acted upon his promise."

Angela held her hand up. "I understand why you're all so upset. I really do. We agreed to assist with Martinsburg's sentencing because, frankly, we thought we were better qualified than anyone else. We also thought it would be an opportunity to really dig at the roots of the prejudice that all differently biotic people experience. If we can get him to articulate the reasons why he has so much hatred inside him, then maybe we can fight it. If we understand it, maybe we can find a way to help people, traditionally and differently biotic alike, to find common ground."

"So you think you can . . . reason with him?" Karen said.

Angela nodded. "We're hoping. I think we can learn something from people like Pete. I think at the very least we may be able to find ways to prevent others from becoming like him."

"Good . . . luck," Cooper said. "My experience . . . says . . . otherwise."

Phoebe thought of Tommy. Everyone in the class seemed out of sorts and lost without his leadership.

"Look," Angela said. "The way to deal with prejudice isn't to ignore it, or worse, to bury it under a rock. It's to deal with it head-on."

"Tayshawn would agree with you there," Karen said. "He would just have a . . . different . . . definition of 'head-on.'"

"Karen," Angela said, "I would like the chance to talk to Tayshawn. I'd really appreciate it if you would let him know."

Karen paused deliberately before answering. "I will."

"Thank you. Now . . . I'm sorry, Melissa. Did you have something to add?"

Melissa's arm was raised, and her comedy mask seemed nearly sinister beneath the coppery mane of her hair. When she nodded, her puffy green velvet sleeve drooped a few inches from her wrist, revealing patches of cracked, raw, curling skin that resembled the pages of a book thrown into a fire. She turned her board around.

ANGELA IS RIGHT, she'd written, WE ALL NEED 2 UNDER-
STAND EA. OTHER

"Come . . . on . . . Melissa," Cooper said, leaning toward
her. "You really . . . believe that . . . would work? You think the
people that . . . burned . . . Dickinson House . . . can understand us? Or we understand . . . them?"

She rubbed the board clean and her marker squeaked as she
wrote.

I'D ♥ 2 TRY

"Give me . . . a break."

I'D ♥ FOR THEM 2 C ME

"They'd be . . . glad, Mel!" Cooper said. "They'd . . . be
glad! They wouldn't feel guilty . . . at all."

Phoebe watched Melissa drag the white cloth back and forth
over the white board, erasing the heart, erasing her words. The
room was silent as they all waited for her to write another line.

TOMMY WOULD AGREE WITH ME

"Good for . . . Tommy," he said. "Easy to do . . . when he
isn't . . . here."

"Hey!" exclaimed Thorny, whose idolization of Tommy
was only exceeded by his idolization of Adam.

"She's right," Phoebe said. "Tommy would meet the situation directly. That's why he did things like join the football
team and start the Web site. It's why he's going on this trip."
She wondered if that was why he dated her, "He's going out to
confront the world with his existence."

"You think he'd be okay with Pete Martinsburg working
right down the hall?" Margi asked. It was one of the first ques-

tions that anyone had posed today that sounded more like a question than a condemnation.

"I think he would, Gee," Phoebe answered.

"You're right. He *would*," Karen said. "He thinks that safety is an . . . illusion, anyway."

"Well . . . he got that one . . . right," Cooper said.

"There's only so much you can do to take precautions these days, I think," Phoebe said. "I know not everyone is going to accept the fact that I want to hang out with zombies. Some people just get so crazy . . . it's like there's so much pressure on everyone in our society, no matter what age you are. People break under that pressure. And when they break, they either give up or lash out. Until everyone is okay with the differently biotic, and I don't think that is going to happen for years, a generation, maybe, we're going to be dealing with violence."

"We're zombies, sweetie," Karen said. "Forget . . . differently biotic."

Phoebe shot her a look and would have thrown a pen if she'd had one handy.

"Great," Margi said, "the crazies will hate us, and safety is an illusion. That doesn't mean I have to go playing with rattlesnakes."

"I'll talk to Mr. Davidson," Angela said. "He'll keep Peter out of sight, if not out of mind. I'll understand if any of you are still uncomfortable with the situation and want to withdraw from the class. I'll see what I can do about getting you partial credit."

She was looking at Margi when she said it, and it was Margi's turn to shy away.

"Nobody's quitting," Thorny said.

"I wouldn't blame anyone if they wanted to withdraw," Angela said, as though he hadn't even spoken. "Margi and Cooper both have a point. The path we're on isn't without risks. "

"Nobody's quitting," Thorny repeated. Phoebe was about to say something when Adam's spoke.

"Want . . . to . . . kill . . . him," he said. His slow, uninflected voice lent an even greater degree of menace to the word "kill." The word cleaved through the conversation. Somehow as the debate about Pete went on, everyone had managed to forget that his victim was sitting right in the room with them, and that he might have an opinion on what should or should not be done with and for his murderer.

"But . . ." he said, and though it took him some time to finish his sentence, everyone waited without interrupting. Phoebe watched him struggle to form the words, and she was close enough to hear the raspy wheeze that preceded each sound as he tried to work his lungs to force air through his voice box. She wanted to hug him, but knew that to do so would be a betrayal, a public admission of his debilitated state. He was having a hard enough time forgiving her for the kindnesses she did show.

"Would . . . do . . . no . . . good," he said.

Phoebe allowed herself to smile. Because she was so proud of Adam, both because of the effort it took him to speak and because of what he was saying. More, she was smiling because Adam was choosing to follow Tommy, and not Takayuki.

"Tommy . . . is . . . right."

It was Adam's big moment, but again Phoebe found herself thinking of Tommy, and wishing he was with them.

# CHAPTER
# TWENTY-FOUR

ALISH WAS muttering to himself as he stared at the computer, where long chemical equations scrolled to the bottom of the screen. Thorny, looking like the bass player in an eighties synth band with the cuffs of his lab coat rolled up, sat on the edge of his desk, checking the time on his cell phone every few minutes. Colette sat in a chair, no doubt wondering if Alish would require another hank of hair, vial of fluid, or patch of skin. Phoebe wondered if she would be as compliant if she were differently biotic.

"Correlations," Alish muttered.

"Did you find something, sir?" Phoebe asked, trying to make sense of the strings of data on his screen. She'd been allowed to skip the last couple shifts of the "work" part of the work study requirement of the Undead Studies class, and was confused by what it was Alish was trying to accomplish.

"What? What?" he said, his wrinkled face far more corpse-like than Colette's in the white-blue glow of the screen. He looked up at Phoebe and pushed his wire bifocals up the length of his aquiline nose.

"Well, yes," he said. "But in the fields of scientific inquiry finding 'something' may mean that what you have, in fact, is 'nothing,' as in, the something you thought was something really turned out to be nothing."

"Huh?" Thorny said, dropping his phone into the deep pocket of his coat. He had a game later in the day—the upside of all of the stars of the team either being injured (permanently, in Adam's case) or under house arrest meant that Thorny got a lot of time on the field.

"In this case," Alish continued, "there does not seem to be a correlation between the presence of formaldehyde in the body and a return to existence."

Phoebe thought his choice of words was interesting, not to mention the course of his study. Adam hadn't been dead long enough for a trip to the morgue, never got the ole formaldehyde inoculation, so ruling out formaldehyde as being a "causal agent" of the whole undead thing seemed self-evident.

Dallas Jones, the first known zombie, was killed on camera while robbing a convenience store, then arose a few hours after his death with no visit to the mortician either. Sometimes Alish's "science" was pretty suspect.

"Isn't formaldehyde a compound?

"What? Yes. Yes, Ms. Kendall. It certainly is."

"Is there something in the compound that could be causing the return?"

He frowned, the skin of his face sagging down as the muscles around his mouth pulled. "My studies would indicate no, that that would not be the case."

"This is going to sound rude and I don't mean it to be," she said. "But what have yours, or anyone's, studies indicated?"

Alish smiled, his long fingers tapping on the edge of his desk. "Not much, I'm afraid."

"Can I go, sir?" Thorny asked. "I've got to get to the game."

"Certainly, Mr. Harrowwood," Alish said. "Score seventeen touchdowns for us."

"I'll try, sir," Thorny said, sprinting past the lab equipment.

Alish turned back to Phoebe. "What we know," he said, "is that there are at least fifteen hundred and sixty-three differently biotic persons in this country."

Fifteen hundred and sixty-three seemed like such a small number, especially when she'd met at least twenty of them. She'd never counted the pictures on "the wall of the dead" at the Haunted House but estimated that there were two hundred.

Tommy once told her he had over six hundred subscribers, but didn't know how many of them were dead.

"Of that number, we have some type of reliable documentation on half. All of those we have good documentation for died between the ages of thirteen and eighteen. The verifiable period of 'true death' has been between two minutes, fifty-seven seconds and eight days, three minutes."

"Eight days?"

Alish nodded.

"I was gone five . . . days," Colette called from her chair. She looked bored, but most of the dead looked at least a little bored if they weren't trying to emote.

"Yes. There does not appear to be a relationship between the time spent dead and the amount of functionality the person has. There also does not appear to be a relationship between the time period one exists as differently biotic and the amount of functionality they have."

"Time is not on their side," Phoebe asked. "In increasing functionality."

Alish took his bifocals off and closed his eyes. "It does not appear that way, no."

"What helps?" Phoebe said, thinking of Adam trying to will his body into a karate stance.

"We have not found anything that helps," he said.

"Music," Colette called. Alish opened his eyes and looked back at her. "Hugs."

"I interrupted you," Phoebe said to Alish. "What else do we know?"

"Not much, I'm afraid," he said. "Nothing conclusive. Our friends Ms. DeSonne and Mr. Williams—no offense, dear Miss Beauvoir—appear to be on the higher end of the functionality scale. There is a girl in California who only blinks. Some of the dead appear to regain senses beyond sight and sound. The degree of touch sensation appears to differ among them. We know that if the brain is destroyed, functionality ceases. We know that traditional biology does not seem to apply."

"What do you mean?"

"No heartbeat, no circulation, no respiratory activity," he said, and there were teeth, faintly yellow and crooked, in his smile. "They're dead, Ms. Kendall. It just doesn't make any sense."

"I can . . . smell . . . that perfume . . . Margi wears now," Colette said. "I . . . couldn't do that . . . before."

"Interesting," Alish said, smiling at her. He looked like he wanted to figure out how to fit her inside a petri dish.

"So what are you trying to find?" Phoebe asked.

"Oh, a lot of things," he said. Then he leaned forward and motioned with a crooked finger for her to lean in.

"Miss Kendall," he said, his voice a dry whispery rasp, "I'm trying to find the secret of life."

He laughed then, and lifted the hooked finger he'd beckoned her with to his lips, as though it were their little secret.

"What a . . . weirdo," Colette said from the front seat of Margi's car, "a total . . . creepy weirdo."

Margi was clapping her hands to try and warm them up while waiting for the heater to kick in, her bangles muffled by her mittens and her coat.

"Who?" she said. "Alish?"

"First . . . guess," Colette said. She turned on the radio so that they could listen to the Restless Dead CD that they had listened to only fifty-three times that week.

"Ugh . . . I hated it working in the lab," Margi said. "But Angela is more than a little creepy too."

"What do you mean?" Phoebe said, leaning forward so she could hear over the bass-heavy drone pouring from the speakers behind her head.

"Well, she's perfect," Margi said. "Just look at her. Nobody is that perfect."

"Except . . . me," said Colette.

"I stand corrected. But really, how could she possibly be the daughter of leathery old Alish? He must have conceived her in his sixties."

"Conceived her . . . in a state . . . of scientific inquiry," Colette said. They all broke up.

Phoebe was the first one to control her giggling. "I just don't know what he's really trying to do. It seems so random."

"He told Tommy once that he was looking for a cure," Margi said. "Tommy got pretty mad. He said he didn't have a disease."

"I don't . . . know." Colette's expression was wistful. "I . . . wouldn't mind . . . being . . . cured."

Margi put the car in gear and rolled down the hill to the gate.

"Okay, Duke," she said, waiting for him to trigger the release so they could leave the compound. And then whispering, "Speaking of creepy."

"Yeah," Colette said, "if anybody should be . . . a zombie . . ."

The gate clicked open and began to separate in the center.

"Creeeeeeeeeeeak," Margi said. "So Pheebes, are you hanging out with us today? It's a beautiful gray Saturday. I had my mom buy some expensive coffee, which is perfect for a day like this. We can go through my recent MP3 downloads."

"I can't, Gee," Phoebe said.

"Can't, or won't?" Phoebe knew that Margi had been

aiming for a gentle chiding tone, but she could hear the irritation in her voice.

"I've got to check in on Adam," she said. The silence from the front seat told her how everyone felt about that excuse.

"He's . . . moving . . . better," Colette said after a time.

"Yes."

"And talking . . . too."

"He's really making some progress," Phoebe said.

"Well." Margi pressed the accelerator a little too hard. "How about I pick him up too?"

"I . . . I don't think that is a good idea right now," Phoebe said, wishing that Margi would back off, knowing that she wouldn't.

"Why not?"

"He's still very self-conscious," she said. "Can we take a rain check?"

Margi looked at her in the rearview, and it was obvious she didn't buy it. She opened her mouth to reply, but Colette beat her to it.

"I was . . . that way . . . at first . . . too," she said. "Tell him . . . when he is . . . ready . . . he's always . . . welcome."

"Thanks," she said, deciding that she'd go see Adam when she got home and maybe talk to him about what had happened. Putting off the inevitable hadn't worked so well with Tommy, and she didn't want a replay of that scene.

She regretted her decision soon after knocking on the Garritys' door. Jimmy opened it.

"He's at karate, pretending he's a real person," Jimmy

said, his contempt for her clear in his dark eyes. "Go the hell home."

"Tell him I stopped by, please?" she said.

Jimmy's laugh matched his personality. "Yeah, right," he said. "I don't talk to corpses."

He slammed the door, and Phoebe could hear Adam's mother yelling at him from a room deeper in the house. She sighed and crossed the short stretch of lawn that separated their houses, then went inside hers. Her mother, still in a sharp, blue business suit, was moving around the kitchen and pulling things from various cabinets and drawers.

"Hi, honey," she said, reaching high into the cabinet where her father—who did most of the cooking—had arranged the spices. "How was your day?"

"Filled with wonder," Phoebe said, giving her a kiss on the cheek. "How about yours?"

Her mom smiled and leaned into her daughter's hug. "I don't know about 'filled with wonder,'" she said, "but it could be worse. Your father is going to be a little late, so I told him we'd get dinner ready."

"Sure," Phoebe said, looking at what her mother had spread on the counter: bread crumbs, heavy cream, tarragon, egg noodles. "Tarragon chicken?"

"Tarragon chicken," her mother replied.

"That's fowl," Phoebe said, continuing one of the little goofy family traditions that seemed to hold the internal world together while the external world was making no sense at all. Her mom smiled.

"I know," she said, "and no fuss about it being Thanksgiving in a couple days. More bird won't kill you."

"Unless, of course, it is avian flu—rich bird."

"Miss Morbid," her mother said, "you mind getting things started while I change? Or do you want to change first?"

"I never change, Mom," Phoebe said. She meant it as a joke, but she could tell by the look that crossed her mom's face that she didn't take it that way.

"Is something wrong, Phoebe?" her mom asked, stopping her bustling to move loose strands of ink black hair out of Phoebe's eyes. "Are you okay? Was it the article?"

Uh-oh, Phoebe thought. "What article?"

"It was in the paper. Some undead people went around Winford last night killing people's pets."

"Can I see?" Phoebe asked. She didn't bother to correct her mother's terminology.

Her mom opened the recycling bin and withdrew the paper for her.

"I'm going to get changed," her mom said. "The chicken breasts are in the fridge. They might need to be defrosted a little more."

"I'm going to read this first, okay?" Phoebe said, scanning the front page of the *Winford Bulletin*. ZOMBIES KILL PETS, the headline read, and Phoebe was glad that she hadn't corrected her mother. There was a photograph of a young mother holding two distraught children. The caption beneath the photo said that the Henderson family was mourning the loss of the Airedale Brady, who was "attacked and killed by zombies" sometime during the night.

There was also the photo of George from the Undead States recruitment flyer.

"Oh my," Phoebe said.

The article suggested that the zombie in the poster was considered the primary suspect in the rash of pet killings that had happened over the past few weeks, and she instantly thought of the wet furry lump that had been in George's trick-or-treat bag on Halloween.

Her mother's voice startled Phoebe. "Terrible, isn't it?"

Phoebe looked at her mom, who'd changed into jeans and a loose T-shirt. "I can't believe it."

"Do you know that boy? You know so many of the living impaired people in Oakvale."

Phoebe looked back at the paper; she thought she knew *all* of the living impaired people in Oakvale.

"Yes."

"Really?" her Mom said. "Shouldn't you go to the police?"

"I . . . I can't believe he would do this, Mom," she said, although she really could.

Her mother got the chicken out of the fridge, cut the plastic wrapping, and slid the three split fillets onto a white cutting board. She began trimming them with a knife.

"Is he a friends of yours?" she asked. She wasn't looking at Phoebe when she said it.

"Not really, no," Phoebe said.

"Well," her mother said, plating the breasts and covering them to prep them for a brief spin in the microwave, "let's hope that it wasn't really him, and that something else is going on.

Coyotes, maybe. It wouldn't be good for your friends if this crime was committed by living impaired kids."

Phoebe wanted to argue the point. She wanted to say how stupid society was if they would blame a whole group of people for the actions of a small minority, but in the end she held her tongue, because she knew her mother was not speaking judgmentally, and that she was right. This was going to make trouble for differently biotic people through out the town. Phoebe had visions of a parade of cop cars leading up to the Haunted House, their lights flashing on the dead faces that gathered at the cracked windows to watch their approach.

"What goes better with tarragon chicken?" her Mom asked. "Carrots or peas?"

"Dad likes peas," Phoebe said.

"Peas it is."

Phoebe had trouble sleeping that night, so rather than fight it she lit incense and a few candles, then straightened her room. Her restlessness annoyed Gargoyle, who raised his furry eyebrows as she bustled around.

"Oh, Gar," she said, sitting down on the edge of the bed to mollify him by scratching behind his ears. "I would never let mean old George eat you."

Gar's eyebrow twitched once, then he settled back down to sleep. Phoebe went and sat at her computer. The article, and its accusations really bothered her.

She set the media player on her desktop to cycle randomly

through the thousands of songs stored on her hard drive. The first one that came up was by the Restless Dead, a group that always made her think of Adam.

She had three real e-mails among the advertisements and spammage. One from Margi, exhorting her to not be a lame-o and go to Aftermath. The second one was from Margi, telling her not to be a lame-o, and to go to Aftermath with them. The last one was from Margi, and it asked her to *puh-leeze* not be a lame-o and go to Aftermath with them.

> *Hey, Margi,*

she typed in reply to the third e-mail,

> *I'm sorry I have been such a lame-o. I'd love to go*
> *to Aftermath with you tho I wish that the train could*
> *pick me up at my house becuz in truth yr driving scares*
> *me to death. True and final death. See you in school*
> *Mon. and we'll make plans. Say hey to Colette fur me,*
> *love Pheeble.*

She surfed for a while, popped on and off MySpace addys of bands as the media player selected them. The Restless Dead appeared again after about a half hour, and Phoebe wondered how the "randomizer," or whatever it was, could pick two songs from a band that maybe had twenty total among thousands in such a short span of time.

She popped onto mysocalledundeath.com and reread

Tommy's last entry, the one where he gave a mission statement of sorts. He talked about hitting the road in an effort to "advance the cause of zombie rights." By traveling, he said he had hopes of connecting with zombies who might not have access to technology, and sharing their experiences with the "wired" readers of mysocalledundeath.

He didn't mention Phoebe by name, but he did say that a "traditionally biotic friend" was going to be assisting with the management of the Web site in his absence, and he expressed a hope that "subscribers of mysocalledundeath would join her, Karen, and himself in expanding both their online community and their presence in the world at large." Phoebe thought about the word "presence" and what Tommy meant by it. He chose his words so carefully; she often suspected that the pauses in his speech weren't due to typical zombie lack of control but because he wanted to make his meanings clear to his listeners. She was thinking this when a hand fell on her shoulder, statling her so much she almost knocked one of her lavender-scented candles over.

"Easy," her dad said. She could smell the wine that he and her mother had been sharing in the living room earlier that night. "Didn't mean to scare you."

"Okay,"

"It's pretty late," he said.

"I know."

"You okay?"

"I'm okay. Just can't sleep. Nothing to worry about."

"Okay, then."

"Really."

"I believe you."

"Dad?"

"Yes, Phee?"

"Is it okay if I go to a club in New York with Margi and some girls?"

Her father's sigh sounded like one of those forced sighs that Karen made when she was trying to show how trad biotic she could be.

"New York, as in New York City?"

"Yes, Dad."

"I don't know. Let me think about it. It's an underage club, isn't it?"

"Absolutely," she said. "You trust me, right?"

"Absolutely." He leaned over and kissed the top of her head. "Hey, it's that undead club, isn't it? Afterbirth or something like that?"

"After*math*, Dad!"

"Oh yeah. So you're bringing Adam and Colette there, is that it?"

"Just Colette," she said. "And Karen. Girls' night out."

"No Tommy either?"

"No Tommy. How did you hear about Aftermath, anyhow?"

"I read too, you know. Like I read about what happened to all these pets that disappeared."

"Oh."

"Pretty scary," he said. Across the room Gar buried his

muzzle into his forepaws as though he understood the jist of their conversation.

"The world can be a scary place," she said, "but that doesn't have anything to do with how much you trust me, right?"

"It has everything to do with how much I trust you," he said, kissing the top of her head. "I'll need to talk it over with your mom. I can think of a thousand reasons why it is a horrible idea to have a group of sixteen-year-old girls going to New York City by themselves."

"All of which are overcome by your trust for me, right?" She debated telling him that Karen would actually have been eighteen or nineteen if she were still alive, but decided it wouldn't help.

He patted her shoulder. "I'll let you know in the morning. Why don't you get some sleep?"

"I will. I just want to finish something first."

"Okay. Good night."

When he was gone she focused again on her computer screen. Someone with a screen name she didn't recognize had tried to instant message her, and she told the service to block them. She read a few of the comments on the bulletin board regarding Tommy's last entry, and most of them were very encouraging and supportive of his "quest."

She minimized the online service and opened up her word processing program. She stared at the blank screen for a moment and then typed in a title.

*Words From a Beating Heart*

She thought a few more moments and then started to type with increasing rapidity. The sound of her fingernails tapping on the keys was always a special music to her, especially when it seemed to match the rhythm of the music she was listening to.

*Hello,* she typed, *my name is Phoebe. My friends call me Phoebe or Fee or Pheebes or, my favorite, Pheeble. That's what my friend Adam called me. You know, I typed "called" just then instead of "calls." Sometimes I get confused in my mind over Adam, because Adam is dead. Since Adam is dead, I sometimes think of him in the past tense and it makes me crazy that I do this, because he's dead but he's come back. He's a zombie now. We still spend a lot of time together, but the time that we spend is different from how it was. A lot of things that we used to do, like talk, and drive to Honeybee Dairy to get hot fudge sundaes after tossing a Frisbee around (my favorite thing to do with Adam) are all things we can't do anymore—not yet, anyway. All those things occurred in the past tense, so, as wrong as it seems, I sometimes think of Adam in the past tense as well. I feel really guilty about that. I feel guilty about it because Adam died saving my life.*

*I have one other nickname, one that was given to me by the boy that killed Adam. He called me Morticia Scarypants. I wear black clothes and have long black hair and am very pale, and so I'm Morticia Scarypass. I listen to goth and darkwave and trance and horror punk and even a little heavy metal. I write poetry and at the time I was dating a dead boy—I was dating Tommy, actually. I think this really made the boy that gave me my nickname angry with me. I think that's why he tried to kill me—although I'm not sure if he was trying to kill me or Tommy, or if he really meant to kill Adam.*

*They call me the Bride of Frankenstein now, since I still spend so much of my time with dead guys.*

*Tommy asked me to help with mysocalledundeath when he was gone, and he thought it would be good if I wrote a blog, that it might help connect trads like me with the zombies who read the Web site daily, and vice versa. I know that it's a risky thing he's asking of me, just like it was risky for me to type the word "zombies" just then. I'm sure there are those of you who will read my words and think, "how dare she, a trad girl, call us zombies." I could say in my defense that my friends use the word zombie all the time, but that won't do anything to justify it if you feel that it's a word that no trad person should use.*

*The thing is, most of my friends are dead. Just like the shirt says.*

*Again, this doesn't give me free license to say or do anything I want just because I'm friends with dead people. I mention it only because it's the truth, and because my friends and I are still trying to work through the issues that friendship present us.*

*When I started dating Tommy, I had no idea that people would hate me just for dating him. I had no idea that friends and family might react differently than I would have expected from them.*

*I had no idea that some of Tommy's dead friends would object to it either. All I knew was that I was interested in*

*Tommy, and he seemed to be interested in me, so I thought it would be fun to spend time with him.*

*When I first saw Tommy, he was so confident. He knew that he was taking risks. And I knew soon after meeting him that the risks he was taking were not for his own benefit but really for the benefit of undead people everywhere. I'd never met another boy who was as selfless as Tommy. I admired him greatly for it.*

*There I go, writing about my friends in the past tense again.*

*I already miss Tommy even though he hasn't been gone very long. I hope the road is smooth and safe for him. If you see him on his travels, thank him on my behalf for giving me the chance to "speak" to all of you. Tell him that I hope he was right, and that I hope that the words that I write will help all of us, living or dead, understand each other a little better.*

When she was done she leaned back and stretched. She tried to imagine how some of the zombies she knew—Colette, Mal, Takayuki—Tommy even, would react to what she'd written. What would Adam think, and would he even tell her?

She hovered for a moment—like she did with everything she'd ever written that was of a personal nature—over the thought of deleting the whole thing. Tommy this, Tommy that. She sounded like a mopey schoolgirl. Oh, wait, she thought, I *am* a mopey schoolgirl.

If you missed Tommy so much, she thought, why did you blow him off, practically chase him out of town? If you were so guilty over Adam getting killed, why didn't you go see him tonight after he was done with karate? Just because you tried to kiss him and he pushed you away?

The zombies who read this would probably think she was the worst sort of hanger-on, the sort of kid that's so screwed up and lonely and cut off from her own kind that she was trying to glom onto the little community that Tommy built. But isn't that what all lonely kids do in some way?

She highlighted the entire text and right-clicked "Cut." The thoughts were out of her head, she told herself, that was the important thing.

Her computer told her that she had mail. She maximized the screen and there was an e-mail from WILLIAMSTOMMY @MYSOCALLEDUNDEATH.COM. "The Long and Unwinding Road" was in the subject header.

Tommy.

She clicked the e-mail open; there was an attachment called ROADBLOG1, and she started downloading as she began reading.

*Hi Phoebe—*

*I'm almost in New York and so far the trip has been going well. I walked alongside of 95 for a little stretch and saw about four thousand white vans, but am happy to say none of them stopped with nets and flamethrowers. I've attached my first blog for you or Karen to post on the site. I'm sending this from a church, if you can believe it. With so many religious types of all denominations out there wanting to burn us like a stack*

*of Harry Potter books, it continually amazes me how many of*
*the clergy reach out. Actually, so far the kindness of people—*
*well, you can read the blog. Have you started writing yours yet?*
*I miss you already. Say hi to Adam and the gang.*
*T.*

She clicked reply and keyed in a quick response.

*Hi Tommy—*
*Glad to hear you're safe, everyone here misses you too.*
*We—the Weird Sisters—are going to NYC later this week, on*
*the day after Thanksgiving to go to Aftermath. Want to meet*
*us there?*
*Love,*
*Phoebe*

Despite her sign-off, she thought the e-mail was a little impersonal. She was about to hit send when at the last second, she tapped

*PS: What do you think of this?*

And then pasted the "Words From a Beating Heart" text she had cut into the body of the e-mail. She immediately felt embarrassed and closed out her Internet service, as though by turning it off she could recall the e-mail she'd just sent.

She looked at the clock and was thankful that tomorrow was Sunday. She opened Tommy's blog and began to read.

* * *

The hour was now so late it was almost absurd, but Phoebe went back online. She saw that WILLIAMSTOMMY had beaten her to the punch.

> *Phoebe—*
>> *This is beautiful. I think the zombie community is really going to respond positively to what you've written.*
>> *Love,*
>> *T.*

Love, she thought, he'd typed "love" just as she had. A multifaceted word, *love*, there probably wasn't another word in this or any other language that had so many shades and degrees. She knew that he loved her and she loved him, just as she loved Adam and Adam loved her. But with love, theirs or his, it was always a question of degree, and what one was willing to do to express that degree.

She wondered what Adam was doing right then, and her breath caught in her throat. But then again, it did the same thing when she thought of Tommy. Shades and degree.

She signed off without replying, turned the volume of the speakers down another notch or two, then blew out the sputtering candles. Only then did she crawl into bed and pull the blankets close to her.

# CHAPTER
# TWENTY-FIVE

TRIED TO WORK the remote but the remote was slippery like a fish slipped out of hands once twice three times on the third Jimmy yells from the kitchen will you stop it you stupid ass and Mom yells and Joe yells and Johnny yells and they're all yelling but this is a pretty typical Thanksgiving.

Mom wanted me at the table but Jimmy freaked said it was bad enough he had to look at me and it ruined his appetite are you trying to make me puke. Felt kind of sad looking at all the food can't eat looked at the table for a minute before they sat mashed potatoes stuffing turnip. Never thought would miss turnip.

Johnny's brought a girl with him for dinner Susan and Susan seems nice but she's scared. Scared of FrankenAdam. Should be. Reached for the remote got it changed the channel the Patriots are winning the Jets are losing and wish wish wish could play.

Next year. Next year. If Tommy why not FrankenAdam? Could play again.

Sure.

Jimmy yells again and storms out and Mom starts crying didn't even know dropped the stupid remote again. Think can smell turkey for a little while but maybe it is really just wishful thinking. Talked to Karen and to Colette about this for a while and they both say it will come. Karen says she can smell just about everything and maybe more. Don't know what she means but Karen isn't really on the same playing field as most zombies anyway. Then Karen started talking about how she thinks she can taste some things and Colette makes a stupid joke about how Karen tastes and then Phoebe came over and for some reason we all stop talking.

Phoebe.

"You okay, son?" Joe asks, florid from holiday wine Hey, Phoebe florid does that count? He reaches for the remote but FrankenAdam is quicker. Quicker!

"I'm . . . fine, Joe." Shorter pause maybe.

He nods, goes back. Johnny is telling Mom that Jimmy is just an a-hole like he thinks that will get her to stop crying and Susan is crying too. Wishing could play some football when there is a knock on the door and Joe lets Phoebe in. Saw Phoebe at school walked with Phoebe to classes sat together on bus but different now. Doesn't touch, doesn't hold my hand.

Phoebe apologizing. FrankenAdam should apologize. Scared shamed Phoebe should apologize.

"Is this a bad time?" she said.

When is it not. Johnny tries to be gallant and introduce crying girlfriend Mom runs to bedroom and slams the door. Fridge opens and another beer is cracked.

"Hi, Adam," says Phoebe, Phoebe so pretty in a silky blouse, light green, shiny, reflecting perfect skin and eyes two shades darker and green, the color of her skirt. Soft suede boots, chocolate brown, just below her knee, with heels. Phoebe.

"Hi, Fee . . . bull." Nervous or dead? At least always have that excuse now.

She sits on the sofa across, green eyes turned toward the game for briefest of seconds. "Holidays can be fun, can't they?" she says. "We have Gram over, that can always be a trip."

Gram is Phoebe's grandmother. Remember she made good pies, pumpkin pies. Used to have a piece of pumpkin pie with Phoebe and her Gram in her kitchen Thanksgiving night.

"Fun. Did . . . Jimmy . . . run you . . . over?"

"He tried," she said, "I'm too quick."

"How . . . was . . . dinner?"

"Oh, it was good," Phoebe said she eats like a bird. Not like Margi that girl can really pack it away but Phoebe always quit before she got full. She'd eat a hot fudge sundae but that was about the only thing. Sad. Sad remembering thinking about all the time wasted with airheads like Holly when could have been having sundaes with Phoebe.

Joe stands in doorway with his beer and that is his way of telling to vacate his seat, so vacate his seat. It takes a little time but almost got it when Phoebe reaches out to help. Wish she wouldn't do that and tell her so. Somehow can't move or talk fast enough unless it is to say or do something that hurts her.

"Why don't you two go for a walk?" Joe says. Johnny and Susan are already leaving and Mom is down the hall with the door closed. Joe pouring beer onto a fire that he does not want to get out of control.

"Let's go . . . for a . . . walk."

"I . . . I just came over to say hi," Phoebe said. "I'm going to go back."

See the hurt in her eyes, hurt that FrankenAdam put there. Don't do much right anymore.

"I'll . . . walk . . . you . . . out."

"We're still planning on going to New York tomorrow," said Phoebe. "If you want to come."

She's not looking at me when she says it. Phoebe was changing right in front of me, I realized.

Realized that finally might have pushed her away.

"No . . . thanks."

She knew anyhow. The wind is sweeping her hair up and can imagine the scent of flowers being drawn forth by the breeze. She doesn't have jacket on and she is shivering. Want to tell her to go home but guess already done that really.

"'Bye, Adam," she said. "I'll see you Monday."

Monday, three days away. The longest gone without seeing Phoebe since death is about twenty-four hours.

"Bye . . . Pheeble,"

Watched her walk away but turn before she gets to the door because don't want her to see watching her. Suppose should be happy, because have been trying to get her to leave alone and live for weeks now, been trying and finally succeeded but no sense of triumph. Could have apologized at least.

Inside the house Joe is watching some team, Patriots or Jets or Giants achieve some objective; scoring of a touchdown or completion of a pass. Feel no sense of accomplishment for achieving my objective, only a pervading sense of loss. Objective of finally pushing her away.

Pervading. Didn't think dead body possessed sense motor impulses but turned reflexively back toward her house. She was already inside.

God, I thought. God, I love her.

Spent the rest of Thanksgiving doing karate in the backyard, barely noticing when a light snow began and stopped a few hours later.

Snow began to fall. Couldn't feel it.

# CHAPTER
# TWENTY-SIX

"WILL YOU STOP . . . apologizing?" Colette said. "And please . . . watch the . . . road? I don't want to . . . die . . . again."

"Okay, okay," Margi said. "Chill out. Is that truck still behind me?"

Phoebe watched the conversation from the "safety" of the backseat, trying not to be distracted by the big pink bubbles that Karen was blowing, or by the other cars on the highway that Margi seemed to be in perpetual danger of drifting too close to.

Margi's parents had given her an eight o'clock curfew, so the girls' decided to go to the city during the day, something that Margi felt compelled to apologize over ad infinitum.

"Don't worry about it, Margi," Karen said, snapping her gum. "I have to work tomorrow morning anyhow. And I need my beauty sleep."

Colette turned around in her seat—Margi had done an exceptional makeup job on her.

"Do you really . . . sleep . . . Karen?"

Karen reaches over and patted her hand. "No, sweetie. I was just kidding. Your eyes are really pretty, BTW."

"Really? Thank . . . you. I . . . do . . . sometimes. Sleep . . . I mean. Not sleep really . . . more like . . . hibernate."

"Really?" Karen said, sucking in a bubble. "Mal does that too. I zone out sometimes, but it isn't really like . . . sleeping."

"I don't know . . . what it is . . . it's weird. It's like I'm . . . awake . . . but dreaming . . . at the same time."

"Weird. George was talking about that the other day."

"George? Old-school George? He . . . talks?"

"Mmm-hmm," Karen replied. "He does to me."

"Ick," Margi said.

"George isn't so . . . bad," Karen said. "I think the . . . old-schoolers . . . are just . . . misunderstood."

Phoebe was about to comment on the fact that they were currently being misunderstood by the local police, but Margi beat her to it.

"Isn't George the one gnawing on pets?" Margi asked. "I haven't let Familiar out of the house in a week."

"What do you mean?" Karen said.

Phoebe realized that Karen was wearing Lady Z; she could smell it mixing with the scent of bubble gum.

"You didn't see that article in the paper?" she asked. She gave a summary of the article when Karen gave her a look of confusion, ending with the photo of George.

"You're kidding," she said.

"That's what the paper said."

"No way. George wouldn't hurt a fly."

"Tak would," Colette and Margi said in unison.

"So would . . . George," Colette added. "He probably . . . thinks . . . he is . . . supposed to."

"I don't believe it," Karen said. "There's no way. No way. George is a little too interested in roadkill, but there's no way he'd do this. He's not *fast* enough. He'd get . . . caught . . . the moment he tried."

Phoebe thought that Karen was trying to convince herself, which made her want to drop the subject. The other girls in the car must have had their telepathetic powers working, because they let the matter rest.

"And Tak wouldn't . . . *kill*," Karen said again. The next bubble she blew made a noise like a gunshot as it popped. "Not even an animal, no way. No . . . way."

"There's the . . . train station . . . exit," Colette said. Everyone seemed glad for the interruption.

New Haven was the first stop, but there were plenty of people who stayed on, wanting to get into New York City for the holiday weekend. Margi ushered the girls into a quartet of facing seats.

"Oh, I can't ride . . . backward," Colette said, "I get . . . motion . . . sickness."

Only when she forced out a laugh a moment later did the other girls realize she was kidding.

She was wearing a black Restless Dead sweatshirt that

Phoebe had given Margi for her birthday a year or so ago. The sweatshirt had a hood, which Colette pulled up so no one could see her face. Phoebe knew that her constant wisecracking was just a cover for a deep-seated self-consciousness.

Karen, her platinum hair trailing down the shoulders of a smart, black leather jacket that tapered at the waist, was sometimes not self-conscious enough. She would look into the eyes of anyone who passed, drilling into their souls with her bizarre diamond eyes. Phoebe watched a young woman pushing a stroller freeze in her tracks before turning around to find a seat in a different car. Beside her, Karen gave the impression of being oblivious to people's various reactions, but Phoebe thought she could see a light dancing in the diamonds whenever she provoked one, good or bad.

And there were other reactions besides the fear. A pair of boys hopped on to the train just before it left the station. One of them had long black hair and a leather jacket, and for a moment Phoebe felt her heart beating in her chest because she thought it was Takayuki, but when the boy looked up she saw that he had blue eyes. His companion was dressed in a similar fashion, with ripped denim jeans and a faded Zombie Power! T-shirt on beneath his motorcycle jacket.

The blue-eyed boy saw Karen and smiled.

"Hey," he said.

"Hello," Karen answered, her voice cool, bordering on blasé.

The other girls, even Margi, who had been chattering away, fell silent when the conversation began. Colette wouldn't even peek out from beneath her hood.

"I like your eyes," he said.

"Thank you," she said. "Yours are nice too."

His buddy thought that was pretty funny, but Phoebe could tell he was also trying to decide which one of them he would try and talk to now that his friend had engaged Karen. He stared past Colette to Margi, who managed to affect a glare that was three parts contempt and one part provocation. Phoebe knew from seeing the look in action that it turned off most of the boys she met, but a certain segment—like poor Norm Lathrop—fell for it utterly and completely.

The train jerked into life and the boy introduced himself as Dom and his friend as Bee.

"Where are you ladies headed?" he said, including the rest of them in the conversation. When his eyes met Phoebe's she felt her heartbeat again; his facial features were angular and handsome, his smile the only soft thing about him.

"We're going to Aftermath," Karen said, sounding both matter-of-fact and bored. Phoebe thought of a cat batting around a ball of string.

"No kidding," Dom said, flashing white teeth. "We are too. Are you looking forward to dancing with the dead?"

He was smiling when he said it, his voice free of sarcasm. Was he unaware that Karen was a zombie?

"Sure," Karen said. "We like to dance. There are a bunch of db kids at our school who go to the club, so we thought we'd go out and have some fun."

"Yeah? What school do you go to?"

"Oakvale High," she said, and there was a momentary

pause. "We're graduating . . . in the spring so we want to make sure we're having as much fun as possible . . . in our last year."

A look passed between the boys. "Seniors, huh?"

Karen nodded.

"Yeah," Margi challenged. "Where do you go to school?"

"Yale," Dom said, sighing like he was ashamed of it. "We're only freshmen, though."

"Oh," Karen said, "are you in . . . the Skull and Bones society?"

Dom and Bee laughed along with them.

"Something like that. We're in a band called Skeleton Crew, so that's pretty close."

"Skeleton Crew?" Margi said, interest suddenly replacing abrasion in her voice. "So you sing 'Living is like Dying'?"

In response, Dom started to sing, "Living is like dying, all over again, all over again, like dying, all over again . . ."

"You're not the singer," Karen observed.

Dom ran his hand through his hair, revealing that it had been razored to a thin dark stubble over one ear. "Boy, you're tough. No, I'm the guitarist. Bee plays bass."

"And your singer," Margi said, "DeCayce. He's a . . ."

"Zombie," Dom finished. "Yep. A dead guy sings for us."

Even Karen seemed intrigued by that.

"So listen," Dom said. "I don't even know your names. How can I get you on the guest list if I don't know your names?"

"You're playing today?" Margi asked.

"You bet. If DeCayce and Warren manage to get our equipment there, yeah."

"I'm Margi Vachon."

"Who's your shy friend?"

"Colette Beauvoir."

Dom withdrew a small wire-bound notebook and a black pen from a pocket inside his jacket. "Hold up. Is that spelled B.E.A.U.V.O.I.R?"

"Wow, you really do go to Yale," Karen said. "I'm Karen DeSonne. D. small e. capital S.O. double N. E."

"French girls," Bee said, grinning.

"I'm Italian," Karen said with a withering glare.

"I'm Phoebe Kendall," Phoebe said. Dom looked up at her with something like interest for the first time.

"Phoebe Kendall," he said, writing her name in the book and then flipping it closed before withdrawing a cell phone from his other pocket. "Hey, Serena?" he said into the phone. "Hey, it's Dom. I've got a few people I want you to add to the guest list for today." He read off their names, starting with Margi and ending with Phoebe. Something Serena said must have been funny because he was still laughing when he said good-bye and hung up.

"Well, Bee," he said once the phone was away, "let's go grab a seat. Hopefully we'll be seeing you girls later today. I'm glad I met you."

Colette peeked out of her hood to watch them swagger down to an empty pair of seats in the back, and retreated like a turtle back into her shell when Bee waved at her.

"I've never been on a . . . guest . . . list . . . before."

"Oh, honey," Karen said, reaching over and tapping her

knee. "That's just because you haven't met enough people yet."

"You're amazing, Karen," Phoebe said. "You were so confident. No wonder they were crazy about you."

"Me?" Karen replied, and when she turned toward Phoebe, the diamonds glittered. "You didn't say a word, but you're the one who has all the boys back home chasing you."

She knew Karen didn't mean it to hurt, but Phoebe couldn't help but feel stung. Currently there were zero boys chasing her. The one she wanted to chase her, she chased away. Actually, she'd chased both of them away.

Karen must have sensed everything that was roiling in her mind because she gave her a gentle push.

"Hey, I didn't mean anything by that. Nothing other than you're hot, that's all."

The train pulled into the next station

There was traffic on the street and sidewalk in front of the squat building where Aftermath was housed, but none of it seemed to be leading to its single door, a massive gray-green slab of metal that looked to Phoebe as though it could withstand a direct missile assault. There were only two decorations on the windowless building: a sign that hung from a metal pole recessed into the building's concrete about twelve feet off the ground bearing the name of the club, and a second sign in the same white script on a black color scheme that read, ENTER FREELY . . . AND OF YOUR OWN FREE WILL. This sign was secured to the door with four heavy bolts.

"Nice," Margi said upon reading the "welcome."

"It looks . . . closed," Colette said. She hadn't taken her hood down the entire time they had trekked through Grand Central Station and into the street where Margi finally got a cab to stop for them. Phoebe didn't think she looked much different from many of the younger people they'd passed.

"I hear music," Karen said.

Phoebe listened. She may have heard a low bass throbbing, but it could have just been the breath of the city, in and out, the sounds of thousands of cars rolling on the streets, the rushing of liquids through thousands of underground pipes, the sounds of a million words being spoken at once.

"Do we just go in?" Margi asked, looking around as though expecting a list of instructions to appear, like the menu boards of a drive-through.

"I think we do," Karen said, tugging the handle of the blast door open. What they saw inside Aftermath was not at all what Phoebe had expected.

The door opened into a sort of lounge area that had been covered floor to ceiling with vibrant swirls of color: a bright, kaleidoscopic display that was a far cry from the featureless dank warehouse Phoebe had been expecting. She followed a flaring curve of yellow ribbon that began somewhere on the plush shag carpet up one wall and then onto the ceiling, where it's varying thickness gave it the illusion of undulating over their heads before curving down the opposite wall. There were symmetrical bursts of multiple colors atop some of the curving bands; they looked like tie-dye designs pressed onto the wall.

The riot of color distracted her, momentarily, from the dozen or so people in the room, some of whom were sunk into formless plush furniture that floated like giant amoebas on the swirling sea of color.

Phoebe looked at Colette, a dark black blot against the brightness of the walls. She watched her lower her hood, and then she watched as the color seemed to flow into her rapidly blinking eyes. Her look of astonishment morphed into a wide smile.

"Welcome to Aftermath," a dead girl said, hopping up from a counter near the door in a way that reminded Phoebe of the baristas at the local coffee franchise whenever a quiet customer disturbs their study time—half-embarrassed, half dutiful, and trying their best not to look wholly annoyed. "We have a . . . ten dollar . . . cover charge."

Phoebe was already opening her purse when Karen stepped forward and said she thought that they were on the guest list.

The dead girl gave a fair approximation of a smile. Her hair was stylishly cut, a soft-looking blond that had been chemically enhanced, probably to hide the gray streaks that were sometimes a natural consequence of death. Colette's hair had been streaked with gray for quite a while, but was now closer to the dark brown it had been when she was alive. The dead girl was wearing a white tank top with the Aftermath logo in black, black jeans, and boots. Her bare arms were pale and smooth.

"Let me check . . . the list," she said. While she was checking, Phoebe took a quick scan of the people hanging out in the lounge. There were a couple of zombies, two boys, playing one of those fantasy card games across a glass table with silver legs. Phoebe never quite grasped how to play beyond the basic concept that whoever could afford the most cards usually won. A girl sitting beside one of the gamers on the pillowy futon gave a bemused whoop when her companion played a card, flipping it with decisive vigor. His zombie opponent leaned back in his seat and gazed up at the Technicolor ceiling, his mouth open and gray-pink tongue lolling out in a half comical re-enaction of his death.

"Are you . . . Karen?" the zombie hostess was saying.

Karen said she was, and then she introduced the other girls, adding, "I really like your belt."

The girl looked down, as though surprised by the strip of silver studded leather around her waist.

"Thank you . . . Karen DeSonne," she said, extending a hand that ended in long white fingernails. "I'm Emily."

She's pretty, Phoebe thought, watching them shake hands. Colette and Margi drifted toward the hallway where the music would periodically blast forth as people opened the glass door.

"There are . . . lockers . . . in the locker room," Emily said. "For your . . . coats and . . . things. Five dollars . . . to rent. Dancing, down the main hall." She pointed with both arms as she gave the directions, like she was trying to bring an airplane into the gate. "There is a . . . snack bar . . . and vending machines . . . upstairs . . . next to the gift shop," she said, giving a final wave at a garish lavender stairwell. "The bathrooms . . . are down the hall . . . past the locker room. Have . . . fun."

"I need to use the restroom. Thanks, Emily." Phoebe said.

"I'll go with," Karen said. Phoebe didn't realize it, but she must have given her a funny look because a moment later Karen added "to check my makeup, silly!"

"Oh," Phoebe said, feeling foolish. "I'll see if the girls want me to put anything in the lockers."

She came back with Margi's coat and ten-pound purse and Colette's black hoodie.

"We're going to need two lockers," Karen said. She nodded back over Phoebe's shoulder. "Look how happy Colette is."

Phoebe looked back. Colette and Margi were on the periphery of an animated discussion occurring at the entrance of the hallway that led to the dance floor. One of the zombies was waving his hands in the air in front of his face to illustrate his point. His left hand was not as obedient as the right. Regardless, one of his companions, a trad boy holding a bottle of energy drink, laughed loud enough for them to hear even over the hivelike buzz of music and conversation.

"Just look at her . . . smile," Karen said. "Could you hear what they're talking about?"

"Books," Phoebe said.

"Books?" Karen shook her head. "Cool."

They started toward the locker room, the swirl of colors abruptly ending at the mouth of a long gray corridor lined with framed posters.

"The guy talking said the best thing about being dead was that he had tons of time to read. He said the worst thing was that the dead can't get library cards."

"That's pretty funny," Karen said. "So is that."

She pointed at the first of the posters, which was for *Night of the Living Dead*. Facing it across the hall was one for *Dawn of the Dead*, beside it the grinning skull from the first *Evil Dead* movie

"Wow," Phoebe said. The next one in line was a promo for a video game entitled *Zombie Apocalypse*, which depicted a man wading into a mob of zombies with a chainsaw. A severed arm went skyward in a spray of dark, ocher-hued "blood."

"You don't find it offensive?"

Karen shook her head. "I like irony. Oh, look, *Return of the Living Dead*. That was always my favorite." She started singing. "*Do you wanna paaaaaarty? It's party time!* Remember that scene?"

Phoebe blushed. She remembered. "That's a 45 Grave song."

Karen was less interested in music trivia. "How could I get offended by this?" she said, pointing at a pair of greenish zombies, the male Mohawked and skeletal and wearing a dog collar, standing over a gravestone, with the movie title being sprayed on it in red by a third zombie burrowing up from the ground beneath. "It's like the music you listen to, right? Zombies and monsters and whatever else, being hunted down by you trads?"

"The monsters usually win in the songs I listen to," Phoebe said. The last poster was the front cover of *And the Graves Give Up Their Dead*, by Reverand Nathan Mathers. The girls stopped and looked at it a moment, and at the photo inset of the author whose severe ice-blue eye gazed at them without pity.

"As long as they don't win in real life," Karen said. "Speaking of . . . monsters."

The zombie staffing the locker room gave them a bored wave as they entered.

"You'll . . . need . . . two," he said, looking at the mound of stuff in Phoebe's arms. He'd had a weight problem in life that had followed him into death, the stool he was perched upon creaked in protest as he leaned over to pluck two keys from the Peg-Board with his stubby fingers.

"Ten . . . bucks," he said. "Or . . . no lock . . . and take your . . . chances."

"Thanks," Karen said, handing him the money and a bright smile. "I'm Karen."

"B . . . Billy," he said.

"Thanks, Billy," she said, taking the keys, and leading Phoebe through the numbered rows of lockers.

"Let me give you some money for the lockers," Phoebe said, once their coats and bags were stowed.

"Don't worry about it," Karen said. "I've got that highly lucrative second job at the mall. I'm flush." On their way out she favored Billy with another killer smile. "Bye, Billy!"

Farther down the hall they found the bathrooms. There were four doors, two on the left that said "Boys" and two on the right that said "Girls." The word "Dead" was above one of each, and the word "Trad" was above the other two.

"More irony?" Phoebe said.

"At least I didn't have to sit in the back of the train."

They pushed their respective doors open, and stepped into

the same room. There were a row of stalls and a row of sinks. A dead girl was applying lip gloss from a black tube that had the distinctive Z logo that appeared on almost all of the Slydellco Zombie cosmetic products.

"Hi," the girl said, looking at them in the mirror. Phoebe thought that maybe she stared at her a beat too long, and it made her uncomfortable as she went into one of the stalls. She heard Karen ask her a question about the lip gloss.

"'Kiss of Life,'" the girl replied. "Sometimes . . . Skip is . . . so corny."

Phoebe heard the dead girls' laughter echoing in the tiled room.

When they returned to the lounge, Margi and Colette were nowhere to be seen.

"Probably burning up the dance floor," Karen said. "Let's go."

The sound hit them like a physical force when they stepped into the club proper, as did the assault of color and light strobing and flashing.

"I'm glad I don't have epilepsy," Phoebe said, blinking against a red strobe that seemed to be aimed directly at her retinas.

The dance hall was smaller than she expected, but only because every other dance she'd ever been to was in a school gymnasium. The dance floor here was far smaller, it looked like a sheet of opaque white plastic beneath which lights of green, yellow, blue, and red glowed with muted color. Margi and Colette were indeed burning up the dance floor, moving in rapid time with the Guy Who Can't Get a Library Card and his friends.

The floor was packed. There had to be thirty people on it, jumping and swaying with the music. Karen leaned over Phoebe's shoulder, her breath cool on her ear.

"We're here to dance, right?" she said, taking her by the hand and leading her down the carpeted steps to the floor. Colette gave an off-note cheer as they joined them, and Phoebe laughed when the eyes of both the deads and the trads bugged out as Karen twitched her short leather skirt.

The smell of Z hung heavy on the air as spotlights from above raked the crowd. Phoebe gave herself into the music, a heavy industrial song by a band she liked called the Seraphim. Then the lights cut all at once, plunging the hall into total darkness for a moment before hot white strobes flickered from all sides. Phoebe couldn't tell who was living or dead in that light; the rapid flashing made everyone's movements appear stiff and jerky. The room went dark again and then the floor lights returned, as well as the overhead spots. Lifting her arms above her head and laughing as Margi executed a few gypsy-like steps, she saw that some of the lights playing on walls and skin were butterflies, or flowers or stars.

She realized a zombie boy was mumbling something at her.

"What?" she yelled.

"I said," he screamed back, "loud enough for you?" Looking closer she realized he wasn't dead after all, he just had bad skin. She nodded and spun away.

The machine-heavy track segued into a crunky rap song

that Phoebe didn't recognize but could understand instinctively, the bass and drum wash infusing her limbs with their energy.

Is this what it's like for them? she thought, feeling the rush and watching Colette laugh at something the Library Card Guy said. She found that she could use music as fuel, like a candy bar or an apple. Without the latter two options, was sound what the dead needed to power them? She thought of Kevin and his jerky scarecrow dancing at the homecoming dance. Here, even the most sluggish of zombies in the room appeared to be moving at normal speeds.

Above the dance floor was a sort of catwalk that led to a perimeter of booths with more of the pillowy blue furniture that was scattered around the club. There were dozens of people loitering around, many watching either the dancers or the pretty colored lights that played across them. There was a DJ in an enclosed booth at the far end of the catwalk, and below that was a platform raised up from the rest of the dance floor that had a drum set and a few stacks of amplifiers. There was a yellow smiley skull—a giant emoticon—on the bass drumhead with the words "Skeleton Crew" written in letters made out of bones.

"Oh, man." Margi slumped onto a futon after a third extended club remix song ended. "I'm all out of breath."

"Me too," Colette said. The people that could hear her over the music thought that was pretty funny.

Margi led a haphazard parade up to a ring of couches on the catwalk. She and Colette introduced Karen and Phoebe to some of their new friends.

"I can't believe how many people are here," Phoebe said.

"How many dead people, you mean?" the boy on her left said. This was Trent, the Library Card Guy.

"No, just people," she said, not sure if he was trying to be confrontational or if he just wanted to start conversation. "We thought the club was closed when we first got here."

"Ah."

Colette said that it was sort of overwhelming, being around this many zombies. "I think the most we've ever had at the Haunted House was twenty-three," she said.

Phoebe turned toward the dance floor. She spotted one of the zombies out there looking as though he'd just crawled out of a three-year-old grave; his clothes were shredded and stained and the skin on the side of his head looked like it was flaking off. He was the only old-school zombie she'd seen, the only one that would not have looked out of place on one of the posters in the hall by the restrooms. Like George.

When she turned back, everyone was leaning in their chairs a little closer to Colette.

"The Haunted House?" Trent asked.

"Um . . . yeah," she said. "That's just . . . just what . . . we call this house we . . . hang out . . . at."

"Where did you say . . . you were from?"

"Connecticut?" she said, like she was being quizzed. "Oakvale?"

"No way!" Trent said, excited now. "Tommy Williams? Mysocalledundeath.com?"

Colette, suddenly a celebrity, smiled at him without answering.

"Wow, that's . . . incredible," Trent said. "Do any of you . . . go to . . . the Hunter Foundation?"

"We all do," Margi answered. She was trying to look like she wasn't interested in Trent's living friend, but she *was* interested in Trent's living friend.

"Unbelievable," Trent said. "Skip has . . . told us . . . a lot . . . about what you are . . . doing there." He paused for a moment, looking at each of them with new interest, which made Phoebe want to sink into her plush cushion until it enveloped her completely.

"Did . . . Tommy . . . really leave . . . like it says on the site?"

"He did," Margi answered.

"Wow," Trent said. "It isn't . . . easy . . . being young and . . . undead . . . in America. Lots of the . . . kids . . . here had a long . . . distance . . . to travel."

"I came here from . . . Iowa," one kid said.

"I'm . . . sorry," Colette said, making him smile.

"Hey," Trent said, "that stuff about . . . dating . . . a trad chick . . . was that true?"

You would think that someone like Colette, who had to make a conscious effort to speak and move their limbs, wouldn't have been so quick to give Phoebe up, but not so. The smile left her face as Colette looked right at Phoebe. Bad enough, but Margi and Karen did the same.

Phoebe made a clicking noise with her tongue and looked away.

"Oops," Trent said. He had trouble cutting off the "oo" sound.

"Um, yeah." Margi seemed to notice Phoebe's discomfort.

"Maybe we could talk about something else? Where are the rest of you from?"

Most, like Trent and his pal who hailed from Staten Island, were from New York City or the environs.

"But who . . . cares about that," he said, even though Phoebe did. "What's going to happen to mysocalledundeath . . . without Tommy? Do any of you know? Just about . . . everyone . . . here reads it."

"How?" Karen asked.

"Computers, upstairs," he answered. "Skip prints out the blogs and . . . hands them out."

"It'll still happen," Karen answered. "Tommy is going to be sending his blogs in from the road. Phoebe and I . . ."

The music cut out and the room went black. Phoebe shrieked.

"Some of you have been waiting an eternity for this, I know," the brash confidence of the voice cut through the darkness. "And you will now know that eternity was not spent in vain. Marking their record seventeenth appearance at Aftermath, please join me in putting claws and paws together in welcoming the band that you've been clamoring for, dead or alive. . . . Skeleton Crew!"

At the stroke of a razor-sharp opening chord, lights came back on. Phoebe looked below and saw Dom standing in front of a microphone. Next to him stood a short, shirtless, rail-thin boy who wore bright orange surfer shorts that ended below his knees. The thin boy was leaning on his microphone stand like he needed it to prop him up. Bee stood on the other side of the stage thrumming the low string on his bass guitar.

"Aftermath! Make some noise!" Dom yelled as Warren, hidden somewhere behind a ring of cymbals, began to play an escalating roll on his snare and double bass. Phoebe thought the greeting uninspired, but it provoked a healthy reaction from the crowd.

"Good . . . day . . . .everyone," the thin boy said, his voice somewhere between the somber intonations of Peter Murphy and Morrissey, "My name . . . is . . . DeCayce . . . and we are . . . Skeleton Crew."

He's the dead one, Phoebe thought. Dom hit another blaring chord and the dead boy leaped three feet in the air without flexing his legs as Bee and Warren erupted into song.

Phoebe was dead tired on the ride home, although Margi was still bopping around in the driver's seat, reliving each moment of their club adventure with minute detail. On the train she was a bundle of energy, even when Karen and Colette seemed to be holding their strength in reserve.

"He was so totally into you, Colette," Margi said. This idea more than anything else seemed to be the wellspring of Margi's energy, and as such Phoebe didn't get tired of hearing it, even though she'd already heard it at least two dozen times.

"I . . . don't . . . know," Colette said. Her denials became weaker each time Margi repeated the statement. Phoebe smiled; it was good to see Colette so moony.

"Yeah, you do," Margi said. "Totally."

The "somebody" was DeCayce. When their set was over Dom had brought his band over to talk to the girls. As raw as

DeCayce was onstage, he seemed very shy in person, and barely added to the conversation—which was mostly Dom bantering with Karen. Trent and his crowd drifted over, and the more people that were around, the more Phoebe noticed DeCayce retreating into himself. Trent was going on and on about what a groundbreaking band Skeleton Crew was, as Colette leaned over and said something that only DeCayce could hear. Whatever it was, it must have been pretty funny, because DeCayce laughed like the idea of laughter was new to him. They were inseparable for the rest of the night; Phoebe would catch glimpses of them talking animatedly, off by themselves in the hidden corners of the room.

Animatedly, Phoebe thought. Wrong word. Definitely the wrong word.

"Hey, Colette," she said. "What was it that you said to DeCayce that made him laugh so much?"

Colette turned back to her, smiling. "That . . . annoying boy . . . kept saying the word . . . 'groundbreaking.' Not good . . . word choice . . . for a zombie."

"We couldn't even find you when it was time to go," Margi said, her pink-shadowed eyes glancing up at Phoebe in the rearview. "Just what were you doing, huh, kid?"

"Stop it," Colette said. She was smiling. "We were . . . dancing."

"We were," and here the pause Margi took was three times as long as any that the New Improved Colette took, "*Dancing*. Is that what you call it?"

"Stop it!" Colette said, nudging her.

"Careful, Colette." Karen said. "She's liable to . . . kill us all.

Besides"—and here Karen leaned forward in her seat—"she's just jealous."

"Of course I'm jealous," Margi said. "Who wouldn't be jealous? Did you see the way he was looking at her? Just once, I'd like for someone to look at me like that. Just once."

"I don't know," Phoebe said, "Bee seemed pretty interested in our pink-haired girl."

"Sure," Margi said, "all I get is the bass players."

"Big Christmas sales at Wild Thingz ! tomorrow," Karen said as Margi pulled into the driveway of the DeSonne home. "A great chance to stock up on all of your Z brand cosmetics."

"Colette will be needing some of those now that she has a boyfriend," Margi said, pretending to think aloud. "But I just don't think Santa is coming for her. She's been naughty."

"Will you . . . stop," Colette said, clearly not wanting her to.

On their way to drop Phoebe off, Margi and Colette started making plans about going to the mall, the people they needed to buy Christmas presents for, and what those presents would be. Phoebe sat in the backseat and willed herself invisible just so she could listen in on their conversation and the easy friendship it represented.

"What about . . . Norm?"

"What about Norm?" Margi replied.

"Don't . . . snap. And don't be . . . mean . . . to Norm."

"Being encouraging would be mean."

"You know he's going to get . . . you . . . a present."

"Tell him to save his money."

"It doesn't . . . work that way."

Phoebe was happy for them, but she was a little sad too. It sounded a lot like the conversations *she* used to have with Margi.

"Well, it needs to work another way. Norm is a really nice guy but I don't feel *that way* about him. I don't feel the way DeCayce, the sexy undead rock star, feels for you."

"Don't change . . . the subject."

"Who's changing? It's the same subject."

"I just . . . think . . . you might want to get him . . . something. Something . . . small. A CD."

"Then he'll read all sorts of deep meaning into the song titles and it'll be even worse than it is now."

"No love songs."

"All songs are love songs," Margi said. A car passed them going the other way and Margi checked her rearview to watch it recede. "What do you think, Phoebe?"

"Colette is right," she said, shocked that her veil of invisibility had been penetrated so easily. "A CD. No love songs. Maybe the Skeleton Crew CD?"

"Great idea!" she said. "Colette can probably get me a case of free copies!"

Adam was in the yard working out when they rolled up the driveway. She saw him revealed briefly in the bright swath of light beaming from Margi's headlamps, turning on his heels from left to right, his fists rotating from his hips to strike unseen assailants.

Margi had seen him too. "You going to go practice your ninja skills with Adam now?" she said.

Phoebe started, but it was just a question. Sometimes she forgot that she hadn't told Margi what had happened. She got out of the car and watched her frosted breath curl in the air before her. Adam was just a vague shadow in the darkness, a flickering ghost half seen through the ambient glow of Margi's headlights.

"No," she said after a time. "I think he's probably pretty deep into it by now. You know how intense he gets."

Margi rolled down her window as Phoebe slammed the door.

"You guys are okay, right?"

Please, Phoebe thought, let's not spoil the evening. "We're fine."

Margi looked at her a long moment. "Thanks for coming today," she said, finally.

Phoebe leaned down and gave her an awkward half-hug through the open window, reaching over to grip Colette's shoulder as well.

"Thanks for having me after all," she said. "You guys are really good friends."

Margi waited until she was on her steps before backing out. Phoebe waved to them from the steps, and then she waved to Adam, but she couldn't tell if he waved back through the darkness.

# CHAPTER
# TWENTY-SEVEN

"SOME OF THE Undead Studies students said that they've seen you working here at the foundation."

Angela had this trick she did when they were in session, where she sort of cocked her head while brushing her long hair behind her ear with her fingers. Pete thought it was supposed to signify how interested she was in what he was saying.

"Am I supposed to start talking about that?"

She smiled at him.

"I don't know what to say. Am I supposed to hide or something when they come?"

She shifted in her seat. "I don't know. Do you think you should?"

He sighed. "No."

"Don't you think your presence might be . . . upsetting to some of them?"

"Maybe. So you think I should hide."

"I don't think we're talking about hiding. I think we're talking about not making yourself so . . . conspicuous."

He hated the pauses in her speech. It made her sound like a worm burger. "Conspicuous."

"You were staring at them when they arrived at the foundation the other day, Pete. I would call that . . . making yourself conspicuous."

"Fine. I'll make myself scarce when they're here."

She held his gaze. "Why were you staring at them, Pete?"

He shrugged.

"Is it because you want to say something to someone?"

"Like who?"

"Adam? Or Phoebe?"

"What would I say to either of them?"

"I don't know. What would you?"

He shifted in his seat. "What, you think I should apologize or something?"

She didn't answer, her smile and gaze remained steady.

"If you are asking me if I feel bad about what happened to Adam, if I'm, like, *remorseful*, the answer is yes. Yes, I'm sorry he died."

She nodded.

"I wasn't trying to hurt him. Her, either. They were just in the way."

"In the way?"

"Yes, in the way." He looked right at her. "In front of the corpsicle."

"Tommy."

He shrugged.

"Why do you think you're so angry with Tommy, Pete?"

"We've already been through all this."

"Please sit down. Let's go through it again, okay?"

"Okay." He sat down. He hadn't really been aware of standing in the first place. "Okay, fine. I don't like zombies. I hate zombies. We talked about a girl I used to know, Julie, and how she died and she didn't come back and that probably fuels my anger. We talked about how my parents are separated and my father doesn't have any time for me and how I don't approve of my mother's choices or her second husband. These facts, or so you seem to think, contribute to what you consider to be my irrational hatred of zombies."

She nodded, her smile widening, as though they were getting somewhere. Pete couldn't wait until his six months were up.

He sighed. "So now we know . . . we sort of know . . . why I hate zombies. But I don't know what to do about it. I see them and I start getting angry all over again. I know it isn't rational. I know that they—the zombies, I mean—aren't really responsible for what happened to Julie. But I don't know what to do about it.

He looked back at her, afraid he'd laid it on too thick. He knew it was important for Angela to think her ridiculous "therapy" was rehabilitating him. Duke had been right, it was stupid for him to try and intimidate the necrophiliacs like he had been; Angela must have seen him on one of the security tapes. Stupid.

He looked at her, affecting a hangdog, contrite expression while trying not to overdo it.

"Pete," she said, "I think it's time we start discussing some coping strategies for you to deal with your feelings about zombies."

He made as if the tension was slowly going out of his shoulders.

"I'd like that. I really would."

He hoped that she didn't notice him gritting his teeth the moment the words were out.

Pete cursed under his breath as some of the bleach slopped over the sides of the mop basin. The wringer didn't want to slide onto its mounting. He kicked it and it clattered to the ground.

"Tough session?"

Pete started. Duke stood behind him, his large frame leaning against the wall. Normally the echo of Duke's heels filled the corridors he patrolled, but when he wanted to, the big man could move in total silence.

"Oh, it was great."

Duke laughed. He reached for the mop wringer and planted it effortlessly in place on the side of the rolling bucket. "I can tell. Isn't head-shrinking fun?"

"I'll be done with it in a few weeks."

"Sure." Duke pushed the bucket to him with the toe of his boot. Bleach water sloshed over the sides and onto Pete's shoes. "Oops, better mop that up. So you think you'll be all done hating zombies when it's over?"

Pete dunked his mop, then wrung it out. "I love zombies."

"I can tell."

Pete let the mop fall against the cement wall. "Look, is there a point to all your insinuations? Every time I come out of my sessions, I try to get to work right away and not bother anybody. And every day, you have something to say to me. Except I never know what you're saying."

There was a flicker of amusement on the pale man's face. "No?"

"No, I don't. Except you seem to be interested in what goes on in there." He ducked his head in the direction of Angela's office down the hall.

"True, very true."

"Well, why the hell should you care? Don't you have anything better to do than mess with me?"

"Sure I do," Duke said. "Like hunting."

"Hunting? What do you mean, hunting? Like, animals?"

"Domestic animals, mostly."

"Domestic . . . ?" Pete stopped. He'd heard about the recent pet disappearances around town. The papers had been quick to blame the zombies.

Duke's smile had grown wider. "A whole bunch of them have died in town recently."

"What are you saying? That you . . . that you killed them?"

Duke shrugged.

"*You* killed those dogs? Not the zombies?"

"Dog. One dog. A couple cats. Mostly it was just creative use of roadkill."

"You're serious? You killed them?" Pete laughed. "Why?"

Duke shrugged, a gesture of false modesty. "Doesn't matter who kills them. It matters who gets blamed."

Pete couldn't believe what he was hearing. He knew Duke was sick, he just didn't know how sick.

"The zombies. The zombies get blamed."

Duke clapped his hand on Pete's shoulder and squeezed. "Of course the zombies get blamed. They're already out there causing trouble, acting clever with these little pranks they're pulling, the graffiti and the stupid posters. They think they're being cute, "raising consciousness" or whatever, but that kind of activity just scares decent living folk. It isn't that much of a stretch to picture them killing the family pet, is it?"

"I don't even believe it. I don't even believe you're the one."

"Believe it." Duke let go of his shoulder. "Even better, it's your good buddy that's going to be left holding the bag on the crimes."

"My good buddy?"

Duke brought his hand up to his cheek, a gesture Pete instinctively copied, and he felt the rough threads of his stitches beneath his fingers.

"Yeah, your buddy. He's the main prankster."

"Good," Pete said, lowering his hand, "I'd love to see that scary dead bastard get his."

Duke raised an eyebrow so high it was almost comical.

"You would?" He leaned in close enough for Pete to smell the spearmint on his breath. "How badly?"

# CHAPTER
# TWENTY-EIGHT

From: WilliamsTommy@mysocalledundeath.com
To: KendallPhoebe@mysocalledundeath.com
Hey Phoebe—
Here's my latest "adventure." I'd really appreciate
it if you could check it over for mistakes before posting it.
How is everybody? Still dead?
Love,
Tommy

DEATH ON TWO LEGS: Aftermath
I stopped at Aftermath during my stay in New York City,
which I'm told has more zombies per capita than any other
place in the country. If that rather unscientific statement is
true, they must all stay in the club itself, because I didn't see
any zombies on the streets of New York. Either that or the
zombies I did see were indistinguishable from the traditionally
biotic people.

*Readers of this blog know that at times I have been critical of Skip Slydell and his company, Slydellco, who I have seen as profiteering off the undead without regard for the repercussions of that profiteering. I've been concerned that his cosmetics and clothing trivialize our cause rather than advance it, but after meeting Skip in his club I'm convinced that that isn't his intention. I won't go as far as to say that I am a supporter, but he isn't the greedy robber baron I originally pegged him for. His methods may be suspect, but I do think he has undead interests at heart.*

*Aftermath is in an unassuming three-story building off the Bowery. In much of his media material, Skip calls the club evidence of a "cultural revolution." Typical Skip, he goes too far with his own hyperbole—but it's hard to deny that some form of cultural change is taking place there.*

*The club departs from the typical cavelike, warehouse decor of most clubs, favoring instead bright primary colors that cover every visible surface (with the exception of the corridor to the bathrooms, but I'll get to that later).*

*"You have to go with what's stimulating to people," Skip told me as we sat on leather chairs in a small office he keeps above the DJ booth. "Dead kids like light, they like color, they like three hundred beats per minute. We've done theme parties, ones where we keep the houselights on for the whole dance. Living kids, they dance in the dark. Why? The dark is exciting to them. It's thrilling. Dead kids, some of them spent too much time in the dark, alone. They don't want to be back there. I went to a rave in an old brick warehouse a few weeks ago*

*looking for ideas. I looked around and said: I'm in a crypt.
Some of these kids have actually been in crypts; who wants to
dance in one?"*

*"Take our furniture. All overstuffed, comfortable. Velour.
Fake fur on a lot of the pillows with nice bright colors. Soft
things, comforting things."*

*I ask him how the club makes any money when it runs
twenty-four hours. Earlier in the day I talked to Simon from
White Plains, a zombie who told me he'd been at the club for
"at least six days."*

*"Yeah, we have about twenty-five people living here," Skip
said, and for a moment I think he's going to dodge the question.
"I have outside funding," Skip tells me. "You'd be surprised how
many people, people with means, are sympathetic to the plight
of the undead. I get money from Hollywood, I get money
from Washington. I kick money from my product line into
the kitty; we're set up as a not-for-profit. The labor is all
volunteer; the expenses are low. Electricity and rent are our
biggest headaches."*

*"What do you do if a dead kid can't pay the cover?" I
asked.*

*"We let him in," Skip said, smiling. "Living or dead. We'll
take a partial donation if they can't pay up in full.
The living kids always, always have the money, though.
And they all buy T-shirts and snacks while they're here.
It works."*

*We watched a band called Skeleton Crew performing
from the window of his office. The members all hail*

*from New Jersey, and, their lead singer, DeCayce,
is dead.*

*"I don't pay the bands either," Skip said, as we watched
Skeleton Crew launch into the first of a set of
eight songs, which were an interesting mix of the bands'
competent speed punk with DeCayce's slow, dirgelike
vocals that hover like the wings of bats. "They play for
exposure."*

*I ask Skip if there's really that much exposure to be found
within the walls of Aftermath, which some people may never
leave.*

*He thought the question was funny.*

*"It's an investment," he said, "I think it's a good one.
Cultural credit is different from financial credit; you build
cultural credit by trading credit with other brands and
products in the hopes that they add to your own."*

*I'm told I have a good poker face, but Skip could see my
confusion.*

*"Look," he said, "did Michael Jordan make Nike, or did
Nike make Michael Jordan? And does it matter?"*

*Skip has a real Michael Jordan fixation, I've noticed, even
though the man has been retired for years. He pointed
out a few kids in the audience who were wearing shirts
that had the Skeleton Crew symbol, a yellow smiling skull
emoticon.*

*"It's like when certain designer clothes started appearing in
retail stores, the stuff was getting shoplifted by the closet load.
The designers thought they had a real problem, but then they*

*realized something. The clothes were getting boosted by fashion-conscious gang kids, and every one of those hip gangsters was like a walking billboard for their product. So the designers said, let 'em steal. They did subtle things to tie their brand into what was happening with urban chic; they did some branding with the rap stars of the day, and pretty soon the clothing was in such demand it wouldn't matter how many outfits they lost from their retail outlets.*

*"Aftermath is going to be like that. Undead culture is going to be the next pervasive phenomenon in the United States and the world. Six months from now this band is going to be able to tell all the people that want their songs for movies, for television, for commercials, that they were once the house band at Aftermath. And Aftermath is going to be able to say they put Skeleton Crew in the public eye. It's like that skull T-shirt you see everywhere, the Misfits one? Where were the Misfits until Metallica started wearing their shirt onstage and talking about what a "seminal influence" they were? They were a small local band with a small cult following, right up until Metallica went crazy and became one of the biggest music acts of all time. And then the Misfits were cool because Metallica wore their T-shirts. And Metallica was cool because they were part of that select cult following of the Misfits. It's all about cultural cred."*

*Skeleton Crew was a good band, the flat, pause-heavy intonation of DeCayce an element unique enough to set them apart from the dozens of bands that played in the same style.*

*"You don't know how lucky you are," Skip said, and unlike*

the songs that DeCayce sang, his words were free of irony, "To be dead in America at this point in time. This is your time."

I didn't know how to respond to that, so I just stood in his high office and watched all the lucky people on the dance floor below as they tried to have some fun.

I spoke to DeCayce sometime later, long after the rest of his band had left, presumably to get some sleep, to dream of being the vanguard of a new cultural revolution.

We talked about many things—how we died, how those around us reacted to our returns. I think it's funny how we rarely reveal the circumstances of our deaths to trad people we meet, but it is usually the first thing we exchange with fellow undead, and I said so.

DeCayce picked up on this instantly: "It's sort of the 'what do you do for a living' for the dead set," he said. "Instead, we ask, 'So, how was it that you stopped living?'"

He told me that the other members of his band were his best friends, and had been prior to his death.

"They all stood by me when I came back," he said. "My family had a much harder time of it—they still do. My friends, though . . . they were there through it all."

I asked him how long it took him to get the control over his speech and body.

"I'm still trying," he said. "I'm better onstage than I am one-on-one, as you can probably tell. Something about the crowd, maybe."

My last question was whether or not he thought there was a message in his music.

"No," he said first, but then thought about it. "Well, I guess there is, but not an overt one. I guess the message in the songs is that it shouldn't matter if someone moves differently, or looks differently, or talks differently. Is biotic differently. What matters is that we're all thinking beings, and if we are thinking beings we ought to be able to find common ground somewhere. Maybe if people can see us playing, three beating hearts and a dead guy, it will inspire a little more tolerance in the country."

Tolerance. I thought that his statement was similar in sentiment to the ideals of the Hunter Foundation. And I wondered, as I did when I first heard the Hunters speak of it, if tolerance was going to be enough.

Phoebe read the blog a second time before typing a reply.

Tommy—

Everyone here is fine. Except for George, who might be in some trouble. Something or someone has been killing animals in Winford and the police are blaming him. Karen says there's no way he would do something like that. What do you think?

When were you at Aftermath? Was it on the 28th? That was when we were all there. Margi, Colette, Karen and I. We had such a great time dancing and meeting so many people. I couldn't believe how many trads were there!

Did you see us?

Phoebe

# CHAPTER
# TWENTY-NINE

KAREN CALLED HER the next day and asked if she wanted to work on the Web site with her after school on Monday.

"I'd love to," Phoebe said.

"Great. You can come over after Undead Studies. You can eat here. I'll watch you, living vicariously the whole time."

Phoebe smiled. "We have the field trip tomorrow, right?"

"I know. I've got a bunch of . . . work to do for that . . . too. We're going to have an action-packed day."

"Okay," Phoebe said, wondering what a meal at the DeSonne household would be like.

"Sounds fun."

"I got Tommy's e-mail last night," Karen said, "the little . . . creep. Sometimes he makes me so mad."

"It was a good blog, though," Phoebe said.

"I can't believe he didn't come talk to us," Karen said. "Don't tell me it doesn't burn you up."

"A little." She was more sad than angry, though. Tommy was avoiding *her*, not them. She'd hurt him deeper than she'd realized.

"Well," Karen said, "I've got to get back to work. I'll see you at school tomorrow."

"You're still at work?" Phoebe said. "How late is the mall open?"

"Until ten, even on Sunday," she said. "This is my second double shift. Craig asked me to stay because two people called in. I figured it was the least I could do after going dancing on the biggest shopping day of the year."

"I should get a job," Phoebe said, thinking out loud. Really the work-study hours were enough; she could wait until the summer.

"Wait until I open up my business," Karen said. "I'll hire you."

"Your business?"

"Tell you later. Craig is giving me the . . . evil eye. I have to go. See you."

"See you," Phoebe said to dead air.

"Field . . . trip!" Cooper said as he took a seat in the back of the bus. Phoebe thought he was pretty pleased with himself for having arranged it.

Cooper claimed to have suggested the field trip so they could get out of some class time, but Phoebe suspected that he'd really done it because he knew Melissa wanted to go to the Haunted House, but had difficulty getting around. She'd worn her comedy mask today, and almost looked happy as she lurched into a seat. Alish and Angela were the last two to get on the bus, and they took the seat directly behind the driver. Phoebe figured that they would be the first adults ever to be invited to the Haunted House. Unless you count the police, who were called there on the night of Adam's murder.

She slid in the seat next to Karen, after a quick glance back at Adam, who sat in the back with Thorny and Kevin.

"Do you really think this is such a great idea?" she asked. "Inviting Angela and Alish?"

"I don't know, really," Karen said. "I don't know if I trust the foundation completely. I e-mailed Tommy, though, and he thought it was okay."

"You e-mailed Tommy?"

"Yes. That was okay, right? Me emailing . . . Tommy?"

Phoebe whirled to face her. "Of course it is. Why should I care?"

"I don't . . . know," Karen said, and Phoebe thought she was using more speech pauses than usual just to be irritating. "Why . . . should you?"

"Should I find another seat?" Phoebe asked.

"No," Karen replied, patting her on the shoulder. "I still love you. We're going to have . . . a blast tonight, aren't we?"

The bus pulled away from the curb, and the chatter grew in volume to compete with the dull growl of the engine. Thorny was telling Adam and Kevin about some phenomenal play he'd made on the football field, practically shouting about his gridiron prowess even though the dead, despite their many issues, were not hard of hearing. Margi was laughing about an e-mail DeCayce sent to Colette with an MP3 attachment of a song they'd added to their live show, a cover of "So Alive" by Love and Rockets, a band they'd known from Colette's brothers' vast record collection.

"He's totally singing about you," Margi said.

"Is . . . not."

"Is too!"

"Is . . . not!"

Melissa was sitting alone a few seats behind them, looking out the window. Karen called over to her.

"Hey, Melissa," she said. "Are you excited?"

Melissa scribbled on her board and held it up. She'd drawn a large and blocky exclamation point.

"There are lots of kids there. Hopefully you'll get to meet Mal. He's one of my best buddies. He used to stay at St. Jude's too."

Melissa erased and wrote.

FR. FITZ TALKS ABOUT MAL

"He does? Father Fitzpatrick seems to be a pretty nice guy, for a beating heart," she said, nudging Phoebe with her elbow. Phoebe nudged back.

I ❤ FR. FITZ

"Tayshawn was at St. Jude's for a while," Phoebe said. "Will Takayuki and his boys be there, you think?"

"I think so," Karen said, "They live there. So to . . . speak. I think it will be more . . . interesting . . . for everyone if they are."

A banner that read WELCOME ALISH AND ANGELA hung from the slouching porch of the Haunted House. It was Karen's idea, executed by some of the zombies with black paint on an old sheet. Alish took Thorny's arm as they went up the rickety steps of the front porch.

"Amazing," the old man said. "Simply amazing."

There were about twenty zombies waiting for them in the foyer. Phoebe watched Karen move to the front of the group, where she asked for silence even though none of them had made a sound. She did a quick scan for Tak, but didn't see either him or Popeye, although there were a handful of the other old-schoolers around, George among them. She was surprised and happy to see that Tayshawn had stuck around to see his old classmates.

"Hello, everyone," Karen began, "I'd like you all to meet Alish and Angela Hunter, who began the Hunter Foundation for the Advancement and Understanding of Differently Biotic Persons. That means us dead folk."

Karen smiled, and Phoebe was gratified to see more than one stony face twitch in an attempt to smile along with her. As irritated as she was with Karen, Phoebe had to admit she'd put a lot of planning into the event. Now that they had chosen to fully accept the Hunter Foundation as a source of funding and support for the Haunted House, she'd thought it made sense for them to try and cement their relationship in a way that went beyond the typical student/teacher relationship. To schmooze them, in other words. Skip Slydell would be proud.

"I would like to introduce each of you . . . to the Hunters," Karen said. "One at a time. We've also brought some new friends along from our class, Cooper Wilson and Melissa Riley."

Cooper waved, but Melissa looked like she was trying to hide behind Adam. Karen didn't force the issue.

"I appreciate your patience . . . in advance for helping make everyone feel at home. And for you . . . living . . . folks, we have some refreshments in the . . . unliving room. Soft drinks and chips."

"Really?" Thorny asked, suspicion evident in his voice. "Where did you get the snacks?"

Karen gave him a droll look. "From the cemetery, Thornton," she said. "Where do you . . . think?"

Karen stood by the Hunters and introduced them to each zombie in turn. Phoebe could tell that Alish wished that he was able to take notes to record his impressions, his hand shook as he clasped each cold, dead hand that was offered to him. His eyes kept drifting to George, who was shambling around the periphery of the gathering like a boy at a party too shy to ask a girl to dance. George made no attempt to hide the physical aspects of his death, the rents in his skin, his missing ear, the ribs visible beneath his ripped and muddy clothing. The funny thing about George was that, unlike zombies like Tak and Popeye who used their scars for effect, it didn't even occur to him to cover them up.

"This is Jacinta," Karen said, introducing a young girl who was still wearing the pink dress she was almost buried in. "She's a newlydead."

As Angela shook the blankly staring girl's hand, Phoebe took another quick scan of the room. Kevin and Thorny were looking at the CD rack by the stereo, and Margi and Colette were already making a loud nuisance of themselves with a small cluster of zombie girls in the corner. George had stopped his circumlocution of the room and was staring openly at Melissa. He took one dragging step toward her, then froze when she looked over at him.

Oh no, Phoebe thought, hoping that the shy girl wasn't spooked by the most zombie-esque of all zombies. They couldn't be more different. George, in truly dead fashion, had no compunction at all about revealing the evidence of his death; she took as much care as possible to hide her own scars, even from herself. Phoebe wondered how many people had figured out she was wearing a wig.

Melissa wrote something on her board and held it up in front of George.

"And how long have you been dead?" Phoebe heard Alish ask Jacinta. Karen and Angela exchanged a quick look, as though neither could believe the question he'd just asked.

"Three . . . weeks . . . sir," was the slow, slow reply.

George was staring at the whiteboard, his tall gangling frame like a six-foot-tall undead question mark.

"What was it like?" Alish asked. Jacinta didn't answer right away, either confused by the question or by its inherent rudeness.

Tak and the rest of his crew made an appearance just as the party was winding down. Phoebe watched Karen fix Tak with a withering glare.

"Nice of you to show up," Karen said to Tak.

"We've been . . . busy," he said. Despite his promise to "be good," he made a point of not shaking hands with Alish. He looked at the Hunters as though the sight of their living flesh was repellent to him. He did his stupid little trick with his cheek too, keeping it hidden from view until he was a couple feet away from them, brushing back his lank black hair with a bare-knuckled hand so they could get a good up-close view of his teeth. The Hunters both flinched, and Karen told him how clichéd he was becoming.

Phoebe noticed something in Angela's expression, though: recognition. Angela, unlike Alish, did not offer her hand to be refused.

"You aren't . . . doing enough," Tak said.

Alish asked him what he meant, but Tak had already turned away. Karen was about to apologize for him when Popeye pushed his way over and thrust one of his recruitment posters into Alish's shaking hands.

"Be all . . . that you . . . can be," he said. He lifted his right hand, the one with all the skin removed from knuckle to wrist, and reached for his glasses.

"Thank you, Popeye!" Karen said, trying to interpose herself between him and the Hunters.

Alish didn't notice her alarm. "This is wonderful!" he said, looking at the poster.

Popeye stopped. "What?"

"This poster," Alish continued. "It's brilliant. The way it captures the grim reality of the undead experience."

Popeye removed his hand from his glasses and peered over Alish's shoulder. "Really?"

"Oh, yes," Alish said, his bony fingers passing along George's image. "The colors, the way it shows the boy's obvious pride in being a zombie . . . even the font and the fine print. It is a remarkable composition."

"You really . . . think so?" Popeye said. "I . . . created it."

"Really? This is a fine piece of work. A fine piece. Such a powerful message. May I keep it?"

"Yeah! I mean . . . sure. The more people that see . . . my work . . . the better."

"Would you do me a favor?" Alish said, gazing intently into Popeye's dark lenses. "Would you inscribe this for me?"

"Um, yeah!" Popeye said, patting the pockets of his leather jacket. "I think . . . I've got . . . a marker . . . upstairs."

Phoebe watched him rush away, in search of his marker. When she turned back to Alish and Karen she almost laughed out loud at Karen's expression.

"Mr. Hunter," Karen said. "That was . . . that was . . ."

"Ms. DeSonne," he said, "in my position, I have to deal with bullies of all stripes. He smiled at her, his eyes twinkling beneath their furry brows. "It gets easier and easier each day."

She smiled back at him, but Phoebe thought she looked uneasy.

"Phoebe, would you come with me a minute?" Karen said, leaving the Hunters socializing with Tayshawn, who had reluctantly promised to talk to them. "I want you to hear something."

Phoebe followed her over to Takayuki.

"Do you have a minute, Tak?" Karen asked with mock sweetness.

"For you," he said, "I have an . . . eternity." Phoebe couldn't tell if he was trying to be charming or sarcastic.

Once they were in the kitchen Karen asked him about George, whether or not he could be responsible for the animal slaughters in Winford.

"George?" he said. "Impossible. George is not . . . fast . . . enough. Just to get to . . . Winford . . . is a major . . . ordeal."

"One of your other . . . pals?

Tak shook his head. "The Sons of Romero . . . would not . . . butcher . . . house pets."

"Sons of Romero?" Phoebe said, wondering if being a Son of Romero meant they were going to act like movie zombies. Tak pretended that she hadn't spoken, that she wasn't even in the room.

"That's cute," Karen said quickly, as though trying to defuse the tension between them. "You think of it . . . all by yourself?"

He shrugged, only one shoulder raising. "Of that crime . . . we are . . . innocent."

Tak was a lot of unpleasant things, but Phoebe didn't think he was a liar.

"Karen," Tak said, "why don't you . . . come with us . . . next time?"

"Please. I have a . . . job. Two jobs."

Tak showed his teeth. "We'd love . . . to . . . have . . . you."

Phoebe watched Karen cast her diamond eyes toward the heavens, but again she had the feeling that Karen was amused, maybe even charmed, by Tak's actions.

She herself was less amused when she saw Tak and his cronies leading Adam and some of their guests upstairs.

# CHAPTER THIRTY

AD TROUBLE WITH the stairs right leg left but made it. Made it in time for Tak Smiley's speech.

Cooper whispers. "Is that . . . Tak? Is that the . . . guy . . . Karen talks about?"

"Smiley." Last stair.

"This is . . . the wall," Smiley said, waves bare knuckle hand at the photographs. Cooper, Melissa, Smiley, Popeye, George, Thorny. Popeye stands next to Thorny shows knuckles shows ribs looks dead. Deader than dead. Thorny leaves.

Smiley continues. "These are . . . your people."

Hundreds of photos. Zombies, deadheads, corpsicles. Poloroids, jpeg printouts. Kids looking scared. Step. Cooper and Melissa looking.

"Our . . . people. The . . . returned dead. Zombies." Dragging the "Z" like drag left leg. *Zzzzzombies.*

"Here . . . I am," Cooper said, pointing at a curling sheet of computer paper. Smiling at Smiley.

"Thought you . . . looked . . . familiar," Popeye said, Popeye clapping Cooper on back, all smiles and light now.

"The beating hearts . . . want us . . . gone," Tak said. "The ones . . . downstairs . . . are no . . . different."

Melissa, writing.

"Not all trads are . . . bad." Cooper said, shaking his head. "Alish and Angela . . . are good to us."

"Like they are . . . good . . . to pets." Tak tapped on the wall.

Melissa writes, holds up: LIKE U?

Tak smiles. "We had nothing . . . to do . . . with . . . the incidents . . . you refer to. All part of the . . . bioist . . . conspiracy . . . to destroy us."

Tak waited, no reply. Turned back to the wall. "Half . . . of these . . . kids . . . have been returned to death. True death. And what . . . have they done?"

Melissa crossed-out writing, started again. Cooper's answer never came.

"You know . . . zombies . . . that have been destroyed. You . . . lived . . . with them. Does the . . . foundation . . . protest? Do they . . . demand justice? Do they do anything more than . . . hold you captive . . . and stick you . . . with needles?"

"I'm not . . . a captive . . . I'm . . ."

Melissa flips sign. George stares so hard, almost funny.

FATHER FITZPATRICK

Tak shakes head, lank long hair flicking against leather, tendons creaking. "You can't look to . . . the beating hearts . . . for sanctuary. In the end . . . they just make it easier . . . to round us up."

"What about the work . . . that Tommy . . . is doing?" Cooper said. Strength there beneath goofy exterior.

Tak looks at Cooper. "I wish . . . Tommy . . . well. My hope . . . is that . . . he reaches . . . Washington. I fear . . . he will not."

"What do you . . . think . . . we should do?"

"I think . . . you should be . . . with your people. With . . . us."

Popeye put his arm around Cooper's shoulder, squeezed. George reaches out, touches Melissa's mask. Gently. She doesn't flinch.

"We will be . . . ignored . . . by our country . . . no longer. We will . . . continue . . . to make noise," Tak said, "until . . . they . . . can no longer . . . destroy us . . . at will." Taps wall. "For . . . them. For our . . . people."

Want to clap. Don't. Look at wall instead. Have no idea what Tak thinks he is accomplishing.

Call from below, time to go. Popeye and Tak thank Cooper and Melissa for time. George waves. Follow them out. Smiley stops at top of stairs, turns.

"You, Adam . . . you should . . . be with . . . us."

Contact. Eye contact. Smiley doesn't look deranged. Looks concerned. Earnest.

"I'll think . . . about it."

Smiley nods, claps arm. Small gesture, big impact. Tayshawn at bottom of stairs like standing guard. Angela waiting, says van has to go.

See Phoebe in doorway. Phoebe turns away.

# CHAPTER
# THIRTY-ONE

PHOEBE WENT over to Karen's house when Undead Studies was over. She was fairly exhausted after the Haunted House event, but Karen was still in go mode, talking about all she felt they had accomplished with the visit. As she watched the dead girl talk about how important it was that the Hunter Foundation spent its money on the right things, all Phoebe could think was how wrong Karen had been when she told Tommy she didn't have any leadership skills.

Dinner at the DeSonne household was strange indeed. Karen's father did most of the cooking, although Karen helped him chop vegetables for a salad. Mr. DeSonne insisted that Phoebe not help them but instead "relax" in the living room, where Karen's little sister, Katy, was playing with a trio of small stuffed bears.

"Mommy has to work late," Katy told her. "Can I touch your hair?"

"Sure," Phoebe said, leaning forward so Katy could drag stubby fingers through her hair. Her mother would be eating at the office, her father said, and would not be in until later.

When dinner began, Karen sat at the table watching them eat spaghetti and salad, listening without comment as her father asked Phoebe some questions about school and the work study, which he referred to as the "special class." Karen would lean over to wipe her sister's face with a napkin whenever the tomato sauce threatened to cover it.

When they were done eating, Karen helped her father clear the dishes, another activity he forbade Phoebe to help them with. Phoebe noticed that Karen didn't speak much as they worked, and her motions were almost mechanical as she moved around the kitchen. Maybe she was reading too much into things, but Phoebe thought that Karen's father was doing everything he could to keep from touching her.

Katy used their absence to lean over and touch Phoebe's hair again.

"They say my sister's dead," she whispered, "but I think she's the prettiest girl in the world."

When the dishes were away, Mr. DeSonne had Katy say good night, which for Katy was a gentle hug and a kiss on the cheek for her sister and for Phoebe.

"I like you," she said, her breath warm against Phoebe's neck. "Come back and play with Karen?"

"I will," Phoebe promised, and Katy bounded down the hall after her father.

"Cute kid," she said to Karen when her chores were done.

"The best," Karen replied. "She was born nine months after I died. Kind of weird, huh?"

Phoebe didn't know what to say to that. She followed Karen to her room in the basement. The room was colder than upstairs, and the cellar floor was hard beneath the thin carpet. There was a musty scent in the air that Karen had tried to cover with various scented candles and plug-in air fresheners.

"The basement used to flood," she said, reading Phoebe's mind. "Sorry."

"No worries," Phoebe said. "It's a little dark down here for work, though. We don't want to go blind."

Karen turned on a few lights, and they sat on the edge of her bed. She saw Phoebe staring at a small silk pillow atop a pair of normal pillows.

"Yeah, it's the one from my coffin," Karen told her.

"I'm sorry, Karen. I . . ."

Karen waved. "Don't worry about it . . . really. My parents bought me a really nice one, lacquered wood with a white satin lining and pillow to match. I came back before I got to use it. And guess what? The funeral home had a 'no returns' policy! So I kept the pillow. Sometimes I lie down on the bed and put my head on the pillow, and I daydream about dreaming."

"What did you do with the coffin?"

Karen shrugged. "I wanted to keep it, but my mom thought it was too morbid. She didn't even want me to have the pillow, but I was . . . insistent. I think they sold the coffin on eBay."

Phoebe took her printed copy of "Words from a Beating Heart" from her bag.

"Karen," she said, "I'm sorry I was so cranky with you today."

Karen smiled. "You wouldn't be saying that . . . just because I'm about to read . . . your story, would you?"

"No."

"Hey," Karen said. "Don't worry about it. You've got a lot on your mind. You're entitled to be cranky."

She nudged Phoebe with her shoulder. "I remember what it was like to be alive too."

"Karen . . ."

"Kidding, I'm kidding. Now are you going to let me read that, or . . . what?"

Phoebe reluctantly handed over the papers. She looked around the room while Karen read, trying and failing to keep from looking for Karen's reactions to her words, and then trying and failing from being disappointed when there weren't any.

"I really like this, Phoebe," Karen said finally. Phoebe let out her breath, realizing how much Karen's approval meant to her.

"Really? You think so?"

"I really do. I wasn't...sure if Tommy's idea of having a . . . living . . . person write for the site was such a hot idea. After reading this not only do I see why it was a good idea—but I think you're the perfect person to do it."

Phoebe thanked her and paused.

"I wrote Tommy a poem when we . . . when we first really became friends."

"I know. He had it in his locker."

"You knew?"

"Everybody knew, honey. The community of the living weren't the only ones scandalized at first, if you must know. Tommy had dead people calling him a sellout even then."

"Tak."

"Not just Tak. Not everyone is as moderate as you think. There's a lot of jealousy and bitterness among 'my people.' And Tak isn't really such a bad guy."

"He's not?"

"No. He can be quite . . . sweet . . . sometimes."

Something in Karen's tone stopped her. Karen was rereading her blog entry, her smooth white skin spectral in the glow of the computer.

"Karen?"

"Mm-hm?"

"Did Tommy talk about it with you? About me, I mean?"

Karen turned toward her, her eyes seeming to hold the glow of the monitor a moment too long.

"He did."

"And?"

"And what?"

"And what did you think?"

"About him dating a beating heart?" Karen said, her pale lips in a thin smile. "I didn't have a problem with it, actually. And that was before I really knew you, even." She shrugged, her shoulders rising and falling in perfect sync. "People should be happy."

"And once you did get to know me? What did you think then?"

"I thought he had great taste." Karen looked at her, and

Phoebe had the same sensation of falling that she'd experienced when looking into Tommy's eyes that first night in the woods.

"Why do I feel like I'm not really answering . . . your question," Karen said, lifting her hands in exasperation. "What is your question, Phoebe . . . Hello, Phoebe?" Karen said before realizing why Phoebe had hesitated. She lowered her arm, too slow a gesture for it to be reflexive.

"Karen, I . . . did Tommy tell you how he felt about me?" she said, stumbling.

"Yes, he did." Karen said, crossing her arms in front of her, picking at the cuff of her sleeve with her fingers

"He told me he was in love with you, Phoebe," she said, her expression not changing, making Phoebe wonder if the subject was causing a rare emotional retreat in her. Then her face softened and her diamond eyes sparked and flared with a sudden and momentary white light.

"I think he meant it too."

Phoebe turned away. "Sometimes I thought . . . I thought that it wasn't *me*, you know? It wasn't *me* but the idea of me. Like I wasn't really important. What was really important was that I was alive."

She looked back, feeling shy and self-conscious, and Karen's pursed lips did nothing to relieve those anxieties.

"Because you were living," the dead girl repeated. "Phoebe, maybe that was . . . part of it. Is part of it. But the two of you had just met, right? You're sixteen. Didn't you ask yourself the same question yourself?"

"What do you mean?"

"Well, how do you know you weren't going out with him just because he was a zombie?"

"I wasn't."

"Are you sure? Dating a zombie really takes the whole edgy goth chick thing up a whole new level, don't you think? How many of the other little goth girls can say that they dated a zombie?"

"It wasn't like that," Phoebe said defensively.

"I know it wasn't, honey," Karen said. "Tommy's a loveable guy. He's brave, he's handsome—if he were still alive he'd be every girl's dream. And you're pretty lovable yourself, you know. I sometimes wonder if you have some kind of chemical or mutant pheromone or something you put out that drives everyone crazy."

"A mutant pheromone?" Phoebe smiled.

"Hey, stranger things . . . But look: you took interest in him as a person, Phoebe," Karen said. "Sometimes that's all anyone really needs to fall in love. Wasn't that what you were trying to say in your blog?"

"I guess so."

"I think it was, Phoebe."

"What else did he say?" Phoebe asked, hoping she didn't sound too eager .

"Not much else," Karen said, but Phoebe thought she could detect a far-off twinkle in her crystalline eyes, like the flare of some distant sun. "He's a very private person despite that . . . blog. Plus he probably didn't want to hurt my feelings."

"Hurt your feelings? Were you in love with him too?"

"All of us dead girls were a little in love with Tommy," she said, "but how do you know I wasn't in love with you?"

They both laughed at that. At least, Phoebe thought Karen was laughing. Phoebe's cheeks felt warm.

"Anyway," Karen said after a time, "I wish I could write like you. I think that was part of why Tommy is so into you. He likes the arty types. Music and poetry, deep feelings."

"You aren't arty?"

"Not very . . . creative, I'm afraid."

Phoebe caught a hint of sadness in her voice, ever conscious that whatever inflection and emotion she saw was a conscious decision by Karen. Looking at her, at her platinum blond hair swept over her shoulder, her diamond eyes sparkling above pale high cheekbones, Phoebe wanted to tell her that it didn't matter if she was "arty," because she was *walking* art. But she wasn't sure how Karen would take the comment, so she kept it to herself.

"Tommy wanted me to kiss him," she said instead.

"That would be a typical thing, yes."

"He thought it would bring him back to life. Or partly back, or something."

"Well, you did, I hope."

Phoebe looked up at her with confusion.

"Kiss him?"

"Oh. No, I didn't."

"You're kidding."

"No, I didn't kiss him."

"Why not?"

"I don't know."

"Why? Because he's a zombie?"

"Well, yeah. That's part of it. But it was just weird, anyway," Phoebe said. "I've never kissed a boy. Not really."

"You're kidding."

Phoebe bit her lip, thinking about her botched attempt with Adam.

"Phoebe," Karen said, her eyes glittering, "you had a boy believing that your kiss would bring him back to life, and you didn't kiss him? That takes playing hard to get to a whole new extreme."

Phoebe started to laugh, and when she did, Karen leaned in and kissed her on the side of the mouth: a cool, feathery kiss that was over before Phoebe could react. "There," Karen said, sitting back. "You kissed a zombie and survived. Next time you see Adam give him one of those, but with more feeling. Who knows? You might even bring him back from the dead."

"I didn't kiss a zombie," Phoebe said, resisting the urge to wipe her lips. Karen wore peach lip gloss. "A zombie kissed me."

Karen thought that was hilarious. "Whatever," she said. "I'll let Adam know he'll have to make the first move." Phoebe could no longer hold her gaze, and turned away.

"I don't think so."

She said it softly, because she wasn't really sure that she wanted Karen to hear her.

"What do you . . . mean? Adam is absolutely crazy about you—you must know that."

Phoebe shook her head. "No."

"Phoebe." Karen gripped her arm. "He's been all puppy dog . . . for you since . . . forever. You're joking, right? He told me . . . he was."

"He told you? When?"

"The night he . . . died." She didn't look away when she said it. "He was going . . . to tell you."

Phoebe's breath caught in her throat, the only reply she could manage was shaking her head.

"What . . . is it? Did something . . . happen?"

When words came, they did so in a rush and a sob. "I tried to kiss him! He . . . he pushed me away! Tommy told me . . . he told me a kiss would bring him back to life, but I tried, and Adam . . . Adam pushed me away!"

Karen's arms were chilly around her. "Oh, honey." Karen rocked her, and Phoebe felt so stupid and helpless.

"I guess he'd rather be dead than be with me."

Karen held her up straight. "No, sweetie. Don't you think that at all. That isn't it. He loves you, I'm sure of it."

"Then why would he *do* that?" She looked around the room for some tissues, but Karen didn't really have a great need for them. Finally she found a package in her backpack. "If he's so crazy about me, why would he practically *shove* me on the floor when I tried to kiss him?"

Karen smiled at her as she wiped tears from Phoebe's cheek with her cool fingers. "Phoebe, you have to think like a guy for a minute. Worse, a zombie guy. One of the most confused and . . . confusing . . . beings on the planet."

"What do you mean?"

"Look at it from a guy's point of view. Here's . . . Adam, superjock . . . extraordinaire . . . and not only can he barely walk, or talk . . . or anything. Even when he was in . . . full command . . . of his game, he couldn't express his feelings, could he?"

"He always had girlfriends."

"Yeah, he was really serious about those . . . airheads, too, wasn't he?"

"I think he was expressing himself pretty well when he pushed me onto the floor."

Karen's look was so deadpan at the bitterness of Phoebe's words that Phoebe couldn't help but giggle. Karen laughed with her.

"Phoebe, does Adam know about what Tommy said to you? About kisses bringing the dead back?"

"I don't know. Maybe."

Karen nodded. "That might be it too. He might not believe that you really . . . love him. He might think you're just going through the motions to try and resurrect him. He might think that what you feel is guilt, not love. Think about it—he's loved you for a billion years, and you never seemed to notice until he . . . died."

"How do you know he's loved me for a billion years? Did he tell you that?"

"Not with words."

Phoebe was skeptical. And, she realized, a little jealous. What did "not with words" mean?

"Phoebe?"

"What?"

"Do you . . . love him?"

She had an answer prepared for that question; she knew it would be coming as a normal part of the conversation they were having, but as soon as the question was asked she forgot the answer.

What she remembered instead was the way she felt when Adam appeared out of nowhere to save her life. She remembered what it was like when they were together, when they were younger, reading comic books or going swimming at the Oxoboxo. What she remembered was how strong he was, what he looked like in his suit, and how he was always, always there for her when she needed him.

And then she remembered how she felt when she was with Tommy, and confusion crept in.

"I . . . I don't know," she said. "I think so . . . I really think so, but I'm not sure."

Karen nodded. "I think maybe you are."

"But I'm not sure. How can I be sure?"

"You'll get . . . a chance. Adam will . . . come around. He just needs to get . . . his confidence back."

"You think?"

"I'm sure of it. And forget . . . about kisses and all that stuff. That isn't really what's going to bring him back. Love will bring him back. Love works."

"You seem to know a lot about guys."

"I know some things." Karen winked, and it was a perfect,

flawless wink, as if she'd been practicing. It startled Phoebe so much she laughed out loud.

"Karen," she finally said, to break the awkward silence, "we were supposed to be working on the Web site, weren't we?"

"Oh yeah," Karen said with an exhalation that was very much like a sigh. "Maybe we should just wait until our next work study at the foundation," she said. "At least then we'd get paid for it."

# CHAPTER
# THIRTY-TWO

"AGAIN," MASTER Griffin said. Did same form one hundred and seven times, counted. One hundred and eight.

"Again."

One hundred and nine. "When . . . will . . . I . . . be . . . ready?"

Griffin squints, reaches, adjusts arm. Lift arm.

"When you can grab the pebble out of my hand. Again."

One hundred and nine. Stare.

"I'm kidding, Adam. Is something the matter? You seem distracted today."

Distracted, he said. Not distracted, dead. Been a zombie for weeks and can barely move. When living, mastered this form on day one, two or three tries. One hundred and ten.

Griffin crosses arms. "Adam, let's take a break."

One hundred and eleven. Look at Master Griffin never

took a break not once in whole year of practice. Griffin sits on the mat, motions to sit in front of him. Griffin crosses legs, lotus. Can't do that. Can't even sit. Sort of flop.

Griffin waits, stares. "Adam, something is troubling you."

No joke, sensei. Dead, or hadn't you noticed? Griffin smiles. Everyone's a mind reader these days.

"The girl who brought you to the dojo," he said. "It's her, isn't it?"

Stunned. Stunned so only the truth will come out.

"Yes."

Griffin nods. "You have had feelings for her for a long time."

Not a question. Statement. Griffin looks, laughs.

"Don't look so surprised. You've studied with me for months now, and I've heard her name a dozen times. 'I played Frisbee with Phoebe.' 'Phoebe likes milk shakes,' 'Phoebe likes strange music.' When you are quiet, you hear things that other people don't actually say out loud."

Shut my mouth. Master Griffin not a talker. Says "again," "again," "again." Higher, faster, use the instep. Quiet.

"Listen more. I haven't heard you say her name since she brought you here last, and today you have trouble with the most basic forms. And not because you are a zombie. Because your mind is elsewhere. With her."

With her. Yes, with her.

"I listened to her when she was here, also, Adam. I watched you both."

Breathe. Tried to breathe.

"What . . . should . . . I do?"

Griffin shakes head.

"I don't know. You made a choice on the night you died, no? A choice for her. You cannot let the results of that one choice absolve you from choosing for the rest of your life."

Smile.

Griffin returns smile. "Sorry. Existence, whatever we term it. I am glad you are listening!"

"She . . . needs . . . to . . . live."

Griffin sits, patient and frowning, waiting for me to finish.

"She . . . needs . . . to . . . forget . . . me."

Griffin inhales. "Is that what she wants, Adam? More importantly, is that what you want?"

Don't answer. Can't

Griffin, serious. "You have a choice to make. Your heart, beating or not, will tell you what to decide. Keep listening."

"How was karate?" Joe asks, driving home.

"Good."

Choices. Pushed Phoebe away. Hurt her. *Chose* to hurt her. Chose to die for her. She chose . . . what? Chose to waste time on FrankenAdam.

"Phoebe hasn't been around a while." Just drive, Joe.

She chose, why? I thought guilt. Think guilt. Who am I? *What* am I?

"Kind of strange, when she was over every day."

Won't quit.

"Hurt . . . her . . . feelings."

"You hurt her feelings?"

Nod. Manage smooth nod.

"Well, you better apologize, and quick."

Joe's right, Master Griffin's right. FrankenAdam's wrong.

Choice would be Phoebe. Choice always was Phoebe.

"You listening to me? You need to apologize to her right away."

"Miss . . . her . . . cooking?"

"Do I *what*? Do I miss her *cooking*?"

Joe hits, actually hits, with knuckles on my arm. Don't feel it. Funny.

"You love her, you big idiot!" Ramped up, now. "And she loves you! You're smarter than that."

Real smart.

"Was . . . joke."

"Real funny. You better apologize to her."

Apologize. Choice always was Phoebe.

"I . . . will."

"You better."

"I . . . will."


Phoebe was surprised to see Adam at the door. He hadn't crossed the thin patch of grass that separated their yards since falling on Mischief Night. "Hey . . . kid," he said, "can . . . I . . . come . . . in?"

"You never had to ask before," she said, holding the screen open for him.

"We need . . . to be . . . invited," he said, his hand slapping at the screen and stepping inside.

Phoebe turned so that he couldn't see her smile.

"So," he said, "what are you . . . up to?"

"Just getting ready for school, same ol' same ol'."

"Doing anything . . . after . . . school?" he said.

"I'm supposed to have a driver's lesson," she said. "But I'll be home around five. Why?"

"Funny," he said, "I always thought . . . I'd be the one . . . teaching you . . . how to drive."

"Me too," she said, sitting down at the kitchen table and taking her bowl-size mug in both her hands. "The gearhead next door."

"Me," he said, pointing at himself, his thumb about even with the bullet hole over his heart. "Want to . . . toss . . . the disk around . . . sometime?"

He stopped his shuffling to look at her.

"I'd love to," she said. "Getting a little cold, though."

"Good," he said, "that's really . . . good. Frisbee . . . I mean . . . not . . . the cold."

She sipped her coffee. "Taking the bus today?"

"Yep."

"Can I sit with you?"

"Well," he said. "I . . . guess . . . so."

"It doesn't have to be in the same seat. If you're afraid of your dead friends seeing you."

"You know . . . how they can get," he said, smiling at her. She thought that even his smile looked more like it had in his pre-death days, much less a rictus. "All bent . . . out of . . . shape."

"Okay," she said, "I'll try to be discreet."

There was a lot they could say there, she thought, in the quiet kitchen, a lot that had gone unsaid and a lot about what had been said, but for the first time she felt that nothing needed saying. The link, the bond—call it friendship, call it telepathetic—that had been broken was there again, radiating in the air between them as palpably as the aromatic steam rising from her cup.

"It is . . . almost . . . time," Adam said. "Can . . . I take . . . your . . . bag for you?"

Her negative reply was reflexive, but the bond enabled her to catch it before it was out of her mouth. Adam, who in a hundred small ways, through opening doors and driving her to work and carrying bags and holding coats and letting her pick songs on the stereo, had not been able to do a single thing for her in the past two months.

"That would be great," she said, nudging her heavy bag from its place beside her chair with the toe of her boot, "because it is pretty heavy."

"Good . . . thing," he said, "that I am . . . pretty . . . damn . . . powerful."

"Good thing," she said, and excused herself to get her coat, hat, and gloves.

"Phoebe." He touched her arm.

She turned, and when she did, he leaned forward and he kissed her.

Kissed phoebe gently gently didn't want to hurt her. Can't

hurt her hurt her enough already. Kissed her. Long but not too long.

Steps back is she angry is she horrified is she happy?

She's shocked.

"Adam," she says, and she's sad. Made her sad crying tears and then "Adam" again and she hugs, her arms are tight around and she's holding like she doesn't want to let go. Like she never wants to let go.

Hug her back. Gently.

She looks up. Kiss.

No magic. No instant resurrection, no return from the dead. No bolt of lightning that starts the heart and pumps the blood. Can't move faster, can't speak more clearly.

But

Oh the kiss.

# CHAPTER
# THIRTY-THREE

**H**E KISSED ME, Phoebe thought, as they walked to her locker. It's all she could think about.

Adam had to duck beneath some poorly hung strands of garland as they walked. Phoebe again fought the urge to mother, to take the bag from him at the door so he would have time to shuffle (walk, she reminded herself, *walk*) down to his own locker and have a chance at getting to class on time. But she didn't. Adam was a big boy and being dead made him slow physically but not mentally. He wanted to do this for her and she needed to let him.

"Company," he said. She looked through the puffy-coated crowds milling through the hall and saw Margi waiting for her at her locker. She waved and Margi blew them both kisses.

"Thanks, Adam," she said, accepting the heavy bag back. He nodded and blew a kiss back to Margi, managing a fair approximation of a sneer as he did it.

They watched him walk back down the hallway, where he was joined by Thorny, whose red-and-green elf hat looked oddly appropriate on his curly head.

"Hey, Pheebes,"

"Hey, Gee."

"Good to see you and the Lame Man all chummy again."

"Yep. We're chummy."

"Did he ask you to the Winter Jubilee yet?"

"No," Phoebe said, a quip about Adam probably having a healthy aversion to school dances dying on her lips. "Where's Colette?"

Margi sighed. "She didn't finish her algebra assignment last night, so she got to class early to work on it."

"She doesn't have to sleep, but she still didn't finish her homework?"

"I know, kind of crazy. If you didn't have to sleep you'd probably have a sequel to *War and Peace* written by Thursday," Margi said. "But we got to talking last night, and you know how that goes."

Phoebe paused in the careful stacking of her textbooks to look at Margi and saw that the darkness around her eyes wasn't all eyeliner.

"Uh-oh," she said.

"Nah, it was good," Margi said. "Deep but *sans* drama. We've all had enough of that lately."

"Mmm. So what did you spend all night gabbing about then, if I may ask?"

"Well, we started off by talking about you and Adam, if you really want to know."

"Margi," Phoebe said.

"No, hold up, it wasn't like that either," Margi said, leaning into her and giving her a nudge. "It was all hugs, smiles, kittens, lacy underwear."

Phoebe slammed her locker and waited for her to finish.

"And then Colette said, 'You know, Gee, you haven't spent any time with Phoebe lately. Just the two of you. We've gotten together, the three of us, and that's been a hoot, and we've gotten together with the Dairy Queen—"

"The Dairy Queen?" Phoebe said.

Margi bit her lower lip. "That's what we call Karen."

"The Dairy Queen? Margi, that's terrible!" Phoebe said, but she was laughing. "I know. I know, I know. It's wrong. We don't mean anything by it, other than she's well, a little frosty. And very, very, white."

"Terrible."

"I know. We're just evil. Well, C.B. is more evil than I am ' 'cause she thought it up. Anyhow, she was saying how we all get together, but you and I never get together anymore, just the two of us. And how, before she, like, died, and Adam died, you and me used to hang out all the time."

"Colette is a good friend," Phoebe said.

"She really is, Pheebes," she said. "And she's sharp. She said that you and I ought to go out and do something together, you know, and not bring her along."

"That would be great," Phoebe said. "I mean, it's great when she's along, too, but it would be fun to be just me and you."

"Yeah," Margi said, taking her arm, a bauble from one of her bracelets snagging on the frilled cuff of Phoebe's blouse. "Us beating hearts need to stick together."

Phoebe tried to detach the charm, a gloomy-looking pewter teddy bear. "Not tonight, though. Adam and I are going to play some Frisbee."

"Holy crow," Margi said, "you guys are really back on track, then?"

"We're back on something," she answered, smiling.

"That's great!"

"Yeah, it really is."

She could feel the weight of Margi's stare upon her.

"What?"

"You tell me what. You've got this goofy, faraway look on your face. You look like you just landed on the moon."

"Oh."

Margi stamped her foot. "Come on, Phoebe! Give!"

Phoebe lowered her voice. "He kissed me, Margi. Adam kissed me."

Margi shrieked and clutched her arm. "Adam *kissed* you?"

"Shhhhh!"

"What was it like?" A little thrilled, a little scandalized, a lot curious. "Come on, Phoebe, tell me!"

There was so much that Phoebe thought she could tell her. How different it was when Adam kissed her than when she had tried to kiss him.

Phoebe was going to tell her, but then the bell rang, and the girls ran down the hall to their class.

There was little of the sense of moral outrage that had followed the news of Tommy and Phoebe's relationship once word about her and Adam got out, at least at school. Phoebe thought there were a few reasons for this, the first being that she and Adam were friends, and people were used to seeing them together.

Unlike Tommy, who was an outsider, an alien, Adam had been a favorite son of the community prior to his death, and as such, was exempted from the hatred that many people reserved for the undead. He was also exempted from blame, as it was common practice for bioists to blame zombies for the "crime" of being undead, as though they'd chosen such a fate. They knew Adam had been killed, and many people, while not knowing who specifically he was trying to protect, knew that he died trying to save someone.

Even when Phoebe and Adam chanced a trip to Winford to see a movie, people mostly ignored them, which was about the best reaction that a mixed living/dead couple could hope for.

"I'm amazed no one is saying anything," Phoebe said. "The popcorn guy didn't even blink when you handed him the money."

Adam was having a difficult time folding himself into the narrow theater seat, and Phoebe was glad the movie they'd chosen was sparsely attended.

"Played . . . football . . . against . . . him."

"Really? Maybe that's why."

"Maybe . . . people . . . are getting . . . used . . . to . . . us."

She wasn't sure if the "us" meant "zombie" or "Adam and Phoebe." They stopped by the food court after the movie to check in with Mr. Kendall, who was sipping a soda and reading a paperback, ready to spring into action if any of the traditionally biotic denizens of the mall chose to make trouble for his daughter and her date. Phoebe tried to talk him out of staying, feeling both foolish and guilty that her father should feel he had to chaperone them in such a manner. Not so foolish and guilty that she didn't ask for more time.

"Hi, Dad. Can I bring Adam over to Wild Thingz! before we go?"

"Did you have any trouble?" he asked.

"No . . . trouble."

"We'll only be a few minutes, Dad. We'll be done by the time you get the car."

Her father bent the corner of his paperback down, a practice Phoebe hated. "Okay. Ten minutes, okay?"

"Thanks, Dad."

The main reason that she wanted to bring Adam to Wild Thingz! was so he could see the line of Slydellco zombie hygiene products. Body spray, lip gloss, hair gel—she always got a kick out of the display, even though Tommy was the only zombie she'd known who actually used any of the products, most of which probably went home with trad kids trying to be edgy. She herself had a tube of Kiss of Life, a dark crimson lipstick "especially formulated for the differently biotic."

She had just begun showing him the rack when she noticed Karen standing behind the cash wrap, apparently working.

"Oh, my gosh," she said, gripping Adam's rock hard bicep. "It's Karen! I totally forgot she worked here!"

Karen saw her and held up a finger, asking for a moment. She spoke to a frowning, acne'd guy with a ring through his eyebrow who Phoebe assumed was her boss, and a moment later Karen joined them at the display.

"Hey, guys," she said, "don't you look cute together. Off . . . on a date?"

Phoebe blushed without knowing why. Adam's "yes" sounded like a tire slowly deflating.

"Listen," Karen said, drawing close. "Don't let on . . . I'm dead. They don't know."

The news stunned Phoebe, but Adam seemed to take it in stride.

"Does this . . . stuff . . . work?" he asked, holding up a can of aerosol zombie deodorant. "I don't . . . smell . . . do . . . I?"

"Of course not," Karen said. "It's really an . . . antibacterial spray. If you've been in the ground too long, I think. Try the Z if you want a . . . cologne."

"You didn't tell them you're a zombie?" Phoebe noticed that her eyes were blue instead of their usual diamond color. Was she wearing contacts?

"We all have secrets. Don't . . . out me, though, okay?"

"I wouldn't do that."

"I know you wouldn't, sweetie." Then, loud enough for her scowling boss to hear at the cash wrap, "We also have the Z in a six-ounce bottle if you'd rather, sir."

Adam smiled.

"Perhaps a T-shirt, then?" she continued, her voice ringing out over the loud horror-punk music playing from the store's sound system. "We have, just in, baby doll tees with the 'Some of My Best Friends Are Dead' logo. Very . . . popular."

Phoebe couldn't keep herself from laughing, and she held on to Adam for support. Karen smiled sweetly at her grumpy boss, fluttering her long eyelashes as she did so.

Phoebe thought it felt very natural, very real, to be having fun with her friends. Very normal. She looked at Adam and he was smiling at her, and she squeezed, not wanting to release him, not wanting to let that feeling go.

# CHAPTER
# THIRTY-FOUR

DUKE SHOWED UP at exactly two a.m., as promised. His huge black truck, sleek and reflecting moonlight, was almost soundless as it rolled up to the curb.

"Hey," he said as Pete climbed in. "Have any trouble getting out?"

"Are you kidding?"

Duke smirked and gave him the once-over. He'd worn exactly what Duke had told him to—black sneakers and jeans, a dark, hooded sweatshirt. Duke was dressed almost the same.

"So where are we going? You know you have to go back the way you came, right? This just goes into the development."

"I know." Duke slowed down a few streets away and pointed at a house near the end of a cul de sac. "Is that where Evan Talbot stayed?"

Pete noted he didn't say *lived*.

"Yeah."

"Got away with that one, didn't you?"

Pete didn't reply. Duke smiled at him, and then gunned the engine, and soon they were on the back roads of Oakvale.

"Did you know that there are twenty-seven cemeteries in Winford? And another seven just in Oakvale?"

Pete shook his head. "No, I didn't know that."

"True fact. That's almost three times as many cemeteries as liquor stores. That's a lot of dead people."

"Are we going to a cemetery?"

"We certainly are. There's a bag under your seat. Open it up, would you? I brought you a present."

Pete found a green canvas bag by his feet. He opened it and a pair of rubber masks fell out.

"You get the one with the long black hair."

Pete spread the mask on his knee.

"Zombies? We're going to pretend to be zombies? In a cemetery?" His mask had a long slash on the left cheek that exposed cracked yellow teeth along a gray gum line. The eyeholes were cast to make the mask look faintly Asian. It was a cartoonish likeness of the zombie who had maimed him.

Duke was smiling. "Fun, huh? Go ahead and try it on."

Pete held the mask stretched out before him a moment longer, then he pulled it on his head. The latex was moist and cool against his skin.

"That looks great." Duke reached over and ruffled the long black hair. "You, son, have just joined the ZLA."

"What's the ZLA?" Pete's voice echoed against the mask

and he adjusted it slightly. Already the trapped heat was making his stitches itch.

"The Zombie Liberation Army." Duke grabbed his own mask and pulled it on with one hand. Pete looked back at a bald zombie with pockmarked skin and round, crazed eyes, its mouth drawn back in a wet looking snarl.

Liberation, Pete thought, excitement and nausea welling up within his stomach in equal amounts. "We're going to dig up some graves, aren't we?"

The mad, slavering zombie face turned toward him.

"Oh yeah," it said.

There were three other vehicles at the cemetery, two white vans and an American-made sedan. Pete saw a half dozen or so figures milling about in front of one of the white vans, each with a shovel.

"Holy crow." He lifted the neck of his mask up because he thought he was starting to hyperventilate in the latex. "We're so close to the main road. What if the cops come?"

"The cops won't come." Duke brought the truck to a halt on the shoulder of the gravel path.

"How do you—"

"I know. The cops won't come. I've got a shovel for you in the back. And put your mask back on, we don't like to show each other our faces."

Pete scrambled out the door and joined Duke at the back gate of the truck.

"What about the zombies? Isn't this the place they put all those posters up?"

Duke unlatched the gate; the shovel he selected rasped against the bed as he drew it out, like a sword. He handed it to Pete.

"I like you, kid. You're observant."

"But what if they show up?"

Duke paused, and Pete could almost picture his bemused expression beneath the garish zombie mask.

"You aren't afraid of some zombies, are you? Big Pete, zombie killer?"

Duke's words made his stitches itch even more. "No, I'm not afraid. I just don't want to get caught."

Duke slid his own shovel out. "Quit acting like a girl. We know where the zombies are. They're busy with their own pranks tonight, so don't worry about them."

He dropped his free hand on Pete's shoulder and pulled him close, so that their masks were almost touching.

"Don't think we're a bunch of stupid rednecks going off half-cocked, Pete. Don't confuse our actions with yours. This is a very carefully thought out operation. The key to destroying your enemies is knowledge and planning. We've got both."

"Who's we?"

Duke let him go and rose up to his full height. He was bigger than any zombie Pete had ever seen.

"Just keep your mouth closed and your eyes open, Pete. I'm giving you a great opportunity here, but you're the one that's got to take advantage of it. Now don't say a word."

With that, Duke called over to the men from the other

vehicles, shouting naturally, as though they weren't about to desecrate a cemetery at two thirty in the morning.

"Gentlemen," he said, as they formed a loose ring around him. Pete counted seven other figures, all men by the looks of it, but he wasn't entirely sure because they were all wearing zombie masks. Each mask was designed to frighten, each having a macabre or grisly detail like a severed ear, missing nose, or wild pop eyes to make the wearer look insane or dangerous, or both. Someone made a comment about the long hair on Pete's mask, another whistled. The weight of the shovel felt reassuring in Pete's hand.

"Hey," a "zombie," definitely male, his large gut hanging over the waistband of his black jeans on all sides, called. "Who's your date?"

Duke pointed a finger at the fat man. "Shut up. We don't have time to be screwing around. Everyone know their parts in this?"

Zombie-masked heads nodded.

"Just to be sure, I'm going to break it down."

The respect that Duke commanded from these men was obvious, even through their disguises. When he spoke, all chatter and joking ceased, and they all milled in a little closer as Duke began to break down the plan. Pete gathered that he was supposed to dig graves along with the men while Duke supervised and took pictures.

"Read the tombstones before you dig," Duke said. "What we want is people with families, hopefully with one name on the marker not yet buried. Kids are okay, but stay away from teens."

"Don't want to catch a live one?" the fat man said. "I mean, a dead live one?"

No one laughed, maybe because Duke leveled his shovel at the man's protruding gut.

"That's the last time I'm warning you. You want to see if you can be the first person over eighteen to come back from the dead?"

The fat man shook his head, his zombie mask twitching back and forth so fast it would have been comical if it wasn't abundantly clear that Duke thought the time for jokes had passed.

Duke lowered the shovel and nodded at another zombie-masked man. "What do you have for us?"

He came forward with a large duffel bag. The man unzipped it and withdrew a stack of paper sheets similar to the "Undead States" posters that the real zombies had used when they decorated the cemetery. They had the same picture of that really, really dead-looking zombie, but the words had been changed to "ZLA—Rise up and Destroy the Living!"

Duke nodded. "Nice."

The man with the duffel took out an old grayish bedsheet. He unfolded it completely until it lay atop a grave like a picnic blanket. The words, "Zombie Liberation Army—Destroy the Living!" had been painted in dripping crimson letters.

Duke laughed. "Put that bad boy up on that mausoleum over there. Okay, people. Let's dig."

The men, even the fat comedian, rushed to obey. A few had already picked out their graves; Pete heard the unmistakable sound of blades biting into the frosted turf. He was aware, suddenly, of the crazy eyes of Duke's mask staring down at him. He almost flinched.

"You okay, son?" he said softly.

Pete nodded, hefting his shovel.

"Attaboy. Why don't you get started on that one over there?"

Pete walked over to the grave Duke had indicated. There were two names on the headstone; the woman had died last year, in her forties. Her surviving husband, a few years older, was still out and about.

He looked back at Duke, who was leaning on his shovel to balance the camera he pointed at him.

Pete started to dig.

# CHAPTER
# THIRTY-FIVE

TAKAYUKI LOOKED back to the edge of the parking lot, where Tayshawn stood under a high streetlight. Tayshawn's job was to watch the mall entrance for prowling police cars, and signal the remaining Sons of Romero with an air horn that he had "liberated" from the hardware store. They had been in the mall lot for an hour now and not a single cop car had swung by. Tak couldn't believe their luck.

He looked back at the mall entrance, where Popeye was putting the finishing touches on his latest art installment. George and Karen stood with four mannequins propped up on the front steps under the unlit neon sign, each bent into stiff, awkward poses meant to parody the languidly unnatural poses of fashion models. Popeye had used papier mâché to give the mannequins a rough, old-school zombie appearance; one even had a strand of latex skin hanging down from its cheek in what was perhaps a sly tribute to Tak himself. Tak thought it looked like someone had plastered shredded wheat to its wooden face.

"Move her over . . . to the left . . . George," Popeye said. "Just a . . . hair. No, my . . . left."

The mannequin had one of the newest shirts from the Slydellco line, the words "Just Dead" in block letters on a white background. The zombie mannequins were all smiling, and all of them sported Slydellco shirts that Karen had picked up for them at her job. The two girl mannequins were wearing cosmetics from the Z line; Tak had watched Karen apply "Kiss of Life" lipstick to one of them from her own personal tube. Tak thought that the crimson lips and the other liberally applied cosmetics—the eye shadow and blush—combined with the grayish papier mâché made the figures look like garish undead clowns.

He thought "Kiss of Life" looked really good on Karen, though. He wasn't sure but he thought she used the eyeliner as well, and he once thought he smelled flowers when standing next to her—his sense of smell was so tricky, and he was never sure if he wasn't imagining scents rather than experiencing them.

George knocked off the zombie's wig as he moved the mannequin.

Tak wished they would work faster, but he was also glad that Popeye took things so seriously; his creativity had been a real boost to the Sons of Romero, who responded to the various projects with eager enthusiasm. And there wasn't much that any of them were enthusiastic about.

"Let me help you, George," Karen said.

Tak watched her bend down to retrieve the wig, her short plaid skirt hiking up on her thighs. She glanced back at him and a wry smile crossed her lips.

"Here we go," she said, straightening the wig on the mannequin. George gave her his version of a smile, and the result was horrific.

"There," Popeye said. "It's . . . perfect. Let me take . . . a few . . . pictures."

He withdrew a camera from his backpack and urged George and Karen to stay in the frame for the first few shots.

"Why don't you . . . join them . . . Tak?"

"No."

Popeye's eyes were unreadable behind his thick wraparound glasses. He turned and snapped a few pictures with Karen and George in the background.

Tak watched her pose, and he could tell she was aware of his attention. She leaned over and mimed a kiss to the mannequin with the slashed cheek. Popeye snapped a few more with them out of the frame, then popped out the memory stick.

He held it out to Karen. "Do you have . . . pockets . . . in that skirt? It's . . . awfully . . . small."

Karen took the stick and dropped it into the pocket of her white blouse. "Don't be cheeky."

Tak watched the exchange, wondering if Popeye got away with his innuendoes because he was gay. He looked back at Tayshawn, still under his spotlight.

"Are we . . . done . . . here?"

Popeye cast his hands heavenward. "Are we done . . . here,

he . . . says. Not . . . 'Popeye, you . . . genius! You've . . . done it . . . again!'"

"Popeye, you genius, you've . . . done it . . . again. Now . . . can we . . . go?"

Popeye shook his bald head and shouldered his bag of supplies, muttering about the lack of respect. Tak watched Karen help George down the stairs; fearsome as the boy looked, he was easily defeated by a simple staircase. His left leg just wasn't working the way it was meant to.

They started across the lot.

"I'm really . . . glad . . . you came with us, Karen," Tak said, once they were out of the spotlights and into the woods. "Thank . . . you."

"Why, Tak. You say the . . . sweetest . . . things."

Tak looked over his shoulder, making sure that George wasn't lagging too far behind. He felt Karen's hand brush against his, and wondered if she'd felt the hard bones of his knuckles where they protruded from the skin. His sense of smell may have been dull, but his hearing was excellent—he could hear the rattling of the equipment in Popeye's bag, the scrape of George's step as he dragged his foot along the trail, and above it all the swish of Karen's skirt as she kept pace beside him.

He cleared his throat. "Will you . . . be late . . . for school?"

She shook her head, and he was almost certain he could detect floral traces in the air around her. "I'll walk . . . straight there. It's . . . closer . . . than home."

"Karen . . . I . . ."

He didn't get to finish, as Popeye trotted up beside them, angling his thin body between them.

"I can't . . . believe . . . no cops . . . the whole night," he said. "We were . . . wicked lucky."

Tak wasn't so sure. "Yes . . . lucky."

"And Karen, thanks for . . . getting the . . . shirts. That really made the . . . piece . . . I thought."

"Sure, Pops. Anytime."

Tak wanted to trip Popeye, who stood between him and the memory of flowers. "You risked . . . your job . . . for us."

Karen smiled at him. "You mean you aren't still . . . mad at me . . . for taking the job?"

Tak looked at the ground before their feet. He'd argued with Karen when she told him about how she was passing, going as far to say that she was setting their cause back to the days of Dallas Jones, the original zombie, by her actions. But the more he thought about it, the more he realized that Karen had a right to live her own undead life. Besides, he'd thought, there were ways that her actions could be useful to everyone.

"I was . . . wrong," he said. "It . . . happens."

Tayshawn, who had stayed back with George, called for them to wait up, and the trio stopped at an intersection of paths.

"Was it hard . . . stealing the shirts?" Popeye asked.

Karen looked offended. "I didn't . . . *steal* . . . them, Popeye. I . . . *bought* . . . them. I have two . . . jobs, you know."

"Really? You . . . bought . . . them?"

"Yes, really."

Tak frowned. "At the same . . . time? I would . . . hope no one connects . . . your . . . purchase . . . with . . . the installation."

Karen looked unconcerned as she took a seat on the remains of a stone wall that had once marked off some Connecticut landowner's plot. "We sell so many . . . of them," she said, "and I've bought . . . a bunch more. I think I'm . . . safe."

"Good," Tak said, watching her smooth her skirt on her pale legs. "We want you . . . to be safe."

Tak knew that that was what had fueled his initial rage when she told him about her job at the mall. Working in a public business was different from her working at the foundation, where there's at least the pretense of a shared beating heart/zombie worldview. If her zombie nature was to be discovered while she was working at the mall, Tak thought she ran the risk of being dragged out into the parking lot and destroyed. It had happened to zombies across America for lesser offenses.

"Does this mean . . . you are . . . a Daughter . . . of Romero . . . now?" Popeye asked.

Tak thought he detected a slight note of jealousy along with the excitement in Popeye's voice. He knew Popeye was fond of him, but he also knew that what drove Popeye's train most of all was his "art," and if Karen was on the team he'd be able to accomplish a lot more because of her access to computers, photocopiers, and things that could be bought in stores. And besides, Tak had made it as clear as he could without saying it out loud that he thought Popeye a trusted friend, but that was as much as he'd ever think of him.

Popeye, he knew, wasn't really deterred. That was one curse that didn't leave when you died. The curse of hope.

"I don't think I'm . . . ready for a . . . commitment yet," Karen said, her eyes that flashed in the darkness still locked on Tak's.

"Your presence is . . . enough," Tak said, "for . . . now."

Karen smiled, and in her smile Tak realized that he was still cursed as well.

Tayshawn and George caught up a moment later, and then they continued through the dark wood.

# CHAPTER
# THIRTY-SIX

UNDEAD STUDIES. Alish looks grave (ha) when class enters. He and Angela are talking to a pair of tall men in suits, some type of law enforcement. Duke Davidson was there as well, his expression and pallor could make him and the gray cop cousins. The men both have zombie eyes. Gray Suit turns, and although Thorny spends much of his day around dead folks, the man's stare is enough to kill the laughter in his throat. Feel Phoebe's hand on arm, her touch a vague sense of pressure. She could be gently resting her hand or squeezing with all her might. Touch could be one of compassion, or affection, of alarm—can sense none of these gradients.

"Guest speakers?" she whispers. Try to shake head. The presence of men like these indicates that Something Has Happened. First thought is of Tommy. Sitting—unaided—can see by the way Karen goes to the beverage service that she is having similar thoughts. Wonder what it is about the presence of certain types of authority that triggers a rebellious response in her. The fact that she can drink liquid, and does so to distract the living people around her, is something of a defense mechanism. She does it in the same way that a juvenile delinquent would clean his nails with a knife.

Angela speaks to us first. She looks as though this class has aged her; the radiance in her smile has diminished.

"Class," she tells us, "this is Detective Gray and Detective Alholowicz. They are here to talk to each of you. About . . ."

"Ms. Hunter, if I may?" the gray one, Detective Gray, said. It wasn't really a question. "We're here to talk to you about a crime." He looked at everyone in the room, but he seemed to find me particularly interesting.

"A terrible crime. A felony. Grave desecration."

"And you think one of us . . . did it?" Karen asked, pouring at least an inch of sugar into her coffee cup.

Gray turned toward her. He was a thin guy; the suit jacket made him look bigger, but when he turned you could see how thin he was.

"We know at least one of the perpetrators of this heinous act was dead," Gray said, and for the first time I saw a flicker of reaction in his pale eyes. I think it was because he'd assumed that Karen was alive when he first walked by. "Ms. Hunter, I think I'd like to begin the interviews right away. Adam Layman, you're up first."

Might have blinked.

\* \* \*

In Angela's office, a little room off the clerical offices that had a couple leather chairs and shelves filled with books. Three chairs stood on a red oriental rug.

Alholowicz kept dabbing at his left eye with a handkerchief. The eye was tearing and glassy looking. He was lumpy around the middle in contrast to his partner, and there was a coffee stain on his white shirt that his tie almost covered.

"You want to stand?" he asked. "You guys don't get tired, right?"

"I want him to sit," Gray said before I could answer, pulling the office door closed with a little more emphasis than what I would have thought necessary. He waited, then he took the other leather chair, pulling it a little closer.

"Do I . . . need . . . a lawyer?" Probably sounded guilty, or worse, scared.

Gray didn't blink. "You don't have any rights," Gray said. "You're dead. You're not even a citizen."

"Jeez, Louise," his partner said. "Give the kid a break, will ya Steve?" Good cop said. "It doesn't have to be like that, does it?"

Gray's eyes were like drills as he reached inside his suit jacket. Inside was a gun in a holster and for a moment I thought he was reaching for the gun and now I'm sure that is exactly what he wanted. Instead he took out a photograph.

"You tell me," he said, holding it out in front of me. "You tell me how it should be."

Looked at the photograph. It was of a murky dark hunched figure heaving a shovelful of earth from a grave.

"Real nice, huh?" Gray said, slapping the photo on the table beside us so hard that Alholowicz had to steady the lamp before it fell to the ground. There was another chair behind Angela's desk, but he remained standing. "That's Chesterton Cemetery, right over the Winford line. You want to tell me who that is in the photo?"

"Have no . . . idea."

"Do you always talk that slowly, or just when you have something to hide?"

"Don't . . . have . . . anything . . . to hide. Didn't . . . do it."

"You didn't do it. He didn't do it, Agent Alholowicz." Gray leaned forward, his elbows on his knees and his hands tented as though to keep them from shaking. "I guess we can just go. He didn't do it."

He got up quickly, his whipcord body brushing against the table. Alholowicz replaced the lamp again.

"Look, kid," he said, "we know you didn't do it. Agent Gray has a niece that's a whatchacallit, a zombie, and he gets really angry when a zombie does something like this because he knows you all don't have, um, any constitutional rights."

"Every time one of you maggot brains screws up like this," Agent Gray said, "you get that much closer to sending people wild in the streets. We're talking chains and torches, smart guy. Eighty percent of America is just waiting to light you guys up in one big bonfire, you hear me? And what do I got if they do? What can I arrest people for? Public disturbance? Fire code violations? I do not want some crazy mob burning up my sisters' kid."

He slapped the table in case I didn't understand how passionate he was about the subject.

"You . . . are in . . . the FBI?" It took a while. Gray, undead niece or not, wanted to hit. He turned away, thrusting his fists on his narrow hips.

"Yeah, we're FBI," Alholowicz answered. He walked over to the shelves of books and tried to look like he was scanning their spines. "We're a new task force, actually. Undead Crimes. No disrespect intended if that isn't, whatchacallit, politically correct. You know better than anyone that people don't really know what to do with you fellers."

"Undead . . . crimes?"

"Yeah," Alholowicz said, lifting a glass paperweight off the bookshelf with one hand while dabbing at his eye with the other. "Yeah, absolutely. Lots of undead crimes. We started out investigating crimes *against* you people, you know? The burnings and the lynchings and the getting dragged behind cars. We cracked this one case where this group was actually crucifying dead folks. Nailing 'em up on crosses and leaving them there. Didn't kill 'em or anything, but left them hanging there in fields for days. Remember that, Steve? That case in . . ."

"I remember," Steve said.

"Anyhow, that's how it started. The Bureau figured that even though you people were dead already and didn't have any legal rights or anything, it wasn't exactly something we wanted to condone. I mean, crucifixions! Jeez, Louise!"

"Can we get on with this, please?"

"Sure, Steve, sure. Take it easy. Anyhow, kid, that's what we were supposed to do. Investigate groups of people that were getting together and committing acts of violence on dead people. But then a funny thing happened. Not so funny, really. More and more we got called upon to investigate crimes of violence committed *by* dead people."

Agent Gray turned around then, no longer looking angry, but just looking tired. "And that isn't good, Layman," he said. "It isn't good, because like it or not—and I don't like it—you and your friends don't have any rights. Zero. The laws aren't there to protect you. Which means that the laws aren't there to protect *from* you either, and the last thing we want is people going to look for some street justice.

He leaned close again, but this time his intimacy was free from rage.

"I don't want to see that happen," he said. "It's wrong."

"Steve's a patriot," Alholowicz said, fumbling the paperweight before navigating it back to the shelf. "He really is. And he loves that little niece of his."

Gray leaned in a little closer, close enough to count Adam's eyelashes

"So let's cut the crap," he said, "Tell me about this guy with half a face."

The dead were always given some distance in the halls of Oakvale High, but once the news of the grave desecration came out, students were literally turning around and running the other way. The incident was all over the news, with the families of the people whose graves had been disturbed making tearful pleas for the police, the government, anybody to do something about the "evil zombies" who would commit such blasphemy. One man, the scab of his grief not yet healed from having lost his wife to a drunk driver the year before, was stone-faced as he called for "the eradication of the zombie menace" on national TV.

The fear the incident had caused was so disruptive that a notice was posted mandating that all differently biotic students needed to be escorted from class to class by a teacher.

"Come on, Layman," Coach Konrathy said, meeting him at his locker before the first bell. "Show some hustle." Phoebe couldn't decide who looked more pissed off about the arrangement.

Some trad students, ones that had been in the pink of health just twenty-four hours before, were absent from school entirely. Norm Lathrop told Phoebe that there was a petition going around school to ban undead students from common areas like the foyer and the cafeteria.

"Boy," Karen said to Phoebe in the hallway as she waited for her to retrieve her books. "Dig a few . . . graves and the whole world comes down on your head. Could I get . . . arrested for digging out of my own grave?"

"Don't even joke. This is too weird," Phoebe said. The flow of traffic had moved all the way to the other side of the hall to keep from getting too close to Karen. "We're getting together at Margi's after school. You want to come?"

Karen shook her head. She was staring over Margi's shoulder, as though her diamond eyes were recording each and every one of her classmates who was now shunning her.

"I'm going to try to . . . talk to Takayuki . . . and the boys. Find out what the story is. Tak swore that George didn't hurt the animals. Maybe they didn't do this either."

"Karen, they were showing pictures of someone that looked a lot like Tak."

"The pictures were grainy. And I know the boys had nothing to do with those flyers."

"How do you know that?"

"Because I didn't make them." Karen's expression went blank. "This time."

"Karen! *You* made those flyers?"

"The first ones, yeah, I . . . used the computer and the . . . photocopier at the mall, when I was on break. It was . . . a joke. A funny one too. This wasn't . . . funny."

Phoebe didn't know what to say, she just stood there with her mouth hanging open.

"Miss DeSonne!" Principal Kim called. "You have a date with history!"

"There's my escort. At least she doesn't . . . pretend these new rules make sense. See you."

"See you."

Phoebe was halfway to her own class when she saw a group of boys standing around Kevin Zumbrowski. His books were on the floor, his shirt was untucked, and one point of his shirt collar pointed at the ceiling. His cheek looked dark, as though it had just been slapped, or punched.

"Hey!" she said.

The boys, she was surprised to see, had Denny Mackenzie

and Gary Greene among them. She heard someone make a joke about the B.O.F.: Bride-of-Frankenstein.

She took Kevin's arm.

"Are you okay, Kevin?" she asked. "Where's your escort?"

He shook his head from side to side violently, like a dog with a new chew toy.

"What is it, Kevin?"

"He . . . wouldn't . . . take . . . me," he said, making a noise like a sob.

She put a steadying hand on his shoulder, shushing him. He looked so pitiful leaning against the wall, unable to cry real tears.

"We're going to be late, honey," she said.

"Don't . . . leave me!" he wailed.

The final bell rang, and for a moment she didn't know what to do.

But then she hugged him, holding him until he calmed down.

"I won't leave you," she said, holding him tight. "I won't."


"They actually gave you a detention?" Margi said, incredulous. Phoebe had gone over to Margi's after school to vent her rage. She hoped some time with Margi and Colette would help her feel sane again. "And Kevin too? That's the stupidest thing I've ever heard."

"I know," Phoebe replied. She was thinking about Kevin. One of the teachers had started yelling at them when he'd discovered them in the hall, and had already vowed to have them both expelled, when Principal Kim arrived and told the teacher to get back to his room and shut up. "It was stupid."

"Principal Kim is making you serve the detention?"

Phoebe nodded. She said that it would be in everyone's best interest if Phoebe accepted the wrist slap, as a complete lack of punishment might be perceived by the student body as special treatment for differently biotics. She didn't actually come out and apologize, but Phoebe could tell from her tone that Principal Kim wasn't happy about the decision. Phoebe accepted the punishment without comment. Kevin didn't say another word the whole time they were in the office, even when Principal Kim called the Hunter Foundation and asked that they send a van.

"That is so unfair."

"I regret nothing," Phoebe said. She was worried about Kevin, worried he'd go to the foundation and shut down, fearful of trads. He'd made some gains over the past few months, and it would be a shame for all his progress to be erased.

"My only great . . . regret . . . in life," Colette said, "is that I was not able . . . to get . . . my brothers' LPs before . . . my parents threw me out of the house."

Phoebe smiled at her from her seat on the floor, at the exotic way "LPs" sounded in her whispery voice. Colette was stretched out on her stomach and hanging over the edge of Margi's bed, a glossy black LP jacket in her hands. The gray was all but gone from her hair, but Phoebe thought that might have been because Margi was dyeing it.

"Why?" Margi asked, taking the jacket from her. She'd bought it at a yard sale ages ago because she liked the cover. "We don't even have a record player, and I've probably got his stuff on MP3."

"I'm feeling . . . retro," Colette said, reaching for Margi's cat, Familiar, who shied away from her.

Phoebe thought it didn't have anything to do with her records but instead had to do with her brother himself.

"Have you heard from him?" Phoebe asked. "Your brother, I mean?"

Colette shook her head. "I don't even . . . know . . . where he . . . is," she said. "He's probably . . . still on . . . foreign soil. He could be . . . dead, for all . . . I know."

"Oh, Colette."

"Well, he could. He's past the age of resurrection too. I think he turns . . . twenty-five . . . this year."

"Twenty-five?" Margi said. "Might as well be dead."

Colette threw a pillow, but it went wild and knocked an unlit candle off Margi's shelf. The clunk it made sent Familiar into a corner, and the much heavier clunk that Colette made when she slid off the bed sent the cat into a frenzy.

"Will you quit it?" Margi said. "My parents are liable to think you've finally turned into an eighties horror movie."

Colette's fall had been way more than awkward; the akimbo way she lay reminded Phoebe of a big Raggedy Ann she'd had as a child, and the boneless contortions it would make when thrown. Colette was not quick to untangle the knot of her own limbs, and she was more than a little disturbing to look at, especially given the unnatural angle of her neck.

"I've got . . . no . . . strings," she said, finally rolling onto her back.

"Couldn't you find him?" Phoebe asked, managing to get skittish Familiar to come into her lap, where he perched with his eyes bright and focused on Colette. "Through the Web, or something? A government agency?"

"No rights," she said, "and my . . . parents . . . don't, do not . . . ack . . . knowledge . . . my horrific existence."

"We're going to see them this summer," Margi said without looking up from her computer screen, where she was scrolling through her playlists. A song from Skeleton Crew was playing at the moment. "They still live in Tennessee. I checked."

"Sure . . . we . . . are," Colette said, looking away. Phoebe could feel Familiar tense up under her hands as she rose to a sitting position.

"We are," Margi told her. "I've got my license and we're going. That's final."

Colette looked back at Phoebe, rolling her eyes up in their sockets until only the white showed. For a terrible moment, Phoebe thought they wouldn't return to normal.

"Whatever."

"You want to talk to your brother, don't you?" Margi said.

"Of course . . . I do," Colette replied.

"How else are you going to do that? The rest of your crackpot family has already written you off. Your dad is the weak link and we're going to get him to talk."

"What if . . . Cody . . . doesn't want . . . to talk to me . . . either?"

"He will."

"How do you . . . know?"

"I know all," Margi said.

"Sure . . . you do."

"I think it's worth trying too," Phoebe said. "I think Cody would want to see you."

"He thinks I'm . . . dead," Colette said, and than tried to giggle. "Oh, wait."

"I've Googled the guy a bazillion times," Margi said. "Nothing. There's some Cody Beauvoir that I guess is a lacrosse hotshot at some high school, that's all I get when I Google him."

"I wonder if Cody . . . ever Googled . . . me."

"He wouldn't get anything but your obituary," Margi said.

"Hey," Phoebe said, "what if we put you up on mysocalledundeath? A picture and a request that if anyone knows Cody to have him contact you through the Web site."

"That's a good idea," Margi said. "Let me get the digital camera."

"Oh . . . no," Colette said, "can't we use a pre-death photo? I want him to . . . recognize me."

"Anyone who knows you would recognize you," Margi said, but even as she said it she was reaching for a photograph that was framed and sitting on her shelf. It was the same photo that Phoebe had hanging in her locker, the three of them standing outside the Cineplex in Winford. Colette's eyes had a thick streak of dark eyeliner in the corner, so that she looked like an Egyptian princess, her arm was gauntleted in a dozen or so shiny bracelets. Her mouth was open in laughter.

"We should Photoshop us out, Pheebes," Margi said, sliding the photo free of its frame.

"Then I . . . would look . . . like an insane . . . freak," Colette said.

"Welllll . . . "

"Look how I'm . . . laughing."

"Okay," Margi said. She found her digital camera and took a photo of the photo, "the Weird Sisters stay together, then. I'll e-mail it to you, Pheebes, and you can put it up on the site, okay?"

"Absolutely."

"Do you really think . . . he'll see it?" Colette said.

"Someone will," Phoebe said.

# CHAPTER
# THIRTY-SEVEN

WALKED THROUGH the door into a hug from Mom. So worried, she says. Always worried, but what is the worst that could happen now?

Okay, Phoebe okay, everybody okay. Don't worry so much.

"The school called," she said. "I spoke to Principal Kim and she told me what happened. About the graves."

Bananas in a bowl, cookies in a jar on the counter. Used to come home and make a sandwich. Sandwiches and ESPN after school. Miss many things, but miss sandwiches most of all. Since making up with Phoebe, anyhow.

"Adam," Mom at arms length, squeezing shoulders as though checking if real. Real or unreal? Fingers kneading, flesh unyielding. Hard. Stone cold, like rock.

"Adam, do you know who vandalized the cemetery? Was it your friends?"

"Don't . . . know."

Looking like she can't believe her son is in the room with her. Maybe not wanting him in the room with her.

"You didn't have anything to do with it, did you?"

Stop, look. Words take time take longer when emotions come first.

"No."

Smiles nervously. Lets go of shoulders, hands shaking as she lights a cigarette.

"There was a boy here to see you earlier, Adam. At least I think he was here to see you; he left when he saw me looking at him through the window. A boy with long, black hair and a terrible scar. He was just standing at the edge of the woods in our backyard and watching the house. Do you know who I'm talking about?"

Nod. Nod.

"Is he a friend of yours, Adam?"

Says name over and over, like she's afraid to forget it. Or afraid that son will forget it. Is he a friend? Complicated. Not friend, but he is a zombie. That makes us something. Decide to assent.

Nod.

Exhales, smoke leaving lungs like the soul leaves the body. What replaces?

"That boy scares me, Adam."

"Me . . . too."

After, left leg right walk to bedroom, think about Phoebe. Phoebe has the night off, going with friends. Margi and Colette, Weird Sisters. Good. Glad. Glad for Phoebe, happy happy glad. Happy.

But worried too. Killing house pets, digging graves. Dangerous activities sure to end in tears.

Like dating the dead.

Right leg left hoof it outside to practice. Around car on blocks, across grass. Practice, practice, focus. Forms coming easier now bend leg flex wrist. Focus.

Phoebe almost died because of date with a zombie. Became zombie because of Phoebe's date.

Forms. Concentrate on the forms.

Phoebe. In danger all over again.

Takayuki doesn't wait long. Comes out of woods like he's made of collecting shadows. Wastes no time.

"Adam. I wanted . . . you to know . . . we did not . . . desecrate . . . the cemetery."

"Didn't . . . think so." Didn't, really.

Tak, nonplussed. "It is . . . part of their . . . plot . . . to destroy us."

"Stop . . . helping them. No . . . pranks."

Tak would spit if he could. Can't. "The 'pranks,' as you . . . call them . . . are our way . . . of telling . . . humanity . . . we will not . . . go away."

"Not . . . working."

"You haven't a right to . . . accuse." Leather creaks when he walks. "You, who . . . fraternize with . . . the living."

"My way . . . of . . . telling . . . humanity . . . I . . . won't go . . . away."

Lie. No politics. Just love. Love Phoebe.

Tak looks, doesn't answer. Scared? Not scared. Shrewd.

"Regardless. I didn't come . . . to argue . . . but to . . . ask."

"Ask . . . away."

"You should . . . be with us . . . Adam. The others . . . would welcome . . . your presence. Your . . . strength."

Very shrewd.

"It does not . . . matter . . . that we . . . disagree. It's . . . healthy. I disagreed with . . . Tommy. But in the end . . . we're both . . . zombies."

"In . . . the . . . end."

Stands, folds arms. See his teeth moving. "I'm not . . . looking for a sidekick. Most people . . . zombie or beating heart . . . want to follow. I'm looking for . . . a partner."

"Flattering."

"Think about it." Eyes are dark but clear through his straight hair. "Decide . . . before . . . the living . . . decide for you."

Gone, back to the woods. No trace, never a trace.

Decisions. Master Griffin encouraged decision, best ever. Or is it—Phoebe in danger? Bend knee, arms out.

Decide.

# CHAPTER
# THIRTY-EIGHT

"DID YOU KNOW the real witching hour is at . . . three a.m.? That's in seventeen minutes," Margi said, looking back at one of the few light sources left in the room. Colette's face looked smooth and flawless in the spectral light as she leaned against the foot of Margi's bed. There was only room for one and a half people in the bed, so in a show of solidarity the girls joined Phoebe on the floor with sleeping bags.

Familiar meowed, content to have the bed all to himself.

"But really it feels like . . . any other . . . hour . . . to me."

Phoebe yawned. She had started to make a comment about how nice this was, how long it had been since the three of them had a Dawn Patrol, but then she realized that Margi and Colette had done it every single night since Colette moved in, although only one of them slept.

"I don't know," Margi said. "Some hours seem a little more magical than others."

"If you . . . say so."

"You aren't getting depressed again, are you?" Margi said. "I'm fresh out of zombie Prozac."

Colette tossed a pillow at the burrito-like shape Margi represented in her sleeping bag, where it landed with a soft plop.

"We used to play board games," Phoebe said

"And make . . . s'mores." There was a hint of sadness in Colette's voice.

"God, we were corny." Margi wriggled in her sleeping bag. "Hey, C.B., you up for a game of Life? We'll spot you a couple of those little peg-people."

Colette stuck her tongue out at her. "And then Margi . . . would tell us about all the boys she was crushing on."

"I did not!"

"And that would take up half the night," Phoebe said, stifling a giggle as Margi popped up, her spiky hair matted and flat on one side.

"Which would end . . . the Dawn Patrol," Colette said, "because she would . . . put us . . . to sleep."

"Har har," Margi said. "You used to fall asleep before eleven o'clock anyhow, so what would you know?"

"Remember the time . . . we each drank . . . like . . . a pot . . . of coffee?"

"Phoebe's dad actually yelled at us," Margi said, laughing. "*Phoebe's* dad. Mr. Low-Key himself. He had his pj's on."

"'I have . . . to give a . . . lecture . . . tomorrow,'" Colette said, in a fair but off-tempo rendition of his speech.

"We used to tell ghost stories," Phoebe said.

There wasn't any immediate reply. Phoebe wondered if there would ever be a time where she could get through the night with Colette or Adam without every other thing she said being ironic or tragic.

"That was . . . fun," Colette said, letting her off the hook in her soft, gentle way. "You always had . . . the best . . . stories."

"Aw, thanks."

"Mine were . . . boring. And Margi's always had . . . a guy with a . . . hook . . . and too much . . . sex."

"A matter of taste."

"I liked Margi's stories," Phoebe said. "Yours too."

"Hey, C.B.," Margi said, "why don't you tell Pheebes about dying?"

Phoebe tensed up while waiting for a reply. Tommy had shared the manner of his death with her on the night Adam had been shot. He died in a car crash that also killed his father—only his father didn't return. The fact that Margi already knew Colette's story caused the sadness to flare in Phoebe's chest; it was another reminder of the closeness her two best friends shared, and how she was on the outside of that closeness.

"It was . . . weird," Colette said. "The after part. The death itself . . . was stupid. I drowned. I might have . . . had a seizure . . . or something. Who knows. One minute I was breathing . . . the next I . . . wasn't."

"You were wedged in a branch," Margi said. "That fallen

tree we used to jump off. You already weren't moving by the time I got to you."

"Yeah. Stupid. Anyhow . . . I was floating after that. I mean I was . . . already dead . . . but it was like I was floating. Well, sinking. There was this blue light about . . . a mile away . . . and I was just sort of sinking toward it. I remember I . . . looked at my hand and it was . . . blue . . . too . . . but I could see . . . through it."

"Were you scared?"

"No, not . . . really. The water was cool . . . not cold but cool . . . and I was going down to this . . . blue light."

"I read this thing about how when people die and come back—not zombie people but like heart patients and stuff—the light is really this chemical thing in your brain," Margi said.

"Now why would you . . . even say . . . that?"

"Sorry, I just thought it was relevant."

"It's my . . . story. I'll decide what's . . . relevant."

"Jeez. Don't get huffy."

"Anyway," Colette said, her eyes tracking the arc of Phoebe's throw pillow to Margi's head. "This . . . floating . . . to the light took about a day. But I wasn't . . . impatient. It was weird, because it . . . wasn't boring . . . either. But the closer . . . I got . . . the faster . . . I sank. And when I was near . . . the light . . . my grandmother . . . floated up to me out of . . . the light."

"Really?"

"Really. You wouldn't . . . have recognized her . . . because she was young . . . and made of light. But I did. She hugged . . . me."

"No way."

"Way. But not really . . . hugged . . . because our light bodies kind of . . . *mixed*. There were other . . . people . . . around. . . . too. One of the things . . . she said . . . was that I couldn't stay. She was . . . sad. I asked her why I . . . couldn't stay, but then . . . she disappeared. The light disappeared, everything. All . . . at once. And then I was . . . going up. Like I was dust being . . . vacuumed. It . . . hurt. I was losing . . . pieces . . . of light."

"What do you mean?"

"It was like . . . I was shedding . . . beads . . . of light. It was . . . freezing. And then I was . . . back."

"You were back. As in, back in your body?"

"Yes. And I . . . was . . . naked. In the dark. On a long . . . metal . . . table. It was dark . . . and I could . . . see. I tried to . . . move . . . and I couldn't. At first. It took . . . hours . . . I guess. I got . . . off . . . fell . . . off . . . the table. There was another . . . body . . . under a sheet."

"You were in a morgue?"

"Funeral . . . home. I got up . . . took one step . . . toward the door. And then . . . someone . . . came into . . . the room."

"Oh, God," Margi said. "I hate this part."

"He . . . started screaming. He was young. College boy, maybe. He was screaming so . . . shrill. I wanted to ask . . . for help. My mouth opened and . . . water came out."

"Ugh."

I've never . . . heard . . . screaming . . . like that. He grabbed a . . . push broom . . . and started hitting me . . . with it. Like I was a . . . monster. He broke it . . . on my . . . back. I couldn't even . . . feel it."

"Oh, Colette."

"He . . . jabbed . . . stabbed, really . . . me with the broken handle . . . in the side. He was still . . . screaming. He was going . . . to do . . . it . . . again . . . when a man . . . in a suit . . . ran in . . . and . . . pulled . . . him away."

"Welcome back," Margi said.

"It was horrible . . . the way he screamed."

Phoebe didn't know what to say.

"The man in the . . . suit . . . put his coat . . . over me. He tried to help me . . . sit."

"And then it sort of went downhill from there," Margi said.

"Colette," Phoebe said, crawling out of her bag and over to her. "I'm so sorry. That's terrible." She sat next to her and put her arm around her shoulder, and Margi came over and did the same.

"Not . . . fun," Colette said. "But I'm here . . . now. With my . . . friends."

"Better late than never," Margi said, yawning.

Phoebe thought Colette's smile was tinged with sadness, as though she was leaving a part of the story out, but it was hard to tell in the green light.

They were quiet for a few moments. They were well into the witching hour by now, and Margi had closed her eyes and was snoring softly against her dead friend.

"Colette," she said, "do you ever think of the blue light?"

"Every . . . day."

"Do you think it was heaven?"

"I don't . . . know," she said, "but I know . . . my grand-mother . . . was there."

After getting Colette her iPod so the music wouldn't disturb their sleeping friend, Phoebe checked her e-mail on Margi's computer.

"I've got one from Tommy."

Colette was so intent on working the selector wheel to queue up a new playlist that she didn't hear her. Phoebe turned back to the screen.

*From: WilliamsTommy@mysocalledundeath.com*
*To: KendallPhoebe@mysocalledundeath.com*
*Dear Phoebe—*

    *I wanted to let you know that I really loved your second "Words from a Beating Heart" column. I've talked to a number of people our age, living and dead, about the site, and everyone was very excited about "Beating Heart." One dead friend I met while I was staying in New Jersey said that your voice has really done a lot to "humanize" the Web site. A funny comment, considering.*

    *BTW, I sympathize with you about trying to get Karen to contribute a little more with the site. Her "I'm not creative" schtick is really tired. I've sent her some harassing e-mails, but I don't think I'll be any more successful at getting her to do it than you were.*

    *I'm not so sure about her T-shirt idea, though. Did she*

*talk to you about that? While I think she's right about it
helping get the message out, I'm really not sure the db
community needs any more Skip Slydells. What do you think?*

*Anyhow, the story that follows is about a side trip I took
to Scranton, Pennsylvania. It's a little rough. Please don't be
worried after you read it, and please tell all "the kids" not to
worry. This stuff is still happening in the world and they need
to know.*

*I miss you.*

*Love,*

*Tommy*

Phoebe read the attachment, which was a long report from
Tommy about a "station" somewhere in Pennsylvania for a sort
of underground railroad for the differently biotic. Tommy
stayed with a young couple who would pick up zombies that
were fleeing Pennsylvania and points south and drive them to
undead-friendly locales in New Jersey. They drove some of the
zombies straight to Aftermath in New York.

Phoebe's mouth went dry when Tommy wrote about a side
trip the couple took so they could bring him to a fire pit
surrounding a row of stakes in a field outside Scranton. Phoebe
knew what the purpose of the pit was even before Tommy
started to write about finding bone chips among the ashes.
When he mentioned finding a melted locket it became too
much for her, and she had to put the story aside for a moment.

I worry about you, Tommy, she thought, picturing him
hitchhiking down into Maryland, slowly working his way to

the state capital. Reading about the horrors that people could enact on the zombies—their *children*, for God's sake—it made her worry about all of them. Colette, Karen, Melissa.

Adam.

She read the story, which ended with Tommy talking at length about the kindness of the young couple, a testimonial that not all traditionally biotic people were madmen bent on the destruction of zombiekind. She set it aside and started typing a reply.

*From: KendallPhoebe@mysocalledundeath.com*
*To: WilliamsTommy@mysocalledundeath.com*

*Dear Tommy,*

*Your story is absolutely terrifying and sad. I'll post it immediately; I think anyone who reads it will be sympathetic.*

*I'm very worried about you. Please take care of yourself.*

*A little news: we brought Alish and Angela and the Undead Studies class over to the Haunted House so they could meet everyone. I'm sorry if Karen already told you all of this. I know earlier you guys wanted to keep the HH a secret, but the secret was pretty much out anyway after Adam was killed. The visit seemed to go really well, even Tak and Popeye were polite. Well, actually, polite may be a stretch, but they weren't as offensive as they usually are, so that's a plus.*

*Tak is still bringing the old-schoolers out on little prank missions. They did the recruiting posters that you know about, and they did another one where they took store mannequins and* zombified them and left them out in front of the mall entrance in Winford. Pretty funny.

Not so funny is that someone dug up some graves in one of the cemeteries in Winford. Tak insists "his people," as he likes to call them, had nothing to do with it. Karen believes him, and I sort of do too. It makes me nervous, though, because whoever did it really did a good job of throwing the blame on Tak— there were photos in the newspaper that looked like him digging. The article made it sound as if zombies were taking "recruiting" to a new level by digging up the graves. It seems like someone is spending a lot of time thinking about how to frame them.

Which reminds me, Pete Martinsburg is working off his community service at the Hunter Foundation. I think it's the most idiotic thing possible, but Angela thinks the best way to overcome "the enemy" is to include and educate them. Most everyone seems to agree with her, and Karen says you would too. Do me a favor and don't tell me if you do.

Also, Tommy, I wanted to let you know that Adam and I are dating. I guess you probably figured that we would, but it's official now. We get the same reaction from people that you and I did for the most part, except in school. I guess people are a little more used to seeing Adam and me together. Except for his old girlfriend Tori Stewart, who I'm told became physically ill when she saw us in the hallway. We're actually going to Aftermath again tomorrow, with Margi and Colette. Karen couldn't make it, she's working (that's another story entirely, but I'll let her tell it). I can't believe Adam is going dancing, *but we've seen all the movies in the theater, and it doesn't really make sense to go out to dinner. We tried bowling but that was a total fiasco. Not much else for a girl and a zombie to do on a Saturday night, is there?*

*I don't know where it's going—you never really do, do you? But it feels right. I'm happy and Adam seems the happiest he's been since his return. I just thought it was fair to let you know.*

*Stay safe, please! We all miss you.*

*Love,*

*Phoebe*

Phoebe looked at what she'd written for a long time before deciding to delete the two paragraphs about Adam. She told herself that if Tommy was still depressed about their breakup she didn't want to add to his misery. Then she changed the "Love" to "Best," because writing "Love" made her feel unfaithful to Adam. Then she decided that she was being ridiculous and changed it back to "Love."

She hit "Send," and then went to her sleeping bag praying that she wouldn't dream of fire pits.

# CHAPTER
# THIRTY-NINE

"So," DAVIDSON said, his large feet up on the desk, while Pete stared at the monitors, especially the one that showed the Cooper kid in his room. Cooper watched television round the clock, except for the twenty minutes each day when he walked to the fence and back. Just about every time Pete looked at his monitor, Cooper was watching television, usually Cartoon Network. SpongeBob and old Tom and Jerry cartoons.

"So, what?"

"So what do you think?"

Pete looked over at Davidson and felt a flicker of anger spark within him. "Are you a head shrinker now too?"

"Not me. I'm a mind expander. What do you think about our prank?"

Pete wasn't sure what he felt. He'd dug the grave all the way down to the casket liner when Duke finally told him to stop.

He wasn't sure what he'd have done if Duke *hadn't* told him to stop.

"Does it bother you, what you did?"

"I don't know. I don't think so." The truth was he'd felt sick to his stomach standing there in front of the headstone, but the feeling went away the moment the edge of his shovel bit into the earth, because he pictured it sinking into the Japanese zombie's—Tak's—chest. It was unnatural to be digging up a grave, but each shovel of dirt felt like a blow against Tak and his kind.

Duke slid his feet off the desk. "Good. It shouldn't. You've got to keep our goal in mind at all times. As long as we're focused on the goal, we'll be all right."

"The goal," Pete repeated. "The goal of killing all the zombies."

"Destroying the zombies." Duke's tone was firm, that of a teacher correcting a promising student. "Destroying them. Some of the things we do will seem a little unpleasant."

"Yeah, unpleasant." Pete smiled.

"Hey, it isn't like we killed anybody." Pete shot Duke a look and Duke covered his mouth with his hand.

"Oops," he said. "Look, to me your only crime is bad aim. If you'd shot Williams they'd be giving you medals instead of making you scrub my floors."

Pete looked back at the monitor. The zombie hadn't moved from his chair. He only had another twenty hours left on his community service, but he spoke anyway.

"Why are you riding me?"

Davidson laughed, drained the last of his coffee. "Don't be so sensitive. If I were 'riding' you, you'd know it."

Pete didn't reply. He looked away but could feel Duke scrutinizing him.

"Are you worried they'll come after you?"

"Who? The zombies?"

"Who else? They're going to be pretty upset when they realize they got punked in the graveyard."

Pete looked away. "No. I'm not worried"

"Really? I would be, if I were you."

Pete shrugged. Part of him wouldn't mind seeing Tak again.

"In fact, I'm worried it's only a matter of time before they come after me too."

"Really?" Pete said. "Why would you worry about that, when you work for this wonderful zombie-loving institution?"

"Things aren't always what they seem," Duke said.

"I'm kind of tired of this cryptic crap," Pete said. "I've got that blond whore trying to shrink my head, and you keep saying this crazy *X-Files* stuff. Like you want to tell me something but you never tell me. I dug up somebody's *grave* last night and I don't even know why, except you think it's some practical joke to play on the zombies. I can't figure it out and I don't want to try anymore."

Davidson stood up. "You're a smart kid, Martinsburg," he said. "A really smart kid. Let's go."

"Go?" Pete said. "We're going to fight?"

Davidson shook his head. "You're a really stupid kid, too. No, we're not going to fight. We're going to discover why things aren't really what they seem. Turn the monitors off."

"Turn them off? But . . ."

"Just turn them off. The fifteen minutes they aren't record-ing is going to be an equipment malfunction. It happens. Now move your ass."

He followed Davidson to Alish's lab. Davidson checked his watch.

"We have eleven minutes. Don't dawdle."

He waited until Pete caught up before walking to the door in the back of the room.

"You know what this room is?"

"I thought it was Alish's office."

"You ever see Alish go in there?"

"No."

"You ever wonder why Alish's office is the only place on the entire grounds that doesn't have a camera on it?"

"Yeah," he said. The thought had occurred to him.

"Well," Davidson said, smirking, "here's why."

He keycarded the door, which made a sound reminiscent of the vacuum tubes they use at the bank drive-through. The lights in the room triggered automatically and revealed a small, dingy-looking lab.

There was a girl, part of a girl, strapped to a vertical table that faced the door. Another part was attached to a machine on a counter by the sink on the wall, a few feet away.

"Meet Sylvia," Davidson said.

Pete didn't scream until she opened her eyes.

\* \* \*

Pete's hand shook as he lifted Duke's coffee cup to his lips. Duke hadn't bothered to wash it and Pete was too numb to care.

"Fourteen minutes, thirty-seven seconds," Duke said, turning the monitors back on. "Equipment back online."

Pete, shivering in Duke's chair, watched him as he took his seat on the edge of the desk. The smirk was gone.

"Are you okay?" Duke asked. He poured the last of his coffee from the Thermos into the cup Pete held with two hands.

"She was . . . she was trying to talk," Pete said. He didn't even remember his flight back to the monitor room. He'd dug up a grave the other night, and he'd been ready to open the casket if that was what Duke had wanted, but all he'd felt was numb. But seeing the girl . . . he thought it was far worse than desecrating a grave. It was like desecrating a grave where the person inside knew you were doing it. Knew it, and couldn't do anything about it.

"She does," Duke said. "You could hear her before Alish went to work on her lungs. She used to say, 'Help me.' You ever see the movie *The Fly*? The original one?"

Pete couldn't focus fully on what Duke was talking about; the image of the girl in pieces filled his brain.

"What," he said, "what is he trying to do with her?"

Duke laughed. "He's trying to cure death."

"Cure death?" He thought of Julie, somewhere deep in the California soil.

"Sure. Why not? The dead are up and walking around, aren't they? Maybe, just maybe, we can cure them."

"Cure death." Pete said.

Davidson grunted. "Don't hold your breath. Alish is crazy."

Pete leaned back in his chair. He drained the last of the coffee, hoping the dark liquid would untangle the images of Julie and Sylvia from his mind.

"He is?"

"Of course he is. You saw that mess down there. He thinks he's going to put her back together again and everything will be all peachy keen. But he needs to get some results pretty soon or he's going to have the plug pulled on his funding. And then things would get really messy."

Pete didn't know what he was talking about. The girl had brown eyes. She had looked right at him and moved her lips.

"Alish thinks he's being clever," Duke went on. "He thinks we don't know what he's trying to do. He's a scared old man who wants to stay alive, and he thinks he's going to find the answer in the dry veins of one of the worm burgers. But the cure he's looking for is not the one that we are looking for."

"It isn't?"

"No," Duke said. "He's trying to treat a symptom. We're looking to cure the disease."

Duke must have seen the confusion on Pete's face. "He wants to cure death," he said. "We just want to cure the dead. Like polio and smallpox. That's what Alish is *supposed* to be looking for."

"We," Pete said.

"We," Duke repeated, nodding. "You and me." Duke clapped his shoulder with a firm hand. "There are some people who want to meet you, Pete. And you will want to meet them. You have a lot in common."

Pete didn't say anything. Duke's hand was on his shoulder, and Duke's pale eyes stared at him with almost fatherly affection. The girl in the laboratory was like a squirrel that Pete had backed over a few weeks after Darren had bought him the car. Clipped by a tire, it's back half was crushed and it flopped around in the pine needles and dirt of one of the make-out spots around Lake Oxoboxo, not aware that it was already dead. Although Pete's date begged him not to, Pete got out of his car and put the little rodent out of its misery with the heel of his high-top sneaker. It took a while, but it was his responsibility to make sure the job was done right.

He'd been to the spot many times since, although never again with that girl. Looking up at Davidson, he realized that his hands had stopped shaking.

# CHAPTER FORTY

"ARE YOU . . . SURE . . . this . . . is a . . . good . . . idea?" Sitting in the bleachers above the field. Phoebe said it's cold outside can't tell too cold for Frisbee another bright idea. Phoebe wears heavy coat with the fake fur lining on hood and cuffs, black mittens hard-to-play-catch-with mittens. Hood up, black fur framing white face. Like snow. Her eyes. Her pretty green eyes.

"What do you mean? Our big date?"

Hard coming to the field. Don't need to close eyes to imagine the snap of the ball and the crack of hitting shoulder pads. Can hear the crowd, smell the turf and sweat. Shake head, shake.

"You . . . and . . . me."

Phoebe takes hand. Strokes cheek with other mitten.

"Adam, you aren't going to break up with me, are you?"

"No," too quickly. "Don't . . . want . . . to."

717

"Then what is it? Are you afraid of what people would think?"

Hardly. "Afraid . . . of what . . . people . . . will do."

Phoebe turns thinking. Looks at field into the past sees Adam running blocking winning. Looks at field sees into the future sees what?

"Adam," holding arm, huddling against as though for warmth no warmth to give. "Are you happy?"

"Happy as . . . a dead . . . guy . . . can be."

"Being with me, I mean?"

"Being . . . with . . . you." Only with you. Feels more than happy. Feels like life.

"I'm happy too. Happier than I've ever been, I think."

Crow flies across field. Ungraceful but swift.

"It won't be easy, Adam. It never is."

"Scared."

"You're scared? Of what? Me getting hurt?"

"Yes."

Had to say it. Didn't want to say it admit it but Phoebe needs to know. Phoebe thinks fearless but not true. Terrified.

"I'm scared for you too, Adam. The way the world is now there is a much better chance of something happening to you than to me."

"Not . . . true. Worst . . . already . . . in past."

"No." Wish could feel mittens as they hold cheeks. Wish could feel smell her breath as she looks into eyes. Cinnamon. Phoebe liked cinnamon gum. Can only imagine. "The worst would be that I lost you, really lost you, without having given us a chance."

Kiss, light. Close eyes and alive again, Phoebe alive in my arms and hold her and kiss back and breathe her and don't let her go.

Open eyes, still dead.

"Okay?" Light snow starts to fall, tiny flakes settle in fur lining.

Nod.

"O . . . kay."

Pats hand, gets cell phone from deep pocket. "I better call Margi. I don't want her to have to drive us when this starts to stick. Good thing we all live so close."

"Good . . . thing."

"I hope this lets up by tomorrow, otherwise Margi's parents won't let her drive to the train station." Brushes hair back. Pretty. Listens to phone, Margi's voice. Margi's loud voice. Be there in five, hang up. Quick call.

"Wish . . . wish could stay . . . longer."

"Me too," Phoebe, snow melting on cheek, catching hair. Shivering. "I wish it wasn't so cold."

Wish.

Wish could warm her. Wish could chase the shivers away.

Can't.

# CHAPTER
# FORTY-ONE

"CAN'T . . . BELIEVE . . . I let . . . you talk . . . me . . . into this."

Phoebe leaned against Adam in the backseat of Margi's car, resting a cheek against his unyielding arm. They were just outside of New Haven on their way to the train station for another trip to Aftermath.

"I can't either, but I'm glad I did." She was nervous, though, because Adam hadn't gone any farther than Winford since becoming a zombie. "You'll have fun, you'll see."

"Too bad . . . Karen . . . couldn't come," Colette said from the shotgun seat as she toyed with the radio dial. Margi snorted.

"Less competition." Margi gave Colette a wicked grin. "Not that *you're* worried about that."

"Is Karen working today?" Phoebe asked.

"Christmas . . . season. Never get . . . away . . . now."

Margi ignored this thread and addressed Phoebe and Adam in the backseat.

"Did you guys know that DeCayce has e-mailed Colette like seventeen times since they met? Which was what, three weeks ago?"

"Seventeen times?" Phoebe leaned over and caught Colette smiling.

"Who's . . . DeCayce?"

"Just . . . ignore her, Adam," Colette said. "Besides, it was . . . nineteen . . . times."

"Oh, excuse me, nineteen times. Colette's getting ready for some zombie lovin'."

Colette slapped her arm, and Margi looked into the rearview at Phoebe and mouthed the word "sorry." Phoebe stuck out her tongue at her and squeezed Adam's arm more tightly by way of reply.

"Are Skeleton Crew playing tonight, Colette?" She'd noticed that Colette was wearing makeup and a new-looking silky blouse. Her hair was brushed back and had a glossy shine—Phoebe wondered if she was using products from the Z line. Whatever she was using was working. She looked great.

Margi answered before Colette could get a word in. "Are you kidding? Do you think we'd be going if they weren't?"

"They are . . . playing. Last night . . . before . . . road trip."

"Send him off smiling, C.B.," Margi said. "Send him off smiling. Are you going to dance tonight, Lame Man? Or are you going sit in the corner like a giant wallflower?"

"He'll . . . dance . . . won't you, Adam?"

"I'm a . . . dancing . . . machine." He looked at Phoebe and tried to smile.

Phoebe was thinking that he didn't really get a chance to dance at homecoming, having ditched his date to take her and the rest of the crew over to the after-party at the Haunted House. But then she remembered that he did dance—with Karen, once they'd arrived.

"You'll dance with me, won't you, Adam?"

"You'll . . . owe . . . me," he said.

She leaned her head back down against his hard shoulder.

"I already do," she whispered.

The club was jumping when they arrived, the dance floor packed with what looked like twice the people than had been there on their previous visit. The increase in population was due almost completely to trad kids—there were loose groups of trads dancing by themselves without any zombies in their midst. The zombies, she noticed, also had a tendency to cluster together. She held Adam's hand as they walked in. Margi and Colette brushed by them, looking for DeCayce.

"Wow. Look at all . . . the zombies."

"Isn't it amazing?" Phoebe squeezed his hand, and leaned closer so he could hear her over the loud trip-hop that pulsed from invisible speakers. "I can't believe what Skip has done here."

"Skip? That's right . . . this is . . . Skip's . . . place."

She nodded. "Tommy did a nice interview with him. I posted it on mysocalledundeath."

Adam looked up, scanning the room and taking in the sights and sounds. A trad couple walked by and gave them an odd look, which Phoebe decided to take as "good for you!" She felt Adam's hand tighten over hers.

The lights were like blue and white rain splashing on his skin. "Want to . . . dance?"

"I'd love to," she said, and let him lead her out into the throng on the dance floor.

They were joined three songs later by Margi and Colette, who had managed to find DeCayce and Bee. Bee paired off with Margi, although neither of them looked thrilled. Colette and DeCayce, on the other hand, were dancing with their faces only inches apart, although the song that was playing wasn't a slow one. Phoebe watched them, fascinated by their obvious chemistry. She wondered if the people who stopped to watch her and Adam did so for the same reason.

"They look . . . happy," Adam said, reconfirming her belief in telepathetic bonds.

"I think I look happy," she replied, stepping into him for a hug. His arms were slow in enfolding her, but she knew that wasn't the same thing as hesitation.

"I think . . . you look . . . beautiful."

"Aw, I bet you say that to all the trad girls."

She was always amazed by how his embrace was firm yet gentle at the same time—she knew he couldn't really feel how tightly he was holding her. He was probably strong enough to snap her spine or crush her ribs; his arms felt like steel clamps as they went around her waist.

A song or two later, Dom, the guitarist for Skeleton Crew, came over to tell DeCayce and Bee that they were on in ten minutes. The boys said their good-byes, DeCayce with a quick kiss to Colette's cheek and a promise to see her after the show. Dom, turning, caught sight of Phoebe and asked her how Karen was doing.

"She's great." Phoebe replied. "She got a job at the mall, if you can believe it."

Dom looked puzzled. "Why wouldn't I believe it?"

"Well, not a lot of zombies work at malls." When Dom just stood there looking stunned she realized she may have said something she shouldn't have. "You knew she was a zombie, right?"

"She said she was," he said, his voice barely audible above the music. "I thought she was kidding." He shook his head, his thick hair waving as he stared at the floor. "Wow."

"I'll tell her you said hi?" Phoebe asked, hoping Karen wouldn't want to kill her.

"Oh, yeah, absolutely! Would you do that for me? That would be great," he said, answering the question behind her question.

"You know, she has e-mail too."

"Yeah," he said, gathering himself as though suddenly realizing how cool ne was. "I'm not much on teledating."

"Seems to be . . . working . . . for your . . . singer," Adam said.

"Yeah, well. Tell her I said hi, though, okay?" Dom said, and then started angling through the crowd.

When Skeleton Crew hit the stage, they hit it hard. They led off with a new song DeCayce announced as "The Dead Living," and Dom's shredding opening riff could blow the dust off a tired soul. The drums came in a moment later like a nest of machine guns, and Bee's bass line was a cavalry charge. The crowd's response was immediate. Phoebe looked around her to see dead bodies pogo-ing and slamming into each other, although with considerably less velocity than their living friends could muster. She saw a girl lifted up over the crowd, her body rigid, as many dead hands passed her to the stage. She looked like she had rigor mortis. Phoebe felt the tug of the music on her body, but when she looked at Adam he seemed to be unmoved, even when DeCayce's chorus sailed out over the fast rhythm of his band.

> *"We are the dead living*
> *Up from underground*
> *Went through hell getting out*
> *You won't put us back down!"*

Other bodies were borne aloft, and the whole crowd was singing along when he repeated the chorus a second time.

"There's . . . Margi," Adam said, pointing at a body bobbing like a cork on the sea of hands.

Phoebe squinted against the glare of the stage lights.

"Colette too! See her, just stepping onto the stage?"

Adam nodded. DeCayce, his sinewy body twitching as if he were being electrocuted, waved at Colette and then Margi to join him at the front of the stage where they sang the next chorus with him, Colette almost managing to sing the words in the proper time with the music. When the song was over they both returned to the crowd, and the lights were cut to a single spot that bathed DeCayce's bare skin with a bluish glow.

"Thank . . . you," he said to the cheering crowd. "And thank you to our . . . beautiful . . . backup singers, Colette . . . and Margi."

Adam bellowed an incomprehensible cheer, which pleased Phoebe to no end.

"This is our . . . last night . . . at Aftermath . . . for a while," DeCayce said. He folded his skinny arms to his chest, hugging himself while the crowd moaned in disappointment. "But we'll be . . . back. Hell, if I can return . . . from death . . . I can make it back . . . to Aftermath."

He was a natural performer, Phoebe thought. The melodrama of his movements, the easy banter with the crowd—she couldn't help but wonder what he'd have been like onstage when still alive.

"We've got to hit . . . the road," he continued. "We've got to bring . . . our music . . . and our message . . . to the rest of the country. So that trad people will know . . . we're not . . . monsters or . . . grave robbers. We're not what that old gargoyle . . . Mathers . . . says we are. We're just . . . people, man."

The crowd settled into a disgruntled mumble at the mention of Mathers's name, and DeCayce used the lull to deliver his message full force, his voice rising in tone and timbre to match the best of the fire and brimstone preachers, to rival even Reverand Nathan Mathers himself.

"We've got to let people know that . . . what they are saying about . . . our brothers and sisters . . . in Connecticut...that they are . . . killing pets and . . . wrecking graves . . . is a bunch of bullshit, man! Straight up . . . bullshit!"

The response was thunderous, and the stage lights returned as Dom hit a random chord.

"This one is for . . . Tommy Williams," DeCayce said, pacing along the lip of the stage. "It's called . . . 'Headshot.'" Skeleton Crew kicked in with a brutal wave of noise that sent the club dwellers into another frenzy of motion and screaming. Phoebe started dancing in place, her skirt and long hair whirling as she thrashed. It was some moments before she realized that Adam was standing still beside her, watching.

"You really . . . like this . . . stuff?" he said, something like a wry grin on his face.

She slapped his unyielding bicep. "Don't be a lump, Adam. Move that body."

His response was to start headbanging. Adam headbanging was funny enough, but because his body couldn't quite master the motion, he looked more like a chicken pecking for loose grain in the barnyard than a metalhead. Phoebe thought it was absolutely hilarious.

"Here," she said, taking his hands in hers. "Move with me."

Skeleton Crew wasn't exactly playing dance music, but there was enough energy in their playing to get her hips swaying and her shoulders rocking. She held Adam's hands and swung his arms from side to side, but beyond that he didn't move—he just watched her moving in front of him.

Phoebe thought that was just fine.

* * *

They found the girls by the stage after the show. Colette was deep in conversation with DeCayce off in a corner, and Margi was with a few people Phoebe remembered from their last trip to Aftermath.

"Hi, Trent." The boy looked thrilled that Phoebe had remembered him. "How's it going with the library card?"

His grin was charming, if lopsided.

"No . . . go. I haven't left . . . the building."

"We need to get going soon," Margi said, pushing herself up from her perch at the lip of the stage. "There aren't a lot of trains later in the day, and my mom will kill me if we're not home by midnight."

"Ready when you are." Phoebe had laced her fingers with Adam's, which were pleasantly cool. The air in the club had grown warm and humid, which meant that there had to have been quite a few trads jumping around on the dance floor during the show. "What did you think, Adam? Did you have fun?"

"Had . . . fun. Could watch you . . . all . . . night." Phoebe thought his smile had become more natural, his face more boyish as the night went on—but maybe it was just the heady club atmosphere playing tricks on her.

Phoebe, blushing, was glad for the dim lighting of the club. She was also thankful that Margi didn't comment beyond a loud "Awwww."

Colette and DeCayce walked over, also holding hands.

"Ready to go, C.B.?"

Colette looked at DeCayce, who tightened his grip on her hand. She looked like she was about to cry, if she could still cry.

"I'm not . . . I'm . . . not . . . going back . . . Margi."

"What? What do you mean?" Margi said, but Phoebe could tell from the quaver in her voice that she knew exactly what their friend meant.

"I'm not . . . going back," Colette repeated. "I'm going with . . . Skeleton Crew . . . on their . . . tour. With . . . DeCayce."

Margi looked like she was going to cry too. She lifted her hand to her mouth like she was trying to hold her words in, and Phoebe, as happy as she was for Colette, suddenly felt terrible for Margi. She looked so forlorn standing there, with her hair matted and her shirt clinging to her skin with sweat. She looked like a puppy that had been abandoned in the rain.

Colette felt the same way, Phoebe could tell. She was crying in every way except producing tears when she spoke again.

"We might . . . try . . . to find . . . my brother . . . or my parents. Or . . . or . . . I'll just . . . travel, I don't . . . know."

The silence grew awkward, and the zombies Margi had been partying with started to drift away to give them their moment.

"Wish me . . . luck . . . Margi . . . .please."

Margi nodded, but she didn't remove her hand from her mouth. Adam was the first to speak.

"Good . . . luck." The low rumble of his voice seemed to kick Margi into action, because she ran to Colette and wrapped her in a forceful hug, finally releasing the emotion she was trying to hold in. Colette hugged her back, making strange hiccupping sounds as Margi poured out her grief.

"I will take care . . . of her," DeCayce said, turning to Adam and Phoebe like they were Colette's parents on prom night. "I'll make sure . . . she's safe. We don't take chances when we are . . . on the road."

"We know you will," Phoebe said, watching her friends. She looked at Adam, who released her so she could join their embrace. When they got control of themselves, Margi dried her tears and forced herself to speak, her voice choked with emotion.

"I'm happy for you, C.B. I really am."

"Thanks . . . Margi. You know . . . you know . . . how much . . ."

"Shhh." Margi put her finger to Colette's lips. "Don't say it. Don't make it feel anymore like a good-bye than it has to."

Margi released her and went to DeCayce, kissing him lightly on the cheek.

"Good luck," she said. "Both of you. Good luck."

DeCayce looked relieved. Actually, Phoebe thought, everyone looked relieved.

They said their farewells, made promises to stay in touch, then said some of the things people wish they said to loved ones while they were still alive. Margi managed not to cry again until their train was pulling out of Grand Central Station, but even then it didn't last long. Phoebe offered to drive once they were back in New Haven, but Margi said she could handle it.

"Aren't you a needy little boy tonight?" Phoebe said, picking

Gargoyle off the floor and squeezing him to her. Gar licked her cheek and then her ear. She dropped him on the bed, where he curled up on her favorite pillow.

She walked to the window and looked down to where a large shadow was moving through the Garrity's backyard. Adam, doing his exercises again. Her lights were out, with only the soft spectral glow of the computer behind her casting any illumination. She didn't think that he'd be conscious of her—the night was practically moonless, so she could barely see him. But she waved anyhow.

Her room had grown chilly, and she had put her terry cloth bathrobe on over her pajamas. She sat down at her computer and went online. There were a number of e-mails to mysocalledundeath.com, one of which had "RE: Colette Beauvior" in the header line, and also one from Tommy. She knew she was being selfish when she chose the one from Tommy, but Gargoyle was her only witness, and he wasn't going to tell anyone.

*Hi Phoebe,*

he'd written,

> *I've made it safely to DC. I think I'm going to be staying at least until springtime. There's a lot I want to do here.*

Great, she thought, one line and I'm already starting to tear up.

*I wanted to let you know I think you guys are doing a*
*great job managing the site. I also think it is a great idea*
*having the "I'm back" section. I had no idea that Colette*
*had a brother and that he might not be aware that she's*
*differently biotic. I saw that you had two more postings from*
*db people the next day. I really hope someone figures out a way*
*to get the picture uploaded for the girl in Omaha. I'm really,*
*really excited about the things you're doing with the site; I'm*
*leaving stacks of the cards we printed up everyplace I think*
*people might use them.*

She whistled for Gar, and when he wouldn't come she got
up and captured him, sitting down with him on her lap. He
gave her a grouchy look but didn't move, probably because she
started scratching behind his ears.

*I have a list of people I want to talk to and places I*
*want to go. Most of my agenda involves talking to people who*
*could help us, or talking to people who refuse to help us, but*
*there's also some other things I want to check out. On my way*
*down from Pennsylvania I met a zombie who told me*
*that there's a zombie gang—as in actual criminal street*
*gang—who gets recruits by encouraging trad kids who want*
*to join to shoot each other. If you come back, you get to be*
*in the gang, and if you don't, game over. I can't see*
*why anyone would willingly choose this existence over real*
*life, but the kid I met insisted it was true. He said his cousin*
*tried to get him to join, but he turned him down. He said*

*they're "crazy fearless" because they're dead, and apparently they have all the other gangs scared witless of them. Do me a favor and don't tell any of this to Takayuki or the other old-schoolers, because I think he'd come down here and be leading them within a few weeks. How is Tak and the whole dead crew, by the way? Is Karen keeping everyone in line?*

Phoebe smiled at the thought of Takayuki and George and the rest of his crew catching a bus down to DC so they could join the fun. But Tommy's next line erased the smile: *Phoebe*, he wrote, *I wanted to let you know I've met a girl.*

She read the line a second time. Gar had begun to growl because she had stopped scratching his ears. He had written *Phoebe*, as in "Phoebe, listen up, because this next bit is serious. Very serious."

*Phoebe, I wanted to let you know I met a girl. A zombie girl. I don't know if it's going to go anywhere, but since I met her here we've been spending a lot of time together—time is something we've both got a lot of—and I like being with her and I think she likes being with me. Her name is Christie Smith.*

I don't want to know her name, Phoebe thought. Tommy, why would you think I would need to know her name? Christie Smith, Christie Smith. Sounds like a weathergirl. Or a porn star.

Why do you even care? she thought. You're happier with Adam than you ever would be with Tommy. With Adam, you never have to guess how he really feels about you.

She pushed up and away from the desk with an abruptness that surprised Gargoyle, who let out a little yelp of surprise. She went back to the window. Adam was still working in the gray grass below.

Christie Smith, she thought. And then: wasn't it *you* that broke up with *him*? *Adam needs me. I don't have any time for you,* you said, or something equally stupid. *I don't have time* to a boy who has nothing, nothing in the world *but* time, an eternity of endless sleepless hours waiting, like waiting for the phone to ring when you know it never will.

After a while she sat back down at the computer. There wasn't much left to read, and she was determined to get through the rest of it even though her hands were shaking and she could feel a rush of tears ready to spill from her eyes. She didn't know if she was angry or sad or both. Probably both.

*I still think of you a lot,*

he wrote,

*all the time, really, except some times when I'm with Christie. I haven't talked to her about you yet, but she's been to the Web site, so she knew that I had feelings for a living girl.*

A living girl. Not a Traditionally Biotic Girl or a Beating Heart, she thought. For someone who chose his words so carefully, how could Tommy not know that each one he wrote was like a razor blade being dragged slowly across her heart.

*I feel like you're still in my soul, Phoebe. And I haven't told her about you because I feel like in doing so I would be letting you go, and I'm just not ready for that yet. It probably isn't fair to her, or to you, even, because I know how you feel, but just not ready.*

He thinks he knows how I feel, she thought. She closed her eyes and was more than a little surprised when the rush of tears subsided.

*Anyway,*

began his final paragraph,

*I hope you aren't mad at me for writing about this. I just wanted you to know that I really am trying to let go like you wanted, so you don't have to worry that some creepy, love-struck dead kid is going to show up under your window some night playing a mandolin. I'm trying, Phoebe. But it isn't easy.*
*Love,*
*Tommy*

She was hot all of a sudden, and she wriggled out of her bathrobe and threw it onto the bed, where the belt fell across Gargoyle, whose ears pricked.

"I know," she said, "you're wondering what's gotten into me tonight. I'm sorry, baby boy."

Somewhat mollified, Gar put his doggy chin on his forepaws. He was too dignified to try to move the belt.

"So you think you know how I feel," Phoebe said, the fingers of her now-steady hands tapping but not depressing any of the keys on her keyboard. She looked back at Gar, who seemed to raise one fuzzy, questioning eyebrow at her. "Well, how about I tell you how I really feel?"

Her fingers were like long, vicious knives stabbing at her keyboard.

> "Dear" Tommy,
>    I'm so, so glad that you have met someone new. And I'm so, so glad that you made the brilliant decision to tell me about her, but not tell her about me, because that once again under-scores what a self-centered, manipulative jerk you can be. I'm still "in your soul," am I? Well, let me out, please. Evict me.
> Adam and I

She stopped typing a moment, suppressing the cry of frustrated anguish that was welling in her chest.

Eyes burning, she resumed typing with a steadily increasing rapidity.

# CHAPTER
# FORTY-TWO

"SO THIS IS IT," Duke said. "After tonight your debt to society is paid. What do you think about that?"

Pete shrugged. "I've still got to do the counseling for the rest of the year."

"Cry me a river. You really aren't glad you don't have to work here anymore?"

"I don't care about it either way." Which wasn't exactly true; being home-schooled was duller than actual school, and he hadn't seen or talked to TC since the trial. He didn't think Stavis's parents would let TC talk to him anymore.

"Really?" Duke said. "That surprises me. I'd think you'd be pretty eager to get away from all of these dead people. All of these insane experiments. You must be completely rehabilitated."

Pete didn't answer, nor did he return Duke's disturbingly reptilian smile.

"Buck up," Duke said. "What's the matter?"

"Nothing."

"Nothing, huh? Are you thinking about that creature in the lab? Thinking you want to put her out of her misery?"

Pete looked at the monitor screen where Alish was bustling back and forth between what looked to be a microscope and another machine that looked like a microwave. After he'd thought about it a bit, he realized he had no wish at all to end the zombie's misery, if that is what it was. The disgust he'd felt when he initially saw it there gave him a reflexive urge to destroy it just like he would any other aberration of the natural world, like finding a bug as big as your hand, or a green mold covering the last piece of cake. He hadn't really thought that the zombies could feel anything, but that one looked as if it was in pain. And that was just fine by him.

"No."

"No?"

"No."

"Hmmm. What did you think of that book that I gave you?"

"I liked it," Pete said. Duke had given him *And the Graves Give Up Their Dead*, by Reverend Nathan Mathers. He hadn't much cared for the biblical references that backed up Mathers's arguments, but he definitely enjoyed reading the sections where Mathers urged his readers to "send the dead back to hell." There was a whole chapter on why it was necessary to burn the corpses, even if they had become inanimate after a head shot.

"You liked it? You didn't think he was a little too over the top?"

"No," Pete said. "He didn't always go far enough. He gives an awful lot of Biblical evidence and warnings, but he never actually recommends an action."

Davidson laughed out loud. "You are an odd duck, Peter Martinsburg," he said, "an odd duck."

On the screen before him, Alish was closing up an experiment and dousing the lights. He walked past the door to his "office" four times, but never went in.

"Alish is coming," Pete said. For some reason Duke always wanted to know when Alish was getting ready to check out. Probably because Duke was supposed to be doing something other than hanging out, drinking coffee, and having study groups with Pete.

"You want to meet him?" Duke asked.

"Who? Alish?"

"No, stupid. Reverend Mathers."

Pete looked back at Duke, trying to see if he was serious. He looked like he might be.

"I don't know," Pete said.

"The Reverend is an amazing person," Duke said, "absolutely amazing. A man of intelligence as much as faith."

"You've met him?"

Duke nodded, with what Pete thought was exaggerated solemnity. "Oh yes," he said, taking a swig from his Thermos cup.

"Really? Where did you meet him?"

"I've seen him a couple times, actually."

"You're kidding. The foundation know about this? I wouldn't think they would be too happy knowing you were hanging out with 'The Scourge of the Undead.'" Pete had done more than read the book. He'd gone online and read some other material about Mathers, his church, and his activities.

"Oh, they know," Duke said, taking another swig.

Alish arrived at the door to the monitor room just then, and he paused, as though aware of the sudden silence that greeted his arrival. His gray eyes regarded Pete the way they always did, which was as if he wasn't—or shouldn't be—there.

"Hello, Mr. Hunter," Duke said.

"Hello. I will be teaching with Angela today. Please vacuum the carpets in the encounter room before the students get here, and see to it that the lab floors are cleaned. Those shoes that the Wilson boy wears leave black marks all over the tile."

"Will do, Mr. Hunter," Duke said. "Pete here will take care of it. It's his last day, you know. The last of his two hundred hours of community service."

"Really," the old man said. He looked at Pete for a moment, but didn't say anything. Then he turned and started back to his daughter's office.

"He's not using a cane today," Pete said. "Why doesn't he need it every day?"

"You're pretty observant," Duke said. "Listen, I'm giving you a going away present. I'm going to talk to Alish. He and I need to meet about a couple of things, so I'll let you work your last shift without me hanging over your shoulder all night. I'll have the radio on, so if you need anything just give me a call. Otherwise, enjoy yourself. Just get the carpets and the floors done like the old man said."

"Okay." Duke was a permanent resident at the foundation, like the stupid Wilson kid and his stupid streak-leaving sneakers.

"Lock up the labs when you're done, all right? You know how to do that?"

Pete nodded.

"Okay," Duke said, smiling. "Have fun."

As he said this, he placed his keycard on the edge of his desk, pressing it down with an audible click.

Still smiling, he turned and left the monitor room.

What the hell? Pete thought, first watching Duke head down the corridor on the monitor screen, then turning back to the keycard on the desk. What is this, some sort of stupid test? A dare?

Whatever it was, Pete wasn't playing. He was just going to get the floors done, keep his head down, and get the hell out of there, "fully rehabilitated," as the man had said.

But filling up the mop bucket, he started thinking about the thing in the lab, how he could see its spine twitch when he was looking at it.

He added some chemicals to the hot water.

What did Davidson mean by leaving his keycard there? Was he trying to goad Pete into doing something?

He mopped the entrance hall, then vacuumed the carpet in the encounter room. Angela had dropped a few hints about having him sit in on one of their sessions, but that had never materialized. Her legs, and the look of annoyance she gave him when she caught him staring at them, were the only things he'd miss about this place.

He went back to the supply closet, changed the mop water, and did the hallway outside the encounter room and the short hall to Angela's office. The keycard, he realized, would let him into her office as well as the main office, two areas of the building that were off-limits to him after hours. He could use the card to go in and get his files.

Not like she wouldn't have backups, he thought. He went back to get his soda and sandwich from the small fridge in the monitor room. He had one more corridor to do, and then he could watch the clock until it was time to go.

Time to go, he thought. Don't do the crime if you can't do the time.

Well, he'd done the time. He knew, despite the wrist slap the judge had given him, that what he'd done was a crime. And despite appearances to the contrary, he did feel guilty for what he'd done. Adam hadn't deserved to die.

But the zombies did.

They deserved to die, die and stay dead. If it wasn't for the zombies, Adam would still be alive, and Pete would still be in school and playing football and getting an endless supply of tail, rather than getting homeschooled by a balding guy in his thirties who smelled like menthol and started shaking every time Pete reached for his pencil. He wouldn't be spending all of his free time in this cave, listening to Duke's rambling. He'd be hanging out with Stavis and getting drunk and playing Xbox or cruising around the streets of Winford looking for even more tail.

Pete ended up throwing half of his sandwich away. His

mother had made him a salami sandwich. No matter how many times he said, "I hate salami, please give me ham," salami ended up in the bag. The Wimp must like salami.

He saw the keycard on Duke's desk.

He swore under his breath and got up from his chair. Just the lab hallway and he'd be done.

The lab hallway, he thought, looking at the keycard.

He switched off the monitors, thinking that maybe he ought to at least say good-bye.

Phoebe and her friends stopped in their tracks when they saw Pete Martinsberg waiting in the front corridor as they entered the Hunter Foundation. Phoebe instinctively moved in front of Adam, as though by doing so she could rewind the past. She felt Adam's heavy hand on her shoulder. Margi and Karen moved beside them and stood glaring at Adam's killer.

"I don't want any trouble." Pete raised his hands. "I was just leaving. Today was my last day of community service, and I won't be bothering any of you again."

Adam, gently but firmly, drew Phoebe back and stepped forward at the same time, his big body casting a long shadow from the sunlight streaming through the foyer doors over Martinsburg.

"I just want to leave," Pete said, looking at each of them in turn, as though unsure of who was the greater threat. From the corner of her eye Phoebe could see the other girls; Margi looked positively feral, a cat poised to spring. Beside her, Karen was the implacable ice princess, looking as though she could kill merely by narrowing her eyes. Even Kevin Zumbrowski, standing behind them, looked vaguely threatening.

"Can I go?" Pete said. He didn't say "please," but Phoebe thought there was a pleading tone to his voice.

"Go."

The word rumbled up from Adam's chest, and he moved aside, shielding Phoebe, in order to let Pete pass.

"Thanks," Pete said, looking contrite. He ducked his eyes as the Undead Studies students watched him pass the way they'd watch a snake slither through the garden.

He stopped once he had the foyer door open.

"Oh, I almost forgot," he said. "Mr. Hunter said he had a surprise for you, something about one of your classmates being back. He said to meet him at the lab at the end of the east corridor. The one on the right."

He might have smiled as he turned, Phoebe wasn't sure.

"Grrr," Margi said, watching until Pete was out of sight. "I really want to scratch his eyes out."

Phoebe squirmed past Adam, feeling partly annoyed and partly proud of the way he'd tried to protect her. "At least he's done."

Karen was already walking down the hallway. "His kind are . . . never done. Come on, let's go see Sylvia."

"Syl-vi-a!" Kevin said, drawing out all three syllables.

They followed her down the hall, but Margi wasn't done with Pete. She held her arms out in front of her as they walked.

"Look at me, I'm vibrating, I'm so mad. How can you not want to beat him up the moment you see him, Adam?"

"I . . . do."

"Why don't you?"

"Some . . . day . . . maybe."

"I really hope so. I really mean it. Let me . . ."

Phoebe cut her off. "Margi, I really think it's best if we forget about Pete Martinsburg. The sooner, the better."

She started to explain why, but Karen had reached the lab door, which was open. And then she screamed.

Phoebe had never heard a zombie scream before, and she never wanted to again. The shrill noise was the sound of a choking animal being tortured—it rang out and echoed through the hallways of the entire foundation at what seemed an impossibly loud volume.

Phoebe ran the short distance to Karen, and she saw why she was screaming, and then she was screaming too.

Karen was the first to recover.

"Give . . . me . . . your phone," she said.

"What?"

"Your . . . phone, Phoebe . . . give it . . . to me!"

Phoebe went digging, the phone suddenly a wriggling fish swimming at the bottom of her bag, but then she caught it, turned it on, and with shaking hands passed it to Karen.

Margi was clinging to Adam, who stood in stunned silence.

"She's . . . she's been taken *apart*," Margi whispered.

Kevin, distraught, shuffled from side to side, his left leg dragging behind him, his stiff arms waving.

"Help . . . her . . . help . . . her . . ."

Karen held up the phone and started snapping photos. On

the third flash, Sylvia opened her eyes, and Phoebe and Margi both shrieked again. Karen ran to where most of the girl hung, and when she spoke her voice was reassuring and steady.

"We're going to get you out of here, honey. Don't . . . worry."

Sylvia's mouth moved, but no sound came out. It looked like she might have been trying to speak. Across the room, her arm twitched twice and then lay still.

"Phoebe." There was an element of command in Karen's voice now, and Phoebe forgot about her fear when she heard her name. "Help me with these straps. Adam, wheel that gurney over here. Margi and Kevin . . . collect . . . the rest of her."

"Oh, Karen, I don't know if I can . . ."

"Do . . . it, Margi! Phoebe, get that . . . scalpel."

The voice at the door froze them all where they stood.

"I wouldn't do that if I were you."

They turned, and Alish stood in the doorway, the sadness on his face deepening the many wrinkles there. Duke Davidson stood with him, holding what looked to Phoebe like a Taser, or a gun.

"You . . . monster. We . . . trusted . . . you." Karen said.

Phoebe watched Karen walk toward Alish and Duke. She'd plucked the scalpel from Phoebe's hand without even breaking stride. Duke stepped forward and braced himself in front of Alish. The old man waved his hands, one of which still held his cane.

"Please, please," he said. "Hear me out. Please. This isn't what is seems."

"It . . . seems . . . you . . . are . . . *dissecting* . . . her. *Vivisecting* . . . her," Karen said.

Phoebe gasped as Adam and Kevin began to surge forward. Duke's voice was a gunshot, and they halted, as though by supernatural command.

"Not another step!" Duke's body was tense with the promise of easy violence. He was smiling.

Time seemed to freeze, and in that moment, when all eyes were on Karen, Phoebe reached over and palmed her phone. Karen had left it on the table beside Sylvia. She was pretty sure that Duke wouldn't let them leave with the phone—if he would even *let* them leave.

"Please, please," Alish was crying, and Phoebe could hear the tick tick tick of Angela's heels as she ran down the hall. "Please, just listen to me."

Karen held the knife, and there was nothing like mercy in her diamond eyes. There was no fear. When she spoke, her voice was a voice from the grave.

"Speak."

"You can't move her," Alish said. "Not when she's like this. She'll reterminate. She needs the fluids we're giving her."

Phoebe looked behind her at Sylvia, although it was difficult to do so. She saw curling plastic tubes attached to her friend, each pumping a violet fluid into or away from her.

Karen pointed at Alish with the knife. "Put her . . . back . . . together."

"We will. That was the purpose all along, you see. We . . ."

"Now."

Alish looked at her. By this time Angela had joined them in the lab, and Phoebe thought the expression of sympathy on her face was the most hypocritical thing she'd ever seen.

"It isn't that simple, Miss DeSonne. The procedure is a lengthy one, and delicate, and . . ."

"I'll . . . wait."

Alish shook his head. "You couldn't stay. It would be very, uh, unpleasant for you."

"Unpleasant? Un . . . pleasant?" She took another step forward. "I'm . . . dead, monster . . . you don't know . . . what . . . unpleasant is."

Another few steps and she would be within Duke's striking distance, and had settled into himself, as though preparing for her attack. He watched the dead girl, his face blank.

Alish's whining grew louder. "You don't understand," he said. "We're helping her. We're really helping her."

Angela walked forward, shrugging off Duke's hand as she moved past. "Karen, please. I know what this looks like. But my father is right, we really are helping Sylvia. When the procedure is done she'll be better. She'll be like you, able to speak and walk and everything else. You need to trust us."

"Trust . . . you."

"Yes, Karen. Trust us. We've always only had your best interests at heart. Please put the knife down."

Karen looked back at Sylvia, whose mouth still worked soundlessly.

"You expect me . . . to trust . . . you."

"I do, Karen. Put the knife down."

Karen hesitated. "But just . . . *look* . . . at her." The scalpel slid from her fingers and struck the tile with a hollow clink.

The zombies wanted to stay until Sylvia was reconstructed, but Alish, backed up by Davidson, insisted that it wasn't possible. They were actually in the middle of the process, he said, which they expected to last another week. Alish blew his nose on a handkerchief and told them that Sylvia would be returned to them for the next class.

"There won't be . . . another class," Karen responded. "Ever."

Thorny was waiting in the encounter room with Cooper and Melissa, and Phoebe would have found their obliviousness hilarious if she wasn't still reeling from the discovery in the lab. Karen, sparing no detail regarding Sylvia's condition, told them what they'd just seen. She told them that Undead Studies was canceled, permanently. She didn't need to take a vote, the consensus was immediate, if unspoken. She advised Cooper to leave the foundation with them, and the dead boy agreed.

"Can I . . . stay . . . at the . . . Haunted House?"

Karen looked back at the door, where Angela stood sucking on her lower lip.

"For . . . now," Karen replied. "I think we'll need to . . . move. Ms. Hunter, would you please get the van to pick us up? As in . . . right now?"

Angela, sighing, said she would.

"I can't believe it," Thorny said. "I can't even believe it."

"Believe it," Phoebe told him.

The students decided to wait for the bus in the foyer. Most of them were all too eager to get on the bus and leave what they'd witnessed or heard about, but Phoebe hung back so she could hear Karen's parting words, which she delivered with ice-cold brevity right to Alish.

"I'll be back in a week for . . . Sylvia," she said. "I'll be bringing . . . friends."

Alish assured her that he'd have Sylvia ready, and then they joined the others, who sat in a cluster toward the center of the bus.

Phoebe took her seat next to Adam, who looped a heavy arm around her shoulders. Karen sat apart from the others, a few rows up.

"Are you okay, Karen?"

Karen ignored the question. "He got us . . . again. Damn . . . him."

Phoebe was confused at first, wondering how the comment applied to Alish, but then she recalled the ghost of a smirk on Pete's face as he'd exited the building.

Karen punched the seat in front of her, and it sounded like she'd used enough force to splinter bone.

# CHAPTER
# FORTY-THREE

"*All differently biotic students are to report to room one eleven for study hall . . .*" Phoebe was late to the cafeteria, having tried to spend a few extra minutes in the hallway with Adam before Principal Kim reluctantly chased her away. Margi was at their usual table, sitting by herself.

"Just you and me today, kid," Phoebe said, smoothing her skirt. "Anything good to eat?"

"You can have whatever you want, I'm not very hungry," Margi said. "Where are Adam and Karen?"

"You didn't hear the announcement? Zombies aren't allowed in the cafeteria anymore. They have to go sit in a study hall with Principal Kim."

"You're kidding."

"Does that sound like something I'd kid about?"

"Jeez. Actual segregation. Unreal. I think trads should be the ones that get segregated."

"I guess we are, by default."

Margi hadn't really eaten anything, her bag of cookies was unopened, and her sandwich had been picked at, but all of the parts seemed to be present on the napkin spread before her. "You want any of my stuff?"

Margi shook her head. "I used to think being dead might be the way to go."

"Oh, Margi . . ."

"No, no. I mean zombie dead, not dead dead. I just thought it might be cool, you know, never having to sleep, being invulnerable to pain, going out at night and basically doing whatever you want. That's all. That freedom, to be outside of society."

"I don't think many zombies are enjoying that freedom right now, Gee."

"I know, I know. It wasn't like I was going to kill myself or anything."

"That's good, because not everyone comes back. Especially . . ." Here Phoebe was going to say, "especially suicides," but Karen was an exception to that rule. "Especially because you have so many people who love and care about you."

"Ease up, Pheebes. I told you I wasn't really thinking about it. And now, after seeing Sylvia, there's no way I'd want to be a zombie. I still can't believe what they did to her, even if it was in the name of science. Do you believe what Alish was saying? Do you really think he was trying to help her?"

Phoebe thought about it. "I believe that Alish thinks he's helping, that the ends will justify the means. The problem is, I don't think he knows what he is doing. How could he?"

"I thought the needles and the reflex tests were creepy

enough, but this—this is just crazy. Do you think . . . do you think Sylvia's the first zombie they've experimented on?"

"I don't know. Probably not."

"Me neither."

Margi looked over at the next table, where a bunch of trad students were laughing and carrying on as though nothing in their world had changed. Phoebe realized that nothing *had* changed—for them.

"Makes you wonder where the ones before Sylvia went."

They ate in silence for a moment.

"Karen sent the photos to the *Winford Bulletin* and a bunch of other places," Phoebe said. "It took us forever to figure out how to get the photos from the phone to the computer."

"I saw them on mysocalledundeath, but I really couldn't look at them. They're too horrible. I was surprised the Web site was still up, though. Doesn't the foundation control it?"

Phoebe nodded. "I was locked out this morning. There's a big ole 'under construction' banner there."

"Nice. How will you get in touch with Tommy?"

Phoebe wondered if Margi could detect the wave of guilt that rose up in her upon hearing Tommy's name. She'd be lucky if Tommy read another e-mail from her ever again after the flame-mail she sent.

"I've got a private e-mail address. Karen and I are going to have to set up a different site. Luckily we have all the photos kids sent backed up." She could tell Margi had more Tommy questions, so she quickly changed the subject. "Hey, that reminds me. Have you heard from Colette?"

Margi smiled. "She called me from Dom's cell phone the other day. She's in New Jersey for a few days, and it sounds like she's having a blast."

"That's great. At least someone's happy."

"Yeah. She sounded so good, Phoebe. So *alive*. She wants us to call her together in a few days." A cloud crossed her face. "Oh, man. We should probably call her today. I don't want her to find out about Sylvia on TV. I didn't even think about calling her I was so upset."

"I know what you mean. I went over to Adam's last night and all we did is watch the news. We never watch television."

"Oh no? What do you usually do?"

She said it casually, but Phoebe caught the evil glint in her eyes. "We take long walks in the woods. We walked all the way to Oxoboxo Lake the other day."

"Long walks, huh?"

"Yes, Margi. Long walks. Very long walks." She leaned back in her chair. "It's starting to get really cold, though. It doesn't bother him, but I can't stand it when it gets cold and windy. I don't know what we're going to when we can't walk."

"You'll think of something."

"Margi! Stop it!"

"Whaaaaat?" Feigning innocence, which she couldn't quite pull off. "I'm just saying, you're very creative, and . . ."

"Margi! Not another word!"

Margi laughed and put her peach pit on her napkin. "Okay, okay. Did you hear the latest? Zombies come back from the dead because of vitamin C deficiencies."

"That isn't even close to true. You're thinking of scurvy."

"You're no fun," Margi replied, pouting. "I know what I'm going to do when I graduate."

"Thanks for that message from far left field, Margi. What do your future career plans have to do with anything?"

Margi cleared a space in front of her and folded her arms on the table, then rested her head on her arms.

"I'm going to work with the undead. Really work with them, *for* them, not like the foundation. I want to be the one to discover how they come back, and I want to be the one that discovers how they can come back even more."

"I think you would be great at that."

"I think I can make a difference. I know that sounds clichéd, but I believe it. Once I got over my guilt and all that yuckiness, I think I really helped Colette. She'd 'returned' quite a bit by the time she left with DeCayce, you know?"

"You were wonderful with Colette," Phoebe told her. "She's happy now because of you."

Margi sat up and rubbed her nose. "I can talk to people, and I'm a good friend. I think I just need to learn the science stuff so I can help people like Sylvia."

She looked out over the cafeteria, where the trad kids talked and joked and ate and were mostly unaware that the zombies weren't present in the lunchroom today.

"I better get cracking, though. I'm getting a C in biology."

"Are you . . . sure . . . you want to go with us . . . tonight?" Tak said to the beautiful girl beside him. They were sitting in back of the Haunted House, alone except for Mal, who had been staring into the sky since Tuesday.

"Oh, I'm . . . sure." Karen said, and he heard it again, the subtle hitch in her speech that conveyed how emotional she was. How angry.

When he first heard her story about Sylvia, a girl he had barely met, he'd been secretly thrilled, his mind leaping instantly to all the different ways that the Sons of Romero could make use of not only the story itself but the wellspring of fury that was flowing from Karen. But the more she told it, the wilder she became. She had so much rage inside her that it almost scared him.

Almost.

"What do you . . . think . . . he thinks about?" he said, nodding to Mal, who was sitting on his rock. Tak had tried many times to recruit the boy, but he didn't seem interested in anything but the sky since Tommy had left.

"Who? Mal?"

"Yes."

"He's praying."

"Really?" There was still an edge in Karen's voice, so Tak wasn't sure if she was kidding or not."

"Really."

"He . . . told you that? He . . . talks to you?"

"He used to."

Tak looked at Mal, at the light frost that covered his body. George shambled out of the woods just then, clutching something to his chest.

"What did you . . . see when you . . . died, Karen?"

Karen looked at him.

"Did you see a white warm light like some of our . . . family? Did you see . . . the faces of those that went before . . . or did you feel . . . an elation, like every happy memory you have . . . ever had was being . . . recalled at once? I have heard . . . our family . . . tell stories . . . like these."

Karen shook her head.

"Or did you see . . . a blankness . . . a void . . . a void that swallowed up your screams . . . without even . . . the gift . . . of an echo?"

He held out his hand to her. She stared at it a moment, then took it. He helped her to her feet.

"Tak," she said, "We don't know what we . . . saw . . . when we died . . . was real. We just . . . don't know. Kevin said . . . he saw a baseball field. Green, the grass cut just so. I saw . . . I saw . . . Mal said . . ."

She stopped for a moment, as though collecting her thoughts, or catching her breath.

"Mal said he saw God. He said that . . . God . . . spoke to him. He's been looking for . . . Him . . . since."

Tak smiled. "Really?"

She surprised him then by laying her hand alongside his ruined cheek. Her face softened, as though the anger had finally left her. She stepped forward and hugged him, tightly.

"Don't do it, Tak. Don't . . . give in . . . to despair. I gave in . . . in life . . . and now I've got a second chance."

"Is that was this is?" he said. His cheek was a chiseled piece of ice next to hers, but he held her as tightly as she held him.

"A second . . . chance? Does your friend . . . Sylvia . . . think this is . . . a second chance?"

She held him. "We have to . . . believe it is, Tak. We . . . *have* to."

"Why?" he said. But it felt good holding her. In fact, it felt better than anything he'd experienced since his return.

"Why," he said. "Why . . . didn't I . . . see?"

"I don't know, Tak. I don't know why we all saw what we saw. But we're here now. Isn't that . . . good enough? Maybe next time . . . maybe next time we'll get to see if . . . if there is a God."

"If there is, Karen . . . don't you see how that's worse?" he said. "It's so much worse if He exists."

"What . . . what do you mean?"

"If there is a God," he told her, "if there is . . . he turned us away. We were there . . . and he . . . turned us . . . away."

She held him tighter then, as if for a moment he was the rock that anchored her from spinning out into the universe. She buried her face in his shoulder, and he thought he could feel her lips moving against his neck, like she was praying. He could feel her against him. He *felt*, and the feeling was so strong that it actually made him question, if only for a moment, the nonbelief he'd carried so strongly since picking his broken body off of the Garden State Parkway and limping down the exit ramp.

"You're trembling," he said. "How is it that you can . . . tremble?"

They stood like that for some time.

# CHAPTER
# FORTY-FOUR

PETE FELT STRONG hands grip his shoulder the moment he was swung around into the wall of his garage, and all he could think was "they finally caught up to me."

Half-winded, Pete struggled to his feet, expecting to see the slashed face of the Japanese zombie. Instead he found himself staring into the cold blue eyes of Duke Davidson.

"Oh." His voice was raspy as he tried to regain his breath. "It's you."

"Think you're pretty clever, don't you?" Duke said, shoving him back against the wall. Pete found himself wishing the Wimp was home, at least then he might get the pleasure of seeing him get his ass kicked along with his own. Duke tapped him on the side of the head like he was trying to get his attention. "Don't you?"

"I'm . . . really clever," Pete said, deflecting a second tap to

759

the head with his forearm. He could feel spittle on his cheeks when Duke laughed in his face.

"I've got to hand it to you, Martinsburg." He stepped back and leaned against Pete's car, which Pete hadn't driven anywhere other than the foundation and back since his sentencing. "One impulsive act, and you throw away months of planning. A year, even."

"Planning what?"

Duke made as if to strike him, and Pete flinched.

"What do you think, Martinsburg?" He shook his bald head. "The destruction of the zombie plague."

Pete rubbed his shoulder where Duke had shoved him. "You left me your key. And then you practically came out and said you were going to be distracting Alish."

Duke's grin grew wider, and he spread his hands in a "you got me" gesture.

"Am I in trouble, then?" Pete said. "I figured I was doing something you wanted me to do."

"Pete," Duke said, and reached out to grip the shoulder he'd just shoved. "Relax. You passed the test."

"I did?"

"Flying colors, son. You can follow orders, but you can also take initiative—you'd be surprised what a rare combination that is. You're exactly who we need. The Reverend is very pleased with you.

"The Reverend? Reverend Mathers?"

Duke went on as though Pete hadn't spoken. "Your pals got a real eyeful at the lab. The pictures they posted have really polarized the issue. The war is on, Pete. The foundation, the primary zombie-advocate organization in the country, will be seriously discredited. Funding will vanish. And the undead, once they see what has been happening to them behind closed doors, are going to run wild in the streets."

Pete doubted that. Somehow, the idea of the zombies doing anything beyond lurking in the shadows wasn't something he could picture. There could be a couple, the Japanese guy and a few of his cronies, who might do something drastic because of what happened at the foundation, but Pete seriously doubted that there would be any mass uprising. "The zombies are like undead hippies. There are only a few that are going to do anything about it."

Duke smiled as he reached into his pocket. Pete thought that he was going for a gun, and that in a moment he'd be past the point of worrying or caring what Duke did. He only hoped that Duke put the bullet in his head so he wouldn't come back.

What Duke withdrew was not a gun. It was the mask that Pete had worn on the night they desecrated the cemetery. Duke slammed it against Pete's chest.

"That's where you and I come in, my friend." Duke pressed the mask against Pete's chest with the palm of his hand until Pete took hold of it.

"The Reverend is expecting big things from you, Martinsburg. Big things. You start tonight."

Pete looked at him and then looked down at the mask spread out on his fingers. The knobby teeth jutted out through the molded tear on the latex cheek, and Pete could feel the scar where his stitches had been itching; he tried to erase the thought that he was staring at a warped mirror image of himself.

"What are we going to do?"

"We're going to take it up a level," Duke said. "The time is right to blow the whole idea of zombie rights and peace sky high."

Duke took one of the yard tools hanging from hooks on the wall of the garage, a splitting maul. He ran his thumb along the edge of the blade, and Pete wondered if he knew that the maul was the tool Pete'd used to destroy the zombie that had been staying in his neighborhood. He couldn't remember his name, Evan or Kevin or something like that. The kid's family, who lived a few streets over, had put their house up for sale.

Duke replaced the maul. "Thanks in part to you, Pete, we've got the world believing that the zombies are willing to dig up graves as part of their recruiting mission. The Hunter Foundation scandal, which we also owe to Mr. Peter Martinsburg, thank you very much, makes this a perfect time to show the living world just how serious the zombies are about swelling their ranks. And when we show them, the living will rise up and destroy the dead."

Pete felt chills along his spine. The light in Duke's eyes bordered on fanatical, but there was something else there too. Pete thought it was pride—pride for what Pete had done.

And maybe even affection. It had been so long since someone had looked at him with that emotion, Pete really wasn't sure.

Duke's words scared him, but they excited him too. When

he thought that he might actually have a hand in bringing about the destruction of *all* zombies, and not just the couple dozen worm burgers haunting Oakvale, he felt something beyond mere rage and revenge.

He felt *relevant*.

Duke put both his hands on Pete's shoulders.

"If the zombies are willing to dig up graves to get more of their kind," he said, "how hard is it to imagine them using more . . . *direct* methods of recruiting?"

Pete was smiling as he pulled on his mask.

# CHAPTER
# FORTY-FIVE

POPEYE WAS actually singing "The Twelve Days of Christmas" as they approached the lawn of St. Jude's. He and Takayuki were far ahead of the other zombies, each of whom was moving even more slowly than usual since they were all hauling bags stuffed with Popeye's gear. His singing was off-key, and lacking in rhythm or melody.

"Will you please . . . shut up." Tak said.

"So I'm not . . . Pâvarotti," Popeye said. "Sue me."

"Your lack of talent I could . . . put up with," Tak said. "It's your . . . song selection . . . that grates."

They stopped about twenty feet from the manger, which was illumined by a pair of bright halogen lamps. Inside the manger a plastic baby Jesus was attended by Mary and Joseph, and they were surrounded by the Magi, a shepherd, two sheep, and a five-foot-high camel.

"The baby is still . . . there," Tak said as Popeye completed a line about lords a leaping. He wished he had an iPod like Tayshawn, who lugged his burden a few steps behind, blissfully unaware of Popeye's singing.

"And it better stay there too," Popeye answered. "The whole . . . effect . . . of this piece will be ruined if . . . there is any vandalism."

Tak noticed that Popeye had begun calling their statements to the beating hearts "pieces" soon after they put up the Undead Army recruitment posters. Or maybe it was the visit from the Hunters that put delusions of grandeur in his bald head, Tak wasn't sure. But Popeye had more of Tommy in him than he realized, because he wanted the bleeders to think.

Tak just wanted them to be afraid.

"Set the bags . . . over there," Popeye was saying. "George . . . how many times . . . do I have to tell you . . . to pick it up . . . not . . . drag it?"

Tak watched Karen cross the road with George. Tak much preferred going in smaller groups when they went into Winford; he thought that for everybody they added, they were doubling their chances of getting caught. But selfishly, he thought Karen's presence made it worth the risk. She was probably faster than all of them, so if there was any trouble, she'd be the most likely to get away.

He set his own burden down and looked at the manger, thinking about Christmases past. When he lived in New Jersey there was a church a few streets over that put out a nativity scene year after year, and year after year the baby Jesus was stolen. One year it was replaced with a dead cat, another time someone demolished the whole scene, going as far as to kick in the pressboard walls of the stable and break the heads and hands off the statues. He remembered, as a boy, looking at a photograph of the destruction in the newspaper and wondering what sort of misanthropic idiots would commit such a senseless act.

That was before he died.

There was condensation on some of the statues, probably caused by the cool mist hitting the painted cheeks and then being bathed in the warmth of the halogen lights. The Magi were bearded, and they were carved and painted with somber, dignified expressions. Tak involuntarily lifted his hand to the space where his cheek used to be, his fingers grazing exposed molars.

"George! Hurry . . . up!" Popeye yelled. The church and the mission were at the far end of a busy street. Three a.m. was not a popular hour on a weeknight, but all it would take is the passing headlights of one car for the whistle to be blown. Tak looked back as Popeye started giving instructions to Tayshawn on how to set up. Karen was already busy.

"How are . . . you?" Tak asked her.

"Better," she said, smiling at him as she tied a knot around one of the figures. "I'm still angry, but I . . . feel better."

"Anger is . . . an energy," he said, but even as he said it he knew that something had changed inside of him after their embrace. Even the meaning of the piece they were about to construct had changed for him.

"Tak, are you . . . helping?" Popeye asked. They'd practiced the setup all week in the backyard of the Haunted House so that they could get in, do the deed, and get out.

"Coming," Tak said, looking away from the manger.

When he died, Tak didn't see loved ones who'd passed on before him or bright lights in the distance. He didn't feel the "warm, womblike glow" that one dead girl described. He'd listened to more than a few tales of a reassuring vision of an afterlife from the zombies that had made their return to the Haunted House, but to him the only afterlife was the one he was "living" now. He died on a busy stretch of the Garden State Parkway, where he lost control of his motorcycle in the rain and broke his neck. He came back three days later with no memory of being gone, just a blankness where so many others reported brightness, love, and joy.

He was convinced that these people were delusional, and that these "visions" were the products of minds desperately in need of some piece of sanity to cling to when faced with the fact of their return from death.

Karen looked up from her task.

"Are you okay, Tak?"

"I'm . . . fine. Why do you . . . ask?"

She shrugged. "I just thought you looked . . . funny. That's all."

Tak looked back as George finally made it across the road, an enormous sack slung over his back.

"I'm . . . fine."

"Okay."

"Hey, look," Tayshawn said, catching sight of George. "It's undead . . . Santa."

"Less talk," Popeye said. "More work. The charred sticks for the fire go here, not over there."

"Hey, Santa," Tayshawn said, "looks like . . . your girlfriend . . . made it."

Tak looked across the lawn to the mission. The girl Karen had brought to the Haunted House the other day, Melissa, was walking in their direction, her white mask reflecting the moonlight.

"Hey, Melissa!" Karen called. Tak was glad Karen kept working while she called to her; he thought that six zombies congregating on a church lawn in the dead of night would be seen by the beating hearts as more than a gathering, they'd think it was an uprising.

Tak watched George, who started walking toward Melissa as she waved, the board that she wrote on under her other arm.

"Let's . . . hurry up," Tak said. "This isn't supposed . . . to be . . . a party."

"You're supposed to be . . . helping, George," Popeye said, managing to sound irritated as he set up one of the gaunt, shrouded figures he'd constructed out of old denim and pieces of the shutters they'd peeled from the Haunted House. Their garments were made from black garbage bags.

"Let him be, just get it . . . done," Tak said, starting to arrange the figures according to Popeye's design.

The work itself didn't take very long, even with Popeye crabbing at George and Tayshawn every few moments. Melissa walked over to watch them, and George tried his best to contribute by moving the figures according to Popeye's direction. Takayuki thought that he might actually be trying to show off for the masked girl. They'd arranged five figures, all smaller and less substantial than the comparatively robust figures of the manger scene. Rather than robes of purple and red, Popeye's figures were all in black, and their stick figure limbs and bodies were visible in the rents of their clothing. Whereas the figures in the manger were all gazing with reverence at the pink-cheeked infant in his straw crib, four of the five Popeye figures, their bony shoulders stooped, were gazing forlornly at the charred remains of a campfire that had gone out. Two of the figures were on their knees, and each wore an expression of abject despair as they stared into the ashes or, in one case, their hands. The faces themselves were spare, Popeye having drawn them with a black marker on beige sackcloth.

The fifth figure stood slightly apart from the circle at the fire. Its back was stooped like the others, but there was something in its carriage, a subtle tilt of the hooded head, that set it apart. It was looking into the direction of the manger scene, and its posture suggested either hope or defiance, or both.

When it was done, Popeye made everyone stand back to look. "Let me explain . . . my work . . . to you," he said, speaking to Melissa, but really to the whole group.

Pompous ass, Takayuki thought, but he also thought Popeye had done a bold and powerful job. The figure looking over at the manger—what was it thinking? Was it leading its people, or considering abandoning them? Did looking at the manger bring it hope, or a more complete sense of despair?

Popeye never got the chance to tell Melissa about his work, not even the title, which he'd told Tak was "The Thirteenth

Day of Christmas." They heard the gunning of an engine followed by a squeal of tires, then they were bathed in red, white, and blue light. The zombies froze, standing as still as the figures they'd just spiked into the earth.

"Oh no," Karen said, rising to her feet.

"Don't move! Police!"

Two police cars had stopped in front of the church lawn, and more sirens whined in the distance. He realized that one of the cars must have been close by, watching them and waiting for backup, as there were only one set of tread marks on the road. The policemen were out of their cars, standing behind the open doors with their guns drawn.

"Get on the ground now!"

Tak knew that the others were waiting for his cue. There was so little cover, and so much ground to cross to get it, but he didn't think getting arrested was an option.

"Tak?" Popeye said. A third car, and then a fourth, sped to the scene in the moment that Tak took to decide, blocking the road.

"On the ground now!" The first cop yelled. "This is your last warning!"

"Tak?"

"I . . ."

He didn't get the chance to speak.

He saw George moving at the corner of his vision, moving with a speed he didn't know George was capable of. The dead boy lurched forward. It looked to Tak like he was trying to move in front of Melissa.

The police didn't see protectiveness in the gesture. They

saw only a shambling zombie lurching toward them, its arms raised and forward, as though grasping for their necks.

Without another word, they opened fire.

The explosive sound of the guns split the night. Tak watched invisible fingers pluck at the back of George's jacket, but the dead boy continued down the hill, closing in on the police. Melissa fell to the ground, her board flying out of her hands as she hit the grass. He heard Popeye swear, and someone went over backward onto "The Thirteenth Night of Christmas," splintering some of the despairing figures. Tak heard the humming of bees and felt—although the feeling was far away, as though through a thick haze of painkiller—a sting. He looked down in amazement as a second bullet slapped against his chest, puffing out his shirt, and causing a thick trickle of dark sludgy ooze to drip out.

He looked over at Karen, standing among the effigies, and as she met his gaze he saw something he'd never seen in the diamond sparkle of her eyes: fear.

"Run!" he yelled, but the word had little power, as the bullet had done something to his lung. He heard one of the spikes on his shoulder *ping* as a bullet snapped it off, and then another bullet hit the soft wood of the manger as he ducked behind it. He ran, and he looked to his left and saw Popeye moving as fast as his dead legs could carry him, going for the stone steps of the church. Popeye tripped, or was knocked over by a bullet, but he got to his feet quickly. Tak thought they might have a chance of getting away, if they could get up the steps and around the wall of the church.

They made it to the wall, but when he looked back he saw Karen running the opposite way. A strangled cry was wrenched from his chest as he saw her lifted up and then thrown to the turf.

She didn't get up.

None of the cops were following, and Tak peered around the corner and saw why.

George had made it as far as the sidewalk. One of the cops shot at him from about ten feet away, but he was either shooting to disable or was unaware that the only surefire way of putting a zombie down was to shoot the head. One of the other cops tried tackling George around the ankles, and he went down in a heap.

Tak knew this would be his best, and maybe only, chance of getting away. Popeye was almost at the wall, and he saw Tayshawn cutting across the lawn to a row of houses. Karen had taken the path with the most open ground, as though she were trying to draw fire.

She still hadn't gotten up.

He looked back. Melissa's fiery red hair was lying in the grass like a tangle of copper wire a few feet away from her, her bald head a ruin of burned and puckered skin. The frame of her white board had splintered when she fell.

She lifted her head, her tragicomic mask hanging askew, revealing the charred skin of her forehead above a fear-crazed green eye. She reached toward him.

On the far side of the field, Karen still wasn't moving.

Tak started back for Karen, ignoring the bullets from the

one cop who wasn't in the scrum around George. He went three steps and felt something tear at his leg, and then he was flat on his face on the stone steps.

"Stop!" Takayuki heard from behind him. "What are you doing?"

It was the priest, Tak realized, the one who had given shelter to Melissa and other zombies like Mal. He was padding across the lawn in bare feet, his bathrobe flapping over his pajamas as he ran.

"Stop!" he cried. "They're human beings!"

Tak got to his feet, but the leg that had been shot wasn't working right. He thought Karen might have started crawling, but then again it might have been the wind whipping her hair and white shirt. He went another step and would have stumbled if Popeye hadn't returned to grab him around the shoulders.

"We've got . . . to go, Tak!" Popeye screamed. "We can't lose . . . you . . . too!"

Tak looked at the carnage on the church lawn. George was being clubbed with nightsticks, and then they tried the Taser. Takayuki saw his friend stiffen and jerk as the current went through him. He had no idea how a weapon like a Taser would work against the undead, but George dropped to the ground, rigid and unmoving.

And Karen . . . was she moving? Was she crawling to the shrubbery that marked one of the sidewalks leading to the church? He struggled in Popeye's grip, but the boy dragged him back, and with his leg disobeying him, Tak couldn't get the leverage to fight.

The priest was at Melissa's side. As he held her, he caught sight of Takayuki.

"Go, son!" he called. "Go!"

"Karen!" Tak yelled, as Popeye pulled him back.

"She's up . . . Tak," Popeye said in his ear. "She's . . . up. They will . . . follow us . . . instead."

Tak looked at Popeye, who'd lost his glasses in the fray. There was no way to tell in the wild bug eyes if he was telling the truth.

He fought back the desire to hobble back down the hill and fight the police, to fight until they disabled or destroyed him. His last sight before Popeye dragged him back behind the stone wall was of George, unmoving and on the ground, and of Melissa huddled in the priest's arms, her hand scrabbling for the wig she'd used to hide her scars from the world.

"We have to . . . go, Tak," Popeye said, quietly.

Tak said a quick prayer in his mind to the God he thought had rejected him.

Then he muttered a curse and limped after Popeye as he ran down the back alley behind the church.

"What . . . was . . . that?" Popeye said. They were standing in a wooded clearing within sight of Lake Oxoboxo, a place Takayuki had picked as a rendezvous point in case they were separated during one of their social-protest runs. Something like being fired upon by the local police. Dawn was beginning to break, turning the clouds above the color of cotton candy.

Takayuki didn't answer. He was thinking about Tayshawn and wondering how long they should wait for him before going on to the Haunted House.

"They didn't even . . . give us . . . a . . . .chance!" Popeye said. "They just . . . started . . . shooting!"

The existence of the Haunted House stopped being a secret when Adam was converted. Tak wondered if there were police—or white vans—headed there now.

"They shot . . . they just started . . . shooting!"

"Something's happened," Takayuki said, his voice a whisper, probably due to the bullet that had hit his lung. Nothing they'd done would have caused the cops to act like this.

"I can't believe . . . this," Popeye said. "I'm lucky . . . I wasn't . . . shot."

"You were," Tak said, "In the . . . ass. Right cheek."

"Really?" Popeye said, running a hand down the seat of his jeans. "Aw, hell!"

"Let's go to . . . the Haunted House," Tak said.

"I can't believe . . . I got shot," Popeye said. "I just . . . can't believe it."

"We all . . . got shot," Tak said, starting to walk. Popeye hurried up to join him.

"You . . . did? Where did you get . . . hit?

"Leg, obviously." Oddly, the leg was bothering him less than it had when the bullet first hit him. He was still limping, but the limp was not as pronounced as before. "Also chest. And . . . stomach."

"Damn. Damn! I can't . . . believe this."

"Popeye," he said. "Did you . . . really . . . see Karen . . . get up?"

"I . . . think . . . so," was his reply, but he didn't look at Tak when he said it.

Tak was angry with him, but he knew his anger was misplaced. The tactician in him knew that Popeye had done the right thing; if the Haunted House community were to lose him, Karen, and Tommy, they'd be decimated in no time. If in fact the police hadn't decimated them already.

He quickened his pace. The human in him, whatever small part that was left, wished he'd died the final death with the others.

"I . . . I think . . . George is . . . dead, Tak," Popeye said. "Like . . . really . . . .dead."

Tak nodded. He'd had the same suspicion. Tayshawn was probably a goner too. Maybe the priest was able to save Melissa, but it was just as likely that they'd knocked him aside and shot her like a dog.

But please, God, he thought, please not Karen. Please.

"Did you feel the . . . bullets, Tak?"

"A . . . little," he answered.

"Why did . . . they . . . do it?"

"Something's happened," Tak repeated. But what it was, he could only guess.

He didn't have to wait long for his answer. When they arrived at the Haunted House after the long walk through the woods, the "something" was on everyone's minds. There were over a dozen zombies in the unliving room when he and Popeye arrived. The boys from the foundation, Kevin and Cooper—

were all waiting for them. Even Mal, who rarely budged from his rock, was there. Many of the zombies rushed at them as soon as they saw them, as opposed to waving, or ignoring him, like they usually did.

The questions and comments came all at once.

"Why . . . did you do . . . it?

"The . . . police . . ."

"Murderer . . ."

He couldn't make any sense of the undead chorus until Anna, a girl whom he barely knew, made her way to the front and told him without pause, in a clear voice, that he had doomed them all.

"What the . . . bloody . . . hell . . . are you talking about?" Popeye said, sounding exasperated. "*They* shot . . . at . . . *us*."

The girl trained her pale gray eyes on him. "Because you . . . killed . . . that family."

"*What?*" Popeye said. He looked at Tak, his mouth open wide enough to show gray gums and beige teeth.

"Why do you think . . . we killed . . . someone?" Tak asked.

"It was on . . . the radio," said one of the other boys. "Every . . . fifteen minutes there is . . . an update. They give . . . your . . . description."

"The radio," he said. He had to laugh in spite of himself. "Who did they . . . .say . . . we killed?"

"A lawyer . . . and his family," was the answer. "Children."

Then he did laugh. One lie, one false accusation, and zombies everywhere are instantly discredited. To think that Tommy thinks he can actually make a difference, that he can effect change through discourse and nonviolence, when his enemies have the means to erase everything he's done in the moment it takes for a beating heart to exhale. Power in America, real power, the power to annihilate and erase would always be in the hands of the living.

"Zombies," he said. "We have . . . not done . . . what they are saying we have done. I've always said that death . . . is a gift. But it . . . is not . . . ours to give."

Even as he said it, Tak was reconsidering his position. He looked at each of the zombies gathered around him in turn.

"The beating hearts . . . are lying."

His whispered words silenced them. He knew they wanted to believe—there may have even been some who hoped he *had* committed a violent crime against the breathers, but for the most part the others would take Takayuki's word over that of a disembodied voice from the radio.

"We walked to Winford," he began, and continued to relate everything that had happened that night. His audience was dismayed to hear that George—a favorite around the Haunted House—had been taken, but they were devastated when he said that they weren't sure if Karen got away.

"What . . . do . . . we . . . do . . . now?" Anna asked. "The radio . . . said that . . . the police . . . were searching . . . for three. They gave . . . your . . . descriptions."

Popeye groaned.

"The police . . . will . . . come here," Tak said. "You . . . should not . . . be here . . . when they do."

"Where can . . . we go?"

Takayuki looked at Jacinta, who had been at the Haunted House only a week or so before the Hunters visited. Takayuki looked at her and thought that his heart would break, if he had one.

"I know . . . a place," he said. He turned to the zombies shuffling around. "We will . . . take you . . . there. Bring whatever . . . you think . . . you need. Tell . . . whoever else . . . is here. Be back . . . in five minutes."

Tak went upstairs and checked each of the rooms for zombies, but everyone had been downstairs. He stopped in the room with the wall of the dead. Downstairs, there was a crash and a thump and the sounds of slow, scared people trying to hurry.

He debated trashing the wall, thinking that maybe it wasn't such a great idea for the authorities to get so many mug shots, but then decided that he'd rather leave it. One of the recruitment posters with George fluttered in a breeze of unknown origin.

He found one of Popeye's markers and wrote on the poster, then went to join his people downstairs.

When he got there, Popeye was hugging Tayshawn, who had apparently just came through the front door

"Sorry . . . I'm late," Tayshawn said, shrugging Popeye away.

"Better late . . . than never," Tak said. He was glad Tayshawn had made it, but not glad enough to hug him. "Did you see . . . Karen?"

The look on Tayshawn's face reminded him what a curse hope was.

"I . . . didn't . . . see her."

Tak tried not to let his emotions show. His voice, made

more hollow and raspy by the bullet that had passed through his lung, betrayed nothing. He was aware of the zombies gathering behind him, awaiting his instructions

"Don't get . . . comfortable," he whispered to Tayshawn. There were a few of their people, Anna and a newlydead boy whose name escaped him, standing apart from the others. "See if you . . . can convince . . . the others. If you can't . . . after . . . a few minutes . . . leave them."

"Where are we . . . going?" Popeye asked. He'd found another pair of sunglasses, with big round John Lennon–style mirrored lenses that looked almost comical on his pale white face.

"You'll know . . . when . . . you get . . . there."

Tak turned, and the undead eyes of their community all trained on him. He'd thought of this moment often, the moment they would recognize him as their leader. Tommy's leaving had made it inevitable.

But when he'd thought of it, he'd always done so with Karen in mind. Just as he'd always known that circumstances would force the zombies to his side, he'd known that Karen would realize that Tommy's methods would not accomplish what needed accomplishing.

And now, looking into their faces and not seeing hers, he felt an emptiness unlike any he'd ever experienced before, save that of when he'd first returned from death.

He sighed, air passing in a wet wheeze from his punctured lung, and addressed his people.

"We have . . . to go."

# CHAPTER
# FORTY-SIX

PHOEBE WONDERED where all the zombies had gone.

She'd taken Adam's hand when they were walking to class, a rare public display of affection, but she was unnerved and a little nervous by the stares they'd been getting, stares that had begun the moment they'd gotten on the bus. She'd have thought everyone was pretty much used to the idea of her and Adam being together by now.

Margi had prattled on during the bus ride as though nothing was amiss, but even she had quieted when she noticed the tense hush that swept through the corridor as they walked.

"What's the deal?" she whispered.

"I have no idea." Phoebe looked up at Adam, who tried to shrug.

Principal Kim ended up pulling him out of their homeroom. Phoebe watched him struggle out of his desk to join the principal and Detective Gray, one of the men who had interrogated them in Undead Studies. Gray closed the door behind Adam once he was out, and Phoebe craned her head to try and see where they were going.

When they were out of sight, she realized that the entire class was silent and staring at her, even Mrs. Rodriguez.

"What?" Phoebe said. "What's going on? Where are all the zombies?"

Many looked away, but Mrs. Rodriguez held her gaze. And then she told her.

Pete sat in the warm cab of Duke's truck, watching the small screen of the wireless television Duke had propped up on the dash. This was the third channel they had tuned in, but the news was all the same.

"Attorney Gus Guttridge, lawyer for the defense in the well-publicized Oakvale zombie murder case, along with his wife and two children, ages nine and twelve, are missing and presumed dead after an apparent hate crime committed by living impaired persons. . . ."

"They're differently biotic now," Duke said to the screen. "Get with the times."

Pete looked over at him over the rim of his Styrofoam cup. Duke took another sip of coffee and winked at Pete.

Pete turned back to the screen just as the photograph of his lawyer was replaced by a close-up of the zombie from the fake recruiting ads.

". . . unidentified living impaired man allegedly responsible for the crimes was apprehended late last night, along with . . ."

"What's going to happen to Guttridge and his family?" Pete asked, not really caring who among the worm burgers would go down for his crimes.

Duke sipped his coffee. "You've heard of witness relocation? It's sort of like that."

"Why would Guttridge do that?"

Pete didn't think an attorney would be all that eager to give up his lifestyle in the name of zombie elimination. The Guttridge home was one of the largest and most opulent he'd ever been in, more impressive even than his dad's place out on the West Coast. Pete supposed he should have felt remorse for all the destruction he'd caused in the home—following Duke's orders, he and the other men smashed furniture and took knives to the trad figures of people in the artwork and photographs around the home. And then came the blood.

"We can be very persuasive."

"I guess you'd have to be," Pete said, watching the video Duke's people had released to the media, which showed a trio of zombies—really Pete and two of the men from the group wearing their masks—shambling from the Guttridge home. "Considering that there weren't any bodies."

The zombies were carrying what appeared to be a body wrapped in a blanket over their shoulders in the grainy, jumpy video. Long hair and a pale arm dangled from Zombie Pete's blanket, which in reality had been a blow-up doll and not Mrs. Guttridge. The "bodies," all four of them, were now deflated and folded in the tool chest of Duke's truck. Pete wanted to think about that even less than he did the buckets of blood that they threw around the Guttridge's bedrooms. Duke had assured him that it had been real human blood.

"Pays to have friends in high places," Pete said.

"The murder and abduction of the Guttridges is considered to be in retaliation for Attorney Gus Guttridge's role in exonerating a minor youth of murder in a zombie-related crime . . ." the voice on the television informed them.

"Zombie-related crime," Duke said, snuffling with mirth into his coffee cup. "You popped that kid."

". . . and for recent developments at the Hunter Foundation, which is alleged to be conducting experiments on the living impaired. Photos depicting an unidentified living impaired girl in a partially vivisected state have been circulating on the Web, where . . ."

"Enough." Duke switched the television off. "Mission accomplished."

Pete grinned, admiring his easy confidence. Duke was a man who was fully aware of the power he wielded, sort of like a coach who could back up his talk with action on the field. After they'd vandalized the Guttridge home, they watched from the safety of Duke's truck as the white vans rolled up. The lead van had the FBI seal stenciled on the door. Duke told Pete about the special "Undead Crimes Unit" of the FBI that would be taking over the case.

Pete had thought that the outside world might think it was a little fishy that there just happened to be an FBI van nearby when the crimes occurred, but Duke assured him that no one was going to be all that interested in investigating those angles.

"Is the whole FBI in on it?" he asked.

Duke held up his hand as he listened to the newscaster rattle off a list of crimes that Oakvale zombies were alleged to have committed.

"Sexual assault," he repeated, plucking the crime out of the ten or so she'd named. "Rumor spreads like cancer, huh? Now, what was it you asked me?"

"The FBI. Is the whole Bureau in on the anti-zombie thing?"

"The 'anti-zombie thing,'" Duke repeated, shaking his head. "You make it sound so respectable. The answer is, of course not. There isn't a single organization in America—governmental, corporate, or otherwise—where all of its members are on the same page. Except, of course," and here he grinned, and switched on the ignition for the truck, "my 'anti-zombie thing.' Put the TV on the seat, will you?"

Pete did as he was asked. "Where are we going?"

"We're going to your house, so you can pack and say good-bye to your mom. The Wimp isn't home, I hope you don't mind."

Pete felt a nervous smile creep across his face. It pulled at the scar he still hadn't gotten fixed.

"What are you talking about?"

"Youth ministry," Duke said, pulling off the shoulder and onto the road. "Your mother took a phone call from a very well-respected and important man last night, Pete. The good Reverend Nathan Mathers. He convinced her that the direction your life was taking was not a good one, and that you needed to fill the emptiness you felt with purpose. The purpose that only Reverend Mathers and his youth ministries can provide."

Pete laughed out loud. "She actually fell for that?"

"Like I said, we can be pretty persuasive. The Reverend especially. Just wait until you meet him, Pete. You've never seen such a commanding, charismatic presence in all your life."

Pete heard him as though from a million miles away. He knew that Duke was laying it on thick about the ministry, but the truth was that Pete *did* feel as if he had found purpose in life. And Duke felt so strongly about him that he was able to have the Reverend—the Reverend!—call on his behalf. The respect these men were showing him combined with the self-respect he had from all he'd accomplished in the past few weeks was an intoxicating mixture. He saw himself reflected in the visor mirror, literally blushing with pride, his face bright pink but for the thin white line of his scar. When he felt Duke's massive hand on his shoulder in a fatherly pat, emotion almost burst out of him.

"Welcome to the team," Duke said, the pat turning into a firm grip. "Son."

The ride home was an eternity, almost as bad as the school day had been. At lunch, Margi had told Phoebe all the rumors she'd heard—zombie murder spree, zombie massacre—so now they were mostly silent, along with the rest of the students sitting on the bus, who all sat far, far away from them.

"We've got to get to the Haunted House tonight," Phoebe whispered.

Margi chewed her lip. "You don't think the cops have been there?"

"Even so. We've got to make sure."

"Okay." Margi looked out the window as the bus rolled up to Phoebe's stop, and the first smile of the day appeared on her face.

"Hey, look! It's Adam!"

Phoebe looked out the window and saw him standing at the edge of the driveway. He waved. She ran off the bus to meet him, knocking him back with the force of her hug.

"I thought they'd taken you!" she said, squeezing him tight. "I was so worried."

"Re . . . manded . . . to . . . custody," he said.

"Remanded to custody? To your mom?"

He nodded. "Zombies . . . with a . . . responsible . . . parent . . . are being . . . freed. Others . . . not."

"Have you watched any of the news? What happened, exactly?

He told her what he knew, that zombies in Winford—and other parts of the country—were supposedly committing crimes in retaliation for what had been done to Sylvia. George was in prison for his alleged role in the murder of attorney Gus Guttridge and his family.

"George is in prison? Margi heard he'd been destroyed. Tak too."

"Tak . . . is . . . at large. America's . . . most . . . wanted. Not sure . . . about . . . George."

"This is awful. I can't even believe this is happening."

"It gets . . . worse," he said, leading her by the hand to her door. "It is now . . . illegal . . . to be . . . undead."

"What do you mean?"

"Martial . . . law. All undead . . . who do not . . . have a . . . parental guardian . . . are to be . . . imprisoned."

He told her about watching the news with Joe, who'd been called from the shop to pick Adam up. The news had shown footage of a police raid on the Haunted House, where a girl named Anna, and Kevin Zumbrowski were taken away in handcuffs. Adam told her that at one point Joe took off his work boot and hurled it at the television, on which the Reverend Nathan Mathers was exhorting lawmakers to "take control of our country . . . before it is overrun with the evil dead!" Locally, Father Fitzpatrick was given much less camera time to explain why he was refusing to turn "an unnamed zombie" over to the authorities.

Phoebe listened to the story with an increasing sense of horror, thinking of Tommy, thinking of Colette and DeCayce, who were all on unfamiliar roads somewhere within the country. Worse, Tommy would probably delete all messages from her unread and unlistened to.

"Have you heard from Karen?" Phoebe refused to believe anything other than that Karen was safe.

Adam shook his head.

"Hopefully she's with her family," she said.

"Hopefully."

"We've got to get to the Haunted House."

"They . . . raided . . . it."

"We have to be sure. Come on, let's call Margi, she should be home by now."

Ten minutes later Phoebe had Margi on the phone, but Margi told them not only could she not take the car, she was grounded. Her parents, no longer influenced by Colette's strange but oddly comforting appearance, decided that she'd been spending altogether too much time with zombies.

"I tried calling Karen," Margi said, "her mom said she didn't come home last night."

By the time she hung up, Phoebe had a sick feeling at the pit of her stomach.

"We've got to go to the house," she said.

"Phoebe . . . it's . . . freezing. Let . . . me . . ."

"I'm going."

"Don't . . ."

"I'm going, Adam! They'd try to kill you if you went alone!"

Adam didn't have anything to say to that, so he waited patiently in the kitchen as Phoebe went to find a heavy sweatshirt and warmer boots.

"They . . . boarded . . . it up."

Phoebe shivered, looking at the plywood sheets that had been nailed across the front door and the first floor windows. It had taken them nearly three hours to trudge through the woods to the house, and the already overcast sky was still darkening.

She looked at the boards, which had been stickered with police crime scene tape. "Let's go around back."

Adam fell in step beside her. Cold and fatigue had slowed her to his pace. She swore when she saw that there was planking over the back door as well. Adam looked at her, then walked up the steps, getting his fingers under the crack between the wood and the door.

"Watch . . . out," he said. He pulled, and boarding tore free, the nails seeming to shriek as they were yanked swiftly from the frame. Adam tossed the big board, sailing it halfway across the yard the way he used to toss a Frisbee.

"Wow."

"Told you . . . I was . . . powerful."

Phoebe'd had the presence of mind to bring a flashlight with her. Switching it on and stepping into the dark, long-unused kitchen, she thought that this was the first time that the Haunted House truly lived up to its name. She could practically feel the spirits of the undead moving in the shadows from her light.

"They're . . . gone." Adam said.

"We need to be sure."

They crept from room to room, finding evidence that people had been staying there—a pile of clothes, a CD, a stuffed bear with the button eyes removed—but no actual people.

"Let's check upstairs."

The stairs didn't seem to mind her, but they groaned in protest when Adam followed. Crime scene tape stretched across the doorway facing the top of the staircase. She shined her light in, cutting across the gloom to reveal the faces of the dead staring out from the photographs still hanging on the wall.

"I'm surprised the cops didn't take them," she whispered.

She heard a light ticking noise against the thin plywood boarding the windows and realized it had begun to snow outside.

"I think . . . they are . . . coming back." Despite this sentiment, he reached out and ripped the tape from the doorway.

"What are you doing?" she asked as he walked into the room. She was thinking of the first time she'd been here, when she and Adam went with Tommy and Evan to meet their zombie friends. Tommy had made her lie down in the darkness so she could understand what it was like to be dead.

*Tommy*, she thought, suddenly convinced she would never see him again. *I'm so sorry.*

"Saying . . . good-bye . . . I guess." The papers on the wall rustled in the cold wind that blew through the cracks in the shutters.

She played the light over the photos, trying to make it easier for him to see the photographs. He reached out for one, but passed his fingers over it. Then he tore a sheet of paper, the Undead States of America recruitment poster, off the wall and crumpled it in his fist.

"Souvenir." He shoved the paper into his pocket.

"I could have folded it for you."

"It's . . . okay. I'll join you . . . in . . . a minute."

They were back in the foyer, just in time to see the bright lights of a car coming up the gravel driveway through the cracks between the boarded-up windows.

"Out . . . the . . . back," Adam said, taking her arm.

They heard the slam of car doors just as they were disappearing into the woods behind the house.

# CHAPTER
# FORTY-SEVEN

PHOEBE'S PARENTS were furious when she finally got home. Joe was pretty pissed too but think he understood.

Snow falling heavy now, well after midnight. Look up at her window and think what couldn't say.

Good-bye.

The danger is too great, now more than ever. Nothing to give.

Long walk ahead. Right left smooth enough now, prints streak in the snow. At the Haunted House standing in front of the wall of the dead saw his message, put in pocket. OXO spaced out along the bottom of the poster. Not hugs and kisses. Message. TOOK THE POSTER SO AGENT GRAY WOULDN'T FIND.

Snow falling in darkness. The snow is good, covers tracks.

Lot to think about on long walk. Phoebe, warm in bed and dreaming. The dead don't dream. Tried to think about something else but without dreams too hard. Oxoboxo woods silent but for the sound of snow and left right scraping along.

The lake isn't huge but it isn't small either. Not sure where Tak is but have a hunch, an idea. Where Colette drowned. If Tak knows the spot that's where he'll be.

Snow-covered lake appears all at once, just beyond a last hill. A flat disk empty of trees, glowing blue white in the cloud-streamed moonlight, not like summer when all can see is an elusive glimmer through thick foliage. Crested the hill and then stepped on matted leaves slick with snow.

Slick. Fall over backward like a rotted oak.

Slide. Slide all the way to the icy shore of the lake, stop at the base of fallen tree. Abruptly stop. Glad Phoebe didn't see.

Phoebe.

Flat on back, eyes wide open, moon veiled. Snow pooling in unblinking eyes. Pain worse than death when think of her and think of her all the time. What could have been, what should have been, what never will be.

Stay down.

Didn't move for don't know how long. Should stay down. Should stay down from jump. Football told tackled kids Just Stay Down, should listen to own advice. After taking the bullet should have stayed down, avoided this pain pain worse than death. She we could have been together but dreams die with death and . . .

"Get up."

The voice, like a knife blade in the dark. Clear snow from eyes and Takayuki looms above blotting out what little moon remained. Smiling but not smiling, icicles in long lank hair.

"Get up."

Speak. Takes effort so cold don't know how long stayed down.

"Hey . . . Smiley."

Smiley straightened, bones and tendons creak like birches in the wind.

"Got . . . your . . . message."

"I wish . . . you'd . . . get up." Looks down. Smiling his non-smile.

"Wish I'd . . . never . . . gotten . . . up."

He shakes head and hair frozen clicks and clacks.

"You're thinking . . . about her . . . again, aren't . . . you? What is it about . . . her, anyway?"

"Phoebe." Saying her name hurts.

"She's like a reverse . . . Dracula . . . one that beguiles the dead . . . instead of the living."

"No," Sit sit sitting up takes effort. "I . . . dug . . . her when I was . . . alive too."

Tak, creaking, sits on the fallen tree.

"You're . . . doing . . . the right . . . thing. She . . . would always . . . be . . . in danger."

"I know." Didn't feel right, felt like death. "Where are . . . the others?"

Looks at frozen lake. "Safe."

"Karen?"

Shakes head. Clatter, click. Like wind chimes. Looks sad. Didn't think Tak could look sad.

"George is . . . in prison. Not . . . reterminated."

"Unless the . . . breathers . . . lie," Tak said.

Thought of the video of George, caged. Thought of other video.

"What about . . . the murders?"

"We had . . . nothing . . . to do . . . with that," he said.

"Because you believe . . . in the sanctity of . . . life, right?"

"No. Because I believe in the . . . sanctity . . . of death. I don't believe . . . any . . . of us did . . . it. But they . . . the beating hearts . . . believe we did," he said. "And that is all that matters. They will be coming for us . . . for you . . . and they will not be stopped . . . with words. Or even laws."

Want to tell him he's wrong. Can't.

"The girl . . ." said Tak. "Phoebe. She watched you . . . die . . . once. Do you want . . . her . . . to go through that . . . again?"

Don't. Want her don't want her to suffer through that. Don't.

"What . . . are you going . . . to do?"

Tak showed his teeth. "Go . . . underground. Bide . . . our . . . time."

"George? The others . . . ?"

"We will . . . liberate them. Or . . . avenge them."

Blanket of snow around Tak's shoulders.

"I want you . . . to come with me, Adam. With . . . us."

Underground. Underground, like the grave.

"I . . . love her, Tak."

Saying it out loud to Tak made something snap inside chest. Cold inside cold outside cold like the grave.

Tak half-skull grin not mocking or malicious.

"If that were . . . true," he whispered, "you would come . . . with me."

Tak stood, offering hand. Two gray-white knuckles where Tak was missing a patch of skin, and a row of long tarsal bones, like the bars of a prison in hell.

Took it. Rose.

And then heard her voice on the wind.

*Adam.*

# CHAPTER
# FORTY-EIGHT

"ADAM," PHOEBE SAID.

The dead boys turned. She was standing at the crest of the hill, just above the long trench Adam's body made when he'd slid down. She was shivering in black sweatpants and her heavy faux fur–lined coat, a gray scarf trailing from her neck.

"You weren't planning on leaving me, were you?"

She didn't need telepathetic powers to read his mind. Something woke her in the dead of night, a feeling that compelled her to go to her window where she'd sometimes watch him as he tried to master the poses and exercises that Master Griffin had set before him. She'd looked down and saw the long slashes of his footprints in the porch light, already half filled with snow.

Once she realized what Adam was planning to do, she'd pulled on her boots and warm clothes and rushed out the door with her flashlight. At first, his tracks, his dragging feet cutting long runnels in the snow, were easy to follow, but as the snowfall increased, the trail became harder to discern in the poor illumination. Eventually she stopped trying entirely and moved to where she thought he was going, which was the lake.

Just follow your heart, she'd thought.

"Phoebe," Adam said, "it . . . is . . . freezing."

She started down the hill, choosing her steps with care, not sure if she wanted to hug him or reterminate him.

"You think?" Her teeth chattered and she hugged herself for warmth.

"You have . . . to go . . . back."

"I'm not going anywhere without you." She slipped a little but caught herself, and soon was at the bottom of the hill with the snow-covered boys. The flakes fell on Adam's cheeks and hair and didn't melt. She looked up at him and saw what she needed to see in his eyes, something that drove the chill out of her body.

"Phoebe," Adam said, drawing out both syllables, "things have . . . changed."

She clapped her mittens together, telling herself that her fingers weren't tingling and her face wasn't numb. "Have they changed, Adam? Have your feelings changed?"

He couldn't meet her gaze. "No . . . never."

"Then why are you planning on leaving me?"

"You are . . . in danger."

"When have I *not* been in danger, Adam? Do you think I entered into our relationship lightly?"

"No."

"Why would you leave me then? Without even saying good-bye?"

Adam looked back at Tak, who brushed his frozen hair back, an almost sympathetic look on his asymmetrical face.

"My . . . anger . . . with you . . . is spent," Tak said. "I really . . . don't want . . . any more . . . of my people . . . hurt."

"They aren't your people," Phoebe said. "That thinking is exactly the problem. They're just *people*."

Tak raised his shoulder, which Phoebe saw was missing one of its metal spikes. "Semantics. If everyone . . . agreed . . . there would be . . . no issue. I'm bringing my . . . the zombies . . . underground. Somewhere . . . safe. I thought . . . we thought . . . you would be safer . . . if Adam . . . came with . . . us."

She turned back to Adam. "Is that what you thought?"

He raised his arms skyward. "Yes. I . . . want you . . . to . . . be . . . safe. Is . . . that . . . so . . . wrong?"

Phoebe noticed that the pauses between his words were longer than usual, which meant that he was getting upset—or that the cold was affecting him. But then again, she was freezing, and at the same time her blood was boiling.

"I don't want to be safe! I want to be with you!"

"Phoebe . . . I'm . . . dead . . . or . . . hadn't . . . you . . . noticed?"

He might speak slowly, but Adam had no problem with volume. Tak looked skyward and then sat back down on the fallen tree.

Phoebe was so angry she stamped her booted heel. "I thought we'd been through this already? You're still here, aren't you? Why do you still keep bringing something up that I don't care about?"

"You . . . should . . . care."

"No, I shouldn't! I care about *you*. Don't you care about me?"

"You . . . know . . . that . . . I do."

"Then why do you want to leave me?" She held out her hands. "Again."

"I don't . . . want . . . to leave . . . you . . . Phoebe. I . . ."

She held up her hand, cutting him off. "Then don't. *Don't.* Don't go 'underground' or wherever else Tak is taking our friends. Don't do it."

Tak looked up at the sound of his name and stopped picking at the entry wound just above his left knee.

"Not everybody can run and hide, Adam. Some people need to stay and fight. The strongest, the bravest, the best and brightest—whoever—some people need to stand and fight. They need to fight for what's right, and they need to do it for all of those that can't."

Phoebe walked to him and took the frozen lumps of his hands. "Tommy. Karen. *You*, Adam. You don't really have a choice. You are the strongest, bravest person I know."

"Not . . . the bravest," Adam said, looking into her eyes.

But she wouldn't be sidetracked. "You're the most dependable, the most responsible, the most admirable . . . and you're getting stronger every day. Every day. Will that continue if you go underground? Without your example, I don't think the zombies have a chance. Let Tak lead the others for now. They don't need you for that. But they will need you when it's time for them to come up again. Let Tak do his job, and you do yours."

She looked back at Tak, defying him to contradict her, but he kept his own counsel. She'd like to think that it was because he could hear the truth in her words, but she rarely could figure out what Tak was thinking.

"You think . . . they need . . . me . . . above . . . ground." Phoebe knew Adam believed her, regardless of what Tak was thinking.

"I do, Adam. I do. But it's more than that," she said, stepping into him, pressing her cold cheek into his chest.

"*I* need you. I really, really need you."

She felt his arms go around her, gently, as though he were afraid he would break her if he held too tight. It made her feel safer than her own words ever could.

"It . . . will be . . . difficult," he said.

"I know. I know it will." She squeezed him more tightly. "But we'll face it together."

The stood like that for some time, and Phoebe felt as though she were warmer even though Adam generated no heat. She heard the creak of leather as Tak slid off the tree, and she braced herself for whatever snarky comment or mocking rebuttal he would surely throw at them.

"I have . . . to . . . go," was all he said.

She saw that she had been wrong, because he didn't say anything else but instead headed to the frozen surface of Lake Oxoboxo.

"Tak." Phoebe could feel the vibration of the word

rumbling up from Adam's chest. The dead boy, already ten feet onto the ice, stopped and looked over his shoulder.

"Take care . . . of them."

Tak nodded, and the rasp of his voice reached them over the quiet ticking of the falling snow.

"Good luck," he said. "To you . . . both."

They watched as he walked farther out, until he was a dark blot on the bluish landscape. When he was a fair distance out she saw him lift his foot and stomp on the ice, the sound of his boot heels echoing back to them across the distance.

"What is" don't . . . worry. "he doing?"

Tak continued his stomping until finally he leaped straight into the air and came down heavily with both feet. There was a crack like thunder splitting the sky open, and he went down through the hard surface of the lake in an icy spray.

A cry rose up in Phoebe's throat, but Adam, still watching the spot where Takayuki disappeared, pulled her closer to him.

"We have . . . to . . . go," he said.

"But Tak . . ."

"He's . . . fine. But you . . . you . . . are . . . cold."

She *was* cold, no matter how much his words warmed her. And it wasn't going to be easy getting back up that hill.

"You're right, I'm cold," she said, teeth chattering. Then she laughed as they started moving.

The going was slow, but they managed to crest the hill by leaning on each other for support. They stopped for one last look at the Oxoboxo, the dark circle where Tak had gone through like a freckle on the blue-white disk of ice. Phoebe turned back and looked up at Adam. When she spoke, she managed to do so without chattering.

"I love you, Adam."

His smile touched his eyes with real expression

"I love you . . . too . . . Phoebe."

The sky clouded over and soon she could no longer see more than a few feet in front of her, but Adam took her hand and led her through the darkening forest.

# CHAPTER
# FORTY-NINE

From: PhoebeKendall@aol.com
To: TommyWilliams17@aol.com
SUBJECT: Updates
Dear Tommy,

By the time you see this e-mail, you should have already heard the news about what has happened here in Oakvale and in Winford. I'm sorry that I didn't e-mail you sooner than this, but it has been a crazy couple of days trying to check on everybody.

Where do I even start? There's just so much. The worst thing is that we still don't know where Karen is. We know she was with Tak on the night the police came, but we don't know if she got away or taken or what. The television stations like to run video of incarcerated zombies, but she's never in the shots. No one wants to think the worst, but Tak did say they were shooting at her. I pray every night that she escaped and that she's out there somewhere, maybe looking to catch up with you.

The Hunter Foundation closed its doors, but you probably know that already, just like you know that Sylvia is being fought over in court right now. What you might not know is that Oakvale High went further than disbanding the Undead Studies program—they went as far as to ban zombies from attending school. Principal Kim was crying when she made the announcement.

Not that there are many of them left to go to school. The Haunted House is quiet now. Everyone there left with Tak and Popeye to go "underground." Sick pun I know but those were his words. I don't know exactly where "underground" is, but even if I did, I don't think I'd write it in an e-mail because who knows whether or not our e-mails are being monitored. But Cooper went, and Mal, and just about every other zombie we know except for George and Kevin and a few others who are in prison or worse. Melissa is still at St. Jude's, and that's become a huge controversy too because Father Fitzpatrick refuses to turn her over.

I hope some of the things that have happened are useful to you as you look for help in Washington, but I guess after the Guttridge family murder that's wishful thinking.

BTW, Tak swears he and the old-schoolers had nothing to do with the murders, or the grave digging of a few weeks ago. For what it's worth, I believe him. He's one of the strangest people I know, but he has a sort of moral code, if that makes sense. I heard that he's on the FBI's Most Wanted list. They're calling him a terrorist.

*I'm glad Colette escaped all of this turmoil. I don't know if Karen told you, but Colette stayed with DeCayce and the Skeleton Crew. She's going to go on tour with them and maybe try to locate her brother. Margi says she might even try to find her parents.*

*So now it's just me and Margi and the other trads here.*

*And Adam. Adam the rock. Strong Adam, Adam who is always there for me.*

*Adam, my love.*

*Yes, Adam and I are "together" now. It's really weird, because in some ways it feels as if we've been together forever, but on the other hand, everything—everything—is brand new. It's going to be super weird now that he isn't allowed to go to school anymore, but we'll manage. We'll have to.*

*I also wanted to apologize to you, Tommy, for all the things I wrote in the e-mail I sent you. It was wrong of me, and I didn't really mean it; I was just hurt and confused because I didn't know how I felt about you, and I didn't know how Adam felt about me, and everything else that was going on. And of course I was jealous because you'd found somebody else, and I have no right to be. You deserve to be happy, Tommy. You're a really great guy and what you do is important, and it might end up being the most important thing for zombies everywhere. Don't stop trying.*

*Sometimes it's the little things that make the difference in this world, little things like writing a poem or picking up a football when everyone says you can't. Or giving someone you love a kiss.*

*Sometimes the little things aren't enough, though, and
that's why I wish you the best of luck. If anyone can make a
change you can.*

*I'm using your private e-mail address because I saw that the
foundation already pulled the plug on mysocalledundeath.com.
I hope my note finds you safe and sound.*

*So, good luck, Tommy. Give my best to Christie.*

*Love,*

*Phoebe*

Phoebe hit send and checked the clock. There was just enough time to make a cup of coffee before the bus came. She'd been drinking a lot of hot coffee in the past few days, as though she needed it to keep her body temperature up after that night/morning in the woods.

She was adding the sugar when there was a light knock on the door. She opened it and there was Adam standing on her doorstep, holding a candy cane and wearing a red Christmas elf hat. He was also wearing his enormous backpack, and coupled with the cane and hat the overall effect was that he looked like a goofy undead Santa Claus.

"Morning . . . sunshine," he said, holding out the candy cane.

Phoebe laughed as she took it from him. "Silly. What are you doing over here so early?"

"Couldn't . . . sleep. Besides . . . it's time . . . for school."

She unwrapped the candy cane and stirred her coffee with it, peppermint mixing with the rich smell of the liquid. "Adam, you can't go to school—Principal Kim announced it on Monday, you know that."

He shrugged, the shoulder with the heavy bag rising and falling in slow motion.

"I . . . feel like . . . going . . . to school."

His grin was so much like the old Adam that her protests died in her throat. "That's a first," she said, reaching for her coat.

"Come on . . . it's widely . . . known . . . I love . . . school."

She laughed. "Yeah, I seem to recall hearing that somewhere."

His face grew serious. "I'm not planning on . . . taking . . . things . . . lying down . . . ever again."

She touched his cheek, feeling for the first time as if she really had made good on her promise to bring him back. He gazed back at her with a steady confident intensity that made her think he'd come further than either of them would have expected.

Breath turning to vapor in the cold air, she took his hand and joined him outside, where the bus was just beginning to chug down their street, ready to carry them off to school.